THE DRAGON STORM

GATES

ANTHONY DIPAOLO

DRAGON STORM

ISBN : 978-1-7374849-2-9

First Paperback Edition

STORM DRAGON HOLDINGS LTD

Illustrations by Scott Trerrotola

~

For my beautiful wife, Michelle. If not for your unwavering love, support, patience and occasional whip-cracking, Alexander Storm would have remained trapped within the dark recesses of my mind.
Thank you.

~

The Dragon Storm
GATES
Book I

1

The invitation was printed on what appeared to be ancient Egyptian papyrus. Delicate at first glance, but in fact strong and durable, Kate held the postcard-size sheet in her hand and gazed down at the artistically drawn letters. Just moments earlier, a tall man shrouded in a cloak of black as dark as a moonless night had knocked on her family's front door and handed Kate the wax-sealed envelope containing the invitation. Kate didn't have a chance to question the man before he slipped away into the night—seemingly disappearing before her eyes. She shut the door and returned her focus back to the invitation in her hand. It read:

Dragon Loch Castle
Kate Winters, Your Presence is Requested on the
Evening of October 17th – 6:00 p.m. Sharp
For a Private Meeting of the
Egyptian Tomb Explorers Society
Yours,
Alexander Storm
*A Private Car Will Pick You Up at Noon—No RSVP Required

Kate stared down at the invitation. She had never heard of Dragon Loch

Castle, nor was she an official member of the ETES. Kate had submitted several dozen papers to the organization and had even corresponded with members via e-mail. She was never, however, offered full membership status into the prestigious group of scholars.

"Dragon Loch Castle," she mumbled to herself. The strange invite and its even odder method of delivery had Kate swimming in excitement. Perhaps one of her papers on Ancient Egyptian mythology had sparked some interest from one of the editing members of the Egyptian Tomb Explorers Society. Her latest analysis of the similarity between the Osiris resurrection myth and modern voodoo's so-called zombies had been returned to her with a big red line through it. Still, she must have caught a member's eye. Why else would she receive this personal invitation to a "private" meeting?

She grabbed the envelope off the floor where it had fallen and raced down the stairs to her basement apartment. Kate's apartment was different from most other twenty-three-year-old girls she knew. It was cluttered with books and papers on topics ranging from ancient cultures and religions to chemistry and physics. Her room, or "The Study" as she referred to it, was like the non-fiction wing of a library. That is, of course, unless you took into account Kate's massive collection of books and papers on such obscure topics as vampires, ghosts, and UFOs. Some would surely argue these titles would be better suited for a comic book store. But Kate knew better. She considered herself a historian by day and a parapsychologist by night.

Kate hopped into her chair and pressed the power button on her oversized flat-panel monitor. Light poured out into the dim room from the screen. On her PC's desktop was a full-color photograph of Bran Castle in Romania. It was rumored that Vlad the Impaler once called Bran Castle home-sweet-home. Bram Stoker, who fashioned portions of his character, Count Dracula, on aspects of Vlad the Impaler's mythology, used Bran Castle as his model for Dracula's castle. Kate, however, had a different castle on her mind at the moment. She pulled up Google and typed in the words "Dragon Loch Castle." As usual, the search returned several hundred results. Kate weeded through the first page without success, but found the entry she was looking for on the second page of her results. "A Complete History of Dragon Loch Island" was located on DragonLoch.com. Kate clicked on the link with growing excitement. The page opened with a renaissance era-type painting of a castle, a knight, and a watery beast resembling a dragon.

"Awesome!" Kate yelled as she reached into her pocket for her cell phone. "Keith is going to get a kick out of this!"

Kate dialed his number and scrolled through the site, intently waiting for her sometimes research partner, maybe boyfriend, always best friend, to pick up. She got his machine instead.

"You're never going to guess where I'm going next week..." she started to leave a message on the antiquated machine, but was interrupted by the sound of a clanking phone as she heard Keith breathing with excitement on the other end.

"Dragon Loch Island," Keith whispered into the phone. Kate could picture him holding his fingers up to his head as if he were a psychic.

"How did you know," she asked slowly, with some obvious degree of amazement?

"'Cause I'm going, too, apparently"

There was a moment of silence on the line.

"Are you there?" Keith asked loudly.

"Yes, I'm here. I'm just wondering why the ETES would invite you to a private conference." Kate heard the shifting on the other end of the line. Keith was getting ready for some long-winded explanation. "No offense, of course."

"Of course," Keith replied quickly.

"It's just that you aren't even an *unofficial* member, whatever that really is. In fact, if someone had asked me, I would have said your interest in "Egyptian Antiquity" is minimal at best. Am I wrong?"

Kate tried not to sound too condescending, although she knew there was a tinge of it in there.

"You're right. But don't forget I worked on the Tanis paper with you, and you submitted it with both of our names—"

"So what does that—"

"So maybe *that's* why they want us to attend. Maybe the big private "hush-hush" party at the old castle is about Tanis or something, and naturally, if they were going to invite one author, they would invite the other."

Keith paused momentarily. "Why is this bothering you so much? I figured you would be happy to go on a little adventure with me."

Kate thought for a moment about the right way to say what she was feeling. "It's not that I don't want to go with you. I was just excited to tell you, and you kinda took the wind out of my sails. All right, rockstar?" Kate had to recover so as not to thrust a sword through Keith's often thin armor that surrounded his ego.

"No problem...I understand."

He didn't. But that was okay. They were going to move on anyway.

"So, you think it's the Tanis article, huh?" She got up to find a copy of their manuscript from her piles of un-filed papers strewn about.

"Yeah. Makes sense to me. They liked that article. At least liked it enough not to draw a line through it. I think it was probably the section about why the Tanis-era Egyptians were hoarding their silver that was a problem for them." Keith laughed.

"Or burying their Pharaohs in it," Kate added.

"Right. But our research was solid. The writing was better than good. And they even thought enough of it to post some of it on the ETES web site." Keith loved to point out how well the two of them worked as a team. And Kate really couldn't argue. They definitely kept each other in check.

"Oh, right. The web site," Kate mumbled. "Let me go there. I can't find a copy around here, but I think I can get it from their submission database."

The second the words left her mouth, she wished she could have pulled them back before they made it to Keith's ear. She could picture him smiling and shaking his head in that paternal way she hated. She waited for it. She waited for the comment about her faulty filing system or disorganized reference material. But it didn't come.

"What's the short address again?" Kate asked. She knew it, but she wanted to keep the discussion going.

"I think it's etesociety.com," said Keith. "Oh, no...maybe it's .org. Yeah, I'm pretty sure it's www.etesociety.org."

"That's it," Kate replied. "Now, let's see if they have a copy of the submission somewhere. It's been a while since I was here."

"Yeah, what, like yesterday?" Keith joked.

"Very funny, wise guy. It's been over a month. I like the new look. They redid a bunch of stuff. What do you think?"

"I'm not on." Keith said quietly, as if ashamed.

"Why not? Let's go. I want you to go to the castle site, too, and see what we can find out," Kate said with the voice of a very feminine drill sergeant.

"I can't get online," Keith said. "My provider must be down, or it's my connection or something."

"Keith?" Kate said amusedly.

"Yes?"

"You don't have a 'provider.' You swipe your service from one of your neighbors. What, are you talking to a stranger here?" Kate asked with a big smile.

"Oh, yeah, well *their* provider must be down, then. Hey, it's not illegal, you know. At least I don't think it is. I'm not really sure, to tell you the truth. But if they don't want to share, they should take five minutes to set up the security. I mean come on, already. Besides, I'm just trying to save a few bucks here for tuition and books and food and—"

"Okay!" She cut him off before he got on a roll. "Then come over here, and we can go over this stuff together. I'll wait for you."

"Cool. I'll be there in a few. Let me get a few things together. It's pretty nice out, so I'll walk it."

Kate laughed. "It's cold out. You want to save gas, you mean. Don't take too long, okay? I want to check everything out. Wait 'til you see the new site. I really do like it."

"Okay. I'm leaving now. See you in a few." Keith hung up the phone and turned toward his PC to turn off the monitor.

"It really *is* a nice new design," he said with a big smirk as he shut the system down.

2

The zipped file extracted itself so quickly from the IM, Samantha was sure her laptop was infected. She couldn't fathom how it had made it through her firewalls. She had top-of-the-line hardware and software systems in place, and she had modified them herself to ensure the highest level of security from the outside chaos of the Internet. She had been on a private message board with other programmers—or hackers—depending on which side you were on. The private message came from a username she'd never seen in the group before.

"What was the name?" she said out loud. Closing her eyes, Sam tried to picture the screen. "Drakon something. Oh, I don't know." Slamming her hands on the desk, she returned her focus to the laptop.

She had been expecting an attack of some kind after exposing that DoubleZ hacking and security group as a bunch of frauds. But this was fast. And truthfully, it seemed a little too stealthy for them. Perhaps she had underestimated their skills.

"They probably sent that new *Magik1 Worm* through. I'm gonna have to act fast."

Sam immediately ran log files to trace the worm's attack on her systems and initiated Antivirus and Spyware scans. Sliding across the room on her chair and leaping up toward the mass of wires and lights that made up the switch and routers, she shut them down to keep the outside out and her data in. But when she looked at her laptop, the screen went black.

"That's it!" She huffed in frustration. "It's fried!"

Strangely, the screen flickered and glowed neon green. A small dot appeared in the center of the screen, and it quickly expanded like a balloon until a three-dimensional black envelope beckoned Sam to click on it. The luminescence of the background shimmered, and the envelope appeared to float magically before her eyes. "This is no virus," Samantha whispered to herself. "This is something else."

Her curiosity piqued, she brought her chair back to the laptop and sat down. The envelope was obviously begging to be clicked, but would she take the chance? She slid the switch that disabled the system's internal wireless card, then reached around to the side of the machine and removed the network cable running to the router. If she was going to chance this, she was going to completely isolate the laptop from the rest of her network. Apparently, she didn't need the Internet anymore since whatever this was had downloaded itself onto her system.

"Well, here goes..." She held her breath and slid her pointer finger across the laptop touch pad until a small icon appeared, replacing the pointer. It was an eye of some kind, and she was pretty sure it had something to do with Egypt. When the eye reached the center of the envelope, she raised her finger and, holding her breath, tapped the pad once. Hard. Fixated, she watched the image begin to spin wildly in place, and then, like a flash, it flew off the screen. But it left something behind, and she swiftly read over the words.

Dragon Loch Castle
Samantha Sinclair, Your Presence is Requested on the
Evening of October 17th – 6:00 p.m. Sharp
For a Private Meeting of the
Egyptian Tomb Explorers Society
Yours,
Alexander Storm
A Private Car Will Pick You Up at Noon—No RSVP Required

*S*am exhaled and sat back.

"How clever," she said with a smirk, regaining her composure having surmised she wasn't actually under a cyber-attack. "And who is Alex Storm?" Sam was both amused and intrigued at the lengths this person had gone through to pass her a note.

She let out a little laugh and went about getting her network back online. "Sounds like fun."

3

Abigail was scared. The visions that had flashed in her mind's eye were both confusing and horrific. The castle with the burning walls overlooking the sea. The hordes of expressionless corpses marching toward the castle and through its walls of flame. Lightning. Wind. Crashing waves. Through these images of darkness and chaos, a face had appeared. It was the calm and intelligent face of a young man. Abigail thought she had seen his face before, but couldn't remember where or when.

She closed her eyes and tried to picture his face again. It was hard work to wipe away the images that plagued her mind, and try as she did, Abigail couldn't do it. She opened her eyes and ran her fingers through her long black hair, brushing it to one side of her face. She let out a gasp of air as if she had been holding her breath for hours, turned, and walked back into the foyer of her old New Orleans home. There it was—just as she had left it on the crumbling ceramic floor. She had dropped it several hours earlier and had not returned to the entranceway since. The feelings that had drenched her like a storm when she last made contact with the envelope had been overwhelming. Abigail approached the envelope and crouched down above it, holding her knees to her chest. Her hair fell forward and shrouded her in its dark veil. Slowly she extended her hand toward the envelope. Her fingers trembling, she reached for it further, waiting for the images to come rushing back to her. But nothing came. No castles or zombies. Abigail squinted, expecting a mental blow at first touch. But still, the images stayed at bay. She grasped it and stood up quickly, not wanting to waste a moment in case the visions returned. The wind had picked up outside, strengthening, and the branches of the trees and shrubs tapped and rubbed on the sides of the antebellum house. Her eyes darted around the small, dimly lit hallway, and she decided to make for the brighter, inner sanctum of her home before opening it.

She crossed the threshold into the kitchen and flicked on extra light switches. Abigail held the envelope by the corner and waved it back and forth nervously. She slid into the large wooden chair at the head of the kitchen table and stuck the pink nail of her pointer finger behind the envelope's flap. With one smooth move, she quickly tore it open and removed the card from inside. It was parchment paper of some kind, and Abigail immediately noted its thickness and quality. Although she did not have much experience with exotic papers or expensive stationary, she clearly recognized this was both. She hastily threw the empty envelope to the side and grasped the card with both hands. Abigail bowed her head ever so slightly and closed her eyes, waiting for the flood of imagery, just as she had done so many times before. It had been like this since she was a little girl.

When she was just six years old, she woke one morning to Mr. Shag— the family cat— cleaning himself on her bed, purring contently. When Abigail pet him, visions of the night before hit her with blinding force. She watched as Mr. Shag cornered a tiny field mouse and ferociously tore it apart, creating a bloody mess right in front of her. It felt so real. When she was nine and Mr. Reynolds had paid her for his Junior Girl Explorers cookies with a crisp new ten-dollar bill, Abigail watched a series of violent bank robberies unfold, and mild-mannered Reynolds was the perpetrator. She watched, horrified, as Mr. Reynolds flashed a lion-sized grin, then pistol-whipped the clerk into submission. Yes, Abigail Wendell had always been able to see the bad—both past and future—in anything or anyone she touched. She had the "dark touch" as her great grand-nanny had called it.

So, she waited for the initial images to return, perhaps with more clarity and detail. Nothing. She peeked out of her left eye down at the card in her hand. It looked like an invitation of sorts, and when she finally had the courage to read its content, her eyes widened.

Dragon Loch Castle
Abigail Wendell, Your Presence is Requested on the
Evening of October 17th – 6:00 p.m. Sharp
For a Private Meeting of the
Egyptian Tomb Explorers Society
Yours,
Alexander Storm
*A Plane Ticket Will Arrive Shortly—No RSVP Required

4

Alexander Storm ran his finger across the spines of several books before he paused on *The Book of the Dead*, translated by Budge. He pulled the oversized volume from the shelf, blew a thin layer of dust from its cloth shell, and descended the ladder back to the main floor of the library. Dragon Loch's library was like no other. Its massive dimensions fell somewhere around one hundred yards long, sixty yards wide, and three extraordinary stories high equaling over sixty feet to the ceiling. The library was the heart of the castle, quite literally and figuratively. It was the largest room in the ancient structure with sixteen fireplaces, several miles of wall-to-wall, floor-to-ceiling bookshelves, twenty-six three-story domed windows, and over 300 lights. Over the centuries, the library's volumes had been expanded and updated to a monster of unmanageable proportions. An actual count of the books contained therein was somewhat difficult, but Alexander was working to correct this and better organize the entire cataloging system. He had computerized the library's inventory and setup laptop workstations throughout the stacks on all three levels. Alex had also created the audio/video archiving system, taking over the adjacent great hall. He set up a massive network of servers and storage units that fed not only the library, but also provided access to the entire castle as well as a secure wireless transmission. Alexander could access his growing digital archives from anywhere in the world.

Although there were many desks and work areas throughout the library, he had setup his "office without walls," as he called it, right at its center. The area had a massive u-shaped dark wood desk, fifteen feet long in any direction. On it perched several oversized monitors, piles of books and papers, and dozens of random artifacts, trinkets and the like. To one side of the desk was several sets of barrister bookcases with glass fronts, a dozen or so curio cases filled with yet more artifacts, ancient texts and scrolls, a half dozen aging steamer chests, and several standard bookshelves lined with volumes that had been removed from their rightful homes amongst the stacks for research, repair, cataloging and eventual return.

Alexander approached his work area with his newly acquired copy of Budge's translation of ancient Egyptian funerary texts and slid into his high-backed leather chair equipped with rollers that allowed Alex to fly quickly around his office, and at times the entire library. As the sun descended toward the horizon, Alex flipped a few light switches under one of the desks to illuminate the room. Out of the corner of his eye, he saw Phillip, the castle's long-time caretaker, across the room, moving some boxes; or at least attempting to. Alex mused at the accompanying groans and moans that dramatically and sporadically filled the air.

"Hello, Phillip!" Alex shouted. "How are you doing?" There was a brief silence as Philip placed the box he was carrying back onto the floor.

"Quite well, sir. May I get you anything?" Phillip was quite knowledgeable about the library and its contents; he spent all his free time there reading about whatever topic tickled his fancy. Alex liked him immensely.

"No," bellowed Alex. "All is well. Shall I give you a hand with those?"

Alexander listened for a second and heard Phillip mumble as he bent to pick it back up. "I'm not as old as I look you know." Swelling pride evident in his tone, even at the low octave.

"Yes, you are." Alexander shouted with a smile and turned back to the book he had just retrieved. He was sure there was a mistake in the modern, re-edited version he was reviewing.

To no one other than the library's walls, Alex said, "This first edition, combined with an image of the hieroglyphics in question, should help me clear this up." He determined to quickly access a picture from www.kmt-bod.org which had a searchable index of all the texts that comprised the so-called *Book of the Dead*. It would give him a jpeg of the exact section he was working on, and he could translate it himself if need be since he was quite well-versed in ancient Egyptian hieroglyphics. He would use Budge's translation as a guide.

Alex focused on his screen and typed in the domain, taking him to the organization's main page. The letters "KMT" translate to "Egypt" in the ancient tongue and "BOD" is short for *The Book of the Dead*. However, it's not one book, but rather a collection of many different writings found within tombs and written in and on coffins. The words provide spells and charms as well as a guide for the dead to travel to the other side. Alexander was particularly concerned with a verse in a group of writings known as *The Book of Gates*. It is separated into twelve chapters known as "Hours"— quite literally the twelve hours of the night. Each hour instructs a departed soul how to pass safely into the next world. Alex's research over the past months had brought him to *The Book of Gates* and was the impetus in the formation of his emerging group of guests.

Suddenly, laughter, like that of a child, echoed ever so softly. It interlaced with the howling wind whipping the old stone walls of Dragon Loch Castle. But he was certain it was laughter, and the hairs on the back of his neck prickled in agreement. He sprung to his feet, desperately looking for its source. As he suspected, his futile attempts to spy some figure within the confines of the great room yielded nothing. Yet there was something odd occurring in this massive catacomb of knowledge. Alex sensed it. His eyes trained harder on his surroundings. Each of the massive ornate wood pillars supporting the second and third walk-around floors of the library displayed a carved scene; each portrayed history, legend, or myth, and represented various time periods and cultures. One depicting ancient Egypt, by some strange coincidence, incorporated several relief representations of The Book of the Dead. It was here Alex saw the shifting shadows dance as if a candle flicker instigated their unearthly animation.

Alex, filled with no small measure of apprehension, made his way toward the pillar as the forceful wind's cacophony increased. The swirling pressure of the night air rattled the windows, threatening to burst into the room, invading its solemn ground and having its way with the priceless volumes of books. Alex turned once more toward the spot where Phillip had stood a few moments before, hoping a human presence in the room might slow his increasing pulse. But Phillip was no longer there.

The laughter again. Slight. A giggle, perhaps.

Alexander's head spun back around to the Egyptian pillar. This time, the soft whisper no longer swirled with the wind. It had grown closer, more defined, and more malicious. steely eyed, Alex charged toward the noise, his steps echoing through the library. He could hear his own breath sounding in synch with the powerful gusts outside. He had seen and heard many strange things in his years. Things that would drive a normal man, a common man, mad. His tolerance for the unknown, be it supernatural or otherwise, was a discipline he had learned at a young age, and he had carried this fearless nature throughout his life. The fact that his near flaw-less control of his emotions was failing him at this particular moment compounded his growing sense of dread, so much so that the two began to meld together.

Alex tried to escape, but he found himself petrified as Egyptian symbols danced on their wooden canvas, every inch of it crawling with movement, every shape contorting, increasing in tempo, every hieroglyphic racing around the pillar, every image tempestuously tormenting him as the shrill, childlike laughter resounded its maniacal cry louder and louder and faster and faster. Then it stopped. But one section in particular continued to morph. He could see the carved reliefs assembling into something new, and as he cocked his neck to the side, inching a little closer, and squinting to figure out what it could be, it hit him. His eyes snapped wide open, he stumbled backward, reeling in space and time, trying to steady his footing, but suddenly his head wrenched back in disbelief—he knew what it was. It was the judgement scene in The Book of the Dead. A dead man's soul is weighed against Maat—the feather of truth. Also, Alex could make out the great devourer Ammut waiting in the wings to eat the souls of those sentenced to damnation. It was a famous and standard depiction of ancient Egyptian beliefs; however, in this newly formed scene, it was Alex and his freshly recruited group of hopefuls who were being judged. And Ammut was staring out of the wood pillar right at Alexander. Through its exposed teeth, the creature spewed forth the diabolical laughter Alexander had heard before. Ammut's glowing eyes, sunk deep in its leathery, scaled crocodilian-like face, were fixed on Alex; its gaze bored into his soul. Weakened by his fear, he prayed for release from Ammut's glare; within those burning eyes Alex saw the horrible images of his past, but also others foretelling the future. He began to struggle, attempting to free himself from the unforeseen force at his back, locking him in place. The invisible foe persisted in its efforts, there was no freeing himself of Ammut's stare. As if locked in a nightmare, Alexander stared in disbelief as the creature's body began to grow and separate from its wooden prison. It was coming out of the pillar. It was coming for Alexander. His mind raced. How could he defeat this enemy, or at least break free of its grasp long enough to escape? The beast was upon him, face to face, inches away; its breath overtook Alex with a hot, rancid growl. The smell of putrefying flesh and dirt cloaked the creature. The flaws in Alexander's analysis of the laughter became evident as the hollow sounds were now discernible as faint screams oozing out of every pore of the devourer's body. The screams of the millions of souls that had been consumed over the millennia. Alexander could feel the pain of their tortured bodies writhing in agony in the dark eyes of Ammut.

"Be gone, you foul beast!" a voice bellowed from behind Alexander. "Back to the depths from which you came!"

Alexander felt his being diminish as a din of ancient Egyptian chanting began to emanate from behind him. It was the voice of Asar. The man who was always there when he was needed most. The man who had saved his skin far too many times to recall. The man who caught him now as he fell backward toward the ground, exhausted. Asar's archaic dialect belting out powerful commands over the apparition, chasing it back to the nether from which it had come. Alexander's mind became hazy and his vision quickly dimmed. His last sight being that of Ammut disappearing into a mist around the Egyptian pillar. Then Alexander blacked out.

5

William Decker nudged the tip of his boot under the sheet of rotted plywood, then shot his leg out, flipping the board over to expose the dark hole in the ground beneath. The smell of sulfur grew even stronger, and he brought the back of his hand up to his nose to block some of the stench. He quickly composed himself and knelt down to get a better view of the catacomb entrance he had just exposed. The native guides he had brought into the jungle with him spoke in whispers amongst themselves, and he could tell from prior experience they were unnerved and ready to hightail it out of there.

"Aan die brand steek!" William shouted with authority, instructing the African guides to shine some light into the hole. They quickly responded with a battery-powered spotlight whose beam filled the area completely. He quickly popped off his lens cover and took the opportunity to document the opening into the Earth with some digital photos. William Decker, or "Decks" as most knew him, looked the part of most other photojournalists in warlord-torn Africa. He was equipped with the standard issue khaki vest lined with dozens of pockets and compartments rendered useless with the age of digitalization. On his head rested a dirty, sweat stained fedora, and strapped around his neck was an expensive digital camera, its design reminiscent of a less advanced model, which leant some degree of comfort to his often technologically ignorant senses. Balmy and elusive, the breeze teased him with gentle hints of relief. But it disappeared as swiftly as it came. He turned to find his guides had withdrawn some distance back; they knew what was down there. They had propped the light up on the ground with some stones, and the dust and dirt created a beam of filth into the opening. Decks took a step back from the hole as well and dropped to one knee again. He reached under his T-shirt and pulled out a heavy silver chain from beneath. On it were several items, including a crucifix, Saint Patrick and Saint Anthony charms, and other religious symbols. He kissed the cross and dropped the chain on the outside of his shirt.

Decks reached into one of his many pockets and drew out a faded antique matchbox. One side displayed the printed words "Green Goddess" with an image of a green-tinted woman sitting Buddha-style. Printed on the reverse side were two stunning green and red dragons facing in opposite directions. He stared into the hole before him as he brought the box up to his ear and shook it several times. It made a peculiar sound, like dried beans in a paper cup, and he smiled. Using his finger and thumb to slide it open, he exposed a crumpled ball of red tissue paper. Decks delicately pulled it out of the box and placed it in the palm of his left hand. He could hear some movement and shifting behind him as the locals got a little closer to see what he was up to. Didn't they know curiosity killed the cat? He smirked to himself and closed his fist around the box's treasure.

"Boo!" Decks shouted as he spun around on his haunches, springing into the air like a monkey jumping across trees. The men began to shout and run, their dark skin going pale. Decks saw at least two of the guides sprint screaming into the night. Still two others had dropped pretty far back and were huddled together like two kids around a campfire being told ghost stories, their eyes darting in all directions at once, waiting for some unknown, lurking creature to emerge from the dark. Decks laughed out loud and began to turn back to the business at hand when he caught his head guide and assistant Mambaua out of the corner of his eye. He had only retreated a step or two back and looked intently in Decks's direction. His face stoic, his eyes large, Mambaua brought his fist up to his face and extended his pointer finger up to his lips.

"Shhh," Mambaua whispered, "or you're sure to wake that there demon,

Doc." Decks's smile faded quickly, he squinted at Mambaua, then turned his head back toward the hole in the ground.

"And ya surely don't want to be doing that. Aye, Doc?"

Decks turned back to his guide. "No, Mambaua, we surely don't want to do that, at least until we are ready for the bastard, anyway." He turned and trudged back up to the hole. Looking in, his veins surged with adrenaline as he hunched down, turning his attention back to the crumpled paper in his hand.

William Decker was no ordinary photojournalist out on the African plains on a quest to capture stereotypical images or produce commentary on the human condition. Decks had begun his career of "documenting" the unknown, the inexplicable, almost thirty years earlier. He had been attending the Pontifical University of St. Anthony, a prestigious seminary school in Italy, when he was approached by emissaries from the Vatican. He had developed a bit of reputation among both his instructors and peers as having more than a passing interest in the paranormal and the occult. Decks was extremely knowledgeable on the myths and legends of many cultures and had studied most of the church's modern reports of supernatural occurrences, including possessions. The two Vatican representatives offered Decks the opportunity to do some real hands-on investigation in Germany under the auspices of the Church, after which he would report his findings directly to them. Words like "fast track" and "consider it a favor" were thrown about, and Decks, blessed with the ignorance of youth, had eagerly accepted the pair's offer.

After several weeks of intense research and observation in Germany, Decks had drafted a preliminary report and returned to Rome to meet with his superiors. He had envisioned a grand inquest-type proceeding in which he would report his stunning findings to a group of wise and elderly church officials. Afterward, he would be praised for his fine work and perhaps invited to stay on at the Vatican, investigating any supernatural claims that might arise, feeding his ego and stirring his excitement. What he got instead was a cold, cell-like debriefing room where he was told why his findings were false by three people—the two recruiters and a man he had never met before. This third individual wore the garb and demeanor of a high-ranking church official, however, he never identified himself. Decks tried desperately to convince the trio they were mistaken, but his arguments fell on deaf ears. He was escorted back to St. Anthony's, and the next morning he received a note asking him to pack his bags as there was no longer a place for him there.

Decks returned to the United States and his native New York where he began attending St. Joseph's Seminary in Yonkers. Although he tried his best to remain focused on his studies, his work in Germany, and its utter dismissal, consumed his thoughts. It was a short time after returning to New York that Decks was introduced to Alexander Storm and the two became good friends. It seemed the Storm family had quite a history in the fields of paranormal study and the occult. Storm made Decks the editor of a paranormal watchdog publication known as *The Supernatural Sentinel*, enabling him to travel the world following up on reports of the paranormal, the strange, and the downright evil. Decker had soon discovered that most of the tips and all of his publication's funding continued to flow from one man, Alexander Storm. Storm even maintained the project's web site at www.supernaturalsentinel.org.

At the cavern's entrance, Decks began to unwrap the delicate tissue paper, tipping the contents over into his palm. It was a large rattlesnake rattle. Gently, he cupped the curious treasure and shook it, and the small fragments danced in their serpentine shell. He looked around and listened, eyes fixed on the hole's opening. Nothing. He closed his fingers around the rattle in frustration, completely enveloping it, and shook it harder. This time, he heard the unmistakable moan rise from down below. He turned, smiling toward Mambaua—but the man was gone. Slightly panicked, Decks scanned the landscape. Everyone was gone.

6

Keith Zauberer's interest in ancient Egypt was purely the product of his feelings for Kate. At her suggestion, he had happily co-authored one paper and researched several others for her. The topics always addressed the obscure, as in the largely unpublicized Egyptian city of Tanis, to the use of spells and magic in every day ancient Egyptian life. The two worked well together, there was no mistaking it, and Keith loved the extra time he got to spend with Kate. Their writing always applied some type of supernatural spin to a seemingly mundane issue. It was this, the paranormal and bizarre, that was more up to speed with Keith's own interests.

As he pulled his apartment door closed behind him, he wondered if it was the Tanis paper that was responsible for the invite to a very select meeting with the Egyptian Tomb Explorers Society. They had certainly flushed out some great historical points, but their analysis of the mystical aspect of their supernatural findings never made the pages of the intellectual publication. Keith turned his key in the door and heard the dead-bolt slide into place with a click. He unzipped the side pocket on his knapsack, shoved his *Lord of the Rings* keychain in, and slid the bag onto his back. He turned to face the night, which was actually pretty cold, and began walking toward Kate's house. Keith remembered when the two had first discussed working on the Tanis paper together, well over two years ago.

"Keith, my dear," Kate had blurted out over burgers at the local diner. "Do you want to write an article with me?"

"No," Keith replied with a mouth full of fries.

"Why? Come on. It'll be fun! It's a great topic."

"Let me guess. Some ancient civilization like Greece, or Rome—or, of course, Egypt. And some dusty old dirty thing that professor 'I'm an old geezer' found after digging for ten years. Right? No way." Keith looked down at the burger in his hands and sunk his teeth in for a huge bite. He knew he might not get another chance for some time to come.

"What?" shouted Kate as she tossed a fry at Keith from across the table. He bobbed his head in avoidance and continued chewing.

"Is that what you think of my research? Old and useless?" Kate said, feigning emotional injury, while reaching for her diet soda.

"No." Keith finally swallowed and looked up at Kate. "Listen, you do research on lots of topics, and I think that's great. It's what makes you who you are. But I have a hunch when you ask me to work on something, it's gonna be some historical mumbo-jumbo, and between school and work, I don't have a lot of extra time."

"Work?" Kate laughed, flinging another fry in Keith's direction. This one found its mark, hitting him in his forehead and dropping to his lap.

Oh, no, here it comes, Keith thought.

"What work would that be?" Kate inquired with a grin.

"Well, it's funny you should ask. To start with, I've just recently been hired by the managers of this very establishment to clean up after you," Keith said with a smile, picking up the fry from his lap and eating it.

Kate let out a slight laugh and regained her composure. She didn't want to encourage him. She tried to shift back into serious mode.

"Listen, it's a great topic—the ancient city of Tanis," Kate said with enthusiasm. So much enthusiasm, in fact, that Keith really didn't want to bust on her again. But he couldn't resist.

"Tanis, huh? So we're going to write about things like snake pits and Indiana Jones?"

Kate looked at him straight-faced. "I'll just ignore that and continue.

That was a make-believe Tanis in a movie. I'm referring to the real Egyptian city of Tanis."

"Oh, sorry." Keith knew when to quit. "So, what's so exciting about the real city of Tanis?"

Kate smiled. She had been waiting for him to ask. "Well, how about the fact that the people of ancient Egypt saw fit to bury their Tanis pharaohs in solid silver coffins?"

"Really?" Keith sat forward slightly in their little diner booth.

"Or the fact that many of those same kings have statues of themselves looking suspiciously like giant wolves." Kate said this with great satisfaction —she knew it would reel him in, hook, line, and sinker. Keith's interests ran a little darker than basic archaeology and history. He liked to read about the supernatural and the occult, magic and mysteries. She knew ancient Egyptian werewolves would certainly float his boat. She was right.

"Okay, sounds like it might be cool. I'm in," Keith said with some degree of subdued excitement.

"I know you're in," Kate whispered with a devilish grin. "You'll do whatever I ask you."

"You got me." Keith whispered. This time *he* threw the fry.

~

He had walked five or six blocks while reflecting on their conversation and was about halfway to Kate's. As he rounded the corner onto Willow Drive, Keith smiled at the memory of the fry throwing fiasco, as it had become known amongst their circle of two. His thoughts, however, were snapped back to reality as a wicked sensation rippled through his body. It almost felt like someone had tapped him ever so slightly on the shoulder. A soft touch, barely discernible through his heavy wool coat, but a touch nonetheless. He spun around expecting to find someone there, perhaps Kate, who had a penchant for sneaking up on him, meeting him half way. But there was no one. He swung his backpack around to make sure all the pockets were closed—maybe someone was trying to pick his pack. He chuckled at the sound of "pick his pack," which was good. It helped him relax a bit. After scanning his surroundings, he determined everything looked normal. However, it was a bit too quiet. Come to think of it, he hadn't seen many cars pass by. At least not that he could recall. He started to walk again, trying to keep his imagination at bay. Why hadn't he just taken his car?

"Cheap fool," he muttered to himself. He picked up his pace a little, mainly due to the fact he was sure he was being watched. He could feel it— after increasing to a full-blown run, he was sure whoever or whatever had been watching was chasing him.

Never run from a dog—it'll just chase you, boy. He could hear the words his father had told him as a child in his head for no good reason at all. *Where did that memory come from?* he thought as he ran harder *It must be that damn Tanis article – silver coffins and fucking werewolves.*

It touched him again!

But this time it wasn't just a little tap on the shoulder. No, this time it felt like someone had pushed their fingers into his hair and ran them down his neck, trying to drag him backward.

"Oh my God!" he shrieked. Refusing to turn around he tried to run faster now, as fast as he could. He couldn't turn around; he wouldn't turn around. He'd have to stop to do that, and no way was he stopping. He didn't need to see what was chasing him, toying with him. His imagination was doing a great job of conjuring up images of the creature-feature character on his tail. He saw the corner of Vine Street ahead and considered just running right into someone's house. Banging on a door, breaking through a window, whatever it would take to escape the clutches of the phantom on his heels. But, then again, would some measly pieces of wood and glass really protect him?

"Just keep running," he desperately groaned out loud, barley able to breathe, but unable to stop. He made it to the corner of Vine. He felt the touch of icy fingers at the nape of his neck again. His blood ran cold. Eyes wide with panic, Keith would have to turn and face his attacker—he was out of options. Just then, the fingers grasped tightly around his hair and snapped his head back. Hard. Keith's body followed his head and he landed flat on his back with a bone crunching smash onto the cement below. There, on the corner of Vine Street, one block from Kate's house, Keith was sure he was about to meet his end. He had hit his head hard enough on the cold concrete to be knocked out and he could feel himself slipping in and out of consciousness. He tried to keep his eyes open, tried to push himself to get up. To fight or to run. But from what? Try as he might, it was hopeless. He couldn't move. And now he smelled the stink. His eyes flickered with recognition as his stomach turned on itself. It smelled like that raccoon that had died in his Grandfather's attic a few summers ago. Except this stench, though akin to the creature's rotting carcass, was a thousand times worse. The sweet and putrid stink of death poured into his nostrils, and all he could do was try not to pass out. Slowly, two gleaming red dots moved menacingly into view and toward his face. Two glowing red eyes—crimson pupils with deep black slits in the center like a snake. The eyes seemed to float in on him from the dark sky until he had nowhere else to look. He had to move.

"Help me, someone! Please!" he cried out with his last gasp of energy. There was no answer, only a hollow nothingness. It was too late, for the hands were upon him, squeezing mercilessly, clamping cruelly. Keith instinctively closed his eyes, but he couldn't block out the bright light radiating through his lids, and it occurred to him this could be it. The end. Suddenly, the blaring of a car horn pierced the silent night, forcing the deadly fingers from his throat. Then someone shouted from a distance, "Hey, you okay over there?" Keith felt some movement around him, but at least he knew it was human. The smell of death had dissipated, so he decided he could let go of the last thread of consciousness and allow himself pass out. And he did.

Alexander tried to focus on the objects around him, but his vision was still a bit hazy. He sat up and rubbed his piercing blue eyes in an attempt to remove some of the remaining fog, then realized he was on the large leather couch in his study. He could make out the fire crackling and roaring in the great fireplace across the room. Alexander felt the flames' radiance flicker on his face, and it comforted him to some degree. It highlighted the intricately carved stone mantel over the fireplace depicting the head of a great dragon at the center, its wings stretched out in either direction. The dragon's head looked down from on high, its beastly snout protruding out into the fireplace, creating the illusion of flames spiraling from its nostrils.

Taking a deep breath, he removed the blanket Asar must have covered him with and got to his feet; even though he still felt a trifle woozy, he would tough it out. He brushed his jet-black hair to the side and walked over to the desk located to the right of the fireplace. This desk had survived the generations at Dragon Loch castle and held a special place in the heart of its current resident. The oversized roll-tops deep wood tones and fine craftsmanship made it one of the most stunning items in the entire castle. Alexander sat, retrieving a sheet of fine parchment and pen from the wood and tusk inlaid box on the desk. He set pen to paper and began to write. Transcribing as much as he could recall regarding the incident at the Egyptian pillar. Alexander viewed the event, aside from being a bizarre tryst into the realms of the paranormal, as a warning of some sort and he needed to record the details while they were fresh in his mind. A deeper analysis of the foreboding visions was called for and he approached the endeavor through the scientific method; paying heed to not focus on the metaphysical aspects of the episode. This was the way he had always approached his run-ins with the inexplicable. This objective often presented its own set of difficulties. How does one proceed in a logical fashion when the very substance of the matter defies all logic?

"Ahem." Asar cleared his throat at the entrance to the study. Alexander looked up at him and nodded with thanks and invitation.

"Always so proper, Asar," Alex smirked. "Please, barge in for once."

"I see you are feeling better, Alexander. I am glad," Asar crossed the threshold of the study and approached the seated Storm. He was an Egyptian native, born and raised in the shadow of the great pyramid in a small village on the outskirts of Giza. His build was strong and his olive skinned, bearded face was kind, yet stern. He reached out his hefty hand and placed it firmly on Alexander's shoulder. Pursing his lips together, Asar nodded once. That would be the extent of it—they could get on with the business at hand.

Alex turned and rose as he asked, "So, Asar, tell me—why do you think Ammut saw fit to pay us a visit this bleak night?" His study had been constructed in the center of the castle, safeguarded from outside walls, so he could not see or hear the current weather conditions. Alexander began to pace the floor, a habit he exhibited when in deductive thought.

"Tell me, Asar, is the weather still ablaze with despair?"

"Not as bad, I believe, but still some wind. Perhaps the storm is passing?" Asar's fine English accent, which he acquired through his studies at the University of Cambridge many years earlier, seemed seeped in worry and disinterested in purveying thoughts on the current weather conditions. Although he had resided in the United States for many years now, the thick tones of his British influences remained intact. A noble trademark, Alexander believed.

"Do you think the weather has something to do with the creature's visit?" Asar puzzled at his colleagues line of inquiry.

"No, not really. Just wanted to know."

Alex stopped pacing and looked at Asar. "So, what do we know about Ammut? What is this creature's modus operandi? I, myself, have always considered Ammut one of the good guys meting out justice in a most powerful and absolute manner, wouldn't you say?"

Asar pondered the question. He never answered too quickly, yet another of his noble qualities; a sigil of refinement. Hints of anger began to peek through as expanded on the line of inquiry, as opposed to rendering an answer. "And moreover, what does he want with you, Alexander?"

"Well, although I am somewhat skeptical, it would appear Ammut wants the same thing every filthy, vile, evil entity in our world wants. To see me come to an end."

M oloch sat outside the crowded terminal area of the Long Island Rail Road at Penn Station. From his vantage point, he could watch all the passengers arriving at the station as they exited the various track gates. He had been waiting patiently for Dr. Ebbers to arrive from the Hamptons for several hours now, and he was beginning to think the good doctor may have changed his mind about selling the ancient documents.

"Spare some change buddy? Nickel, dime, quarter? Dollar if you're feeling generous." Moloch glanced at the tall beggar and quickly looked back to the gates, dismissing the filthy rogue.

"Hey, man. You deaf?" The vagrant raised his voice slightly and stepped a bit closer. Moloch turned and fixed his eyes on those of the man for no more than a second, but it was long enough. The man's head snapped back, away from Moloch, and his gaze fell to the floor. His brow wrinkled tightly, and a deep frown emerged as the panhandler stumbled away in a fog of confusion.

Moloch sat motionless, watching the new herd of travelers pile into the station. He wore a dark wool overcoat with six red and green ruby-encrusted buttons. His black hair was long and straight, and it seemed to blend into his jacket like a hood. Moloch's eyes, chillingly dark blue, like the fathomless depths of the Arctic's icy waters, penetrated the droves of commuters in search of his prey.

Finally, spotting his target, Moloch stood up and began to move toward the scattering mass of lemmings. Ebbers had arrived on the 1:46 p.m. train from Babylon, three hours later then agreed. Shoving his way through the crowd, he moved quickly toward the doctor, who was moving slowly through the crowd, scanning his surroundings with apparent apprehension. He looked to be in his sixties, with hair meticulously unkempt and a gray beard trimmed into various states of disarray. Moloch noted his finely tailored suit and surmised that it represented the air of refinement the doctor must have once possessed. In his left hand was a black leather briefcase, in his right, a sheet of paper. Moloch found himself a few feet from his target when he caught site of the two ethereal figures rushing in from either side straight at Ebbers. They were coming in quickly, pushing rudely through people in their path. Their movements, phantasmic like as they were, appeared to pass right through those in their path. Ebbers spotted Moloch and raised the briefcase up in front of him with a nervous smile of relief. The crowd was tight at this juncture of the station, and Moloch wanted out—fast. His dark eyes darted from side to side as he tried to calculate a possible escape route. Ebbers followed his glance to his right, immediately catching sight of one of the shadowy figures closing in, and whirled around to dash back to the safety of the departing train.

"Doctor," Moloch hissed to the frightened shell of a man. "Don't move." He swooped in with an unnatural motion and held open his long coat, engulfing Ebbers in its folds. Their faces inches apart, the doctor finally got a good look at Moloch, and his body began to tremble. He looked down at the floor for an instant, and when he raised his head, Moloch was gone. Dr. Ebbers looked to his right just in time to see the phantom figure hurtling toward him. He turned his head away and squinted his eyes, bracing his body for the inevitable impact. The figure smashed against him like a wave kissing a wall of breakers...then vanished in a whirl of mist. Ebbers, still bracing for an impact that never came, opened his eyes just in time to see the other apparition burst into a mist of nothingness around him. The cowering man began to whimper. He swung his head from side to side looking for more ghostly figures, but found only scurrying commuters moving in every direction, oblivious to the otherworldly act that had just played out. Oblivious to the fact that events had just transpired, right before their eyes, which would threaten their very existence. Oblivious to the war which had just begun. Ebbers looked down at his hands. It took a moment to register in his confused mind, but he finally realized the briefcase was gone. Moloch had taken it.

"What have I done," cried the doctor? "My God, what have I done?"

9

Samantha pulled into the parking lot of the local Quickie Mart convenience store and dropped the stand on her new Harley. She had picked up the motorcycle for herself a few months back after a huge corporate coding job paid off big. Her windfall had inspired her to splurge on something she would never normally even consider buying, but always secretly wanted. She had walked into the showroom and seen the bike on the floor. Glacier white pearl with a black leather seat and chrome everywhere the eye could see. It looked sleek. It looked fast. And quite frankly, it looked fun. So, after contemplating for a few minutes, she gave the pimple-faced salesman following her around the easiest sale of his career. She had called her father that night, excited to share her news, and all she got was a half-hour lecture on the inherent dangers of motorcycles and the benefits of saving unexpected income for retirement or a rainy day or whatever people her father's age think it should be saved for. She didn't let it spoil her fun, though. It was nights like tonight that made her really appreciate her lack for frugality. Cool and clear. Great for riding, even if it was only three blocks for beer and chips. Sam had bought a black helmet at the same time, and her friend Matt had painted lightning bolts and an artistic mass of wires and glowing colors on it. She loved the helmet and decided to top off her flashy setup with a plate which read WIRED4SPD.

Samantha turned off the engine and swung her denim clad leg over the seat. Freeing it from the prison of her helmet, her long blonde hair cascaded across the sides of her face. Off to the side, a group of teenage boys had been eyeing the motorcycle, now they were eyeing the driver, whistling and mumbling unintelligible cat calls. Sam ignored them and headed into the store. She stepped into the florescent lights, and her nose was assaulted with an unappetizing mix of coffee, nachos, and those hot dogs that just keep rolling. She looked at two men behind the counter, who seemed to be arguing over something in their native tongue. Samantha wasn't sure if it was Indian or Pakistani, but she knew it was something along those lines. Although she frequented the establishment, often for dinner unfortunately, there always seemed to be different people behind the counter. She turned and headed toward the back row of refrigerated cases.

"No! No!" one of the men shouted from behind her. She looked over her shoulder and saw the two continuing to argue. One of the men was tapping the back of his hand into the palm of his other and pacing side to side, while the other, the one saying no, was waving his hands around wildly. Sam felt her cell phone vibrate in her pocket, and she slid it out. Even though the screen read "unavailable," she accepted the call.

"Hello?" she said. Nothing—dead air. "Hello?" she said again. "You'll have to call back. I can't hear you." Sam ended the call and went to put it in her pocket when it began to vibrate. Annoyed, Sam answered again. But this time, she quickly pulled it away from her ear. Nothing but static, and loud static at that. She must have audibly reacted because the two men behind the counter stopped their bickering and turned to look at her.

"Everything okay, miss?" the hand slapper asked.

"Can we help you with something?" the wild waver added.

"Ice cream?" she said, even though she knew where it was. She slid her phone back into the pocket of her jeans and waited for a response.

"Yes, we have many kinds—all are very good," said the hand slapper, using them now for pointing rather than slapping.

"Thanks." As she turned back toward the ice cream, she felt her phone vibrate yet again.

No reception in here. They'll have to leave a message or call back, she thought. As she reached her destination of frozen delights, she heard one of the men yelling something else to her that she couldn't make out.

"Got it! Thanks!" she yelled back, and she went about the business of picking a tub of ice cream from their "many kinds" which only equated to five.

"Coffee looks good tonight," she said to herself, reaching for her prize, she paused in her descent into the freezer burnt depths as her cell vibrated *again*. Shaking her head, she ignored the dull hum. Sam grabbed the icy container and let the glass door fall closed. As the glass came back into view, she found herself staring face to face with the hideous and repulsive reflection of a creature. Burning red eyes pierced her own; rows of gnashing teeth protruded from its jaw to form an insidious grimace. Shrieking, she dropped the ice cream onto her foot, instinctively forcing her to look down. When she glanced back, the beast had vanished. Searching up and down the rows of chips and candy, she was unable to locate any traces of the ghastly beast. Heart still pounding, she ran along the wall of frosted glass doors, scanning each, hesitantly at first, for the toothy apparition. Sam's commotion must have sufficiently alarmed the pair of arguing counter jockeys, as the hand waver was hurriedly making his way to the refrigerated section of the store.

"Is something wrong, miss?" he whispered soothingly in an obvious attempt to curtail Sam's mounting state of excitement.

"Yes," Samantha snapped back, her facial color presenting signs of embarrassment. "I saw something."

"What did you see?" The clerk replied.

She paused for a minute. *I saw a monster, and I'm very scared, and you don't look like you or your buddy will be of much help*, she thought to herself.

"I saw a big bug," escaped her lips instead. "A big, giant black bug, and it ran into the cooler."

The clerk looked at her for a moment, then turned to pick up the fallen tub of coffee ice cream. When he stood up to face Sam, his eyes burned red, and he smiled at her—the same rows of sharp, distorted teeth clogged with rancid pieces of meat and debris now painted his unnaturally wide grin. Terror overwhelmed her and almost rendered her frozen in place, but after her instincts to flee kicked in, she howled with dread and whirled around to run...run as fast as she could toward the door, and hopefully, escape. Her legs propelled her past the chips and around the corner where she noticed the clerk had not moved; he was standing there dumbfounded, holding the melting tub of ice cream. His face had transformed back to its normal Indian or Pakistani self. She had had enough, she wanted out. But after she rounded the corner of the last isle and dashed past the front counter, something within caused her to pause just short of the door. Perhaps it was the unknown that awaited her in the darkness beyond the threshold that betrayed her muscles.

"He awaits you, Samantha. He waits for you in the darkness where screams are silenced and time is no more," whispered the hand slapper, still behind the counter.

"What?" screamed Sam in disbelief as she pivoted around to meet his words. He wore a mask of shock and confusion, obviously dumbfounded at the words that had just departed his lips, and backed away from the counter. *That's enough! What's happening?* And with that, she bolted out the door into the night, the convenience store door smacking the brick-wall in response to her forceful exit. Retrieving her helmet from the handlebar grip where she had hung it, she pressed it over her head with force, paying no mind to her long blonde hair which flowed out the back like a gilded cape. The bike responded with growl as she pressed the ignition button. Shifting her weight, she righted the motorcycle, freeing the kickstand from the pavement, and heeled it securely back. Glancing up, she noticed the group of boys who had whistled at her on the way in. They were huddled together with their backs to her, messing with something on the ground. As Sam focused on them, she quickly realized they appeared to be violently kicking at something. She could now make out their monotone, mid-pubescent laughter, giggling at whatever mindless nonsense they were up to.

"Hey! What are you punks up to?" The group did not respond. She gently throttled the bike and pulled it around to the gang of hoodie-clad teens. Their laughter growing louder as she approached until the din of their communal enjoyment exceeded sound of her bike's exhaust.

"What's so funny?" she yelled. She watched as they stepped back from the target of their group attack in slow unison, laughing, their hoods obscuring their faces from her view. Samantha walked her bike forward, parting the dispersing circle of teens at its center, and looked down at the ground. *Oh my God!* There was a person lying face down on the pavement. She jumped off the bike, paying no mind to the grinding echoes of impacting chrome, and dropped to one knee over to the helpless victim of the hoodlum's assault.

"Oh my God!" she yelled. "Are you all fucking insane?" She knelt down and touched the body—it was a woman. Something looked familiar about her, and she grabbed at the fallen women's shoulder and rolled her over. Sam's eyes snapped opened at the revelation of the horror beneath her. Samantha's mind reeled in disbelief and confusion as she starred down at her own beaten body. Her face bruised and bloody thanks to the kicks and punches of the teenage boys. Her long hair matted in blood and torn from her scalp. She felt her head begin to swim and her vision begin to blur. Rising to her feet, her balance quickly gave way to stumbling as she lost her footing and fell forward. Samantha could still hear the echoes of the group's awful laughter all around her as she passed out on top of her beaten and bloody doppelganger.

10

William Decker heard the discord of sliding dirt and stone behind him before he saw it, and he spun around to face the dark hole he had exposed a few minutes earlier. He had been thrown off by the apparent mutiny of his entire guide crew and had lost track of the gaping cavern burrow but for a second. The malignant demon had snatched the opportunity to forge into the night air from its dark, damp hiding spot. Decks felt the tight grasp around his right ankle, the bony fingers digging into his skin. His face flushed with blood as the tentacles of panic attempted to take hold of his being. Fighting the roots of fear back with a burst of assuring breath, he peered down at his imperiled limb. Spinning slightly to the left, he allowed the rays from the propped light to hit his body, exposing the wretched hand and arm pulling on his leg. Decks could not resist—he raised his camera and managed to get a burst of shots off. The white heat of the flash illuminated the gash in the earth and bounced colorless light off the devil's eyes.

"Wait 'till Storm gets a load of these!" Decks growled in a tone drenched in enthusiastic accomplishment. With the skill of a Rockstar spinning a guitar around his body, he whipped the camera to his back and fumbled with the reptilian cartilage that was still in his hand. Holding the rattlesnake rattle loosely, he began to shake it again. Softly at first, then with increased fervor as he felt the demon's grip loosen. The vigorous rhythm of his hand came to a climax as the creature retreated back into its lair. Loud moans emanated from the mouth of the dark hole. Groans so hideous and violent they made Decks's blood ice-over in the African heat. The realization that he was free of the fiend came as a sudden shock and Decks stumbled backward causing the rattle's intensity to slow. The momentary decrease in the snake tails spellbinding song was all the demon required in order to break free of its trance. Decker did not panic. It was all part of the plan – part of the process of exercising the evil from this plane of being. With renewed confidence, he inched backward allowing the monster to come forth from the hole, vengeance burning in its cold, dead eyes. Intense concentration crept across Deck's brow as he drew it out into the open. He was well aware of his singularity of chances to accomplish the task at hand. By the deceptive light of the night's sun, he finally got a good look at the demon which had parasitically twisted and withered the body of its host. According to Decks's research in the local village, a young man named Tador had been stricken ill over two months ago. He had been brought to the local infirmary, and shortly thereafter, had morphed into the creature Decks saw before him now. The teen was possessed by an Abiku— an ancient African demon known for its extremely ravenous appetite for human flesh.

Decker had come prepared. He was not about to become some ghoul's goulash. He smirked at his witty wordplay and reached for his largest vest pocket with his free hand. Without warning, like a lion stalking its prey, the Abiku leaped from its crouched position in front of the hole and violently snatched at Decks, barely missing its mark. The demon had desecrated the young villager's body; its skin was consumed with pussing sores and rancid lesions. Not unlike a spider empties the inner fluids of the webbed butter-fly, the Abiku had drained the color from the teen's hair leaving it white as snow. Having undergone a golem-like transformation, the beast no longer possessed the qualities of its former self. The malicious spirit lunged at Decks with wild abandoned burning in its deeply sunken dead eyes. The creature's mouth drawn wide; Decker gazed in disgust at the possessions effect on its host. A split and rotting tongue was framed by rows of rancid, decaying teeth. He blinked once to clear the imagery from his minds eye and fumbled to open his pocket. With eyes transfixed on the monster, his fingers fumbled about his pocket. Decker smirked as the nerve endings on the tips of his fingers finally identified their objective. He began to shake the rattle with increased strength as a heightened sense of resolve took root. Removing a large, rectangular block of red wax from his pocket, he shifted his body forward. Shaking the rattle with Dervish intensity to hold the apparition at bay, Decks brought the wax block up to his mouth and bit into it, exposing the tip of the glass vial that had been entombed within. He tried feebly to use the thumb of his right hand to peel away the rest of the wax, but was unable to accomplish the task one-handed.

"Shit!" Decks yelled, tossing the rattlesnake tail to the ground to free his other hand. Like a child on Christmas morning, Decker went to work on the wax shell. Encasing the glass vial in wax to protect it seemed like a great idea back in the States; however, it now proved far too cumbersome in the field. With Decks preoccupied, the Abiku, free of the snake's charms and sensing its prey's mounting fear, seized the moment and charged forward. Teeth gnashed up and down from within its demented smile, manic eyes bulged from sunken nests and the demon raced forward with a blood-curdling cry. Decks removed the last patch of wax which had been stuck to the neck of the vial and flung himself forward to engage the raging creature. The Abiku was on him now and Decker struggled to maintain the focus of his objective as its jaw contorted in metaphysical ripples and dislodged. Decks could see the multiple rows of teeth lining the inside of the Abiku's oral cavity, and the fatal flaws in his timing became all to evident as he prepared to be torn apart.

Like the powerful clap of igniting dynamite, the shot rang out from behind Decker with thunderous echoes, throwing the Abiku back with the impact of the blast, stunning it, and rendering it pliable to Decker's counterattack. A stunned Decker smiled with relief as he righted himself. There was no need for him to investigate the source of his rescue. Without turning, he raised his arm in thanks. Mambaua standing several feet behind him, shotgun in hand, allowed a rare wide grin to form.

"I thought you had left me as well!" Decks shouted thank you in his savior's native tongue. "Dankie!"

"Don't mention it, Doc," replied Mambaua, raising the gun again and leveling it at the creature beginning to stir on the ground. "Abiku only down for a second. Better do your thing."

Decks turned back to the creature and lifted the auburn vial up to the light. He quickly unscrewed the silver top and tossed it aside. As he walked toward the beast, Decks pulled out a dagger-like contraption with a threaded cylinder at one end. Bringing the two items together, he screwed the dagger like a spout onto the top of the vial. The demon gained some sense of lucidity again and was up on all fours like some primordial quadruped. *86[Decks grasped the vial like the handle of a knife and began his move forward to meet the Abiku. Sensing its prey's new found confidence, the monster cried out and rushed at Decker on all fours like a scurrying rodent. Mambaua raced forward and fell in at his friend's side. Decker glanced over, and grew puzzled watching Mambaua drop to the ground flat on his stomach.

"What the hell are you doing? This is no time for lying down! Get up and get out of here!" Decks yelled. Before he could even finish his cautionary directive, Mambaua fired another shot into the chest of the demon, sending it reeling backward, flipping it like a tortoise on its shell.

"Now you finish him, Doc," Mambaua said with quiet intensity. "Now you send him back to Kuzimo."

Decks nodded and leapt forward, landing on top of the Abiku that was struggling to recover from the firearms blast. Straddling the creature, he thrust his left hand down and grasped the demon's neck, pressing it flat to the jungle's damp, fertile ground. Clutching the knife, he lifted his free hand up into the African night and prepared to deliver a powerful blow to the fiend's chest. Decker paused momentarily, causing Mambaua to call out in puzzled encouragement. Out of the corner of his eye, Decker had sensed the slightest hint of movement in the dark jungle before him. He squinted for a moment, arm still stretched above his head, and strained to make out the faint silhouette of a lion-like creature in the distance. As the distant apparition came into focus, Decker could make out its blazing red eyes and its face encrusted with green scaly skin. Shaking off the vision, Decker returned his focus to the more immediate threat; the Abiku writhing below him. Now was his chance—he could delay no more. With one smooth, forceful thrust, he plunged the silver blade of the dagger into the demon.

Relinquishing his hold on the beast's neck, he placed both hands on the top of his metaphysical weapon and held it in place. For what seemed an eternity, Decker watched the contents of the vile empty into the demon chest. The Abiku suddenly began to buck wildly, sensing its own impending demise, and knocked Decks to the ground.

"Don't shoot!" he commanded as he began to scramble around the jungle floor in search of the snake's tail, "you'll knock the vial out!" Mambaua nodded and relaxed his tension on the trigger.

"Gotcha'!" Decker yelled, rising to his feet. He scanned the area for any traces of menacing figure he had seen seconds earlier, but it had disappeared. The cries of demonic agony drew his attentions back to the task at hand and he resumed his orchestration with the rattle.

"Keep an eye on our surroundings, Mambaua, will you?"

The guide nodded. Decks turned back to the demon. It was no longer convulsing. Instead, its head was titled back, and its mouth was fixed open widely. Glowing mist wafted out of every orifice in the poor villager's face. Decks, sensing the final act was at hand, stepped forward and shook the rattle vigorously.

"Insit sonder uitgaan. Insit sonder uitgaan. Insit sonder uitgaan!" Decks chanted over and over, demanding the creature "enter without exit." The ethereal haze began to dissipate and pull away from Decks as if it was still made of flesh and bone.

"Insit sonder uitgaan. Insit sonder uitgaan!" Decks held out his clenched fist and opened his fingers, exposing the rattle in his palm. The spirit tried to resist the magnetism pulling it closer and closer to reptilian cartilage. Once again, with well practiced movements, he swiveled the camera around his body and captured the demon's floating essence.

"Insit sonder uitgaan!" The mist funneled down to the rattle like a genie into a lamp. Relief swept over Decks—it was over. The final movements in this dark dance of the macabre were coming to conclusion. Pressing his luck, he captured one more burst of images. Bad move – he quickly surmised. He released the camera, allowing it to slam into his hip, as the lingering tail of phantasmic mist wrapped around his neck like a python around a rat. Mambaua leaped to his friend's aid, but Decker staved off his approach, stopping him dead in his tracks with an outstretched hand.

"Insit sonder uitgaan! Insit sonder uitgaan!" Decks gasped the words, forcing them through the assault on his throat. At last succumbing to the incantation, the demonic mist relinquished its last vestiges of physical being and disappeared into the rattle.

Decks rubbed his throat and stretched his neck.

"Close one. Aye, pal?" he asked turning to Mambaua.

Mambaua said nothing, starring at him stoically. Spinning from Decker, he lowered his weapon and began to walk back toward the expedition's camp. Decks smiled and reached into his vest, pulling out the matchbox. He slid it open and unraveled the delicate red tissue paper. Gently, he placed the rattle containing the essence of the demon into the folds of the paper and slid shut the cardboard sarcophagus. Placing the matchbox in his pocket, he tapped the outside of his vest victoriously.

"I think we'll just hold onto you for now," Decks said. Turning his attention to the dead villager, he bent down and gently rolled the limp body into the hole in the ground.

"Sorry buddy," he whispered as he placed the board back on the opening and stuck a large branch into the ground next to it. Using a white handkerchief he carried with him, he tied a makeshift flag to the branch. This would allow the man's fellow villagers to either come get him in the morning for a proper burial or stay clear of the area; the more likely of the two options he surmised.

"A contagious demon! Ha!" Decks laughed out loud. He bent down and picked up the light from the ground and set out in tow behind his friend. But the hairs on his neck caused his body to halt—there, in the darkness where he had seen the strange beast earlier, something shifted. He quickly shined the light into the night. Nothing!

"Doc! Come on now, man," Mambaua shouted from further up the trail. Decks shook his head and fell in behind.

"I'm coming, Mambaua!" he shouted back. "Just checking for contagious demons." A thought he was now finding much less humorous.

11

Alexander Storm approached the steep cliff overlooking the Atlantic Ocean at the north end of Dragon Loch Island. He peered over the edge, down into the water over two-hundred feet below and watched as the waves crashed against the side of the island with a thunderous roar. His ebony hair blew to one side as a westerly wind swept across the landscape, kicking up leaves and debris. He turned his back to the gusts and looked up at the sky. There was a new chill in the air brought about by the previous night's heavy rainfall. Alex pulled his long jacket tightly around his chest and neck as he watched a small patch of clouds sail by. In under twenty-four hours, his guests would be arriving. All except Decks, who was running a day behind. They were Alexander's group of hand-picked individuals. Each of them was bright and young, with their own special set of skills. He had researched and investigated them all for well over two years, and, at this point, felt as if he knew each intimately, though they had never met. Conversely, his imminent guests had zero knowledge of him and would not bear the same kinship he felt, at least not at first.

Dragon Loch Castle, situated approximately twenty-five miles east of Montauk Point, New York, is an oddly shaped island. With rounded cliffsides to the North and an inlet, also called a loch, to the South, it was just under a mile from east to west and a bit over a mile from north to south.

The sheer northern-coast cliffs gave way to beautiful green landscape which, like a giant ramp, sloped almost to sea level at the island's southern coast. The loch, from which the island got its name, ran a little over halfway into the island's interior. At the inlets's widest point, it was one hundred and six yards wide, its depth at times, unrecordable. The island's eastern coast was a dense, tree-lined forest of pines, oaks, and small foliage growing in the beds of pine and debris. Some of the trees in the area dated back hundreds of years, and to guess an age would be purely speculation. The loch terminated interiorly in an intricate set of docks and loading areas. Over the years, the island's interior waterway had been redesigned many times, each architectural upgrade endeavoring to create a structure that could withstand the massive surges from the Atlantic Ocean. Even on a calm day, the waves carried through the loch and collided against its inner shore line. The island's helipad and fueling station lay to the west of the inlet dock, while the massive city of generators lay to the East. Most of Alex's guests would be arriving by boat, brought over from the salty shores of Montauk, traversing the loch to the castle. Decks would arrive by chopper. Alexander knew questions would be abound once the travelers had arrived. Many questions, of that he was sure. How would he answer? How much he would share upfront had been an issue plaguing him for some time, now.

Alexander thought about how he would begin his initial conversation with each guest. He had decided to meet with them individually at first and then assemble the group for a meeting of sorts. The web of false pretenses employed to lure each of his visitors to the shores of Dragon Loch plagued him. The deceit was undoubtedly necessary, but was a poor way to begin their relationship nonetheless. The purpose of their gathering was intricate, and at times, wholly unknown to Alexander himself. He needed this discussion to be face-to-face. He needed his audience "trapped" for lack of a better term, unable to retreat from the revelations at hand. The fabricated meetings and conferences employed to summon his guests would certainly make them leery of him, and he would have to work hard to gain their trust.

Alex turned toward the massive structure to the South—magnificent Dragon Loch Castle—and began to walk back. The castle and the island would gain him some respect at least, some semblance of legitimacy. Hopefully enough to buy him some time to explain his work and the purpose of the meeting before they turned and hightailed it out of there. He laughed out loud. "This is not going to be easy. Not with this group." A drift of wispy clouds passed over the October sun and Alexander pulled his coat tighter against the chill. "I wish Decker was here to help me explain a bit. Two men telling ghost stories are better than one." But his smile faded as he approached a rear entrance to the castle.

12

The manuscript had proven well worth his effort to obtain. Moloch studied the aged and fading documents with a gleam in his fiendish eyes. At some point in history, one of the manuscript's caretakers had the crumbling papyrus sheets sealed in some form of paper-thin coating. While this had certainly achieved the objective of protecting the ancient documents, it also made it impossible to ever remove them from their shell without destroying them utterly and completely. The Dark Letters, as it had come to be known, was believed to be nothing more than a myth by most who had heard the tale. But Moloch certainly knew better. He had risked exposure—quite possibly worse—to obtain the two pieces of papyrus from Ebbers, but he knew they were the keys to his purpose. Each sheet contained six riddles written in a mix of several ancient languages including Latin, Greek, Hebrew, and Egyptian hieroglyphics. To solve these meant to discover the secret locations of twelve separate pieces of an even older document that would reveal the true prize in this quest.

Moloch rose from his stately leather chair and crossed the study to the fireplace. Opening his left hand, he waved it swiftly back and forth in front of the smoldering embers of the dying fire. The flames surged and darted toward his fingers like metal to a magnet, and soon it was raging once more. He turned, walked back to his chair, and picked up one of the papyrus sheets. Pivoting back to the roaring fire, Moloch held the sheet up to the bright light created by the blaze.

"Let's see if the legend holds true," Moloch whispered to the violently flickering flames—as if responding to the excitement in his words. "Reveal your secrets."

Heeding the menacing figures command, the glowing firelight exposed small, faint pictograms after each section of riddles. Moloch squinted slightly and focused on the first of the images. A slight smile crept along his jagged lips as his eyes widened with complete understanding. Suddenly, his head snapped back, and loud, blood-curdling laughter filled the room.

13

Alexander had just received word the boat had departed Montauk Point and would arrive at the shores of Dragon Loch within the hour. He rose from his chair in the study, crossed the room, and exited out into the hallway that separated the castle's library from the study and laboratory wing. He hurried down the hall, passing the second of two castle labs, and made a left toward the exhibit hall at the center of the massive structure. Alex stopped short when his cell phone vibrated against the inside breast pocket of his coat.

"Hello?" he said with some degree of urgency. It was Asar—he was on the boat. Alex had sent him to assess each guest's frame of mind and to ensure they arrived on the island safely. He also wanted Asar to do his best to keep them apart until he had a chance to speak to them individually.

"Alexander, how are you doing?"

There was a short pause, and Alex waited for Asar to continue.

"We should be arriving in about an hour or so," he finished.

"Yes, I know. Captain Mills already informed me."

"Oh, good. Glad to hear it."

"What's wrong, Asar?" Alex paced back and forth between the hall walls. "I can hear it in your voice. Are you able to talk, or do we have an issue?"

"No, no. Nothing like that," Asar said quickly. "Nothing to worry about like that, my friend. Although, we did have a young couple who claimed to be tourists board the ship—"

"It's a *boat* Asar. A boat," Alex interrupted.

"I know!" shouted Asar.

"Sorry. What about a young couple?"

"Yes, they said they thought it was a tour boat, whale watching or some nonsense. I am not sure whether I believed them or not, but they left without incident."

"Okay, so what's the problem?"

"Well, it proved to be quite difficult to—"

Asar pulled the cell phone from his ear to escape the amplified howling and bellowing of Sam and Frodo, Alexander's feisty pair of beagles.

The doggy duo ripped around the corner of the hall following the echoes of Alexander's footsteps and headed right for him. Alex spun to meet the over-excited barking. "Frodo! Sam! Sit!" he shouted. The two dogs who had been nipping and razzing each other as they darted through the castle looked up at the sound of their master's voice and came sliding to a halt just inches from his feet. Alexander returned to his conversation as the dogs took turns nudging one another when they thought Alex wasn't looking.

"Difficult to what, Asar?"

"Well, Alex, it was difficult to keep the group from talking to each other."

"Go on."

"Abigail and Samantha had arrived at the pier early and, as I was made to understand it, got out of the cars to stretch their legs. The two wandered into each other, and a conversation ensued." He paused momentarily to allow Alex to comment if he desired. He did not. "They spoke only about the fact they were both attending a function on Dragon Loch before they were separated by a call to board."

"All right, that's not so bad—"

"You did not let me finish."

"Please get to the point, Asar, before I start running through these hall-ways baying like my two moon-weary friends here."

"They spoke again on the ship...sorry, *boat*...and they were all in on the conversation this time. One of them was really giving us a problem, demanding we turn around and screaming things like 'kidnapping' and 'death penalties' and—"

"Okay, okay! Relax. You're underway. Don't turn around, of course. Who was it? Keith?"

"No. It was Samantha."

"Miss Sinclair? Huh, obviously," the amusement in Alex's voice evident.

"I have locked them in the main cabin and—"

"Don't do that, Asar! Go unlock the cabin and just make something up to set their minds at ease. Tell them they have been selected to be on one of those horribly tedious reality shows and you are not supposed to discuss it, but you don't want anyone getting frightened or upset. Tell them all will be revealed when they arrive at the island." Alex smiled to himself. That was thinking on his feet.

"Well done, Alexander. I think that just might work."

"Of course, it will, go take care of that, and I will make the necessary changes on this end. When you arrive, bring them all directly to the library through the exhibit hall entrance."

"Very good. I do apologize for the mix up here."

"Don't think twice about it, Asar," said Alex with sincerity. "It might even be better this way. Ring me when you arrive. Goodbye."

Asar sighed a bit of relief. He had expected Alexander's wrath at his failure to keep the group separated to be severe. Suddenly, a surge in the sea threw him off balance, and he caught himself on the back of a nearby chair. Regaining his footing, he smiled and headed toward the main cabin to unlock their guests.

Back at the castle, Alexander slid his phone into his pocket and tore off down the hall toward the library, his long black coat flying behind him like a cape. He could hear the clicking of the dog's nails on the ancient stone floor behind him as his loyal companions swiftly followed their master to whatever end they did not know, nor care.

14

Moloch's six-vehicle motorcade pulled away from the Mena House Hotel in Giza and merged onto Sharia El Ahram road toward the plateau. He rode in the back of the black sedan at the center of the group. Two Suburbans led the motorcade, with a pair of identical vehicles to the rear of Moloch's car, a hulking van sped ahead of the cluster of five, paving the way to Moloch's destination. All of the dark vehicles moved with the camouflage of the moonless night above them. The group passed the police station and the ticket building as they approached a fork in the road. The Great Pyramid of Cheops filled the horizon before them.

"Nehmen sie das links!" Moloch shouted into his radio, and the six vehicles turned left, winding around the pyramid. He looked out the side windows at the massive Egyptian structure.

"Such grand power," he said to his driver. "Reaching towards the heavens."

"Yes, sir," the driver responded nervously, looking back and forth between the road and his rearview mirror.

"And now what? What did they get for their efforts, for their sacrifice? A dirt-water-back-end country. That's what they got." Moloch spat with disgust as his driver continued to look back and forth nervously, not wanting to show disrespect.

Moloch hissed, "They should have built down instead of up. Then they would have been rewarded for their efforts, I can guarantee you that." He stared forward into the rearview mirror at the driver. "Yes, I can guarantee you that."

The driver looked at Moloch, and this time he did not show fear, but instead understanding. He smiled a sinister grin and nodded almost uncontrollably in agreement. He looked like a demented bobblehead.

The caravan continued on, passing the row of smaller structures known as the Queen's Pyramids on the left, while Cheops' feat of unparalleled architectural splendor, continued to unravel on the right.

"Ein anderes links!" Moloch demanded as the first truck approached another split. The vehicles all veered left as the back of the Great Sphinx came into view. "Anschlag!"

The vehicles came to a harsh stop as Moloch's driver rushed to exit the vehicle to open his master's door. Moloch quickly stepped out into the uncharacteristically balmy Egyptian night, grasping the handle of a black leather attaché. "Wait here for me," he commanded, towering over his driver, then hurried to the front passenger side door of the first truck. It flew open, and a young man in dark military fatigues jumped out. The soldier stood at attention in front of Moloch, who moved past him and got in the front seat.

"Go stand guard by my car." The soldier looked at him, perplexed. Moloch shook his head. "Schützen sie mein auto, uhr." The soldier pulled his automatic rifle from his shoulder, nodded at Moloch, and ran back toward the sedan. Pulling his door shut, Moloch turned to the driver.

"I speak English, sir," the driver blurted out before Moloch could say anything.

"Excellent. Drive to the Sphinx. Get as close as you can. Oh, and send someone to relieve that soldier—someone who understands English."

"Yes, sir," the driver said, repeating Moloch's directive to the others in German.

The truck lurched forward and turned, leaving the road behind for the sand and stone of the desert. Almost immediately, shouts could be heard coming from the direction of Chephren's pyramid to the rear of the Sphinx.

Armed guards ran down Chephren's Temple causeway toward Moloch and his men.

"Take care of them!" Moloch ordered. The driver radioed the last truck in the caravan; it stopped, and its rear window rolled down. The guards continued to chase after them, their attention centered on the vehicles traveling alongside the Sphinx. As such, they did not notice the dull gray barrel of the GAUSE-17 Gatling gun protrude from the back of the stopped truck. The Giza guards were only yards from the Suburban when one of them noticed their impending doom and stumbled forwarded over his own feet, crashing to the sand. As he lifted his face from the ground, his desperate screams of warning were quickly drowned out by the spitting thunder of the monstrous weapon spitting out 4,000 rounds of ammunition per minute. The barrel slid back into the truck as it pulled away from the red-stained sand to join the rest of the raiders.

Moloch stepped out from the stopped vehicle, feet sinking down into the fine granules of sand below, and looked back into the truck at the driver.

"Tell your men to hurry. The Egyptians will send reinforcements. Have them set up around the Sphinx so they can cut down anyone who approaches. We need only minutes."

The driver nodded at Moloch and quickly began barking directions to the others. The trucks commenced to circling the Sphinx like a band of Indians around a horse-drawn wagon in some celluloid rendition of the Wild West. Stopping, they positioned themselves at the four points of the compass. Several mercenaries exited each vehicle and made ready for battle with whatever the Egyptian government could muster up in such a short time.

Moloch walked to the side of the van, which slid open, and several men piled out. He motioned for them to follow as they made their way to the Sphinx. Standing at the front of the ancient structure, he ordered his men into the trench between the beast's paws to where the famous Dream Stela of Tuthmosis IV stood. The stela, a large stone tablet, was placed between the paws of the Sphinx to tell the story of Tuthmosis's rise to Pharaoh by clearing the sand and debris away from the Sphinx. Moloch stared at the tablet momentarily, then shifted his gaze up to the eyes of the stoic man-beast. His hypnotic connection was shattered by the clash of gun fire as the Gatling guns began to spin from several different locations.

"Rip it down!" Moloch shouted with fury through grinding teeth. "Remove the stela and expose the stone behind it!" Moloch took a step down into the crowded space as several men with digging tools and sledge hammers took the tablet down in less than a minute.

"Pull it to the side, and scan it to be sure." Moloch motioned the field sonar tech forward to run his portable system over the fallen stela to make sure it contained no pockets or secret compartment.

"Quickly, clear the ruble from the front of the beast!" Moloch ordered as he moved in closer to the chest of the Sphinx.

"All clear, sir." The sonar technician had finished his scan.

"Excellent," Moloch muttered to himself. "I would not have expected to find it there."

The clang of machine guns mixed with screams of pain and agony continued to wretch the air above. Once the front of the Sphinx was cleared, Moloch sent the technician in to scan for the compartment which held his prize. In no time, the tech yelled out, "Gefunden ihm!" He had found it already.

Moloch moved to the scanning device LCD and was able to discern a small square chamber, no more than a meter in each direction. He grinned wide and patted the technician on the back. "Well done!" He directed another group, who had been waiting in the rear, to excavate the chamber. The technician reached into his pants pocket and pulled out a large permanent marker, looked again at the LCD, and traced the position of the square on the chest of the Great Sphinx. He smiled at Moloch, who gave him a paternal nod, then stepped away so the excavation could begin.

The two archaeologists quickly applied hammer and chisel to the technician's defined outline of the chamber and began chipping away layers of the sandstone structure.

From over the radio, Moloch heard, "Sir, you need to hurry!" He raised his hand to his ear piece to hear better over the continued gun fire and the banging and chatter of his group. The panicked voice continued, "They are sending in the heavier troops! Military will be here soon..." The voice trailed off into a hail of gunfire.

"No time to waste!" Moloch yelled. "Get it open now!"

The next swing of the hammer met with no resistance as the chisel slid through the stone into the ancient air behind the chest wall of the Sphinx. Moloch stepped forward, pushed the scientists out of the way, and shoved his extended hand into the exposed slot. Closing his fingers around the slab of stone, he pulled, snapping the front of the stone off with a grunt. He let the rubble fall to the floor of the desert and peered into the hole he had widened. His eyes grew wide, and a serpent's smile crept across his face. He reached in and withdrew a metallic box from the chamber, dropped to one knee, and opened the attaché he had been carrying. He placed the object into the case and stood, eager to depart.

"We are done here! A success!" Moloch cried. The group cheered, waving shovels and hammers in the air.

"Now scatter, and return to me tomorrow." Moloch barley finished his words as he spun calmly and floated out across the desert sand toward his waiting car. He moved without urgency and without harm through the battle which was ensuing around him on the Giza Plateau. Unfazed by the rapport of arms or the ordnance whizzing by his body, he approached his vehicle, the soldier standing guard quickly opened the rear door, and the driver started the engine. Moloch slid into the back, throwing his case on the seat beside him.

"Did you get what you needed, sir?" the soldier inquired before closing the door.

Moloch nodded, "close the door and let us be gone," smiling now, "the end has begun."

15

Alexander paced back and forth between the library stacks and his newly constructed group work area. Phillip had done a great job following his specifications for designing the section. Situated near his research desk at the center of the library, it would allow the others to work comfortably and efficiently with him. Several large wooden desks, arranged in a circular fashion, were sectioned off from the rest of the library by bookshelves, large tropical plants, strange artifacts, and ornate Japanese shoji screens. Alexander wanted to give the area a sense of separation from the rest of the library, without the need to construct walls. Phillip had understood his conceptualization and had configured the area perfectly. Alex made a mental note to praise the old bird for a job well done. Phillip had also taken it upon himself to set up a group area at the center of the formation which consisted of oversize Italian leather couches and a regal wooden table and chairs, as well as a small refrigerator, coffee machine, and water cooler. It offered all the comforts of home—to some degree, at least. Most importantly, Phillip had assembled the one thing Alexander had requested be present at the group's nucleus—an obscenely large smart board. Here they would be able to brainstorm and post ideas and information. Alexander knew there was nothing like having the physical images and words on both a large and constant scale.

Alexander bent over to pick up a scrap of paper left over from the furniture packaging, then stepped to the first desk to his right, Samantha's, and threw it into the trash bin at its side. Each desk had a personal laptop on it. They were wired into the castle's mainframe, which had been programmed to grant different levels of access to each user depending on their particular specialty. None of them had been granted access to everything, but one or two of them were close, and as trust was gained, Alexander would expand their rights. The archives of Dragon Loch contained a spectacular amount of information. Not the run-of-the-mill knowledge which was available from any internet abled device, no the information contained in these archives was largely unknown to the rest of the world. In fact, some of the castle's secrets were so obscure and unfathomable that Alexander would never allow them to be revealed.

Alex hoped that all of them would agree to take part in this critical venture, for lack of a better word, thus assisting him in his self-appointed duties. He had researched and chosen each of them very carefully. With unique talents, they were each valuable in their own right, and as such, were integral to making the project work. There were no backup players here. If one of them bowed out now, it would weaken the group. He had been studying each one of them for over two years. He knew their strengths and their weaknesses. He knew their secrets and their pasts. He knew what made them tick and how to appeal to their individual desires. The problem was persuading them to work together. If things had gone as initially planned, it would have been a much easier task. He knew he had some hard sells here, but Alex felt he had a better chance of securing their loyalty if he spoke with them one-on-one. At the moment, though, he was unsure, and he didn't like that feeling. Not at such a crucial point in time. He ran one finger across the desk, tapped it with a closed fist, and walked out into the open library.

If it wasn't there already, the boat would be arriving in minutes, and he would have to begin the process of revealing his true purpose in summoning them to Dragon Loch. He would have to tell them there was great evil in the world, and by his estimation, it was growing stronger every day. He would have to try and explain to them how for hundreds of years his family had been entrusted with keeping this growing evil in check, and that he now required assistance in this task Alexander pushed his palm through his hair as he often did when in rapid thought, and he paced furiously once more.

The announcement, "Alexander, the boat has arrived," echoed through the library over the castle's intercom system. He stopped, took a deep breath, and turned toward the staircase leading to the library's second floor. He would situate himself at a vantage point that allowed him to watch them enter the library. As he ascended the spiral staircase to the second level, Alex reached into his pants pocket and took out his cell and dialed.

"Hello, Mom? Can't speak right now," said Asar announced robotically on the other end.

"So I surmised," replied Alex, his excitement betraying his attempt at sounding calm, cool, and collected. "Bring them to the group area and let them settle in a bit. I'll be watching from above for a few minutes. I will join you straight away."

"Very good, Mom." Asar continued the charade, looking around at the others who were debarking from the boat. His bellowing voice brought attention to an otherwise inconspicuous conversation.

Keith nudged Kate. "Mom? What's she, like, two hundred years old?"

Kate smirked back at him with a shushing glance.

"More like Mum, right? *Mummy* that is." Keith continued chuckling to himself.

"Don't be mean," whispered Kate. "Make yourself useful and take this bag. Asar seems very nice."

16

Moloch placed the leather bag on the table in his study and crossed the room to the bar. He flipped a rocks glass upright and pulled the stopper from a diamond-cut crystal snifter of scotch. After pouring himself a quick shot, he raised the glass in the air. "To continued success, my lord," he whispered, and downed the exquisitely aged malt.

A voice answered in return, "Let us hope your success continues...yes."

Startled, Moloch spun round to face the heart of the room, scanning the dimly lit quarters for the source of the statement.

"The master will have it no other way, my old friend," continued the raspy feminine, voice.

Moloch shifted forward in the room, moving swiftly, like a shadow. He could make out a silhouette in the easy chair at the opposite side. Without removing his gaze from the figure, he waved his right hand in the direction of the fireplace. The flames jumped to life with a blazing explosion sending a mortally blinding flash of orange and yellow light into the room. When the initial burst of light faded, Moloch was no longer by the fireplace, but had slipped like a ghost to the corner, standing over the chair.

"Naamah?" Moloch whispered, staring down at the woman lounging in the chair below him. Except for her long, shapely legs which were spread and draped over the arms, her slender body was all but lost in the fur-lined chair.

"In the flesh." She snapped her legs shut and rose from her seat. Moloch took several steps back. Her dark dress and features had hidden her well in the dim light. She let out a slight laugh at Moloch's apparent surprise.

"Why Moloch, you look as though you have seen a ghost." She brushed past him as she crossed the room to the bar. Pouring herself a drink, she turned back to him. He had been studying her intently. She raised her glass and corrected him. "To *our* continued success." She laughed again and brought her glass to her lips.

"Although I do so *enjoy* your company, Naamah, I do not need any help here," Moloch replied with both lust and contempt for his uninvited guest. "How did you find me, anyway?" Moloch inquired as he took the seat Naamah had relinquished. It was warm, and he could detect the sweet aroma of honey and flora.

"Oh, that was easy my dear. That sniveling fool Ebbers gave me what little information you had passed to him in your efforts to obtain the riddles, and I pieced it together from there." She smiled and took a seat on the leather couch across from him. Curling her long legs so the spiked heels of her black leather shoes pressed against the back of her thighs, she sipped her drink, watching for Moloch's reaction.

"What is it I can do for you?" he asked, doing his best to avoid falling for her demonic temptations.

"I was surprised to hear you had been able to purchase the papyri from Ebbers, seeing as how he and his ancestors have sworn to protect them for several hundred years." She leaned forward, raising one eyebrow as she whispered, "Do tell how you did it."

Moloch loosened up a bit, rising to refill his drink. "Superior bargaining skills, that's all. You just need to be able to read people—really read them—and then you will know what they want. What they desire."

"Spare me the philosophical mumbo jumbo," hissed Naamah, growing annoyed at her effect on him—or lack thereof. "Is there a point here some-where? How did you get Ebbers to hand them over?"

"Ebbers is a very bad man," said Moloch with a smile. "His extracurric-ular activities as a younger man would make some demons blush."

Naamah's interest piqued. She sipped the rest of her drink and dropped the glass to the floor. "Go on."

"As evil as he is, Ebbers has one little problem." Moloch grinned. "The sniveling dog doesn't want to spend eternity in Hell."

Naamah laughed out loud. "*That's* how you got the riddles? You promised that idiot his soul?" She stared at Moloch in disbelief while Moloch wore a smile of pride.

"Well, that's how I got him to take the papyri out in public. The good doctor got cold feet, it seemed," he said, then paused for effect, "right there at the zero hour. I was pretty sure he was going to run away and hide. So, I took them from the fool before he knew what happened."

She rose and crossed the room to the table. "You are nefarious, Moloch. You should be congratulated. Many have tried to obtain the riddles for hundreds of years now. All have failed where you have succeeded. Well done." She looked down at the attaché on the table. Reaching out, she touched the leather with the long red nail of her pointer finger and slid it across the length of the case.

"I believe his ancestors may have joined our little swaray as well." Moloch rose and headed for the table. "The angry spirits would have tried to stop him. Either way, I would have just taken the riddles. This way his soul is safe and sound where it belongs."

"Yes, where it belongs." Naamah looked back to the case, curiosity building. "Is one in there?" The words fell from her lips so quietly they barely reached Moloch's ears.

"The first of twelve," he said, reaching out and grasping her wrist to pull her away from the table toward him. "Right where the riddles foretold it would be." He pulled her closer, the eternal chemistry between them brew-ing. "What do you want here, Naamah?" Their faces were mere inches apart.

"I want to help you," she whispered, her lips brushing his as she uttered the words, "I want to help you free the infernal one." Her eyes grew narrow, apprising the gaze of her companion. "What is it *you* desire Moloch?"

17

Abigail felt a sharp pain in her right temple, just above her eye. It wasn't the worst migraine she'd ever had, but it was pretty close, and its throbbing intensified as they approached the imposing wooden doors of Dragon Loch Castle. She was eager to meet with Mr. Storm, and she wasn't going to let a stupid headache ruin it. There was such an odd mix of characters here, and she was positive there was more going on than met the eyes —even *her* eyes. She grasped her forehead between her thumb and pointer finger and rubbed back and forth trying to shake the stubborn pain.

"Are you all right, young lady?"

Abigail opened her eyes to find Asar standing in front of her.

"Yes, I think so. Just a bit of a headache. Most likely from—"

Before she could finish, Asar had taken her by the wrist. Abigail braced herself for a debilitating flash of visions. What was he doing? She began to pull away. Asar seemed to recognize her reaction, and he squinted at her curiously.

"Just checking your pulse my dear, nothing to be afraid of," Asar assured her.

"I'm really okay. Just a little seasick from the ride, that's all." Why couldn't she read him?

"Nonsense." He huffed. "Your face is quite pale. Your heart is racing."

She jerked her arm away from him this time, not wanting to risk the possibility of reading him any longer.

"I'm fine," she protested once more as she rummaged through her small black purse for a tiny mirror she kept. Grasping it in her hand, she looked up toward the others who had stopped outside the doors, waiting for Asar.

"Are you two coming?" shouted Keith.

Asar turned to look at Keith, but said nothing. Abigail opened the mirror and held it up to her face. Her rich, dark skin did look pale, almost white around her lips. She peered over the top of the case at Asar. Her head was swelling with thunderous palpitations now.

She softly admitted, "It appears I do look a bit pale. Perhaps I *could* sit down for a moment when we get inside."

As she brought the mirror back to her face for one more look, horror filled her heart. She spun around, dropping the mirror to the ground with a shriek of terror. Where was it? She pivoted back and forth. Where was that hideous face she had seen directly behind her in the mirror's reflection?

Asar stepped to her quickly. "Are you okay my dear? What is wrong?"

"I'm *fine*." She responded firmly. "Can we just get inside, please?"

"Of course." Asar bent and picked up the mirror, dusting it off on his jacket as they walked. It wasn't broken.

"Here you go, young lady," Asar said gently as they joined the group of others at the doors. "It's in one piece. No bad luck shall befall you."

"That remains to be seen, now doesn't it?" she replied.

～

*P*hillip heaved the arched wooden doors of the castle open to greet Asar and their guests. Sunlight drenched the grand entrance hall, which was adorned with ornate jade and marble sculptures. Some sprang from the floor like great white oaks, rising up to the heavens; others were mounted on the walls which were constructed of slabs of pale beige and gray marble veined with rivers of brown and rust formed by the passage of time. The late autumn sunlight caused the quartz and minerals dispersed throughout the walls to sparkle and shimmer. Further within the hall was a brilliantly designed staircase spanning the entire length of the hall. It started at both sides of the room and ascended up in an arch to arrive at the middle in the hallway above. Asar crossed the threshold first and summoned the others in.

"Hello, Phillip," Asar said with a nod. "My friends, this is Phillip. He is the caretaker of Dragon Loch, and quite often, of its inhabitants as well. He is fairly old now." Phillip scowled at him and huffed a bit under his breath. Asar continued, "In fact, he has been here so long I believe he may have come with the castle." He finished with a smile, which Phillip returned, momentarily.

"Speaking of which," blurted out Keith, "how old *is* this castle? And I mean, *where* is this castle? I've never heard of it. Have you? Have you?" He turned to the others for some sort of validation.

"All in good time, Master Keith," replied Asar. "I am sure Alexander is looking forward to providing you all with a history of the castle and his family."

"Where is Mr. Storm?" Keith asked having already dispelled any hope of his initial questions being answered.

"We will be joining him in the library," Asar said with an amiable smile.

"Where are the cameras and the film crew?" asked Samantha dryly.

Phillip looked noticeably puzzled. Asar spoke up before the caretaker could respond to Sam. Storm was quite literally minutes from unveiling the truth to their guests, and he didn't need a mutiny now. "They are all waiting in the library."

"Must be a pretty big library," said Kate, laughing.

"Actually, you jest, but it is probably one of the most comprehensive libraries of its kind in the world, at least since the fire in Alexandria, that is," replied Asar with an air of seriousness the group had not seen in him before. "Its dimensions are two-hundred by sixty."

"Feet? Aw, that's not that big," said Kate, waving her hand at him.

"Yards, Miss Kate, two-hundred by sixty *yards* are its rough dimensions. Three stories high. Its volume count is well into the millions, and now, with the added computer-based archival system, you can access almost every work ever published from within its walls."

Kate's jaw visibly dropped. Keith reached over and comically pushed it back up. "She really likes books." He stated matter-of-factly.

"And I'm really into tricked out systems," added Samantha. "Any chance of sneaking a peek at the hardware for that bad-boy?"

"I am sure Alex would love for you to have a look," Asar quickly responded, glad to have diverted attention from the reality show hoax. "Shall we proceed?"

Asar noticed Abigail had wandered to the marble bench in the center of the hall below the staircase wall. "Feeling any better, miss?" Asar inquired.

"A bit, thank you."

"Phillip, please bring Miss Abigail some of Alexander's mint and chamomile tea in the library when you can." Phillip nodded and exited out a door at the side of the staircase.

"That's really unnecessary, Asar. I'm fine now."

"Nonsense," he replied. "Shall we continue, then?" The group followed him up the stairs and through the main entranceway into the upper hall of the castle. Everywhere, they were met by sculptures and artifacts, paintings and tapestries. The walls were made of solid blocked stone, and the overall immense stature of the castle noticeably intimidated them all.

Kate stopped at a three-paneled mural mounted several feet up on the stone, a large spotlight illuminating its mystical strokes. "My God," she exclaimed. "Is this a Bosch? I mean, it *is* a Bosch, but which Bosch is it? I've never seen it before."

Keith stepped up beside her and tilted his head sideways. "Can't say it looks familiar to me, either." Kate smacked him in the chest with the back of her hand. He crossed his arms to protect himself from the next blow if one were to follow. "No, I'm just saying it doesn't look like any I've seen, either. Not like I know all of Hieronymus's work or anything, but I have *never* seen this." Kate shook her head and looked back at the paintings.

"You are, in fact, both correct," said Asar, laughing. "This mural was a gift to Alexander's family. It is a private work. Never photographed. Never published." He turned to Samantha, giving her a wink. "That means no snapface photos, please." To which Sam rolled her eyes at her seniors' ignorance.

Looking back up at the three panels, he continued, "It depicts a battle between angels and demons, the slaying of a great dragon or serpent, and the punishment of the accursed ones in Hell."

He turned to continue their trek deeper into the castle. "It is one of my favorite pieces in the whole of the castle. Good eye, Kate."

She smiled proudly as the group resumed its trek towards the library.

"*Good eye Kate,*" Keith mimicked their guides praise, and once again braced his body for Kate's petite, yet powerful, retort.

18

Alexander's cell vibrated in his pocket, a damn annoyance as far as he was concerned, at the exact time he heard his visitors making their way through the library. He remained poised and out-of-site of the others from his vantage point behind a stone pillar.

"Damn," he whispered to himself as he slid the phone from his pocket. It was Decks. Alex touched the side button to ignore the call—Decks was most likely just giving him an updated ETA. He would call him back after this long-anticipated meeting. He put the phone away and turned back to the small group making their way towards him. Peering around the curved stone which was obfuscating him from view, he could make out their faces as they got closer. Asar was leading the way with Keith and Samantha right on his heels. Kate was fairly close, but appeared to have trouble walking with her head spinning in every direction. Alex could hear them clearly now.

"This is unbelievable!" shouted Kate. "I mean, I believe it because I'm standing here, but honestly, this whole thing is really rather unbelievable."

Samantha was clearly still agitated and was asking Asar something about cameras.

Abigail was quite a few steps behind as well, and, like Kate, was looking around, astounded by the athenaeum's massive size.

Asar ushered Keith and Samantha into the newly furnished area Phillip had assembled and directed them toward the center. He waited for the other two to catch up and guided them in as well. Abigail sighed a breath of relief and made a beeline for one of the deep leather couches. Asar walked over to the refrigerator and pulled the door open. Reaching in, he withdrew a bottle of cold spring water and headed toward Abigail.

"Help yourself, my friends," he said to the others. "Alexander will be joining us momentarily." He twisted off the top and handed the bottle to her.

"Thank you, Asar." She took the bottle and ran it across her forehead. Cool beads of condensation stuck to her skin, and she wiped them away with the palm of her hand.

"This is all very nice, Mr. Asar—" began Samantha.

"Just Asar."

"Yes, fine, this is very nice. Very big and beautiful and all that." Her tone became more animated. "But what the hell are we doing here, and who is this Alexander Storm guy?" She strode right up to Asar, eyes blazing. "I want answers now, or I want the damn keys to the ship."

"It's a boat." Alexander interjected softly.

"What?" Samantha turned with a start as Alexander walked briskly into view.

"I said it's a boat, not a ship, Miss Sinclair." Alex walked past her and sat on the couch next to Abigail. "Abigail Wendell, I presume?" She nodded. "Alexander Storm." He extended his hand. "Pleased to make your acquaintance. Are you feeling all right?" Catching himself, Alex withdrew his offer of salutation and winked at Abigail.

"Very nice to meet you as well, Mr. Storm. I'm okay. Just a bit of a migraine."

"Oh, well then I should have Philip fetch you some of my famous mint and chamomile tea."

"Phillip is already on his way with it," Asar said as he moved toward a chair at the table to finally sit down.

"It's quite soothing and will help your head," Alex said, rising up from the couch to greet the others. Extending a hand to each, he greeted them. "Kate, Keith. And Miss Sinclair, it's a pleasure to finally meet you."

"Have you been waiting long?" Samantha replied.

"Excuse me?" said Alex with a slight twist of his head.

"Have you been waiting long? To meet me, that is."

"Well, actually—" Alexander started.

"Oh, great. What are you? Some kind of stalker?" She whirled around on her heel. "See? I warned you all there was something weird going on. Something fishy with this whole thing. First a conference. Then a game show or whatever. We're in trouble here. Surrounded by fucking water no less!"

"Miss Sinclair!" Alexander shouted. She spun around again, this time glaring at him straight in the eye. "Miss Sinclair, please relax. You are in no danger here. None of you are," he added, trying to reassure them. "Please, sit down and close your mouth."

"What!?"

"Listen," the word sailed from his lips softly and demanded a sea of calm from his nervous visitors.

Keith and Kate, obviously worried, took a seat next to each other on one of the couches. Samantha began to back up toward the seat next to Abigail. "Okay, but I want some answers. Now."

"Fine. I understand, Samantha," Alex said. He walked over to the wood table, slid out one of the chairs, and spun it around to face the four puzzled faces.

"To start with, Samantha, I *have* been waiting to meet you. You completed an important security programming job for me back in February."

"What do you mean, for you?" she spat out with disbelief. "That was for a company called SHL."

"That's right," Alex responded. "SHL—Storm Holdings Limited. You programmed my security system for this library's archive servers and interfaces." Alexander glanced around at the others to see how they were reacting. "And you did a stellar job, by the way. Works quite astonishingly. Thank you."

Sam squinted sideways at Alex. She was letting her guard down slightly, just enough to notice Alex was quite handsome and bore no resemblance to a stalker or pysco-killer.

"Each of you has already been asked, or will be shortly, to play an important role in my research work here at Dragon Loch. Let me explain—"

"Your tea, miss," Phillip interrupted as he handed the cup and saucer to Abigail. "Alexander, Mr. Decker is on the phone for you, and he stated it is of the utmost importance he speak with you now, without delay."

Alexander looked at Phillip. "What does he want? Did he say? I'm in the middle of something here."

"He said to tell you it was a matter of life and death—many lives, at that. I have transferred the call to your private study."

"For Christ sake!" Turning to his guests, he said, "Please forgive me. I will be as quick as possible, but I must take this call." Without waiting for an answer, he dashed past a bookshelf than around a corner, out of view.

"Well, that went well," Alexander mumbled to himself as he sprinted toward the side exit of the library toward his office. "You best be in the thralls of imminent peril, Decks old pal."

19

Moloch stared down at Naamah as she lay sleeping, her tan body interwoven with the red satin sheets of his bed. She seemed so tame now, so serene. But he knew better. The ruthless spirit contained in this magnificent exterior wouldn't think twice about crushing anything that got in her way. He, of course, did not fear her. But he certainly did not trust her. She stirred slightly, sliding her long leg up to her side, her breath speeding up slightly. Moloch grabbed his stylish black jacket hanging on the velvet-lined desk chair and walked in front of the ornate oval mirror hanging opposite the bed. He slid his arms into the immaculately tailored jacket and adjusted the knot on his black and red silk tie. In the reflection, he could see Naamah's eyes were open and fixed intently on him.

Without turning, he said softly, "I need to run a few errands, my dear." He paused, awaiting a response. She said nothing.

He continued, "Please make yourself at home. Joseph will be at your beck and call." He faced her, brushing imaginary lint from his sleeves. "Don't hesitate to make use of his services."

Moloch strolled to the side of the bed and leaned over, lowering his face to hers. "I will return for you within three days' time," he whispered into her ear. Naamah nodded, still starring into the void he a had filled moments before. Moloch withdrew from her, kissing her thigh as he rose.

Before he could take his leave, she spoke up, "Where are you going, exactly?"

Moloch turned to find her sitting up, leaning on her elbows, her body exposed to him.

"Jordan, if I am not mistaken. Yes, Jordan." He began to hum "Swing Low, Sweet Chariot," waving his finger back and forth in time.

Naamah, laughing, dropped back onto the bed and turned on her side. Pulling the silky red sheets up over her lower body, with a little smirk she softly said, "Happy hunting, then."

20

A lexander grabbed the phone from the desk in his study and spoke quickly, but calmly, into the receiver.

"Hey, Decks. Is everything all right, my friend?" he asked.

"There's not a lot of time, Alexander," Decks shouted with an intensity Alex had never heard from him before. "Listen carefully!"

"Go ahead." Alexander didn't like the fear or urgency in Decks's voice.

"I was awaiting passage to the U.S. in Sierra Leone. I had made arrangements to have a private plane get me back as I told you when last we spoke." He paused.

"Yes," Alex said, urging him on.

"I ended up at a tavern called The Bori for some drink and a little seclusion—"

"You know the Bori are a secret society of witches in Africa," Alex interrupted.

"Please, Alex, just listen," Decks implored.

"Sorry. Go ahead," Alexander replied quietly.

"Well, I got to talking to some locals—one in particular was an old gentleman by the name of Totana Sid. We discussed some of Africa's more colorful myth and lore. He was extremely knowledgeable on the subject. Anyway, after talking and drinking for most of the night, he told me he wanted to share an important secret with me." Decks paused for a breath.

"Go on, Will," Alexander encouraged his friend to continue. He was concerned about getting back to the library before his guests really started to give Asar a hard time.

"Yes, well it was *some* secret," Decks continued. "Moloch has returned." Decks whispered the name as if saying it out loud would conjure him.

"What?" Alexander's heart chilled at the utterance of the name. "What are you saying?"

"Totana Sid told me the wretched demon walks among us Alex, and with purpose. He intends to free Samael from the fires of hell, Alexander."

Alexander felt a lump form in his throat, and he swallowed hard before responding to the accursed tale.

"And just how does Moloch intend on freeing the beast?" Alex asked, already sensing the answer.

"He has the riddles Alex. He means to reassemble the *Book of Gates.*" Decks's voice was trembling.

"How?" responded Alex, feeling a little off balance and pulling the chair away from his desk to sit down.

"He apparently ascertained who the current keeper of the riddles was and convinced him to relinquish their burden to him." With hurried speech he continued. "One of my sources in the States confirms the riddles were apparently taken from a Dr. Ebbers right there in the Hamptons, Alex. They were right there in the Hamptons all this time."

"Why did you wait so long to tell me all this, Decks?" Alexander was annoyed at a delay which was most likely none existent.

"Delay? I wanted to confirm things, but there was no delay brother," Decks responded. "I wanted to make sure it wasn't a ruse to distract you from other issues of course."

"We knew something was coming," Alex said sharply. "It's the motivating factor behind assembling this team."

"I know," concurred Decks, "but it wasn't until I saw the Egyptian news, that I realized it was actually already happening."

"What Egyptian news?"

"Haven't you been watching? You're always on top of world events!" said

Decks in disbelief, confused by Alex's ignorance of details concerning a major incident unfolding in the Near East.

"I've been busy preparing for the meeting," explained Alexander. "Things changed. Plans changed. I've been—"

"Turn on the news, Alex," Decks interrupted. "Moloch has already laid siege to the Giza Plateau."

Alexander picked up the remote control from his desk and clicked on the LCD mounted on the wall to the right. He flicked through the channels to Eagle News, which was broadcasting a map of Egypt in one corner of the screen and a shot of the Pyramids of Giza in another. Alex raised the volume.

"Once again," news anchor Harold Smith said dramatically, "a well-armed group of gorillas has led an all-out assault on the Pyramids of Egypt, more specifically the complex's iconic Great Sphinx. An unknown number of heavily armed assailants stormed the tourist mecca several hours ago, killing an estimated forty people including guards, military personnel, and tourists. Although their objective is not known at this time, reported activity at the front of the Sphinx by witnesses and the remnants of digging indicates the group may have been attempting to extract some mysterious object from the ancient structure."

They cut to a live shot of the Giza Plateau where flashing lights and scattering people, both official and civilian, cluttered the scene. As the camera panned to the front of the Sphinx and zoomed in, the hole Moloch had torn in the lion's chest became apparent. Alex clicked the screen off.

"God save us," whispered Alexander. "He already has one."

21

Moloch paused at the entrance to the dimly lit bar and slowly scanned the tables. The subterranean décor and secluded sitting areas that made up The Cave Bar outside the Crowne Plaza Resort in Jordan made it difficult to get a fix on everyone in the room. The magnificent structure was over two thousand years old and had been carved, like many other locations in Petra, directly into the rock. This archaic little watering hole, once a sacred Nabataean tomb, was now reduced to a tourist trap for rich millennials. Moloch smiled at this thought. The desecration of any holy relic did not offend him in the least. Rather, it made intermingling with these quasi-aristocrats bearable for the moment. A lack of punctuality, on the other hand, was something he found deplorable, to say the least. Noting the time, he swiftly moved deeper into the bar in search of his connection in this ancient city of stone.

The small tables and accompanying wrought iron chairs that cluttered the bar were packed with tourists of all nationalities. As they sat there indulging themselves in drink and hookah smoke, the fools were oblivious to the evil slithering among them. Moloch weaved in and out of the tables, making his way to the back which housed the deeply carved, private catacombs. Each alcove contained its own set of table and chairs. He would have to stealthily peer into each one to find Martin.

As Moloch passed the final table of bar patrons, he felt smooth fingers tighten around his wrist. He stopped and looked down into the bloodshot eyes of an exotic looking brunette who spoke to him in French. She was inviting him to join her and her friends. Moloch looked around the table at the four or five women giggling at their friend's unbridled display of brazenness. Moloch turned back to the woman and locked eyes with her. She started to breathe heavily, her free hand running through her hair and then down her body. As her mouth fell open and her eyes began to roll back, Moloch tugged his arm free.

"Perhaps some other time," he softly suggested to the confused woman. "Ladies," he said and nodded a gentleman's farewell, then resumed his path to the back of the bar. He approached the first in the set of secluded niches in the stone, and there he spotted Martin sipping what looked like red wine, smiling at Moloch.

Martin took a swig, placed his glass on the table, and rose to greet his guest. Wiping the crimson remnants from his mouth with his finger and thumb, he motioned for Moloch to enter the room.

"Please, come in. Sit." Martin's Middle-Eastern accent was thick, but he looked either British or American. Moloch pulled out the chair across from Martin and sat down. Before joining him, Martin stepped out of his sanctuary and waved to a waiter across the room. He turned back to Moloch, nodded, and reclaimed his seat and drink.

"I have requested the waiter, sir," he spoke jovially "I take it you are quite thirsty after your long journey." Martin raised his eyebrows and tilted his head slightly to the side, waiting for a response.

"Yes. Quite thirsty," Moloch responded.

"Excellent. Here he is now." Martin turned to the waiter. "Please indulge my friend here with whatever he needs."

Moloch stared at Martin. "What do you suggest?" he asked.

"The 'Dark Tomb' is quite good." Martin smiled at the waiter who jotted down the request. "It has Cognac and some other tasty things all mixed together. Prepare that on the rocks for my friend." The waiter nodded and swiftly departed.

"So, I take it your trip was satisfactory," asked Martin, lighting an unfiltered cigarette with the candle from the table. Moloch nodded. A puff of deep rich smoke emanated from his mouth as he picked stray strands of tobacco from his lips.

"Good, good. And your suite at the Crowne?" Martin took another drag. The glow at the end of the cigarette intensified from a dull umber to a bright orange, illuminating the pock marks scattered across his dark, oily face.

"More than sufficient," said Moloch, leaning forward in his seat. Martin exhaled out of the side of his mouth so as to not offend his guest—his master.

"Enough niceties, Martin," hissed Moloch. "What are the results of your site survey?"

"Yes, of course." Martin dropped the cigarette to his side and worked the toe of his brown leather shoe into it momentarily. The embers scattered in the soft breeze moving through the bar.

"I was able to discern some of the points, but I need to review the material with you a bit." He paused, awaiting a reaction which did not come. "I am sorry to say I do not understand some of what you have given me, and I need your help and ancient wisdom."

Moloch leaned back in his chair. All signs of pleasantries disappeared from his face. "Tell me what you have learned thus far."

Martin lifted the palm of his hand toward Moloch, who squinted back at him.

"Thank you. That will be all." Martin instructed the waiter even before Moloch's drink hit the table. Sensing the unprovoked aggravation in Martin's voice, the waiter turned and left without uttering a word.

Moloch lurched forward again, this time nearly across the table. Glaring into Martin's eyes, he commanded in a harsh whisper, "From the Valley of Moses, treading the sands of the gorge, arrive at the rose mountain's open mouth and pass through to the land beyond."

"Yes. The 'Valley' refers to Jordan, the 'gorge' and the 'rose mountains' are as discussed. Even the rest of the riddle—"

Moloch interrupted, "Seek out the paper room in the paper church to the North—beneath its floor, a metal door lined with the keys to the stars. Pluck a star and travel not far to the castle built by pharaoh for daughter," he recited from memory as the reflection of the candle's flame danced across his eyes.

"Yes, the 'paper room' and 'church' I interpreted," Martin said with some degree of self-congratulation. "It is the 'metal door' which is the issue here." Martin paused and looked out into the bar and then back at Moloch. In a strained, quick whisper, he said, "I cannot just waltz in there and rip up the floor. And if I cannot rip up the floor, I cannot make the connection to the 'castle' because I have no idea what the hell the 'keys to the stars' are, so I don't know what I am even looking for!" Martin ran out of breath as he pled his case and he inhaled a large gulp of air before dropping back in his seat. His panic apparent, he sighed, "I cannot rip up the floor."

"But *I* can." Moloch smirked at his frightened companion. He picked up his "exotic" drink and took a sip. "Not bad," he said holding it up. "Relax, Martin. You are at a very happening night club you know." With that, Moloch shifted his seat so he could see back into the heart of the bar. The woman he had toyed with several minutes ago was still sitting with her friends, laughing and whispering among themselves. She stopped and looked toward the back of the bar where she caught him staring at her. Moloch raised his glass at her and smiled. "A *very* happening club."

22

Abigail's hands trembled, and she found it hard to grasp the china cup Philip had brought her. She lifted her arm to take another sip of the pleasant-tasting concoction and noticed the cup was actually ivory, and the intricately carved decorations appeared to be Egyptian.

Perhaps hieroglyphics, she thought to herself. *Or even some ancient spell.* She twisted the cup back and forth so she could see all the markings before raising it to her lips for another taste. *I could use some ancient Egyptian magic right now,* she thought.

"You all right there, Abigail?" Kate asked from across the room. "You don't look so hot." Kate rose and hurried across the large oriental carpet that separated the two sets of couches.

"I feel a little weak," Abigail whispered, swallowing the last of her tea.

Samantha stood up next to Kate to get a better look at her new friend. She tossed her long blonde hair to one side and bent down to feel Abigail's forehead with the back of her hand.

"You're burning up!" Sam exclaimed. "She's burning up!" she repeated to Kate.

Abigail blinked her eyes several times and looked up at the pair. "I just feel a little weak. It's something that happens to me from time to..." Her words trailed off as her gaze drifted to the cup in her hand. The tiny carved reliefs appeared to rise out from the china and float in the air like a bee hovering above a flower. Abigail's eyes widened as she watched the apparition begin to animate before her. She felt her body weakening more and more. She gazed up at Sam and Kate and could see the confusion in their stares. Abigail wasn't sure if they saw what she was seeing, too, or if they were just reacting to her increasing lack of control over her body. Either way, they knew something was afoul and hopefully they would help her. She struggled to free the cup from her fingers, and it dropped to the floor with a thump.

"Asar!" Kate yelled in the direction of the great stacks where he had been moments before. "Asar, come quick!" She looked back at Abigail who, impossibly, levitated above the sofa just slightly. Dumbfounded, Kate yelled for Asar again and found he was standing right next to her.

"Miss Abigail! Can you hear me?" Asar asked.

From behind them, they heard a terrified cry. Samantha's voice trembled as she pointed toward the ivory teacup laying sideways on the burgundy rug. "What the hell is that? And what the fuck is it doing?" Sam took several steps back and looked to Asar for answers, but he offered nothing more than a blank stare. Mist began to pour out in a stream from the inside of the cup, and Kate stumbled backward. The spiraling haze, draped in a greenish glow, separated Abigail's floating body from the rest of the group. From the center of the expanding cloud, the rough outlines of a figure started to take shape. Asar quickly leapt back, shouting, "Protect yourselves now, ladies!" He turned to look back at Keith and found him scrambling backward on the couch, pointing at the cloud.

"That's it, Kate!" Keith screamed. "That's the friggin thing that attacked me!" Keith pointed at the creature materializing before them.

Asar whirled back around to Abigail. "Abigail, can you hear me?" But she floated several feet off the couch, unaware, legs crossed like a Buddha, facing the figure in the mist. *138 As if a giant fan, like one found on a movie set to create the illusion of wind, had been turned on, the mist blew off into the library, revealing the creature within clearly.

"Ammut!" Asar hissed, and the demon turned its crocodilian head toward the sound of its name.

Sam and Kate flew backward, nearly crushing Keith on the couch.

Trembling, Sam whispered to herself, "I know that face, too." Kate and Keith, sitting on opposite sides of her, both turned their heads at the same time, looking at her in disbelief. Sam said, "I saw it in the ice cream cooler door reflection before I found myself dead."

"Uh, what?" coughed out Kate, raising one eyebrow in Keith's direction.

"I warned you profane serpent! Be gone!" Asar demanded, but Ammut fixated its slitted reptilian pupils on Abigail. "I command you to return to the depths from which you crawled!"

"No! Wait!" Abigail's eyes shot open, and she stared at Asar. "Wait, Asar. You have misjudged the its purpose." She turned her attentions back to the creature. Her body still levitating, and began to speak to Ammut. Her voice echoed with something otherworldly, unnatural.

"Ammut means you no harm." Abigail coughed and spat. "Ammut means to help you. The sixth commander of hell has returned. Moloch has returned from aeons of sleep."

What? Asar mouthed the word, but no sound escaped his lips.

"Ammut knows its plan. Ammut knows its wishes." The creature of myth faced the others as the message continued to flow from Abigail.

"Moloch wishes to invoke *The Book of Gates... Toth has sent his messenger to us*...Moloch has the riddles...evil intends to set forth a greater evil upon mankind...the demon intends to open the twelve gates of night and end our time."

Abigail's body slowly rested back on the couch as Asar moved toward her, his hands at his side, not wanting to threaten Ammut with his advance. Keith and the two girls had gotten up from the couch and stood waiting. Abigail's eyes closed as her body went limp in the leathery folds of the couch. Ammut backed away from the group into the darkness of the library until all that could be seen were its piercing red eyes. Then even those were gone. Asar fell to Abigail's side and grabbed her wrist to check for signs of life.

"She's alive!" he shouted as the others rushed to assist. Suddenly, her body shot straight up, and her eyelids snapped fully open to reveal fiery pupils, smoldering with the same intensity as Ammut's.

A voice, not her own, growled. "Know this and take heed. Fail to stop the beast, and your fragmented souls, and the souls of all, will burn for eternity."

Kate let out a guttural scream, crying, "Is it gone or not?" as she retreated toward the other side of the room again.

"I believe it is," answered Asar.

"It's gone," whispered Abigail. She had regained consciousness, but she remained terrified nonetheless. Drained, she looked up at Asar. He grabbed her forearm and helped her sit up. "That creature spoke to me ... through me," she told them. "It has been trying to warn us. Help us."

"It has a funny fucking way of helping, that's for sure!" snapped Keith.

"Keith, go and get Abigail some cool water," Asar suggested to diffuse the tension.

"On it." Keith moved quickly and returned with a bottle of water for Abigail. "Here you go. You all right?" he asked, twisting the cap loose and handing her the bottle.

Abigail took a long drink and caught her breath before answering. "I think I'm okay now." Rubbing her temples, she said, "My headache even seems to have disappeared." She attempted to stand but wobbled and tried to keep her balance.

"Easy, easy," encouraged Asar as he and Keith both caught one arm, helping her land safely on the cushions. "Just relax a minute."

Asar turned to Kate. "Go to your desk—you'll know which one it is— grab a blank journal and pen from the desk and come back here." He paused as she looked at him with some confusion. "We need to record what Abigail has revealed to us for Alexander." Kate shook her head and dashed off.

Samantha's eyebrow raised up, and she asked, "Translated? What do you mean?"

"Abigail's special talents allowed her to hear what you and I could not," he said, walking over and picking up the cup on the floor. "We thought the devourer meant us harm. Abigail translated its ancient language of death into that of the living so we could hear its message. Hear its warning."

"What talents?" Sam and Keith asked in stereo.

"Well, that is for her and Mr. Storm to explain," Asar said, turning to greet Kate as she returned. She held up the blank journal and pen over her head.

"Got it! Figured it out!" she announced, a little out of breath.

"Good. Let's try to record what Abigail has told us before we forget," Asar encouraged. This really wasn't his area of expertise. It was Alex's, but he knew how to proceed until Alexander returned.

"Don't you want to know how I guessed which desk was mine?" Kate interrupted.

"I think I know," said Asar with a smile.

"*I* want to know," Keith quickly chimed in.

"You're gonna love this, Keith," Kate said. "There is an old French map of the Tanis excavation framed over the desk."

"Oh, yeah?" said Keith. "That's cool."

Kate opened the journal and dated the top of the page, "October 17, Library—Ammut Visitation."

"It said something about a...Moloch," Samantha said, hurrying to Kate's side to help.

Bursting through the door on the other side of the library, Alexander proclaimed, "Moloch has returned," walking swiftly across the carpet toward the desks. "He has returned, and he intends to do very bad things—"

"We know," the others interrupted.

Alexander stopped dead in his tracks and studied their faces. Tilting his head to one side, he inquired, "What's been going on here?"

23

Moloch's body swayed back and forth in rhythm to his horse's slow, yet purposeful, gallop across the Jordanian sands. The jet-black creature's muscles extended and contracted with every stride, revealing the horse's impressive equestrian physique. Moloch had named the horse Rommel after the infamous Nazis field marshal. The psychotic Rommel had once uttered, "In the absence of orders, find something and kill it." A sentiment that tickled Moloch's fancy so much that he was inclined to grant the "the desert fox's" plea for more time on Earth, granting him a hundred-year hiatus from an eternity of torture and damnation.

Jordan's blazing sun beat down on horse and rider, and Moloch tapped the steed's side with his boot to drive him quickly into the shade of the jigsaw puzzle of stone that comprised the passageway's ceiling. Kicking up sand from the ground below as the horse's pace accelerated, they moved out of the direct rays of the sun and quickly through the passage known as Al-siq.

Moloch could see the sharp bend ahead and this time gave the horse a stern kick, compelling the beast to a sprint. As they rounded the curve of the mountainous valley, Moloch found himself face-to-face with the spectacular stone ruins of Petra. More precisely, the carved structure known as the Treasury. This magnificent marvel of stone craftsmanship had been carved directly into the face of the mountain and appeared to be a two-story palace. On the ground level, a large doorway was set behind six columns. A façade of a peaked roof line separated the two levels and gave way to ten more columns above. The second level of the structure was a mix of ornate designs and finely carved statues with the center of the level culminating in an intricate crown-like peak, all set in the natural rose-colored stone of the countryside.

As breathtaking as the vision was, Moloch had not the time, nor the appetite, for gazing upon its splendor. He dismounted Rommel and dropped the worn leather reins to the desert floor. There was no need to restrain the animal; it would not move from the spot until its master commanded. The rider reached around the horse's back and detached a military-grade, tan canvas backpack from the saddle clasp. Moloch flung the pack sideways over one shoulder and turned to face the entrance to the Treasury. He could make out some of the statues visible in the stone monolith, including a host of Nabataean gods and mythological creatures. He quickly recognized the Greek pair Castor and Pollux. Also known as the Dioscuri, the role of these equestrian figures in the Greek myths was to guide the souls of the dead to the Elysian Fields.

In Arabic, the Treasury is known as Khaznet Far'oun—Pharaoh's Treasury. This mysterious name is derived from an ancient tale of a powerful sorcerer of black magic who is said to have hidden a pharaoh's treasure in the massive stone structure. And although no one has ever found gold and jewels behind the walls of the Treasury, Moloch knew all too well that there was indeed a treasure concealed beyond its entrance.

He approached the steps and climbed up toward the masterpiece of ancient design. Dropping to one knee, he pulled the bag from his shoulder and let loose its metal buckle with a snap. He withdrew a worn and tattered leather journal. Sliding the elastic band off the book, Moloch quickly thumbed through a few pages until he found what he was looking for. The second of the twelve riddles.

"'From the Valley of Moses, treading the sands of the gorge.'" Moloch read the words aloud, and they echoed within the eerie dessert silence. "'Arrive at the rose mountain's open mouth and pass through to the land beyond. Seek out the paper room in the paper church to the North—

beneath its floor a metal door lined with the keys to the stars. Pluck a star and travel not far to the castle built by pharaoh for daughter.'"

"Take me to this 'paper church'", he yelled to Martin. "Then I must return to the States."

Martin dismounted, his feet sinking into the sand, and ran to Moloch's side.

"I thought we were just surveying the ruins today." Martin's worry wrinkled his forehead. "There are many armed soldiers scattered about, and we would do much better under the cover of darkness."

"Relax, Martin." Moloch laughed. "Take me on the grand tour, show me what I need to see." Moloch began to scale the stone steps. "I will then take my leave and return with an army of my own."

24

Naamah crossed the threshold of the book store, closing the door behind her. The makeshift bronze bell fastened to the ceiling above rattled out a tinny song as the door latched shut. Taking a step forward, she turned her head slowly from side to side, measuring her surroundings much like a wild animal does crossing into uncharted territory. She was surrounded by the musty pulp of rare and ancient books. Several dozen rows of shelves were fortified by piles of yet more weathered and aged volumes. Still more books were strewn in the exposed rafters on the back wall and across the sills of the two large windows on either side of the rear of the store. The deceptively large building known as The Wings of Horus Bookstore was the home of some of the most unique and mysterious titles in all of Europe. Naamah moved with shadow-like purpose toward the center of the establishment where a desk and some tables sat. Again, she stopped and listened, waiting to pick up some trace of movement in the shop. But nothing stirred. She shrugged her shoulders and shook her head.

"That's bizarre," Naamah whispered to herself as she turned to walk toward a random section of shelves.

"What is?" came a raspy voice from behind her. "I should say *which* is, perhaps, since most things here are quite bizarre, to say the least."

Naamah whirled in the direction of the voice with a bit of a start.

Behind the desk was a small man of advancing years whose brown tweed suit, bushy white beard, and ornate tobacco pipe reminded Naamah of centuries past.

"I was commenting on how strange it was that a store with such treasured items be left unmanned. At the mercy of—"

"At the mercy of a beautiful woman?" He finished with a wink.

Naamah shot the old man a quick smile as she glided toward him, but it quickly faded, the seriousness of her business evident in her eyes.

"I seek an ancient text. Both the original work which was written around 10 BC and the translation which was assembled over several decades in the 1400s."

"My goodness," responded the old man with a hint of amusement in his voice and a smile on his lips. "A young woman who knows what she wants."

Setting his pipe down in a tarnished brass ashtray, the curator made his way around to the front of the desk where Naamah stood. Extending his hand, he spoke proudly, "Allow me to introduce myself. Maxwell Chichester the Third, at your service."

"Chichester." The words emerged like a slow hiss off Naamah's tongue. "I knew your great grandfather quite well." She allowed the words to sink in for a moment. Chichester's smile slowly dissolved into a stern frown as he processed the revelation. His eyes darted toward a plain wooden side table several feet from where he stood. The drawer.

"The drawer..." Naamah could sense his thoughts. When Chichester's gaze returned to Naamah, she was smiling so wide her dimples seemed to be protruding from her face and up into her eyes. Her features morphed and twisted into an unnatural excuse for a smile. He stepped back instinctively, visibly disturbed by her utterly freakish expression.

Leaving a trail of blurred reality behind her, Naamah moved in a fraction of a second to the small antique table. Tapping her open hand on its surface, Naamah's lips parted to expose two rows of razor-like teeth causing Chichester to grimace in fear.

Naamah's composure, and her serene, seductive features, resurfaced as she drew in a deep breath.

"What's in the drawer, Maxie, baby?" she asked in a deep, sultry voice. She brought her fingers down to the time battered wood and began to run them around the frame, tracing its outer ridge. Her pink tongue peeked out from between her lips as she grabbed the handle and tugged it open.

"Wait!" yelled Chichester, lurching toward Naamah.

"What have we got here?" She reached in and brought out several sheets of papyrus. Each sheet was protected within a sheet of laminate material. The pages were filled with the beautiful lines and curves of Hieratic, a shorthand script version of Egyptian Hieroglyphics.

"Well, this isn't what I was looking for. But let's see what we have here, shall we?" Naamah waved one hand in a nonchalant manner, and a high-backed antique chair slid across the store's weathered wood floor, slamming into Chichester's legs and back. The sheer force of the assault sent the bookstore owner's body solidly into the chair. With another wave, the solid maple arms of the chair began to vibrate and hum. The cacophony of metaphysics came to a climax as the arms lifted and spun themselves around Chichester's arms as if made of wet clay, locking him firmly into place.

"You sit, my dear, take a load off ... I will read." Naamah shuffled the papyri. "Hmm. What will I be reading exactly?" she asked as she searched the documents for a starting point or an identifiable title or phrase.

"Ah, here we go," she whispered with a smile of content. "I will read the tale of Amenna, son of Ameny." And with that, she focused her attention solely on the ancient documents in her hands.

25

The Tale of Amenna, Son of Ameny:
   I was on my way to the Pharaoh's mines on a fine ship in the company of one hundred fifty of Egypt's best sailors. As we approached land, the winds picked up and the waves grew high and soon our ship was lost. I managed to seize a piece of wood to save my very life. All the other sailors had been lost, drowned by the sea.

   The waves carried me, and soon I was washed ashore on a deserted island. Saved when all others had perished. The island was unknown to me, but luckily, I found plenty of food—figs, melons, fish, and fowl—and I lacked for nothing. As such, I lit a fire and made an offering to the gods of Egypt. All of a sudden there was a noise like thunder—

The ringing of the small doorbell broke Naamah's concentration, and she looked up toward the entrance to the shop. A young couple, hand-in-hand, entered. The girl was visibly excited, incoherently chattering naive comments as her companion looked mildly interested. Naamah moved swiftly in front of them and with a smile, stated, "We are closed."

The girl looked as though she would cry and turned to her friend with a pout. He had already started to leave when she grabbed his arm. He spun around and looked at her.

"Ah, oh, yeah. Can't we just look around a bit? It would mean a lot to—"

He realized something wasn't quite right. "What the hell is that?"

Naamah didn't even bother to look. She assumed the man had spotted Chichester being actively restrained by an inanimate object. The girl's eyes shot open wide, and she sucked in just enough air to let out one hell of a scream.

"I have no time for this," Naamah said with a shrug. She brought one finger to her lips and then waved it out in their direction. Her timing was perfect. The couple dropped before the budding scream ever had a chance to pass the girl's lips. Naamah returned her attention to the ancient story.

All of a sudden, there was a noise like thunder; the trees shook and the ground trembled, and there before me I saw a huge serpent. It was mighty, blue as lapis lazuli and all overlaid with gold. It drew itself up before me as I cowered on the ground, and three times it asked me, "What has brought you here, little man? If you don't tell me I will make you vanish just like a flame." And then it snatched me up and carried me away in its mouth.

I told the great serpent about my voyage and the shipwreck. And it said to me, "Fear not. If you have come to me, it is the gods who let you live and brought you here to this mysterious isle."

A small puff of air escaped Namaah's nose as she pondered the childlike narrative and fiddled with the loose sheets of papyrus. The story sounded vaguely familiar. She was sure she had heard it in some form or another over the centuries. However, she was not clear how this simple Egyptian tale was linked to the book or the papyrus she was searching for. But Chichester's concern regarding its discovery was sufficient for her to humor the premise of a connection. Namaah continued shuffling the sheets, reading the first few lines of each as she moved through them.

"Okay! This looks right!" She looked up proudly, raising the next page of the story up above her, but her pathetic audience consisted of no more than a squirming curator and a pair of dead lovers at her feet.

"Oh, well." She shrugged it off and slinked over to a green and brown tweed loveseat placed caddy-corner in the West side of the store. There she could see everything going on in the room. She sat and tossed her ebony hair behind her shoulders, sending waves of brunette dancing across the air as if floating, semi-frozen in time. She lifted the next page and began to read, out loud this time. And for absolutely no reason at all, she was reciting the lines in her best French accent.

The great serpent said that I would remain on its island for four months until a ship came bearing sailors from my own land to take me home to my wife and children.

The serpent seemed to enjoy company and conversation, and it talked at length with me. It told me how it lived on the island of plenty with its kindred, and how there were seventy-five serpents altogether.

I bowed and told it that it would be rewarded by the pharaoh with gifts of perfume, oil, and ships laden with treasures. But it just smiled and said, "I am the Prince of Punt, and I already have such riches. When you depart from my island, you will never see it again, for it will be transformed into waves."

Time went by, and just as the serpent had said, after four months had passed, one day I saw a ship. I climbed up a tree so I could see who was aboard, and then rushed to tell the great serpent what I had seen in the distance.

It already knew all about it, and said, "Farewell, farewell. Go home, little one. Within two months you will be at your home once more. Embrace your children, know thy wife, and may your name be blessed amongst your people."

I bowed and thanked the serpent, and it gave me parting gifts of perfume, sweet wood, kohl, incense, ivory, a cape made of shed snake skin, a ring of platinum, and secured between two large, rectangular plates of gold, was a single sheet of papyrus.

I went down to the shore and met the sailors, who took me aboard their ship. Just as the serpent had said, after two months, I arrived home. I sought out the pharaoh's courtiers, and before the whole court I presented the pharaoh with the serpent's gifts, except for the papyrus between the sheets of gold. The serpent had warned the papyrus was for my eyes, and those of my kin, only. After presenting the gifts to pharaoh my story was heard by all in the pharaoh's court.

26

"So, let me get this straight," Namaah said to Chichester as she placed the sheets on the cushion next to her, bringing her hands together and to her lips as if praying. *157 "Amenna, the great and hip son of Ameny, was given 'The Papyrus of the Twelve Gates of Night' by a giant snake on some dissolving island?"

She paused to think.

"Amenna, either having been told the power and worth of the spells by the serpent, or simply guessing their value, kept this great prize from his king."

Namaah rose to her feet and walked toward the chair that still held Chichester in its embrace.

"Well, I guess I don't need you anymore, old chap," Namaah announced in her best British accent this time. "I will trace Amenna's lineage and find what I need at the end of the line."

Raising her hands above her head with palms out, Namaah closed her eyes and began a slow and purposeful chant. Chichester, sensing the end was near, wiggled and squirmed against his restraints, his muffled cries trying to cut their way past the antique wood covering his mouth.

"Namaah!" The curator managed to fire out his strongest and last scream for attention, muffled as it were. It worked. She opened her eyes and looked at Chichester, curious to hear what was so important in these, the final moments of his pathetic life. His facial expression demanded conference with the ancient evil before him. Namaah dropped her arms and nodded her head triggering the wood covering Chichester's mouth to slither away like a snake, allowing him to take a deep breath before he spoke.

"There is more to, to the story…"

Chichester could barely get the words out, choking as he went, "You need me…you still need me."

Namaah smiled a skeptical grin. "Go on, make it fast. It's almost tea time." British again.

"That is not the end of the story," beseeched Chichester.

"It's not? Well, do I *need* to know the end of the story, or are you just trying to buy time here?" Namaah squinted her eyes at Chichester, trying to get a read on him.

"You *need* to know. But I want to make a deal."

"What are your terms, book seller?" hissed the demon.

"I want to live," he stated with a nervous giggle. "Let me live, and I will supply you with the last page of the story. It is here. It is near." He paused to maximize the drama. "And I can promise you, no one else has this information. No demons. No scholars. Not even Alexander Storm." Chichester paused and watched her closely.

"Storm!" the name rattled down her spine like fragments of rusted chain. "What does Storm have to do with any of this?"

Chichester studied Naamah's face for a moment.

"You mean you don't know?" he asked with daring condescension.

"I know he likes to stick his nose in where it doesn't belong, and one of these days someone is going to cut that nose off and feed it to him," Namaah said, growling. "Now I am getting bored with you. Give me the page, and I will let you live."

Namaah clapped her hands together, and the chair let go of Chichester, morphing back to its normal state. He dusted himself off and stretched his back, turning to face Namaah.

"Where is it now?" she asked, frustration building within her.

"There, behind the painting." He pointed across the room to a large framed work hanging on the wall.

Namaah's long legs took a runway march towards the mounted work of art. She would be cautious. She was an old demon, and she had not managed to survive for aeons by ignorantly walking into traps. Standing before the canvas, she began to smile.

"Hieronymus Bosch! How perfect, Maxie. I love it." Namaah looked back at him. "*The Temptation of Saint Anthony*, I believe." Returning her gaze to the masterpiece, she reached up to touch the canvas and frowned as her fingertips withdrew, repulsed. "Oh, Maxie. It's a copy. Very disappointing, I must say. I was hoping to partake in some of anguish and pain that radiates from the artists original works. The pain of his repression and self loathing drips from the canvas like fouled marsh water." She paused. "Oh well, I will just have to indulge my needs elsewhere."

She moved to the side and motioned for him to come forth and examine the painting. He looked up at the large canvas before him. The scene depicted St. Anthony praying while lying on the back of a demon flying through the void. The Saint's eyes stared to the heavens praying, no begging, for strength as he is besieged by all manner of demons and bizarre creatures.

Chichester thought the imagery was quite fitting, and he managed a narrow smile and, perhaps, even a tear.

"Well," Namaah said. "Do your thing. Let's get going here, Maxie."

He nodded to her and reached up to the left-side bottom corner of the painting. Grasping the canvas, he pushed up twice, left once, and there was a click. He turned back to Namaah and smiled a sheepish grin; she nodded him on again. He pulled down on the canvas, and it slid towards the floor by means of a hidden track until it was directly in front of them. Reaching out and grasping the right-side edge he tugged the painting forward. The canvas, as if on a hinge, rose from the wall like a door being opened. It came around full tilt so the back of the painting was the only portion facing the room. There, in the wood catacomb of the canvas frame, was a stone cylinder. He turned back to her again for approval—the she-demon's eyes were on fire.

"Very good, Max," she hissed. "Now bring the prize to Momma."

He reached out and grabbed the cylinder. It was heavy for its small size. He had almost forgotten the powerful feeling it had always instilled just by holding it.

"I haven't held this in my hands for many years," he said excitedly—giddy, almost. "I nearly forgot its power, its beauty, its force!"

Chichester pointed the marbled stone at Namaah and began to read from the Ancient Egyptian carvings on its sides.

"Sesh per Ankh. Sesh per A—"

Something slammed across Maxwell's face so hard that it sent the majority of his teeth to the back of his throat. His eyes, which had instinctively shut in response to the force, popped open in a crazed state of pain and confusion. It was Namaah's black, dead hand over his mouth, and her foul rotten breath.

"Foolish little man," she snarled and spit. "I would have let you live."

Chichester's eyes widened with pain and fear. She snatched the stone cylinder from his hands and pushed him to the floor. His hands immediately fumbled for his broken and bloody face, as cries of agony spilt out into the bookstore from his gaping hole of a mouth. Namaah backed away and looked down at the carvings in the stone. She laughed out loud. A simple Egyptian exorcism spell. He had almost gotten her with a two sentence Egyptian spell. It wouldn't have killed her, but it would have given him some time to hide himself and the contents of the cylinder. With that thought, she opened it and peered inside at the contents. She wasn't taking any chances. She wanted to be sure it contained something before she annihilated Chichester. There was a scroll in there. She felt it on her fingers and she sensed, by touch, it held great power. Satisfied, she turned back to Max. He had managed to get to his feet by grasping the painting and, with great difficulty, pulling himself upright. Unfazed, Namaah flicked her fingers in his direction and magically spun him around, pinning him against the wall to face her, causing the macabre painting to flip over again so the images were visible once more. Namaah gazed at Bosch's handiwork.

"You know, I speak to him from time to time, Maxie, Maximillian, Maximus. Bosch, that is, not that asshole Saint Anthony," she clarified with a snicker. "He is sick and perverted—and tormented—just like you will be. He fears the plague. Can you imagine? So, we put him in with the rats sometimes, and other times we blacken and swell his body with puss and blood. Then we like to make him paint for us with his own rotted fluids. Wait a minute." She paused for a moment in contemplation. "Maxwell, I have decided you have given me what I asked for, and as such, I will uphold our bargain. You have truly inspired me; my artistic beast has been set free. You are quite a muse Maxie. Damn."

Namaah turned and walked toward Chichester.

"We will just go ahead and ignore your little transgressions, buddy boy," she said in her best Groucho Marx impersonation, using the cylinder as a cigar.

She slid the stone vessel into the folds of her clothes and clapped her hands together above her head. She began to sway back and forth like a Bali dancer—hips rounding, arms, neck, and shoulders moving in synch.

Her erotic movements came to a sudden halt as she ended her mock dance. "Just kidding!" she said with a chuckle, pointing at Chichester. Just as quickly as her laughter had started, it stopped; her face grew dark and her eyes ignited with the flames of Hell. She parted her flushed lips ever so slightly and whispered something foul into the air. The whisper took on a form—a glowing mist of black and purple haze as the words echoed in on themselves over and over, ad infinitum, growing in intensity and pitch until deafening heights were reached. Chichester screamed as his ears spewed forth a crimson river of blood. Flames now surrounded his body and veins of dark, heavy clouds of matter stretched out like skeletal fingers, invading every orifice of his body with their vulgar intent. He could feel his insides being twisted and contorted. He could feel his skin tearing and changing. He could feel all of this, but could not see it since his eyes had been ripped from his skull. Maxwell Chichester screamed and screamed until something shut his mouth with a violent snap. Then Maxwell Chichester made no more sounds.

Namaah laughed, spit on the ground, and was gone.

27

"A strategic response is required at this point, Decker." Alexander Storm spoke softly, but the purpose behind his words was sternly echoed in his tone. "The cogs and gears of this plan must be set to spin with some urgency you understand."

Alex was pacing back and forth amongst the desks in the library work area. He could see the confused expressions plastered on the faces of his newly assembled fellowship. He was more than certain that each of them was questioning why they had been summoned to Dragon Loch, and whether their host was nothing more than an eccentric madman. Alexander was disappointed he wasn't going to be able to introduce himself and his purpose in the manner he had planned, but there were more pressing issues at hand, and the group would instead be forced to get some on-the-job training.

"Trial by fire," Alexander half-whispered to himself.

"What's that, Alex?" asked Decks.

"I said, trial by fire." He lifted his chin to motion to Decks towards his visitors' questioning stares. Decks, tilting his head to one side and squinting slightly, shifted his gaze from Alex to the small group.

"That's fine, Alex. They'll figure it out."

William Decker walked swiftly to his friend's side. He was close now.

Close enough to whisper to Alexander. Close enough to see the concern in Alex's eyes.

"Don't worry about them right now. You worked very hard to find this group. To bring them here. Put them to work, Alex. They might surprise you."

Alex turned to Decks and smirked. "I have no doubt they will live up to expectations."

"Settled," Decks continued to whisper, "and that being said, we need to formulate a plan of attack. We are about to enter into a war, perhaps the greatest war of all time, and speed and accuracy will be the key to victory."

"You are right, my friend!" yelled Alex with new fervor, breaking free of the clandestine conversation. "Asar, come here, please!"

Asar, who had been waiting for direction in the wings, quickly sprang to attention and awaited Alex's directive. As a loyal soldier awaiting his command, enthusiasm and unquestioning servitude radiating in his expression.

"Asar, we are going to be traveling to the main land," Alexander spoke quickly, euphoric on his minds cognitive escalation. "We may need weapons. Light fare for now. Also, have a vehicle waiting that can fit a few of us comfortably for some distance." Alexander spun around to look at his team. They were rising and milling about—they sensed the excitement. Some more than others, but it was there.

"Excuse me, sir?" Keith called from the front of the group. "Excuse me?"

"One moment, Keith," replied Alexander somewhat impatiently. He was trying to gather his thoughts. "I will be with you momentarily."

Turning back to Decks, he placed one hand on his shoulder.

"Decks, are you familiar with the Ebbers family on Long Island?"

"Of course. Legend and rumor have it they were entrusted with fragmentary information regarding *The Book of Gates*—"

"Yes, yes, yes." Alex interrupted him before he could continue. "All of you, gather round quickly," he yelled to his guests, who in turn sped to his side.

"How do I explain this?" Alexander pondered out loud.

"Just spit it out," Kate suggested.

"Excellent advice, Kate," smiled Alex. He liked her very much. Kate was smart and tough. Her innocent beauty, often overshadowed by an unquenchable thirst for knowledge. She reminded him of her mother.

"We have a bit of an unplanned, but certainly not unforeseen, predicament as it were—we have several different, um, 'beings' for lack of a better term, searching for a series of papyri whose content could amount to catastrophic results if they were to fall into the wrong hands. The papyrus is commonly referred to as *The Book of Gates,* and it's an ancient Egyptian manuscript said to have been entrusted to mankind by the god Isis after she resurrected Osiris, freeing his spirit from the underworld. Everyone following me so far?" asked Alex. Hesitantly, they all nodded, their skepticism as to what was coming next was abound.

"At some point in history, three brothers figured out just how dangerous *The Book of Gates* was. In the wrong hands, it could be used to raise all manner of filth and evil from the depths of the underworld, from Hell. So, the brothers decided they would destroy it." Alexander lowered his voice to almost a whisper. "However, try as they would, the three brothers could not destroy the papyrus."

Kate raised her hand as if in a classroom. She was taking notes in a leather-bound journal.

"Yes, Kate?" asked Alex, trying to restrain his annoyance at being interrupted.

"You don't mind if I take notes, do you?" she asked.

"No, I don't mind," replied Alexander. "I prefer it." He shot her a smile, which she reciprocated shyly. It lasted no more than a millisecond, just long enough for it to register to Keith.

"Also, what were the brothers' names? Would we know who they are? Which century was this?"

"You do not know them, and their identity is unimportant for the time being." Alexander turned to face the rest of the group to finish his tale.

"The papyri could not be destroyed, but two of the brothers visited an old and powerful holy man—an ancient—and together they broke the papyri into twelve parts. These parts were then scattered around the globe."

"So, we are talking about a scavenger hunt!" Samantha blurted out. "I love a good treasure hunt!"

"A treasure hunt it is, my dear," Alexander said with quiet purpose. He turned and began to walk toward Samantha, and their eyes locked. Samantha could feel the soft hairs on the back of her neck stand up. Alexander's eyes were alive with fire and energy. She could feel the power in his stare—he bored right into the depths of her being. Alex strode to her side, reached out, and touched her hand.

"But this treasure hunt, my dear girl, is like none you have ever been on...like *no one* has ever been on." Alex paused for a second, still looking into Samantha's eyes. His own narrowed to an intense squint. His sharp, handsome features faded from Sam's vision until all she could see were his eyes.

"I do hope you are up to the challenge." Breaking the ocular link with Sam, he spun to face Abigail, who was obviously still shaken. Her eyes veered away from his, and with a sharp laugh, Alexander moved back to the center of the group.

"What the hell was that?" whispered Keith out of the side of his mouth.

"Shh," smiled Kate. "He's eccentric. I like it."

Keith raised one the corner of his lip and lowered his eyebrows. "Oh, is *that* what you call it? Eccentric?" He crossed his eyes at Kate. She giggled and once again shushed him.

"Where was I? Ah, yes," Alexander began again. "So, the papyrus was split into twelve parts and divided between two of the brothers. Each brother took his six pieces and traveled the world. For hundreds of years, the brothers sought out unique locations to hide the fragments of the ancient work. They traversed the globe, from remote islands to barren desert wastelands. Climbing the highest mountains and descending into the lowest depths in search of the perfect hiding spots for the disassembled *Book of Gates*. After each brother had completed his task, they came together one last time. Realizing that it might someday become possible to destroy the papyri, they felt it best to leave a map to the twelve pieces. But they needed to do it in such a way it could not be easily deciphered if it fell into the wrong hands. Together, the two brothers drafted their map of riddles upon a sheet of ancient papyrus. On this document lay the key to *The Book of Gates*. Twelve riddles crafted for only the strongest of mind and heart." Alexander ran his hand through his hair and looked off into the distance for a brief moment. He reached out and placed his hand upon Decker's shoulder.

"*The Riddle of the Gates*, as it became known, was entrusted to a blood-line of Paladins—or holy warriors—who swore upon their very souls to protect the riddles at all costs...until the end of time." Alex pushed his lips together in a sullen smile which was directed at Decks, squeezed his friend's shoulder, then looked back at the group.

"The riddles themselves were written in an ancient script, already long dead at the time the brothers' drafting. They then returned to their home-land and sought out their brother. They told him their tale and spoke of their travels. They did not tell their other brother the secrets of the hidden locations." Alexander paused as he listened to the gusts of wind picking up strength as they crashed against the castle walls, forcing him to pause his explanation. His hands came together as if in prayer.

"As I was saying," he continued, "the third brother knew nothing of the locations of the fragments. They did, however, tell him of *The Riddle of the Gates* and identified the bloodline entrusted with its protection."

The others had inadvertently moved in closer, and Alexander noticed a few of them reacting to the symphony of wind pounding the walls with growing fervor.

"That night, the brothers celebrated with a great feast. They danced and drank until the sun rose the next morning. Then, without word or warning, the two brothers who had hidden the twelve pieces took sharp steel to their own throats and severed all knowledge of their secrets."

"Well, except for the riddles, that is." Kate moved towards Alexander. "Except for the papyrus they gave the Paladins, right?"

Alexander smiled at Kate once again. "Yes. Except for the cursed riddles."

The large stained-glass window just to their right began to rattle, almost imperceptibly at first. Alex's eyes darted from face to face looking for any signs of concern. More noticeable, though was the ticking chatter of nails on the stone floor as his dogs charged into the library, coming to a sliding halt at their master's feet. Samantha bent down and began to rub under Frodo's chin. The dog licked her hand, then both canines began to whimper and bark.

"What is it, boys?" coaxed Alexander. Then he caught sight of Abigail's face. Terror. Her eyes transfixed on the sixty-foot high clattering window threatening to shatter into fractals any second. Its colorful swirls and lines depicted a splendid rendition of King George and the Dragon. The commotion of the shaking and clamoring far outweighed the turbulence of the winds, and Alexander turned back to Abigail whose face was twisted in a silent shriek.

"What's there, Abigail?" Alex yelled as he nodded to Decker. "Abigail, what has come to pay us a visit on this most dark of nights?"

Alexander moved to the right with impressive agility, and as his long black cloak sailed through the air, draping behind his body, he reached for the throat clasp and released it into the air, exposing a brilliant silver sword strapped to his leg. His strong hand grasped the ornate dragon head handle, and the ruby-red eyes inlaid in the sword glowed furiously. With a smooth arc of his shoulder and arm, he drew the blade from its sheath and raised it toward the menacing glass.

"Well!" he screamed into the night. "Let's get on with it!"

With that, the great panel bowed and roared like some great leviathan from the depths below, and the wind lashed its fury against the castle wall. There was an incalculable moment of silence, then a deathly sucking as the pressure finally gave way to the battering forces of nature, exploding the ethereal art into thousands of pieces. The shards jetted inward like an assassin's razors but came to a dead stop midair. The group of initiates stared in disbelief as thousands of colorful daggers floated in suspended animation.

"Asar!" called Alexander. "Take them to the ship! Take them all and get to the mainland!" Asar dashed to Alex's side.

Dread marked his face, but determination fueled his soul. Asar cried, "I must stay and fight! I must—"

Asar was cut off by Alexander's grasp on his jacket.

"You must do as I say," said Alex, "and you must do it now!" Alexander's voice deepened with conviction. "Or else, I fear all is lost." He shoved Asar back to quickly herd the group together and away to some semblance of safety. For Alex knew there was no long-term retreat from the evil that had besieged them.

"You must follow me!" Asar yelled to the others. "Stay close and be silent!"

As Asar began to lead the way, Alexander shouted to him, "Wait for us on the other side! Decker and I will..."

His voice trailed off when the floating glass decided to start moving again. Something else, something even more dangerous, was coming.

"Alexander!" Decker shouted.

"I see it, Decks! I see it!"

Following behind the glass, slithering in from the darkness, was a black cloud in the form of a massive serpent.

As Asar hurried the group through the nearest passage out of the library, he and Kate paused just long enough to see the glass exploding against the castle floor and the great serpent coiling into strike position, head and fangs aimed in Alexander's direction.

"We have to help them!" shouted Kate, attempting to push past Asar and back into the library. But he grabbed her firmly and pulled her back to him.

"Young lady," he shouted, his frown turning to a smile. "It is the serpent that could use your help, not Alexander." He shook her a bit and laughed— a big, hearty laugh. Kate smiled back. A broken and stunned smile, but a smile just the same. She turned and looked back at Alexander once more. He was staring directly at her—he winked, flashed a wry smile, and raised his sword above his head, poised to engage the serpent. But before she could witness the fantastical clash, Asar pulled her through the door and out of sight of the battle. It was in that instance that Kate realized her life was changed, forever.

28

The hull of the ship cut through the white caps of the rough water with ease. The wind had largely retreated, but the swells still made for a choppy ride. The *Tiamat*, however, was built for turbulent seas. Stretching over 240 feet long, Alexander had built her to be a castle at sea, and had spared no expense in this endeavor. The deck housed an array of high-tech gadgetry including a helipad, upon which sat a small chopper. To the stern lay a massive mechanical arm which held, suspended, a side-launch turbo explorer boat. There were rows of sonar, radar, and communication dishes and antennas. The captain's helm rose from the ship's forward deck and was wrapped in brilliantly etched glass depicting all manner of sea creatures in vivid detail. The quarters of the *Tiamat* were just as impressive. With twenty-six state rooms, a captain's quarters, a full galley and dining area, laboratory, and library, the vessel acted as a floating Dragon's Loch. Her power and stature enabled Alex to travel to the four corners of the globe.

Asar stood at the helm with binoculars in hand. He raised the night vision-equipped Sightmark Ghost Hunters to his eyes and scanned the horizon, cutting through the pitch black. Once satisfied there was nothing waiting on the other side of darkness, he began the whole process over again.

The *Tiamat's* first mate, Samuel, was at the wheel to Asar's left. He was relying on the ship's state-of-the-art navigation equipment to travel the dark sea, never looking out the glass pane before him. Samuel's tanned, leathery hands grasped the ornate wood wheel tightly. He had been fore-warned of the possible dangers that could befall the crew of the *Tiamat* on this particular excursion. Having helmed Alexander Storm's ships for many years, he had become quite accustomed to the bizarre, the danger-ous, and the unexpected. His thoughts drifted back in time to a particular trip to Easter Island in the South eastern Pacific. His shoulders lifted a bit as a cold chill ran down his spine. Samuel Windsom was not a timid man. He had been raised in the Nordic tradition of the sea on a small island off the coast of Finland. With his first breath the hearty salt air had filled his lungs. Of his fifty-some-odd years, Samuel had spent nearly every one of them on the water. The sea had taken his father, a village fisherman, when he was only six years old. An influenza outbreak on the island claimed his mother and younger brother only three years later. Alone and penniless at the age of nine, Samuel took to the very sea that had begun his youth's path of tragedy, and he never looked back. It was some years later when he and Alexander had crossed ways on a Polynesian voyage, that his life's true adventures began. He had been piloting Alex's former ship, the *Leviathan*, which now lay under 35,000 feet of salt water at the bottom of the Pacific Ocean. Alexander had become obsessed with locating the fabled "place of departed souls," which had been mentioned so predominantly in Easter Island lore. After two weeks on the island, Alexander and company returned to the *Leviathan*, demanding a hasty departure. They had brought something back to the ship with them, and with it followed evil. After only an hour out at sea, the side of the ship was hit with such force it almost capsized the hulk of a vessel. The hull had been ruptured, and the *Leviathan* immediately began to take on water and sink. The crew had scrambled to the launches and abandoned ship. Samuel remembered the look of terror in his mate's eyes as the deep-sea sharks began to breach the surface of the water. Soon, their fear of what awaited below changed to a fear of what descended from above. A large winged mass had streaked across the sky high above the rafts. Its black-as-night features stood in extreme contrast against the crystal blue Polynesian sky. The apparition dove at them, and in a black blur, crew members began to disappear from the life boats. Once, twice, three times the creature descended, and each time a man was lost. Panicked, two crew members fell over the small boat's sides into the water. They were immediately converged on by the sharks, whose numbers had grown so numerous that their movements created a sea of white caps around the small boats. The water would burst into a frenzy of ivory mist which quickly transformed to red as another mate was lost to the predators. Samuel recalled how Alexander had risen to his feet, arms outstretched, and began to chant into stinging whip of the sea's salty wind. He had not been able to make out the words, or even what language Alexander was speaking, but after several seconds his din of metaphysical prose caused the air around the winged creature to ripple as it does over asphalt on a hot summer day. The effect expanded inward, eventually engulfing the black mass in a bright flash of light—so bright that the men watching the awesome supernatural spectacle had been rendered temporarily blind. Samuel, having averted his eyes from the display, watched as Alexander sat back down, folding his arms across his gut as if in excruciating pain. He watched as Storm closed his eyes, spoke several unintelligible words, then extended his arm toward the water. The men in the other two boats shrieked and yelled in Alexander's direction as dozens of oversized dorsal fins breached the water's surface and set a course towards a handful of men huddled together in the water. In sheer panic, the sea bound men besieged Alexander's boat. The desperate swimmers kicked and tugged at each other in self-preserving attempts to flee the open water. Samuel had seen how Alexander's eyes popped wide open as he lunged to the boat's side and pressed one extended finger below the surface of the water. The sound that followed, like a giant bell rung deep below the water's surface, thundered and produced massive shock waves. The echo of the suboceanic bell quickly faded, and with it, the onslaught of fins vanished and dematerialized before their eyes. "Meke-Meke," the mate next to him had whispered. It wasn't until sometime later that Samuel learned what the words meant. It was the islanders' name for the great demon fabled to haunt the skies above them. In fact, the inhabitants of Easter Island feared this creature so much they spent an immeasurable amount of time constructing massive stone figures with the sole purpose of warding off the creature.

"Meke-Meke," Samuel muttered with contempt.

"What?" yelled Asar as he lowered his binoculars and spun toward Samuel.

"Why in God's name, Sam, would you mention that accursed creature here and now?" Asar asked in disbelief.

"Eh," Samuel replied waving one hand at Asar. "Besides, Alexander put that big turkey in its place."

Asar shook his head. "Yes, my friend. But Alex is not here with us now, is he?"

Samuel's smirk faded from his weather-beaten face, and the sea dog turned back to the wheel mumbling some insult under his breath.

"That's what I thought," scolded Asar as he returned to surveying the waters ahead of them. The ship pounded on through the waves as the two men swayed back and forth in silence for a time. The rhythm of the water lulling their nerves a bit.

"So, what are you two looking for?" The men turned to see Kate at the base of the helm, her hands on her hips. "And where is Alexander?"

Asar nodded to Sam, who returned to navigating the *Tiamat*. Kate ascended the stairs and filled the open space between the two men.

"How are the others, Miss Kate?" Asar asked with paternal curiosity.

"They are settled in and resting," she replied. "They are, of course, curious as to what the hell is going on."

Asar smiled at the young woman. Her beauty was exotic, thinly veiled behind her exterior innocence. Her stern tone emanating from her slight stature made him smile, marveling in her courageous tenacity. Asar liked her.

"Did they send you to inquire?" he asked.

"Inquire?" she paused. "No. They sent me to find out what the hell is going on, like I said."

"Ah, their fearless leader," Asar replied with a grin.

Kate crossed her arms and moved closer to Asar. "And where are we going?" She uncrossed her arms and thrust her hands into the tight pockets of her frayed jeans. "And again, where is Mr. Storm and the other guy?" She leaned back against a tall swivel chair and hopped up into it. This time she whispered, the masked terror cracking her voice inadvertently, demonstrating she was obviously more frightened than she was letting on. "And what are you looking for out there?"

Asar paused for a moment to collect his thoughts. He preferred Alexander explain things, but he was not there, and the group was worried and tired. He shared in their sentiment.

"Well, young lady, it seems we have some things to discuss."

"That's right. You bet we do," she replied. Her confidence returned, and her stern eyes and demanding demeanor impressed him once again.

Asar walked over to Kate and took the chair next to her. He leaned forward, resting his elbows on his legs.

"Where to begin..." he exhaled with force as the ship barreled on through the night toward the sleepy eastern shoreline of Long Island.

29

Moloch gazed down at the small box on the table. It was constructed of a dark metal, reminiscent of aged silver, or something akin to it. The vessel had tarnished with time, but not as one would expect silver to age. Rather than developing a brown hue, the box had simply grown dark, resembling pewter. Moreover, there was a strength and mass to the metal which defied the common properties of ancient silver. Moloch reached forward and grasped the box in his timeless hands, balancing it in the center of his palm, he bounced his arm up and down. Moloch nodded, appreciating the supernatural weight of the box.

"The strength of steel," he said out loud, turning his attention to the soldier of fortune standing on the other side of the table, "with the weight of platinum."

Moloch placed the box back on the table. "What do you suppose it's made of, Joshua?" he asked the soldier as he crouched down to look across the top of the box. He could make out faint etchings in its surface, nearly worn bare by the passage of time.

"Well, I am sure I do not know sir," Joshua replied in a perfect southern drawl. "But if anything comes out of it that you disagree with, I can kill it," he added with a momentary smirk.

Moloch snorted in amusement as he rose to face him.

"I like you, Joshua. How did you get involved with the Germans?" He strolled toward the other side of the table. Reaching into his jacket's inside pocket, he withdrew a dark burgundy cigarette case. He pressed his thumb on the case's latch button, and the top sprang open. Moloch plucked out an expertly rolled cigarette, then tapped it against the case, shifting the tobacco inside to one end.

"How did you end up in Egypt with us? Or assigned to my car for that matter?" *180 Moloch stopped several feet from Joshua and placed the smoke between his lips. Joshua caught a glimpse of the razor-like teeth behind Moloch's smile. He shouldered his rifle and stuck his hand into the pocket of his fatigues.

"Well, sir, I am exceptional under fire." With dexterous precision he whipped a match from his pocket and snapped his fingers together, igniting it in a burst of smoke and sulfur. Cupping the match with his other hand, he gingerly lit Moloch's cigarette. As its glow intensified, Moloch smiled and blew the match out with a sharp burst. Joshua withdrew back a step or two, a slight gasp of air escaping his lungs as he moved. In the match's flare, he was sure he had seen the tormented, screaming faces of children in the dark pupils of Moloch's eyes.

"Something wrong, Joshua?" Moloch asked with a sarcastic grin. "Catch sight of the future?"

Joshua said nothing.

"Well, I do hope you are up for the challenge. We have much work to do."

Moloch returned to his place before the box. He reached out and ran his hand across its top. From where Joshua stood, he could make out faint reliefs or carvings in its top. He ventured forward to get a better look.

"What is that?" he asked Moloch. "There on the top?"

Moloch exhaled but did not look up at Joshua.

"That, my dear boy, is a dragon."

30

Completely drained, Abigail lay on the bed of the stateroom she and Samantha had ducked into. Sam, noting her weary companion's state, had suggested she rest a bit. The others, preoccupied with the events transpiring, seemed oblivious to Abigail's mental and physical breakdown, so Samantha had led her there in hopes of helping the poor girl and perhaps getting the answers to a few questions. Abigail seemed attuned to what was going on, but Sam was still unsure about what her involvement was, exactly, in the grand scheme of things.

The stateroom was just that—stately. A large king-size bed, private bathroom, dressers, and a computer station fit in there comfortably. Sam guessed they were in Alexander's room. She reached out and touched the bed. In a harmless attempt at camaraderie she climbed in to the bed next to Abi. Abigail was lying on her back, eyes shut, hands crossed on top of her chest. Her long white dress was bunched up all over and hoisted up to the middle of her thighs. Sam could see faint beads of sweat on the dark skin of her legs. She reached out and touched the top of Abigail's hand; it was warm and clammy, even though the room was cool. Abigail opened her eyes in response to Sam's touch.

"You okay, girl?" Samantha asked.

"Yeah. I think so," she said, nodding her head slightly.

"You don't look so hot."

"I'm fine. Just tired," she said, closing her eyes again.

"What's going on, Abigail?"

Abigail lay motionless, her warm skin heating the cool sheets of Alexander's bed.

"I'm not sure, Samantha. I can feel the danger—the impending doom—but I don't know why or from what."

Sam giggled nervously. "Great." Then she lowered her head into her hand and rubbed her forehead. She could feel the hard motions of the ship deep in her stomach. She didn't have to be psychic or a clairvoyant—or whatever the hell Abi was—to feel the danger. She thought back to the group of kids the other night. Their faces. She hadn't felt right since then. And it was only getting worse.

"That was some sick shit back there at the castle, huh?"

Abigail didn't respond. She had dozed off again and was dreaming dreams of a great hole in the Earth and Hell flowing up from its depths. A solitary tear pressed free of her sleeping eye, and ran silently down her cheek.

31

"We are arriving at port," Samuel announced over the PA system. Keith got up from his chair and exited the small room, which served as the ship's library. He had been waiting for Kate to return, but she never came back. He pulled the door of the library closed behind him and turned to head up the corridor toward the bridge. He stopped dead in his tracks. Something had moved just ahead of him in the dimly lit hall.

"Kate? Is that you?"

No response, just a fleeting shadow up ahead.

"Who's there?"

Still nothing. Keith turned to go back into the library. The handle was locked.

"Shit, I must have hit the lock," he mumbled to himself. He turned and walked in the opposite direction. Slowly at first, he rounded the bend of the ship and followed the corridor deeper into the *Tiamat*. His ears registered a faint shuffle triggering his heart rate to increase. Something moved behind him. He began to quicken his pace.

"Where the hell is everybody!" the words left his lips in transition from whisper to yell. Fight or flight kicked in, and Keith chose flight. Scared to look over his shoulder, he barreled through the vessel's narrow halls.

"Help!" The words clamored out from deep within him, echoing around the rocking ship's passageway. Keith was in full sprint, still fleeing from the unseen force behind him, but he wasn't going to stop. He would keep running forever if he had to.

"Oh God!" he gasped. Something was coming out from the wall of the corridor just in front of him. He couldn't stop.

"Must keeping running...beat it...blow by it...run faster... forever," his mind reeled. He willed his adrenaline laced legs to pump as fast as they could, shutting his eyes as he met with the terror before him. Then he felt it. The sheer, unadulterated terror coursing through every fiber of his being as something grabbed his arm and spun him around. The momentum of his running coupled with the centrifugal force of his spin, hurled his body up against the inner wall of the corridor. He screamed.

"Hey! Killer! Open your eyes, tough guy!"

It was Kate's voice coming from up ahead.

"Kate!" Keith opened his eyes and saw her laughing. "You scared the crap out of me!"

"Obviously! Do you need to change your undies there, big guy?" Kate continued to chuckle.

Keith slid down the wall, head hung, to the floor. The adrenaline pumping through his veins quickly converting to muscle exhaustion. His breathing slowed a bit, and he actually laughed. A weak laugh, but a laugh all the same. He was relieved, as always, to see her.

"You're an ass," he said with, courage resurfacing in his chest. "You know there are real monsters this time, Kate. You don't need to screw with me."

"Okay, okay! Take it easy. Let's go grab the others." She extended her hand and hoisted Keith to his feet. Once up, she ran her hand across his back as they started back toward the front of the ship.

"How the hell did you get in front of me so fast?" Keith asked.

"Huh?" replied Kate.

"In front of me, you were right behind me, then you came out from in front of me."

Kate's smile faded.

"I was never behind you Keith, I came from the other direction. I heard your racket and stepped in the shadows to goose ya."

"Oh, crap, Kate."

"Yeah...let's get the hell off this ship before we end up at the bottom of the Atlantic."

The two of them looked at each other; Kate glanced over her shoulder briefly and nudged Keith to move forward as they sprinted towards the bridge. Perhaps it was the ever-famous power of suggestion, or perhaps it was the rocking vessel's use of light and water bouncing in through the ship's portals; either way Kate was sure of one thing, she had seen movement in the shadows behind them as well.

32

"What do you think you are doing, Naamah?" demanded Moloch. The demon was on top of her naked body, straddling her and holding her arms down at the wrists. She squinted up at him and struggled to raise her arms. Each time she got close; Moloch pressed them back down into the mattress.

"Get the fuck off, Moloch," she demanded. "Or, or I swear—"

He lowered himself toward her. "You swear what?" he whispered, inches from her face. His bourbon and tobacco laced breath invading her nostrils. She bucked again, and Moloch's body snapped upright. He looked deep into her eyes, and he saw familiarity. Tilting his head slightly sideways, he never broke their connection. "You swear what?" he repeated calmly and snapped his hands from her wrists. Naamah lay there for some time, not moving, staring at his face. Slowly, a smile crept across his lips. His gaze relaxed and wandered across her body, the familiar terrain of an exotic isle. She was an exquisite creature; the master had truly created a mechanism of temptation in her form. His eyes floated across her breasts, and soon his hands followed. Naamah smiled, biting her lower lip, over acting her part as the consummate seductress. Moloch did not mind the show. His hands glided down her body, which reacted by arching up towards his touch as a moan of pleasure escaped her slightly parted lips. She reached up and wrapped her arms around his body, pulling him closer, their mouths finally meeting in an unholy union as Naamah's long legs encircled his hips, squeezing him against her velvet skin.

"You were saying?" She toyed with him, pulling away from their embrace. Moloch grabbed the back of her long black hair and forced her back to him. His other hand reached back and grabbed her ankle, driving it up into the air.

"Later," he whispered. "We will address that later." He grasped her hair even tighter and held her face against his own. "But we *will* address it." Once more Moloch pressed his lips firmly on hers as they resumed their dark waltz.

33

"Make haste if you will please" shouted Alexander to the group of nervous travelers as they disembarked the *Tiamat*. He was standing under the flickering light of a lamp post at the entrance to the dock, his long black coat wrapped tightly around him to fend off the cold of night.

Kate, who had just stepped foot on the docking plank of the ship, looked up in disbelief.

"Alexander!" she cried out and ran towards him. His presence had an inexplicable reassuring effect on her. The excitement of the moment mixed with the salty cold night air took her breath away. Kate's chest heaved up and down as she walked the last two steps to him. She looked at his smiling face and sensed the slightest manifestations of apprehension behind the confident mask he had donned for his guests.

"What happened?" Kate started. "What was that thing? How did you get away?" She swallowed and raised her hand and poked Alex in chest. "And how in God's name did you get here before us?"

"Easy, Kate." Alexander demanded, sensing a second poke coming. He reached out and caught her hand, cupping it in his own with a soft grasp. "Easy now." Something about Alexander's voice calmed her, and Kate could feel her composure returning.

Kate snapped her hand away from his and leaned in closer. "What the hell is going on?" The words each fell like the blow of a powerful hammer.

Keith watched the bizarre interaction between Kate and Alexander, and he felt a hollow, sinking feeling in his gut.

"Who is this guy," he thought? He walked quickly toward the lamp post and grabbed Kate by the shoulders, pulling her back a few steps.

"You heard her, Storm," he said, snarling. "What's your game?"

"Wait, Keith," Kate started, but Keith raised his hand up, silencing her pleas.

Alexander raised one eyebrow and lowered his chin. "This is no game, I assure you." He reached out and placed a comforting hand on Keith's shoulder. "And I promise to answer all your questions and more," he said as he looked over at Asar. Alexander nodded and smiled humbly at his old friend.

"Are the vehicles ready?" Alexander asked Asar.

"Yes," he replied. "And I am very glad to see you."

"You as well, Asar. I am glad to see you as well."

"Where is Decker?" Samantha suddenly spoke up. "Did he make it?"

"I assure you, William is unharmed, Sam." Alexander turned to meet the tough computer guru's gaze. "He has gone ahead on another leg of our treasure hunt." Alex smiled and began to turn back to Keith, but quickly returned to Sam, adding, "Your words I believe."

"So..." Keith attempted to regain Alexander's attention by waving a hand in front of Alex's face.

"So. We have much to discuss," Alex answered as Keith tried to interrupt. "And yes, I will answer your questions. But we must get on the move here. The hour is already late. We will talk on the ride over."

Alexander turned toward the worn wooden steps leading away from the docks.

"Where are we going, Alexander?" demanded Kate. Alex turned back to her and smiled.

"To the island residence of Jonathan Ebbers." He paused a moment then turned back to the stairs. "And in the words of my favorite crime fighter, the game is afoot."

34

W illiam Decker's plane touched down at Cairo International Airport. As the landing gear hit the ground, the breath he had been holding in since the pilot had begun his descent escaped his lips with force. Decker wasn't fond of flying. In all honesty, he hated it. Asar would often make fun of him, laughing at the fact that Decks could walk into a pitch-black room and do battle with all manner of beasts, but flying scared the crap out of him. Wherever feasible, Alexander would make special arrangements when it came to Decker's travels in order to reduce his time in the air. Trains, boats, cars, and even a dusty old camel were preferred by Decker over air travel. Alexander had decided to send him ahead to investigate the events that had transpired in Egypt. In an effort to have the group cover more ground, Alex had made the decision to let Decker take a separate path. Besides, Alexander had no idea where they might be heading, so he liked the idea of having an emissary in this part of the world for quick deployment purposes should the need arise. Decker reached into the inner pocket of his tattered black leather jacket and fumbled for his cell phone. Grappling with it, he turned off airplane mode and waited for the messages to pour in. Nothing.

Decker stood up and retrieved his bag, which he had secured in the overhead compartment. He flipped the bag's strap over his shoulder and made his way into the line of lemmings waiting to exit the aircraft. Decks gazed at his watch. The well-worn brown leather band seemed to scream for reinforcements, while the deeply etched glass face almost obliterated the Roman numerals beneath.

"Six-twenty," he mumbled to himself. "made good time." He shifted back and forth in the exit line as impatiently as a child waiting for the bathroom.

"Very good time," came a soft feminine voice from behind him. Decker peered over his shoulder. She continued, "Sorry, I heard you commenting on the trip time ... to yourself"

Decker turned to face his fellow traveler. She was petite and pretty. Her dark features and facial structure led Decker to assume she was a local returning home.

"No problem," Decks replied. He was able to get a better look at her. Her long black hair and dark eyes were mesmerizing, and he found himself transfixed by her gaze. Suddenly, the woman smiled and nodded her head, motioning his attentions to the departing passengers in front of him. He smiled back for a moment, caught in the moment, before the meaning of her gesture dawned on him. He quickly looked back toward the front of plane and saw the line had moved a bit.

"Oh, sorry," he said while taking a few steps forward. He felt foolish and was sure he was blushing. He looked at his watch again, not knowing what else to do with himself.

"Are you on a tight schedule?" she inquired.

"Somewhat," he replied as he turned to face her again. She was smiling at him, and it was sexy. That's the only way he could describe it. She wore the smile in her eyes, not just her lips, and it gave him butterflies in his stomach.

"You have a beautiful smile." The words just flew out, and the forward-ness was a little out of character for Decker. She didn't turn away or seem embarrassed, though. In fact, her smile seemed to grow bigger.

"You're not so bad yourself," she replied while raising both her eyebrows in unison. Decker grinned at her for a few moments, but it didn't seem uncomfortable or awkward this time. The line started moving again, and she motioned him forward. He took a few steps and turned back round to face her.

"Anika," she said with an extended hand. He reached out and took her hand. It was soft and warm.

"Decker," he said, "William Decker. But my friends call me Decks."

They were still holding each other's hand. The butterflies were fluttering stronger than ever.

"Well, William," she said with a bit of a laugh, "what brings you to Egypt? Sightseeing? Business? Pleasure?" The word *pleasure* seemed to flit from her mouth, beginning with a very exaggerated movement of her tongue and ending with her full lips in the shape of a kiss. Decker smiled. "Business," he replied still eyeing her perfectly formed lips.

"Oh, what a shame," Anika said with a theatrical pout. "I was going to offer to buy you a drink." She motioned him forward again, and they dropped each other's hand. Decker turned and moved up more. They were almost at the exit of the plane.

Great, he thought to himself. *I'm always avoiding planes at all costs, and now I don't want to get off this one.* He turned back to Anika.

"To tell you the truth—"

"Please do," she interjected in jest.

Decker smiled. "Well, I *have* been traveling for some time and could use a meal. And surely a drink."

Anika smiled.

"What say I buy you dinner?" he asked.

Anika nodded her head in agreement. "Fine. As long as you let me buy you a drink."

"Sounds like a plan. Where are you staying?"

"At my house," Anika said with a smirk. "I live here."

"Oh, yes. I thought as much but didn't want to assume."

"How about you?" she asked, signaling to Decker they were about to exit.

"I'm over at the Mena," he said with some urgency. "It's right on the other side of the pyramid complex..."

His voice trailed off when she snickered at him and nodded her head. "Yes, but of course you know where the Mena House is. This is your home."

"This is my home." Anika smiled back at him with some amusement. "I will meet you in the lobby in an hour. Does that work for you?"

"Ah, yes," he said, a bit nervously. "That works just fine for me. Anything you say is fine with me."

"Well, then it's a date, Mr. William Decker, a.k.a. Decks." Anika extended her hand again as he inched his way backward toward the exit. He reached out and took her hand in his once more, and once more he could feel the warmth of her body. Suddenly, Anika squeezed his hand with some force and pulled him toward her until they were inches apart. Decker was taken by surprise and his eyes widened, again fixed on hers. She leaned in to his shoulder to whisper in his ear.

"You almost fell down the exit stairs, William." Now he was sure he was blushing.

35

Naamah stood over the wooden bar in her suite and turned over two high-ball glasses.

"Ice?" she asked without turning round to face him. She was racking her brain, preparing herself for whatever questions Moloch might toss her way. She was sure he would ask about Chichester and bookstore incident. How did he know? He was in Jordan at the time, wasn't he?

"No ....," he was eyeing her intently, "no ice. What are you considering over there, my dear?"

"Nothing," she quickly answered. *Too quick*, she thought to herself. *You answered too quickly. You sound defensive. Fix it.*

Naamah slid the decanter of scotch forward and removed the glass stopper.

"I was just replaying our latest carnal escapades in my mind's eye." She spilled a drop of the fragrant alcohol on her hand and ran her palm down the sheer hip-length robe she had thrown on. Moloch watched her from the bed. He could clearly see her body beneath the thin tan fabric and became aroused again at the thought of touching her. Her long legs seemed to go on forever, melding into her perfectly formed bottom. Most exciting to Moloch was the tattoo of a spine running the length of her back and disappearing at her neck under her silken hair.

"So, what happened with Chichester?" he asked in a quiet, almost whisper of a voice. His tone disturbed her, and she turned to face him. Naamah's robe was open in the front, and she stood, staring at Moloch, two drinks in hand, waiting for something more to be said. Nothing more came.

"Chichester," she repeated the name as she moved toward the bed. "Why are you interested in that old fool?"

"Really?" he said, squinting his eyes at her; she stopped moving. "Are we going to play this game? I can make it very uncomfortable for you in this room tonight. Is that to be our ultimate destination?" Moloch began to rise from the bed.

"No," Naamah said with a smirk. "I was looking for the riddles, okay?" Moloch settled back into the bed but remained propped up on his elbows. It made the muscles in his upper body bulge and flex. Naamah looked at his chiseled features and his steely eyes. She decided to end the game quickly and climb back onto his body for another round.

"I had heard Chichester possessed either some or all of the riddles, and you were not including me in anything, so I was determined to get at least one riddle, solve it, and retrieve a piece." She continued without taking a breath, "I figured if I was able to recover at least one piece of the papyrus, you would consider me a worthy partner. I told you I want in on this."

Naamah dropped to her knees on the mattress at the base of the bed. "I want to be a part of this—not just a bystander."

"Well?" Moloch said.

"Well what?" she responded, reaching forward and handing him his drink.

"Did you find what you were looking for?"

"No," she said, obviously annoyed. "That old bag either didn't possess anything or refused to give it up." Naamah paused and took a swig. Lying to a fellow demon was hard work. They could smell fear, and hesitation quickly bred paranoia.

"That was some show you put on there," Moloch laughed and took another drink. Naamah sighed a deep, but silent, breath; it was over.

"A plague mask, huh? You turned Chichester into plague doctor? Brilliant! Hideous and chilling, to say the least." He finished his drink and tossed the glass to the floor. "I love it," he growled with an unearthly voice as he rose to the side of the bed and walked around to Naamah, who was still on her knees.

"Consider yourself my partner in crime, as it were." He reached out and removed the glass from her hand, then violently tossed it against the wall, shattering it into pieces. He slowly placed the palm of his hand on the center of her back and moved it back and forth gently. He stopped moving his hand and forced her down onto her hands. She was on all fours. Moloch walked behind her at the base of the bed and leaned down over her. Naamah could feel his fury pulsing behind her.

"Tomorrow we return to Jordan," he whispered in her ear. She let a slight gasp escape her lips as her breathing grew deep and short. "We will raid the ancient city of Petra and acquire the second papyrus."

Moloch grabbed the back of Naamah's hair and pulled her back to him. "But mark my words," he murmured with a guttural growl. "Cross me, and it will be the last thing you ever do."

36

"We are on our way to the home of one Dr. Ebbers on this cold and dreary night," Alexander announced to his entourage as the van pulled away from the docks. Asar was driving, and Alex sat in the passenger seat, facing the back rows, his features barely visible in the dim light of the interior.

"Who is he?" Kate called out from the dark recesses of the van. She sat with Keith in the second row, while Sam and Abigail leaned forward to listen from the back.

"Well, that is a good question Kate. Allow me to elaborate."

"And where is Decker?" Samantha interrupted.

"Yeah, where's Decker," Kate turned to Sam in support of her inquiry, "did he make it?"

"All right, all right." Alex put his hand up to stop them before they got out of control.

With some hesitation and what could only be characterized as a timid tone, Keith asked the question plaguing all of their minds, "Are we in danger?"

Alexander turned to him, "Of course you are, Keith. But that's why you're here isn't it?"

"Uh, no," Keith quickly replied, shifting in his seat. "I'm here because *she's* here," he continued, nodding sideways toward Kate. "Maybe *she's* here for the danger, but *I'm* here to keep her out of it."

"Well," Alexander said with a smile, "that is very noble of you. You are a good man Keith, and I am glad you are amongst our ranks. Now, please, everyone. Listen. We haven't much time before we arrive."

The group seemed to settle down, all but forgetting their questions regarding Decker's status. Asar looked through his rearview mirror to make sure everyone was paying attention. "Listen up now, my friends," he called out and shifted his gaze to the side mirror to make sure the other vehicle was still behind them. The second van was close behind with Samuel at the wheel. It was packed with all manner of supplies and equipment.

"To begin with, Decks is fine. I sent him ahead to Egypt to investigate the incident at the Giza Plateau." Alexander grinned and said, "I am sure, however, it would please him to know all the young ladies are concerned about his well-being."

"What was that at the castle? What happened there?" Kate interrupted.

"Please, Kate," Alexander implored. "I am not going to get into that now as it is not relevant to the task at hand." Kate crossed her arms and shoved herself back in the seat, obviously dissatisfied with the lack of explanation on Alexander's part.

"We'll revisit it," he said to Kate. "I give you my word, okay?"

Alexander looked back to the group as a whole. They were waiting.

"Ebbers's bloodline was entrusted with the keys – the riddles, the two brothers I spoke previously of, left behind. I believe he has been a very bad boy and struck up a deal with the devil, if you will. I surmise the enemy has acquired the riddles, and it will only be a matter of time before they decipher them and reassemble *The Book of Gates*." Alexander's eyes glowed as whispers of moonlight beamed through the windows of the vehicle. "We cannot allow this to occur. We are the only defense against this unimaginable evil, and we must find a way to stop it or risk the release of Hell on Earth." The group was silent.

"No pressure or anything," Samantha blurted out from the back in a chortle of nerves.

"No pressure, Sam," Alexander replied. Kate was sure she saw a tear form in the corner of Alex's eye. Was this a manifestation of sadness or fear? Or was it his pride in those he had chosen to accompany him on this grand endeavor? Kate was pretty sure it was the latter. She didn't believe Alexander Storm felt fear.

"So, we are on our way to the doctor's residence to get a copy of the riddles. I am sure he has one. We will ask nicely at first. If we are met with even the slightest hint of resistance, we will take them by force. Please be prepared to search and to do it quickly. We haven't much time here. If the dark one's pull too far ahead in this race, I fear we will not be afforded an opportunity to recover."

37

The world-famous Mena House hotel rests in the shadow of the Great Pyramid at Giza. Originally, "The Mud Hut," as it was known, was nothing more than a two-story hut for hunters. The grounds had passed hands several times between 1869 and 1886, at which time it opened as the Mena House Hotel. Its close proximity to the pyramid complex, as well as the old-world flair for style and service, have made the Mena a must-stop attraction in Egypt.

Decker exited the cab and quickly approached the front of the hotel. The enormous chandelier hanging overhead at the front entrance turned the night into day and instilled in Decker a warm, welcoming feeling. He had stayed there on several occasions through the years and was thrilled Alexander had booked him a room. He passed through the center doors and entered into the great reception hall. The decorum and architecture created the sensation of stepping back in time to when the Egyptian craze engulfed the globe and words like "Tut" and "Carter" were on the tips of everyone's tongues.

"Mister Decker?" inquired a voice from behind the reception counter ahead. "Over here, Mister Decker. I will help you." A short, middle-aged Egyptian man waved his hand excitedly. "Over here, Mister Decker."

Decks stopped at the counter and placed his bag down on the floor between his legs, a trick he had learned from visiting less hospitable locales.

"How are you, this evening? Mr. Storm said you would be in hurry, so I have everything ready for you. I am Siad, the night manager here at the Mena House, and should you need anything at all, please do not hesitate to call upon me." Siad raised one hand over his head signaling the bellhop to assist them.

"Let us get your bags for you, and we will have you settled in no time." Siad peered over the counter, "Where are your bags, sir?"

"This is it," said Decker with a smile. "Traveling light this time."

Siad waved off the hop and turned to grab an envelope from the counter behind him.

"Here you are," said Siad passing the envelope to Decks. "Your keys and a map are in there. You have the Presidential Suite, and I am sure you will be quite satisfied with your accommodations."

Decker smiled and thought to himself, *Good ol' Alexander*. He picked up his bag. "Thank you, Siad." He started to walk in the direction of his suite when he stopped, turned, and jogged back to Siad.

"Yes, Mister Decker?"

"I am expecting a young lady to join me for dinner in about half an hour. Can you call up to me when she arrives?"

"Of course," replied the manager. "We will see to her comfort until you join her."

"Thanks." Decker made his way to the presidential suite, humming as went. Fumbling with the key card, he swiped it four ways before the light turned green. He pushed the door open and entered into what oasis, best described as an Egyptian palace. The Presidential Suite was located in the old palace section of the hotel and featured beautiful traditional detailing, murals, ornate wood paneling, gilding, fine upholstery, and a tremendous canopied bed right out of a harem fantasy. The suite's original wooden balustrade and arched windows finished off the illusion.

"Wow." He threw his bag on the bed and headed to the largest window. With some degree of drama, he grasped the gold and maroon floor-to-ceiling curtains and parted them down the middle. Like Moses parting the sea, he exposed a miracle out of time. The Great Pyramid was so close,

Decker was sure he could reach out and touch it. He drew in a deep breath as he soaked in the grandeur. Although he had been to the complex more times than he could remember, it never failed to strike awe in him. He looked down at his watch and caught sight of the flurry of emergency lights still flashing at all corners of the plateau. Local authorities were still engaged in their investigation of Moloch's handiwork. He needed to get in there, up close and personal with the Sphinx. He walked over to the side of the bed and sat. *193 Pulling a slip of paper from his shirt pocket, he picked up the handset of the phone next to the bed and dialed out the number he had scribbled on the sheet.

"Yes, hello?" he said. "Susan, please."

There was a pause.

"When will she be returning?" he inquired. "It's quite urgent."

Decker stood up as he listened. He peered at his watch for the umpteenth time. Anika would be arriving soon. Butterflies again.

"My name? Yes, my name is William Decker." He thought for a minute about how to phrase the next line, then said, "I am in the employ of Alexander Storm."

Decker could hear some muffled speaking on the other end.

"Hello?" he called out. "Thank you. My cell number is 917-866-3030. Have Susan reach me there when she returns please."

Decker hung the phone up and headed to the bathroom to wash up. He took off his shirt and turned the water on. Catching sight of himself in the mirror, he couldn't believe how exhausted he looked. William Decker was a rugged, handsome man. His body was strong and lean and he wore his years well. But tonight, he looked tired. He thought of Anika and smiled into the mirror. He had just begun to splash water on his travel weary face, when a loud knock sounded on the door to the suite.

"Jeez. Give me a break." He grabbed a hand towel from the counter and dried his face as he walked to the door.

"Yes?" he said with some annoyance as he pulled the door open. "What is it?"

"Very nice, William," said Anika. "I see you dressed for our date." She smiled a sly half smile. "That's not to say I mind you shirtless." She laughed and walked past him into the suite.

"Anika," started Decker with a mix of embarrassment and shock. "What are you doing here? Am I late? I thought we were meeting downstairs."

"Oh my God, William," she said, ignoring his questions. "This place is incredible."

Anika wore a skin tight, black-sheen dress—short but classy—and black leather heels that lifted her petite frame a good foot closer to the heavens. Decker smiled. He could smell a wonderful mix of exotic spice and flora that was her perfume.

"Go finish getting ready," she said, still marveling at the suite. "I will wait here and soak up the grander." She walked toward the open window and peered out.

"Fantastic view!" she called to him in the bathroom.

"Yes. Yes, it is." He finished washing up, wet his hair a bit, and crossed the room to his bag on the bed. Inside was one clean shirt and some after-shave. It would have to do. Anika's back was to him as he fumbled with the buttons over his chest. She was a sight that even the Pyramid in the back-ground had trouble competing with.

"Stop staring, William," she said without turning.

He thought of something to say in response when his cell phone rang.

"Saved by the bell," he laughed and grabbed his phone.

"I have to take this," he said to Anika, who was facing him.

She wrinkled her brow and shook her head in understanding.

"Hello? Yes, hello, Susan. This is William Decker. Thanks for getting back to me so fast." He paused to listen, then replied, "Yes, Alexander gave me your number. Well, I need a favor, and he thought you were the one to ask. I need to get close to the Sphinx for a few minutes."

There was a laugh on the other end of the line. Even Anika could hear it from where she was standing.

"Yes, I know what happened, it's directly related to why I need to get down there. I understand."

There was a long pause while Decker listened.

"Well, I guess I will await your call then," he said, somewhat defeated. "Thank you, Susan."

Decker hung up and threw the phone onto the bed. He walked over to Anika who had made her way to a loveseat in the middle of the room. Her arms were outstretched in either direction over the back of the couch, and her legs were crossed.

"Okay," she started. "Are you ready to go down?" A smile crept across her face, and she blurted out a laugh.

"That didn't come out right!" she laughed, and Decker smiled back.

"Are you ready?" she rephrased.

"Anika, I'm afraid we may have to reschedule. I need to wait for this call and make some contingency plans in case they aren't able to accommodate my request."

She rose from her seat, and as she did, the intoxicating aroma surrounding her floated toward Decker, piquing his senses.

"No, you don't," she said quite seriously. "Let's go."

"Huh?" Decker asked. "You don't understand—"

She raised a finger to her lips demanding his silence.

"We will go eat. Maybe have a few drinks," she continued.

"But—" Anika put a finger to his lips this time, quieting his protests.

"After which," she continued, "I will call my godfather, and he will get you in to see the Sphinx."

"What?" asked Decker, taking a step back.

"Well, I heard your conversation, William," she said. "I was sitting right here."

"Yes, but how are you going to do that? Who is your godfather?"

"The Minister of Antiquities."

"What?" Decker asked with surprise. "Your godfather is Hazi Zawai?"

"Yes, he is William," Anika smiled, "and he always does what I ask of him."

"I'm sure he does," said Decker rather dryly. "I'm sure everyone does."

Anika laughed. "You're silly, William."

Decker put out his arm, offering it to her.

"It seems my dilemma is resolved. Shall we go, my lady?" he asked in his best British accent.

"We shall," she replied mimicking his British drool as they locked arms.

"You are full of surprises, Anika."

"You have no idea, William. You have no idea."

38

"Asar," Alexander whispered. "You take Sam, and find your way around to the back entrance of the house."

Asar shook his head and nodded to Sam, who walked up beside him.

Alex continued, "My research shows there is a back exit, a sliding door, right about dead center in the rear of the house. Text me when you are in position."

Alexander turned and pressed the button on a laser pointer.

"There is the path—it will lead to a patio, and the door should be right there." Alexander moved closer to Sam and Asar. "Be watchful. I don't know how paranoid Ebbers has become. Could be booby traps, or at the very least, surveillance."

Alexander waved the two on, and the rest of the group watched them disappear into the night. He turned back to the others and looked them over, mentally trying to pair them in the most efficient manner. Behind him loomed the darkened estate of Dr. Ebbers. It was a modest size ranch-style architecture common to the shore line of the East end of Long Island. *199 Alexander had been able to locate blueprints for the property a few years ago, and his only hope was that Ebbers had not made any changes to the floor plan since.

"Okay, Samuel. You and the brave and noble Keith will take the side door off the kitchen."

"I stay with Kate," Keith said a little too loudly for Alexander's comfort.

Alexander put a finger to his lips, indicating to Keith to keep his voice lower. Keith was having none of it.

"Don't tell me to keep quiet." Keith stepped forward to within inches of Alex. "You call us to your castle for God knows what, and now you essentially want us to break the law and burglarize some old dude's house? I'm not going for it! And Kate stays with me."

"Keith." Kate moved toward him. "It's okay, Keith."

"No, it's not Kate," he said, pivoting around to face her. "We've been blindly following this guy, and there's real danger, Kate. *Real* danger and who knows what the hell else."

"I assure you, Keith," Alexander said with growing impatience, "if you don't lower your tone, you will find out exactly what is out here."

A single chime rang from within Alexander's long coat and with it the sharp sound of a twig snapping in the near distance. Alexander's head whirled in the direction of the noise, and he shot both arms out to the sides to silence the others. Alex looked toward Samuel, who was staring directly at him. He had heard it as well.

"I fear we are not alone." Alexander reached into the inner pocket of his jacket and withdrew his cell phone. He quickly read the text from Asar. *In position.* Alexander looked away from the phone and scanned the darkness surrounding them before composing his response. *Chng plns—not alon—we r goin in frnt door—b redy 4?* Alex hit send and replaced the phone. He then released the one button holding the front of his coat closed and flipped the left side open exposing the handle of the long blade hidden at his side.

Snap.

It, what ever *It* was, was close now. Alexander considered the amount of ground it had covered in only a few seconds.

"Samuel," he called him closer as he walked behind the others and ushered them toward the front of the house. "Samuel, it's not human—it's too fast. Take them in through the front door if it's open; I will be right behind you."

"Are you sure?" Samuel responded with concern.

"Yes. It will be easier to defend ourselves if we're not out in the open."

Alex motioned them on, harshly whispering, "Go!"

Samuel turned and moved sure-footedly to the front entrance of the house. Abigail, Keith, and Kate followed on his heels, and the four stopped at the front door, glancing back at Alexander. Then they saw it. Red eyes glowing. Hot breath steaming around its head. The moon providing just enough light to illuminate the great bulk of its form emerging from a thicket of bushes and overgrowth.

"Hell hound." The words escaped Samuel's lips, and as they did, the beast's head twisted and focused on him rather than Alex, its lips raised in a snarl, exposing rows of razor-sharp teeth. The most notable being two large, boar-like canines. The head of the hound was enormous and disproportionate to its body, as was its grotesque, protruding snout. The creature's legs were as thick as tree trunks, and its body arched with the akin nature of a screeching cat rather than a dog. Out of its spine sprang a row of bony spikes that swayed as it moved as if the vestiges of some medieval armor. And moving it was. It had refocused on Alexander and was approaching much like a lion padding toward its prey.

Alexander turned for a split second to make sure the group had made it to the door. But they were still outside, locked out.

"Break it down, Samuel!" he yelled. "Break it down, and reunite with Asar!"

Snap.

It was on him. Alexander didn't even look. He grasped the handle of his sword and drew it from its sheath. The moonlight shimmered across the blades edge and he raised it high above his head. His body snapped into a warrior's defensive position. His lips parted, exposing his teeth to the beast and his eyes grew wide and wild.

"Alex!" cried Kate as she rushed from the shelter of the house toward him. Samuel bent his leg and snapped it forward with surprising force onto the center of the door, splintering it into the interior of the house with a violent crack. The distraction provided Alexander with the opportunity he required. The beast, which had already sprung to the air above him, propelled by its massive hind legs, glanced in the direction of the crashing door. Seizing the moment, Alexander leapt forward to meet the fiend's assault as the lunar rays danced off his blade.

"Back to Samuel!" he shouted at Kate as he brought the blade down against the head of the beast.

"Alex! No!" screamed Kate. Her movement came to a sudden halt as Keith's arms wrapped around her from behind, lifting her several inches off the ground and moving her toward the safety of the house.

"Put me down, Keith!" she demanded, twisting and pushing to escape. Keith held his ground and carried her, kicking and flailing, back to the threshold where he was met by Abigail who did her best to calm her.

A horrible wail broke the couple's struggle as Alexander drove his sword up into the creature's skull to the hilt. Twisting to one side, he unsuccessfully attempted to hurl his body from the path of the slain beast's fall. An audible groan escaped Storm's lungs as the hound crashed down on top of him, engulfing him in fur and the stench of decay.

"Oh my God," Kate whispered. "Keith, help me." She charged from the front of the house back toward Alexander, who was trapped under the hulk of the Hell hound. Keith and Samuel raced behind her to Alexander's side.

"Alex!" Kate screamed. "Are you okay? Are you alive?"

"Get this filth off of me, please," came the muffled response from below the slain creature. The fur on the hound began to smoke and sizzle like bacon in a hot pan.

"Hurry!" Alex shouted with legitimate concern for his wellbeing. "It's about to disincorporate!"

"Push with me, Keith," Samuel yelled as the two skidded to the side of the beast. "We *must* get it off him!"

The two began to shove at the hound's ribs, attempting to roll it over, but it was too massive. Suddenly, the hound burst into flames, burning on its back with such immediate intensity Keith was forced to avert his eyes.

"Push, damn it! *Push!*"

Then, as if by divine intervention, the Hell hound lifted off of Alexander and rolled to the side of the two men. The carcass emitted a grotesque sucking sound and then a deafening snap.

"Look away!" screamed Alex, rising from the ground. He took two steps and dove onto Kate, driving her to the ground beneath him. Keith and Samuel turned away as the hound exploded—and then imploded—in a blinding burst of light which generated enough heat to scorch the trees and grass around them. And then it was gone.

"Glad I could be of assistance." Keith and Samuel raised their heads from the ground to a pair of large boots standing in front of them.

"Asar!" yelled Keith.

Alexander turned toward the group.

"Thanks for checking on us, Asar," said Alex with a sense of relief.

Keith rose to his feet and dusted his pants off a bit.

"A bit strong, aren't we, Asar?" said Keith jokingly.

"To say the least," Abigail concurred having been the only member of the party to witness Asar's feat of strength.

"I work out," Asar replied with a wink.

"Hey," yelled Kate, "can you get off me now?"

"My apologies, Kate," started Alex. "I meant no disrespect. I was merely—"

"Uh, Alex?" said Asar, walking up to his friend.

Alex and Kate rose to their feet and looked each other. Alex with some confusion, and Kate with some anger.

"Well, then," said Alex, breaking their connection and walking to the smoldering ashes of the Hell hound. Bending down to the blackened remains, he grabbed the blade of his sword and raised it up. He banged its flat edge against his jacket to knock away the debris and slid it back into its sheath.

"Shall we go see a man about some riddles?" he asked as he walked toward the house.

"Sam and I have already secured Ebbers," said Asar with pride. "The young lady, who is quite resourceful I must add, is holding him at gunpoint in his study."

Alexander looked surprised, raising his eyebrows and pursing his lips.

"Very well, then. Good job to all. Let us acquire what we came for and be on our way."

The rest of the group fell into place behind Alexander as they entered the home.

"Let us be quick here," Alexander said with quiet urgency. "I fear the night has more surprises in store for us."

39

"William ... over here!" Decker looked past the military barricade and spotted Anika waving her hand high in the air. She had left him for a short time after dinner to finalize his trip to the closed area surrounding the Sphinx. She must have stopped home first. She had changed out of her dress and into a pair of military-grade khaki pants, combat style boots, and a ribbed tank top. Anika's hair was pulled back in a ponytail, and she wore sleek leather work gloves on her hands.

"Hello!" Decker waved back at his archaeological angel. He smiled, knowing he'd be on the other side of the barricade with her soon. She smiled back and walked swiftly to meet him at the military checkpoint. As she grew closer, Decker noted a laminated card hanging around her neck, much like a backstage pass at a concert. He could make out the seal of the Department of Antiquities on it.

"Hello! Everything is in place." Anika reached into her back pocket and pulled out a laminated pass like the one she wore. A guard stepped between the pair, interceding in the exchange of the pass. Anika withdrew her hand and the pass. The guard spoke to her in Arabic which rapidly flew off his tongue. Anika stared at him a moment, her eyes pressing together in apparent agitation. Finally, she reached into her front pocket and withdrew a folded square of paper. She said nothing and handed it to the guard. The soldier took the paper and unfolded it with contempt. Decker saw his eyes moving across the paper quickly, and his expression instantly changed from anger to worry.

"Sorry." It was his only word. He carefully folded the paper back up and gingerly handed it back to Anika. She smirked, replaced it in her pocket, and handed Decker the pass.

"Come on, William," she said, and the guard stepped aside, letting Decker cross into the secured area.

"Nice job, Anika," he said as they walked. "If you don't mind me asking, what did you show him?"

"It states I am making a survey of the damage for Zawai, and you are my American assistant," she said, laughing out loud. "How about it, William? Are you up for being my servant?"

"You said assistant," Decker said jokingly.

"Really?" Anika stopped and looked at him. "Are you really going to pass up an opportunity to be my servant? Tending to my every need and desire?"

Decker stammered a bit. "Well, since you put it that way."

Anika laughed and began walking again, a rich, hearty laugh. She seemed to be in her environment, and she moved sure-footedly through the sand and rubble toward the eternal lion.

"My godfather knows of you. He says you have quite a reputation."

Decker laughed nervously. "All lies, I assure you."

"He says you deal in ghosts and zombies."

"The supernatural." He smiled at her. "The supernatural is what I call it."

"Ghosts?" she responded with quick jest. "Are we looking for Boris Karloff?"

"Ha ha. I wish my mission involved the simplicity of a dusty old mummy."

She stopped again. "He also said you work for someone named Storm. Alexander Storm."

"With him," he corrected. "I work *with* Alexander Storm."

"Wow," Anika said. The smile on her face widened. "You seem to have a real problem with servitude."

"You are very quick, Anika."

"Quick? Oh, you mean like our dinner?"

"Listen...I'm sorry about that," Decker said, becoming more serious. "I really am on a tight time constraint, here."

"I am teasing, William," Anika said soothingly, sensing his worry. "There will be plenty of time for eating and drinking once work is done."

Anika stopped. "Here we are." Decker had been so engrossed in their banter he hadn't realized he had gotten so close to the legendary monolith.

"Wow." He stared at the beast's head. "He snuck up on us quick."

"She," Anika replied. "*She* snuck up quick."

"She?" Decker repeated. "You believe the Sphinx to be a woman?"

"Strong and beautiful," she started. "Guardian of her family of pyramids, resistant to time and the elements of life. Yes, William, I have no doubt she is a woman."

Decker smiled. He really liked her. Not just her beauty and charisma—he enjoyed speaking with her immensely.

"Shall we?" Anika guided Decker down to the space between the paws of the Sphinx. There was bright light emanating up from up above, and as the two walked toward the arms of the lion, Decker saw half a dozen workers. They had set up large work lights all around the damage, which was immediately noticeable.

"Jesus," Decker said gritting his teeth. The workers stopped their various tasks and turned to him and Anika. A guard grabbed her pass and lifted it to examine it, then turned to Decker and did the same with his. The guard nodded and settled back on his perch, holding the arm of the Sphinx up with his back. Seeing the guard relax, the others returned to their work. Anika touched Decker's forearm.

"How long do you need?" she asked.

"Oh, I don't know. Five or ten minutes?" he replied.

Anika stepped forward and addressed the group in Arabic. They stopped and looked up at the two of them again.

"What'd ya say?" asked Decker, a little unnerved at the sight of the guard moving toward them again.

"I said they were doing a great job, but now would be a good time for them all to take a fifteen-minute tea break."

Decker laughed. "Great! But they don't seem thirsty."

Anika shrugged her shoulders and rolled her eyes. With a huff, she reached once again into her front pocket and pulled out the note from Zawai. She handed it to the guard, who opened it, read it, and gave it back to Anika without saying a word.

"Let's go!" he shouted in English and then again in Arabic. The workers remained in place; a look of confusion filled their dark Egyptian faces. Their failure to comply with his command caused the guard's chest to visibly swell and he took a single step in their direction and yelled the directive once more. The workers literally dropped brushes, cameras, and papers then hurried past Anika and Decker. The guard nodded at Anika as he passed.

"Take as much time as you need," he said and then followed the others out of the area.

"What the hell did he say to them?" Decker asked with a laugh.

"He said we work for Hazi Zawai directly, and if they did not vacate the area, they would have to answer to him."

"Wow," Decker replied. "Is it better to be feared or loved?"

"My godfather is both feared *and* loved," Anika said, defending her godfather's honor. "His bark is much worse than his bite. But it's a loud bark all the same."

"I'll say," Decker agreed.

"The writer Elizabeth Peters—" Anika started.

"Oh, I love Peters," he interrupted.

"So do I," she said with a big smile. "Anyway, as you know, then, Peters created a character named Emerson."

"The Father of Curses," said Decker.

"Exactly to my point, William," she said, taking a step toward him. "I am sure Peters modeled this character's personality on that of my godfather's."

"Ha ha. Enough said."

Anika turned to the Sphinx, and her face grew stern.

"What a disgrace," she said. "We lost sixteen soldiers as well. Of all the treasures to steal in Egypt, why such an operation to deface the Sphinx?"

"Oh, this wasn't about damaging the Sphinx, honey," said Decker, walking past Anika and up to the center of the damage.

"No?" she replied moving to his side.

"No." Decker reached out and put his hands in the opening created by Moloch's henchmen. "This was a recovery operation."

"What?" Anika stared at Decker. "Are you saying they took something from here?"

Decker felt around in the hole. It was empty. He grabbed a penlight from his pocket and shined it in the hole, illuminating its interior. Anika moved in, and with her face close to Decker's, and peered into the hole.

"What is that?" Anika exclaimed. There was a colorful painting on the inner wall of the opening.

"Well, if I'm not mistaken, that's Isis standing over her dead husband, Osiris."

"What's she holding?" Anika could barely contain her excitement.

"That would be *The Book of Gates*."

"Are you sure? How do you know?"

"Oh yeah," he smirked. "I'm pretty damn sure."

Decker retrieved a small digital camera from a pocket in his cargo pants and took several photos of the image at the back of the opening.

"Here...give me the light," Anika said, reaching out her hand.

She took it and aimed it at the back of the small crevice, further illuminating the tunnel enough for Decker to get some vivid close-up shots.

"So, Isis is resurrecting Osiris," Anika said in thoughtful cadence.

"So the story goes."

"Hey!" Anika pointed to the inner base of the opening. "What is that? Get a shot of that, William."

Decker put his arms and the camera into the hole and snapped several shots of the area than withdrew from the damage a bit.

"Let's have a look," he said, opening the images on the camera's LCD screen. "Hmmm."

"What is it?"

Decker held the camera in front of Anika. It was an image of what appeared to be a giant serpent and a female deity, most likely Isis again, using a sharp object to skin the snake.

"How bizarre," Anika said, looking up from the camera. "What does it mean?"

"I'm not sure." He powered the camera down and put it back in his pocket. "Not sure at all, but it may prove to be of importance down the road."

Decker ran his hands over the stubble that was developing on his cheeks, and he stared up at the stars, deep in thought.

"I wonder if Moloch saw it?" he said to himself.

"Who's Moloch?" Anika snapped. "William, do you know who did this? If so, you need to tell me so I can tell Zawai."

Decker looked at Anika. "I do know who did this," he said with some reservation, "but I can't tell you as of yet."

Anika looked furious. She stepped up close—extremely close—to his face.

"What was in the hole, Decker?"

Just then, all of the lights went out.

"What's going on, William?" There was growing concern in her voice.

Decker reached out and grabbed her hand, then pulled her to him.

"Let's get out of here," he whispered in her ear. "Stay close to me."

Anika turned first to exit the area, and as she did, she came face to face with a ghostly version of what appeared to be an ancient warrior.

"Decker!" she yelled, and he pivoted around to face the horror that was unfolding before their eyes. The one apparition had become two, and then eight, then at least forty spirits filled the small area. The cloud-like spirits, each glowing with an unnatural red hue, were closing in on the couple. Decker fumbled for his camera when Anika grabbed his arm.

"Look, William," she said in disbelief. "They wear the two crowns of Upper and Lower Egypt."

"My God," Decker scanned the ghostly beings—Anika was right. "These are the ghosts of the dead kings of Egypt!"

The spirits continued to multiply around them. Anika and Decks huddled together as the area swelled with the undead.

"What do we do, William?" Anika yelled.

The dead pharaohs were but a few feet from them, and Decker could see their eyes clearly, glowing with a blue radiance. A realization suddenly overcame him.

"They mean us no harm."

"How do you know that, William?" pleaded Anika.

"I've been doing this a long time," he said, laughing nervously. "I just know."

"So, what do we do?"

Flash

"Did you just take a freaking picture?" Anika's typical calm demeanor was fleeting. "I can't believe you just snapped a picture."

Flash

"Are you nuts?" she screamed.

Decker reached out and grabbed Anika's hand again.

"There's only one way out," he cried, pulling her close to him. Decker moved her around to his back.

"Wrap your arms around me, and close your eyes."

Anika followed Decker's instructions and wrapped her arms around his chest. She could feel his heart pounding and wondered if it raced with fear or excitement.

"Let's go! Walk steady and hold on."

Decker guided her forward. The spirits did not move from their path, and Decker decided he would simply press on. He stopped for a moment and stood but an inch from the closest pharaoh's face. He looked briefly into the brilliant, blue-lit eyes, then he lowered his gaze and kept walking through dozens of apparitions, chills running up and down his spine as the cool mist that composed their being brushed over him, filling his nostrils and clouding his vision. The sheer power of their presence pulsed through him. Thousands of years of power and knowledge.

"Almost there, Anika!" he yelled. "Hold tight!"

Anika let out a gasp. Even though her eyes were closed, she was experiencing much of the same sensations as Decker.

"Just a few more steps!"

Anika squeezed him even tighter. Decker could feel her heart beating against his back. He reached up and grabbed her hands from his chest and spun her to his side.

"Open your eyes!" he commanded. Anika did as she was told and jumped forward to hug him. He squeezed back for a second.

"No time for love, Dr. Jones," he said, smiling, in his best Short-Round voice. "Run!"

The two sprinted past the barricade and out into the damp night air of Egypt.

"What the hell just happened?" Anika demanded in between gasps for air. She was bent slightly with her hands on her hips. She stood up and looked at Decker.

"How did you know they wouldn't hurt us?"

"I just did," replied Decker, also trying to catch his breath. "They were there to warn us, Anika. Warn us of something so bad that Amun Ra himself sent two thousand years of Egyptian pharaohs back to make his point."

"Point taken," replied Anika. "But warn us of what?"

Decker looked at his watch.

"I have to go, Anika," he said without looking up. "Time is of the essence here."

"What?" she yelled. "Are you kidding?"

Decker hated himself as the words came out. "I need to meet up with the others and review this material." He patted the camera in his pocket.

"No way, mister." She grabbed his arm. "What is going on?"

Decker turned from her and walked toward the Mena House to grab his bag. Anika ran up to him and grabbed his arm again, spinning him to her.

"Since you're so fond of Indiana Jones quotes," she said with a smirk, "remember this one, 'I guess you got more than you bargained for—I'm your goddamn partner!'" Anika let go of his arm and began to jog toward the hotel. Decker stared at her for a moment, and a small smile crept across his face.

"Hey, wait for me!" he yelled as he took off after her.

40

"Where is it, Ebbers?" demanded Alexander. "I know you have a copy somewhere."

Alexander paced around their captive, who was tied to a kitchen chair in the middle of his study.

"I'm telling you," Ebbers pleaded. "Moloch took it. He took my only copy. I can't help you."

Alexander turned to the others, who had congregated together at the room's archway entrance. They were staring at him, counting on his success in persuading Ebbers to supply them with a copy of the riddles he had handed over to the demon.

Alexander walked back to Ebbers and crouched down to look him in the eye.

"I know *you* know that what you did was so very wrong."

Ebbers tried to turn away from Alexander, but Storm mirrored his movements side to side.

"What did he promise you? Eternal life? Wealth? Women?" Alexander's voice grew in intensity. "What in God's name did he promise you to convince you to sell out the entire human race?"

Ebbers looked up at Storm. There was terror and remorse in his gaze. He bowed his head and shook it despairingly.

"He promised me," He paused for effect. "He promised me my soul."

"What?" Alexander jumped back. "Is that even his to bargain with?"

Ebbers looked up into Alexander's face.

"Yes, it was." He averted his eyes once again. "I forfeited it some years ago. Youth tends to play us the fool. I wanted something. He could give it to me. In exchange, I signed over my soul at the end of a fifty-year moratorium."

Alex looked Ebbers over. Was he being truthful? Or was he just toying with him? A good poker face is often hard to break, and Alexander had seen quite a few in his lifetime.

Ebbers said, "I have nothing to offer you, Storm."

Alexander could wait no more. He turned to the group.

"Leave us," Alexander demanded. "Go start searching the house."

When he was sure they were alone, he strolled up to Ebbers, who shuddered at the thought that his life was now in the hands of Alexander Storm.

"You can kill me, Storm. I'm not afraid. My soul has been forgiven, and I have made my peace with God and—"

Alexander reached out and grabbed Ebbers by the throat, squeezing just enough to stop him from talking or screaming.

"You fool," Alexander whispered. "Do you honestly think God will accept into Heaven the very man who unleashed carnage and unbridled evil on his children, who brought about the very end of this world?"

Ebbers stared at him with revelation brewing in his eyes.

Alexander released his choke hold, stepped back a bit, and unleashed a powerful blow across his jaw. Ebbers's head snapped back and then shot forward again thanks to the sheer force of the punch.

"Here's the deal," Alexander growled. "You will give me a copy of the original riddles, and I will not summon a soul stalker here to reap your soul and leave you in oblivion for all eternity." Ebbers's eyes flashed with fear.

"You were entrusted to guard those writings," Alexander continued. "Not use them as your private bargaining chip."

Alex's fury was peaking again, and he strode back to Ebbers with fist in hand, prepared to deliver a damning blow. Alexander wound up.

"Wait!" He was weeping like a child with a scraped knee. Alex had him.

"Tell me, Ebbers! Tell me now!"

"Wait! Wait!" He gasped again. "Wait!"

Alexander paused and then let his fist snap again, this time landing on Ebbers's chest. The restrained man cried out in agony. Alexander bent in close once again as spittle popped from his gasping mouth and ran down his chin.

"Have you had enough? Tell me!"

Alexander heard a noise behind him. He turned around and peered across the room at a large glass framed print on the wall. In the soft light's reflection, he could make out Kate's face watching him from the opposite side of the room. He wondered how much had she seen.

Ebbers bounced his head back up. He was sobbing and coming very near the end of what his meek stature could endure.

"Tell me now," Alexander demanded once more towering over his prey.

The broken man shook his head in defeat. "I don't have the original riddles—"

Alex, eye's aglow with newly kindled fury, prepared to deliver another blow.

"Wait! Wait!" He cried. "I have something better!"

"Really?" Alexander lowered his fist slightly. "And what might that be?"

Ebbers swallowed hard. "I have a *copy* of the twelve, translated into English."

Alexander Storm smiled. He looked back at the glass frame across from him, but Kate had slipped into shadows and was gone.

~

*T*he Twelve Riddles of *The Book of Gates*

1: The guardian of the three, your quest's beginning with its end in me, my stone eyes see the eons as they pass between my paws of dust and rubble, descend into my chest and you will find my heart as it pounds to the rhythm of the sand, my stone eyes fixed on the horizon waiting for time to end.

2: From the Valley of Moses, treading the sands of the gorge, arrive at the rose mountain's open mouth and pass through to the land beyond. Seek out the paper room in the paper church to the North—beneath its floor a metal door lined with the keys to the stars. Pluck a star and travel not far to the castle built by pharaoh for daughter.

3: To the home of the Seven great rulers and a passage to the cosmos and beyond. Rivers run cold and silent beneath the ground in the place where the jaguar sits perched upon a throne of stone. At its center, a castle's temple and a staircase to the North—follow the serpent when day and night are one, and take its head before it can run.

4: Cast upon my shores a broken oar, a broken wench, a broken hole, a broken thief may add his gold to my treasure which has always been on the side of the broken hole. Six men down and fifty-five men home.

5: Looking down on all the world, wondering if it will ever rest, lies the land of the wild horse, with the lair of the kat to the Northwest. Find the caves, many they are, hidden by time, forgotten by all. Search through each until one finds a prophet marked by sorrow, his treasure hid behind.

6: A cage for an entire land, ripe with fury, stone and sand. A keep without a castle door, a home with frame and nothing more. When sixty-seven make it whole, the sixty-sixth is the one to know. A sacred serpent guards this, guard's retreat, and guards the truth beneath its feet.

7: I am the fisherman, Simon, one of the twelve. Visit with me beneath the eighth Clement, hesitate not and begin your further descent. Move quickly through the darkness to the tomb of the Nile, find the Westerner's bird and remove its perching tile. Take the prize and rise like the Morning Star. Search your quarters and you will find a space for all and the answer you seek.

8: Floating south in the Caribbean lies a city of heroes, their skulls carved in stone built by the architects of zero. Within this jungle, a city does rise to conquer the beasts of stone and serpents of vines. A wise man, a sacrificed man, a holy man will find his demon knelt on a throne and steal his royal scepter, cracking the T in stone.

9: South of Heaven, but within its walls no evil lies. Carved in a slayer's memory for helping a dragon meet his demise. From sky across—from land it's lost—within a holy altar does reside.

10: Ripped in the face of the Earth, a giant wound since its birth. In a land known to few men, a key in stone hidden well, ride the water and scan the walls for a tell. Once you find this cavern in time, follow its passage to the nights aligned. There you will find that which they guard, marked with Osiris's seal in a place so odd.

11: In the Holy City of the land which in winter feeds the starving Mekong, seek ye out the ancestor of Brahma. In the temple where the trees eat the stone, locate that which should logically house what you desire. If perplexed by many, remember to always first center yourself. Find the stone with serpent's seal, the truth beneath Buddha had hoped to conceal.

12: In the olive-skinned land of all ports, beneath the wine and the hum of the sea, lies a world as above except void of sound and of love, but still they continue to be. As a pupil of Anubis might thrive, so, too, must the dead teach the live. Find him who has waited the longest, be sure your math is true, for this is the last of the journey; a mistake may end all of you.

41

The sub-door to the hangar flew open with a whoosh of air. Moloch ducked his head and stepped over the threshold, his wide strides carrying him forward with a purpose. Naamah moved swiftly to keep pace with her nefarious partner. The finely crafted leather case slung over her shoulder twisted and swayed with the harmony of her movement.

"Hello!" Moloch shouted out, clapping his hands together for effect. "Are we ready?" he called out rhetorically. He glided to a table in the middle of the hangar, and with a sweep of his arm, sent everything on top of it crashing to the ground.

"Set everything up here," he instructed Naamah. She walked past Moloch, setting the leather case down on the table. Her nimble fingers made quick work of the two straps which secured the top of the bag. Reaching in, she pulled out a large roll of paper, a notebook, and some photographs. She flipped out the rolled document across the table, exposing a large map of Petra. The weathered and worn chart was littered with scribbled notes and illegible markings. The soldiers of fortune who had been scattered about the hangar made their way towards Naamah. Moloch looked around at his small army of battle-hardened mercenaries.

"Yes, come." He waved them in. "Let us review our plans."

The men had been waiting for over twenty-four hours for Moloch to arrive and their bloodlust was visible in their eyes. As was their annoyance at the delays that had kept them coped up. Naamah glanced at Moloch, then back to the sluggish movements of the hired guns.

"Let's go!" Naamah belted out in a startlingly powerful voice. "You are being well compensated! Now fall in!"

The troops took heed of Naamah's demand and quickly gathered around the table. Any traces of lustful intent Moloch had noted in the men's stares, quickly deflated to the business at hand.

"Nicely done," Moloch whispered to Naamah. "They seem to really like you." He let out a loud, sarcastic laugh and walked to the head of the table.

"Come, Naamah." He motioned her to his side, and she smiled at him. She was hoping to earn his trust, and taking control of the subordinates would help. Moloch was keeping the riddles and their secrets close, only telling her what she needed to know. She would need more information, though, if she was ever going to pull ahead of him in this quest. For little did Moloch know, but his new partner had every intention of taking him out of this race. Then the prize would be hers and hers alone. She would open the final gate, allowing the First Angel Samael, to rise from the fiery depths from which he was cast so many eons ago. Samael would reward Naamah by making her his queen on Earth, and the Earth would become a living Hell.

"I take it all of you have familiarized yourself with the location," Moloch began. "This mission is more than just combat and protection. We are looking for several items." He paused to make sure he had their undivided attention. "We have a treasure map, if you will, and before anyone gets any crazy ideas, we are looking for something valuable to *me*. It has no value on the open or black markets, and I am paying you a hundred times more than what you'd get if you happened to find someone to buy it." Moloch paused again and let his words sink in. He was in no mood for mutinies; he was at the beginning of the pursuit and would not stand for interruptions. Unlike the soldiers at Giza, these men were not loyal followers with knowledge of the mission. He would make use of the faithful once again, but this particular phase required operatives who were expendable; as he was already resolved to expending them as needed. His resolution was predicated on the inevitability of a clash with the heavily armed Jordanian guard currently occupying the Petra complex. The sites limited egress and ingress created a fertile area for pinning down an enemy on the valley floor. Moloch also knew there would be intensified patrols at the ruins in light of the aftermath at the Sphinx, as all archaeological sites in the region were now on high alert.

"I believe we are all on the same page," he continued. He noted the majority of the heads nodding in agreement. One gruff individual to the rear of the crowd bore a twisted scowl on his face which spoke volumes to Moloch.

"You there, in the back." Moloch pointed at the angry looking soldier. "Is there a problem?"

The soldier looked surprised and pointed at himself to confirm Moloch was addressing him.

"Yes, you," he said. "Come forward, please."

The mercenary pressed through the ranks of his fellow militants until he found himself face-to-face with Moloch. He stared at his employer with distain, clearly fighting back some mixture of emotions which were surely linked by rage.

"Speak your mind, soldier," Moloch prodded him in an even, almost concerned, tone, "I would like your input here." Moloch smiled—a sly and forced smile—and waited.

"You people are all the same." The soldier's English accent was broken and dirty. "You hire us and think you can control us. What say we take your maps and crap and go grab this treasure for ourselves?" The impertinent soldier's voice got louder and rougher as he spoke. "You waste our time make'n us wait for your ass like we got nothing else to do. Like you're better than us, like your royalty." The man turned to the others and became very animated in an attempt to rile up his brother's in arms. "This sorry sap prances in here and thinks he gonna tell us what's what. Am I right, boys? He tells us there is a treasure that's worth nothing, but he will spend a small fortune to get."

Naamah began to move toward the man, but Moloch reached out and grabbed her arm. She looked at him and shrugged her shoulders.

"Wait," he said to her softly. "Wait."

The soldier spat out, "I say we have our way with the hot slut and drop this bloke in a hole." He was sweating—beads ran down his temples and the back of his neck. "Then we ride into the shithole hunk o' rock and take the treasure – splits it even."

Moloch could see the sweat and smell the fear beginning to resonate on the interloper. The rebel wasn't getting the reaction he had expected from the others. They were going to let him be the test pilot on this flight to nowhere.

"Oh, bollocks! I will take them out myself!" The soldier reached for his side arm holster, which appeared to contain a Desert Eagle pistol, and spun back round to face Moloch.

Naamah looked at Moloch with burning intensity in her eyes. "Now?" she asked, staring at Moloch, her black fathomless pupils dilated wide. The renegade soldier's arm began to rise from his side until his weapon was leveled on Moloch who remained stoic, motionless.

"Now." Moloch nodded. In a blur of black, she was on the insolent fool. Grabbing the hand which grasped the gun, she snapped it at the wrist. The cacophony of splintering bone and tearing flesh echoed through the deadly silent hangar. Naamah's free hand was cocked behind her with such force that the fields of muscles hidden just below the surface of her soft skin bore themselves to the surface. She looked into the doomed soldier's eyes and saw confusion and pain drift across them like storm clouds in a murky sky. Catapulting her fist forward, she shattered his rib cage, driving her petite hand deep into his chest. Blood issued from the mortal wound, atomizing into a red mist onto the remaining mercenaries. Naamah opened her hand until her slender fingers could make out the last vestiges of life thump from her victim's heart.

"Yummy," she whispered, smiling at her prey. She wrapped her extended digits around the pulsing muscle and ripped it from his chest. The streams of blood that had been spraying across Naamah's face and body, immediately ceased with the removal of the body's pumping system. Naamah released dead soldier's mangled hand and let his lifeless carcass fall to the floor of the hangar. Releasing the crushed organ from her other hand, she watched as it splattered on the floor at her feet in a splash of gore. Raising her crimson painted face to the others, she darted her tongue around her lips, savoring the metallic dew that had collected there. Their faces said it all. Mission accomplished.

"I am going to go clean up," Naamah stated matter-of-factly to Moloch.

"By all means, my dear," he said with a smile and a nod. "Go wash this vile dissenter's essence from you."

She turned back to the gaze upon the faces of the shocked soldiers who continued to remain silent and motionless; awe dripping from every pore of their bodies.

"It was the slut comment," she said to them with a laugh. "That was supposed to be a secret." She winked at a tall, rugged soldier, and he quickly averted his eyes, preferring to assess the state of his boot laces rather than lock eyes with the succubus.

"Does anyone else have any questions or concerns?" asked Moloch. "Some grand idea that you wish to share with the group, perhaps?"

The grizzly assembly of hardened killers shook their heads in unison; several of them, brave enough to vocalize their subordinate position sounded off, "No, sir."

"Very good." Moloch returned to the table. "Let's get back to the task at hand then, shall we?"

"Oh, just one more thing," Naamah called out from behind the men, who snapped to attention at the sight of her blood-splattered body. "Can someone point me in the direction of the little girls' room?"

42

The time weathered sheet of paper containing Ebber's translations rustled in the autonomous wind produced by Alexander Storm's incessant pacing. He had read through them several times and had already formulated ideas based upon some of the obscure clues in the text. Likewise, there were passages in the text which seemed more-or-less, self evident. At least if one is to trust one's own gut instincts he surmised. Alex's movements came to a halt and he surveyed his group of super heroes. The thought made him laugh out loud, but isn't that what they were? Superheroes? A group of unlikely outcasts who had been brought together for an ultimately divine purpose, and perhaps the supreme sacrifice. Although he understood that this fact was wholly possible, that one, or all of his newly acquired compatriots could cease to be at the end of this, he decided to banish such thoughts from his mind and concentrate on the task at hand. Alexander had grown quite fond of them all, rather quickly, and he did not wish to entertain the prospect of any of their demises.

"Tea, coffee, and sandwiches," came Ebbers's voice from behind Alex, akin to a roving vendor at a ballgame. "You must come and eat to keep your strength up." Ebbers had held out for as long as possible, however, once faced with the threat of his eternal soul being devoured he found himself quickly abandoning all resistance. He had guided Alexander to a hardbound copy of *Egyptian Magic* by Dr. Bob Brier tucked inconspicuously away on a bookshelf in the study. Alex's spine bending page acrobatics quickly produced a yellowed envelope which dropped to his feet like sails drifting through a crosswind. Retrieving it from the floor, he was pleased to find the copy of the riddles as Ebber's had promised. The good doctor had pleaded with Alex to give him an opportunity to make amends. He explained how he had changed his mind at the railroad station that night, but it had been too late. Moloch had tricked him, and he had set into motion a course of events to could very well lead to the imminent destruction of mankind. He implored Storm to grant him the opportunity to assist in the quashing of the rising evil that threatened to plague the land. To let him redeem himself to the world and to God. Alexander wasn't sure if he trusted Ebbers or his purported desire to be forgiven, but he had decided to give him a chance, at least for the time being. Besides, Ebber's historical knowledge by way of his pedigree, could prove useful in the coming battle.

Alexander turned back to the others, who were milling around the study. "Go ahead and have something to eat and drink," Alex suggested as he walked toward the bulky antique table in the center of the room. Ebbers had already begun to pass sandwiches around the table, and soon Asar sat down.

"I, for one, am starved," he proclaimed as he took a seat, "oh and look, bologna!"

"How can you eat right now?" demanded Samantha.

"Well, because I am hungry," Asar roared like a bear diving into a picnic basket. "And if I don't eat now, I will grow weak and tired, and I may not get a chance to eat ever again." He smiled and sunk his teeth into a well stacked bologna and cheese sandwich.

Samantha wrinkled her brow and considered Asar's words.

"Oh," she suddenly blurted out. "I get it." Sam pulled out the chair next to Asar and sat down. She grabbed a tuna fish sandwich from the quaint platter Ebber's had prepared and began to eat. She was famished, too, she realized as her mouth salivated before even making contact with the bread.

"You a very wise man," she commented to Asar through her manly chews. Asar smiled at the young woman. Soon, everyone had taken a seat except Alexander and Ebbers.

"Perfect," Alexander said with no small amount of enthusiasm. "Now that I have your undivided attention, I can explain to you what we have here, and what we are going to do," he said, holding up the page of riddles.

Ebbers tried to leave the room.

"Where are you going, Doctor?" Alexander called out without turning to face him.

The doctor stopped and looked at Alex. "I was going to make my exit since you intend to discuss your plans."

"You begged me for a second chance," Alexander replied quite harshly. "If that is really what you are looking for, redemption, then your help may prove invaluable to our mission."

Ebbers stared at Alexander in disbelief.

"Alexander!" Asar began to rise from his seat.

"Asar, please sit back down and enjoy your meal, old friend." Alex gestured with the palms of his hands for Asar to retake his seat. "We will see how Dr. Ebbers does, his trust must be earned, his allegiances flushed out. I will apprise his actions and go from there." Alexander nodded at Ebbers. "You should know, Doctor, there will be no more chances for you. Your ninth life, as it were, is at hand. Cross me, and you will know what true vengeance is."

"Understood, Mr. Storm," Ebbers replied, taking a seat next to the others at the table. "I will not let you down."

"That remains to be seen," Alexander assured him, "your actions here will dictate your future ... for eternity. Then it's settled. Our numbers continue to grow and evolve. Now, let us get on with the business at hand."

Alexander pulled out the vacant chair at the head of the table and sat amongst them. Laying the riddles down before him, his eyes methodically darted about the page. Several times he nodded to himself, mumbling incoherently, then he began to address the table.

"These twelve riddles are the keys, verbal maps if you will, to the globally scattered pieces of papyrus that make up the notorious Egyptian *Book of Gates*. If all of the pieces are acquired, one who is skilled in the ancient ways can reassemble the archaic spells and call forth a passageway to the underworld, and what follows will be Hell on Earth."

Keith stammered and choked on his food. His face growing red with embarrassment, he maladroitly swiped across the table, groping for the cup of water before him. Kate, without turning her attention from Alexander, reached over and smacked him on the back several times.

"There, there," she said in a mommy-to-baby voice. "Just breathe! It will be fine." Asar laughed from across the table at the display.

"Enough!" Alexander called out. "This is not funny! Not in the least!"

"Sorry, Alex," came the apology in unison from Asar and Kate.

"Are you quite alright, Keith?" asked Alex.

Keith nodded his head and waved Alex off with his free hand. He was still working on catching his breath.

"Very good, so what needs to be accomplished is *not* twelvefold you understand? We need only secure one of the fragments to achieve our goal, for without all twelve pieces, the papyrus is nothing more than a bad bedtime story." Alexander paused. He was sure all members of his party were listening, but he needed to ensure they were all, in fact, understanding him.

"We will need to first determine if our adversaries have located and acquired the papyrus located in Giza. If so, we will make our way to the next location which needs to be discerned from the riddles which have been so graciously provided by our host," Alexander winked at the table, "of this fine tuna and bologna dinner."

After a momentary pause, perhaps awaiting a reaction to his weak attempt at being comical, Alexander picked up the sheet of riddles. He opened his mouth to begin reading them to his listeners, and once again paused before the first word left his mouth. "Also," he looked up from the paper, "you should be pleased to learn Decker is in Egypt investigating the scene of the Sphinx's assault. He will reunite with us soon."

Alexander directed his attention to the verses in front of him. "The first reads, 'The guardian of the three, your quest's beginning with its end in me, my stone eyes see the eons as they pass between my paws of dust and rubble, descend into my chest and you will find my heart as it pounds to the rhythm of the sand, my stone eyes fixed on the horizon waiting for time to end.'"

Alexander grew silent, letting the words take root in his listener's minds. He then repeated the passage.

"It's clearly the Sphinx," Kate spoke up first. "The 'guardian of three,' which are the three pyramids, the reference to paws and staring into the sand."

"The young lady is correct," said Ebbers with approval. "This is clearly the Sphinx, which means—"

"Which means Moloch is proceeding in order," interrupted Alex, "or at least he is for now. And he is at a distinct disadvantage with regards to time since he must decipher each riddle before attempting to resolve its meaning. Thanks to Dr. Ebbers, we are able to bypass this time intensive step." Alex paused again and scrutinized Ebber's face, "you *haven't* supplied the demon with these translations, have you?"

He shook his head violently in a definitive 'no'.

"Yes, thanks to the good doctor," Asar repeated sarcastically.

"I understand your anger," Ebbers addressed Asar's comment as he made his way to Alex. "I will do everything in my power to make up for it." He stopped just in front of Alexander and reached for the paper.

"May I?" he asked.

Alexander nodded, and the doctor took the paper and walked over to his desk. He laid the sheet on a copy machine and began to print copies.

"I believe we should do as Moloch is doing and attempt to retrieve the papyrus fragments in the order in which they have been presented to us. I say this for several reasons, one of which being that I am unsure if there are further clues relevant to future locations present at the previous. You understand?"

Ebbers walked back to the group with a stack of copies and began to pass them out.

"Very good, Doctor," said Alexander. "This will help tremendously."

Alexander reclaimed his copy from Ebbers and began again.

"Okay, let us examine the second riddle, shall we. 'From the Valley of Moses, treading the sands of the gorge, arrive at the rose mountain's open mouth and pass through to the land beyond. Seek out the paper room in the paper church to the North—beneath its floor a metal door lined with the keys to the stars. Pluck a star and travel not far to the castle built by pharaoh for daughter.'"

Alexander peered up at the group, apprehensive hope in his eyes. "Any thoughts or ideas? Just yell them out if something strikes a chord or makes you think—"

"Rose!" yelled out Kate. "Roses are red."

"Red mountains," clarified Alexander.

"Valley of Moses," added Samantha as she rose from the table. "Your computer on over there, Doc?" she asked Ebbers, pointing to the cluttered desk.

"Yes," he crossed the room with enthusiastic energy, "by all means young lady."

"You online?"

Ebbers nodded, "the password is *alphaomega*, all lowercase."

Sam slid the chair out and dropped into the seat in front of the keyboard and shook the mouse. The screen flickered to life, and she entered the password. Sam opened the browser and typed in 'Valley of Moses' in the search bar.

"Anything?" called Keith.

"Gimme a second, will you?" She shook off his impatience.

"It's returning things like Jordan and Petra!" Sam shouted to the others. "Does that mean anything to you Storm?"

"Everything Samantha," replied Alexander looking at Kate. "The rose-colored mountains of Petra in Jordan!"

Alexander sprang from his seat as he uttered the words, invigorated by the speed at which their concerted effort had produced results.

"No time to waste!" he exclaimed. "Our destination is the ancient city of Petra nestled in the dusty backdrop of Jordan."

Alexander gathered up the team's materials as he spoke and, without further delay, made his way to the door.

"Wait!" yelled Abigail. "What about the rest of the riddles?"

"No time to sit idly by, researching each location my dear girl," replied Alex. "We will endeavor to clash with the mystic prose of the riddles as we proceed to our destination."

The others were already to their feet, scrambling towards the exit. Alexander noticed Ebbers was lagging behind, and he recoiled back into the room.

"Are you not coming, Doctor?" Alex called from the room's threshold into to the study.

Ebbers ambled his way to Alexander, his deportment penitent. "If you will have me."

"Secure anything you think may prove germane to our quest, Doctor," Alex instructed. "Any research you may have. I will wait two minutes, then we must be underway." With that, Ebber's was off.

Alexander grinned at the doctors enthusiasm, his loyalty, however, remained a question mark in Storm's mind. He retrieved his phone from his pocket and dialed Decks. The call instantly went to voicemail.

"Decks. Hello. We have acquired the riddles. Change in plans. Abandon your efforts in Egypt, I fear they will prove futile at this juncture, and meet us at the ruins of Petra in Jordan."

43

As the plane sat on the tarmac; Decker's phone alerted him to the presence of a new voicemail from Alexander. He lifted the phone to Anika and pointed at the screen, "Storm," he advised her.

"Check it silly," she said, lightheartedly nudging her companion.

"I would," he smiled and shook his head, "but there is no reception on this damn plane. I can't get a connection to the message."

He rose from his seat and flashed a quick smile. "Be right back. I'll come get you if there are any issues. Don't let them take off without me please."

"Don't worry," she said with a laugh. "You're not going to get rid of me that easy. If they get ready to take off, I'll get off, and we'll catch another flight."

Decker smiled. "Okay. Back in a sec."

He walked down the aisle between the rows of seats, glancing back over his shoulder at Anika at least twice. Each time, she was watching him, smiling. He got to the cabin door and looked back one last time. She was still smiling, and this time she waved him on and mouthed the word *go*.

Decker stepped down the stairs onto the tarmac and made a bee-line to the closest doors into the terminal. He needed to get away from the noise of the planes and stay in an area where reception was sufficient enough to access his messages. He pulled the large glass door open and stepped inside. Once the door snapped shut behind him, sealing the noises of the airport on the other side, he dialed his voicemail. As he listened to Alex's voice on the message, he nodded his head. They had the riddles and were apparently ahead of the game. He ended the call and slid the phone back into his pocket.

"Petra!" he exclaimed to himself. As he stepped toward the door, he glanced up and saw his plane taxiing away.

"Anika!" He slammed his hands against the release bar on the door and it flew open with such force it crashed against the outer wall. Decker ran toward the plane, but it was too late. It had already reached the runway entrance and was pivoting for entry.

"Hey!" he yelled as he ran. "Hey! Shit!"

It was hopeless. The pilot couldn't hear him, of course, and even if he could, he wouldn't have stopped. More likely they would have radioed in to have him shot for being on an unauthorized run of the pavement.

"Oh, Christ," he gasped as he ceased sprinting after the jet and rested with his hands on his knees.

He stood up straight and ran his hand up over his face and through his hair, realizing that all of his gear was with Anika. He turned back toward the terminal door and took a mental inventory of what he still had. Passport, wallet with funds, cell phone, notepad, and pen. He figured he'd be all right. It just wouldn't be the same without Anika, the only non-replaceable thing on the plane. He had grown very comfortable with her in a few short hours, and even though he protested her demand to tag along, he couldn't have been happier to have her with him.

He got to the door and heard the jet accelerate overhead. As he reached for the handle, he paused as his plane passed overhead, casting a shadow on him from above.

"Looking for someone, William?"

Decker pivoted around, nearly loosing his footing.

"Anika?" he yelled. There she stood; both their bags slung over her shoulders. Decker reached forward and grabbed her hand.

"I thought I'd lost ya' kid," he said with returning composure.

"Nah. Figured I stick around a bit."

"I'm glad."

"Do me a favor," she said, somewhat seriously.

"Name it."

"Take your darn bag!" She laughed, turning her shoulder to him. "It weighs a ton. What do you have in it, rocks?"

Decker laughed and grabbed the bag's strap from her. "Yes, as a matter of fact, there are some rocks in there."

Anika walked up next to him and bumped her butt into his hip as she passed.

"So, where are we headed?"

"Jordan," Decker replied as he swiftly stepped around her and opened the door, allowing her to pass.

"Jordan," she echoed, turning to face him.

"Yes. Petra, to be exact."

"Excellent. My third cousin on my father's side is a commander with the Jordanian police force."

"Of course, he is." Decker kidded as he followed Anika into the terminal.

"I will call him while you book our flight and let him know we're coming."

"You may want to alert him to expect other visitors as well," Decker said solemnly. "And these chaps are a bit more hostile than you and I."

44

E bber's home was only a short distance from the Montauk Airport, and Samuel managed to get them there in record time. Storm kept a private jet fueled and ready to go in a hangar several hundred yards from the strip, which runs northeast to southwest between the Block Island Sound and Lake Montauk. His longtime pilot and friend, Lobo, was always on call and arrived to the airstrip minutes before the others.

"Montauk Airport is the most easterly airport in the United States," Alexander commented as they boarded the jet. "Make yourselves at home. I need to speak to our pilot regarding our destination, fuel capacities and headwinds."

He moved up the aisle, passing the two spacious leather couches that lined the center of the Challenger 601 jet. To the front of the plane were more leather seats with wood tables. To the rear, a galley and bathroom were directly behind more chairs and tables.

"If you push the green button on the wall behind the couches," Alexander informed them, "desks equipped with laptops will rise from the cutout outlines in the rug. Please feel free to start researching our destination—Petra." With that, he opened the cockpit door and disappeared into the nose of the jet.

Alexander sat in the co-pilot seat. "Lobo. How are you, my friend?"

"Great. Love getting pulled out of bed in the middle of the night."

"Ha," Alex tapped him on the shoulder, "were you not alone?"

"No comment," Lobo smirked while fiddling with the jet's instrument panel.

"Well then," Storm laughed, "you weren't actually sleeping then. So, no harm done."

"Where we headed?" Lobo ignored his employer's defective rationale and turned his attention to the mission at hand.

Lobo was a no-nonsense ex-Marine pilot who had flown missions in Desert Storm. Alexander had met him by chance while Lobo was applying for an airplane maintenance worker position at the airport. They talked for quite a while that day, after which Alexander offered Lobo a job as his "pilot-on-call," and Lobo gladly accepted. Although the missions were more often than not quite perilous, he had a lot of downtime in between, for which Storm compensated him none-the-less.

"Our destination is one of your old haunts," Alexander paused. "Jordan."

"Excellent," Lobo replied as he continued to flip switches and turn knobs. "You got it, chief."

"Very good," Alexander stated, rising from his seat. "And when you are finalizing the flight plan, get us as close to the ruins at Petra as possible. Landing strip optional of course."

45

Moloch steered his horse through the narrow rock formed pass leading to the ancient city of Petra. The great stone walls blotted out what was left of the late day sun and cooled the air surrounding his small army. Naamah rode several yards in front of him, and Moloch enjoyed the sight of her body bouncing up and down in the saddle of her steed. He found her company to be pleasing, but he was wise to her ambitious nature and knew better than to trust her. She had existed much longer than he had, and he could not lower his defenses in the face of her timeless charms. Charms which had been honed to perfection on the backs of countless souls. Naamah had been one of Samael's four brides, and she possessed a strong connection to the high demon. At the present, she served a purpose, and as long as she continued to assist him, he would allow her to be part of his unholy crusade.

"It should be just ahead," Moloch called out to her.

"I think I see light!"

Naamah's horse picked up its pace as she prodded it on with her heel.

"Easy does it," Moloch shouted to her in a low, but powerful, voice. "We have no idea what is waiting in the clearing."

The long, thin passageway they were traveling was known as "Al-Siq," and it was literally cut through a mountain providing the only source of egress and ingress to the ancient city. The "Al-Siq" ended in a clearing at the grand entrance into Petra known as the Treasury. Built by the Nabatean's around 312 BC, the Treasury was a huge, three story, castle façade carved directly into the face of the mountain. In Arabic, the Treasury is known as El-Khazneh, or Khaznet Far'oun, which means Pharaoh's Treasury. This name comes from an ancient myth that treasure had been concealed there by a powerful black magician who is often identified with a wicked and very wealthy Egyptian pharaoh. The legend had been correct; however, it was not gold or rubies that had been buried at Petra, but instead a treasure of ancient and forbidden knowledge.

Moloch eventually saw the light of the clearing ahead as well, and soon Naamah was covered in the hot sunlight of the desert. She stopped her horse and peered over her shoulder at Moloch, flashing a devious smile his way. Moloch nodded back at her and trotted to her side. He took a piece of paper from his saddlebag and unfolded it.

"'From the Valley of Moses, treading the sands of the gorge,'" Moloch spoke reading the second riddle aloud as the others joined them in the clearing, "'arrive at the rose mountain's open mouth and pass through to the land beyond. Seek out the paper room in the paper church to the North —beneath its floor a metal door lined with the keys to the stars. Pluck a star and travel not far to the castle built by pharaoh for daughter.'" Moloch finished and lowered the paper to his side. He was staring at the Treasury, watching his men scour the area for guards and cameras.

"What does it mean?" Naamah broke the silence, softly.

Moloch turned his gaze to her and pointed at the paper. "Well, the first part brings us here, and the second part references two locations within the city of Petra." Moloch dismounted and walked to Naamah's horse. "The first of these locations, 'the paper room in the paper church,' is a reference to the Church of the Papyri, and more specifically, the Room of the Papyri within the church."

"I see," she said, smiling. "Papyrus is ancient paper. It becomes quite simplistic once we arrive at a starting point."

"Yes, a bit of research, and the vaults open before you," Moloch stated, perusing the notes in his hand once more. "And the second location, the Castle of the Pharaoh's Daughter, is another structure located within the stone walls of the city."

"Elementary." Naamah laughed as she hopped down from her horse.

Moloch walked over to her. "Yes, that was the easy part. Now the hard part."

"And that is?" she inquired.

Moloch began to read again. "That is, 'beneath its floor a metal door lined with the keys to the stars. Pluck a star and travel not far to the castle built by pharaoh for daughter.'"

"Oh," said Naamah with less enthusiasm. "so, the verse is still a mystery I assume." She walked around Moloch and elevated herself on her toes to peer at the document over his broad shoulders. "You don't know which location. The church *or* the castle."

"No," he replied and withdrew the paper from Naamah's sight. "The castle is the zenith, I have no doubt, but we will have to explore the ruins and ascertain exactly what the terms 'metal door' refer to. Then we must tackle the question of keys or stars, and how the process will play out in the castle."

"Well, what are we waiting for?" She approached the Treasury entrance, which offered passage to the rest of the city. Her strut, diminished not in the least by the sand beneath her feet, beckoned Moloch's mind elsewhere for but a moment.

"What, indeed?" Moloch replied finally replied.

"All clear, sir!" one of the soldiers shouted from the steps.

"Very good," Moloch responded with a smile which quickly faded as he turned from the men. The locations lack of both guards and tourists made him very weary. He had expected a welcoming party of firepower and force after the Giza incident. Moloch would have to stay sharp, something was surely amiss.

Moloch watched the soldiers gather round, gravitating toward his authority. "Your job is to make sure my companion and me are not molested by guards, military, or even tourists. All of which are curiously absent at the time. I do not care how this is achieved. We require uninterrupted time at two locations which are located on opposite ends of the site. We will begin at a restored church structure to the North and then travel across the city to the ruins of an ancient castle in the South. I want to stress to you the importance of our mission and our need for solitude." Moloch paused for effect. "If you cannot contain this situation, thus ensuring our success, there will be no payday."

Moloch walked toward Naamah, who was waiting at the immense carved doorway to the Treasury. He stopped and turned back to the men. "Proceed, we shall wait here in the outskirts until we receive the all clear".

The soldiers hurried past them, passing through the doors of the Treasury. Moloch nodded with encouragement at the motley horde as they passed and then strolled over to join Naamah.

"Let's give them a few minutes, then we commence our exploration at the Church of the Papyri."

Naamah smirked at him. "I do love me a good ol' fashion treasure hunt," she said, running her fingers over his shoulders and down his muscular arms. Without warning, the tomb-like silence of the city was shattered by a barrage of gun fire.

"Looks like the boys are securing the city," Naamah said with a grin and a snap of her finger.

Static broke out from the radio clipped to Moloch's belt.

"Sir!" a harried voice cried. "Sir, you copy? Over."

"Yes? What is it?" Moloch replied. "Can we proceed? Over."

"No, hold your position. I repeat, hold your position. Over."

Moloch waited with the radio by his ear. He was staring at Naamah. His eyes looked intense. Concerned even.

He brought the radio back to his mouth and depressed the side button. "What is the situation? Come back? Over."

More gun fire rang out. Clearly, an exchange had commenced based upon the resonance of the shots.

"I repeat, what is going on? Over."

The silence of the radio finally broke. "Ambush. They were waiting for us, sir. We've taken casualties. Snipers, sir. A bunch of them. Up in the hills I believe. We're separated and pinned down." Gun fire blared over the radio, and Moloch pulled it away from his ear.

"How?" Moloch demanded moving into the inner sanctum of the Treasury. "How did they know we were coming? This was a trap. Not merely increased security due to Giza."

"Storm!" Naamah replied, hurrying behind him. "It must be Alexander Storm."

46

Alexander Storm's black leather boots hit the ground with an audible thud as he exited the jet onto the Al Manzil airfield in Jordan. He rushed so quickly toward the three Jeeps waiting for them that he left a plum of rose-colored dust in his wake. Asar was next to exit, his hulk-like body moving astonishingly fast in an effort to keep up with Storm. Ten minutes before the flight had landed, Alexander had received word there was a firefight underway at the ruins of Petra. There was no time to spare.

Alexander was already belted into the passenger side of the first Jeep when Asar pulled open the driver's door. Alexander waved him away from the vehicle to no avail.

"No, Asar!" Alexander yelled.

"Get out!" Asar yelled to the driver as he plucked him from the seat as one would a feather from a chicken. "Out, now!"

"No! You must stay with the others!"

"Nonsense," Asar replied, already behind the wheel of the Jeep.

"Stay with them, I tell you!" Alex grabbed Asar's arm. "You must protect them!"

"There is no danger here, Storm." He turned to the driver, who had regained his footing in the desert sand.

"Go," Asar instructed the driver. "Lock down the jet. No one gets off. Do you understand? No one gets on either. If the situation calls for it, you instruct Lobo to put the bird in the air."

The driver looked at Alexander.

"Don't look at him!" demanded Asar. "Do you understand me?"

The driver looked back at Asar and nodded.

"Go and radio in to the tower for a fuel truck." Asar turned the key on the Jeep and the engine cranked into a low hum. "Have the plane refueled and inspect it for departure."

The driver turned to run back when Asar called after him. "Hey! *No one off the plane!*" The driver trotted away, but Asar called out again, with even more emphasis, "And most importantly, no one gets *on!*"

The driver stopped and looked back at Asar. He understood the charge and rested a hand on the pistol holstered at his hip. Nodding once more, he resumed his path toward the jet, waving Kate and Keith back up the steps. Kate placed an open hand above her eyes in an attempt to see through the blaring desert sun. She could make out Alexander and Asar in the Jeep. They appeared to be arguing.

"Back inside, miss." The driver had arrived at the base of the steps. "Please return to your seats." He walked toward the cockpit and ushered them inside.

"What about them?" Kate protested. "Where is Alexander going?"

"Please," the driver replied with more force. "Get back in the plane. It's not safe."

Kate threw her hands down and disappeared back into the jet's cabin.

"Get out now, Asar!" Alexander demanded. "I don't need you here!"

Asar was ignoring him as he reached around and grabbed the seatbelt to strap in.

"Get out! I order you!"

Asar stopped and turned to Alexander. He stared at him for a moment and then burst into a hearty laugh.

"Ha!" Asar engaged the vehicle's clutch and shifted. "You *order* me?" He laughed once more and hit the gas. "Hold tight, old boy!" he shouted to Alex. "We have nine kilometers to cover in record time."

Alexander crossed his arms and looked forward. "Fool!" he shouted at the windshield.

Asar burst out laughing once more.

47

Moloch and Naamah stepped out of the Treasury and into the dusty, arid air of the ancient city. Naamah scanned the landscape in every direction for any sign of their hired guns, but she only saw three or four dead or wounded on the ground. The cowards had launched their attack from the cover of the stone cliffs and ruins, pinning the mercenaries down. Naamah heard several shots ring out and located an indentation in the hills to her left that obscured the sniper from view. She stopped and let Moloch continue ahead. Naamah waited patiently, the heat coming up from the ground and rippling over her silhouette. Finally, she watched as the barrel of a rifle extended from a space within her focal point, and a momentary glint of light from the scope's reflection hit her eyes. She followed the intended trajectory to a half wall some fifty yards from where she stood. Naamah looked at the ground at her feet and spotted a golfball size stone at her side. She bent down and picked the rock up, bouncing it in her hand like a child would a ball. She stared down at the stone in her hand.

"Incendia! Ignis! Flamma!" the demon shouted. The words echoed off the mountains, and she could feel the sniper's gaze redirect on her.

"Incendia! Ignis! Flamma!" This time the stone in her hand began to glow red hot and quickly burst into a ball of fire.

Naamah's other hand, open with palm out, came up facing the direction of the hidden sniper. A shot rang out almost simultaneously—the bullet's trajectory was the demon's head.

"Desino!" she hissed, and the bullet froze midair, inches from the palm of her hand. She could hear chatter from the hill and looked back to the sniper's roost. With a swift and furious motion, Naamah launched the flaming stone at the hill, and with surgical accuracy, it hit its intended target and detonated with a massive explosion. Rock and debris showered down, and Moloch turned to Naamah with a grin.

"Nice shot, my dear!" he yelled back to her. "I think you got him!"

Another shot rang out. Moloch's arm darted out to his side, and he grabbed at the air, closing his fist around over what appeared to be empty space. He opened his hand, dropping the lead slug to the hot sand below, then turned back to Naamah, who had already set a new stone ablaze. She hurled the explosive rock past Moloch and into another secluded section of the hills bordering the archaeological site. Once again, the rock and sand exploded with the force of a missile detonation. Turning to Moloch for his approval, he nodded in appreciation and continued toward the Church of the Papyri.

Naamah surveyed the half wall where she assumed their men had been pinned down and saw four or five mercenaries emerge. The soldier in the front of the group raised his hand and gave Naamah a thumbs up as they continued in her direction. Swiftly turning her attention back to Moloch, she saw he was about to enter the target structure. Proceeding at an unnatural speed, she reached his side in seconds.

"Nicely done," Moloch commended her. "That should buy us some time."

The pair of demons disappeared from view as they passed under the modern canopy that was built to protect the entrance to the archaic Church of the Papyri.

48

Asar brought the Jeep to a sharp halt just outside the entrance to the curved canyon leading into Petra.

"On foot from here," Alexander shouted as he jumped from the vehicle.

Asar exited and moved to the back, unsnapping the clear plastic window that secured the rear area of the Jeep. Reaching into the compartment he withdrew several rifles.

"Alex!" he shouted. Alexander turned to Asar, who tossed him an ominous looking automatic weapon.

"Right." Alexander nodded and strapped the gun over his shoulder. "Let's go!" The pair began to jog into the mouth of the canyon.

"Has Decker arrived?" asked Asar with no small degree of hope, huffing in the furnace-like air.

"No. They are en route."

"They?"

Alex smiled. "Yes, they. Our friend Decks is in love, I believe."

"Really?"

"Yes, really." The two continued jogging the long path. Gun shots echoed in the distance.

"Why?" asked Alexander. "You have an issue with that?"

"Issue?" Asar's breathing was becoming more labored. "No, no issue. It's just this is going make for one heck of a date night."

Alexander turned to Asar as the two continued their forward momentum.

"Yes." He grinned. "Agreed. It will be a date to remember."

Their concerted laughter began low at first, muffled by the strenuousness nature of their movements, but soon grew, fueled by nervous tension, until it echoed through the canyon entrance. It ceased altogether, however, as gun fire broke out anew. Closer this time.

"A date from Hell, you mean," Asar added.

This time, their laughter was replaced by silence.

49

"So, are we supposed to just sit here and wait?" Kate harassed the driver and Lobo, both of whom were asking her to stay calm and have a seat.

"This is nuts!" she shouted.

"Yeah!" Samantha joined into the mix of complaints. "I thought we were here to help!" She looked to the others for support. "This is not helping. Sitting in this heap being babysat by the flying wolf."

"What?" Lobo darted Sam a dirty look.

"Maybe we should just relax and wait for Alex," Abigail suggested softly.

"Not maybe. That is what you are *going* to do," Lobo's annoyance was becoming evident in his tone. "Sit down and shut up!" he shouted at Kate and Sam.

"Hey!" Keith yelled, rising from the couch. "Don't talk to them like that."

"Don't get your panties in a bunch, Romeo." Lobo waved Keith off.

"I need to monitor the communications and make sure this aircraft is ready for flight when Mr. Storm returns." Lobo, relaxing his tensed muscles slightly, considered the discussion to be over and started to make his way back to the cockpit. "So cut the crap and stop acting like spoiled children. Relax, and do what you're told." He turned back to them once more, standing in the doorway of the pilot's quarters, shook his head, and slammed the barrier door to the cockpit shut.

Kate and Sam dropped back into the comforting folds of the couch with defeat. The driver, who had clearly been instructed to guard the group, moved back into position in front of the side door. He wore a genuine look of relief on his tanned Jordanian face.

Sam reached back over her head and smacked the button on the wall. The sound of pneumatics resonated, and she moved her legs to allow the workstation to rise up in front of her.

"Let's say we have a look at the rest of those riddles, Doc," she motioned to Ebbers, who had secluded himself in the small strip of empty space in front of the galley. He nodded and rose to join them.

"Good idea, Samantha," Kate said. "If we can't offer assistance to Alexander in the field, perhaps we can make some headway here."

Sam winked at her. "That's the spirit."

"No spirits, please." Keith joked as he sat down next to Kate. "No monsters, demons, UFOs, or freaking sasquatches, either, alright."

50

"Follow me," Moloch instructed Naamah. "This way." The two figures moved silently through the Church of the Papyri, traversing several stone-carved sub-rooms, and stopped at a gated threshold.

"Beyond this gate is the Papyri Room referenced in the riddles." Moloch reached up and wrapped his thick hands around the pitted iron bars. "The paper room."

Moloch's body tensed, and with a quick jerk, he ripped the gate from its stone footing.

"Oh, my," Naamah said in her best bimbo voice. "Aren't we *so* strong?"

Moloch shot her an unimpressed glance and tossed the gate to the floor of the church. He entered the chamber farthest to the West, and Naamah followed close behind. The air was dense and damp—a noticeable change from just a few steps back. The darkness of the room made it impossible to make out anything more than outlines and soft shadows.

"A little light here would prove useful my dear," he said without looking at her. "Perhaps you can whip up something a little less lethal for our needs?"

Naamah reached into her pocket and withdrew something in her closed hand. Moloch turned around and waited for the display of magic. Naamah lifted her fist to her full red lips and seductively blew on it. Her fingers opened one by one in spider-like motion, exposing her upturned palm.

"Poof!" she shouted, and with the finger from her other hand pressed the switch on an LED penlight. The intense glow filled the small room, and she let out a small laugh, her mouth half upturned in a sideways smirk.

"Your humor is fathomless," Moloch admitted as he reached out and snatched the light.

"Hey!" Naamah shouted.

"Do you know what you are looking for?" Moloch asked sarcastically as he broadcasted the light around the room, taking in every nook and cranny of the stone chamber.

"No," Naamah replied, "but neither do you."

"I don't?" asked Moloch, shining the light at his feet.

"No. You don't. You just told me outside—"

"I am a liar! A great deceiver. Do you really believe I would come here, unprepared, without the knowledge to complete our objective?" Moloch glanced over at her. "Really, now?"

"Okay," she quickly responded. "If we are being honest now, what's in the box?"

Moloch darted his gaze at her. "What box?"

"The small metal box you retrieved at the Sphinx." She watched his expression closely. "The one with the dragon engraved on it."

"I have no idea what you are referring to, my dear," the demon exuded mocking innocence. He turned and went back to surveying the floor around him. It was lined with ornate tiled frescos.

"Oh, back to deception, are we?" she said, clearly annoyed.

"Who says I ever stopped?"

"My dear." She mimicked him, and he nodded with indifference.

"Well, I faked my orgasm."

"Which one?" Moloch replied dryly.

"All of them."

"No, you didn't."

Naamah's giggle was deep and sultry, and Moloch smiled at her obvious tell.

"Here!" he shouted and dropped to his knees. Naamah quickly joined him on the floor, and he handed her the light.

"Here," he demanded, pointing to a cluster of mosaic tiles.

"What is it?"

"Do you remember the riddle? 'Pluck a star.' What is a star, Naamah? What is the key to a star?"

She thought for a moment.

"Incendia," he whispered in her ear.

"Fire!" shouted Naamah. "Stars are balls of gas and fire!"

"And what do you see here," asked Moloch, pointing at a group of ten or twelve tiles in the floor?

Naamah studied the mosaics for a moment and then noticed they were different from the others in the room. In the center of each tile was a metallic cutout in the shape of a flame. They appeared to be brass or copper and were inlaid in the ceramic tiles. Each metal flame appeared identical and was no more than two inches in length.

Moloch, having now completing his lesson in archaeology, lifted his pant leg to expose a hefty blade strapped to his ankle.

"For when magic fails," he remarked to Naamah with a mischievous smile. "Or for when you're not around."

This time, *she* smirked.

Moloch withdrew the blade from its sheath and carefully wedged the tip under one of the flame-shaped inlays. He carefully tilted the knife.

The fragile piece of ancient metal popped, snapping in two, and Moloch let out a growl. Naamah pushed his hand aside and extended her middle finger to him. His angry eyes squinted at her. She smiled and lowered her hand to the edge of another inlay. Gently, she wiggled the edge of her nail under the metal and lifted ever so softly. This time, the metal cutout gave way without a fight, and she lifted it up. She turned to Moloch, who was clearly quite pleased with her display of dexterity.

"For when your knife fails," she said, waving her middle finger at him. He laughed and extended an open hand. Naamah raised one eyebrow and dropped the piece of metal into it.

"Thank you," he said with some degree of sincerity. "It seems I have found yet another use for you. But oddly, both uses seem to be strangely related."

"Ha! You forgot my balls of fire."

"Oh, yes." Moloch laughed. "Three uses for you, and once again they are all related."

Naamah shook her head. She had walked into that one.

"Great. A witty demon."

Moloch was finished playing with her and didn't respond. Instead, he took the light from her hand and held the metal flame up to it.

"Strange. It seems rather unremarkable."

He slid the piece into a small glass vial he had retrieved from his pocket and pressed a cork into the top. With a masterful sleight of hand, it disappeared into his clothing.

"Shall we?" he asked, offering an arm to Naamah.

"Yes. We shall."

They quickly maneuvered through the deteriorating structure to the entrance.

"The sun has gone down," he commented as they entered the night air.

"It will be easier to get to the Castle of the Pharaoh's Daughter without being seen."

They stepped out from under the canopy and onto the cooling desert sand.

"Keep to the shadows, my dear," suggested Moloch as they moved summarily toward their destination on the other side of the city.

"I always do," Naamah replied. "I always do."

51

"Can't you move this thing any faster?" Decker yelled at the driver, twisting and turning in his seat like an impatient child.

"Shhh," Anika hushed him. "He's going as fast as the road will permit."

Decker and Anika had arrived at King Hussein International Airport located in the Jordanian city of Aqaba about thirty-minutes before Alexander's jet had set down. Upon arrival the couple had been met by a member of the Jordanian National Police force who informed them he would be taking them part of the way to Petra. A transport from the Desert Police Force would transport them the last leg of the journey. They had only been on the road a short time before the officer received a radio call reporting an attack was in progress at the ruins. Decker had reached out to Alexander immediately to informed him of the events which were transpiring at their destination.

He wondered if Alexander had made it to the site yet, praying he had the good sense to have Asar accompany him. Decker knew Alexander Storm had the habit of ignoring the danger signs that proved to be blatantly obvious to everyone else around him. He was always mindful of others' safety, but like the clairvoyant who could not foresee his own demise, he often missed the portends of risk to his own well-being.

"We will be meeting with the Bedouin Police Force in a few moments, madam," the driver spoke while peering at her through his review mirror, only addressing Anika. "Please be ready to make a quick transfer, as the agents picking you up cannot delay returning to Petra."

Anika nodded at the mirror. "We're ready, sir. Just tell us when to jump out."

Decker looked out of the dust-coated front window and could see the waiting truck in the distance. They were currently traveling in some type of modified van that looked more like an ambulance than a police vehicle. As they grew closer, Decker was glad to see a more suitable mode of desert transportation.

"That will get us through this sea of sand faster," Decker announced.

The driver looked at Decker in his mirror but said nothing. He obviously did not appreciate the cowboy-like attitude of his American passenger and was doing all he could to completely ignore him.

The police van skidded to a stop a few feet from the side of the four-wheel drive equipped patrol truck. Anika and Decker grabbed their bags, which had been propped between their legs on the floor, and scurried to depart the vehicle.

"Go! Go!" yelled Decker as Anika opened her door. "We have to get to Alex and the others!"

The pickup vehicles passenger jumped from the door and grabbed the handle on the back door. Anika threw her bag in the back and followed it into the truck. Decker couldn't help staring at her body as she hoisted herself into the seat.

"Hey," whispered Anika, turning and catching him red-handed. "Mind on the mission, William."

Decker smiled at her and jumped into the truck as the door slammed shut behind him. Within seconds, the officer had returned to the passenger seat, and the truck was away through the dense sand.

"Strap in, William," said Anika as she adjusted and locked her seatbelt. "This is going to be a rough ride."

"Hey!" came a woman's voice from the driver's seat. "What are you trying to say? I'm a great driver."

Embarrassed, Anika tried to rehabilitate the situation. "I was referring to the road ma'am, not your driving abilities."

"Gotcha," the driver laughed, looking over her shoulder.

"Mariah!" shouted Anika. "How have you been?"

"Good, good," replied Mariah.

"Decker, this is Officer Mariah Aabula of the National Police Force."

"Pleasure," replied Decker. Mariah had her hair tucked up under her official hat and Decker had assumed the driver was a man. Her face was tight and strong, but there was an attractive softness to her nonetheless. She turned back again to acknowledge Decker, and the truck began to veer sharply.

"Ahh! The road!" yelled Decker, pointing to the front window.

Mariah looked back in front of her and righted her direction with a jerk. She looked at Anika in her rearview mirror.

"Worrier, huh?" She joked. Anika just laughed.

"There is, technically no road you understand?" she laughed addressing Decks directly.

"So, do you know *everyone* in Jordan and Egypt?" Decker whispered out of the side of his mouth to Anika.

"No!" shouted Mariah from the front. "Just the important people!"

Mariah laughed. "Who's your friend, Anika?"

The conversation was interrupted by the truck's blaring police radio.

"We're taking severe losses here! Over!" the tinny voice blared. "We need backup! Military grade ordinance being used against us, and we're taking losses! Over!" The sound of gunfire and explosions rumbled through from the radio's speakers. Mariah's passenger began to shout in his native tongue, his body completely animated as he slammed his hand on the dashboard.

"If you can hear me," Mariah shouted into the radio's handheld, "we are en route. ETA fifteen minutes, heavy reinforcements being airlifted from the North. Over." She let go of the handheld's button and waited for a response. Nothing.

"Repeat, we will be there soon! Hold tight! Over."

Mariah latched the handheld back onto the radio and slammed the gas to the floor.

"So, Anika," Mariah repeated, her voice now devoid of wit. "Who is your friend, and what has he gotten you into?"

52

"All right, Mr. Ebbers." Samantha rested her hands above the keyboard before her. "Read me the next of those riddles."

"That's *Doctor*," Ebbers his voice resounding with condescending annoyance.

"Excuse me?" Samantha looked away from the monitor. "What was that?"

Ebbers shifted from one leg to the other. The young blonde was rough, and he sensed a verbal duel would not server his best interests at this juncture.

"I said it's *Doctor* Ebbers." The words, decisively, fell a bit less harsh. "It's Doctor. You said *Mister* Ebbers."

"Seriously?" Sam's irritation became evident to everyone in the cabin of the jet. "You must be joking, right?" She pushed herself back on the seat of the couch, granting her an improved view of the others.

"Can you guys believe this ass?"

"Excuse me, miss." Ebbers was clearly offended. He removed his glasses from his face and began to nervously wipe the lens with a cloth he carried in his pocket.

"Save it," Kate chimed in, raising her hand to the doctor. "You are at a slight disadvantage with us, obviously, so you just have to take your knuckle sandwiches, as my grandfather used to say. You betrayed your bloodline. You betrayed those who believed in you and trusted you." Kate stood up, and Ebbers instinctively took a step away from the oral onslaught. "And from what I understand of this story, which isn't a hell of a lot, I admit, you betrayed all of mankind."

Ebbers replaced the spectacles atop his nose and placed a hand on his forehead. Taking another step away from Kate, he was oblivious to the obstacle in his path of retreat. Losing his balance, he fell back until he was sitting on the edge of the couch running parallel with Samantha.

Kate continued her bout of anger, as Samantha watched the scene unfold with mob-like enthusiasm.

"So, I don't think you get to be sensitive about the prefix of your name. I don't think you get to be upset about anything. You should be grateful and humble. A lesser man then Mr. Storm would have put an end to you. So be appreciative. Sit there. Shut up, and answer Sam's questions so we can undo the mess *you* created."

"Yeah!" Sam yelled out. "What *she* said!" She turned and gave Kate a thumbs up. Kate smiled at Samantha, her face flushed crimson and her breathe moving at a thoroughbred's pace, she fell back into her seat. She could feel Keith's eyes boring a hole and finally turned to face him.

"What?" She laughed.

"Nothing," Keith said slowly. *But I love you*, he finished in his head.

Samantha returned her focus to the monitor before her. "Can you read me the next riddle, Ebbers?"

Ebbers reached over and grabbed the sheet from the small table on the side of the couch and began to read it aloud.

"'To the home of the Seven great rulers and a passage to the cosmos and beyond. Rivers run cold and silent beneath the ground in the place where the jaguar sits perched upon a throne of stone. At its center, a castle's temple and a staircase to the North—follow the serpent when day and night are one, and take its head before it can run.'"

Ebbers finished and looked up at Sam. She was typing the riddle. When she finished the last line, she read it back to Ebbers, who confirmed its accuracy.

"Okay," she said, "let's get to work here. Open the rest of the work stations and everybody take a verse of the riddle to research. If we split up the work amongst ourselves we may have better results." Sam clicked keys and tapped the touch screen display with lightning fast fingers. "All right, I have shared this riddle on the jet's private network. Let's get it loaded on all the machines and get to work."

"How did you do that so fast?" asked Keith with astonishment. "How'd you get into Alex's network?"

"Seriously, Keith?" She laughed, "Why do you think I'm here? My charming personality?"

Keith laughed. "Yeah, I see your point."

53

A momentary hiatus in the explosions and gunfire presented Alexander and Asar the opportunity they were waiting for. Cautiously, they stepped out into the courtyard clearing in front of the Treasury. Night had wholly taken the day, and they employed bright halogen flashlights to illuminate their path, as well as the fronts of the carved stone structure, on the interior.

"Even by the dark of night, Petra is nothing short of an awe-inspiring masterpiece," whispered Asar.

"Indeed," replied Alex. "An underrated archaeological marvel if ever there was one."

"Let's see if we can keep it in one piece."

"Ha! Let's see if we can keep *us* in one piece."

Alexander shook his head in agreement. The ceasefire ended as swiftly as it had begun, and a firefight broke the temporary silence. The two retreated back to the cover of the chamber from which they had entered.

"I believe it would be prudent to pursue a forward advance at this juncture," Alexander suggested, walking back out into the clearing. "as the action appears to be on the other side of the Treasury for the time being."

Asar, nodding, moved forward with Alexander, crossing the red stone and sand desert floor that led to an intricately designed rock staircase. The pair vigilantly ascended the steps and entered under a grand stone archway.

"Douse the lights," Alex whispered, "and don your night vision."

"We don't have any night vision with us, Alex."

"Oh, right." He smiled and continued, "Douse the lights, and open your eyes very wide as to absorb the highest concentration of available light."

"Not funny, Alex," Asar snapped back at him. "Nor is this the appropriate time for humor."

"Quite the contrary, Asar," Alexander replied. "This is the perfect time for a little levity."

"Oh, really? Well, then, I guess I will let you know when I finally hear something amusing."

"There you go, Asar!" Alexander tapped him on the back. "That's the spirit."

Cloaked in the cover of darkness, the two used their hands and feet to navigate their way to the other side of the Treasury. The uneven floor stones and debris in the path constituted their own set of problems and the pair nearly fell on more than one occasion.

"Beware of scorpions, Asar," Alexander advised his friend with a chuckle.

"I grew up on the streets of Egypt during the day and amongst the desert ruins at night. Are you really telling me to watch for scorpions, Alex?"

"Yes." Alexander continued to press forward through the stone structure. "And watch for cobras, asps—"

"And bullets," interrupted Asar. "Now mind your tongue before you get us killed."

It had been several minutes since the last burst of gunfire. Alexander and Asar reached the back exit of the Treasury and peered out into the open city beyond. Only the faint light of a quarter moon illuminated Petra, and Alexander was optimistic that the low light might provide them the cover they needed to move about unseen.

"Where do we need to go now, Alex?" inquired Asar in a soft, husky, whisper.

"I honestly am not sure. We really didn't complete the research necessary to traverse this location under these conditions. If the others were correct, we should head to the church. However, I have a feeling the enemy might be beyond that step. Kate believed the last reference was to a ruined structure."

"Pharaoh's daughter's castle or something along those lines, correct?"

"Yes. And if I recall, the city should be in that direction."

Alexander moved to the right of the doorway and stepped out. Before he could take another step, Asar grabbed him by the body of his jacket and yanked him back. Alex felt at least one bullet fly by his face, and he stammered backward into Asar. They fell back into the safety of the Treasury as a barrage of bullets ricocheted around the walls in front of them.

"Many thanks," Alexander said. "Guess they know we're here now. Who do you suppose is taking pot shots at us? The good or the bad?"

"Perhaps it is the ugly."

"There you go," Alexander laughed. "More of that signature Asar humor. Does the comedian possess any ideas?"

"Yes. Don't step out there."

"Seriously, Asar, we need to get to those ruins, or we are going to lose another fragment to the enemy."

The two friends stood there in silence as the gunfire died down and eventually came to a halt. Suddenly, Alexander sprang forward.

"I have an idea, Asar," Alexander's voice was filled with the echoes of hope. "Follow my lead, funny man, and keep your head down lest it be blown off."

"Discernibly not funny Alexander."

54

"'To the home of the Seven great rulers and a passage to the cosmos and beyond. Rivers run cold and silent beneath the ground in the place where the jaguar sits perched upon a throne of stone. At its center, a castle's temple and a staircase to the North—follow the serpent when day and night are one, and take its head before it can run.'"

"Any insight, Ebbers?" Keith prodded the reluctant witness. "Come on, you must have read through these a zillion times. Your ancestors read them. There must be something."

"Perhaps." Ebbers repositioned himself on the couch and looked around the cabin at the others. He seemed to linger on Abigail, who sat in one of the standalone chairs close to the cockpit door. He studied her as if he noticed she was amongst them for the first time. Abigail's eyes were closed, and her breathing was short and rapid.

"Hey!" Sam shouted. "Eyes over here, you perv."

"What?" Ebbers seemed outraged by the comment. "Really, you are beyond repair, young lady."

"She didn't mean it," Keith said quickly turning a chiding eye to Sam. She wrinkled her nose at him and mouthed the word *what* with a great deal of facial exaggeration.

"We're all uptight, Doc," Keith began again, "but we have a common goal here. We have to help. And figuring out the next location in these riddles will go a long way in doing just that."

Ebbers turned back to Abigail while continuing to nod in agreement to Keith's words.

"My arrangement, if you will, is with Storm," he said with certainty. His demeanor had changed a great deal since back at his home when his forced servitude came across as pathetic and needy. Perhaps his stripes were beginning to surface.

"Tell us what you know," Kate added. "We'll tell Mr. Storm you helped if that's what you're afraid of."

"You don't understand!" he shot back at her. "Storm is not here, and he may never return." Ebbers's eyes drifted back to Abigail. Her face looked familiar to him. Her dark skin and the features of her Cajun ancestry intrigued him. Then, Abigail opened her eyes. She opened them and looked right at Ebbers as if she had felt his stare all along. She looked into him, and her pupils swelled with revelation.

"Monster," Abigail whispered. Only Ebbers caught it, and he jumped to his feet.

"Who brought her on this aircraft?" Ebbers demanded. "Do you have any idea who she is? *What* she is?" Ebbers reached near panic and his voiced boomed throughout the steel cabin. "I didn't sign on for this!"

"Sit down!" yelled the soldier standing guard, finally asserting his control over the banter that had been transpiring amongst the occupants of the cabin. Ebbers had forgotten he was there. In fact, everyone had forgotten he was there. Kate turned to look at him. He was advancing into the group when she heard the pilot's voice.

"What's the problem?" Lobo asked, shaking his head. "How's a guy supposed to get any shut eye around here? Enough!" Lobo turned back to the cockpit. "Next one of ya to sound off can *get* off. You all get it? LOL and WTF and all that other crap." Lobo slammed the door behind him.

Samantha giggled. "Uh, *WTF* was that?"

Ebbers settled back into his seat, and the guard moved back into his position as sentry. Kate got up and walked over to Abigail. She looked down at her and touched her arm gently. Abigail opened her eyes and forced a smile.

"Are you okay?" asked Kate.

"Yes," she said as she shifted up in her seat. "He freaks me out. I mean, he made a deal with the devil for God's sake. Why has Alexander brought him here?"

Kate walked past Abigail and sat in the empty chair beside her.

"I'm not sure. I'm not sure why he brought us here, either, for that matter. I *do* know that whatever is going on is real. I've seen enough to cast away any doubt of the dire situation we are in; we are *all* in."

"I agree," Abigail conceded. "But what are we supposed to do? Sit here?"

"No," Kate said with certainty. "He brought us together to help him. I think he expects us to take the initiative, and I assume Ebbers is here because of what he knows. It's obvious, at least to me, that Alexander isn't a stupid man. All of us have a purpose. I have some familiarity with the ancient Egyptians. This *Book of Gates* is how Isis brought Osiris back from the dead; resurrection. She guided him through the underworld. If these spells can open a portal to Hell—and Hell is real—well, I guess that's everyone's problem, right?"

Abigail nodded. "But why am *I* here?"

"Girl," Kate smiled. "You clearly have some outrageous talents. I know you're aware of this. Am I right?"

Abigail looked away.

"Maybe there are some things you don't know about yourself yet. Maybe that is part of why you are here, to learn about yourself and how you fit into this all."

"What's *his* interest in me?" Abigail looked toward Ebbers and lifted her chin.

"I suspect he senses you can see him clearer than the rest of us. Heck, I sense it, he must."

"Huh?" asked Abigail, as if she wasn't aware of the truth.

"I think you understand, Abigail," said Kate as she rose to her feet. "And do me a favor—keep your eyes on him."

Abigail nodded.

"I mean *all* your eyes."

Kate began to walk back to the others when Abigail reached up and grabbed her wrist.

"I still don't know what we can do," she said and shook her head. "And I am tired, very tired, and I don't know why. Ever since I arrived at Dragon Loch, it's been growing in me, exhaustion ... draining me."

"I don't know what's making you feel that way, but I suspect you're feeling a sense of impending doom, and if we sit here and do nothing, I think it's only going to get worse. So let's get something started." She walked to the middle of the cabin. "Dr. Ebbers, are you willing to offer any insight into this riddle? The third one specifically for the time being?"

Ebbers looked up at Kate and then at Abigail, who was staring at him through eyes that none of the others had. Stern, hard, and flickering with a flaming glow. To the others, her gaze was soft and natural. Ebbers quickly averted his eyes and tried to slow his racing heart.

"As I said, why should I help you?" asked Ebbers with arrogance.

"Well," Kate began as she walked to Samantha, "because I asked nicely."

Ebbers's expression did not change. He found no levity in the stupid girl's childish innocence. He did, however, feel it was a good idea to appear like he was assisting should Storm return.

"Well, in that case," Ebbers said, rising to his feet and walking back to the rear of the cabin, "in the third riddle, the quote 'Seven great rulers' refers to Mexico. Its quite obvious." Ebbers lowered himself into the chair. "You figure out the rest."

55

Moloch and Naamah moved effortlessly over the fallen stones and debris that surrounded the Qasr al-Bint Firaun. The free-standing fortress was built with massive blocks of yellow sandstone, and all but one wall of the structure was still intact. Legend states that the monument was built by a great Egyptian pharaoh for his daughter.

"What leads you to believe these are the ruins in the riddle?" Naamah asked as the couple reached the fallen wall.

"Qasr al-Bint Firaun," stated Moloch, matter-of-factly.

"Little rusty, big guy. Let's not play professor and pupil."

Her words brought a smile to Moloch's face.

"Oh, we can play *that* professor and pupil." Naamah paused and quickly added, "But not right now."

"It translates roughly to the Castle of the Pharaoh's Daughter," Moloch said and turned to the South. "The riddle stated the 'castle built by pharaoh for daughter.'" He turned his head in the opposite direction. "Seems to match...*down!*" he yelled to Naamah.

A shot rang out, then another.

"Their aim is improving!" Naamah shouted, clearly exhilarated.

"They are getting too close," Moloch added as he scanned the landscape for the source of the shot. Without much light, the hills of Petra were pitch black to human eyes unaided by the likes of flashlights or night vision. Moloch and Naamah, however, could see in the dark as clear as they could in the day. Their demonic eyes sucked every last vestige of light from their surroundings, resulting in a distinct advantage over their pursuers.

"There!" Moloch pointed to an area beyond the fortress in the cliffside. "In one of those caves."

The mountainside was flat and riddled with small openings which had been carved by the Nabataeans.

"Storm's here," Naamah suddenly hissed at Moloch. "I can smell his foul stench in the air."

"No time!" he ordered. "Take out the whole mountainside."

With that, Moloch forged forward into the sanctum of the castle's walls, leaving Naamah to deliver her unique form of devastation.

Without missing a beat, Naamah crouched down and began to wave her open hands over the ground. As if she were gracefully dancing, her arms crossed and swayed, vibrating with the sheer power of her intent. Suddenly, stone and sand together began to levitate and form before her as she rose completely upright. Her arms continued to twist and sway, gaining momentum and force. Her long black hair began to lift and fly as the clusters of debris proceeded to whirl around her with tornado-like force, lifting her body up off the ground with it. As the funnel rose, so did Naamah, until she was fifty feet in the air. The rocks and sand whipped into a cloudy blur. Then came the fire. It ignited at the base of the cyclone and shot up over Naamah to the top of the funnel. She stilled as the flaming pillar of molten rock and sand continued molten metamorphosis over and around her. Turning her head, she raised one finger and made a flicking motion at the flames. They heeded her will and launched a burst of flame and rock some hundred yards toward the exit of the Treasury. The fiery projectiles hit their mark only a short distance from where Alexander and Asar stood, pinned by the demons and the soldiers. The shower of fire and light produced by Naamah, quickly exposed their position to the others, and a barrage of gunfire broke out. Naamah's eyes were drawn to Storm, and he to her. The nemeses locked onto each other over the vast distance for no more than a split second, but it was powerfully primal nonetheless. Alexander blinked first and ducked back into the safety of the Treasury's walls. Naamah returned her focus to the mountain. Flashes of light radiated from several of the small caves as bullets whizzed toward the demon's whirling weapon of destruction. The speeding lead found no purchase though, and was quickly absorbed into the spinning mass, becoming part of the molten tornado.

"Fugo tonare!" The demon's words commanded the funnel to unfold into a massive sheet of fire which hurdled like a tsunami toward the mountainside. Blanketing the cliffside, the impact of the fiery spell unleashed the echo of a hundred crashes of thunder all at once. The ancient city of Petra shook at its foundations as stones crumbled and structures fell, and within the blink of an eye, the mountainside was annihilated. Molten rock and sand showered down on the area behind the castle like a biblical storm.

As Naamah descended back to Earth, she saw Moloch disappear into a thin doorway which was carved directly into one of the structure's walls. She steadfastly made her way there to find a steep, narrow staircase. She ascended the steps, reaching the top in seconds. Naamah turned to her left and was immediately met with another set of stairs. Moloch was just reaching the top, and Naamah could see the small metallic cutout they had found at the Church of the Papyri glowing bright red in his hand.

Moloch caught sight of Naamah's movement and turned to her.

"Come quickly, Mother of Destruction!" he yelled to her. "The prize awaits."

Moloch turned and disappeared around the bend of the upper wall of the castle built for pharaoh's daughter. However, Naamah could still hear his voice echoing.

"The prize awaits..."

56

The turbulent ride through the rough desert terrain was akin to a small vessel being tossed about on an angry sea; and it made Decker sick to his stomach. As his head bobbed and weaved in the uneasy rhythm of the truck's motion, he tried in vain to formulate a plan to render assistance to Storm and the others. He had no idea what to expect when they arrived at the ruins. Decker surmised that Alexander was already on location and hoped his friend had not placed himself in harm's way. He found his thoughts drifting back to an excursion the two had made some years ago to a village in Fatges, Spain which was purported to be haunted. Japanese investors had hired Decker to investigate the validity of claims made by locals involving specters inhabiting the small settlement. The businessmen hoped such tales would bolster their capitalistic pursuits into themed amusement monstrosities and wanted the validity of the legends solidified by a respectable scholar in the field of paranormal investigation. Legend held that a series of unexplained murders had transformed the village into a ghost town. Spending the night in the ill-fated Spanish ruins purportedly guaranteed a daring individual's unnatural departure from this world. Alexander and Decks had arrived in the failing light of dusk and had barely set up camp before the blood-curdling screams and wails began to echo from the crumbling town's ruins. Alexander would have none of it, and Decker remembered him rising to his feet and marching off toward the nearest structure.

"Poppycock," he had exclaimed in his oft-used fake British accent. "Do they take us for fools?"

Decker had chased after Alex, begging him to take a moment and gather his thoughts, but Alexander had ignored his pleas.

"This is nonsense, my friend!" he had replied. "A poor excuse for a Hollywood set."

Alexander had stopped at the threshold of the crumbling stone building and continued, "And I will not have some theme park investors tarnishing your good name and reputation to further their marketability."

But rather than heed Decker's warnings, Alexander charged into the ruins, yelling, "Show yourselves, you dime store charlatans!"

Well, they had shown themselves all right—just not in the way Alexander Storm had anticipated, that's all.

"Good God, man!" he had shouted. "Don't enter this house!" All traces of British voice play had fled with the color in his complexion.

Decker remained vigilant in the doorway of the dilapidated structure as his mentor had instructed. He watched as Alexander spun in all directions as a circle of fiendish spirits imploded upon him. The ghouls floated across the broken wooden flooring, surrounding Alex. Their phantasmic forms exuding menacing contempt for the interloper. Their menacing form was only outmatched by the spectacle of their heads which were tilted all the way back, exposing large gapping holes in their throats from which leached forth all manner of foul creature, stench and smoke. Shrieks and wails emanated from the openings in their necks as well and each one held in its spectral hands the weapon of its demise.

"Get out!" Decks had screamed at Alexander. He recalled how he had been sure the great Alexander Storm would die amongst the ruins in that forgotten rat hole in Baix Camp, Spain.

Alexander had cried out to Decker, who was clearly battling the weight of his own self interest versus coming to his friend's aid, "Do not enter. Cover your eyes until I tell you otherwise!"

Decker heard his command, but continued to watch the supernatural display nonetheless. Alexander raised his hands above his head. With intense concentration evidenced on his face, Alex turned to apprise Decker's status. He was not pleased with his friend's apparent disregard for his directives and he shouted at him once more, realizing at that point that it was a fruitless endeavor. Storm returned his attentions to the besiegement upon him. His hands, still outstretched, had begun to radiate a thick blue light from his fingertips. Decker watched in astonishment.

"What the hell is happening, Alex?" he had cried out.

"Do it! Do it now!" Alexander cried with great effort, as if he were holding a heavy weight above his head. "Close your eyes now, goddamn it!"

This time, Decker complied and shut his eyes tight. William Decker would never forget what occurred next. Like a massive vacuum had been switched on, he felt all the air around him being sucked away as the night went completely silent. Then, with an explosive gush of force, something completely enveloped Decker's body. It was light. So powerful was the light that he had been able to see it right through the thin, soft skin of his eyelids. A concentrated blue radiance like nothing he had ever experienced before. The luminosity's penetrating radiance did not burn, however. He became quickly overcome with the sensation that he had plunged his body into the dark depths of a still and frozen lake. There was no other way to describe the sensations engulfing him. He had fought every urge to open his eyes, even though he felt the ice blue light demanding to be seen. Calling to him.

His mouth drew open, involuntarily, and screams issued forth as he fought back, throwing his hands up over his shut eyes to add another layer of protection against the onslaught of supernatural brilliance. He felt the air current commence to swirl around him, and he was sure his freezing skin would be separated from his body.

"What is—"

He tried to speak, but the air was sucked from his mouth each time he opened it.

Then, as quickly as it had begun, the wind was gone, as was the freezing sensation. He stood motionless and listened.

"Alex?" he whispered into the still air, voluntarily blinded and still not willing to risk further exposure, his eyes remained covered and shut.

"It's alright," Alexander voice was calm and soothing as he touched Decker's shoulder. "You can open your eyes my friend."

Decker removed his hands from his face to find Alex standing before him, unscathed, devoid of all manner of apparitional glow.

"What the hell was that?"

"The ghosts were quite real, Decker."

"Yeah, no shit!"

"Ha ha!" Alexander had laughed. "I used some flashlights. I had to scare them off."

"What! Are you kidding me?"

"Oh, stop." Alexander had brushed off Decker's apparent disbelief. "You are well aware that I possess a special skill set which comes in handy in certain situations. Let's not make more out of this than need be."

"Special?" Decker had responded. "Special my ass. Special is being able to find water with a stick or tell my future with a pile of bones." Decker had begun to follow after Storm. "This was more than special, my friend. There's a word for it. Not sure if you're familiar with it. *Supernatural*! Oh yeah," he said with tremendous sarcasm, "you know it...'cause next to the word in the dictionary is a picture of *you*!"

Alexander, standing with his back to Decker, put his hand up, calling for an end to the conversation.

"Be careful what you utter in the moonlight my friend." He had turned to face Decker. "You never know who—or what—might be listening."

With that, Alex turned to walk back to their camp.

"You may tell your employers that this town *is* indeed haunted, as I surmise this will boost ticket sales, which should solidify you as their go-to guy for situations such as this. Only you and I need to know the truth. That this town *was* haunted, and it was a legitimate supernatural phenomenon. Therefore, you should have no hesitation ascribing your seal of approval to the by-lines."

"That was very reckless of you, Alex. Rushing in there like that could have gotten you killed."

"Nonsense," Alexander replied. "I knew you had my back."

Anika's hand on his knee snapped Decker back to the present. He blinked his eyes and looked at her sweet face in the dimly lit truck. She smiled back at him, a concerned smile, and patted his leg.

"You okay, William?" she whispered.

Decker nodded and covered her hand with his. Her skin was warm and soft, and he could sense its touch calming his mounting apprehension.

"It will be okay," she said softly. "Your friends will be okay. We will be there in a few minutes, and you can charge in there like the U.S. Marines."

Decker smiled at her. It was if she could read his mind. Something about the way they communicated made him feel as if he had known her all his life.

"I know it'll be okay." He turned to look out the front window. He could see the opening of the entrance into Petra emerging from the darkness. "I know everything will be alright cause I've got you covering my back."

"I do have your back," she replied. "And hopefully, the rest of you, too."

Decker turned to her and smiled. Their tender moment, however, was shattered by the bullet that ripped through the glass of the truck's windshield with an awesome burst of crystalizing glass.

57

Moloch ran his fingers over the rough stone wall before him. The final row of stairs in the ruins—known as the Castle of Pharaoh's Daughter—led to an open landing of carved stone. Naamah and Moloch stood overlooking the interior of the castle below. The slab floor was situated in the upper right corner of the structure so that the back and side wall formed a ninety-degree angle before them. The two-level run of steps, chiseled from one solid block of rock, loomed behind them, and to their left was the open drop to what remained of the princess's crumbling castle.

"How do we know which one?" Naamah whispered, not wanting to interrupt Moloch's intense study. She took a step closer to him and looked across the back wall. It was riddled with hundreds of small holes and indents arranged in perfect rows, both horizontally and vertically. Upon closer inspection, Naamah discovered the markings were not merely holes, but were, in fact, ornately carved shapes. Crosses, moons, circles, squares, diamonds, and, of course, the silhouettes of flames, made up the array of forms present on the wall.

Moloch stepped back and turned to Naamah.

"What was that?" he asked her.

"I said, how are we going to figure out which hole the key fits in?" She turned and motioned to the vast wall. "The rows run all the way to the other side of the castle. This could take all—"

Moloch reached out and placed one finger over Naamah's lips, effectively silencing her. She looked at him with confusion, one eyebrow raised. Swiftly, he moved his hand from her mouth and slid it behind her head, clutching her long ebony hair. The demon tugged gently, tilting it back, exposing her neck.

"Wait!" Naamah yelled in protest, positive she was about to be torn apart. Moloch ignored her pleas and quickly pressed his mouth against her throat. His lips parted slightly, and he kissed her neck passionately, pressing his tongue against her skin as he did. Chills ran across her otherworldly skin, a feat not so easy to achieve, and she relaxed her body. He worked his way up her neck and behind her ear. She reached up and wrapped her arms around his muscular back and drew him closer to her. Moloch continued his erotic assault, making his way to her earlobe. Naamah moaned as one of her hands released him and dropped down between her legs. Moloch pressed his nose against her hair and neck. He drew in a deep breath, capturing her scent as his eyes slowly closed. His free hand reached down to join Naamah's as he spun her around and walked her back against the side wall. Her body writhed against the cold stone edifice of the ruins.

Their bizarrely timed ritual came to a sudden halt as the echo of a gun shot reverberated through the ancient structure. The fight was moving closer. The single shot was quickly followed by a barrage of gunfire seemingly originating from direction of the Treasury and Alexander Storm.

Moloch paused and whispered into Naamah's ear, "We shall have to continue this later."

He relinquished his erotically fueled grasp of her body and proceeded back to the rows of symbols; Naamah, releasing a pent up burst of air, threw her hands down in frustration.

"Later?" she asked.

"Yes, later," he promised. "A celebratory ritual in honor of our acquisition of the second fragment of papyrus."

"You know where it is, then?" Naamah exclaimed with sheer excitement as she moved to his side.

"Of course, my dear," he replied, removing the metallic flame symbol from his pocket and holding it up to the wall. He moved his hand across the stone, sweeping it from side to side, watching Naamah the entire time.

"Wait for it...wait for it," he said in jest. Finally, as he passed the flame over a row toward the outer ends of his reach, Naamah saw it. One of the holes cut in the shape of flame glowed an auburn hue as the metallic flame got closer, and it continued to emanate slightly until Moloch's hand came to rest directly above it, at which time the hint of light transformed into real flames, darting out from the rock to kiss metal key. Moloch pressed the key into the lock; reunited after centuries of sleep, the two merged together seamlessly.

Naamah looked on with anticipation as a faint glimmer of light began to trace a previously unseen square around the outside of the keyhole. Moloch stepped back as the growing outline became more defined. Then, in the dark of the Jordanian desert, a massive burst of blinding light forced the two demons to shield their eyes momentarily. When they could see the wall again, they were met with a protruding stone block approximately two feet square. Moloch dashed to the wall and grabbed the newly revealed rock relief with both hands, ripping it from the face of the wall and tossing it over the side of the platform to the floor. He extended his hand into the hole, and Naamah watched his face intently. He felt about, grasping at the empty air inside. But his movements suddenly stopped, and she watched as a devious smile crept across his ancient lips.

"What have you found?" she demanded, almost breathless. "Show me. Show me!"

Moloch withdrew his hand, and in it was a small metal box of copper or brass, tarnished green from the ages. Holding it out in his palm, he used his other hand to gently lift its lid, exposing the treasure within.

"And there you have it, my dear," Moloch stated with reserved excitement. "The second prize in our quest."

Naamah moved closer, eyes burning red, and peered into the small box. There, in the ancient vessel, was the second fragment of *The Book of Gates* and the demons found themselves one step closer to the end of time.

58

"What did you find, Kate?" asked Samantha as she paced in front of the computer. Kate was smiling as she read the article she had pulled up on a search for the words "Mexico" and "Seven great rulers."

"I got it!" Kate yelled as she moved out from behind the computer screen and began to pace. Her excitement was overwhelming, and she found it difficult to catch her breath.

"Of course, you did," responded Keith, grinning at her with great admiration. "It's what you do. Storm made the right choice calling on you."

"Nonsense," she replied. "Anyone could have figured this out."

"But *you* did," added Sam, walking to her side. "Now tell us what the hell you found already, girl!"

"Okay. Here goes," Kate began. "The term 'Seven great rulers' in Mexican history refer to the seven great Mayan kings. I recognized this once Ebbers—I mean *Doctor* Ebbers—" she corrected herself and smiled at the doctor, who nodded back to her in acknowledgment, "told us we should be looking to Mexico."

"Go on," urged Samantha.

"Well, I assumed we were looking for some historical structure or monument, so I began searching all the most well-known Mayan ruins in Mexico. One of my first choices was the famed ruins of Chichen Itza."

"Chicken what?" Samantha joked.

"Chichen Itza," repeated Kate with a smirk, "which is also referred to as Uucyabnal in some ancient texts." Kate moved closer to Keith and put her hand up for a high five, which Keith, confused, delivered half-heartedly.

"I don't get it," said Sam dryly.

"Neither do I," came a voice from behind them. Kate turned to see Abigail, who had silently moved back to the group. "What does it mean?"

"Oh, sorry," replied Kate. "Yes, the name Uucyabnal literally means 'Seven great rulers.'"

"Ohhh," responded Keith.

"Got it!" Samantha shouted with a wide smile. "You are *hot* Kate!"

"On fire," added Keith.

"Very good, Ms. Kate," Ebbers called from the back. "Now finish it."

"Hey." Samantha turned to meet Ebbers's glance. "Do you know the answer to these riddles or not? Because it sure seems like it to me."

"I know bits and pieces, you unruly girl." He turned away from her. "Don't you think if I had the answers, I would have collected them myself?"

Samantha shrugged. The doctor's reply seemed reasonable. She turned back to Kate.

"So, you have narrowed it down to this chicken place, but I assume it's a huge site, right? Where do we look once we get there?"

Kate walked back to the couch and sat down in front of the computer.

"The answers are all here," she said, determination in her eyes. "Let's take a look at the next lines: 'a passage to the cosmos and beyond' refers to the Mayan beliefs and study of the space and the cosmos. This confirms we're on the right track. Not sure if there is any further meaning there. We will come back to it if need be."

Kate pounded away on the keyboard.

"The next verse states, 'rivers run cold and silent beneath the ground.' This is also a reference to Mexico, which is littered with underground rivers and 'cenotes'—underground pools of water."

Kate began to type again as Samantha slid in next to her.

"The next part of the riddle is a bit more complicated and I believe directs us to the spot in Chichen Itza we need to look at. 'In the place where the jaguar sits perched upon a throne of stone.' I searched the terms Chichen Itza and jaguar, and came up with Kukulcan's jaguar throne."

"You gotta love the Internet," Samantha whispered, staring at the screen, watching the riddle unfolded before her.

"Don't leave home without it." Keith joked.

"It gets better," replied Kate. "The throne is located on the grounds of Chichen Itza, in an interior structure known as 'El Castillo.'"

"The castle," translated Abigail from the fringes of the group.

"The castle," repeated Kate with building enthusiasm as she placed a pencil in her mouth and gathered up her long dark hair. Keith had seen this ritual a hundred times before, and it meant that Kate was on the cusp of some grand reveal. He watched her pluck the pencil from between her lips and pass it through her hair, forming a makeshift bun. Keith thought it was possibly the sexiest thing he had ever seen.

"So, the next line," Kate continued, "reads 'at its center, a castle's temple.'"

"There's the castle part, I guess," added Samantha. Kate acknowledged her with a smile.

"Yes," she said. "In fact, the site I found says, 'Dominating the center of Chichen Itza is the Temple of Kukulcan, often referred to as El Castillo, or the castle.'"

"My God," Abigail blurted out. "That's dead on."

"'At its center, a castle's temple,'" repeated Keith. "You are amazing, Kate."

"It gets even *better*," she replied, grabbing the mouse and moving about with quick clicks. The printer on the left side of the cabin began to churn and warm up. "Wait 'till you guys see this."

"I'll get it," Keith said as he sprang up to retrieve the page from the printer. He grabbed the edge as it was fed through and lifted it up to show the others. The image was that of a long stone staircase, clearly an ancient structure, with intricate carvings lining its sides.

Kate read from the riddle again, "'and a staircase to the North—follow the serpent when day and night are one, and take its head before it can run.'"

"I see it!" yelled Samantha. "The serpent's head."

Keith examined the printout himself. "Oh crap! There it is!" he yelled, pointing to the large stone head of a dragon or serpent at the base of the stairs. "And if I was a guessing kinda guy ... which I am," he laughed, "I would say if we break the head off, we will find the hidden papyrus."

"Sure Keith," Kate smiled, "we will just make our way to one of the most significant archaeological sites in all of Mexico and start whooping off the heads of the monuments. Should go well for us."

"Sure," he laughed, "why not?"

"Yeah," Kate replied, "think we will leave that task to Storm, okay."

"What's with the 'day and night' stuff, though?" asked Sam.

Kate's smile quickly transformed to a frown and she turned back to the screen.

"What is it, Kate?" asked Abigail, sensing the immediate change in the Kate's enthusiasm.

"Well, this is the crazy part—"

"Just this part?" asked Keith with a laugh.

"Okay, the *real* crazy part. The Mayans were aware of their surroundings. Of time and space, and the nature of the universe. They also understood the yearly equinoxes."

"A time when the day and night are the same length," added Ebbers from his seat.

"Yes," replied Kate. "Exactly."

"When day and night are one," Keith thought aloud. "One in that they are the same length."

"Right," Kate responded as she sat back from the computer. "And that day is tomorrow, March 20th."

Suddenly, the cabin of the small jet began to vibrate violently, and the air became thick and clouded. Samantha and Abigail, who were sitting closest to the front of the plane, felt a powerful rush of frigid air wisp across their faces, and they turned in unison to seek out its source.

"Oh my God!" Sam screamed rising from her seat as if to run, but she instead used her upward momentum to launch her body sideways across the couch, landing in Kate's lap. She threw her arm around Abigail's back and drove her off the couch and towards the floor. Keith turned toward the front of the plane and came face-to-face with that that had stricken such fear in the others. At the side door, Keith found the guard who had been watching over the group. He was twisting and convulsing as a black and purple tornado of mist encircled his body. Keith watched as the guard was lifted off the floor and twisted horizontally in the air. He could see the guard's body morph before his eyes, distracted only momentarily by the screams of the others. He turned to Kate, who was pinned to the floor of the cabin next to Samantha. The sheer force of the cyclonic winds that were wreaking havoc on the interior of the jet precluded any of them from moving. A cataclysmic barrage of gunfire drew Keith's focus from the guard, redirecting his attentions towards the front of the cabin. He turned to see Lobo standing in the doorway of the cockpit brandishing an assault rifle. The pilot was firing at the morphing figure that had once been their guard, his assault, however, appeared futile. Keith continued to watch as the guard's body grew in size, its features becoming twisted and distorted further. As the body reached its growth climax, having exhausted all room for expansion within the cabin of the plane, Keith's feelings of dismay and confusion turned to sheer terror at the sudden appearance of wings. The giant, dragon-like appendages lifted away from the body that was once the guard, and opened into a Lovecraftian display of reptilian grandeur.

"Do something, Keith!" Kate yelled. "You can't let it leave! It knows where the third papyrus is!"

"I can't move!" Keith yelled back. "I can't even lift my arms!"

Shrieking laughter pierced the sound and fury of the tumultuous winds as the creature spread its wings wide. Fully transformed, the demon hovered in the air before them, and the wind and mist subsided. Black as night with steely blue eyes, it glared at them, and its wings flapped rhythmically, suspending it in the air. Samantha tried to rise from the floor, but was met with a piercing scream, the sonic force of which drove her back to the ground. The demonic creature turned and planted its clawed feet firmly against the door to the plane, driving it off its hinges and out into the desert night. Lobo charged at the creature, and Keith could make out the reflective glean of something metallic in his hand. Lobo's charge was abruptly brought to a halt as the creature, eyeing his advance, flapped its wings madly, sending him hurtling across the jet. Having dispatched Lobo, it whirled back to the others, spotting Ebbers for the first time, cowering behind the chairs. The creature and the man locked eyes in what appeared to be a moment of recognition, the ocular union yielding an unnerving moment of complete silence. The terrified passengers watched as the creature raised one hand over its head, then whipped it forward unleashing a trail of force so powerful that it metaphysically rippled the air in a visible path directly to the cowering Ebbers. The demonic fiends ethereal assault found its mark in Ebber's chest. The cacophony of mutilation that followed filled the plane with a chorus of crushing bones and snapping sinew. When at last there was nothing of solid consistency left in the doctor's body, the interior grew silent and Ebber's lifeless form slumped to the ground, and fell limp against the back wall.

Now, having completed its preordained assassination mission, the creature turned towards the gapping hole in the side of the jet, and in the blink of an eye, disappeared into the Jordanian night.

59

"William is in trouble!" Alexander shouted to Asar as he sprang from his crouched position near the rear entrance of the Treasury.

Asar reached out and grabbed Alex by the arm.

"Get down, for God's sake," he whispered loudly. "You're right in their line of sight."

Alexander yanked his arm free of Asar's grasp and moved farther into the structure, away from the dangerous threshold. Although slugs of lead implanted themselves into the wall where just moments before he had stood, Alexander's focus was trained on the opposite end of the stone fortress. His eyes grew distant as he appeared to gaze out past the Treasury and into the Siq and its winding passageway. Turning back to Asar, who had risen and was standing close to him, he could sense his friend's concerns.

"What is it, Alexander?"

"Decker, and those in his company, are in trouble." He abruptly turned and began walking towards the front entrance where they had arrived. "This is over," he continued, gesturing toward the roof of the Treasury.

Asar looked up and saw nothing. He was about to request that Alex clarify his statement, when he heard the distinctive whirl and thump of gunship choppers arriving overhead.

"Who are they?" Asar asked as he trotted to catch up with Storm who was on the move already.

"It's Moloch's exit plan!" Alexander stopped but didn't turn to face his friend. "It informs me that we have failed here tonight, and Moloch has secured the next piece of the puzzle."

The sound of the choppers grew louder as they approached the inner grounds of the Petra ruins. Alexander said nothing further, disappointment exuding from every pore of his being, and continued his egress.

"We must get to Decker!" he desperately yelled, contemplation of his failure finally ending, he broke into an all-out sprint. "We will have ten more chances to deal with Moloch and his minion. We must not despair."

Asar, as strong and agile as he was for his size, watched Alex move like a panther through the night. By the time he exited the Treasury, Alexander Storm was only a blur that disappeared into the canyon gorge that led out of Petra. Asar leaned one hand against the massive stone wall of the building's façade and took several deep breaths to steady himself before continuing on. Drawing in an even-keeled steadying breath, he took a moment to look up at the ancient Nabatean craftsmen's handiwork that surrounded him. It was awe-inspiring, even in this light. Tapping his hand on the stone, as one would an old and trusted dog, he closed his eyes and nodded his head.

"We will prevail, brothers," he whispered to the lifeless stone. "We *must* prevail for all those who have come before us." He pushed off the wall and ascended the steps. "And for all those who will come after, else all is destined to dust and ash."

With these final words, he turned his back on ancient Petra and did his best to run through the sandy gravel to catch up with Alex. His ankles twisted and pulled as he pounded through the soft, uneven ground below him and passed into the Siq. Darkness was all consuming in the narrow canyon. The tall walls of rock that lined the slender passage gave no credence to the moon's attempt at illumination, and Asar moved cautiously. His heart thumped in his chest, and sweat pooled upon his forehead. And even though his muscles screamed to rest once again, he had no intention of allowing Alexander to rush into the desert without him. Asar came to a sharp curve in the path and had to turn his shoulder at the last moment so he wouldn't smash his face into the jagged stone. His efforts to save his face compromised his shoulder as it slammed against the wall and tore a tuft of material from his shirt. The arsenal he had strapped to various parts of his body flew forward upon impact, bouncing against the rock, reminding him of their cumbersome nature. He quickly unbuckled the weapons secured across his back and dropped them to the sand below. He couldn't handle the extra weight of the steel and wood and decided, with some modicum of hesitation, that he was better off leaving them on the desert floor. Shed of the extra weight, he started off again, picking up his pace as best as he could. Asar hurried on, pushing forward no matter how tired he was becoming. As he rounded another sharp bend, he could see the convivial moonlight finally being granted access to the canyon at its mouth. Asar focused on the silvery rays which beckoned him on and out into the desert night. As he approached the final stretch of canyon, he suddenly noticed the shadowy still silhouette of Alexander just within interior of the passageway. Asar moved as quietly as he could to Alex's side. This was no easy task, sneaking up on Storm, compound the attempt with Asar's loud, heaving breaths and it quickly became an impossibility.

"Asar, old man," said Alex, not even turning to look at his friend. "A snake could have heard you coming!"

Asar said nothing, but instead worked wholeheartedly at regaining his breath and slowing his pulse.

"It's a joke, you know," whispered Alex. "Snakes don't have ears."

"Oh, I know!" shouted Asar through gulps of air. "I get it, you fool."

Asar hunched over with his hands on his knees.

"Are you going to regurgitate, Asar?" Alex asked with a laugh. "Perhaps a few less butter, honey and bread sandwiches would serve you well?"

"Really, now." Asar gasped. "Shut up and tell me what's going on. Where is Decker?"

"Well, which is it? Do you want me to shut up or tell you?"

"Really, Storm, I am in no mood for your particular brand of asshole right now." Asar stood with his composure regained, practically. "Tell me what's going on, or I am going to march out of this passage."

"Well, that would not be wise, old friend," said Alexander. A more somber mood overcame him, and he continued, "William appears to be pinned in a vehicle just beyond the walls of this gorge, and he is surrounded by three or four of Moloch's people."

Alexander moved up and peeked around the passage. The men had moved in close to Decker's truck, and their weapons are trained on the side doors.

"Hand me the bolt-action, they should prove to be relatively easy pickings, if you will, from this distance" he requested without turning to look at Asar. He reached his hand back, grasping at the vacant air.

"Give it to me, Asar!" Alexander demanded. "I am sure these mercenaries are just awaiting orders to dispatch the people in that truck, and I don't want to give them the opportunity."

Alexander folded his hand back and forth, beckoning Asar to place the firearm in his grasp. Still, nothing came.

"Asar," he said, grunting as he turned to the large Egyptian. He looked him up and down. "Asar, where are our arms, damn it?"

Asar looked at Alexander with the eyes of a child about to be chided by his mother for some foolhardy set of deeds. The senior man simply shrugged his shoulders.

"I dropped them, Alex," he said with solemn shame in his voice. "The load was too much, and I wanted to catch up to you."

"Seriously?" Storm's voice was angry. Asar's expression, however, forced him to reevaluate his approach. "All right, then. Don't beat yourself up."

Alex withdrew his arm and rubbed his hands on his forehead, grinding dirt and dust into the accumulation of sweat that had gathered across his body. Dropping his hands abruptly, he looked up at Asar.

"Time for plan B!" exclaimed Alexander. "Don't know why I bother making a plan A, as we always end up going with plan B. I should just make plan B plan A—"

"Alexander," Asar whispered, seeking to curtail what could very easily turn into a time-consuming tangent. "What's plan B?"

"Plan B is easy," said Alex with a smile. "You create a diversion, and I incapacitate the foot soldiers."

"What?" shouted Asar, a little too loud. "That's your plan?"

"I said it was plan B. Not quite as good as plan A, but workable all the same."

Asar stared at Alex. "And what is it I am supposed to do to draw their attention and not be shot dead in the course?"

"Oh, I don't know. Try running about, panting like a dog. Shouldn't be too difficult."

"What?" hissed Asar.

"Go!" yelled Alexander Storm as he charged out into the night.

60

Keith rose, jumping from the couch and landing by Kate and Samantha. Sam was still lying across Kate's body, and Keith could see her face peeking out from beneath. Her eyes were filled with terror and tears.

"Get off her!" Keith yelled in Sam's face, causing her to recoil. "You're crushing her!"

"Relax there, Romeo," Sam replied, clearly hurt by his implications, as she rose off Kate. "I was protecting her, you ass."

Kate, who was on her back, quickly rolled to her side and sat up. She looked at Keith but remained speechless. He reached out and grabbed the front of her shirt, pulling her to him. Kate's silent tears turned to all out sobs as he wrapped both arms around her and drew her in tight to his body. She resisted for a moment, as one tends to do while experiencing defensive panic, but finally gave in to his embrace, hugging him back. Samantha walked up behind the pair and reached out her hand, gently running her palm across Kate's dark, silken hair.

"It's all right, Kate," she whispered. "It's gone now. We're gonna be okay."

Kate relinquished her grasp on Keith and looked up at Sam. The terror remained, and although Kate didn't say a word, Samantha could hear her loud and clear. The look in her eyes said it all. *No, it's not. No, we are not safe.*

A hoarse, primal scream broke the girls' silent connection, and their heads whipped around to see Abigail pointing to the back of the plane. Her expressed terror ensued, until her vocal cords gave way to mechanical failure. Slowly, with trepidation, Keith turned toward the area of the jet Abigail was focused on. He half-expected to see the creature advancing from the recesses of the plane, but instead was met with the morbid remains of Dr. Ebber's desecrated body. Whatever supernatural force the creature had employed against him left the doctor's body looking like the victim of a wrecking ball. That is to say, pulverization, as there was no visible external damage. Instead, Ebbers looked like a child's stuffed doll who had seen better days. Keith surmised the force of the impact had crushed the doctor's bones and turned them to powder. Ebbers sat prone on the floor with his legs extended and spread in front of him. His torso was slouched all the way to the floor between his legs. His head, which looked like a deflated beach ball, was bent backward and rested on his back, the pits of his sunken eyes fixed on the ceiling of the plane. He looked like a broken accordion.

"My God," Keith muttered, catching Kate's attention. She righted herself on her wobbling legs and attempted to look back toward Ebbers. Keith leaned forward and grabbed her shoulders, stopping her before she could complete the pivot toward the rear of the plane.

"Wait," he cautiously whispered to her. She glared at Keith and yanked her shoulders to break his grasp.

"I'm fine, Keith," she insisted. "Let me go."

"There's no reason for you to see this," he pleaded with her.

"Hey, I'm not some weak chick who needs to be shielded from what's going on, okay?" She wiggled again, breaking free this time. "I just got scared, that's all. I thought we were going to *die!*"

"Yeah, well I'm not so sure the threat of that outcome has passed," called Sam. She had moved Abigail to the first section of couches and was holding her.

Keith turned towards the sound of Sam's voice, allotting Kate the opportunity she required to break free of his protectionist hold over her.

"Holy crap!" she yelled out. "What the hell happened to him?"

"*Hell* happened to him," the deep voice emanated from the front of the jet. It was Lobo. He stepped over the debris strewn about the floor and walked toward the huddled passengers.

"What happened to you?" Sam asked as he walked by her and Abigail.

"I don't know," Lobo replied, rubbing his head. "I assume the force of the demon's blast knocked me against the wall of the plane." He paused for a moment, peering over at the missing door and the gapping hole into the darkness its absence afforded. "I don't really remember."

Spying Ebbers's body, Lobo made his way to the folded pile of human remains. He stopped in front of the Raggedy-Ann-like body and crouched down. Extending a finger, he leaned closer and poked the skin on Ebbers's arms much like a boy prodding at a dead bird with a stick.

"Don't touch him!" yelled Abigail, breaking her silence and sitting straight up on the couch.

"Relax, sweetheart," replied Lobo without even looking at the hysterical girl. "He's *beyond* dead. Trust me on this one."

Lobo pressed his finger against the skin once more. It was mushy, almost like pizza dough, and he withdrew his hand quickly as a bout of disgust overcame him.

"Creepy man," he announced. "This is friggin' horrible."

Lobo rose and walked up the aisle between the couches towards the side of the aircraft. Running his hand along the frame, he quickly assessed the damage created by the forceful removal of the door. His mind began racing with a multitude of options for its speedy repair, only a few of which he deemed viable solutions.

"What happened here?" he asked of no one in particular, pointing at the gaping hole in the side of the plane.

"The creature ripped the door off its hinges," said Keith.

"Great," muttered Lobo.

Samantha, feeling the thick layer of desperation forming like early morning London fog, let go of Abigail and sprang to her feet.

"What's the plan, people?" she called out, trying to disperse the hopelessness that was clearly taking hold of her companions. She moved towards Kate, a mask of enthusiasm at play on her face.

"What's the plan, nerd?" she asked soothingly. "What does Storm want us to do next?"

"I don't know. How should I know?"

"Well, *he* certainly isn't going offer any assistance, huh," Sam said sarcastically while nodding toward Ebbers's body.

"That's not funny," snapped Kate.

"It's *not* funny. You're right. But I don't find the idea of waiting here, like sitting ducks, the side of the plane ripped open to the night, waiting for a demon to return and smite the rest of us with sonic cannon balls, either, all right?"

"Agreed," said Keith with a solemn laugh.

"So, what would Alexander—"

"No, forget Storm, Kate. What would *you* do next?"

"I don't know," exasperation evident in her voice, her eyes darted around the floor of the plane in confusion.

"Well, think about it a minute, and then *know*, okay?"

"I guess I would go to Mexico." She looked up at Samantha. "I guess I would head to Chichen Itza."

Samantha, clapping her hands together, said, "Chicken eats her it is!"

"What's that?" asked Lobo, returning from checking the damage to the plane. "What did I miss?"

"We're going to Mexico!"

"Mexico?" he replied. "I am not going anywhere without Storm."

Sam got up. "Listen," she said, getting in Lobo's face. "For all we know, Storm is dead. He told us what we have to do—stop the end of the world, for God's sake! And this requires us to think independently and outside the box. So, can you get this hunk of shit off the ground with the side door missing or not?"

Lobo looked baffled at the pretty blonde girl standing before him, ordering him about.

"You're something else, aren't you?" he replied to her with a smirk.

"Yes, I am," she quickly swung back. "My doctors just haven't figured out what that something is yet," she added, batting her eyelashes at him with exaggerated enthusiasm.

His smirk turned to an all-out grin. "No, I can't fly this jet without a door. Pressure issues."

Samantha sighed at his response.

"I can, however, fix the door."

"Of course, *you* can." she said with an air of subdued excitement. "How long will that take?"

Lobo turned and looked over at the opening. "Maybe fifteen minutes."

"Um, oh," Samantha replied again, stammering, noticing for the first time how handsome Lobo was—in a GI Joe kind of way. "That'll work. Get busy, soldier," she added.

Lobo laughed. "I know what you are, miss. Sassy."

"Really? Now? Does this feel like an appropriate time for that?" Samantha shook her head and turned to Kate and Keith.

Lobo's eyes followed her as she marched away, "See what I mean, *sassy!*"

Samantha looked at Kate who was clearly happy to be distracted by Lobo's little display. Sam rolled her eyes at her, and, against every fibre of her being, let a little smirk slip by her steely façade.

Lobo turned from the damaged door frame and called out, "I will require your assistance, Keith."

Keith nodded and shot Kate a look of concern. "You gonna be okay for a few?"

"She'll be fine, Casanova," Samantha said and pushed him forward. "Get to work."

"What do we do with him?" asked Abigail, who had been quietly studying the remains of Ebbers from a safe distance. "What do we do with the body?"

"I only fly the living," called Lobo. "Dump it before I seal this hatch."

"What?" exclaimed Abigail and Kate in unison.

"He's got to go," said Lobo, and by his tone the subject was obviously not up for discussion. "We can tack a note to him for Mr. Storm should he return."

"*When* he returns," added Kate.

"Yeah, the note can say, 'Here's the new Ebbers doll brought to you courtesy of the Storm Toy Company. We skipped out on you to Mexico. Meet us at Chichen Itza.'"

"Sam!" yelled Kate. "You said it right!"

"Oh, please," dryly laughed Samantha. "Can't you tell when someone is trying to be a wiseass?"

61

Asar was afforded no time to think, as was so often the case when acting on one of Storm's *plans*. Alexander had emerged from the gorge entrance like a shadow in the desert moonlight. With his stealthy movements, he had managed to avoid the attention of Moloch's men who were gathered around the overturned vehicle. Asar's part in the scheme was now required and he sprang into action. Bursting from the stone-lined pathway like a maniac, he ran headlong screaming and waving his arms, directly toward the accident scene, never once raising his eyes to apprise the reaction of the heavily armed men. His weathered brown boots felt like blocks of cement strapped to his weary legs, and every facet of his being told him to drop to the desert floor and lay silent. But he did not. He could hear the gunmen shouting and the rustle of their weapons. He was all-in at that point, his fate now nestled tightly in the hands of Alexander Storm, once again. The thought surged his adrenal gland and a barrage of Egyptian curses bellowed from his lungs with the force of the ancient gods behind them. He could still hear the men's voices in between his theatrical echoes, and he knew he was fast approaching the truck. Finally, he lifted his head and gazed upon the lion's den he was running into full throttle. Their weapons were all leveled on him, having apparently overcome their initial shock at his display quite quickly. In his peripheral vision, he could see the red glow of the men's laser scopes against his sweat and dirt laden white linen shirt. Alexander had never failed him, and he knew in his heart of hearts he never would, but the laser etchings across his chest had brought him to the edge of quasi-suicidal insanity. His mind reeled, he knew Alexander would never put him in this position if he had not gone over every possible scenario in his head beforehand and arrived at a successful conclusion each and every time. Like a man who gives himself up to devotional understanding, he, too, was at peace in his "leap of faith." His body switched to autopilot as the wildly flailing arms and zig-zagging maneuvers continued. He looked up once again to find the men had lined themselves up side by side, prepared to cut down the mad Arab.

From the corner of his eye, he caught a blur of movement that was surely his salvation. A glimmer of steel, a puff of dust, and the first in the line of would-be shooters buckled at the knees and fell back into the sand. Asar could see Alex, his sword in hand, as he rushed up behind the second assassin, the stealthy lion had made his way behind them. Like the strokes of a homicidal artist, Alex's blade painted a mortal stroke across the neck of the second man who instantly relinquished his firearm to the sand below and wrapped both hands around his spurting throat in a futile attempt at salvation. The blood flowed black in the moonlight, squirting out from between his fingers, and in seconds he dropped to the ground.

The flame that had been the element of surprise was extinguished. The remaining two gunman, realizing they had been ensnared by a master hunter's trap, turned to meet their enemy head on. The mercenary closest to Alexander began furiously firing his weapon, even before he had finished pivoting in the sand, and the bullets sprayed in all directions. The air parted as lead whizzed past Asar's ear and he froze in his tracks.

"*Down!*" ordered Alexander.

Asar let his body go limp and he dropped to his knees.

Another bullet flew by Asar's head. This one closer still. The fourth gunman had turned away from Alex, and was attempting to align his laser sight on Asar's new elevation. He took a step back, towards the overturned truck, to facilitate the new angle, his laser now trained on Asar's knelling body. Asar saw two things before he threw himself facedown into the sand and stone of Petra's desert floor. First, he saw Alexander lunge forward and drive his sword into the gut of the third gunman. Second, Asar saw the soft features of a woman emerge from the darkness behind the assailant focused on him. She lifted her arm and brought with it an automatic pistol, which she aimed at the back of the shooter. Asar's face was already in the sand when he heard the shot. The sound rang forth and then back as it bounced off the stone canyon behind him. Then all gunfire stopped. The air was still and silent except for the distant whirl of Moloch's helicopters.

62

Moloch reached into the inner pocket of his jacket and withdrew a black radio. Lifting it to his mouth he paused for but a moment to smile at the beauty that was Naamah. She raised one eyebrow in response, and smiled back. Moloch pressed the radio's side button.

"Joshua," he said sternly and let go of the button.

"Yes, sir," came Joshua's quick response. "You ready? Over."

"Yes," Moloch replied with a hearty laugh. "We are indeed ready. I hear your rotors. Are you close?"

Naamah gave Moloch a questioning look, and he wrinkled his brow with confusion, not understanding her gesture.

"Over," she whispered.

"Oh, yes," Moloch pushed the button again. "How close are you? Over."

"Seconds away, sir. Over."

"Very good." Moloch turned and headed toward the descending stone staircase. "Retrieve us in the clearing in front of the area I designated as the 'castle' on yours site map, Joshua."

Another moment of silence ensued and Naamah shook her head.

"He won't respond to you until you say—" Naamah began, but was cut off by Moloch's waving arm.

"Over, Joshua. Over."

"Yes, sir, give me a minute to find it in the dark. Over."

"Nonsense, allow me," Naamah said as she sprinted past Moloch and out of the confines of the stone structure.

"Naamah will show you where we are, Joshua," Moloch said as he, too, exited the castle's stairway onto the desert sand. He walked out from behind the collapsing wall just in time to see Naamah fetch a small stone from the ground below her. She held it in her closed fist and brought it to her face. Moloch could see her whisper something into her hand as beams of light began to escape from the spaces between her fingers. She opened her fist and rose it above her head.

"Orior! Oriri! Ortus!" she shouted to the dark sky. "Rise! Become visible! Appear!"

Responding to her demonic directives, the glowing red light in the palm of her hand became a thick cylinder and expanded upward. Up and up it went until its end point became indiscernible.

"Careful, my dear." Moloch laughed as he reached her side and slid the radio back into his pocket. "You don't want to disturb you-know-who."

"He has no interest in this place anymore," she hissed back at him, her eyes transforming into large black orbs filled with primal aggression.

Joshua's voice emanated from within Moloch's jacket. "I see your marker, sir. Over."

Naamah's hair blew and danced around her face as the chopper moved into position above. She turned to Moloch and yelled, "Think fast!" as she tossed the glowing stone in his direction. The beam of light transformed midair into a winged serpent that swiftly soared toward Moloch. He raised his hand and waved it in the apparition's path, bursting it into a million dots of light and dissipating it into the air. Moloch laughed at Naamah's playfulness and walked past her to the chopper, which had landed in the sand. Upon reaching the door of the chopper he paused, closing his eyes. In but a moment, they sprang open, and he turned and smiled at Naamah, who was suddenly at his side.

"What a coincidence your little light dragon was!" he yelled over the whirl of the chopper.

Naamah waited for him to finish. Dust and debris spun around the two demons as they stood under the revolving blades.

"One of my minions has just informed me our next stop is in Mexico, where we will visit with our old acquaintance Kukulcan, the great serpent scourge of the Mayans."

Moloch reached up and effortlessly hoisted himself into the chopper. He turned and extended his hand to assist Naamah, who ignored his gesture, and with the grace of a gazelle, leapt into the helicopter. They each found their seats and grabbed a set of headphones from the back of the seat. Joshua turned from the cockpit to make sure his unholy pair of passengers were in and then quickly pulled the yolk, lifting the copter off the ground. Moloch peered out of the open side of the chopper down at the ruins of Petra.

"Ah, Nabataea," he sighed. "Great you were, but gone are you now."

Moloch turned back to Naamah. "It appears we have some competition as you feared, my dear."

"Storm. But we knew that already."

"Yes. But it is more than just Storm and his idiot few."

"Anyone we know?"

"Apparently, he has brought together a group of unknown misfits to help him fight his battles."

"Really?"

"Although I am informed that there is one among them who may prove to be a challenge."

Naamah waited for him to elaborate, but he simply stared at her. What was he looking for? He still didn't trust her. She could see it. She could feel it behind his cold, steel eyes.

"They are headed to Mexico as we speak. We must beat them there. Eleven fragments are useless."

Moloch leaned forward toward the cockpit.

"Joshua, as we pass over, unleash whatever weaponry this bird is equipped with on the back of the Treasury, over there," he ordered, pointing to the location of the entrance to the ruins.

He sat back in his seat and looked at Naamah again.

"Perhaps Storm is still in the ruins, cowering in the shadows," he said with disgust.

Naamah shook her head and grinned. "You know he's not. I think you just like to destroy everything you touch, Moloch."

"Nonsense, my dear." He smiled an awful smile at her. "I haven't destroyed you...yet."

63

"Asar!" Alexander shouted to his comrade. "Care to join us now?"

Asar lifted his head from the desert floor, spitting sand from his lips, and peered in Alexander's direction. He could make him out standing a short distance from the woman he had caught a fleeting glimpse of before hitting that ground. Alexander's sword was down and at the side of his leg, and he stood motionless, facing the other figure. Asar turned his attention, momentarily, to the overturned Jeep and he squinted in the dim light to identify the markings on its side. From his present distance, the dark night obfuscated his efforts, but he surmised by the general outlines that they were of military origin or the like. Asar rose to his feet and began dusting himself off as he walked toward Alex.

"Alexander Storm?"

Asar heard the woman whisper softly. There was urgency in her voice. She had lowered her weapon to her side, but her arm was not relaxed. As Asar grew closer, the woman's dark, attractive features came into focus and he decided to take it upon himself to break the tension.

"Hello!" Asar called to them. "Hello, miss! Thank you for—"

"Are you Storm?" she inquired again, interrupting Asar's feeble attempt at distraction.

"Indeed, I am." Alexander finally stepped forward and responded. "And you are?"

Suddenly the woman raised her gun and leveled it at Alexander. Her eyes widened as she swung her other arm up to grasp the weapon with both hands.

"Wait!" yelled Asar dashing through sand at her. "Wait! Stop!"

Alexander knew he was defenseless against her weapon; he shifted his weight and lifted his chin. He fixed his gaze on the woman's eyes—there was no escape. His instantaneous assessment of the situation offered no scenario for defense. He was at the mercy of his assassin.

"No!" Asar's pleas grew closer, but still too far to make a difference. The woman did not react to the charging Egyptian, and her attention remained locked on Alexander.

"Well, here we are," Alex said, hoping to distract his assailant for a brief second, hoping his words would cause her finger to relax ever so slightly on the trigger. A brief moment in time, but perhaps, just maybe enough time for him to remove himself from the quandary he had walked into.

Before Alexander could finish speaking, he noticed something odd in the woman's eyes. A connection. Her eyes darted to the desert floor for a split second, but it was sufficient for Alex's keen senses. Giving her a sharp wink, Alexander dropped to the ground as the muzzle of the woman's gun flashed in the night.

"No!" Asar screamed again, confused by the series of events unfolding before him. Stopping dead in his tracks, he saw Alexander lying motionless on the ground. Asar turned and began to run toward his collapsed companion. It was then he noticed the falling body—not Alexander's—and everything began to click in his mind, although the cogs still needed a bit more grease. The woman had not shot Alexander. She had, in fact, saved him by taking out the would-be assassin approaching stealthily from Storm's rear.

"A fifth soldier!" she yelled to Asar. "He was hiding behind the truck."

Asar waved a hand at the woman to signal his understanding and called out to Alexander.

Alexander laughed and, as if doing a push up, raised his body off the desert floor. Asar arrived at his friend's side and extended a hand to help him up the rest of the way.

"Thought you were a goner." Asar laughed a little unconvincingly, tapping Alex on the back a bit harder than he should.

Alexander turned and grinned at Asar. "So did I," he whispered.

Dusting the Jordanian sand from his clothes, Alexander raised an open hand in the woman's direction. "Asar, may I introduce to you Miss Anika Jannah."

64

The noises filling the cabin of the aircraft sent chills through Keith's body. It was as if there were a hundred children on board all screaming out in unison. He turned his head and looked over at the makeshift door he and Lobo had fashioned and prayed it would hold for the journey across the Atlantic. He could deal with the cacophony of madness the air speeding over the door was producing, as long as the damn thing held.

"Can't you do something to stop that?" cried Sam over the shrill sound.

Keith turned to her and simply shook his head.

"Jesus Christ," Sam muttered as she shifted in her seat, "as if the fucking monster wasn't enough."

"Try to ignore it," whispered Kate from the seat beside her. She reached out and touched her hand gently. "Think about something else."

Sam yanked her hand away. "Like what? The demon that pulverized the good doctor maybe? Or maybe the fact that we are traveling thousands of miles in a broken plane flown by some guy named after a wolf or something?"

"That's not his name," said Keith as he rose from his seat and moved toward the girls. His body was unsteady, and he wobbled with the turbulent shifting of the plane. Kate let out a short burst of laughter laden with the release of tension.

Keith wrinkled his brow at Kate. "What?"

"Nothing," she said through almost closed lips, clearly attempting to contain an all-out laugh. "You look like a drunken sailor."

"More like a drunk monkey," Sam added.

"Ha ha. You both think you're so cute," he said as he dropped into the seat next to them. "Let's see one of you attempt to navigate this flying can."

Keith reached down and brushed the legs of his jeans off as if dusting away the pair's insults.

"Navigate, huh?" replied Sam. "Yeah, I don't know, should I get a map or something to 'navigate' my movements?" Sam made a goofy face at Kate, and they both got in yet another laugh at Keith's expense. "I don't know, Kate, do they make a compass for walking? You know, one that tells you when to put one foot in front of the other?" Again, the two girls burst out into uncontrollable laughter.

"That's not even funny!" Keith yelled in his defense while shaking his head slightly as it nodded back and forth with the turbulence.

Abigail, who was sitting across from the group, sprang to her feet. "It's not funny!" she shouted. "None of this is funny. What's wrong with all of you?"

Keith was taken aback and looked up at Abigail sympathetically. "Just a little levity," he said innocently. "Helps calm the nerves a bit, that's all."

"Well, I don't get it!" Abigail shouted over the intensified screaming of air." I don't get it at all." She turned away from the group and walked toward the couch at the back of the cabin.

"I don't know, Keith," Sam said. "Abigail seems to be navigating the plane just fine." There was a momentary pause between the two girls, who were clearly trying to hold back a major outburst. Keith looked at the strained restraint in their faces and rolled his eyes.

"Go ahead!" he finally shouted. "Let it out! I don't care!" And with that, the girl's laughter filled the jet once again.

Keith thew his hands up in surrender and turned to see what Abigail was up to. She was sitting with her head held in her hands and her elbows resting on her knees. Keith could see her lips moving but couldn't make out what she was saying. He didn't know if it was the screaming door or that she was whispering that made her words inaudible. Perhaps she was praying. Not a bad idea, he thought.

"So, super nerd," Sam said, grabbing Keith's focus away from Abigail. "What were you saying about our Mr. Lobo's name?"

Keith turned back to face Sam and Kate.

"Oh, this interests you huh? His name is not Lobo," replied Keith. "It's Lobo."

"Oh, I get it," said Sam staring at Kate again. "What the hell are you talking about?"

Keith smirked. "His name is Low Bo. As in low—L-O-W," he said, spelling out the word.

"His real name is just Bo," he finished.

"I get it," Kate said. "It's a nickname."

"Kinda makes me feel better, to tell you the truth." Sam joked. "And I don't really know why."

"Whatever," Keith said, blowing her off a bit.

"No, really." Sam tried to sound serious but just came across as condescending. "How do you know?"

"When we were fixing the door, I asked him what kind of name Lobo was, and he said it was a nickname. He had earned it in the Air Force years ago and it had stuck with him."

Keith moved in closer to the girls since they had stopped busting his chops.

"Apparently, our pilot up there holds the record for flying an F-16 closest to ground level."

"Really?" exclaimed Kate.

"Yeah," said Keith, "and it's something ridiculous like not more than ten feet off the ground for two miles."

"Wow," said Sam as she sat back in her seat, clearly impressed.

"Yeah, that's no joke." Keith shook his head up and down, still in awe of Lobo's abilities.

Kate leaned in toward Keith. "Well, that actually makes me feel a little better."

"I guess so," said Keith softly. "At least I feel more confident that he can get us all the way to Mexico."

Keith turned to check on Abigail, who was still sitting in the back muttering something to herself and then turned back to the girls.

"Now we just have to figure out what the hell we're supposed to do once we get there," Keith finished, still troubled.

"Well, sit back—" Kate gasped. She was staring over Keith's shoulder; her face instantly went pale.

Keith spun around to see what had startled her to find Abigail standing right behind him, almost right on top of him. Her arms were hanging at her sides with the palms of her hands facing out. Keith raised his head slightly to meet her gaze and was horrified to find her looking down at him with opaque, white eyes, as if they had rolled back in her head.

"Abigail!" Keith shouted. "Snap out of it!" But her trance-like gaze was fixed on them.

"You're all going to die," she hissed. "Your souls are going to be torn from your putrid, rotting flesh..."

Abigail's body went limp and she collapsed to the floor of the jet before Keith could catch her.

Then the plane fell silent, except for the intense screaming of air being sucked through the cabin door.

65

Alexander's knees hit the coarse, warm sand of the Jordanian desert. He crouched down and bent his head sideways to peer into the passenger window of the overturned truck.

"Mariah was shot as we approached, and she lost control," Anika said from the other side of the vehicle. She was staring at the officer's dead body, which hung upside down in the driver's seat, the seatbelt still holding her in place.

"She was shot in the head," Anika whispered. "She's gone."

Alexander stood up straight. "So to is her partner I am afraid. Dead, that is, and shot in the head as well."

He looked at the rear doors of the police truck. The passenger side door, as was most of the truck, was dented and smashed from the vehicle's roll across the unforgiving desert terrain. Alex walked around the back of the truck to join Anika on the other side.

"I managed to kick my side door out." Anika gestured to the truck door. It was still open.

Alex examined the bent edges of the tattered door. "You are stronger than your slight frame would reveal," Alex said, flashing Anika a forced smile.

"Adrenaline," she replied softly.

Alexander nodded and studied the ground at his feet. Even in the poor light, he could make out a set of distinctive drag marks etched in the sand. He turned his head to follow the trail, but quickly lost it.

"Damn the night," he said, gritting his teeth. Without wasting another moment, he shot around to the other side of the truck again, bent down at the passenger window, arched his arm, and sent his elbow through the glass. It shattered with a dull thud. Alexander dropped to the ground and thrust his body into the vehicle. Unexpectedly, a beam of light began to glow in the truck's interior, and Alexander emerged with a hefty black standard police issue flashlight.

"Let's get Decker," Alex stated with confident conviction as he marched past his companions into the open desert.

The two glanced at each other momentarily whereby Asar gestured to Anika to proceed. "After you," he offered and the two summarily joined Alexander and his guiding light. They followed the drag trail, visible clearly in Alex's light, much like a bloodhound stalks a scent, oblivious to the environment around him.

"He was unconscious," offered Anika as they walked, "but he was alive. I wanted to get him away from the danger and find us help."

"I didn't see very much blood in the rear seats or here in the sand for that matter," Alex reported, never looking up from the trail.

"I think he hit his head. I don't think I saw much blood on him, but it happened so fast. I'm trying to picture him, and I am not seeing much blood."

"It would be black," reminded Alexander.

"What?"

"Blood," he continued. "It would appear black in the dark of the night."

Anika said nothing, but appeared to be reimagining the scene in her mind.

Alexander lifted the light ahead into the darkness and spotted a group of boulders and what appeared to be building debris of some kind.

"There!" yelled Anika as she ran ahead toward the stone oasis.

"Wait, miss!" Alexander ordered sharply. "The desert still holds dangers." Anika was not listening to his words, however, and she was already at the mounds of enormous stones. Asar tapped Alex as if to say, "I got her," and sprinted ahead as quickly as his large frame would allow. Alexander, in turn, broke into run and caught up to the pair who were staring down into the sand on the far side of the rocks.

"Right here!" Anika exclaimed. "I left him right here!"

She reached over and snatched the light from Alexander's hand and began to wave it around wildly, spinning in all directions. Alex reached out and grabbed her wrists.

"Hey!" she yelled.

Alex steadied her arms and pulled her closer to him.

"Relax, Anika." His voice was calming, almost musical. "William has endured much, much worse."

Alexander, still grasping her arm, directed Anika to shine the light behind them farther, past the rocks, and stopped.

"Asar," he said, motioning his friend to the end of the beam.

Asar, who had been on his knees fishing around in the sand for hints of Decker's whereabouts, stood up and ran to the focal point of the light's ray. He bent over to examine the ground. Anika softly pulled her arms free from Alex's grip and repositioned the light on Asar.

"I am calm, Mr. Storm," she whispered while tightening her eyes into a squint. "No hysterical women here."

"I was not implying—" Alexander's defense was cut short by the sight of Asar running back to them.

"Tire tracks, Alex! And drag marks like before, but softer impressions!"

"That's because he was dragged by two rather than one."

"Yes," replied Asar as he returned to their sides. "Yes, I fear you are right."

Asar drew himself close to Alex. "And blood, my friend. A lot of blood."

"What?" Anika grew closer. "What did he say?"

"Are you sure?" Alexander asked. Then he put his hand up to silence Anika.

"Yes, Alex," his voice laced with the echoes of sorrow. "It was red...not black."

66

Alexander Storm's jet barreled through the darkness on its trans-Atlantic course. According to Lobo's calculations, they would arrive at their South American destination just shy of sunrise. The pilot had encouraged his weary passengers to get some rest, however the violent screams of air rushing in the sides of the makeshift door precluded any meaningful degree of slumber. Lobo and Keith's impressive handiwork had become further dislodged shortly after takeoff, and the sound was all but deafening. Kate and Keith, unable to speak over the airstream's din, stared at each other in near darkness. Both of them were thinking the same thing, of this each was sure. *How did we get ourselves into this? And what the hell is this, anyway?*

The night's turbulence toyed with the aircraft, and the constant barrage of shaking and shifting sent Abigail into an all-out recitation of chants and prayers, the substance of which was of course, lost to the cries of the wind.

"Cut it out!" shouted Sam, unable to look away from her quickly moving lips and rocking body. Abigail either could not hear her transfixed in her spiritual escapism—or she chose to ignore the pleas.

"Hey!" Sam yelled at the top of her lungs. "Stop that! You're freaking me out, and you're going to jinx us!" Abigail looked across at Sam, clearly shocked out of her trance.

Kate flashed Sam a look, shaking her head side to side ever so subtly. Sam shrugged her shoulders and mouthed the word *what* with the innocence of a child whose mother had caught them doing something foolish.

Kate looked back at Abigail, who seemed unfazed by the exchange. "You go right on praying," she whispered to herself. "We can use all the help we can get."

No sooner had Kate offered her quiet encouragement, then the plane went into a horrifying series of shakes and altitude shifts. The four companions grasped the arms of their chairs, their eyes collectively darting about the walls of the aircraft as if searching for the first signs of it giving way.

"Brace yourselves!" Lobo's shouts penetrated the unnerving noise of the cabin. Kate had not even noticed the door to the cockpit had flown open. He screamed, "Lock in! We're in for a rough landing!"

Kate could see him shouting over his shoulder from the other side of the door, the shape of his body barely discernible in the dim glow of the jet's instrument panels. Her face must have betrayed the calm demeanor she was trying to convey; Keith had risen from his seat and was grasping the top of her arm.

"I'll go see what's going on, Kate!" he shouted over the noise. "I'm sure Lobo has it under control. Storm said he was the best!"

Keith turned from Kate and began the arduous task of navigating his way to the cockpit without being slammed against a wall or losing his balance and crashing to the floor of the jet. Kate watched him with some disbelief. Keith wasn't exactly known for his bravery. She smiled to herself amidst all the chaos. *Maybe there's hope for him yet*, she thought to herself. As if responding to her silent praise, Keith lost his footing and crashed against a row of seats, letting out a laughable whine as he hit. And, despite the circumstances, she did just that—laughed out loud.

"Nope, no hope." She giggled a little bit, and Keith rose to his feet with the help of the sides of the seats and made some gestures as if brushing himself off. He turned, hoping Kate's eyes had been trained elsewhere, and glanced back at her. She was still giggling and he grimaced, nope ... she caught it.

"I knew you were laughing!" he shouted back at her. "I did that on purpose, you know."

"Of course, you did!" Kate shouted back without missing a beat. "Planned the whole thing, right?"

Keith nodded, shooting Kate his best "I'm cool" expression, and turned back toward the cockpit. The door was swinging back and forth violently in synch with the harsh, unpredictable rhythm of the plane's movements. As it banged open and closed continuously, Keith thought to himself how creepy it would be if something other than their esteemed pilot was on the other side of the door when it flew open next.

That's what I would do if this was a horror movie, he thought to himself. "Wait a minute, this *is* a fucking horror movie!" he said out loud.

Pushing forward, he finally made it to the entrance of the cockpit. Keith peered in at the dark figure of Lobo at the controls, then turned his attentions to the pitch black that was the view from the front windshield of the jet. Complete blackness, interrupted intermittently by the silent flashes of what must be heat lightning dancing across the sky. The momentary flashes of illumination allowed Keith the ability to discern the heavy rain pummeling the windshield.

"What the hell is going on?" Keith shouted to Lobo.

Lobo, visibly startled, quickly glanced over his shoulder at Keith.

"Go lock in, kid!"

"What's going on?" Keith yelled again. "We took a vote, and we want to know the plan!"

"The plan?" Lobo shouted back. "The plan is to land this bird. And it's gonna be one hell of a rough landing...in the middle of a jungle...in the dark...in the middle of a goddamn tropical swell...with a busted entry door in my hull blowing all kinda shit up into my works!"

The jet shifted hard again and tossed the cockpit door up against Keith's back. Using the jam of the entry, he braced himself enough to stop from flying face-first into the cockpit.

"Go lock in!" Lobo demanded once more. "If you get tossed out the front windshield, well, that will be one more piece of crap for me to deal with! You get me kid?"

"I get you," Keith replied sternly. Then, with increasing panic and disbelief, hollered, "How the hell you going to land this? How can you see? You looking for lights?"

The pilot motioned to the monitor mounted on the floor to his right. Keith squinted to make out the screen and he realized it was some sort of night vision.

"No lights, son," he said. "This is an abandoned air strip in the middle of the fucking jungle, kid. Cartels used to use it as a drop point before entering the states. Federales grew wise, and there's too many tourists traipsing about these parts these days. Probably been down for twenty years or more."

"Well, how do you even know it's there anymore?" Keith shouted back as the plane took another vicious dip.

"Oh, it's there, man." Lobo nodded at the screen. "I know it's there."

"Oh, so you've landed there before, then?"

"Nope!" shouted Lobo with a grin. "Now go lock your ass in, and shut the fuckin' door on your way out."

67

Alexander's arms dropped to his side, and his fists clenched tightly. Asar could see the grave concern broadcast across his friend's face.

"What now, Alex?" Asar inquired, his patience running low for the night, having had enough twists and turns for one evening.

Alex's head jerked toward Asar, as if snapping out of a momentary trance. He stared at his companion a moment as if to speak, then his eyes darted toward the rock formation barely visible in the night.

"Yes, Storm," implored Anika. "For God's sake, what now?"

Alexander's shoulders rolled forward and seemed to grow slightly taller as his body recoiled and recovered from its temporary wave of despair.

He extended one hand to Asar for the flashlight he was still holding. "Now? Now we apprise the situation methodically."

Alexander raised the light at the cluster of boulders and moved in to get a closer look. His companions quickly fell in behind him, both of them looking past Alex to the focal point of the light.

"Now," he continued, "we will assess the amount of blood loss present in the area..." Alex stopped short and turned to look at Asar and Anika, who had likewise stopped mid-step so as not to slam into their guide. "We will, of course, have to take into account the absorption rates of the sand as they will impact our calculations and determine how far a given amount of liquid will spread. This is a factor which can make pools of blood appear much larger than they actually are."

"Of course," Asar quickly added, turning to Anika briefly. "We mustn't jump to any conclusions." And with a nod, he motioned Alex to continue on.

Understanding his friend's intention, Alexander fondly mimicked Asar, saying, "Of course." Alexander proceeded towards his objective, whispering "of course" to himself once more as he approached. As he grew close, Alex focused the beam of light on the surface of the rocks, as well as the sandy ground around them. His companions stopped a few steps behind him and they could make out the perplexed look on Alex's face. The flashlight cast an eerie upward pool of light across his face, reminiscent of a child telling stories around a campfire and using a flashlight for added effect.

"What is it?" called Anika, stepping from Asar and trodding towards Alexander. As she reached his side, she was taken aback by his sudden and sharp burst of laughter. Horrified by what she could only surmise to be nervous energy, involuntarily released as he contemplated the possible loss of Decker, she turned back to Asar, who seemed just as stunned as she.

"Ha, you old fool!" he shouted whimsically as he turned to face them. "That's not blood!" He bent to one knee and ran his hand across the bumpy ridges of the boulder. "It's red paint!" he shouted. "Red paint!"

Anika and Asar looked completely lost as they watched Alex take several steps backward away from the boulder, allowing the beam of his light to expand over and up the rock's surface. Coming to a sudden stop, Alex let out yet another sharp laugh and turned to the two, waving his free hand at them, directing them to where he wanted them to look.

"You see?" Alexander yelled. "A red scorpion!"

Both of his companions stared at the rocks, eyes squinting in an attempt to bring into focus Alexander's revelation. Then, simultaneously, their eyes widened as they made out the primitive, yet obvious, formation of a scorpion painted across the rock face.

"What of the red in the sand?" Asar demanded, for although he was relived it wasn't Decker's blood, he felt quite embarrassed by his oversight —or "under" sight as it were.

"Our friends were in quite a hurry. They spilled their paint all over the desert floor in their haste."

"Friends?" Asar yelled to Alex, who was now marching back in the direction of the overturned vehicle.

"Yes, Asar." Alex pivoted around to face the duo. "I know exactly where Decks is, and I am free of any worries regarding his safety." He paused with another, more contemplative, snicker. "Or his health, for that matter."

68

The maddening cacophony of scraping metal was brought to an abrupt halt as the jet came to a complete, and perhaps permanent, stop. Except for the constant chatter of falling rain and whispering wind which continued to lay siege to the grounded aircraft, complete silence engulfed the interior. Sam heard nothing but the air entering and exiting her nostrils.

"You guys okay?" whispered Sam into the darkness.

There was no answer. Samantha, who had come to rest on the floor of the jet, raised herself up onto her elbows and squinted into the light void cabin trying to focus on something...anything.

"Hey," her ears registered a faint sound from somewhere in the recesses of the jet and she called out. "Is everyone okay?"

The indistinct resonance of movement from somewhere within the lightless void was her only answer. Twisting her prone body in an attempt to better situate her ears, Sam tried to ascertain the origins of the eerie din. The sounds were growing stronger, their echo drawing near, and she could feel the involuntary thumps of her heart rising in turn. Sam strained to commandeer control of a sense which she had no direct power over, but it was of no accord, and she continued to stare into blackness. Panic gradually began to wrestle its constricting grip around her as her vision and hearing failed miserably to provide insight into the unknown terror that was stead-fastly approaching.

The shuffling, slithering sounds grew louder still. Whatever archaic evil borne of the darkness engulfing them was slouching through the cabin towards her. The panic now morphed to sheer terror, seizing her limbs. Mustering up the inner strength that she so prided herself on, Sam snapped out of the trance and used her feet to slide backward on her butt into the unknown space behind her. Scurrying like a crab, her swift move-ment was met with a head banging thud as she backed into the wall of the jet cabin. Trapped, she could retreat no more. Gnashing her teeth, she steadied herself for whatever approached from the void that was, as far as she was concerned, as expansive as fathomless space.

It was close now, this unknown phantom approaching her. Dragging and sliding. Sam was quite sure that the evil that had almost taken them early in the night had returned to finish its demonic deeds. What could she do? Her eyes remained unadjusted, and she was experiencing a very real and clear understanding of blindness.

The tension was too much. "Jesus fucking Christ. Where is everyone?"

Silence.

"I'm right here." The words floated on the dead air, mixing with the patter of rain, right beside Samantha's head. She instinctively jerked and recoiled away from the sound, smashing her head on the wall for a second time. She recovered quickly and attempted to rise to her feet, only to feel cold, boney fingers grasp her wrist and pull her back down to the ground. Consumed with fear, her balance and reflexes were misfiring in all direc-tions, and she fell back to the floor, unable to stand or fight back.

Her mind was racing. What new Hell had grabbed her? What had crawled onto the jet after it made its emergency crash landing in the jungle of Mexico? Or had just appeared, for that matter? They were no longer dealing with laws of nature here. As Sam tried to gather her cognitive reason, she withdrew her arms and wrapped them tightly around her own chest, pulling her legs upward toward herself in a fetal position. That's when she heard the laughter. Big, booming laughter, coming from some far corner of the jet.

"Hey!" The voice was once again in her ear, no longer a whisper. "Hey, it's me. It's Abigail." The sudden relief of familiarity rushed over Samantha. "It's me, Abigail. You're okay, Sam."

Samantha's hand darted from her chest and reached out into the darkness for Abigail. This time, her grasp was met with a warm and soft embrace as Abigail grasped Sam's trembling hand.

"I got you," she said. "You're okay." The words flowed empathetically. "We're all right."

"Holy crap," were the only words Samantha could get out before the laughter caught a ride on the howling winds and once again filled the cabin from some far-off corner.

"Oh yeah?" Sam started. "Then what the fuck was—"

Her words came to a halt as a loud, powerful hum, like that of a Midwest transformer on a hot August night, surged the silence and then popped to a series of beeps and alarms. The cabin came alive with the bright red hue of the jet's emergency lights.

Samantha quickly turned to the hand in hers and found Abigail smiling on the floor in front of her.

"You all right, honey?" Abigail whispered from behind a huge grin. "You're okay now." Her white teeth looked red in the glow of the cabin.

"I think so," began Sam as she turned to survey the rest of the plane.

"What the fuck, guys?" she yelled, her eyes coming to a stop directly across from her. "Are you two kidding right now?"

Abigail turned to see what Sam was reacting to and found Keith on top of Kate, their lips locked in a tight embrace, both oblivious to what was going on around them. Sam relinquished Abigail's hand, and she sprang to her feet.

"Hey!" she yelled, causing Keith to break the embrace and roll to his side to face Sam. He shrugged at her and smiled.

"Yeah," Kate said. "We were pretty sure we were going to die, Sam."

"I agree! I thought we were all going to be scattered in pieces across the jungle, but you don't see me mounting Abigail like some crazed teenager!"

"Actually," Keith spoke up as he cleared his throat, "I wouldn't mind seeing that."

To which Abigail let out a giggle as she rose to Sam's side.

"Really, Abigail?" chided Sam. "Don't encourage him, please."

"Good evening passengers," Lobo's voice boomed over the intercom system. "Due to some great headwinds and kicking tailwinds—"

He stopped mid-sentence and broke off into a fit of laughter which Sam identified the source of cackle she kept hearing.

"As I was saying," Lobo continued. "Due to some great winds we have arrived at our destination ahead of schedule. Please be sure to remove all your belongings when exiting the plane, and thank you for flying Stormy Skies Airlines." Then, audibly trying to control his laughter, the words finally made it out, "Don't forget to tip your pilot."

69

"What are we waiting for?" demanded Asar. "There really is no time to waste."

Alexander turned to Asar and stared at him for a long moment before replying, "And when was it, exactly, you knew me to be a time waster, old friend?"

Asar let out a grunt and returned to his pacing, stopping every now and again to peer up at the clear desert night sky. He had commented on several constellations over the past hour, and Alex noted he had about half of his identifications correct. He did not have the heart to correct his companion, as Asar was clearly trying to impress their newest addition with his vast knowledge of both the cosmos and everything else known to man.

"Ahem." Alex did his best to clear his throat and mask his reaction to this last thought.

"Very good, Asar," quickly added Alex. "You truly a scholar of the heavens."

Anika slid in beside Alex, who had remained quite stationary for the past hour and leaned in to his ear.

"You do realize he is getting them all wrong, don't you?" Anika whispered.

Alexander noted her soft, yet rugged features as she remained very near him, apparently waiting for him to concur with her observations. He had rapidly surmised her to be an excellent companion for Decker. Her warm Arabian skin gave no indication of her age, which Alex surmised to be mid-forties. She did, however, carry herself like a woman somewhat younger. She had her wits about her, even in this quite stressful situation and clearly had the ability to maintain humor amidst her obvious fear and concern for Decker's wellbeing. Which he also noted, was sincere concern and worry. Anika's natural beauty, which should have been masked by dust and the day which had just unfolded, was intact and unscathed.

"Well, not quite *all* of them," Alex whispered back.

Anika giggled at his response and withdrew to a less intimate distance. She dropped to her knees in the sand and waved the palms of her hands back and forth over the warm desert ground.

"What are we waiting for, Alexander?" she asked without looking up. "Shouldn't we be doing something? Anything?"

"We *are* doing something," Alexander quickly responded. "We are doing *this*."

"Don't bother, miss," Asar said walking back toward them. "He's not going to tell you. He likes the suspense."

"I like to keep my plans close to my chest, Asar," he said with a hint of displeasure at the remark. "You should know that by now. That way, if those plans should require modification, as they often do—in an instant no less —I do not need to reacquaint my companions with the new plan. I can simply instruct them on how we are proceeding in that moment. This also avoids hang-ups, second guessing, and delays based on contemplation of the first, second, or even third plan, as I have now decided to act on the fourth plan."

"Ha," scoffed Asar, turning his attention once again to the night sky.

"So, how many plans do you have for dealing with our current situation?" Anika quickly interjected in hopes of breaking the tension.

"Six," replied Alexander, relinquishing his gaze from Asar to look down at Anika in the sand. "I have six viable scenarios to facilitate success in our current situation."

"And do you favor one of these plans over the others?" She continued her distractive chatter, but with a real interest in the answer.

"I do," replied Alexander, making good use of his extraordinary powers of dissimulation.

Alex crouched down to address Anika. "There is no need to be concerned about our banter," he smiled, and his tone and expression eased her mind. "We are simply passing time, as it were."

"What the devil is that?" Asar cried out, racing back to Alex's side. "It sounds like the beating of a hundred drums"

A galloping beat had shattered the almost serene silence of the night. Anika looked up at Alexander as the rhythmic din found her ears as well. She rose to her feet and dusted her legs off, turning from Alex and Asar to scan what she could see of the landscape surrounding them. Alexander studied her, watching her facial expressions as she banged her hands together, freeing any sand that had accumulated on them into the still air. He noted that although she appeared enthralled, her demeanor was far from fearful. A like appraisal of Asar did not yield a like assessment, as his friend was notably disturbed by the nearing onslaught of percussionary fervor.

Anika's heart raced as the clamoring beat grew closer and louder. Galloping she thought. Yes, galloping. She could now feel the reverberations echoing across the soles of her feet.

Anika turned back to Alex, who seemed unmoved and unafraid. The sound surrounded them on all sides, and she could make out the distinct cries of horses neighing violently as they charged in from all corners of the night. The galloping hooves slammed against the Jordanian sand like sharp cracks of thunder.

"Is this what you've been waiting for?" she demanded of Alex. "Are we in trouble here?"

Alexander stood, stoic, staring into the night. He appeared impassive to the clamor approaching them.

Alex's indifference afforded Anika no comfort, and she backed away from him, her eyes darting around the desert in search of adequate cover should the need present itself. A cursory inquiry of the dim landscape resulted in the harsh realization that no viable sources of cover existed. They were vulnerable. They were sitting ducks.

"What the hell is this, Storm?" she demanded as the ground trembled beneath them. The thunderous assault had reached an apex, the source of which was now upon them. Asar and Anika steadied themselves, steely eyed to hide the fear within. Then, without rhyme, nor reason, silence gripped the threesome. Asar, who had moved to Anika's side, now changed his position in order to stand back to back with her in an effort to eliminate the unknown assailant's element of surprise. Then, in ghost-like fashion, dozens of horse heads floated into view, piercing the event horizon of the night's darkness, encircling the trio on all sides.

"What *is* this, Storm?" Anika cried from beneath clenched teeth, her body trembling in sheer terror.

"This *is* plan number one," replied Alexander, turning to his companions with a grin.

70

Naamah's nude body knelt motionless before a large stone altar in a subterranean room beneath the ruins of Dalquharran Castle in South Ayrshire, Scotland. The eldritch stone ruins towered into the night sky, foreboding and silent, its halls seemingly abandoned to all who pass. Below the ground, however, lay a labyrinth of passageways and chambers reaching out in all directions like the roots of a tree. Moloch had a history with the structure during its heyday and was intimately familiar with the underground byways that flowed just beneath the surface of the outwardly mundane stone and mortar castle. It was, therefore, an obvious choice for his home here amongst the living. The secluded location, coupled with the security and privacy of a subterranean lair, provided him and his minion a prime location for the incubation and hatching of their diabolic campaigns.

Naamah's long black hair flowed down her back and in front of her face. Her lips moved in a foul cadence spewing forth whispering secrets in a shadowy chant. Her kneeling body stretched and arched all the way back so as to sit on the back portion of her heels. This abnormal feat of contortionism proved to be both odd and erotic all at once. Naamah mused with herself as her hips begin to gyrate involuntarily, her senses elevated by the release achieved from the empowering stretch of her taut physique. Flickering candles littered the ground all around her, emitting puddles of molten wax as if phallic pawns in the demon's ritualistic game. The candles luminescence resulted in an ebb and flow of light and shadow that danced across her bronze body. Naamah preferred this room over all others in the castle. Essentially barren, save the archaic stone altar situated in the center of the room. The enigmatic carved rock had existed at the locale aeons before the castle was constructed. Moloch had informed his female companion that Dalquharran Castle had, in fact, been built around the altar, which had been a prevalent source of ritualistic activity during the time of the Druids and beyond. Its origins were a mystery, as were the source of the preternatural carvings and symbols which adorned its every inch. Tonight, she knelt before it in a trance of satanic verses that produced a swirl and rush of air around her nude body. The demon's words formed within the depths of her being and were uttered forth in a sharp cadence akin to the repeated cackles of a wild animal on the prowl for a mate. Her hands pressed tightly together; between them rested the handle to a dagger whose steely blade stretched up between her breasts against her chest. The radiance of the multitude of candles caught hold of the blade's metallic hue, setting off tiny, glittering shots of light throughout the room.

Bound atop the ancient altar, a young woman, devoid of all clothes, lay on her back, her state of consciousness fading in and out. The girl's hands were extended out over her head and secured together with leather straps which in turn were fastened to the altar. Her long, diminutive legs, bound together as well, squirmed about untethered to her bed of stone.

The volume of Naamah's din intensified as her breathing quickened. Her ancient body began to subtly gyrate, working in rhythm with the increasing gusts of air. The unnatural turbulence played with the demon's hair, lifting it softly in waves and dropping it in a scattered fashion over her shoulders and face. Her eyes, which had been clasped tightly shut in meditative concentration, burst open, exposing her expanded black pupils. The mirror-like saucers of her eyes were set aglow with the reflective images of the flames flickering atop the chambers many candles. While repositioning her body over the altar, Naamah thrust the blade out and away from her body and brought it high above her head in exaggerated movements. The air surrounding her enraptured captive responded to every foul phrase that escaped Naamah's lips. The bound girl moaned as the rushing air darted around every curve of her naked body. Naamah's words spewed forth with animalistic frenzy as she positioned the point of the blade over the girl's chest. Jerking her body forward, she extended the dagger up as far as her body would permit and steadied herself to deliver the fatal thrust. Her eyes continued to burn with candlelight and cosmic revelation as her chest heaved violently, her body poised to unleash on her victim below, sending her soul straight to the master.

"What ever are you up to, my dear?" The words emanated from behind Naamah, breaking the spell instantly. She let out an irritated cry and lowered herself back into a kneeling position. The demon's intended victim, clearly oblivious to all else, continued to arch her body and writhe in phantasmic sexual ecstasy.

"What does it look like, Moloch?" she asked with playful irritation. She could feel him moving closer, gliding across the room, his eyes fixated upon her perfectly shaped ass which was perched over the heels of her feet. She seductively arched her back, accentuating her curves, and pushed her bottom out in order to afford him a better view her glistening nether regions.

"It looks like you're about to murder this poor, innocent," Moloch said, then paused for a moment as he surveyed the young woman on the altar, "dare I say, *virgin*, for sport."

Naamah could feel the heat of his body directly behind her, and she was drawn up to him like a magnet to steel.

"This creature is far from innocent," she offered in her defense. "She is an initiate." Naamah did her best not to let him play with her; he was always running some game for his amusement.

She felt a quick brush of fabric across her skin, and in her peripheral vision she could make out Moloch's robe dropping to the cold stone floor.

"She's a what?" Moloch was right beside her, and his lips whispered inches from her ear.

"The girl is, is an initiate," she stammered but for a moment. "A willing participant who wishes nothing more than to offer her body up to Lucifer."

Moloch knelt down behind Naamah, allowing his throbbing member to slide down her back and come to rest up against her wet bottom. Naamah gasped uncontrollably as he wrapped one arm around her waist and jerked her to his body.

"She doesn't look too willing, my dear," he whispered into her ear in reply. "She appears oblivious to what is transpiring around her."

"That is because I offered her a mild tincture to ease her passage." Naamah was uninterested in the conversation at this point and wanted nothing more than to experience him thrusting inside her.

Moloch lowered his head into Naamah's neck, breathing in deeply, his nose gently searching, taking in her intoxicating essence.

"Why would you endeavor to eradicate such an exquisite specimen when so much fun could be had instead? Sacrifices are not required here Naamah. This is *my* realm—this is *my* time."

Naamah playfully yanked her exposed neck away from his lips. She could feel him between her cheeks now, throbbing, and she was losing control.

"We have done so well, thus far," she quickly replied before her will gave way to the beast building inside her. "We have crushed our enemies and been met with success every step of the way."

Moloch reached around and wrapped his long muscular fingers around her throat, extending her neck up and exposing it to his embrace once again. Her eyes rolled back, as an involuntary moan escaped her mouth, her tongue slowly dancing around her parted lips. The blade fell to the stone blocks below with a clang as her hands sprang open to reach and grab at her companions' body.

"That's the spirit," he said with pleasure at her obedience. "Let's talk this about a bit."

With that, Naamah reach behind her and wrapped her slender fingers tightly around him. Tugging hungrily, she gasped as she directed him up between her legs. Her wet, inviting body took all of him in as the pair of demons moaned in passionate release. She allowed one more movement and then stopped his body short, hard, holding him in place.

"A sacrifice such as this keeps up the appearance we wish to foster with those who may be watching." She struggled to get the words out—she could feel him attempting to break away from her hold, and thrusted her body back in response.

"There is no need for that," Moloch replied indifferently to the prospect of offending the powers of Hell with their actions. "We are shielded from their sights here. We are in our own darkness, our own space, and we have nothing to fear or answer for."

Naamah relaxed her tension which held their bodies still, allowing Moloch to begin moving in and out of her again. She moaned with pleasure and raised herself up to let him reach deeper and deeper inside of her. Moloch took her flowing hair in his hand, and clenching his fist, he pulled her head back to him, arching up her entire body, exposing the lines of the hard muscles beneath her skin. Her breasts swayed back and forth in the candlelight. The rushing air and wind in the room picked up again as the unholy union spawned a magic that reached even greater heights. Suddenly, Moloch withdrew from her and grabbed her wrist, spinning her around to meet his eyes. He stared at her longingly, and Naamah thought she caught something greater than lust in his eyes, if but for only a moment.

"I have arrived at a stimulating notion," Moloch said as he released her and walked to the altar. "Why not sacrifice your 'initiate' in a much more pleasurable manner."

With that, Moloch ran his hands down the girl's body, stopping at the bindings on her legs and, with the pluck of a finger, snapped her supple legs free. He waved his hands apart, and the initiate's legs parted and rose to the air in response to his command. Naamah walked over to Moloch's side, running her long fingernails across his back and the initiate's breasts as she passed between them, stopping to stare down at the girl on the altar.

"I would have been just as satisfied plunging my blade into her," resolve filled her voice as the words emanated slowly followed by a fiendishly seductive laugh, "but this works, too."

The girl's eyes opened at the sound of Naamah's voice above her, and she turned and focused on Moloch.

"What happened," the girl asked. "Am I in Hell?"

"Not yet," Naamah bent and whispered in her ear, "but we are working on it."

71

A lexander stepped forward, motioning his companions to join him in his advance. Anika and Asar took refuge in his expression and moved swiftly to his side.

"May I introduce you to the Medjai of Deshret, the keepers of the Red Crown of Egypt, the Red Scorpions," Alex announced proudly as he raised his hands in presentation, bowing his head ever so slightly as a signal of reverence to the mighty clan.

The horses had formed a tight circle in the sand around the trio. From Anika's vantage point, the heads of the mighty steeds played more prominently than their masters atop, thus she could barely discern the outlines of the riders above.

"Friends of yours I assume?" Anika asked.

Alexander turned to her and placed one hand firmly upon her shoulder. "Very old, very dear friends," he replied with a large grin. "*Very* dear friends."

With that, the riders instructed their horses to shimmy to the sides, parting a hole in the center of the circle, opening a space out into the dark night.

"Ah, yes," Asar said with an air of ease. "Serket, of course."

"Serket? The scorpion?" Anika replied illustrating her translation prowess.

Alexander smiled at her with approbation. "Very good."

Anika watched in awe as the massive head of a white stallion came into focus, emerging in the shadowy space formed by the other riders. Puffs of steam bellowed from its nostrils and the immense beasts' eyes reflected red in the available light. The awesome creature hulked forward, every muscle in its legs flexing and bulging. Anika stared in amazement. She couldn't recall ever seeing such a splendid mount in her life. Asar and Anika took a step back, looking quickly over their shoulders as they butted up to the mares to their rear. A shiver ran down her spine as the horse at her back let forth a burst of hot breath that penetrated her clothing, warming the skin beneath.

From their new vantage point at the opposite side of the equestrian circle, the rider of the white horse finally came into view. Anika was shocked to see a person of slight stature atop the white titan. Based upon the physique of the mare, expectations had dictated something more along the lines of a barbarian of a man atop such a creature. Instead, she found a slender figure garbed in colorless darkness. The rider's head and face were swaddled in tufts of blackness which revealed only the large dark eyes beneath to the outside world.

"It's a woman," Anika proclaimed softly, her voice echoing with astonishment.

"Indeed, *she* is," Alexander replied.

Anika's gaze, which had momentarily shifted to Alex, returned to the rider. The beam from his flashlight cast shadows across the circle of horses, but there was just enough light on the white horse rider's face. The woman stared down at Anika. There was both warmth and power present in her gaze which was accentuated by the thick black makeup lines meticulously traced in the stylistic fashion of the ancients. Leaning forward, the rider relinquished the reins and reached up towards her face. Unfastening the wraps from a point near her ear, the rider allowed the sable fabric to fall forward and unravel into the cool breeze of the desert night. Anika could now discern the rider's sun-borne, olive-skinned face. She was stunning and fierce. Her full lips formed a sideways grin as she turned her attention from Anika to Alex.

"Alexander," the rider laughed said with a deep, rich Middle Eastern accent. "What a great pleasure to see you."

"The pleasure is all mine I assure you," he said, moving forward and to the side of the great white stallion. "You have no idea how glad I am to see you, Serket." His voice was both sincere and filled with the air of gratitude.

Alexander reached up and ran his hands along the horse's face, gently tapping the side of the muscular steed. The majestic creature showed no signs of reservation to Alexander's proximity. Anika noted the obvious familiarity that existed between man and beast.

"Alexander," Serket said softly, as if to a child.

Alex said nothing. Rather, he wrapped his arm under the horse's neck and proceeded to squeeze his face against the stallion's head. The horse responded in turn with a gentle neigh and pushed toward Alex, reciprocating his embrace in a remarkably tender display.

"Alexander," Serket repeated, slightly sharper this time.

"Yes?" Alexander finally replied, glancing from the horse up to its rider.

"What have you gotten yourself into this time, Alexander?" Serket shifted in her saddle and leaned down toward Alex.

Alexander ceased his folly with the white stallion and moved to Serket's side so their faces were quite close.

"Very dark things, I am afraid," his words emanated slow and purposeful, his eyes locked on Serket's. "And as coincidence is not present in my vocabulary, I believe the Medjai's time may be at hand."

72

M oloch emerged from the enormous, albeit weathered and aged, wooden door to Dalquharran Castle and stepped out into the bright Scottish sunlight. The new morning radiated across the land, calling forth light, warmth and hope. He hated it. The modest castle, built in 1786, was now nothing more than a hulking shell of stone. The interior and roof had been laid to waste for many years now, and what time had not erased, the elements had finished. Very few souls had any knowledge of the tunnels and catacombs that littered the subterranean recesses of the citadel. Many of the passageways, like the altar room, had existed on the site long before the castle's construction. Moloch had visited the hidden side of Dalquharran on several occasions through millennia and was well versed in both the history and layout of the passageways and structures below the castle. A peculiarly shaped circular staircase in the center of the castle ruins descends to a cellar chamber with a tedious red and ebony door. Behind which, one descends several floors into the damp and musty darkness that lies below the surface, finally arriving at the first of six runs of tunnels. The number of hidden rooms and passages in the castle's subterranean world seemed limitless at times. Most of the alcoves and passageways had collapsed and crumbled through the years, however a large portion of the space directly beneath the castle's structural foundation remained intact and navigable. For hundreds of years, loyal followers, believers in the darkness, had toiled and labored in the dank rot of the underside of the castle, ever expanding Moloch's fortress on Earth. Clearing rooms and tunnel runs, while stabilizing ceilings and walls until a sizable portion of the castle's underground labyrinths were restored for the majesty of their demonic master. Most of these laborers had died in the very blackness they built; their bodies left strewn throughout the decaying structure's interior in chiseled out catacombs. Their decaying flesh and bones assembled in an honorarium to Moloch. The fortification suited Moloch well, and he felt quite content in his dark, stone encapsulated hell.

"What are you up to, my dark prince?" The words, like melodic whispers, came from behind him as Naamah emerged from the great stone archway.

Moloch did not turn to meet his companion, nor was he shocked at her arrival by his side, as he could smell her scent moving toward him long before she spoke a word. Naamah stepped up beside him and raised her head to meet the sun's rays. Moloch peered at her through the corner of his eye. Her inky satin cloak flowed and framed her body, blowing rhythmically in the breeze, hypnotizing him momentarily. Snapping to, he cleared his throat and turned to address her.

"We must move quickly now, lass," he said with a comical drawl. "Mayan stones be calling."

"How quickly?" she asked with a smirk at his Scottish role-play.

"Now," he said dryly, the accent and jest fleeing his voice. "We should be there now."

Naamah nodded. She walked from Moloch's side down the stone steps to the unkempt dirt and grass that lined the grounds of the castle. Moving slowly, her eyes darted back and forth across the terrain at her feet, as if looking for a small item lost among the debris.

"What are you looking for, my dear?" Moloch shouted from the castle entryway.

"Oh, a little of this," she said, pausing to crouch down to retrieve what looked like a small red stone from the ground, "and a little of that," she finished, holding her prize up over head.

Moloch walked toward her, his pace quickening as he grew closer.

"Shall we?" she asked as he approached.

"That's it?" he asked, gesturing to her hand. "That's all you need?"

"That's it!" She laughed. "No virgin blood or slaughtered masses," she said softly as she placed the fabric at the tips of her left gloved hand between her teeth and pulled off the long black gauntlet exposing the bare skin of her hand.

She placed the pebble in the palm of her gloveless hand. Smoke accompanied by an aura of bright, pure white light instantly began to emanate from the diminutive stone.

"All I need is a little piece of home," she flashed Moloch a crooked smile. "And you and I both know that can be easily found anywhere in this world."

73

The metallic echo of raindrops pounding the downed aircraft finally took a sojourn as the first gleams of daybreak crept through the cockpit's windshield. The golden rays of the rising sun flowed through the pilot's door and expanded like smoke in a bottle into the main cabin of the plane.

Lobo had suggested that his weary passengers wait the storm out by attempting to get some rest. Scrunched up in their seats, they had covered themselves with makeshift blankets of jackets and sweatshirts, resting their heads on pillows constructed of folded arms. The pilot's suggestion had sounded quite absurd at the time. Too much had transpired over the past few hours to actually give way to rest, let alone sleep. But after tossing and turning and staring out into the eerie red hue of the plane, each of them had gone mentally kicking and screaming into a deep and necessary slumber.

"Up and at 'em," barked Lobo as he emerged from the cockpit, slapping an open hand against the wall of the main cabin.

A chorus of moans and muttered complaints quickly filled the cabin, and Lobo surmised that this is what a mother must feel like while demanding her children awaken on the first day of school.

"Up and at 'em!" Lobo urged them again.

"Up and at 'em," mimicked Sam as she tossed her body sideways in her seat, turning her back to the pilot in protest.

Kate snickered at her companions's toying. "She's not a morning person, Lobo," she explained, her own eyes still shut tight. She could feel the warm sunlight penetrating the cabin, and she could see it through her thin lids. Finally, stretching her arms out and over her head, she opened her eyes and shifted up and out of her seat. Kate turned and looked through the cockpit door. Through the front window of the plane, she could see nothing but green. It seemed as though the Mexican jungle had swallowed the aircraft up in the night, the vegetation morphing into a carnivorous army, ravenously devouring the plane where it lie.

"How did you land in this ... my God?" asked Kate, still peering out the cockpit door.

"Ah, it wasn't so bad," replied Lobo as he nudged Keith's leg. "We're at the end of it. The full runway is behind us, and its still a fairly clear-cut run."

Keith slowly sat upright and rested his head in his hands; one of his palms slowly rotated around his eyes as he tried to shake the sleep off.

"Guys, we really need to get motivated here if we want to make it to the ruins on before nightfall," said Lobo as he walked around the plane, a large camouflage knapsack in hand. "We're on a tight schedule with the sun."

"Wait a minute!" shouted Kate. "What do you mean?"

Lobo continued to roam from cabinet to drawer, grabbing items from each location and stuffing them into the infantry bag.

"Do you know what's going on here?" Kate demanded as she walked up behind the burly pilot.

"Of course I do, sweetie." He turned to her with a sly smile. "Mr. Storm always has a handle on things."

Kate continued to stare at him.

"Didn't you guys figure that part out yet?" He looked around at the rest of the travelers. "The man is on his game, always, and all you kids need to do is listen and follow his instructions like good little soldiers."

"Soldiers?" Abigail didn't like Lobo's insinuation.

"Soldiers, scientists, adventurers." Lobo paused and huffed. "Just follow his instructions. Nothing underhanded here." He paused again. "Storm is the good guy ... always ... to a fault at times."

Kate had regained her composure. "So, you have a handle on where we are and what needs to be done? Because we did a little internet research. You know, Google knowledge? And honestly, you know what that's worth."

"No, not really," Lobo replied matter-of-factly as he shoved a huge knife into a sheath on the side of the bag. "I've always considered the Internet a useful tool."

"Course you have," Samantha chimed in from the other side of the cabin, and Kate shot her a 'shut up' glance.

"What I'm saying...what I'm asking is," Kate stumbled for the right words as she grew closer to Lobo, "besides the basic premise, I have no idea what the hell is going on or what we are supposed to be accomplishing."

"Easy." Lobo turned to face Kate as he flipped the bag across his shoulders and straps around his arms in one fluid motion, which reminded Kate of a vampire donning his cape. "Ready? Castle...solstice...serpent..." He paused to grab onto the makeshift handle and fasteners holding the side door of the plane in place and gave it a massive tug. The sinuous straps began to snap and pop. "Stone head," he continued as he gave it another heave to slide it open and out. "Secret compartment...papyrus..." The door screeched open and snapped, falling to the jungle floor with a thud as a dazzling flood of light entered the cabin like a wave. "...Save the world..." He paused once again as his eyes adjusted to the radiant glare. Still peering outside, Lobo slowly raised both of his hands straight up into the air and completed his instructional rant. "Mexican drug cartel."

74

Alexander's hands clenched Serket's hips as the pair galloped through the Jordanian desert. Her mighty stallion carried the pair effortlessly on their course to Decker, punching through the hills and gullies of the sand as if running through a flat meadow. Alex shifted his body to look at the horsemen trailing behind them. He was certain he could hear Asar complaining through the din of wind that rushed over his face and into his ears. He smiled, allowing a throaty laugh to escape his lips. He feared the sudden release of tension that he just experienced could very well lead to a bout of uncontrollable laughter and his chest heaved into Serket's back as he labored to subdue what would be an uncharacteristic display.

"You all right, Alex?" she called from beneath her facial wraps.

"Wonderful," he exclaimed as he took in another oversized helping of desert air laced with his companion's exotic fragrance.

Out of the corner of his right eye, Alexander registered a gleaming shimmer, which almost instantaneously morphed into a horizontal line of fire as he turned to face it. The sun was beginning its ascent, and like a phantom pouring forth its formless shape, the light began to stretch out across the desert sand. It was truly surreal, and Alex watched in awe as the expansive black *nothing* of the desert became *something* before his eyes.

"How close?" Alex prompted, the euphoric moment passing and his thoughts returning to the business at hand.

"Close. Only half a kilometer more."

Alex turned to check on the band of riders behind them again. They were completely visible in the new dawn light, but still a distance back as their horses were no match for the spirited power of Amunet. Alex let go of Serket with one hand and reached down to praise the great stallion, tapping her assuredly with his open hand.

"Best hold on tight, Alexander Storm," Serket advised. "We are about to navigate an extremely precarious path."

"Oh, right!" He quickly returned his free hand to Serket's side, grasping her tightly. Alex did not need to be facing her, nor did he require her scarves to be opened to know she was smiling a mischievous smile at the moment.

"Behave, Mr. Storm," she yelled out as she twisted the reins to their left, sending Amunet into a hard, downward turn and onto a new, winding path.

The horse recovered effortlessly, and Alex could see the tension drop from the reins as the great white steed clearly knew its course without rider intervention. They were rapidly racing toward a massive rock formation, jagged and extending out and up in all directions. The horse's pace did not waiver as they vaulted headlong at the mountain side. Fifty meters, forty meters—the rocks were approaching dizzying speed.

"You might wish to shut your eyes," Serket announced.

"Really? No need for that, I am sure!"

Twenty meters. Alex could make out nothing before them now but solid mountainside.

"I thoroughly, and completely trust..." impact seemed all but imminent, *"the horse!"*

His words trailed off and echoed into the endless sand as Serket, Alexander Storm, and the great horse Amunet disappeared into thin air.

75

"What are you—" started Sam as she walked toward Lobo?

She stopped dead in her tracks as she watched the muscles in his right arm, raised high above his head, flex and become taught as his fist closed hard. So hard was this gesture that it caused the skull and cross bones inked across his front forearm ripple and come to life.

Sam was no soldier, but she unequivocally picked up on the universal symbol for "stop!" Or in this case, "Don't fucking move!" No sooner had the words entered her mind did they emanate in a low, stern growl from the side of Lobo's mouth: "Don't. Fucking. Move."

Sam looked around at her companions. They were all frozen in place like a morbid game of Simon Says. With shallow breaths of jungle air, they waited on their pilot's next move.

"Hola, amigos!" Lobo shouted in a firm, yet friendly, voice. "Una tormenta tomó nuestro avión de sorpresa."

Silence.

"Necesitamos llegar a Chichén Itzá ahora." Lobo did his best to hurriedly relay their intent, however the twenty or so soldiers pointing their arsenal of firepower at him did not seem the least bit interested in his plight.

"Perhaps you can help us?" Lobo exhaled without much enthusiasm.

"Inglés?" finally a response, "you Americano?"

Suddenly, the four companions, who were still unable to see their would-be captors, heard a barrage of chatter in Spanish and broken bits of English.

"Sí, amigos," Lobo answered, a glimmer of hope in his voice. He could not see the origin of the question, but the sound of the asker's voice seemed to come from behind the cluster of assassins.

"English!" the voice instructed. "Your Spanish sucks!"

Lobo could see the owner of the voice as he emerged through the center of the soldiers. A short man with a chiseled face and a dirty white shirt approached the side of the downed plane. He paused several feet in front and below Lobo, then reached around to his back waist. Lobo held his breath. His strategic mind began to analyze the situation and attempt to formulate possible scenarios that would facilitate the group's escape. He arrived at none. He may be able to save himself, but his companions were untrained *kids*. They were easy pickings for this battle-hardened militia. If these bandits opened fire now, they were all as good as dead. A wisp of air escaped Lobo's chest as the short man retrieved nothing more than a blue bandana from his pocket.

"Hell of a landing *amigo*," said the man in his best American accent, laughing. "You're the pilot, yes? Where'd you learn to fly like that?"

"Here and there," Lobo replied with a hint of sarcasm, beginning to feel a little less threatened for the moment.

"Ha," snapped the man in the dirty white shirt. "I have been to both of those places myself."

Lobo laughed and began to lower his arms, which were on the verge of spasming at his shoulders.

"Up, up!" screamed a soldier to his right, moving forward to make his intent more evident. Lobo's arms shot back up like rockets.

"Perhaps you drop the bag," said the man, clearly the head honcho, as he swiped the bandana across his forehead and over the back of his neck. "Make things easier on you."

Lobo understood this was more than a kind suggestion to ease his arms. He dropped his left elbow down slowly, notching his shoulder a bit, and allowed the strap of the backpack to cascade down his arm, the bag coming to a rest with a tin thud on the floor of the plane.

The man in the dirty white shirt had paused and to watch this intently, no doubt attempting to gauge his prisoner's resistance level. He smiled and began to pace back and forth in front of the door. "Good, good," he rattled off to himself.

"You armed, mister pilot?" He stopped short and posed the question.

"Not presently," Lobo dryly replied, motioning to the bag at his feet.

"Agárralo!" the man shouted, and one of the soldiers in the front shouldered his assault rifle and ran past the man to the door of the plane. Lobo watched as the soldier tippy-toed up to reach the floor at his feet. Through the corner of his eye, he watched the dirty dry fingers feel around, grasping at the strap of the bag like a drunk tarantula—he couldn't reach it from where he stood.

"For shit's sake," the man in the dirty white shirt finally shouted, nodding at Lobo. "Help a brotha out, will ya?"

Lobo kicked the bag toward the teetering drug soldier who snatched it and pulled it down to the ground with a smug expression as if he did it himself.

A shrill whistle drew Lobo back to the man in the dirty white shirt.

"How many in there, *amigo?*" he asked with a smile and paused as Lobo opened his mouth to answer. "And don't lie to me. I butcher anyone you forget to mention."

Lobo froze, and he considered his options. His passengers were not grunts with tactical training. They would not hide. They would not fight. They would, he surmised, stay frozen.

"Four," he said with a nod. "Five, counting me."

The man in the dirty white shirt took several steps backward until he was behind the muzzles of his dogs' weapons. He retrieved his bandana once more and wiped his forehead slowly. An obvious tell, Lobo thought to himself. *I've heard of wood burning. I guess sweat wiping is its jungle equivalent.*

The man in the dirty white shirt lowered his arm from his head and looked up at Lobo. Staring into his eyes, he snarled. "Don't fuck this up, cowboy."

"You! In the plane!" the man in the dirty white shirt commenced to shout. "Put your fucking hands in air and walk slowly to your shitty pilot's side!" He took another step backward.

"One at a time," he continued. "You fuck this up, I kill you all and go eat breakfast."

76

Alexander relinquished his tight grasp of Serket's hips as the horse came to a slow trot and stopped. He pressed his palms down onto the back of the majestic horse and hoisted his body straight up, flipping one leg over, he dismounted Amunet. The sound of Alex's feet hitting the ground echoed like a hefty book being slammed on a desk. Leaning forward, he dusted the front of his pants off, more in gesture than necessity. He could still hear Serket's giggles.

"I am rather enthralled that I was able to lend to your amusement," Alexander softly retaliated. "Quite a ride though, I must say."

Serket spun to face Alexander, peering down at him from between the cloth of her vailed face. Her eyes were stunning and compelled Alex to catch his breath.

"Heart skip a beat?" she asked softly.

"What?" stammered Alex, realizing his emotions must be self evident in his gaze even in the dim light of the hollow mountain.

With a movement that seemed more schooled in dance than equestrianism, Serket spun from her mount and softly landed on the ground face-to-face with Alexander.

"Did the illusion at the entrance get you?"

Alexander recovered seamlessly. "Ah, yes. Of course. Quite exhilarating." Their eyes remained locked, sizing one another up. "Only so much, of course, as my confidence in your abilities never wavered."

"Of course," Serket repeated as her expression grew narrower. "What did you think I was referring to?"

Alexander stared into her eyes for what felt like an eternal pause. He had missed her and her powerful presence. Serket reached around and released the flowing material from around her head, letting it fall to the side of her body. Reaching around to the other side, she grasped a section of linen and swiftly unwound the wrappings that ensured her hair remained safe from the harsh desert elements. Her long, flowing locks of obsidian flowed down and cascaded across her shoulders in cloud-like fashion. Serket smirked, exposing the dimple under one eye. It was no great feat of the imagination to forget the woman before him was a ruthless warrior.

"Are you trying to seduce me, Serket?"

"Me? Never," she said, laughing, then turned to face the growing clamor of hooves as the rest of their party entered the hidden sanctuary.

"If I want you," she said, turning her gaze back to Alex, "I will just take you."

"There you are, Alexander!" Asar shouted from one of the horses as they rallied into the subterranean labyrinth.

"Here I am!" Alexander shouted with parental jest in his voice. "Swallowed by a whale of mountain." He turned and walked through the hall that led further into the mountain. "Afloat in its belly, but safe all the same!"

Alexander marched forward a bit before stopping and looking back at Serket. "Shall we?" he called to her.

"After you," she replied, taking up pace behind him and arriving at his side.

The two moved forward into a massive clearing within the mountain, the rest of the party in tow. Alexander stared in clear astonishment, lifting his head to look up into the hollowed-out mountain which he surmised must go up half a mile into the dark recesses of the stone. Before him, spread out in all directions, the span was at least equal to the height, if not more. His heart racing harder than before; he broke from Serket's side and ran out into the boundless inner city.

"Now *this* is truly amazing!"

"Always running from me, Alexander Storm!"

Alex paused for a moment, and without turning back, he shouted to Serket, "You are the scorpion! One must always run from the scorpion!" Then, turning to face her, their gaze locking once more, he whispered. "For any other decision would surely mean a slow and painful death."

77

S amantha was the first to unstick her feet and force herself to the hole in the side of the plane. She had only taken a step or two when Keith's arm extended in front of her.

"Let me check this out first," he whispered.

Sam snickered and was about to push past him when she caught sight of his eyes, he was serious.

"Okay, Rambo," she toyed. "Go get 'em."

With that, Keith turned to face Lobo's back, raising his hands over his head, and began walking toward the light which continued to flood the cabin. He was only a few feet from the pilot, but was still unable to make anything out on the floor of the jungle outside.

Lobo turned slightly to his right, just enough to catch sight of Keith's face.

Oh, Jesus, he thought to himself. *This guy is no soldier.*

Keith edged forward until he was aligned with Lobo. His eyes demanded several moments to adjust to the sun's intensity at the threshold.

"Easy does it, chief," Lobo whispered.

As Keith's vision cleared, he could feel a dry lump take root in his throat as if he had just swallowed a spoonful of flour.

"Easy does it," Lobo repeated, recognizing the panic creeping across Keith's face. "Calm, cool, and composed. You hear?"

"Silence!" someone shouted from the firing line. Lobo didn't think it was the man in the dirty white shirt. He was pretty sure he had crept back into the safety of the rear command. Lobo raised his chin toward the voice as if to silently acknowledge the directive.

Samantha moved next. Then much like children closely pursuing their father through an amusement park's haunted house, Abigail and Kate fell in tightly behind her.

"Don't push," snapped Sam. "We'll get there."

The three continued edging forward.

Samantha could clearly hear the shouting as they approached. "Have the rest come! Now!"

"Let go of me, Kate," Samantha instructed. "And put your hands up."

The three girls arrived in train-like fashion at the exit's threshold. Lobo could once again sense them at his side and motioned with his head for Keith to shift over so the girls could move in line with them.

A voice yelled, "Spread out now!" Lobo was sure it was the man in the dirty white shirt this time, and he turned to look at the girls.

"It's all right," he said, trying, unsuccessfully, to soothe them. "Just move forward and spread out. They want to make sure you're not a threat."

As the three women moved to the edge, a cacophony of excited chatter broke out among the soldiers.

Samantha looked out at the hoard of armed men. "Holy shit," the words escaped her mouth as she stared down at the guns. However, she found the stares of the cartel soldiers more distressing.

"Easy does it, Sam," whispered Lobo.

"Fuck you," she whispered back. "These animals only want to kill you. Switch bodies with me and see how fucking calm *you* are."

Keith's jaw clenched. "That's not happening, Sam." He turned to look at Kate and repeated his promise, "That's not fucking happening."

"Oh, it's happening, Rambo!" She felt tears of rage welling up. "And let me cut your cliché short." She paused for impact, then announced, "It *will* be over your dead fucking body."

"Take it easy, goddamn it," Lobo snapped. "Keep your suburban soldier shit in check."

"Easy does it. Easy does it," said the slimy bastard Lobo had dubbed the man in the dirty white shirt. He had re-emerged at the sight of the women and was walking toward them. "We are all friends here."

The man stopped several meters from the plane and looked up at Lobo. "You. Pilot. Down, now." He pointed to the ground under Lobo.

Lobo's eyes blinked hard as he contemplated his options.

"Jump," the man in the dirty white shirt demanded, "or fall," he added.

Lobo bent his knees and launched himself to the ground below. He quickly stood upright and locked his hands behind his head. He stared at the group of killers, and his nose twitched uncontrollably.

What's that smell? he thought as his mind raced.

"You next!" The man in the dirty white shirt commanded Keith.

Keith nodded at him without making eye contact and turned to look at Kate once more. Crouching his hands to the floor of the plane, he lowered himself out the door to the jungle floor. Not as dramatic as Lobo's leap, but it did the trick.

"Very good." Laughed the man in the dirty white shirt. "Now you—join the pilot," he said, pointing over at Lobo. "Both of you—on your knees!"

Keith slowly made his way to Lobo's side and peered up at him with desperation in his eyes.

"Plan?" Keith begged.

"Working on it."

"Shut the fuck up!" the man in the dirty white shirt demanded. "Get on your knees! Both of you!"

Keith and Lobo simultaneously dropped to the ground, hands remaining locked behind their heads. Keith grunted as he came down on the rocky ground of the makeshift runway. Lobo caught the smell again, stronger down on the ground, and familiar.

"Plan emerging," he whispered ever so softly.

"Bueno," the man in the dirty white shirt as he walked over to the door that had come to rest on the ground outside the threshold. He used it as a step to reach up to the three remaining passengers.

"Come now, ladies," he demanded, extending his scarred, dirty hand up to them. "We are no savages. Come join friends."

Kate and Samantha stood motionless, well aware of the horrors that awaited them if they exited the plane.

"We've got this," Abigail announced loudly to her companions. "Alexander Storm would not have sent us here to die."

"What? Who?" bellowed a deep voice from the jungle beyond the clearing.

The assassins snapped to hard attention at the sound of the mystery voice and leveled their weapons at the side of the plane, edging forward ever so slightly toward the wayward group.

Abigail was reaching down toward the hand of the man in the dirty white shirt, but she was unable to steady herself, and he hopped up and took hold of her extended hand.

Her hand clenched down on her captive's grasp, and the snapping of his bones was audible. Her eyes rolled back in her head as she tumbled out of the plane toward the ground below.

Dirty white shirt guy screamed out in agony as he tried to wrestle his hand away from the falling girl. Samantha took advantage of the confusion to leap out, landing solidly on the plane's fallen door behind the man in the dirty white shirt. Her body rose upright behind him just as he got his hand free of her vice-like grasp. The soldiers were closing in on them, not firing yet for fear of killing their Napoleonic leader.

Sam withdrew a long steel blade from somewhere behind her back and wrapped her arm around dirty white shirt's neck, pressing the steel so hard against his skin that droplets of dark red began to form around its edges.

"Alto!" Sam demanded!

"Stop! Alto!" The voice from beyond the clearing was barely audible in the din of confusion.

Abigail's body had sprawled on the jungle floor and was convulsing. The visions of dirty white shirt's lifetime of evil deeds were blasting like a cannon through her mind. Blood, murder, torture, and rape, all marked by dirty white shirt's greasy smile. Abigail was transfixed, and she could not slow her body's movements.

"Jet fuel!" yelled Lobo as he rolled to cover against the fallen plane door.

Reaching down to his boot, he withdrew a Zippo from the flapped pocket sewn into its side. Rising to his knees beside Sam's legs, he screamed, "Gas!"

The encroaching hoard of gunmen came to a stop and again began to fall back.

"Retrocedan! Retrocedan!" dirty white shirt commanded as he struggled on the edge of Sam's blade, his arms extended in front of him, the palm of his unbroken hand pointed out to make clear to his men to stand down.

Abigail continued to moan and writhe in agony amongst the dirt and vegetation that made up the jungle floor. Kate, who was the only one remaining in the plane, looked down at her friend, and although every muscle in her body told her to retreat to the safety in the cabin behind her, she stepped forward and launched herself out. Hitting the ground hard, she let out a groan and rolled in beside Abigail's body. Righting herself to her knees, she scoped Abigail up and cradled her across her legs. Her body was drenched with sweat, yet cold as a block of ice.

"Abi," she whispered. "Abi."

Lobo had risen to his feet, waving his trusty lighter in all directions, his eyes following it, darting about like a madman.

"We all go boom!" Wild-eyed, he continued to command the soldiers' attention.

Keith saw his opening, and he sprang to his feet. Dashing between Samantha's insanity and the side of the plane, he made his way to Kate's side, and together they lifted Abigail up and began to drag her toward the cover provided by the rear of the plane.

"You got this, Kate," Keith encouraged. "Just like getting away from that dog on Williston Road when we were in high school," he smiled at her. "Hey, you remember?"

Kate's mind returned to him, she smirked, then said, "Of course I remember. Got the scar on my ankle to remind me."

The two moved in unison, dragging Abigail, who was starting to break free of the dark spell she was under.

"This is how it is!" started Lobo.

"Tell them how it is there, Cap," Samantha said with strained breath as she struggled to keep her smelly captive close to her blade.

"We're walking out of here with your boss," he continued. "Now! Or everybody goes up in smoke!"

"Ha ha! Very nicely done!" the booming voice commended Lobo. A tall, muscular man emerged from the jungle and walked up to the group of soldiers. Lobo could see him clearly. He wasn't dirty like Sam's hostage. He wore fine clothes, a fedora, and sunglasses. His face was shrouded in a thick, curly beard of peppered gray and black whiskers. He walked with confidence toward the soldiers; they parted for him to pass, and he stepped out in front of Lobo. Withdrawing a cigar from the inner pocket of his vest, he ran it under his nose, breathed deeply, and placed it to his lips. Baring his teeth as if to snarl, he bit the end from the tobacco leaf bundle as smoothly as one may bite a ripe apple. Turning to Samantha, he spit the end to the ground.

"Well done, young lady." He paused and turned to his men behind him. "Perhaps I should let you kill General Miguel and give you his job?" The horde of soldiers grinned and laughed. He continued, "You are clearly a better soldier, and far easier on the eyes."

Kate watched from their position at the plane's tail. She was quite sure these men would smile and laugh at anything that came out of the mysterious man's mouth if it was, in fact, his intention to be humorous. Kate's mind, being a bit unhinged at the moment, wondered what a difficult job it must be for these men to decipher whether "mystery man" was trying to be funny or not. And, apparently, they had a laugh leader. One assassin was charged with figuring out mystery man's intent and beginning the laugh process, then everyone else fell in a split second behind him. She surmised that would mean all the soldiers except for one were actually paying attention to that one, the laugh leader, and not the mystery man.

"Oh fuck! What am I thinking?" She shook her head.

"What?" whispered Keith.

"Nothing. Well, actually, it's kinda funny. Remind me later if we don't die."

"What is *wrong* with you?"

The mystery man moved toward Sam. "Please do not kill him, miss. He's a loyal soldier. I was teasing."

Turning to Lobo, who was still holding the lighter out in front of him, he stopped right at the edge of the plane door.

"So, tell me," the man boomed again. "Where is Alexander Storm?"

"What?" the words hissed from Lobo's lips as he stopped waving the Zippo about and stared at the man, who had stepped up onto the door with the others.

The man leaned in toward Lobo and placed the cigar back between his lips. His expression on his face was fearless.

"Tell me, friend." The man smirked. "Do you have a light?"

78

"This part of Petra is known as the Wadi Ramm," Serket explained as she led the three visitors further into the rock sanctum. "The Medjai discovered this naturally formed hollow mountain thousands of years ago."

"What of all the rooms and passages, though?" Anika asked. "Surely these are not natural formations."

Serket nodded. "Correct, these were carved through the millennia by the Medjai, with the greatest expansion occurring between 333 BC and 160 AD."

Serket paused the group and turned to her right to face an immense stone fortress constructed at the middle of the mountain's clearing. The massive structure stretched several hundred feet up into the darkened void.

"This is a place of magic my friends," she began. "There are five identical monuments erected around the globe. Alex, perhaps you have encountered others on your travels through the years."

"Perhaps," Alex slowly replied and winked at Serket. "Yes, I believe there is some familiarity to the architecture."

"Really?" Anika asked, stepping forward to get a better look.

"Oh, yes, miss." Asar assured her as he shifted to Anika's side. "Mr. Storm has traversed almost every inch of the globe."

Alex let out a stifled laugh. "Not quite, old friend, but I have travelled and explored extensively, and," he said, move close to the marveling pair, "it is quite a unique vision, isn't it?"

"Indeed," Asar agreed softly, mesmerized as he stared at the spectacular structure.

"Thus, one would not forget seeing a beauty that equals it. Much like you will not ever forget laying eyes upon this one."

The towering rock structure was constructed from carved black obsidian bricks, about half the size of the stones used in the building of the Great Pyramid at Giza. Unlike the stones in Egypt however, these appeared to produce a purple luminescence which radiated throughout the immediate area surrounding the fortress. The first level of stone walls at the base rose up as if to culminate in a pointed pyramid structure but stopped about halfway through the geometric shape. Then, from a newly formed base atop this first level, the tower rose up in a reverse spiral staircase winding through the darkness, only visible as it climbed higher due to the faint purple hue which emanated. There were no windows in the rigid walls, and the only opening was a great archway at the base of the first level. This opening, blocked by a material so opaque that it created the illusion of staring into open space rather than a solid wall. This effect was amplified by the fact the door did not radiate purple as all the other parts of the exterior did.

"Yes, I most definitely have encountered one or two of these before." He turned and walked back toward the mountain wall to his left. "But that is a story for another day."

As Alexander strolled up the slight incline toward the dozens of doors and passages that lined the wall before him, Serket called out for him to slow down.

"You have no idea where you are going!" She laughed as she joined him. "Care to let me lead?"

As the pair reached level ground, Alexander came to a dead stop and hung his head down. Closing his eyes for but a second, he quickly snapped to, shocking Serket.

"My presence is required elsewhere," he said quickly and moved even faster. "I shall check on Decker's well-being but for a moment and be on my way. I have no doubt he is in good hands here."

Serket's relaxed expression turned serious. "Yes, of course," she said as she guided Anika and Asar forward. "I'll take you right to him."

Wasting no time, Serket led the three up to the massive wall of passageways.

"It's right up ahead," she said.

Asar, who was doing his best to move swiftly with the others, peered into the entranceways of the various rooms and hallways as they passed. He saw men and women scurrying about, performing various tasks. One room appeared to be a kitchen where people sat at stone counters eating and talking. It was for all intents and purposes its own microcosm within the mountain.

"Lights?" Asar blurted out.

"Yes," Serket called back to him. "I was waiting for someone to inquire," she added as she continued at her hurried pace, Alex at her side.

"Well?" Asar asked after a long pause.

"That, I am afraid, is an ancient Madjai secret, Asar."

"Huh?"

"Magic, my friend," Alex instructed matter-of-factly. "She means it's magic."

"Oh." Asar nodded his head. "Why didn't you just say so?"

The four hurried to a section with rows of long halls disappearing back into the mountainside.

"It's the next entrance, Alex." Serket pointed to the doorway a few feet in front of them, from which emanated a greater degree of light than the majority of the rooms they had passed.

"I hope you will return soon to resume our tour," Serket said softly to Alex. She could sense even though he was walking beside her, his mind was elsewhere. "Since you now know the location of our hidden city."

Alexander stopped at the threshold to Decker's room. "I have no idea where we are, and I could wander the Jordanian dessert for weeks and never locate your entrance again." He smiled and raised his eyebrows. "I do believe you give my navigation skills a lot more credit than they deserve."

Serket smirked at Alexander. "You lie," she stated with curt sweetness and turned to enter the room.

"Only when I sleep," Alex jabbed back.

Serket stopped in her tracks as she entered and turned back to him. "I believe you lie for other purposes besides just sleeping."

Alex laughed at her wit. "I honestly believe we could do this for eternity, and I wouldn't mind," he said as he walked past her into the room. "But I do have the task of quelling mankind's eternal damnation to deal with first."

"Trifles," Serket replied as she entered Decker's room behind Alexander, "such trifles."

79

SEVENTEEN YEARS EARLIER

L ike a bird clearing its wings for flight, Decker grabbed the bottom flaps of his long trench-coat and shook them rapidly. The sudden deluge of rain dissipated as rapidly as it had begun, but not before soaking him to the bone. Feeling hopeless in his efforts to extricate the rain water from his saturated clothing, he settled back against the wall of the tattered apartment tenement and fished around the inner pockets of his coat for his somewhat crumpled, soft-pack of smokes.

"Dry," he huffed with relief as he withdrew the cellophane wrapped pack and applied a well rehearsed shake and jerk. The one-handed move instantly brought a solitary cigarette up through the small opening on the top of the pack. Lifting the pack to his mouth, he lipped the rouge cigarette and withdrew it. He jammed the crumpled pack back into a pocket and began the new tap and rub game known as find my lighter.

Pausing his somewhat comical search efforts, Decker lifted his hat in salutation at an old woman scurrying past on the walkway. The elderly woman was clearly oblivious to his presence due to her preoccupation with her rain water logged attire.

"Buenos días," he exclaimed as she passed. "Lovely weather you have here."

The old woman scoffed at Decker and continued on her way. Without further pause, he returned to his efforts to locate his illusive lighter. Tracing the outer fabric of his pants pockets, he finally drew upon the familiar outline with his fingers. Lighting his cigarette, he took a long, deep drag and leaned his back against the wall.

Where the hell was Storm? he wondered.

Alexander had urgently summoned him to join him in Mexico City. Decker had been forced to part ways with a bottomless bottle of whiskey and a fine-bottomed waitress at Ricky's Tavern in Bayside, Maine.

Now he was on a street corner, in a shitty part of Mexico City, sopping wet and drink-less, waiting on the ever-mysterious Mr. Storm. Decker found himself complaining more often as of late, but honestly, he didn't mind the excitement and the mystery. He found both to be very agreeable, and of course it kept him moving. Rolling stones and moss, and all that happy horse shit.

The tip of his cigarette glowed with intensity as Decker took another long drag. He turned and looked up in an effort to survey the latest location Storm had directed him to. There, amongst the crumbling ruins of a once great portion of the city, lie a ten-story apartment building. He was currently located right outside of Tepito, in an area fondly referred to by locals as, "el barrio bravo," or brave neighborhood. Decker snickered at the moniker now, realizing it had nothing to do with the regal nature of the inhabitants, which had been his original assertion. No, he understood now, standing in the middle of this architectural heap of steaming crap that what it really meant was one needed to be brave to live here.

The building's symphony of faded and chipped pastel paint, may once have been inviting to those looking to settle in the area. Now, however, the only emotions being instilled by the structure were despair. The hulking frame of pitted concrete now served only to compound the overall repressed mood of the locale.

Decker took another drag and dropped the cigarette to the cement walkway. He stared at the billowing smoke for a moment, his weary mind trapped in the expanding puff, drifting everywhere and nowhere at once. Much like himself, he thought. Snapping to, he applied the tip of his boot to the discarded cigarette and extinguish the last remnants of its embers.

"Flask," he whispered to himself, as he resumed the task of rummaging through his pockets. His fingers found his oft solitary companion, and he began to withdraw it from his pocket when a familiar voice beside him caused his fingers to relinquish their grasp of the metal vessel.

"Decker."

He spun around, slightly unnerved, to find Alexander Storm right beside him.

"I didn't hear you coming," he replied, noticeably taken aback.

"Well, that's okay, old friend," Alex conveyed with a calming smile. "I do believe your attentions may well have been directed elsewhere."

Placing his hand on Decker's shoulder, he simultaneously squeezed him in greeting and directed him away from the front of the dilapidated building.

"So," he began, "I was summoned here several days ago to investigate claims of demonic possession of a juvenile subject. I had received some photographs and other *purported* evidence. All of which offered me no more than a hefty serving of skepticism I must say," he continued, "but along with the photographs and drawings was a tiny scrap of paper with one word scratched onto it—"

"How are you, Alexander?" Decker interrupted. "Oh, just peachy," he answered for Alex.

"And you, Mr. Decker?" Decker posed the question to himself, continuing the word play, "How might you be faring?"

Alexander crunched his brow. "Really? Are we doing this?"

"I am quite well." Decks sustained the parody. "Thank you for asking!"

"Come now, Decker," Alex said with complete conviction of progression. "We are well beyond the need for such pleasantries, are we not?"

Decker shrugged his shoulders. "It's been months, Alex," he replied. "Normal people at least say hello when they haven't seen each other for a while."

Alexander stared speechless at Decker.

"What?" Decker asked.

"Are you quite done now?" Alexander had already refocused on his need to convey his story. "Because we have work to do if you are done."

"Done," Decker quickly replied with a huff.

"Good." Alexander didn't miss a beat. He peered over Decker's should up at the center of the apartment building. "Good. And did you just characterize you and I as among the 'normal' citizenry? Really now?"

Decker waved Alex's attention back to him, expressing his willingness to listen to whatever insanity was going to come out of Alex's mouth next.

"Oh, yes," Alex continued. "The scrap of paper which brought us to this dismal display of human decline. There was one word scrawled on it."

"You mentioned," Decker replied with impertinence. "What the hell did it say?"

"*Bathin.*"

80

Lobo calmed his fervor and scrutinized the bearded man's gaze. Surrendering to his gut instinct, he stretched forward and extended the lit lighter up to the man's cigar. The man reciprocated the movement and leaned in to allow the flames of Lobo's Zippo to flicker around the tip of the aromatic tobacco. Puffing his cheeks and lips as if playing a trumpet or horn, the bearded man brought the cigar to glowing life. Flames licked the air as large wafts of rich smoke emanated around the man's face. Sam watched the exchange from a slightly higher vantage point and attempted to gauge the situation. Her captive, sensing her confusion, reached up with his healthy hand and tapped gently on Sam's forearm. The touch startled her, and she tightened her pressure instead of relinquishing her hold. The man in the dirty white shirt—General Miguel, as he was apparently known —yelled out in pain.

"Easy! Easy!" he implored, realizing he was truly within inches of death.

"Shut the fuck up, you smelly bastard!" Sam's response was a combination of adrenaline and fear, and Miguel recognized the danger he was in.

"Everyone relax!" the bearded man yelled. "I believe we are all compadres here."

"Not likely, you douche bag," Sam hissed, her eyes squinted and fixed on the bearded man with the look of a caged animal.

"Oh, my. You are fiery, my dear." His voice exuded the unmistakable tone of admiration as he took a step toward Sam and her profusely sweating captive.

Sam pulled Miguel back and turned to Lobo. "What the hell, man?"

"Put that lighter away, Captain, before you blow us all to kingdom come," the bearded man instructed without looking away from Sam.

"I'm not feeling this, Lobo." Sam's breaths were short and rapid.

"Easy, Samantha," Keith called from the ground. "Don't lose it."

"Yes," the bearded man agreed. "Listen to your friends, Samantha."

The dense forestry that surrounded the hidden runway rustled and shifted as the wind started to pick up. Sam looked beyond the bearded man into the jungle beyond. She could see the trees swaying in the warm air. Insects and light debris rose and fell on the outskirts of the clearing, and she felt herself relaxing the knife's tension on the clammy throat of her captive.

"Where is Alexander Storm?" the bearded man asked, directing his inquiry at Lobo.

"He's not here."

"Are you friends or foes of Storm?" The bearded man tilted his head and squinted his eyes.

"Friends," Lobo answered without hesitation. He was too tired at this point to try and figure out which answer the guy was looking for. "Lifelong friends."

"Whose life do you refer to?" he asked. "Yours, I assume?"

The bearded man turned and jumped down from the fallen door, then continued, "Alex's friends are my friends."

He stopped and pivoted back to the group, which was hanging on his every word. "You are safe now." His voice rang sincere. "Truly."

Sam looked back and forth between her companions on either side of her. She was not about to trash her only advantage until she was certain the threat was gone. Lobo nodded at her, which she found encouraging, but she was not convinced just yet.

Sensing their apprehension, which was evident from their failure to stand down, the bearded man withdrew his cigar from its roost between his lips and opened his arms wide in a surreal group hug gesture.

"I am Ricardo Montalvo," he announced, "but my friends call me El Gato." He paused again for effect, "You may call me El Gato," visually entertained by his own shallow humor.

"How do you know Alexander Storm?" Lobo asked as he lowered his lighter, still burning with an apocalyptic flame. Lobo had been prepared to die. *How many of his young companions realized how close they were to going up in a ball of fire?* he wondered.

"Alexander Storm, and his associate William Decker, saved my daughter's life many years ago."

"Let him go, Sam," Lobo directed. "We're safe here."

Samantha squinted her eyes at Lobo. Did he know what he was talking about?

"You sure about this?"

"Quite sure." The words came like the soothing wind, but short and choppy. "Let him go, Samantha."

Samantha reluctantly loosened her grip and withdrew the blade's sharp edge from Miguel's throat. He leaned over and exhaled.

"You been holding your breath this whole time?" Sam laughed a nervous laugh. "Wow!"

El Gato stepped toward Lobo. "Please extinguish your lighter, sir. Unless you are still intending to deliver us all to the gates of Dios."

Lobo shook his head back and forth slowly. "Just trying to make it through the day, buddy."

"As am I," replied El Gato.

Decker snapped the boxy metal lighter shut with a flip of his wrist. Using his free hand, he checked the temperature of the metal case. It had been burning a long time, and he didn't want to return it to his boot if it was too hot. Satisfied it wouldn't create a fire hazard, he bent over and stashed it away.

Rising upright, he realized El Gato had moved closer to him. Clouds of smoke swirled around his upper body, the pungent odor of the cigar hanging and overpowering the heavy jungle air.

"So," he said to Lobo kindly. "What convinced you?"

"Who said I was convinced of anything?"

"Oh, come now." A smile, partially hidden by his overgrown beard, widened across his sun leathered face. "You were clearly willing to die before asking for mercy."

"Decker," Lobo flashed an uncontrollable hint of a smile. "Moody bastard saved us all."

"Huh?"

"You could've known about Alexander, what he is rumored to pursue, and matters he is known to engage in." Lobo rolled his shoulders forward, releasing the kinetic tension built up inside. "But the chances of you knowing of his association with Decker required knowledge a bit more intimate. He's more of a 'behind the scenes' kind of guy."

"Ah." El Gato stepped back and raised his hands above his head. "Tonight we raise a toast to William Decker, then."

He quickly turned and walked to the center of the runway clearing so all could see and hear him.

"Descansen!" he directed his men, and they immediately lowered their weapons with the synchronicity of a well-trained militia.

"Very good." El Gato tried to coax the others out of hiding. "Everything is good."

Samantha stepped down to Lobo's side.

"You can stop hiding, Keith," Samantha chortled, laughing out loud. "The bad men like us now."

81

SEVENTEEN YEARS EARLIER

The desolate ashen sky, that had appeared to be receding, crept back above them, devouring the azure skyscape without warning. A piercing, cold breeze picked up, unseasonable in nature for Mexico this or any time of year. Alexander paused as he felt an overwhelming sense of despair take hold of his being. He turned from Decker, whose muffled volley of questions had settled into the background of Alex's consciousness and raised his face towards the sullen sky. The effect verged on paralyzing, and he closed his eyes to the cold discourse within. Alex took note of the cries of some unknown species of bird in the distance, undoubtedly sending warnings of Mother Nature's impending onslaught to its fellow avian travelers. The creature's solitary cry augmented the dreary emotions swallowing his soul. As if on cue, the wind whispered and morphed into a roar, taking nips at Alex's face. The bellowing chill sent shivers down his neck and through his spine. The escalating sadness ensued, and he felt himself trapped in a downward spiral of emotional turmoil, the origins of which were of unknown provenance. He opened his eyes to gaze at the sky once more and found the darkness had intensified around them in mere seconds. The sun, which moments before had presented as a concentrated ring of silver fire, determined to scorch its way through the veil of clouds, was at last, vanquished.

"Alex?" Decker placed a hand on his shoulder, gripping tightly with concern. "Hey, you with me buddy?"

Alexander parted his lips, but no words escaped the vacant hole they fashioned. He was aphonic and forlorn; blackness crept into his vision like ink diffusing in water, and with it, panic revealed its gnashing teeth.

Alexander perceived the entire scene as if outside of his own body. In a dream-like state he watched as Decker's other hand swiftly took hold of his other shoulder. With a firm jerk, he spun Alex from his transfixed state, breaking the evil union that had developed between his soul and the sky.

"Snap out of it, man!" Decker implored, and he began to shake Alex violently.

The convulsive motions broke the spell and with it the solitary grasp that had taken him. Alexander's eyes regained focus on Decks's worried features. Alex lifted both arms under his friend's grasp and parted them from his shoulders with force. A snarl crept across his face as he stared at Decker. How could he, Alexander Storm, be nearly swept into the confines of oblivion with such little effort? The thought resonated and angered him deeply.

"Easy," Decker whispered again. "What's the deal, Alex?"

Alexander's anger raged red upon his face and he turned to look up at the tattered apartment building.

"It appears," he proclaimed turning back to Decker, "that I have under-estimated our enemy."

Decker looked somewhat puzzled.

"Bath—" Decker did not have the opportunity to finish the demon's name as Alexander lurched forward and cuffed an open palm against his friend's mouth.

"Shhh." Alex was close to Decker's face, his eyes burned with new-found knowledge, a revelation of the evil that could befall them if they did not tread carefully. "She already knows we are here."

Decker blinked in acknowledgement, and Alex relinquished his hold on his face. Remaining close, he stared at Decker, who was visibly chasing his own thoughts.

"This is an ancient and wise force, my friend," Alex spoke with an unwavering conviction of purpose. "Are you prepared for this battle? Is your *soul* prepared for this battle, William?"

Decker, without hesitation, nodded his head in both understanding and resolute partnership.

"You know me, old man." Decker smirked as he reached out and touched Alex's shoulder, "I would follow you into the very bowels of hell without hesitation."

Alexander smiled, but his face seemed shrouded in sadness as he started off toward the portentous building. Without looking back, he called out to Decker, "Good, 'cause that's exactly where we are headed."

82

SEVENTEEN YEARS EARLIER

As Alex and Decker ascended the winding staircase to the sixth floor, their ears were subjected to a bedlamatic assault of foul noises. Stifled, eerie laughter faded in and out around the duo. The oratory acrobatics beseeched their senses, at one moment the evil mirth was directly beside them, the next, a mile away. The preternatural disquiet steadily began to unnerve the pair as they climbed.

"Shall we recite a prayer, Alex?" Decker asked as he followed a step or two behind. "I have several which may be fitting."

"Such as which?" Alexander's voice was condescending at best. "Perhaps something along the lines of, 'God save your servant, who trusts in you,' etcetera?"

"Yeah," Decker responded with more than a spoonful of irritation at Alexander's tone. "Befitting? No?"

Alexander stopped and peered over his shoulder at Decker.

"No," Alexander emitted an abruptness which signaled to Decker his companions complete return from the void which had strained to overwhelm him. "This is not a goddamn movie." Alex turned and continued his trek onward. "Words will not chase away this demon." His voice did not waver. "You possess no sacerdotal hymns or sermons that can beseech the purveyor of the evil we are about to encounter." He continued, "you may as well brew it a cup of tea and call it Marvin for all the damage your words will do."

"What?" Decker paused his climb and snickered. "What the hell are you talking about Storm?"

Alex paused and lifted his head up, as if annoyed by the chatter.

"My point is, nothing you can say will rile the demon from this poor girl's soul. Nothing that can be recounted from any book or—"

Alexander stopped mid-sentence and sprinted up, hurdling two steps at a time. Decker took to chase, attempting to keep up with Storm.

"No words, yes," Alex excitedly announced again, "but perhaps Marvin's Tea is, in fact, the answer!"

"What?" exclaimed Decker, on Alexander's heels now as they reached the landing of the sixth floor, his chest heaving on the verge of breathlessness. "What tea? And who the fuck is Marvin?"

83

"I cannot express my thanks enough," the bearded man said, his thick South American accent filling the corridor. He extended a hand to Alexander as the two breathless visitors entered the dimly lit apartment. "When Father Quinn spoke of you, he seemed uncertain if you'd come."

The man's broken English was subtle, and his deep, earthy Spanish tones bellowed confidently, in sharp contrast to the uncertainty on his face. Alexander's eyes darted around the main sitting room of the apartment. Modestly decorated, but cleaner and more modern than he had expected from the building's menacing facade. He spotted several religious icons throughout the small area, including a dollar store picture of Christ on the far wall over the couch, a large wood and brass crucifix over the archway leading to another area of the apartment, and a tall statue of the holy Mary, serpent under foot, in the far-right corner of the room.

The laughter and chatter, which had plagued their movements outside the confines of the apartment, ceased as the bearded man shut the door behind them and walked back in front of his guests. There was nothing extraordinary, or foreboding for that matter, in the space before them.

There was, however, the smell. Alex knew that pungent aroma all too well. Decker knew of its origins as well. It turned their stomachs, and they shot glances of recognition at each other, their host, ignorant to their silent communication, was none the wiser. The putrid smell of sulfur, rot, feces, and piss. Asar had coined the term 'demon's cocktail' to describe the amalgam of odors, and a nervous laugh never failed to escape the old boy's mouth whenever he uttered it.

The man turned to face the duo and again extended a hand to each in nervous apprehension. Alex humored him, recognizing that the man's weary mind was concocting paranoid scenarios of behavior that would induce the pairs departure; such as the outlandish presumption that his inability to offer proper salutations may offend Alexander, and in-turn, he would demand their immediate exodus from the wretched apartment.

"Thank you," the man repeated over and over. "Thank you. Gracias."

Alexander made note of the salty water welling up in their host's eyes and swiftly broke away from the barrage of gratitude before the man became inconsolable. Alexander was well aware of what the man experiencing—he must have felt so lost, so alone, up until this point. Nowhere to turn, no one to confide in, no one to assist in his hellish existence. And although the bearded man had no way of knowing whether Alexander and Decker would be able to render any resolution to the matter at hand, at that juncture in time, it mattered not. For at that moment, the man was not alone. At that moment, he had friends in misery, he had amigos in his nightmare. At that moment, he had hope. And Alex knew hope, after all, was all one needed to quell a demon and dispatch it, kicking and screaming, back to its infernal origins.

"I am Alexander Storm," Alex said with a nod. "And this is my associate, William Decker."

The man smiled nervously back and forth between the two.

"Don't mind his appearance, Mister...?"

"Montalvo." He replied, extending his unsteady hand once again, "Captain Ricardo Montalvo."

84

SEVENTEEN YEARS EARLIER

Montalvo led Decker and Storm through the archway, passing under the wood and brass crucifix, past a small kitchen to the left and an equally modest bathroom to the right, and stopped just outside of the closed door at the end of the dimly lit hallway.

"The clerk told me these are the brightest bulbs available." Montalvo pointed to the light fixture on the ceiling above the door. "But it is always *oscuro*—always night here."

Montalvo reached for the door handle to his daughter's room. Alex snatched his arm away before his fingers could close around the knob.

"I prefer to not proceed blindly into the abyss, Captain," his tone was soothing and the look of shock produced by Alex's restraining action quickly subsided from their host's face. "Why don't we go back to the sitting room and talk a bit before venturing further?"

Montalvo nodded in agreement. He turned back and motioned for the pair to follow him back to the sitting room. Alex and Decker sat on the couch under the picture of Jesus, while Montalvo took what Decker surmised was "his" seat in an easy chair to their left. Folding his hands together, he leaned forward and waited for Alex to begin.

"So, Mr. Montalvo—" Alex began.

"Ricardo, please, sir."

"Yes, very good, Ricardo," Alex began again. "If you would, please paint us a portrait of the events leading us to this moment?"

Montalvo nervously rubbed his eyes. Alexander suspected it was a habitual movement at this point, soothing eyes that were far too tired and probably often puddled with welling tears. "Yes, please, I'll explain. My daughter, Anna, she is ten, you see." He stopped for a moment, hesitant to continue.

"Yes?" Alex prodded him on.

"About three month ago, she started to look sick, pale ... blanco. Her mother, God rest her soul," tracing the sign of the cross across instinctively and continued, "she died of the influenza over five years ago now. Anna started to look and act like her madre just before she passed on."

"How do you know it was the flu, Ricardo?" Decker asked.

"Huh?" Montalvo squirmed and squinted at Decker, but Alex encouraged him to ignore the inquiry for the time being and continue.

"I bring Anna to the doctor and they find nothing wrong, but she gets worse and worse. She cannot get out of bed, and she will not eat or wash."

Ricardo paused and took a deep breath. "Then the other things begin."

"Go on," Alex assured him. "We are listening."

"First, she say horrible, ugly things about me, about her madre, about herself. Then she begin to change to look different. She like skin and bones." He paused again, and almost in tears, he said, "She look dead in her eyes, in her face."

There was another pause as Montalvo collected himself and continued his narrative in slightly broken English.

"I pray, I go to the church, I ask God to help me—"

"Who watches the child when you go to church?" Alexander interrupted. "Or to work, for that matter?"

"Sí, sí." The man shook his head. "My wife's hermano, Enrique, would come, but after what happened, he comes no more. I have not been to command in over a month. I don't think I have work there anymore."

"Go on," Alexander pressed.

"He fell asleep, right there on the couch. I was at work. He said he dream of Mary—of the Virgin Mary—she come to him and tell him he must..." Ricardo paused again. "He must kill my Anna!"

"Ricardo, I know this is difficult, but please continue."

"Sí, so he wakes himself and says she's there, right in front of him!"

"Anna?" Decker exclaims.

"No," Ricardo continued. "Mary, the holy mother," he said, pointing to the statue on the floor between them, "and she has a knife in her hand. She tell Enrique, 'Take the knife, slay the beast.' Enrique is afraid. He takes the knife and goes to Anna in her room. She was sleeping. She is coughing and breathing hard. Enrique says he pulls the covers back, and Mary was beside him, demanding him kill her now. Enrique cried. He cannot do it. She tells him he must, or she will rot in Hell, a whore for the demons, just like her madre."

Ricardo's body collapsed in on itself, breaking down in an empty, sullen moan. Alexander gave him a moment to gather his fortitude and then asked if he could go on.

"Sí," Ricardo replied. "I came home, and I don't see Enrique and I hear crying from Anna's room, so I run back there. I find Enrique; he has the knife up in air. I knocked him to floor. He doesn't fight, and he cries, asking what has happened. We sit on floor, and he tells me the tale. When he finish, we stand, and I turn and Anna is sitting up in bed the whole time, staring at us, eyes wide open. It was evil, not Anna. Something else, I tell you."

Ricardo stood up and began to pace. "Her eyes made my blood run cold, Mr. Storm." He halted in front of Alexander, "like she knew something, like she caught us."

His words sent chills traversing over Decker's limbs as he visualized the all too familiar penetrative gaze of the which Ricardo spoke.

"Is there more, Ricardo?"

"Yes, Enrique tell me of the Mary statue, so I run out to see, and there I find at her feet," he said as he turned and pointed to the effigy, "right there I find the paper with the word, the name—"

Alexander sprung up and placed his pointer finger against his lips.

"No need to announce it to world, my friend," he instructed Ricardo.

"Sí. So that's when I ask Enrique to please find Father Quinn. He comes by the next day and Anna is very ill. She is sick, and I must clean her, and Father Quinn wait in here for me."

Ricardo's eyes widened as he took his seat again, the force of emotional gravity pulling him to the chair.

"When I come from Anna's room, Father Quinn was not in here." Ricardo, his mind clearly working into a fervor, sprung up and dashed to the apartment door. Sliding the security lock, he flung the door open and pointed to a spot on the floor right on the other side of the threshold.

"He's out there—on the other side, and he is staring at me Mr. Storm. He is afraid, Mr. Storm. I say, 'Why are you out there? Come back in.' He says 'no, I cannot. I was told to leave.' I say 'by who?' He points to the holy mother and says '*Her* Ricardo. Mary told me to leave or *rot here forever.*'"

Ricardo continued, attempting to calm his tone, "I speak to him at the door. He says he does not know the word on the paper I show him, the word Enrique tell him, and he looked in all his books and the Bible. He find nothing. I say 'I am desperate. You must help Anna.'"

Pausing once again, Ricardo took a deep breath, his eyes filled with torment and confusion, "That's when Father Quinn think for a moment, and he says, 'I know someone who may be able to help you—Alexander Storm.'"

Fatigued from his recitation, Ricardo shut and locked the door and made his way back to his chair. The momentary peace that reflected in his expression, spawned by the promise of assistance, was quickly shattered as the evil sound of child's laughter echoed from down the hall.

An air of confidence permeated Alexander's demeanor and he rose from the couch, walked to Montalvo, and placed a comforting hand on his shoulder.

"Well," Alexander offered, "even though Quinn didn't recognize the name on the paper, I am pleased he knew my name."

Ricardo nodded and allowed a strained smile to form in the corner of his mouth. Turning to address Decker, Alexander crossed his arms and arched an eyebrow at his companion.

"Perhaps Father Quinn should expand his reading to include *The Lesser Key of Solomon*, what say you William?"

Decker smiled at the archaic reference and rose to Alexander's side.

"I take it you are prepared for battle old friend?"

Decker nodded in agreement, yet his words were contradictory. "Nope, let's get on with it."

"Magnificent!" Alexander walked past Decker, ignoring completely the sarcasm radiating from his words and headed down the hallway. "Seize the statute of Mary, and join me in the darkness."

85

In a display of exaggerated movements, General Miguel rubbed his neck with the palms of his hands. His eyes were still transfixed on Sam, casting her an evil glance as he worked at his neck. The bulk of the cartel soldiers had receded back into the jungle, and neither Lobo nor the others could see them anymore. Sam was still quite shaken, and she trembled ever so slightly as adrenaline continued to pulse through her veins. Her eyes darted from side to side and came to rest on her group of friends huddled together at the back of the plane. She jumped down from the fallen jet door and started toward them.

"Come on!" she yelled. "We're on a schedule here, remember Kate?"

Kate relinquished Abigail's hand and rose to her feet. Dusting the jungle dirt and debris from her jeans, she turned to Keith and motioned for him to get up.

"Mr. Storm is counting on us," she coaxed, "and I've come to believe we're on a mission of great magnitude here."

Keith was up and by Kate's side. He looked over to find Lobo still engaging the bearded man in conversation. Mister fat dirty white shirt had joined the two and stood several yards behind his superior.

"Ugh." Abigail huffed while nursing her bumps and bruises. She had taken quite a few falls and tumbles in the last few minutes, more than half of which she could not recall. Hearing her labor, Keith leaned over and extended a helping hand.

"Come on, kiddo," he said, hoisting her to her feet.

"Thanks." Abigail smiled. She smiled a huge, joyous smile that Keith found unsettling. What Keith didn't realize was that Abigail had held tight to both his and Kate's hands, and no bad mojo had rushed her senses. She was smiling because her new friends, her new companions in this quest, were pure of heart. She could not remember the last time she had been in contact with an adult and not had some dark vision of their past overtake her. She smiled and turned to Samantha, who had arrived at her side.

Now this one may be another matter altogether, she thought with an inner laugh.

"This is crazy shit, guys," Sam said. "Cray-cray all the way."

Abigail chuckled at Sam's word which formed an unintentional response to her thoughts.

"Right on cue, Samantha," said Abigail with a giggle.

"Huh?" Sam was perplexed by her statement and felt as though she had missed something.

"What did you guys come up with? Some kind of inside joke in the thirty-seconds I was away from you?" Sam paused. "Ya know, risking my life? For the group? For you?"

"Relax, Sam," Kate said as she brushed her arm and walked past her. "I have no idea what is amusing Abi so much, but it has nothing to do with me."

Kate continued towards Lobo, her navigation of the uneven jungle ground impeding her progress slightly and making it look as though she had had one drink too many.

"You okay, partner?" Keith called out as he sped past the other two and jogged up to Kate's side.

"I got you," he said as he placed his hand under her elbow. She stopped and yanked it away. His eyes widened at the look on her face.

"Sorry," he said before she could open her mouth.

Kate's annoyance at his behavior turned to something else as she squinted her eyes.

"Take it easy on him there, resting bitch face." Sam joked as she walked past Kate to join Lobo.

"What?" Kate bellowed, clearly hurt by the comment.

"She's kidding," Keith stated matter-of-factly and turned to join the others.

"She's calling me a bitch," Kate whispered to herself. "Kettle black much, huh?"

"Stay together, *please*, Kate," Lobo called out.

"Yeah, yeah," Kate replied as she headed toward the group. Her feet stopped dead in their tracks, and she snapped her head around to the jungle behind and across from the plane. She was sure she had heard something, and all of Montalvo's bandits had returned to the cover of the trees on the other side of the airstrip, closest to where she stood.

Her eyes gazed, unblinking, into the green blur of the jungle. The hairs on the back of her neck began to rise and tingle. Her body's response to a threat she could not identify, or pinpoint, made her heart race; she was sure she was being watched from beyond the tree line of the jungle. She could feel it. Somewhere, set back in the overgrowth, a pair of eyes were burning holes into her. Her fear was real, and her gut told her she needed to react to it.

"Come on, let's get out of here!" she called out as she turned and ran toward her friends. "I've got a bad feeling. Let's move."

"Working on it, okay?" Lobo responded nervously as she arrived at his side. He lifted his hand, gesturing to Montalvo. "We're working on it!"

Montalvo stared at Kate a moment. "You are very beautiful, miss," he offered a reassuring smile. "You remind me of my daughter, Anna."

"Thank you," Kate replied as Montalvo returned his attentions to Lobo, as if reinforcing the notion that complimenting a woman's beauty would somehow silence her annoying interruptions and questions—or any free thought, for that matter.

"As I was saying," Montalvo continued, "Mr. Storm and Mr. Decker did me a great service many years ago, risking their own well-being for my family. I owe Alexander an enormous debt of gratitude. I owe them both."

Keith responded, "We are here under Storm's direction to stop something evil from happening."

"Mr. Storm must have immense faith in you to leave such an important task in your hands." Montalvo paused in thought. "Your plane is down, no changing that anytime soon."

"We don't need it," Lobo advised raising his hand to emphasize his words.

"Then tell me what you need, Mr. Lobo," Montalvo took a drag from his musky cigar. "Tell me, and if it is in my power, it shall be done."

Lobo smirked and turned sideways toward his friends. "We need to get to El Castillo at the Chichen Itza ruins, and we need to get there *now*, before the sun sets."

"Ah, some wicked business is at hand, I'm sure," he said, his deep Spanish accent shrouding his words. "I shall get you there safe and sound in no time. We are familiar with the back roads and secret passes through this jungle."

Lobo nodded as Montalvo let out a sharp whistle. Within seconds, a soldier emerged from the jungle's overgrowth and awaited El Gato's instructions. Montalvo, without looking up to confirm anyone had responded, yelled out several commands in Spanish, at which the soldier turned and ran into the jungle.

"Can you have men get there before us and clear the ruins?" Lobo was trying to think like Alex might—not an easy task by any stretch. "We need unfettered access, and I don't want tourists or workers there impeding us or getting hurt."

Montalvo turned toward the jungle with Miguel and the others following close. As they walked to the edge of the jungle's clearing, Kate could not help but peer back over her shoulder several times. She still felt the eyes upon her from the other side of the airstrip; the dread of what was out there was overwhelming, and her fear of the unknown consumed her thoughts.

"I feel it, too," Abigail leaned in close to her. "Come on, let's double time it away from this place."

As the small group entered the jungle, the low hum of personnel carriers and jeeps greeted them. Montalvo's men hustled about the vehicles, which were barely visible up ahead.

"They will get us there safely, and they will clear the archaeological site completely before our arrival."

Montalvo walked to the rear door of the first personnel carrier. A short soldier steadied himself and opened the door for his boss.

"Come, come now." He stepped aside to let the others pass into the truck. Abigail, Kate, Keith, and Sam, one at a time, climbed up the large metal steps and grabbed an exterior handle on the armored infantry vehicle, hoisting themselves through the door and onto one of the spacious seats that lined the interior of the vehicle. Lobo was last, and as he was about to pop himself up and in, Montalvo reached out and grounded his movements.

"Amigo," he whispered. "I will get you to Chichen Itza safely. I will clear the site so your deeds, the ones I prefer to know nothing about, can to be done in secrecy, and I will guard the perimeter and extract you when you are ready."

"But..." Lobo felt it coming.

"But I will not bear witness to those deeds, and you are on your own in the site." He moved in closer for effect. "I will get you there and out safely, but whatever happens in between, well, that? That is on you."

Decker nodded and returned to entering the vehicle.

"One more thing, Captain," Montalvo called up to Lobo.

"What's that?" Lobo paused to listen.

"Let us pray that whatever has been tracking us from the other side of the jungle does not pursue us to Chichen. Sí?"

86

Alexander extended his hand toward the door handle of Anna's bedroom. His long, slender fingers paused with no more than a sliver of air separating his skin from the tarnished brass knob. Pausing for a moment, he turned and looked over his shoulder at Decker, who stood closely behind him.

"Prepare yourself. She will sense the peril to her existence, and she will act quickly."

Decker nodded.

"Steel your mind," he admonished. "The demon will prey on you there. Your resistance is paramount to our success ... understood?"

"I'm ready, Alex," Decker raised the statue of Mary up with both hands. "If all else fails, I'll hit it with Mother Mary. This thing is heavy."

Alexander smirked. He reflected on this quality in William. His ability to outwardly make light of a very "heavy" situation. Exuding calm and confidence to those around him. It was a fine quality, one of several which offset his oft vice-like tendencies.

Alex returned his focus to the doorknob. Closing his eyes and gathering his breath, as if about to take a great leap of faith, he clenched his hand on the handle and spun it open. Confidently, his shoulders snapped back as his stature and physique appeared to grow before Decker's eyes.

"Here we go," Decker whispered. "Once more unto the breach and all that."

Alexander nodded, appreciating the Shakespearian reference, and pushed the door open. Without peering into the room, he took several steps in, looking at his feet until he saw the frame of the girl's bed come into view.

"Are you in?" he asked without looking up.

The only sound—giggling. Bone chilling giggling.

"Close the door behind you!" he ordered.

Alex could feel the hot breath on his forehead now, the smell of rot and decay wrestling itself into his nostrils.

"Uh, Alex?" Decker was sputtering. The degree of fear in his voice made Alex's spine convulse slightly. Decker knew better than to use Alex's name in front of the demon. And he had obviously come into the room eyes forward—another amateur mistake.

"The door!" Alex hissed.

The breathing was unrelenting against Alex's head. It was fast and steady. It had weight, as if a hand was pressed against his head. It was, Alex thought to himself, a parlor-like display.

"Great. Another amateur," the words inadvertently escaping his lips.

Click.

Decker had finally closed the door.

"*I shut the door*, as your companion appears otherwise engaged." The words were garbled as if uttered under water. "You can look up now, pilgrim," the demon instructed.

Alex remained stoic and lifted his head to meet the demon. He saw a child's feet first, bruised and laden with sores. Continuing his eyes ascent, he came upon her white nightgown, soiled with stains of urine, feces, blood, and vomit. Alex noted in disgust that the vestures resembled an overdone movie prop. Finally, the young girl's long black hair came into view. It was tangled and matted, with chunks of strands missing as if a child had taken scissors to it. Alex paused for a moment within a moment.

"Look upon eternal night, pilgrim!" The demon's voice demanded an audience with Alexander's eyes.

Alexander obeyed the inevitable and observed the horrific plague of sores the demon had let loose upon Anna's face. Split and oozing skin, bruised and blackened. Her small, soft lips were bloated and cracked. The inner demon's grotesque, smiling mouth was open to expose the poor child's teeth which sent uncontrollable shivers through Alexander's body. They were decaying, festering with puss and filling the air with their foul odor.

Finally, their eyes locked. Sunken black holes. Anna's pupils dilated so wide that the whites of her eyes had vanished. The demon giggled and tilted its head slightly. Its wretched tongue darted from corner to corner as if preparing for a long-awaited feast. The two remained locked on each other for what seemed like an eternity, but was, in truth, mere seconds.

"Boo!" The demon lurched forward at Alexander, lifting her hands in a menacing pre-reach position, playing with his fear and amusing herself at the same time.

Alexander remained motionless. William Decker, however, cried out like a small child.

The demon fell back into the mattress with a satisfied snicker. She had been successful in her plight to terrify, and, although Storm remained characteristically nonreactive, Decker's reaction was prize enough. Alex remained focused on the small child's body as traces of the demon's true voice could be heard interwoven with the giggles of a little girl. The overall effect was quite unnerving, and the sound became physically painful, to which Alexander shook his head.

"Alexander Storm!" The demon's face lost all signs of the pleasure it had achieved. "Thought perhaps you had lost your nerve. Did you get my note? Knew you would come. Knew I could make you *come.*"

"Not likely," Alexander quickly retorted recognizing the she-demon's double entendre. He relinquished his view of the girl momentarily in order to surveil the rest of his surroundings. The bed was pressed into the far corner of the room so the top and far side were against the wall. The room's light came through a shuttered window on the back wall to the right of the bed, and from a lamp on the floor without a shade. Alex could hear the faint buzz of a bulb reaching the end of its life. The lamp sat beside the only other furniture in the room—a solitary chair. Taking several steps back, Storm quickly moved from the foot of the bed to the side.

"Not likely, Bathin."

A smile crept across the girl's face. She teased her mouth with a finger and began to pout. She slid her knees up in front of her and rocked her legs open and closed under her nightgown. Alexander slowly blinked as if the show was tiresome and trying his patience.

Decker, clearly disturbed by the display, attempted to shift toward Alex. The floor let out a massive creak as he took his first step, and Bathin's head spun toward the sound with a mechanical precision that stopped him dead in his tracks.

"Alexander Storm, my true love!" the Demon announced. "And what is this? You brought another boy for me to play with!"

Decker said nothing and veered his eyes from the evil stare.

"What have you got there in your hands, boy?" Bathin demanded.

Alexander stepped forward, attempting to put himself between the evil entity possessing the girl and William. The demon snapped her head at his movement.

"What are your plans here, Bathin?" his spoke in an even and direct tone in an attempt to divert the demon's attention. "Hasn't the poor child suffered enough? Set her free and move on before the host dies."

"Plans?" the demon asked. "Why, you and I are to wed! Consummate our nuptials, no?"

Alexander sighed. "Again, not likely."

Bathin snarled and snapped her legs shut so hard Alexander was sure he could make out the sound of the girl's brittle kneecaps splintering beneath her dying skin.

Suddenly, the little girl's voice returned. "I have suffered so much, Mr. Storm," she said. "Papa took all my dollies and toys away." She began to mock cry, but then, through her teeth, she seethed, "All because I wouldn't touch his cock."

"Really?" Alexander rolled his eyes, unimpressed.

Bathin sat up and swung her legs over the side of the bed.

"You don't believe me?"

"When opening your mouth lies clamor to climb upon lies." His eyes sharpened on the demon, fearless and confident. "You are a miserable creature. A fallen angel." Alexander paused, then added, "And I fear you are a bit naïve."

"Naïve?" Bathin spat back.

Alexander turned to Decker. "My friend, have you ever heard, in all your travels and existence, such a silly thing as a naïve demon?"

"What?" Decker had lost his ability to respond with anything other than a simple word.

"What game is this, Storm?" Bathin slowly lifted and levitated several meters over the bed.

"What's in your hands, filth?" The demon levitated toward Decker. She snapped both arms backward, and the shutters on the window behind her flew from their perch against the panes. Light, still muted as if squeezing through the finest of silk, shot into the room and upon Decker. The statue of Mary, squeezed tightly in Decker's arms now, became visible to the Demon. She shot backward across the room and rose up to the corner above the bed. Her eyes were no longer black holes of emptiness. They had come alive with a flickering orange glow straight from Hell.

"Smart...filthy...pilgrim," Bathin sputtered at Alexander. "But it is *you* who have underestimated *me*."

With that, the room came to life. Bursts of freezing wind followed by burning rain lashed against the duo, smacking their skin like a leather whip. The sky outside the exposed window darkened unnaturally, and what was left of the room's furnishings vibrated and jolted about.

"Señor Storm!"

Anna's father banged at the door to the bedroom.

"What's going on, Storm?"

"Yes!" the demon screamed out. "Perfect! Let's let Papa in!"

Without thought or hesitation, Alexander grabbed the top of the chair beside him.

"Step back *now*, kind sir!" he ordered Decker.

With one fluid motion, he lifted the chair and whipped it toward the door as the knob began to turn. Alexander's aim was perfect. It landed with precision against the door, as if directed by some unseen force, and wedged itself between the handle and the floor, preventing entrance into the room.

"How the fuck?" Decker stared at Storm.

"Not now, kind sir." Alexander grimaced at his companion as he darted about the room, and all at once was at Decker's side.

"Mother Mary, may I?" he toyed, reaching out and relieving Decker of the statue.

"Filthy pilgrim!" The demon stood solidly atop the bed and warned, "the immaculate whore cannot save your souls." The seething vitriol was almost overpowering—but not to Alexander.

"Now sir," he implored his companion, paying no mind to the demon, "buy me some time, will you?"

Alexander knelt on the floor and laid the statue down in front of him. He quickly reached into the deep caverns of his long overcoat and pulled a metallic object from its recesses.

Decker's head briefly whipped back and forth between the two embattled warriors and stopped on Bathin, who had begun to transform before them. Her child-like features stretched and contorted as the figure of a woman emerged from the vestiges. A magnificent beauty, long black locks of hair flying in the satanic wind that surrounded her. Her garb was torn and falling over her voluptuous body as she floated effortlessly toward Decker.

"Make love to me, William." Her voice was soft and angelic. "Take me. Take me now. I will bring you such pleasure, the likes of which you've never known, that you never even knew existed."

Decker's eyes widened and he looked back at Alex again. He could now make out the metallic object in his hands—a small round case of some kind. Alexander was employing a fair amount of force in an effort to twist the lid off. He paused just long enough to take stock of Decker who was clearly enthralled by the womanly manifestation of the harlot.

"She's a bloody demon!" he snapped at William. "Get your wits about you, will you?"

The room's cacophony increased, and the small lamp flew across the floor right at Alex. He dodged the distraction without even looking up and snapped the top off the round metal case. Decker responded to the crash of the lamp behind him and looked back at Alex, who was now shaking the contents of the metal case out onto the floor. Decker felt a soft finger brush his cheek. She was at his side.

"What are you waiting for, William?" Bathin's lips were warm at his ear. "Fuck me."

Decker stepped to the side in an effort to escape the succubus's touch.

"What are you up to, Storm?" he demanded. "What the hell is that?"

"Marvin's Tea!" Storm shouted as he lurched forward and grabbed the statue of Mary off the floor.

"What?"

"Marvin's Tea!" he shouted over the wicked din, looking up at Decker. "If you don't mind, I'll explicate a bit later!"

Alexander, momentarily apprising the situation between Decker and the Demon, quickly recognized his friend's resolve against the temptress's seductions was failing. He studied the physique of the hell spawned beauty and noted the ethereal undulation toying with her features. She was beginning to morph again into something much more dangerous—he needed just a bit more time.

"William!" Alex called to Decker. "Close your eyes, my friend."

"What the fuck?"

"William Decker!" Alexander drastically emphasized. "*Close your eyes!*"

The tone of Alexander's voice carried a mystical weight and, questioning Alex no more, he snapped his eyes shut.

"Good," he continued. "Now, as I recall, you had some verses, some stanzas, you felt could prove useful!" Alex paused for effect. "Begin them now!"

Alexander rose to his feet, statue in hand. Raising his arms high above his head, he slammed the statue to the ground. The ceramic exploded like a bomb, its splintering fragments scattering about his feet.

"What the hell?" Decker peeked through one eye to see Mary in pieces below Storm.

"Shut your damn eyes man!"

The demon let out a wail and began to circle Decker.

It screeched, "Open your eyes! Open them and peer upon your queen!"

Decker clamped down his lids even tighter. He could feel Bathin's fingers entering his mind, trying to pry open his vision.

"I will make you a prince..."

"In my name," Decker took a deep breath as the words flowed like holy daggers, "so they cast out demons, they shall speak in new tongues, they shall take up serpents, and if they drink any deadly poison, it shall in no wise hurt them."

Bathin, sensing a losing battle in Decker, turned her attentions to Alexander, who was scrambling around on the floor, passing his hands under and over the sharp shards of ceramic fragments. He was spreading the pieces out, trying to detect something. His fingers and palms were tattered and bloody as he located his objective a few feet in front of him.

"Open the door now, goddamn it!" Anna's father continued to wail and smash against the heavy wood frame, and Alex could see the chair approaching the end of its function.

Alexander's hand darted forward at the small velvet satchel he had located amongst the ruins of the statue. Bathin rose in the air above him, and with a blinding fury, clapped her hands together. The room went pitch black.

"Lights out, my friend!" he yelled to Decker, who opened his eyes and dropped to his knees. "Continue if you will, *please.*"

"They shall lay hands on the sick, and they shall recover. The serpent is only brought into the holy sanctum, and only handled..." Decker continued his prayers as flashes of light, akin to the strobes of lightning, began to fill the room in an apparent response to his words.

Decker, assisted by the flashes of light, spied Alex swipe an object from the rubble on the floor. He watched the demon bounce around the room with distorted and macabre movements. He noted his friend was paying no mind to her malevolent display, and it offered him some degree of solace.

"A bag of bones," Alexander exclaimed holding the small bag up. "Or in this case, a bag of stones—eighteen, to be exact."

He tore loose the string that cinched the bag closed and retrieved the open metallic case from his pocket. Placing it in his left palm, he turned the bag over, spilling its contents into the metal box. Decker could discern the clanking sound of stones followed by sharp cracks of thunder. Alex dropped the bag to his side in response to the lightning induced intermittent visions of the demon charging him.

"Please finish!" Alexander commanded turning to Decker. "I believe your words are my lantern in the darkness!"

"Of the holy ghost, of the holy spirit!" Decker yelled as Alex retrieved the cover and placed it softly atop the round case. Another burst of light filled the room as a thunderous rumble threatened to shake the very structure to the ground. The demon was upon him.

"Finish, please!" Alexander Storm's voice trailed off as he slammed his right hand down on the top of the metal box.

"Speak directly to the disciple!"

With the sealing of the lid, Bathin's spectral charge instantly began to dematerialize before them. Her body halted in levitated suspension, she writhed and twisted in screams of agony.

"Fool!" The demon cried. "You should have joined me! I would have loved you for a thousand years, Storm," she hissed as she faded. "You cannot even fathom what you have lost!"

The small box took on a life of its own as it began to glow red hot in Alex's hands. But he did not relinquish his grip. The odor of searing flesh filled the room, and Decker could see the escalating pain in Alexander's face.

"You are incapable of love, serpent," his words came resolute from between his clenched teeth. *Now get in the box!*"

With the echoes of his final words still clinging to the darkness that engulfed the room, Bathin vanished. The oppressive air that had seized their senses abruptly gave way to a flood of amber sunlight and an almost graceful atmosphere of calm. Alex looked down at his ravaged hand. The metal box had already begun to cool, no longer exhibiting any traces of the fiery glow that had threatened to consume not only the vessel, but Alexander's hand as well. Lifting the box up to his ear, he shook it with a short, violent burst and smiled at William.

"Marvin's Tea." He winked at Decker whose face remained plastered with an amalgam of terror and disbelief.

A soft moan from the bed snapped Decker back to reality. Turning towards the sound, all vestiges of fear left his face and were swiftly replaced with signs of hope. There, laying as clean and new as the breaking morning, was Anna.

"Get the door, William." Alexander lifted his chin and motioned him toward the door; it was quiet on the other side.

Ricardo shoved his way past Decker, paying him no mind, and charged at Alexander.

"What the hell have you done?" His words, fueled by the intense anger that was consuming him, were cut short as he spied Anna on the bed. Her transition had been absolute and was immediately evident to her father. He rushed to her side, embracing her tightly in his arms.

"Papa?" She stirred softly, opening her eyes to her father's hugging and kissing. "Papa! Easy Papa!" He ignored his daughter's pleas, overwhelmed with emotion as a mixture of tears and laughter emanated from his exhausted being. The nightmare was over. Morning had come, and Ricardo had no intention of halting his barrage of affection.

Alexander bowed his head slightly. "We will leave you to it, then."

Neither Ricardo nor Anna responded to Alex; they were lost in the euphoria of the moment.

"What's the box?" Decker demanded. "What's the tea? What the fuck?"

"William," Alexander chided, "a gentleman has no use for such malediction."

"A gentleman I'm not," Decker's voice still held traces of the ordeal.

Alexander motioned for him to join him in the other room as the two walked to the front of the apartment. Exhausted from the encounter, they both gave in and dropped onto the sofa.

"Explain!" Decker finally shouted, unable to stand his companions silence any longer.

"Okay, okay!" Alexander laughed.

"First, the box."

"Yes," Alex replied. "Marvin's Tea."

He withdrew the tin from his jacket where he had placed it and held it out for him to examine. Decker noted the blistered and oozing state of his friend's palm and fingers.

"This box was manufactured by Marvin & Son's, Import Export in 1786, London. It is made of solid silver."

"Ah," Decker's eyes bore signs of understanding.

"Yes, then, solid silver through and through. The ornate dragon design on the cover caught my eye many years ago, and although Marvin's Tea has not been in business for quite some time, I still use the box to carry a serving or two of my own blends."

Decker nodded. "Go on," he prodded, hoping to keep Storm on track before he sidestepped into a tangent about tea leaves.

"I surmised the statue of Mary was the issue," he continued. "Everything appeared to have gotten underway after Ricardo acquired it. Now, since we knew the demon's name, and I had extensively researched same, I was aware she used stones to conjure her black magic. The stones are in fact her vehicle for manifestation. They are also capable of inducing portals through space, but not time," he quickly noted.

"Of course not," Decker bantered, "who ever heard of rocks that can propel you through *both* space ... and time."

Storm tossed his friend an ever-so-slight glance of annoyance and continued, "I took an educated guess that the stones were in the statue, and I knew if I could obtain them and seal them in silver in the presence of the demon, I could trap her—*indefinitely*."

Alexander afforded Decker a moment to digest the information. He fished around in his pockets again and withdrew a scrap of folded paper. Giving it a snap, he opened it and handed it to Decker. William gazed down at the notes, reading the words to himself. 'The eighteenth spirit of Lucifer is Bathin. Characterized as a powerful duke of Hell, she is said to often manifest with a serpent's tail, galloping upon a pale horse. The demon is said to be knowledgable in the use of herbs and precious stones; and she possesses the power to transport men from point-to-point. Bathin was granted power over thirty legions of demons. Her seal and sigil are unique and as magnificent as the beauty of her human form.'

"Where'd ..." Decker began?

"Dictionnaire Infernal," Alexander offered, "J. Collin de Plancy."

"Of course," William mused, although he was quite familiar with compendium as well.

"Trapped *for now*, huh?" Decker folded the paper and handed it back to Alex. "Transport men from country to country? Interesting, no?"

Alexander placed the paper back in his coat. "Exceedingly."

Alexander rose when he heard Anna's father approaching from down the hall and signaled for Decker to join him.

"My God, Mr. Storm!" Ricardo cried out in tears as his large arms engulfed Alexander. It was an embrace not to be refused. It was the embrace of an extremely grateful father, and it was not to be denied.

Alexander acknowledged Ricardo's seemingly never-ending thanks and praise as he offered Decker a similar embrace.

"I am a humble, out of work policeman, but if ever there is anything I am capable of...please ...please! I am your servant."

"Don't start down that road, Ricardo." Decker laughed, "Pretty sure a similar promise is what got me here today. Mr. Storm is like the paranormal 'Godfather,'" he winked.

"There is something." Alex moved closer to Ricardo, ignoring his companions lighthearted exchange. "Perhaps you can help."

"Anything!"

"Yes, well, can you tell me about the merchant who sold you the Virgin Mary statue—"

"Gave me," Ricardo interrupted. "He gave me the statue."

"Of course he did," Alex replied dryly. "Where can we find him?"

Ricardo went over to the small table next to his reclining chair and retrieved a pen and sheet of paper. Leaning on the table, he jotted down an address and handed it to Alexander.

"It's only a few blocks over," he said, feeling useful already, even if he had no idea why.

87

SEVENTEEN YEARS EARLIER

Alexander and Decker walked in virtual silence for the entire five or six blocks to the address Anna's father had given them.

"How's your hand doing?" Decker finally broke the silence.

Alexander held his right hand up to illustrate the fine bandage and dressing job Ricardo had done.

"It's fine," Alex replied, "although I fear the memory of this day will be embedded in my hand for the remainder of my days."

Decker shook his head. "Well, at least it was a dragon on the top of the case." He paused for a moment. "I can think of a lot of worse things to have an impression of on the palm of your hand."

"Ha," Alexander replied. "Very good—"

His words were cut short as they arrived at their destination. Alex recognized the tattered red canopy Ricardo had described as hanging over the street vendor's wares.

"Well, there's that." Decker walked past Alex and under the red overhang. The area was in shambles. Tables and shelves were overturned and tossed. The space was completely abandoned.

"Looks like somebody left in a hurry." Decker continued to apprise the remnants of tables and carts, hoping to discern a clue to the space's prior occupants' identity. "You think Ricardo tipped him off that we were coming?"

Alex paused on the outskirts of the red canopy. "Not at all."

Decker walked out to join Alex.

"Nothing." He huffed. "The place is sanitized."

"Good show," Alexander said to no one in particular, "but our paths shall cross one day merchant, and I will hold you to answer for your crimes."

Alexander turned to leave. "Until then..."

88

"How are you faring, William?" Alexander leaned over his friend who lay tattered and bruised on the bed beside him. Decker's eyes sprang open, and his face became animated with signs of joy at the sight of his friend. Alexander reached down with his right hand and clasped the top Decks's hand in a firm embrace.

"I'm fine, Alexander." Decker attempted to use Storm's grasp to hoist himself up in the bed.

"Easy, there," Alex said as he dropped his own shoulder towards the mattress, sending Decker back into his pillow. "Easy, now."

Decker grimaced as he settled back into his puffed-up cluster of pillows. Suddenly, an air of recall washed across his face.

"Anika!?"

"Yes." Alex smiled as he turned his head towards the room's entrance. At that moment, Anika rushed through the archway, arriving at the other side of Decker's bed. Alexander noted a glossiness in her eyes as she reached for Decker. He relinquished his grasp on Decker's hand and took a step back from the bed. Anika had worked her arms around Decker and was in the process of complicating his injuries.

"Oh, God!" She sprang up from Decker. "Am I hurting you? I'm so sorry!"

"I'm fine," he sighed. "Come here and hurt me some more, will ya."

Anika laughed through the start of a cry, fending it off with a sniffle.

"You are not fine," she said, rubbing his shoulder. "Look at you!"

"How are your friends, Anika?"

Anika's lips transformed into a sullen frown as she shook her head back and forth.

"Both of them?"

"I'm afraid so, William." Alexander jumped in to save Anika the obvious pain of explanation.

"I'm so sorry, Anika." Decker's face, bruised as it was, twisted even more with inner pain. "It's my fucking fault." His chest lifted with a heavy breath, exhaling he said, "I should have never involved them...or you for that matter."

"Stop it, William." Anika's voice was compassionate and unwavering. "Casualties of war, as I have come to understand." She looked up at Alexander. "And a rather important conflict, to say the least."

Anika rose and reached out to touch Decker's face. Her hand softly clasped his scruffy cheek, and she gazed down at him. At that moment, Decker wondered when exactly it was that he had stepped into that great big pile of shit. There surely had to be a catch somewhere. Some bombshell she would drop on him, some unpalatable past or subversive present. Decker reached up and cupped his hand over hers. He didn't care. Right now, she was perfect. Right now, all he felt was love and admiration for this strong, beautiful woman by his side.

"Well, I don't mean to intrude on your moment," Alex said. He uncrossed his arms and was about to walk toward the room's exit when Asar, who was observing from the shadows with Serket, stepped forward and placed a firm hand on Alex's chest.

"You have a moment, Alexander?" It was an instruction more than a question, and as this was a rare intrusion by the old Egyptian, he was tempted to comply.

Instead Alexander smiled and tapped Asar on the shoulder. "No, you hopeless romantic, I do not possess one extra moment." He turned back to Decker. "And William, more than anyone, can appreciate that."

"Absolutely," Decker blurted out, attempting to rise up again, this time with the assistance of his bent elbows. "Where are we headed?"

"Ha ha! You, my friend, are headed back to sleep so that you may heal—"

"Come on, Alex," he interrupted. "I'm—"

"I know, I know. You are fine."

"Right!"

"Do me a service, will you Decker?"

"Anything," William smiled, awaiting his instructions.

"*Get* fine," Alexander toyed. "You *are* needed, but I need you whole."

"Wait," Decker said to Alex, who had turned to Serket.

"What?" Alexander didn't look back, however.

There was a brief moment of silence. "Nothing," Decker said, finally acknowledging the seriousness of his present condition.

"Thank you. We have many a dark passageway to venture down in this journey, William. And I will need you in peak operating condition."

Asar turned and tapped Decker on the foot. "You rest. We will send for you when you are well."

"*We?*" Alex asked.

"What?" Asar acted as though the question had no meaning to him.

"*We* are going nowhere." Alexander's tone let them all know he was done explaining and had jumped the ship of reproach. "*I*, however, am going to Mexico." Reaching into his pants pocket, he grasped a chain and yanked a tattered silver pocket watch adorned with a tribal wolf into his hand. Depressing the winding button with his thumb, he popped the lid and exposed the watch face inside.

"And I have a little over an hour to get there!"

"Well, that's not happening, Alex." Serket stepped from the dark corner of the room.

"Quite the contrary, my dear," Alex said as he slid the watch back into his pocket. "It *is* happening. It must. And you will assist me."

"Go on," Serket said, smirking with intrigue. "Tell me how I can help you get halfway around the world in an hour's time, Alexander Storm."

"Very well." Alex nodded at her compliance, and more so at her lack of dallying him with questions and skepticism, although her voice was wrought with the sentiment.

"I will require a dark, private area," he began.

"Easy one," she smiled. "You're inside a mountain."

"Yes, I'm aware of where I am." He paused for a moment. "May I continue?"

"By all means. Continue Mr. Storm."

"Yes. I need a goodly amount of incense or herbs to burn," he said, and she nodded but remained silent. "But no sage, of course."

"Of course, Mr. Storm." Serket was toying now, taking pleasure in his restrained annoyance.

"A handful of candles and an offering of some kind, be it goat or sheep or whatever innocent creature you have lurking in your mountain."

"You going to kill it?" Serket stopped him.

"That's generally the end result of being a sacrificial offering." Alexander threw some of her own medicine back at her, and Decker laughed, grasping his ribs at his involuntary response to their banter.

Serket rolled one side of her lip up at Alexander, exposing some teeth.

"Very attractive." He jabbed back, although he was not jesting. "Oh, and one more crucial component, Serket," Alex said as he moved closer.

"Yes?"

"I will require a chalice of virgin's blood."

Serket lifted one eyebrow. "Really? Well, don't look at me!"

"Ha!" Alex blurted out, clearly more amused than he should be. "Kidding. Slaughter no virgins on my behalf." Alex clapped his hands together hard and began to walk toward the doorway. "I do require all the other items though. Immediately."

"What are you planning, Alexander?" Decker called out before Alex made it through the archway.

"Marvin's Tea!" he exclaimed without turning around, and he exited the room.

Decker shook his head. "Not this shit again."

89

Ricardo Montalvo silently watched Kate as she gazed out her window at the jungle landscape as it flashed by. Her hair blew softly in the breeze, and her eyes intermittently squinted as bursts of sunlight escaped through the dense overgrowth that surrounded their path. The ride was bumpy and uneven, and she steadied herself with both hands pressed down by her sides into the seat. Her presence seemed angelic and soft—innocent—and Ricardo wondered how such a creature could find herself in the middle of the Yucatan sharing a ride with him. El Gato. His thoughts turned to his own Anna and her innocence which had endured, even through her ordeal. He wondered where she was and what she may be doing. Did she marry? Did he have grandchildren? It had been so long since he had set his eyes upon her, since he had embraced her or touched her lovely face. He was dead to her, and for such a pure heart to have uttered those words, he knew they were true. He knew he would never see her again. For even though Alexander Storm had wrestled the evil from her soul that rainy afternoon in Mexico City, he did not insulate Ricardo's from the evils of the world. He was quite sure Storm would be very disappointed at the turn of events, the choices that had been made, that led a humble policeman down a dark path to become one of the most nefarious drug lords the world had even known. Ricardo was also fairly certain Storm was aware of his transformation into El Gato. The enigmatic man was tapped into the rivers and streams of evil that transverse the globe. He must surely be aware of the beast he had developed into.

Ricardo's thoughts were snatched away by the overwhelming feeling he was being watched. He broke his gaze from Kate and looked to his left to find Keith stoically locked on his face. Ricardo, sensing the reason, nodded respectfully and averted his eyes. Engaging the view from his own window instead, he raised his smoldering ember of a cigar and took a long drag. He relished the jungle in the morning. The often-elusive peace he would experience on rare occasions was accomplished by way of an amalgam of scents, sounds and colors. But, as usual, his respite was only momentary, as the silence of the passenger compartment was abruptly shattered by loud static bursts emanating from a cartel radio resting on the seat beside him. Keith listened, but since his Spanish was limited to a couple of curse words and a few tag lines from Taco Bell commercials, he had no idea what was said.

"Very good," El Gato announced. "We are almost there, and the area has been cleared without incident."

"How'd they pull that off, chief?" Sam asked, knowing the answer before the words left her lips.

Ricardo smiled and winked. "My men can be very persuasive, miss."

"I'll bet," Sam added as she turned her gaze back to the window closest to her.

"Thank you for your assistance," Lobo leaned forward in his seat, sensing the tension. "We would never have made it to our destination on time."

Ricardo nodded and shook his head. "I am curious, but I really do not wish to know."

"What did Storm do for you?" Keith asked, still locked on Ricardo. "It must have been something major to stop you from raping and murdering us."

"Hey!" Lobo yelled out. "Cut the shit, now!"

Keith shrugged him off and slouched back into his seat. Kate was gawking at him with daggers in her eyes, shaking her head at his insolence.

"Or," Ricardo growled, "perhaps they would have murdered you *then* raped you."

344 | ANTHONY DIPAOLO

Keith swallowed hard. The tone of the drug lord's voice was humorless and flat. The rest of them swallowed just as hard as Keith.

"But we are all friends here!" El Gato finally said, laughing. "No need to discuss such things or to act like uncivilized swine!"

Keith relaxed slightly and leaned forward in his seat.

"I am speaking to you, of course." Ricardo wanted him to know that right here, right now, he was boss.

Keith looked up at his host and gave an awkward, sour smile. "Of course. Sorry, dude. Uncalled for."

Ricardo raised his cigar again. "A man should think before he acts...or speaks. Such pause often presents us with the best course of action. Wouldn't you agree, amigo?"

"Wholeheartedly," Keith answered without a moment passing. "Enough said. I gotcha, sir."

The vehicle took on several cavernous bumps that launched the riders up from their seats. As they settled back down and found their footing, Ricardo leaned forward to peer out the side window.

"Ah, Chichen Itza approaches," he announced, clearly giddy.

Dropping back against his seat, he looked at Keith. "The details of what Mr. Storm did for me are not important. Suffice it to say he risked, without promise of anything in return, his life—*his very soul*—to protect that which I hold most dear in this world."

The military-like vehicle came to a sudden halt as the radio began to boom once more. Ricardo nodded and tapped hard on his side door. His rapping was quickly answered by a soldier who opened it and stood back.

"We have arrived," Ricardo said and smiled at his guests. "This is where my path ends, amigos. We shall wait here for you should you require a quick escape. Otherwise, adiós and safe travels."

"Thank you for your assistance, once again." Lobo extended a hand as he headed for the door.

"No need for thanks," El Gato replied, offering his hand in return. "My regards to Mr. Storm when next you encounter him."

"Will do." Lobo thrust his feet out and jumped to the jungle below. Standing at the bottom of the door, he assisted the others out one by one.

Kate rose last and nervously nodded at Ricardo as she reached for the doorway.

"You really do remind me of my Anna." Ricardo smiled, and Kate was sure she saw some glimmer of love and humanity in the monster's eyes, and then...it was gone. She carried the cold chill that shook her body out the door with her and did not look back.

The group had only taken a few steps when Ricardo Montalvo leaned out the open doorway of the truck. "Amigo!" he yelled, most likely addressing Lobo.

"Huh?" Lobo turned back to see Ricardo's head protruding from the side of the vehicle.

"Amigo!" He laughed heartily. "If you *do* return to me, be sure whatever you are fleeing from can die by the barrel of my gun or the edge of my blade."

Lobo nodded in both agreement and understanding.

Ricardo's laughter gave way to a stern scowl. "Otherwise, I must insist you find alternative means of transportation out of Mexico."

90

Alexander followed close behind Serket as she led him through the narrow winding passages to their destination. The shadowy, coarse stone walls that lined their path were damp to the touch, and Alex marveled at the fact that in a land so arid, these ancient stones knew the secret of extracting water from the earth. He ran his hands along the wall, toying with the accumulated moisture as they descended further into the Earth.

"It's how we gather all the fresh water we need, you know," Serket stated without glancing back at him. "Even in this inhospitable environment, everything you need can be found...if you know where to look."

Alex watched Serket's slender shape navigate the passages with ease, and he pondered her brilliance, both inside and out. She held a flickering torch slightly ahead of her body, and Alex was sure it was for his benefit, not hers, as she appeared able to move through the passages with ease.

"Hey!" she called out. "Stop staring out my assets!"

"Really?" Alex chortled.

"Oh, come on." She stopped and turned to face him. "Lighten up a bit, Mr. Storm! I'm kidding."

"Very well," Alex replied. "Carry on."

Serket shook her head, amused as always by Alex's steadfast need to control his emotions, and resumed her steady march through the mountain. Alex was relieved the torch light was positioned in such a manner as to cast shadow across his face, thus masking the responsive color that was flushing him from the neck up. As indicators go, his body would have provided all the evidence she required to prove the truth of her assertions. Averting his eyes, he quickly recovered his composure and smiled at their exchange.

"Anytime soon, great Medjai?" Alex quickened his pace to catch up as the narrow passage would not afford side-by-side travel.

"Yes." She motioned the torch ahead of her. "Right around the next bend."

No sooner than the words had been uttered did she come to a sudden stop. Serket lowered the torch towards the ground at her feet and summoned Alex closer to her.

"There are rudimentary steps here, Alex." The torch light reflected off of the finely worked stone on the floor before them. "And it's slippery due to the moisture deposits, so you must tread carefully."

"Understood," Alex said as he raised both of his arms up and let his palms rest against the face of the walls on either side of him. "Proceed."

Serket raised the torch back to eye level and they continued their descent into the darkness. After twenty-six steps, they arrived at a level landing, solid stone encapsulating every side except that of the steps behind them.

"This is secluded as requested, but rather tight, no?" Alexander spun on his heels, surveying the space around them. The torchlight shimmered and reflected off the perspiration of the mountain walls.

Serket shook her head in agreement and stepped forward to the wall directly in front of them. She waved her torch around a bit at the wet stone and silently swapped it into her left hand.

"You are not the only sorcerer in the room, Storm," she whispered as she thrust her right arm forward at the wall.

Alex's eyes widened as her arm vanished into the rock up to her elbow. She turned, and Alex could see her sly grin in the dancing torch light.

"Grab my arm," she instructed, offering him her torch bearing elbow. Alex reached out and took hold of Serket's forearm. Once she felt he had a secure grasp, she lurched forward and pulled them both through a narrow, crescent-shaped gash in the wall that was so perfectly camouflaged a man could stand there, trapped at the base of the stairs, and die of starvation and despair before he located it. It was a grand illusion which employed no magic to achieve its deception. Instead, the walls underlying secret was devised through the skill set of a master stone mason.

"Always impressive," Alexander said as he released his hold on Serket and moved to her side. They had entered into a rather large subterranean room within the bowels of the mountain.

"This is the deepest point within our refuge." She raised the torch up to illuminate the space. Alexander noted the bullet shape of the room as well as the absence of any form of artificial light. He was swiftly engaged by the overwhelming sense that they were sealed in on all sides. It was perfect and would serve his purposes well. At the center of the room, Alex could discern the outlines of a massive carved block, which he surmised served as an altar of some design. Atop it were half a dozen unlit candles and a bushel of herbs and incense tied securely in a fashion akin to a bouquet of wild flowers.

Alex turned momentarily to Serket, and she could see his approval and appreciation at her speedy assistance evident on his face.

"Your sacrifice is in the jar, Mr. Storm," she said. "Sorry, no goats for rituals here. Food and milk, you know."

Alex walked to the altar and located the jar. He picked it up and held it between his eyes and the flickering light of Serket's torch. Inside was a small brown and black desert mouse.

Alexander looked from the jar to Serket's face, which was obviously awaiting signs of approval.

"The fated rodent will serve my purposes." Alexander placed the jar back. "Size is of no consequence."

"Hear that often, do you?"

Alexander ignored the remark and extended his hand, fist clenched, out over the stone slab. Opening his fingers, palm side down, he waved his hand over the unlit candles. The wicks of each sparked to life and light emanated across the surface of the altar.

"There are no smoke and mirrors here, my dear," he whispered, illuminating the difference between magic and craftsmanship.

"Impressive as always," Serket replied. "You have promised to teach me that one several times you know?"

Alexander did not reply as he had already become lost in the mental preparation of the deeds at hand.

"You may return to the others now, Serket," he directed as he moved to the far side of the altar. "Thank you for your assistance."

Serket didn't move. Alex continued to walk around the stone block, searching for some optimal location only he would be aware of.

Seconds passed before he looked up at Serket, who stared at him intently.

"Was there something else?" he inquired.

"No."

"You may go." He once again returned to his preparations. "No need to leave the torch."

"I'm not going anywhere, Storm!" she called out.

"What?" He stopped and stared directly into her eyes although his concentration was only slightly focused on their exchange. "No. It's not safe for you to stay and watch. You must go."

"I plan on it. Going, that is. With you."

"Come now—"

"Does this clandestine method of global travel hold a passenger limit?"

"What? No...well yes, but not at this time."

"Huh?"

"What's your point, Serket? I am pressed for time, and although I appreciate all your efforts, I must make haste *now*."

Serket tossed the torch to the floor and walked to Alex's side. "I'm not sure what is going on or what you've gotten yourself and the others into—"

Alexander attempted to interrupt her, but she would have none of it.

"But I do know that the stars have steered our paths to intersect once again, and my intention is to stand beside you on this journey."

Alexander's expression was unreadable.

"I cannot ask you to bear this burden or take on this risk, Serket."

"I never heard you ask. So, obey the wisdom of an ancient Medjai and do as you are told Mr. Storm. Let's go." She walked toward the altar.

Alex inhaled, then exhaled a deep and pensive breath.

"I have no time to argue with you," he ultimately declared, as he began to withdraw items from within the inner sanctum of his coat.

"No time." Serket repeated. "I'll take it however it comes."

Alexander flicked his wrist and snapped open a blade which resembled a butterfly knife with some minor alterations and placed it on the altar. Lifting the bushel of dried botanicals, he reached forward toward a candle. Stopping abruptly, he looked to Serket.

"No sage," she assured, without provocation.

Alexander smiled and proceeded to set the bushel alight. After a few seconds, he lifted it to his lips and blew hard. The flame retreated and sputtered out, leaving only bellowing, thick fragrant smoke behind to fill the stone room.

"Brace yourself," he advised his companion as he withdrew the silver box from his jacket and forcefully twisted the top loose. "We travel on the wings of Lucifer to our destination!"

"What?" Serket took a step back. She hadn't expected that, and she stared at Alexander with grave concern.

Alexander lifted the top of the dragon-adorned silver box, and Serket was quickly overcome by the stench of sulfur and rot. Reaching into the box, Alexander withdrew two small stones and placed them on the altar. He closed the box, but the unpleasant smell remained. Returning the box to his jacket, he quickly reached for his knife and the jar.

"Sorry, little fella," whispered Serket.

Alexander unscrewed the lid and grasped the rodent by its tail. Holding the mouse above the two small stones on the altar, he began to chant fervently. The din of his words echoed in the chamber, and the smell of the burning incense and herbs, mixed with the sulfuric demon reek, made Serket's head spin.

Alexander's eyes opened wide, and his face twisted into a scowl forged with a mixture of aggression and dominance. With one sharp pull, he slid the blade across the underbelly of the helpless creature and sent blood, black in the scarce and focused light of the room, pooling down onto the small stones.

As if the passage of time came to a grinding halt, the rodent ceased its wrestle with the reaper, the rolling smoke of the burnt offerings froze in midair, and the candles flickered no more.

Serket looked to the far side of the chamber where a purple and green mist was manifesting from the stone chiseled floor.

"Steady now, my dear," Alexander commanded, looking more like himself. "Steady."

From within the spectral formation of exotically colored mist, Serket could discern a shadow rising, growing. The figure first presented itself as an outline void of both light and color, but quickly resolved itself into a definite shape. She watched as the once formless void mutated into a distinct outline which possessed the curves of a human body. A female form. The ethereal matter, having accumulated into an independent mass, separate and apart from the swirling mist, stepped into the natural light of the candles, revealing itself in spectacular fashion, as a naked woman. Long flowing red hair—unnatural red—cascaded across her pale skinned body as she moved forward in a slow slink to the altar. There was no small measure of gracefulness in her movements, however, and as she grew closer, Serket's eyes locked on her glowing pupils which returned her gaze. Her long-fingered hands seemed to float in the air at her sides and long legs carried her exotic body across an invisible floor several inches above that of the chamber's. She could feel the demon traversing her very being, delving into her soul, creeping through every pore of her body. She felt...she felt something. She felt excited...she felt aroused.

"Bathin!" Alexander intervened in the dangerous seduction.

"Storm!" The demon whipped her head around, refocusing her attentions from Serket to Alexander. She drifted toward him; her speed intensified. "My time is almost at hand."

"My level of patience for your oft entertaining game play is zero," Alex said, without looking upon the spirit before him. Instead, he raised his fist above the altar and brought it crashing down onto the two blood-soaked stones. Whether by some preternatural force possessed by Storm, or by way of the powerful spell's invocation, the stones shattered to dust at the command of his crushing fist.

With this action achieved, Bathin emanated an oppressive moan and hurtled herself into his face, nose to nose, eye to eye, the two stood.

"Seven more, Storm. Seven more," she hissed.

"Six," he quickly corrected the demon's mathematical computations. "The Medjai travels with me this day."

"Ha! Even better!" Bathin clapped her hands together, her slow, accentuated movements giving way to sharp, purposeful actions. "I can taste the freedom! It tastes like your blood Storm."

Bathin looked back to Serket, who stood *sotto voce*, soaking in the aberration playing out before her eyes.

"And who is this lovely creature you have brought to my altar?"

The demon was about Serket now, spinning around her body, passing back and forth between ethereal and solid state.

"Those eyes," Bathin said as she turned to Alexander for concurrence. "Those are eyes I would *love* to see staring up at me from between my legs."

The demon stopped circling Serket and hovered in her line of sight. "How I would lavish in that," she continued, "and how I would enjoy carving them from your skull after I came in your mouth, you pretty little slut."

Serket withdrew her face in horror at the sexually charged images of violence and lust Bathin was feeding into her mind's eye.

"Enough!" Alexander cried out. "Chichen Itza! *Now*, demon!"

Bathin spun around. "Going to visit the serpent, are we?"

"It is none of your concern." Alexander stepped around the altar and surreptitiously placed himself between Serket and the alluring succubus. "I have commanded. You will obey."

"You miserable little pilgrim! You lowly filth! You do not command me."

Storm stepped forward. "Today, *I do*. Tomorrow remains unwritten, but today, I do."

Bathin, powerless to oppose his directive, relented to his demand and bowed her head, her fiery strands flew about, reacting with a mind of their own. The mist floated in from behind her and began, as per the demon's command, to engulf Alexander and his companion.

"Close your eyes," he assured Serket. "It is but a mere blink in time."

The mist began to swirl around the two holy warriors, increasing in speed and force. Bathin spread open and crossed her arms in a repetitive motion as she took to chanting fervently. Alexander looked up at the roof of the chamber and watched as the stone of the mountain began to dissolve before his eyes. He felt the very fabric of time and space melt away. And, as on all his previous trips on The Bathin Express through the years, questioned the rationale of trusting a demon to do as commanded.

As rapidly as the manifestation of demonic magic has begun, it ended. Serket opened her eyes, expecting to be in Chichen as Alex had instructed. But they remained in the stone vault of her mountain.

Bathin quickly slithered into Alex's face. The demon's demeanor had changed from its previous insolence to serious urgency.

"Free me!" she demanded. "Free me now, Storm!"

He recoiled. "What? What is this? Do as you were commanded, witch!"

"Free me, Storm," she repeated, her words wrought with panic and urgency. "Moloch and that filthy sweet whore! Free me now!"

"Speak fast, demon—speak coherently." He stepped forward to signal his willingness to grant her an audience. "Lest you forget, I can end you with the remaining stones and my knowledge."

"Our common enemy aligns us pilgrim," she beseeched him, "they mean to free Samael, to crown him the dark lord of Earth. My allegiances lie elsewhere. As should yours ... under these abhorrent set of circumstances ... as peculiar as that may sound."

Alexander lowered his head and squinted at the revelation her words brought.

"Hell is not in alliance?"

"Never," she hissed. "It is the burden of our very nature. But my flag flies with the old guard."

Serket listened in awe of the conversation unfolding before her. She was aware of the spirit world, she was versed in legend and spell, she had fought many a battle with those very legends, and she herself was a product of this magic. However, that which was being revealed to her in this dark mountain chamber was beyond anything she had known before.

"Free me now, Storm," Bathin once more implored. "I will battle this

354 | ANTHONY DIPAOLO

threat to both of our existences by your side," she continued. "I will procure reinforcements from the very lord of Hell himself. You must realize you will need more than your sorry old bones, Storm."

Alexander stepped back and fell in beside Serket. This time, however, he reached down and grasped her hand in his. He remained silent in thought for what felt like an eternity.

"I will consider your request." His stern and unwavering voice shattered the weighty silence that had accumulated amongst the three.

"Don't be a fool, pilgrim—"

"Enough!" He squeezed Serket's hand tighter. "I said I would consider it, and my word is my oath." He stared at the demon without fear. "As your oath is to my word."

Bathin lowered her head, the mist resumed, and the ceiling above them opened to the fathomless heavens. Then stark silence.

Alexander squeezed Serket's hand twice. "Open."

The bright light of the Yucatan flooded her eyes, and as she regained focus, she could make out the pyramidal ruins through the rows of trees in the clearing before them.

"What now?" she softly uttered.

"To battle my dear." His voice changed as he released her hand. "To bloody battle."

91

L obo led the group down the shadowy foliage-lined path that led to the archaeological marvel. A warm breeze jetted through the trees and softly caressed his cheeks. Sam was next to him, keeping pace as they neared the clearing to the Mayan ruins.

"So, what's the plan?" Sam asked as she double stepped to keep up.

"Shhh." Lobo blew her off as one might an insolent child.

Sam shook her head and looked back at the others, who trailed several feet behind them.

"I'm surprised he's not carrying her through the jungle on his back," she mused, staring at Lobo for a reaction.

"Huh?" was the only response his cluttered mind could offer.

"Keith," she clarified, "I'm surprised he isn't carrying Kate on his back."

"Shhh!" Lobo demanded again.

"What's your problem?" Sam's face turned to a scowl, clearly irritated at Lobo's unwillingness to gossip with her on their walk.

Annoyed, he stopped suddenly and turned to Samantha. "My problem is I'm trying to think, okay? I have no idea what to expect up ahead. How can I protect the four of you if I have no idea what we are walking in to?"

Sam attempted to interrupt him but was met with an open palm and a shush once again.

"I'm also going through the words of the riddle in my mind, trying to make sure we haven't missed some important indicator or warning—"

"Listen!" she finally burst through the wall of his words. "I don't need you to protect me. I am perfectly capable of covering my own ass!"

With that, she turned and marched ahead of Lobo. He was growing more and more fond of her and smiled as he watched the rough beauty charge ahead. He stayed focused on her features for a spell and then drifted ahead of her to what appeared to be the end of the path where several of El Gato's men mulled around, awaiting the group's arrival.

Seeing their faces and their rifles at the ready, Lobo had an uneasy feeling, and he broke into a run to catch up with Sam. "Take it easy!" he yelled ahead. "Wait for me! Please!"

Sam continued to press forward, ignoring Lobo's requests. The armed bandits caught sight of Sam's approach and fell in together to meet her arrival. They blocked her movement by spreading out across the path, and she came to a grinding halt.

"Where you running to, chica?" one filthy and sweat-ridden soldier asked. "Wait for you, hombre."

Samantha shook her head and turned to see Lobo arriving at her side.

"What's the problem, amigos?" Lobo inquired in his most manly voice, his obvious concern for Sam evident in his demeanor.

"No problem, ese," one soldier replied and then leveled his AK-47 at Lobo's head. Wild-eyed, the cartel soldier leaned forward, bringing the rifle well beyond point blank range. Lobo threw his hands in the air and took a reactionary step back.

"Hey," he said. "No trouble here."

"Did I fucking miss something?" Sam spit out her words, ready to attack.

"Shhh!" Lobo could find no other words to offer Sam at the moment.

"Goddamn it!" Samantha yelled out. "Stop fucking telling me to 'shhh!'"

The bandits laughed in unison at the argument, and the one closest lowered his weapon then spun it around, offering Lobo its non-lethal end.

"A gift from El Gato." He gestured for Lobo to take hold of the rifle.

Without hesitation, Lobo locked his hands on the wood stock and relieved the soldier of his weapon.

"Gracias," he said as he inspected the firearm and checked its action.

"You!" another soldier yelled from the rear, addressing Sam.

"What?" she replied, unfazed by the entire display.

"You know your way around a gun?" Lobo asked, assuming they wished to supply her as well.

"Don't you wish you knew?" Sam replied in a low, sultry voice.

Lobo said nothing, as his tongue had tied itself into a knot.

She held out her hands to accept soldier's Neanderthal-like offer. He stepped forward and tossed it to her.

"Been shooting since I was twelve, jefe." She checked her weapon in much the same fashion as Lobo. "I think I've got this handled."

Lobo smiled. He was quite sure she had it handled.

"Hey, amigo," the soldier in the back called to Lobo.

Lobo nodded his head in response, still sliding his hands across the wood stock and barrel of the weapon.

"You don't need a gun with this one, no?"

Lobo laughed, he understood the soldier's point.

"What's that supposed to mean?" Samantha asked Lobo.

"He's commenting on the fact that you're tough enough to handle whatever lies ahead without the need for a gun." He paused. "Get it? It's a compliment from these men, believe me."

Samantha laughed and leveled her weapon at the enlightened speaker's head. A smile, ever so slight, crept across her face as she squinted one eye and lined up the pinned sight on her target. The soldier seemed stunned at the display and started to step back.

"Bang!" Sam yelled out in mock gunplay grandeur. "You're dead!"

92

"So, what's up with those two?" Keith asked his companions while watching Samantha and Lobo walk together.

"Who knows?" Kate quickly replied as she looked nervously from side to side. She had yet to shake the ominous feeling that had overcome her back at the site of the downed plane.

"Huh?" Abigail asked with a puzzled look on her face. "You think there's something going on?"

"What's the matter," Keith said, laughing. "You didn't sense it?"

"Nope."

"No 'spidey senses' popping?" he mused, harmlessly.

"No," Abigail sighed. "I tend to miss this sort of thing. Love and happiness aren't on my radar the way evil is."

"Man, that sucks, Abi," Kate said sympathetically in an effort to comfort her, but not really providing Abigail her full attention. The nagging feeling was still tugging at her thoughts. She felt vulnerable, like they were all exposed to someone or something stalking them from a distance. Abigail had shown a similar sentiment back at the runway, but seemed unaffected now.

Kate had to chase the notion away and concentrate on the task at hand, whatever that may actually be.

"He clearly digs her," she said, turning to her companions. "Don't really have a read on Sam, though."

"Yeah, she's tough," Abi said with a laugh.

"In more ways than one." Keith snorted, more amused at his words than Kate and Abigail were.

The faint whispers of something rustling from the depths of the jungle found its way to Kate's ears.

She came to a sudden stop and turned to look behind her.

"You guys hear that?"

"Hear what?" Keith ruffled his brow, trying to recall whether he had heard anything out of the ordinary seconds before. "I don't think I heard anything but trees in the breeze and insects."

"No, no," Kate said. "Listen *beyond* that, Keith."

"But—"

"Just *try,* will you?" she implored.

"Okay." Keith stood perfectly still and closed his eyes.

"What are you hearing, Kate?" Abigail bore a perplexed expression having not heard anything out of the ordinary from the recesses of the jungle that surrounded them. "I think it's just the w—"

"Shhh!" Kate shot her a look, and she fell silent.

Keith's head tilted up, and slivers of bright warm sunlight passed through the trees to caress and warm his skin. The smell of agave and tropical flora filled his nostrils, and for a moment, he was lost in his own thoughts. He might have remained like that for some time had it not been for the rustling sound that finally registered in his auditory senses.

rustle ... rustle

Keith's eyes shot open. "Heard it that time, dude!" He lifted his arms and tapped the others firmly on their backs. "Let's go catch up...now!"

Abigail and Kate picked up their pace in order to stay in tandem with him. Having reached his side, they continued in a jog, as Keith dropped back slightly, peering over his shoulder from side to side. Each time he looked forward to ensure the girls were okay, his stomach would tighten in a knot of apprehension right before he checked the rear again. He was certain there would be some...*thing*...right on his heels. What though?

What was closing in on them? He didn't know what, but he was sure something was headed their way.

The rustling grew louder, faster, bigger. And it was close.

He looked ahead to see Lobo holding a rifle. *Thank God*, he thought. Switching his focus to Sam, he was even more thrilled to see her holding one as well.

"Come on! Pick up the pace!" Keith blurted out in his strongest whisper, just loud enough for Sam and Lobo to hear. They both turned to see Keith, Kate, and Abi charging down the path toward them.

"What are they racing?" Sam said with a laugh. "Really?"

Lobo squinted to see the trio better, and after a moment, snapped into a defensive position.

"Ready yourself, Sam," Lobo whispered. "Something's wrong."

By that time, the threat had already registered with Sam, and she scrambled to her left for cover behind a fallen tree stump.

The group of soldiers behind Lobo, sensing impending danger, slipped away silently into the jungle. They were gone for almost half a minute before Lobo and the others realized it. Keith peered past the point where they had been standing and could make out a clearing through the trees beyond.

"Hey!" he yelled to Sam. She turned, and he held up his hand to her, extending two fingers to point in her direction. He then closed his hand forming a fist, twisted it, and extended the same two fingers to point at the clearing to his rear.

Sam squinted and then nodded to let him know she understood. She sprang up and charged past Lobo to the jungle behind him. As soon as she got to the tree line, she could make out the clearing of the archaeological site right beyond the overgrowth. She stopped in the cover of the trees and turned to face her friends, dropped to one knee, raised her AK-47, and leveled it at the area right beyond the incoming trio.

"Something's out there!" Sam heard Kate screaming—all semblance of covert movement was gone. "It's getting closer!"

Lobo lowered his weapon as they grew near to him. He said nothing, but turned sideways and extended his arm, fingers outstretched, toward Sam.

Kate and Abigail flew past Lobo, darting for the cover of the jungle behind him. Keith, heart pounding and sweat pouring, arrived at Lobo seconds later.

Attempting to catch his breath, Keith sputtered, "Want...me...to...do?"

Lobo said nothing and nodded him toward the others. Once Lobo saw all four of them were secure in the tree line, he began backing himself into the woods to join them. With agile steps, he continued to look to the ground as the trees closed in on him. Once he got to the tree line, he about faced and charged into the wooded area.

"Cover!" he yelled to Samantha as his back was now exposed to the unknown enemy, and she responded with same. Lobo didn't pause when he reached her. Instead, he turned and dropped to one knee, taking Sam's position.

"Listen!" he called to Sam.

"Yeah?"

"Lead them into the clearing!" he directed. "We're entering from the east side of the complex. El Castillo should be slightly to the north. Once you are in the clearing, use the other ruins as cover to make your way to the castle."

He paused and looked at the large faced scuba watch on his arm.

"It's almost four o'clock guys. The solstice is already underway. Don't miss this chance, or we'll have to wait for winter."

"Got it!" Sam confirmed his sentiments and signaled for the others to fall in behind her.

"Why is she leading the way?" Keith asked as if he had been left out of planning a party.

"Ah, yes." Lobo rolled his eyes. "Cause she's got the fucking gun!" He shook his head some more, then he looked to the others in turn. "Really?"

"Forget it!" Keith blurted under his breath, falling in behind Sam.

"Forgotten." Lobo snidely replied and ushered them on.

They had taken several steps toward the clearing when Lobo called out, "Do not wait for me!" He paused to make sure he had their attention. "Understand?"

"For what?" Samantha called back.

"For...anything!"

Lobo stayed low to the ground and emerged at the edge of the exterior tree line. He scanned the path and woods in front of him. The rustling was everywhere, surrounding them.

RUSTLE ... RUSTLE ... RUSTLE

"Fuck. Me." The words came slow and precise. He turned one last time to see his companions exiting the woods into the clearing of the ruins.

The sounds were on top of him, and he snapped his head back around to face the enemy; whatever that enemy was.

"What the fuck?"

Samantha stopped dead in her tracks as the jungle behind them rang out with the cacophony of rapid gunfire. Still hesitating, she tried to gauge the duration of successive firing in order to determine when Lobo's weapon would be spent. She peered down at her own firearm. The curved clip extending from the rifle had been taped to another clip in reverse. Hopefully Lobo was equipped with the same setup, she could not recall.

Smart criminals, she thought to herself and smiled. At that moment, the jungle fell silent.

Samantha, holding her breath, remained poised, rifle ready, prepared to protect her friends.

"Come on, Lobo," she coaxed the empty air in front of her, hoping desperately the words traveled by some magical means back to Lobo's ears. "Flip the clip, buddy."

Three shots blasted nearby, and Sam exhaled. "He's still kickin'," she assured the others as the repetitive music of gunfire rang through the jungle once more. Sam turned and ran to the nearest stone ruins on their left. The others quickly fell in line behind her, and as they rounded the corner of the large stone platform, Sam stopped again and crouched down, providing the others cover as they made their way to the refuge of the ruins.

"This rock," Keith whispered. "It's the Venus something-or-other, I believe."

"Platform," Kate replied dryly.

"What?" Keith called out to her. "Can't hear you over all the gunfire!"

Kate shook her head. "*Platform* of Venus! You heard me just fine!"

Keith winked and smiled. Kate always calmed him down, and he felt a burst of self-assured energy come over him. Stepping out, he moved forward around the others until he reached the stone's end. Making three or four takes at it before committing, he popped his head out to look further into the archaeological complex.

"Get back!" Kate yelled through her teeth. She grew silent when she saw Keith's eyes widen and his expression change.

"I didn't realize it would be so massive," he said to the others, his gaze locked on the great stone pyramid in the distance. "Fantastic!"

Sam stood upright and moved past Kate and Abigail to join Keith at the platform's edge.

"Easy there, Indiana Jones," she whispered, to which Keith smirked and nodded. A simultaneous revelation crept across both of their faces. The gunfire had stopped.

"He's fine." Samantha grabbed Keith by the collar of his shirt and jerked him back and behind her. She took his place and found herself momentarily awe struck by the grandeur of the ruins as well.

"Okay," she said, turning to the others. "Here's the plan. You three use the cover of the wall to the left, run along it, and get to the stairs or the serpent or whatever."

"What are you going to do?" Abigail quickly interjected.

"Gotta get some ammo to Lobo," she said in a tone that forbade negotiation. "Fast. Then I'll catch up with you."

"Sam—" Kate started, but was quickly shut down by Samantha's furrowed brow.

"Go now!" Sam hissed, waving the gun barrel past the stone platform. "Now!"

Kate and Keith walked to the edge and peered around the structure.

"Wow!" Kate cried out, and with a nudge, said, "Let's go!"

With that, the two jutted out from behind the Platform of Venus and made a beeline to the crumbling stone structure lining the path to El Castillo. The ground was unnaturally flat and covered in short, green grass; they were able to move effortlessly across the terrain, then found their seclusion against the next wall.

"Come on, Abi," Kate said, extending a hand back.

Abigail turned to Sam. "I'm coming with you."

"Why?"

"Because I've had some visions—some premonitions—and my gut tells me you're where I should be." She paused briefly, then continued, "Where I will be needed."

Sam shook her head. "Not gonna argue with you, girl." She looked out toward the group of trees they had emerged from. "But we are going to be running into some heavy, unknown shit, okay?"

"Okay." She turned to retrace their steps out to Lobo. "Let's roll."

The girls had taken but four or five steps when Lobo emerged from the jungle overgrowth.

Samantha smiled, and raising her fingers in a loop to her lips, let out a short, sharp whistle. Lobo stopped and turned to Sam and Abigail. He raised a hand as if to acknowledge their location, but something made him quickly transform his wave into a wave *off*, directing them further into the complex. Sam grabbed Abi's wrist and pulled her a few steps back to the cover of the platform ruins. Within seconds, Lobo had arrived at their sides.

"Fucking run!" he screamed.

"What is it? What is it!" Sam smacked her open hands against his chest to capture his attention.

Lobo looked down into Sam's eyes. "Wolves!"

"Wolves?" Sam repeated. "Step back! I'll pick them off as they come into view."

Lobo grabbed her by the shoulder and said, "Not happening, Sam."

"What?"

"My bullets had no effect on this particular brand of wolf."

"What the hell?" She stared at him again, and that's when she saw a brand of fear in his face she hadn't seen before.

"Sam, it's a pack of *ghost* wolves."

The rustling had grown close again, and all three of them heard the approach.

"A pack of giant, white ghost wolves!" Lobo continued, eyes locked on the tree line.

"What makes you think they're ghosts?"

"*That!*" Lobo pointed to the area of jungle he had just emerged from. Sam watched as a great beast charge through the foliage, and without slowing, it turned and headed in their direction. The wolf—if it could actually be called a wolf—was the size of bear. It was covered in long mange of white with piercing red embers for eyes. Steam bellowed from its open jaws, and Lobo was apparently correct in his assertion. It was a ghost. Or a demon. But the issue was not up for discussion at the moment. It was dead —Sam was sure of that. The charging dead she thought to herself. As it grew closer, she could make out great gaps in its fur where rotted muscle and sinew peeked through. *295 Instinctively, she raised her AK-47 and began to punch off rounds at the monster.

Lobo's hand darted out and landed atop the rifle. He pressed down on the gun and mouthed the word, *stop*. Sam lowered her weapon.

"Save your ammo for something you can kill."

Sam shook her head. "Where's your AK?"

"I was out! I threw it at that!"

Another feral creature burst through the trees and took the same route straight at the trio. And then another, and another, and another. In all, six demon wolves were about to tear the three of them limb from limb and then move on to Kate and Keith.

Lobo squinted his eyes tightly together. He had to think...and fast.

"We gotta hustle up a tree!" It was the only idea that popped into his mind. "Dogs can't climb!"

"We'll never make it to the trees, for one," Sam said in rapid fire. "*Two*, these aren't fucking dogs, and they fly for all the fuck we know, and *three*, even if we make it to safety in the trees, Kate and Keith are sitting ducks."

"Dead ducks, you mean." Lobo took a deep breath. He was fresh out of ideas.

The canine hellions were close now. In five or six more strides, the first creature would be upon them. The trio was downwind and Sam could smell them. Rancid and acidic, the air felt charged with their scent.

"Let me pass!" Abigail put her hands on their shoulders and parted the pair. She moved between and past them, straight toward danger.

The first fiend was mere feet from her, and the smoke radiating from its mouth and nostrils was dense and voluminous enough to be felt on the skin of its would-be victim.

Abigail turned around to face her companions. "Join the others now!"

Then she raised her hands in an interlocked position above her head. "I'll deal with these beasts."

"How?" yelled Lobo.

"I'm what you might call a *witch*...and I seem to have a way with animals."

93

"Stay close to the wall, Kate," Keith instructed her for the third time as she persisted on venturing out and across the clearing to the great Mayan pyramid.

"I know!" she snapped.

The two continued along the lines of the ruins like ants following a predecessor's path. Their course was comprised of a great wall constructed of rows of standing columns and rectangular bases. Once they reached the end of the structure, they could check their surroundings and decided whether or not to move into the open and exposed landscape.

"Keep going to the end, Kate, and we'll see if it's safe!" he called ahead.

The wall provided only superficial cover, and at the most would be a stone security blanket if they decided to cross the expansive clearing. They needed to traverse the risky portion of the landscape and make it to the pyramid. Once they made it the towering structure, they could circle around the base to the north or northwest side. Kate looked back and forth between the end of the wall of columns and the south face of the pyramid.

"We should have planned this better!" she called back to Keith.

"Why? What do you see?"

"It's not what I see." She stopped and crouched down as she arrived at the end of the stone wall. "It's what I *don't* see."

"Huh?" Keith said, arriving at her side.

"What I *don't* see is the north face of El Castillo." She pointed around the pyramid. "It's on the opposite side."

Keith shook his head. "Okay, but we really didn't *plan* this did we? At all?"

"You know what I'm saying." Her annoyance was obvious. "Don't be a dick. I was just pointing out where we need to go, and we should have started out at the opposite side of the Platform of Venus."

"Got it," Keith said, paying it no more mind. "Let's go. Now. We're too exposed here, sitting targets."

"What?"

"Get up, Kate. No time to Monday morning quarterback this." He paused and looked down at her, extending his hand to assist. "In fact, there's no time for a plan at all. We run for it!"

Keith took a huge step from the semi-cover of the wall and pulled Kate along with him. Once in the clearing, he let go of her hand so she could run full-force. She complied with his choice and sprinted across the flat land-scape. Keith kept pace as they closed in on the south wall of the ancient monument. Almost simultaneously, they extended their hands out in front of them as they crashed against the new-found security of the north wall of El Castillo.

Winded, Keith leaned over on his knees and sucked in big gulps of the humid Mexican air.

"Come on, old man," Kate said and smiled at him, her face and chest flushed by the exhilaration as well as the exertion. "I have a plan."

Keith laughed, still leaning down on his legs. "Of course you do."

"Up!" she shouted in the excitement of her newly arrived at solution. "We climb. Let's go!"

"Got it," Keith agreed, beginning to regain his wind. "Up and over. Good idea. You first."

"Wimp!" Kate shouted and took to the stone like a spider on a web. She was already fifteen feet above him when he joined in. Looking up into the cloudless azure Yucatan sky, he was able to follow her silhouette against the crisp, clear background.

"Nice view!" he yelled up to her.

"Climb," she instructed. She needed him to remain focused. The climb was sure to be no small feat in the heat.

Keith stretched his shoulders and neck and jumped up to the first set of stone steps. He was amazed at how nimbly he was moving. The ascension was easier than he had expected, and he moved smoothly up at a fair pace gaining ground on Kate as he went. The expertly carved stone steps, although a little narrow, were only slightly taller than a set of modern steps. This height difference gave Keith's longer legs a slight advantage, and by the time he was three quarters of the way up the south side of the pyramid, he was directly behind Kate.

"Move it, move it, move it!" he barked in his best Marine drill sergeant voice.

Kate did not respond. She was within three or four steps of the covered landing at the top, and she pressed forward to get to its safety.

"Wait for me before you head back down," he called to her, hoping to catch his breath a moment at the peak before the steep incline down.

Keith looked up again as Kate reached the landing and disappeared from his view. He picked up his pace and climbed up the steps, arriving where Kate stood. As he did, he was taken aback by the faint, deep whisper of a voice carrying on the wind. The echoing words originated from somewhere in the distance, and he had not heard the sounds on his way up. He was about to ask Kate if she heard the mysterious din, too, when she pointed out a completely different, and much more pleasant, topic.

"My God." Awestruck, she turned in a clockwise circle gazing out onto the land around them. "What an amazing view!" she shouted.

Keith righted himself and clapped the dust from his hands. Lifting his head for the first time at the top, he took in the view and gasped.

"Awesome," he said, bobbing his head a few times. Then he reminded her, "No time. World to save."

Without a word, Kate turned and crossed the landing, passing under a stone roof to the opening on the other side. She walked to the edge of the top step and looked down. Keith watched a familiar expression of fear and concern creep over her.

"What is it?" he moved to her side and peered over the stairway.

The west side border of the north side staircase was alive with movement.

"It's the solstice!" Kate cried. "The great stone serpent is moving!"

The solid run of stone rippled and bounced. This was no intricately planned ancient shadow show as folklore alluded to. The stones were moving, and at the base of the run of blocks that comprised the reptilian body, lay the serpent's massive stone head.

"Look!" shouted Kate, pointing to the serpent's head. "That's what we need to get to, according to the riddle."

Keith stared down as the carved stone skull of the snake began to shift and change.

"'Take the head'—I remember!" He turned to face Kate and asked, "How do you plan on achieving that bit of magic?"

Kate opened her mouth to reply, but she was silenced as gunfire rang out from somewhere below them. Glancing over the landscape, Kate quickly located the Venus ruins.

"There.Do you see it?" she yelled to Keith, pointing to the ruins below.

"Oh, shit! What the hell is it?" Keith could make out one—no two—large animals moving toward the Venus stones.

"If the others are still there," he paused, "they have problems."

"What are those? Bears?"

Before he could answer, the same deep and indiscernible voice bellowed throughout the entire Mayan complex. Keith looked to Kate, and he could discern from her expression that she could hear the unnerving chant on the air as well. It was growing louder, the words becoming clearer, yet the annunciation remained foreign to Keith's ears.

"LIIK'IL KAN ... LIIK'IL K'I'IK XTAABAY ... LIIK'IL KUKULCAN"

"What is it?" Keith shouted over the ruckus of noises filling the air.

"Kukulcan." A look of recognition crept across Kate's face. "It's Mayan!"

Kate instinctively grabbed a small, worn leather journal from her pocket. Using a shard of pencil that was tucked away in the book, she began to jot down the words that floated toward them with the increasing winds.

"Kan," she repeated to herself and scribbled again.

Keith moved closer to her to see what she was up to, and she shooed him away, trying to concentrate on the muffled words.

"Liik'il!" she shouted with a huge grin. "Liik'il means 'rise!'"

"Rise?" Keith once again tried to approach her side, and once again she shot him a glance, fending him off. Kate closed her eyes as her lips moved, repeating the words over and over. Keith tried to make out the words as she mouthed them, trying to discern if she was speaking English or not.

"Blood phantom! Ghost!" she yelled and leapt forward in excitement. "I got it!"

Keith moved in her direction, sensing the waters were finally safe.

"Rise serpent! Rise blood phantom!" She paused and looked at Keith. "Or blood ghost," she argued with herself.

"I don't want to make either of their acquaintances." He nervously jested. "Doesn't matter to me."

"Ha!" Kate finished the chanting words. "Rise, Kukulcan!"

The ground under their feet rumbled and shook, so much so that Kate nearly lost her balance at the staircase edge. Keith reached out and pulled her back in. Locked together, they leaned over to check on the serpent who had detached its head from the massive stone block footings beneath it. It veered up and away from its ancient foundation. Coiling back in striking position, it rocked back and forth, transfixed on a point to the West.

Keith followed its line of sight to the edge of the clearing. He watched as two figures appeared seemingly out of thin air. He blinked several times attempting to clear the stress and heat from his vision that was surely playing tricks on his mind. The two figures were advancing still and he quickly surmised that they must have exited from the edge of some unseen section of the jungle.

The pyramid rumbled harder as the stone serpent became even more agitated, hissing and curling about in response to the pair's arrival from the depths of the jungle. It had yet to detach the entirety of its body from the underlying stone, and only about half of its length was free.

"Look!" he shouted to Kate, pointing out the approaching duo from the West as the Mayan chant continued to spew forth ever louder.

Desperately she asked, "Is it Storm?"

"Not sure," he replied, squinting in an attempt to bring everything into focus. "But I think the fucking chanting is coming from one of them."

Kate shot a glance back to the Venus ruins and was horrified to find them overrun by a pack of the white creatures that resembled massive dogs.

"It's a man and a woman!" Keith announced.

"Is it Storm, goddamn it?"

The visitors were coming into view, and he watched as the female bent over and retrieved something from her feet. Keith tried to make out what she was doing, but they were still too far away to make out the finer details.

She seemed to slow to a crawl as she lifted her hands high above her head. The man continued his forward march to the pyramid, paying no mind to his companion.

"Abigail!" Kate shouted.

Keith turned to see Abigail emerge from the Venus ruins, hands also raised above her head. She dropped to her knees as the charging pale beasts closed in around her.

"What is she doing?" Keith cried out. "She's a sitting duck!"

Suddenly, a blinding white light began to emanate from their companions clasped hands. Its glow rose and expanded around Abigail in all directions. The powerful beam, encircling her in a shell of illumination, stopped the charging creatures in their tracks. Sickening whines and wails filled the hot jungle air, as the creatures threw their bodies to the ground, rubbing their faces in the dirt and grass that lined their surroundings. The baying howls of the immense creatures left Kate and Keith with no doubt as to their identity. They were wolves! And Abigail was employing some form of magic to fend off the colossal apparitions.

Keith looked back at the woman to the West. Debris and fire spun around her as if she stood in the eye of a tornado. As if she *were* the eye of the storm. The scene was reminiscent of images he had seen on the Net when they were doing research on supernatural manifestations in nature. It looked like a phenomenon known as a dirt devil. The mysterious woman remained facing the direction of El Castillo, but had ceased all forward advance. Keith had momentarily lost track of the man who had appeared from the jungle with her. He quickly located him after a cursory scan of their surroundings. A sinking feeling of dread filled him as he watched the dark figure of the man approach the base of the pyramid below.

"That sure as hell isn't Storm," he muttered to himself as he got a better look at the tall, shadowy figure. As if sensing the presence of Keith spying on him from on high, the man froze and turned back to his companion. He shouted to the mysterious woman in a language Keith did not recognize. Turning to Kate, Keith grimaced, finding the annunciation and cadence of the individual below's words physically painful to his inner ear. Kate, reacting to both Keith's expression, as well as the cacophony of jagged dialect, ran to his side. "Latin?" she paused, "Or Aramaic? Not Mayan." Kate nodded to herself as the echo of the man's alliteration steadily rose to an unbearable state within her mind. No, it was none of these dialects.

The pair watched as the furtive woman reacted to the calls of her companion. The dust and debris that had been forming into a cyclone around her, now transformed itself into billowing clouds of smoke and flames. The fiery specter turned her attentions from the pyramid and began to move, floating several inches above the floor of the jungle complex, to the northeast side of the complex. Kate traced her path, and arrived at her ultimate destination with horror in her eyes.

"Oh my God!" Kate cried out. "She's heading for Abi!"

The blazing apparition suddenly advanced, with supernatural speed, to within fifty feet of Abigail's location. The air around her continued to spin as the glowing intensity of its internal flames grew.

"Look!" Kate cried, pointing in Abigail's direction. She was all but gone, consumed in a blinding white sphere of light.

A sudden and explosive sucking noise echoed all around them until all traces of sound had been filtered from the air. The unnatural silence was only momentary as the imploding vacuum reversed with a massive bang as beams of white light and fire projected from the pair of conjurers who were now, quite obviously, locked in battle. The opposing forces generated by Abigail and the fire wielding woman eventually staved each other off in a magical stalemate which held fast in the center of the space between them. A magnificent display developed between the two as white light crashed against the evil sprays of flame. The two forces, still holding each other at bay, continued to grow in both intensity and size until neither could be contained any further. In a momentary flash of brilliance, brighter than a thousand stars, the conflict ended as the light, moving like water traveling in waves, spilled forth and engulfed the entire Mayan complex. ...then all fell silent once more.

94

An unnatural still that had overtaken the jungle to the west of the complex clearing was suddenly broken as the massive tropical leaves grew aflutter with hisses of wind. With increasing intensity, the warm air bounced back and forth in opposite directions, eventually causing the foliage to tear and tree trunks to sway. There was an emerging design, a pattern if you will, to the wind's movements. An organized chaos which first became apparent on the floor of the jungle as small debris lifted and spun. Like a reversed maelstrom in the deepest sea, the air, dirt, and scattered vegetative debris began to rotate, expanding as it went up. There, in the heart of the Yucatan, a miniature tornado hung in place and ripped a hole in the jungle. The sheer velocity of the wind uprooted trees and whipped them to the side, lifted rocks and funneled them up to the heavens, and scorched the sand and earth below it into twisted ruins of glass.

As quickly as the phenomenon had arisen, it dissipated with a furious burst that broke the symmetrical cylinder of wind into nothingness. The particles trapped in the spinning gale shot out in all directions like water fleeing from a stone dropped in a puddle.

In its place, two dark figures appeared from the cloudy mist, their boots crunching down on the splinters and strands of glass that had formed on the ground beneath them.

Naamah stepped forward and reached up to her hood with both hands. She grasped the sides of it and lifted it off her head, allowing it to drop back and cascade over her shoulders.

"Nicely done." Moloch stepped forward to join her.

Grasping her wrist, he spun her around to face him. Leaning down, he brought his lips almost to rest against hers. Naamah's eyes were transfixed on his, while Moloch's eyes strayed elsewhere, focused on the curves of her red lips.

"Whisper those sweet words to me my dear," he said with a sly smile. "You have yet another snake to charm."

Naamah sighed.

"Are my innuendos and advances getting old?" Moloch's tone was comical; his eyes, however, swam in dark, serious waters.

"Of course not, my prince." She leaned in and allowed their lips to touch.

He withdrew with a satisfied smile. "Speak the words now jezebel, lest I banish you back to perdition."

"Wonder how that would work out for you?" Naamah was about to lay out the dangers of carrying out such a threat upon her when she was instantly silenced by Moloch's actions.

Whipping around in the direction of the clearing, he leaned his head back and began to take in large huffs of the air.

"We have company, Naamah." He did not turn to face her, but instead began to move forward toward the clearing. "The words. Now."

Naamah, in a blur of movement, arrived at his side and stopped his forward advance. Lifting herself on her tippy-toes, she rested her lips against his ear.

"LIIK'IL KAN ... LIIK'IL K'I'IK XTAABAY ... LIIK'IL KUKULCAN"

Moloch smiled. "Again."

"LIIK'IL KAN ... LIIK'IL K'I'IK XTAABAY ... LIIK'IL KUKULCAN," she whispered, louder this time.

"Again."

Moloch's lips parted, and this time, as the words left Naamah's mouth and entered his ear, they exited his mouth with an earth-shaking intensity. Naamah dropped from her perch against his body and turned to walk into the clearing with Moloch. The ancient words, welling up from somewhere deep in his demonic being, came forth and burst upon the landscape like birds of prey. Moloch continued his chant as they neared the edge of the jungle.

Their movement was momentarily paused by a short burst of what sounded like echoing gun fire.

"LIIK'IL KAN ... LIIK'IL K'I'IK XTAABAY ... LIIK'IL KUKULCAN," Moloch continued as they resumed their way to the clearing.

As the two demons emerged from the jungle, Naamah was immediately aware of the stone serpent's movement on the northern steps of the pyramid before them.

"It's working!" she yelled to Moloch, who nodded and continued his call to the ancient serpent.

"LIIK'IL KAN ... LIIK'IL K'I'IK XTAABAY ... LIIK'IL KUKULCAN"

The serpent was up and hovering on the edge of the pyramid.

"Shall I slay it?" Naamah called over his words once more.

Moloch shook his head and pointed to their left. Naamah, turning her attentions as he directed, found a growing orb of light expanding in the distance. She immediately surveyed the scoured ground below her. It took mere seconds to locate what she was looking for. Bending her knees to lower herself to the ground, she reached out and plucked a stone from amongst the grass and dirt.

Beginning her incantation, she forked from her dark companion and blazed forward to the left. Moloch continued his march to El Castillo, almost to the base of the great structure already. Gazing up at the massive stone beast with growing excitement, he continued his dark commands.

" LIIK'IL KAN ... LIIK'IL K'I'IK XTAABAY ... LIIK'IL KUKULCAN," he shouted directly at the serpent's veered head, *"Rise, worm, meet your new master!"*

Moloch quickly turned to apprise Naamah's position. She was ablaze before the interloper and her pathetic white orb of light, poised for slaughter.

Moloch peered deeper into the light and smirked.

"A witch," he said with a snicker. "She'll make short order of you."

Confident in his companion's abilities to dispatch the neophyte, Moloch was about to turn back to the task at hand when his peripheral vision picked up on an anomaly behind Naamah, at the jungle's edge. The air there was beginning to ripple, and the landscape behind a small patch of space fluttered as if being cast off a burning surface. Moloch watched pensively as the very fabric of the jungle began to dissolve and become displaced.

"A demon?" The words fell from his mouth as a perplexed whisper.

The space, a completely dissipated rift in the jungle's fabric of reality, was a void of black nothingness. Moloch's face went still and stoic as he watched two figures emerge from the dark hole in the jungle. The newly arrived pair paused momentarily as the blackness of the rift closed in on itself, revealing the picturesque landscape in its place. Moloch strained his vision to discern the identity of the duo. The demon's attempts were thwarted as the pair broke into a sprint, charging directly towards him and the pyramid in his background. Filled with a sudden sense of urgency, Moloch looked to his companion. *307 Both Naamah and the white witch she was confronting were completely engulfed in blinding auras of light and fire.

Moloch turned his back and made haste to the edge of the pyramid's base. Once there, he checked on the progress of the approaching pair of interlopers and found they had covered a sufficient amount of ground for Moloch discern their faces. Moloch's eyes returned to their true form, born of fire and pain. He recognized the charging duo. Or at least one of them.

"*Storm.*" His steely white rows of teeth ground into one another as the words slipped his lips. The demon's jaw popped open and his face contorted into a grotesque visage.

"Storm." He howled again, spit and blood spewing forth with the words.

Alexander, having apparently located his target, withdrew a glimmering sword and wielded it above his head. Moloch bared his rows of now twisted teeth and readied himself to meet the charge of his foe. Mere seconds from impact, all intentions were thwarted as both warriors were overcome by a wave of blindingly intense white light.

The ancient jungle fell silent in the aftermath of the sun-like burst, save for the grinding din of stone on stone as the great serpent broke free of its pyramidal prison.

95

The light was blinding, taking physical form as it boomed against Alexander and his companion much like a wave's swell crashing against a stone laden shoreline. Serket had only taken two or three steps into the clearing of the archaeological complex when her eyes slammed shut reflexively and her body was forced down to one knee. Alexander was mere steps in front of her when the sheer force of the explosion ceased all forward motion. Like Serket, he eventually gave in to the energy of the converging magic forces. He did not drop to his knees, however. Instead, he leaned his body into the onslaught of energy, allowing his frame to hang suspended at a slightly askew angle.

Serket struggled to open her eyes to locate Alex, but her retinas were not equipped to handle the intensity of the light. The glowing white and red swirls beaming through her eyelids were sufficient to cause her physical pain and thus she wisely kept them shut.

Alexander's skin pulled taught on his face and hands as it was stretched to its limit. If the radiance of fire and light didn't end soon, he feared he would be flayed where he stood.

"Storm!"

He could barely make out the trembling intonations of Serket's voice, although she couldn't have been more than a few feet from his position.

"Storm!" she screamed. "Where are you? Can you hear me?"

"Right...here! Shall all be...over...soon!" The intense pressure on his face and mouth labored his speech and his lungs burned as he forced the words out.

Alexander could make out whirling sounds filled with howls and wails, and he surmised Moloch had introduced some hellish creatures into the mix.

Demonic soldiers, he thought to himself, trying to keep his mind focused on the next step and not the current situation. Alex caught wind of more intense howling and the guttural cries of a creature's last stand.

"Wolves!" he called out to Serket. "Watch for wolves! When the spell is broken!"

Serket could barely make out his words. It was if they were atop two tall buildings, crying across the massive expanse to each other.

"What?" She needed him to repeat his words—they must have been important, or why would he struggle so to convey them to her at this juncture?

Then, just as suddenly as it had begun, the light and fire receded to its origins and vanished. Alexander stumbled forward as the invisible wall released him from its impediments. Catching his steps and righting himself before he fell to the jungle floor, he whirled around to find Serket.

"Wolves!" he cried.

This time, Serket heard him and sprang from her kneeling position. The warnings, however, were no longer necessary since the treacherous fire and light appeared to have lifted the creatures into the air and scurried them away to nevermore. They were gone, and the surrounding clearing, as well as the archaic stone ruins, were silent.

"Are you all right?" Alexander grasped Serket's wrist and pulled her toward him. Relaxing his fingers, he looked her up and down. She appeared unscathed, but out of respect for the revered warrior, he waited for a response.

"Fine," she replied after no more than a moments pause, "just another day at the office ... right?"

"Right," Alexander's face lit up at her ability to find humor. "But our job has yet to begin, my dear!"

Alexander circled around in place once apprising their surroundings and the chaos they had walked smack dab in the middle of.

The first thing he saw was Abigail, down on both knees in the dirt. Her face was in her hands, and although he couldn't tell if she was laughing or crying, he was pretty sure it was the latter.

"Abigail!" he instinctively cried out. "Abigail!"

As the words left his mouth, her opposition came into focus.

"Naamah." He spit the words from his mouth like one might spit out rotten meat, or a drink the was far to hot to ingest. "It appears we are a step or two behind."

Serket looked over at Abigail, who was still surrounded by a dying aura of light.

"That one's yours," she surmised, to which Alex nodded.

Naamah turned to Alex and Serket, visibly shaken by her showdown with the mysterious sorceress.

"That one's not!" she cried as she lurched forward in Naamah's direction.

Suddenly, a sharp and grinding sound hovered above them from the direction of the ruins of El Castillo.

"To Abigail's aid if you will!" Alex instructed Serket. "I will deal with Naam—" But he didn't get to finish the sentence. His ears were assaulted by a powerful and purposeful voice creeping through the air like mist on a dark pond at dawn. Alex turned toward the sound only to find the demonic figure of Moloch inching forward in their direction.

"Bastard," he hissed under his breath. "So here is where we shall make our stand!"

Alexander reached into the fathomless recesses of his coat and withdrew a silver sword. The blade shimmered in the fleeting light; its handle bore the tribal dragon crest of his family set in stones and steel and bound in leather straps.

Moloch suddenly stopped on his course to Alex, his head lifting skyward toward the sound of the rumbling stone.

Before Alex could trace the demon's gaze upward, he watched as the sun's rays, which had been bathing the clearing floor before him, disappear. Engulfed in shadow.

"Oh, shit!" Serket cried out, having spotted the enormous stone serpent rising in the air above them, casting a looming shadow across the landscape.

"To Abigail if you will! Moloch is conjuring control of the serpent to destroy her!"

Serket turned from Alex to run to Abigail, but instead found herself face to face with Naamah.

"Love your eyes, bitch," she whispered to Serket. "Too bad you keep such lousy company." Jutting her arms forward, she planted a burst of fire and energy into the center of Serket's chest, hurtling her backward with a thud.

"To your feet! Protect the girl!" Alex yelled to Serket, who shot him a sideways glance before hopping back to her feet.

Naamah spied the serpent—it coiled above Abigail. "Destroy her, winged one," she called to the stone manifestation. "Turn the infidel's bones to dust!"

Abigail was lost in her misery and confusion, overcome by what had transpired between her and the she-demon. In awe of the raw power that had emanated from her body. A power, up until this point, she was unaware she possessed. The serpent's shadow growing over her did not register with her senses and the stone beast positioned itself to deliver a fatal blow.

Alexander, sensing Moloch was intent on murdering Abigail rather than battling him, made his way towards the helpless girl.

"Abigail!" he cried again, but it was no use—she was consumed in her despair.

The stone serpent's long body was close now, and Alex was within feet of its slithering segments of rock which traversed the land like the treads of a tank. His gaze traced the ancient structure's body up to the head and watched as Kukuclan veered back like a cobra poised to strike. It was following its master's commands, which continued to echo throughout the complex. The serpent was positioned to let gravity unleash its fury on the unsuspecting victim.

Alexander froze, and tilted his head to the heavens. The wind around him began to whip and hum with growing intensity.

"What are you doing, Storm? Take him out!" Serket cried from somewhere behind him.

Alexander's eyes shot to the ground around him as he reached forward with his free hand.

"Momentarily!"

Again, Alexander's body stood motionless as dust and dirt whipped by him, headed toward the jungle landscape to his rear. Like a great grizzly bear seizing a salmon from a stream, Alexander reached out gracefully and grabbed at a blur that was passing in front of him with the wind. As his body recoiled from the ground, he emerged with a hare, ears in his grasp, and held it high in the air.

Alex sprinted forward, directly at the stone monster. "Kukuclan! Here is your blood oath, mighty one!"

As Storm reached the side of the serpent's body, it veered its head, rocking to and fro, and repositioned its course of trajectory. It was now poised to lash out at him. Without a moment to spare, Alexander flicked his silver blade with the precision of a seasoned butcher, slicing the rabbit down the center. The snake readied itself to unleash on Alex as he tossed the bleeding remains of the hare against the ancient serpent's stone body.

Alexander roared. "Your blood sacrifice! Now return from whence you came!"

As the blood of the rabbit trickled down the snake's rocky scales, the grand spectacle of animated stone and fury froze solid, and its stone carcass fell to the ground with explosive force. Alexander dove toward the pyramid behind him, narrowly avoiding the rock segments raining down from on high.

Serket had fallen to the ground to protect herself from the barrage of raining stone and was just turning to Alex when Abigail's moans and cries turned to utter screaming as her mind lost hold of madness occurring around her.

Alexander turned to Serket. "Where is Naamah?"

"I don't know," she replied, rising to her feet. "I lost her when the serpent fell."

Fearing Abigail's screams signaled the worst, he took off running in her direction, hopping and sliding over one of the stones from the compromised serpent's body. He could see Abigail as she stood screaming at nothing—and everything.

"Storm!"

Alex turned toward the calling voices. They came from atop the great pyramid El Castillo, and he quickly made out Kate and Keith running down its northern steps.

"Storm!" Kate repeated as she charged down the stairs. "Naamah is at the serpent's head!"

Alexander felt a sharp pang in his gut.

"Take his head!" Naamah's words echoed as Alex turned to the fallen skull of rock behind him just in time to see her emerge from behind it. She held a stone cylinder high above her head, waving it back and forth to signal to Moloch the prize had been found.

Naamah shot forward into the open area of the complex, fifty or sixty yards from Moloch and knelt down.

"Where are you, my little gems?"

Choosing a stone from the ground, she repeated her satanic verses and held the rock in her palm. Moloch was moving toward her, closing the space between them quickly.

Alexander stumbled and broke into a run. He had to stop Naamah from opening a portal, or this fragment of *The Book of Gates* would be lost as well.

Naamah's hand was aglow, and the air spun and churned around her fingertips and wrapped around her wrists. Reaching back behind her, as if to throw a fastball at home plate, she launched the stone at Moloch. It came to rest directly in front of him, landing at his feet.

"A most excellent throw!" he called to Naamah, and she laughed at his praise as she sauntered forward.

The ground in front of Moloch was alive with the demon's handiwork as a funnel of dust, dirt, and fire grew ever higher. Alex watched as Moloch disappeared into the terrestrial blur, engulfed by Naamah's portal.

Alex, realizing he could not get to Naamah in time, looked for Serket, who was already moving forward on a course toward Naamah and the demonic portal.

"Serket!" Alex shouted at the top of his lungs. "*Serket! Take her out!*"

Serket didn't respond or look at him. Rather, she let loose the belt that held her flowing garbs around her waist, allowing the robe to drop to the floor, exposing her sleek-fitting black clothes beneath. Reaching back and across, Serket grasped the handles of two gleaming short swords that had been concealed across her back and withdrew them into the air. Charging with savage intensity toward her target, she closed the distance on Naamah in seconds.

The demon, sensing the oncoming threat, spun around and once again hurtled a blast of fire and force at Serket's body, sending her back and to the ground. Naamah laughed as she turned, and with nothing more than an assured and steady pace, continued her trek toward the spinning portal.

Serket arched her back, and releasing the sword in her right hand, snapped forward and to her feet. Sensing there was no longer any time to make the distance to Naamah before her escape into the dark recesses of the portal, Serket raised her free hand to the sky.

"BARRAH HORUS! BARRAH!"

Dropping her arm to her side and turning it to point to the ground behind her, she called out again, never taking her eyes off of Naamah.

"BARRAH HORUS ... BARRAH!"

Alexander felt the ground around him begin rumble as he watched Serket conjure the ancient powers of the Medjai.

"BARRAH HORUS ... BARRAH ... BARRAH ... RISE !"

The ground behind Serket rose up to meet her words and burst forth like a geyser. Fragments of earth and grass exploded into the air, creating a gaping hole as if a bomb had dropped.

Alexander's heart skipped a beat as a mighty cry came forth from within it, and out from its depths flew the form of a giant falcon. The bird shot from the ground like a blazing arrow and sailed straight up into the heavens, its majestic call reverberating across the ruins.

Without turning her gaze from Naamah, Serket's arm shot forward as the falcon dove to the ground fifty feet behind her and leveled off at shoulder height. The falcon, called forth from the avenging god Horus, flew at Serket as she extended her pointer finger at Naamah.

Serket did not yell her words this time—she uttered them through gritted teeth. "Parodway. *Destroy.*"

With the force of a hurricane, the falcon's span burst open, and with several powerful blasts from its wings it careened toward its objective. Serket stood motionless as the mighty bird passed but inches from the top of her head, blowing her hair forward in its wake.

By the time Naamah registered the incoming danger, she was steps from entering the spinning mass of dust and fire. Her body instinctively whirled around as the falcon tucked its wings in tightly at its sides to reach its maximum velocity.

"*Destroy!*" Serket cried out once more.

Kate, who was almost at the base of the steps, stopped and tried to keep her eyes at pace with the feathered torpedo racing through the air. It was then she saw the glimmer, the gleam, as beak and feather morphed into shinning, shimmering silver.

The impact was massive. The falcon arrived at its target with a force so great it blew Naamah's head off—not from her body, but into a mist of blood and bone, the falcon's metallic form vaporized along with its target.

Alexander cried out. Kate was speechless. And Serket remained motionless except for the smile that crept across one corner of her mouth.

Naamah's body stood upright still, but her knees began to buckle and give way. In her left hand, clenched in a death grip, remained the stone cylinder containing *The Book of Gates's* fragment.

"The cylinder!" Alexander called to all the others. "Retrieve the cylinder!"

As Alexander's companions hurried to respond to his directive, they were met with Serket's cries.

"There! In the portal!"

Alexander froze as he watched a hand protrude from somewhere within the spinning cloud of darkness and take hold of the back of Naamah's falling corpse.

"*No!*" he screamed out, already knowing it was too late.

With an effortless tug, Moloch pulled Naamah's body back, and it disappeared into the spinning mass. Instantly, the portal—and with it, the Mayan fragment of *The Book of Gates*—vanished.

96

"I think you need to fill in the gaps *now*, Alex." Serket softly touched Alex's arm with a look of concern.

He did not respond. Instead, he stared, fixated on some faraway point on the ground in front of him.

"Hey." Her voice was caring and sympathetic, but it garnished nothing more than a "hush up" hand signal from Alex.

Sam and Lobo had finally made it around the base from the far side of El Castillo and joined Kate and Keith, who were hurrying over to join the others.

"Storm!" someone yelled from the group. Alex could barely hear any of them; their voices transformed into background noise in the far reaches of his mind.

"Hey! Storm!"

The din of questioning calls got louder as the group grew closer. Serket, having met none of them before, watched each intently as they arrived. She was trying to gauge their purpose and measure their strengths.

"Give him a moment." She motioned for them follow her a distance away to avoid disturbing Alex, who was obviously either experiencing a mental break or planning their next move. Knowing him as she did, she was quite sure it was the latter. Or, at least she was fairly sure it was the latter. The group ad-hoc warriors had quieted down a bit and were staring at Serket for direction.

"My name is Serket."

"Scorpion?" Kate squinted at her, performing her own bit of scrutiny.

"Yes." Serket was impressed, but she had expected nothing less from a group assembled by Alexander. "Very good. I'm an old friend of Alexander's, and our paths crossed in Jordan and—"

"And how the hell did you get here?" Keith chimed in. "From Jordan. To Mexico. So fast, I mean."

Serket paused and turned an eye to her pensive traveling companion. Obviously, the group was not as well acquainted with Alexander Storm as she thought. She was looking to him for assistance, but there was none to be had. At least for the moment.

"Not important right now." Serket attempted to move on, but the impetuous one wouldn't let it go.

"Uh, kinda important, scorpion," he said and shook his head at her.

Lobo was smirking and shaking his as well, but Serket had a gut feeling that his vaguely familiar face might have more knowledge of Storm than the others.

"Serket," she corrected him. "And Mr. Storm can address your questions when he is ready." Then, leaving no time for response, she added, "Tell me your names, would you?"

Keith attempted to open his mouth in opposition again, but was silenced by Lobo's palm as he moved toward Serket. "Sam, Keith, Kate," he said, pointing to each. "And I'm Lobo, Alex's pilot...amongst other jobs ... we have met before ... several times."

"That's it." She smiled, "I knew our paths had crossed. My apologies," she offered Lobo a wink in consolation. "I am pleased to meet you all," Serket said as she bowed her head slightly and smiled.

"Did you see her head get *atomized?*" Keith was obviously rattled and turned to Alexander, seeking answers. "Hey! Storm! Fucking-A, man!"

Alexander snapped to attention, relinquishing his gaze from the ground.

"Go get Abigail!" he yelled, not looking at anyone, but rather straight ahead. *"Now!"*

"Hey!" Keith said, obviously taken aback. "Some answers here! Don't you think we deserve—"

"Nothing," Alexander answered for him. "Do as I instruct and silence your whining. Get Abigail."

"Alexander," Lobo said as he approached Alex. "They're just scared, you know—quite a show they just watched from the bit I caught."

"Yes," Alexander looked into his eyes. "Pray tell, where were you?"

Lobo stepped back. A look of shock flashed across his face. "What?"

"Where were you when I needed you?"

"Easy does it there, Storm," he replied, stepping even closer to Alex. "We had to go around the pyramid, okay? Shit went down fast!"

"As shit always does." Alex turned to look at Abigail, who still lay huddled up by the Venus ruins. "Would you mind getting her, please?"

"Yeah," Lobo started to head toward Abi, obviously hurt by the exchange.

"*El Gato*," Alex said, spitting the name as if it sickened him to speak it. "Where is he?"

"Back through there." Lobo paused and pointed to the section of jungle from which they had entered the complex. "There's a road on the other side of the jungle border. He's waiting there to see if we need him."

Alexander nodded for Lobo to continue to Abigail. "The coward waits just beyond the line of fire."

Turning to the rest of the group, he said, "Listen up. We are down by three in a race of twelve."

Kate opened her mouth to speak, and Alexander shot her a look that caused her to recoil in silence.

"This race," he continued, "has no second place—cliché, I know—but accurate, nonetheless. We are now forced to transform our strategy, as planning escaped us to some degree due to the reactionary speed that was required. We will not be forced at the same pace. One out of twelve is all we need. One out of twelve breaks the spell. One out of twelve stops Hell on Earth." Alexander smirked to himself at the rhyme, and Serket recognized his color and composure returning.

Alex paced in circles. "So, we are going to split up—"

His thoughts were broken by the sudden outburst of disagreement from the group.

"Enough!" he demanded, and silence returned.

"We will return to Dragon Loch," he continued, "and there we will coordinate the missions and split into two groups, or perhaps three." The plan unfolded as he spoke.

"Kate," he said, striding to her as she looked at him with a twinge of fear in her eyes. "You seem to be well-versed in deciphering the riddles. You will remain at the castle. You will be *accueil*— home-base. You will guide us."

"Hold on a second—" Keith began.

Alexander spun to face him. "You will separate. You will do as I instruct, and you will do it without question going forward, Keith," he said, then squinted into Keith's eyes. "Or there will be no world left for you to love her in."

"Hey," Kate and Keith both responded to Alexander's words.

"Give it a break, guys!" Sam wasn't interested in the high school love charade right now, either.

Alexander winked at Sam, at which she smiled and quite possibly blushed a bit.

"Lobo, Serket, and Keith will go after one papyrus," he said, then he turned to Serket. "You *are* in for the long haul, are you not?"

"Of course," she said with a sly laugh. "I have no idea what we're doing, but you know I would follow you into the very depths of Hell, Alexander."

Alexander smiled back at her. "Let's hope that doesn't become necessary, my dear."

He turned back to the others. "Abigail, Samantha, and I will go after another section of *The Book of Gates*."

"Gates!" Serket's expression was grave. "The Dark Ones have three hours of the night, already!"

Alexander turned to her with urgency radiating through his gaze. "Yes, Serket. Now you understand."

Serket's body tensed up, and the woman who was a desert princess moments before was transformed into a Medjai warrior. "I understand."

"Kate, you will be joined by Asar very shortly, and you will have Philip there as well."

Kate nodded in acceptance.

Alex stepped closer to her. "We need to round them up in Jordan, Serket. Can you arrange transport to the strip outside of Petra?"

"Do you think Decker is ready to move?"

"He has no choice." Alex shook his head, knowing how important Decker's presence on the team was. "He will be fine. Trust me."

"Your call, Alex." Serket knew Alex was a better judge of Decker's condition than she was. "You know what he's up to, I'm sure."

"Yes. They will form the third group. Decker, Anika...and they will need one more set of hands."

"Do you want to enlist one of my Medjai?"

He tilted his head. "Yes. Have your best accompany them back just in case, but I have someone else in mind."

Serket's eyes narrowed as she awaited Alex's reveal. It did not come.

Lobo approached, cradling Abigail in his muscular, tattooed arms.

"She okay?" Sam called to Lobo.

"Shaken up," he answered and smiled at Sam. "But in one piece. She'll be okay."

"Lobo. Yes, she's okay." Alex turned and inspected Abigail. "A bit more than you thought you were capable of, hey young lady?"

Abigail said nothing. She only stared at him. She wasn't really sure how she had done what she had done. She wasn't sure where that power had come from or how to turn it on and off. But she was all of a sudden strangely aware of Alexander Storm's better understanding of herself than she did. And although she was afraid and unsure of the future, she was at the same time comforted by his odd knowledge of her powers and who she really was, who she could really be. She finally nodded at him signaling, if nothing else, her confidence in Storm's understanding of her. He would guide her—she was safe.

"The SAT phone please, Lobo." He held out his hand to the pilot.

"Yeah, yeah." Lobo shifted Abigail to his other side and gently handed her off to Sam, who had come up beside them. "In the backpack. One sec."

"Charged, I pray?" He raised one eyebrow at Lobo.

"No need to pray, Storm," he said with a laugh. "I got it. It's as it should be."

He retrieved the satellite phone from the pack and handed it off to Alexander. In the back of his mind, he was cringing a bit since he couldn't truly recall if it had been on the charger before the plane went down. Alexander depressed the power button on the side of the phone. Silence.

Oh, fuck me, Lobo thought to himself.

The phone came to life with beeps and lights, and Alexander held it up in the air a bit, looking up toward the sky.

"Your *way* clear, Alex. Clear shot," Lobo said with some relief.

Alexander smiled. "At ease sir — your clear as well."

Lobo let out a short laugh, releasing the tension that had built up waiting for the damn phone to turn on.

"You could have just used my cell." Kate held up her iPhone. "We're not exactly in the middle of nowhere anymore."

Alexander pondered her words for a moment. "No, I guess you are right. I forgot how inundated the world is with cellular data receptors."

"Cell towers," Keith said with a laugh. "Yeah, they've been around forever, Storm."

Alex eyed Keith. "Not quite. In fact, their presence is a mere millisecond in time. You're showing your generation's oblivious nature toward history before your birth—"

"And you are showing your age, Alexander." Serket cut him off before he inadvertently divulged more than he intended to, at least at this juncture. "Who are you calling?"

"An extra hand."

"Anyone I know?" she toyed with him as he dialed.

"Perhaps."

The phone rang, and Alexander covered the receiver with his hand. "Lobo, we will have our drug dealing friend supply us with two jets."

"Who are you calling, Storm?" Serket got in his face. "Tell me."

Alexander ignored her and continued addressing Lobo. "You will fly one to the Petra air strip where you last landed our jet and retrieve Decker, Asar, Decker's companion, Anika, and one of Serket's people. I will fly the rest of us back to Dragon Loch, and you'll meet us back there — promptly."

The satellite phone continued to ring.

"We are splitting up," Alexander continued with the phone pressed to his ear. "Serket and Keith are with you."

"Where are we going?" Lobo was all business.

"Not sure," Alex mused. "But I believe Kate will make short order of our new objectives. Isn't that right Kate?"

Kate's eyes grew wide. "Um, I will do my best," she said.

"That's all we can hope for. She will get us to destinations quickly," he said, ignoring her humble subtleties.

"Are you calling Jericho?" Serket exclaimed, unable to take any more.

Alexander blinked twice at Serket, refusing to answer her.

"Goddamnit."

He finally relinquished and said, "Yes."

"Storm, he's a liability! Treasure hunting, fortune seeking, no good—"

"Necessity," Alexander interrupted. "He is a necessity at this juncture."

Serket pressed her lips together as the others watched, clueless.

"He's a pirate, Alexander," she finally burst out. "A goddamn pirate!"

"Be that as it may," he said and leaned in closer to Serket's face, "this pirate flies the Dragon flag."

The Dragon Storm
GATES
Book II

97

F rank Jericho grasped his suspension rope tightly in his left hand as he shifted his weight and drove a long steel spike into the rock with his right. The impact pushed him back from the cliff's side, and his dusty boots dangled freely above the four-thousand-foot drop. Kicking out both his legs in front of him, the soles of his boots came to rest against the stone once more as gravity and his lifeline pulled him back into place. Reaching over his shoulder with his free hand, Jericho retrieved a climber's hammer from the metal ring on the side of his pack. The worn leather gloves that encased his hands twisted around the hammer's handle as he brought it down with precision on the head of the spike. Once, twice, three times, metal on metal echoed throughout the canyon like claps of thunder. Replacing the hammer in his pack, he grasped the metal spike and allowed his full weight to draw down on it.

"Don't go nowhere," he directed the spike, "you bastard."

Reaching to his side, Jericho brought up another line that was attached to his waist with a large clasp at the end. In one smooth motion, as a master tailor may thread a needle, he snapped the clasp over the oval opening in the end of the spike. Testing the stone and metal's tolerance once more, he tugged the newly secured line out toward the open space behind him several times. It did not budge. It was secure.

In sheer exhaustion, Jericho released his grasp from all lines and allowed his body to drop ever so slightly, then hang limp and suspended, secured by his lines above and in front of him. He hung there motionless for some time, arms dangling at his side like the corpse of a recent visitor to the gallows.

Jericho sighed deeply as a bird of prey screeched somewhere in the near distance. His deep brown skin, dripping with perspiration, cooled in the sliver of shade he had secured himself in. Tilting his head back, he allowed his eyes to shut.

A vibration interrupted his reverie. He remained motionless as his satellite phone buzzed against his back.

"Goddamn it, Storm." He huffed, inhaling deeply. "I'll call you. Don't call me."

The phone continued to buzz away, but he had already shut it out of his mind. He had learned to zone out, to compartmentalize his thoughts when engaged in endeavors such as this. This mental zen had saved his ass on more than one occasion and allowed him to become one with the task at hand. It was a skill which had taken many years to perfect, long before he was doing things like dangling thousands of feet above the Grand Canyon. It had been acquired on the tough, unforgiving streets of New York City. It had evolved organically through blood and murder, through sickness and depravity, through every imaginable filth and horror a human being could imagine. Twenty plus years as a homicide detective where he learned to focus on the clearance, the solution, the pieces of the puzzle. It had trained him so well he was without family, without his wife, without friends or companions.

The buzzing continued. *Save Storm's irritating ass. Unbelievable*, he thought to himself.

Snapping to, he fiddled with his pack and withdrew the phone. Clasping the end of a finger of his glove with his teeth, he whittled his way across each finger and pulled it off.

"Annoying fuck," he spat out and pressed the green button on the phone.

"Not now, Storm!" he yelled into the receiver. "Not a good time."

He withdrew the phone from his ear and was about to press the end button, but paused at the sound of Alexander's voice yelling wildly on the other end.

"What?" he yelled, placing the phone back against his ear.

"Jericho?"

"Yes?" The annoyance came through in spades.

"How did you know it was me?"

"What?" Jericho sputtered. "Are you kidding?"

There was silence for a moment. "No, not really."

"Storm, you gave me the damn phone!" Jericho began to sway in place, his anger building. "No one else has the fucking number."

"No need to—"

"This is seriously *not* a good time, Storm. I'm dangling a couple of thousand feet above a rocky death here."

As Jericho pulled the phone from his face in disgust, he could make out Alexander's sarcastic, final words. "Oh, very good."

"Very good my *ass!*" he slammed the phone back into his pack. "How's that cozy castle you prick?"

Before replacing his leather glove, Jericho reached to his side and grasped his canteen. Spinning the top off in a singular movement with his thumb, he took a large swig of water and gulped it down.

Cool refreshment calmed him a bit. He had been waiting to take a drink in order to conserve his fresh water. But Storm's intrusion had sparked a dry patch in his throat. Swaying gently on his ropes, he surveyed the beautiful landscape around him, and was soon back in his state of zen.

He was several thousand feet above the rock and flowing Colorado River below, suspended to the wall of an area of the Grand Canyon known as the Temple of Isis. Several thousand feet above him, at the plateau of the temple, was an Egyptian-inspired, albeit natural, rock formation known as Cheops Pyramid. It was at the base of this pyramidal formation that his main lifeline was secured, and it allowed him to traverse the sheer stone wall back and forth horizontally as he descended. Jericho had spent the last three days searching every nook and cranny of the Temple of Isis for the passageway into the Canyon's interior that Storm had assured him existed.

Jericho sighed once again as he pulled his glove back on. For underneath his annoyed veneer was the face of deep satisfaction—bliss, even.

This is where he loved to be. This is what he loved to do. His years of law enforcement were often hazy memories from another life. He was free now. He was truly free. He was a fortune hunter, a treasure seeker. Frank Jericho was a grand traveler, following legend and lore to the four corners of the globe. And he was damn good at it, having amassed a small fortune in treasure and antiquities over the past ten years.

This hunt was different, of course. This was debt payment. This was Storm collecting on old assists. And there had been quite a few of those through the years. Jericho's career was based eighty percent on his own skills and twenty percent on Storm's intervention. Or maybe it was more like sixty/forty.

Ah, whatever, he thought to himself. It didn't really matter since this wasn't the first time Storm had called in a chip, and it surely wouldn't be the last.

Jericho was distracted from the stunning horizon to movement below his boots. Squinting to sharpen his view, he made out the silhouette of a falcon or hawk circling some two or three hundred feet below him. He watched the mighty bird intently as its call shattered the breezy silence. Suddenly, the winged creature shot forward at the rocky side of the Canyon and disappeared into the rock.

Jericho blinked twice and shook his head as if waking from a dream. He waited several seconds for signs of the bird. Nothing.

He laughed out loud and said, "Holy shit! Looks like Horus has shown me the way in!"

Undoing his waist line, he secured the pulley system that kept him from plummeting down to his death and began to slowly walk prone down the canyon side.

"Okay, Alexander Storm!" he shouted with growing anticipation. "Let's see if the ancient Egyptians really built a temple in the middle of Arizona."

98

Alexander entered the library through the west entrance and paused a moment. Peering down the rows of book stacks to either side of him, he remained motionless and listened.

The sounds of rapid typing echoed through the expansive catacomb. Alexander smiled to himself and slowly made his way through the corridor between the stacks to the open, inner sanctum of the library some fifty or sixty-yards in. He moved silently and kept his presence concealed by proceeding close to the shelf line. Glancing ahead, he caught sight of a figure seated in his work area. Her back was to him, and he watched her shoulders ebb and flow as she typed and reviewed the data on the monitors in front of her.

The sound of the large laser printer leaping into action broke his momentary fixation, and he emerged from his secreted location. With a slow and purposeful march, he continued toward his desk. Kate had not sensed his presence yet, and he wished to keep it that way. Why? He really wasn't sure, but he was achieving some degree of satisfaction as the voyeur here, albeit in the most innocent of circumstances.

Kate was a mystery to him. Her mind was mature beyond its years; however, she continued to portray herself as a young girl in need of some degree of approval and assistance from the men in her life. He had seen it, though—the real Kate. In the short time they had spent together, he had recognized flashes of true strength and leadership. Her deductive skills and knowledge far surpassed all the others in the group. He knew this long before they had interacted together. Years of reconnaissance to assemble the perfect group of warriors had produced a wealth of knowledge on the group members' abilities. None were more impressive than Kate. At least, from a non-metaphysical standpoint, that is.

He was close, several feet from the back of her chair, and he watched as she went about her business. Alexander looked beyond her long flowing black hair to the monitors before her. Leaning slightly forward, he squinted at the array of small windows opened and scattered around the screen. Rock formations and canyons, Egyptian symbolism and old, yellowed maps.

"Good evening, Alexander." Kate's voice was playful, and she did not turn from her work.

"You knew I was here?" Alexander was shocked, and it was evident in his voice. Perhaps his analysis of her metaphysical abilities was inaccurate.

Kate said nothing and fired the printer up again with what appeared to be old newspaper clippings. Grabbing the page from the printer, she spun in her chair to face him. Her eyes were on fire with excitement. Alexander could sense her bursting need to share her findings.

"Mr. Storm breathes so loud," she said with a sly grin. "We could have shot him in the dark."

Alexander clapped his palms together and began to round the desk to join her at his work space.

"Very good! A Tolkien fan after my own heart."

Before Alex could reach her side, Kate held up her hand, stopping him in his tracks. "Have a seat in the comfy chair, big guy." She rose to her feet and continued, "You'll need to sit down for this."

Alexander nodded and dropped into the oversize leather chair in compliance. Folding his hands in his lap, he gazed up at her. "Please, proceed. Enlighten me."

Kate smiled again and turned to grab a few more documents from the desk.

"Okay, I decided to go out of order, to take riddles from the bottom of the pile since you pointed out all we need is one papyri to throw a monkey wrench in the whole demonic occupation of the Earth thing, right?"

"That is correct, Kate," Alexander reconfirmed. "We get one of the 'keys' to the gates, and nothing and no one passes through."

Kate stopped and looked at Alexander sternly. "In either direction?"

"Excuse me?" Alexander was taken aback.

"We take out one of the gates, and nothing or no one can pass from Hell to Earth, right?" She paused again, and Alexander studied her closely. She continued, "Or vice versa from Earth to Hell."

"I don't understand," Storm began, but was silenced by Kate's innocent, yet somehow knowing, expression.

She walked closer to him, leaned in, and stopped just short of his face.

"You understand *exactly* what I'm asking. Care to have me elaborate?"

"That will not be necessary," he replied, hoping to avoid further discussion of that particular topic. "Twelve papyri or no passage." He turned his eyes from hers. "In either direction. Let's move on, shall we?"

Kate returned to a safe distance from Alex. There was some bizarre connection—an attraction—between the two of them, and they both felt it. To overcompensate for these feelings, he behaved somewhat paternally. While Kate clearly found it difficult to keep a straight face when addressing him, even in the most serious of conversations, restrained giggles seemed to escape her. And it pissed her off.

"Okay, so I grabbed this one first," she continued and brought a page from the back of her pile into view then began to read aloud.

"'Ripped in the face of the Earth, a giant wound since its birth. In a land known to few men, a key in stone hidden well, ride the water and scan the walls for a tell.'" She paused and looked up at Alexander, clearly excited by her new-found understanding of the words. "'Once you find this cavern in time, follow its passage to the nights aligned. There you will find that which they guard, marked with Osiris's seal in a place so odd.'"

Pausing to shuffle the papers in her hand, she could feel him staring at her. She could feel her neck and chest flushing. Damn him. *Stop looking through me*, she thought as she composed herself.

"Right," she started again. "Okay. So 'ripped in the face of the Earth, giant wound since birth.' Blah, blah."

"Blah, blah?" Alexander said with a laugh.

She didn't look at him. "For now. Blah, blah for now. I'll get to the rest in a moment."

"I apologize. Please continue." Alexander smirked.

"Right. So, I started running searches on 'wound in the Earth' and got some expected results. Things like the 1908 Siberian meteor hole, blue hole in Belize, and stuff like that. And, of course, the prerequisite trash of the Internet you have to weed through before you get to what you're looking for."

She looked up at Alex, who nodded her on.

"So, I concentrated on the time-line clue, 'since birth,' and realized we were looking for something old, either formed during the start of time or ages ago. I immediately thought of glacial rips."

"Of course you did." This time, when Alex laughed, she smiled.

There was that damn giggle again. She focused on her words.

"*Anyway*," Kate continued, "glacial rip equates to canyons and the like. So, I searched canyons, and of course the Grand Canyon comes up first, so I thought to myself, 'Yeah that looks like a wound from an aerial perspective.' So next I pulled up a detailed map of the GC."

"GC?" Alexander raised one brow.

"Grand Canyon, Storm," she said and shook her head. "Are you even listening?"

"Of course I am, my dear. What else would I be doing?" He shifted slightly.

Kate looked up at him, completely straight-faced.

"My apologies," he said, suddenly feeling quite awkward. "I dislike anagrams. Please do continue."

"Who *says* that?" Sometimes she couldn't believe how proper the words he used were. She shrugged it off and continued her analysis. "Okay, so I pulled up a map of the G—the Grand Canyon—and lo and behold, look at this."

Kate quickly moved in beside Alex and dropped a map of the Grand Canyon in his lap.

She pointed to several spots and said, "There and there and there." Taking a step back, she added, "Temple of Ra, Temple of Set, Temple of

Osiris."

"Yes, I see them and am somewhat familiar with the naming anomalies of the...GC." He smiled, she did not.

"Osiris!" she started pacing, "I saw that and *knew* I was on the right track!"

Shuffling through her papers again, she pulled out the news clipping Alexander had noticed printing when he entered.

"Check this shit out!" She could no longer contain her excitement as she handed Alex the article.

Alexander looked the article over and placed it down on the arm of the chair.

"I am quite impressed, Kate." He was sincerely moved by her innate ability to solve these riddles.

"How could I never have heard of this?" she blurted out as she paced around the work area. "A goddamned ancient Egyptian tomb in the middle of the Grand Canyon!"

"It's unfounded. Quite debunked many times over."

"What?" Kate spun around and rushed toward him.

"Many explorers have attempted to substantiate this find, but to no avail." He pursed his lips together as if to let her down easy. "The Smithsonian even denies the existence of the elusive duo of Professor S.A. Jordan and G.E. Kincaid." He rose from his seat and walked toward Kate, then clarified, "The pair who claimed to have found this hidden treasure."

"This has to be the right location Storm." Her words were fueled, and she waved the papers in the air.

Alexander shrugged.

"I think it is best for you to waste no more time on this riddle and proceed to the next. Of your choosing, of course."

Kate moved close to Alexander—their bodies were inches apart.

"Are you saying we're not even going to *attempt* to locate the hidden cavern?"

"No," Alexander said and smiled. "I'm saying I already have someone probing every crack and crevice of the sheer cliffs of GC."

"Stop it!" Kate yelled. "No more GC! You sound weird when you say it. What's going on?"

Alexander raised an eyebrow. "As I said, I have someone on it. He is excellent. If it exists, he will find it *and* the papyri."

Kate moved in closer still, visibly annoyed, as he rose from the chair. "Did you solve all these fucking riddles already?"

Alex jerked his head back. "Language!" He interjected, and pivoting on his heel to depart, said, "Now that's just puerile, Kate. Why would I have you solve the riddles if I had already performed the task?"

Kate felt her skin flush again, but this time there was no inner giggle. "Storm!" she yelled as he disappeared from her view.

99

"This place is really something." Keith couldn't help himself as he wandered around the huge stone-walled den.

"It's a castle, genius," Sam spurted out without opening her eyes, her body semi-prone on one of the large leather couches that adorned the room. Her right leg, hanging over the edge of her seat, continued to wave back and forth with nervous rhythm. The past two days had been a whirlwind of adventure and tragedy, and she couldn't endure Keith's useless chatter about the obvious. She needed a few minutes of rest and was second guessing having declined Storm's offer of "private quarters" to wash and rest a "spell." Truth was, she didn't want to miss anything. She was pretty sure that was the reason everyone had elected to stay here, together, in this monstrosity of a den.

"I wonder how Kate is making out," Keith said as he took a seat in the lavish leather easy chair by Sam's head.

Samantha's voice rang with sarcasm. "Why don't you go and find her? She could probably use a hand."

"Stop already, Sam." Abigail had listened to enough of the banter between the two of them. "Mr. Storm told us to get some rest. To 'revive.'"

"Sorry." Keith looked at Abigail with exhausted eyes.

"It's not you," she replied, nodding toward Sam.

Sam remained motionless with her eyes closed tight. "I saw that, Abi."

"Humph." Abi grunted as she fell back into the couch. "Well, it is."

"Okay, okay. I'll give it a break. If Captain Obvious gives it a break, too."

"Fair enough," Abi said and smiled at Sam. She had also had enough of his constant chatter, but didn't want to be rude. It was just excited energy and dwindling adrenaline after all. "Keith?"

Keith rubbed his hands together and leaned forward. "Yeah, sure." His mind was clearly elsewhere, pondering all that had transpired and attempting to gain some modicum of control over the immediate future. "But what are we doing? Are we really going to split up and start traipsing all over the globe?"

"Wait for it." Sam said and nodded at Abigail. "Wait for it."

"And why does Kate have to stay here? In the castle?"

"And *there* it is." Sam lurched forward and off the couch.

"Look, Romeo," Sam said, standing in front of Keith's chair. "As I understand it, this is a little bigger than the two of you right now. So, you're gonna have to suck it up and roll with the punches here, okay?"

"Suck it up?" Keith sprang from his seat and got in her face. "Roll with the punches? What are you, a motivational cliché peddler?"

"Woah." Sam's eyes snapped open in surprise. "What the hell does that even mean?"

Abigail was on her feet. "I'll tell you what that means. It means we should stop squabbling amongst ourselves and really make an effort at resting a bit, okay?"

Sam and Keith turned to face Abigail, abandoning, quite effortlessly, their little struggle.

"We have to get some rest." Abigail took their undivided attention as her cue to sit back down. "At any moment, Storm is going to come in here—and I mean any moment cause I'm pretty sure the man doesn't sleep—and tell us grab your stuff we are heading out and none of us are going to be prepared."

"You heard the lady," Sam said with a smirk to Keith. "Sit down, and shut up."

"Sam, gimme a break and stop being a bitch." Abigail had had enough. "Lie down and go to sleep."

Samantha, feigning shock, shook her tired head. It felt like a lead weight.

"Yeah," Sam moved back to the couch. "Let's just lie down *and* be quiet," she quickly added. "I need to rest."

"Fine." Keith couldn't argue anymore. They were right. He needed sleep.

Keith climbed back into the chair and pulled his knees up to his body. He hadn't realized it, but he was well beyond exhaustion.

"We have some time," he said, satisfying his subconscious need for the last word. "Storm said we'd rest until his friend Decker arrives."

"Uh huh." Sam was almost asleep, and her acknowledgment was almost humorous.

"And that's not gonna be for some time since he's injured and on the other side of the world," Keith added.

"Right," whispered Abigail.

Samantha was seconds away from passing through the threshold into deep sleep when she felt a dull vibration, almost like the deep bass of loud music, moving through her bones. She tried to fight the outside world off, but to no avail.

"Everybody up!" Sam exclaimed clapping her hands together. "Hope you had a great rest!"

"What?" Abigail rolled over.

"Yeah," Sam replied, grabbing her shoes and gear. "That's right! Get up."

"Why?" Keith and Abigail replied in unison.

"Looks like flyboy's calculations were wrong." Sam snickered, gesturing toward the ceiling. "Chopper's here. Decker's here. Intermission's over. Back to the show."

"Hello?" Alexander answered the satellite phone as if he knew not who was on the other end.

"Storm!" Jericho's voice was short and perplexed. "Storm, it's me."

There was a brief moment of silence, and Jericho shook his head in disbelief. He was dangling several thousand feet above the Colorado River, and Alexander Storm seemed disinterested at best.

"I know who it is!" Alexander finally snapped back at him. "Have you any news," he continued, "or did you call to make small talk and chit chat?"

"What?" Jericho was stunned at Alexander's response, but not surprised. He was well acquainted with the mood swings and the bottomless pit of Storm's constantly evolving thought processes. He often mused to himself that Storm was the only man he knew who could be in two places at the same time—the physical here and now, and the other world that lived only in his mind. Dozens, if not hundreds of steps, planned out in advance. Jericho had come to the realization many years ago that neither he, nor anyone he had ever encountered, could outplay Storm. No one could ever really know his intentions or what he was thinking. It was okay with Jericho. Storm was one of the good guys. Frank didn't fear his maniacal mind. He only wished he was a little more in tune with it, or at the very least, that Storm would be a bit more forthcoming with his plans. It was all right. Jericho had come to terms with it some time ago, and he had learned to go with the flow. He trusted Alexander Storm, after all, and there were not many others who could lay claim to that trust —if any.

"Jericho, I really haven't got time for this," Alexander crackled across the satellite phone again. "I have several undertakings slated to go off at this very moment, and I must attend to my flock."

"Your *what?*" Jericho's voice echoed with concern. "Never mind. Yes, I have news, Storm."

"You found it!"

"I'm hanging outside the goddamn front door right now!"

"Splendid!" Alexander's voice was elated, "I knew you would! I knew if anyone could find that needle in a giant stone haystack it would be you, Francis. Your exploration skills are clearly set to surpass my own. I don't think I would have been so fortunate."

"*Jericho,*" he corrected. "And I have a feeling you would have recognized this sign as well. It was almost custom made for you," he said with a laugh.

"You will have to tell me all about it, but not today. Today I need you to get in there and retrieve that papyri."

"I'm going, but what am I looking for? The satellite phone isn't going to work in there."

"Ah, yes. I am not quite sure how to have you proceed. This riddle, above all the others, is sketchy, at best."

Jericho shifted on his guide line and swiveled so his feet could rest on the bottom ledge of the opening. He tried to peer in, but was met with a blackness whose tendrils engulfed everything not more than a few feet in.

"Can't see shit," he relayed to Storm. "Odd smell, too."

"Sulfur?" Storm was instantly agitated.

"No, no," Jericho quickly reassured him; he knew where Alex was going. "Foul like decay."

Alexander's voice softened. "Could be bats, Jericho. Best take heed. They can be quite a menace, and their guano can be both caustic and toxic."

"Bat shit," Jericho said with a laugh. "Yeah, I've dealt with plenty of bat shit through the years. I'm all good."

Alexander laughed, recalling several joint expeditions in South America and India that had their fair share of bat incidents.

"All I can tell you is what the riddle maker left for us."

Jericho could hear papers shuffling on the other end. Jericho smirked a little and said, "Storm, you mean to tell me you don't have all this memorized?"

Alex said nothing and continued his paper rustling. Finding what he needed, he recited, "'Follow its passage to the nights aligned. There you will find that which they guard, marked with Osiris's seal in a place so odd.' Of course I have it memorized. I was looking for documents for our resident decipherer, and something just came to mind that she might find useful."

"She?" Jericho toyed with him. "A lady friend?"

"Lady friend?" Alexander echoed. "Seriously, sometimes I do not understand your ribbing."

"I'm kidding, pal," Jericho quickly recovered. "If we have nothing else to say to each other, I'm gonna go. My back's killing me, my arms are dead, and I need to go save the world."

Alexander laughed a hearty laugh. "That's the spirit, my friend!"

"Later." Jericho placed the phone back in his pack and immediately pushed off the ledge with both feet. His muscular legs flexed and strained with dying energy as he proceeded to repeat the same move each time he swung back to the ledge. He was working up his momentum so he could release the line lock and swing right into the cavern entrance. He needed to plan precisely the right tandem movements, or he was sure to lose his balance and fall backward out of the opening.

"One...more...time." He grunted as he expelled his last drop of energy and sent his body soaring away from the opening. Leaning back, as one does on the ascent while riding a swing, he lifted his legs in the air for maximum drive. He waited; his eyes locked on the toes of his boots. He was watching for shadow to overtake light, indicating he was far enough in the opening to release the lock. Milliseconds passed at a pace that felt eternal to Jericho who knew better than to let his mind wander to the results of a failed attempt here. As darkness passed across his feet, he slapped the latch that held his position on the line and watched as the pulley sailed across the opposing line. Arching his back and pointing his feet down, as if jumping from the swing this time, he coasted through the air and into the cavern entrance. Jericho held his breath as he prayed for his feet to plant on the rock surface of the interior of the cavern.

The soles of Jericho's boots came solidly into contact with stone floor of the entryway. He instinctively bent his knees and steadied himself. It would take a moment of orientation before he was out of danger as he was unsure of how far in he had careened. Extending his hands out at his sides, he found his balance and rose back to an upright position. He unsnapped the LED flashlight from his belt and fired it up to illuminate the space in front of him.

"Sweet," he whispered into the darkness. He was on solid ground. Peering over his shoulder, he was pleased to see he had sent himself a good ten feet into the cavern. He was safe. Relaxing his body, he fell to one side and leaned against the cavern's inner wall.

Taking a moment to survey his surroundings, he passed the light back and forth and up and down. The opening to the cavern was about ten feet high and roughly fifteen feet wide, fairly uniform throughout. The inner area he was resting in appeared to expand on a gradual slope up at the top and out at the sides. The walls of the cavern were not smooth. Instead, they appeared hole ridden and porous like a soft rock or piece of coral the sea had sculpted to its liking over many years. Not what he had expected.

The walls in this area were devoid of any marking or unnatural characteristics. Jericho turned and looked closely at the stone he had just been leaning on.

Wait a minute. He pulled his glove off and ran his fingers across the rough surface of the wall. He noted uneven ridges and cuts forming slight, but visible, ninety-degree angles across the wall.

Somebody worked this stone, he thought. *Very subtle remains, but remains of tool marks nonetheless.*

His interest was instantly piqued. Had someone carved this entire catacomb? Turning toward the dark, he decided he had rested long enough and began to venture farther in.

"Don't know what I'm looking for." He joked out loud to himself. "But I'm gonna find it, sure as shit."

Walking forward at a slow but steady pace, Jericho passed the light back and forth across his path. Although it wasn't readily visible to the eye, he was sure he was descending as he moved farther into the darkness. He also noted the increased intensity of the cavern's stench filling his nose.

"What the fuck is that?"

As he approached roughly forty feet in, he noted the sharp curve in the path just ahead.

"Man," he said to himself. "I hate coming around corners into who the hell knows what."

An uneasy feeling came over him as he reached the curved wall. Without thinking twice about it, he took a large outward step and shot his light into the darkness around the curve.

"Shit!" He couldn't control it, and the words escaped his lips. He hadn't really expected to see much of anything but rock in front of him, and he was taken completely by surprise by the tall figure standing at the end of the new run of tunnel. He stood motionless for a seemingly interminable amount of time, then he finally got his nerve up.

"Hey!" He yelled into the cavern. "Hey! Who's there?"

This was madness. There couldn't be another human being in this tunnel. There was no way someone could be down here with him. Rational thought returned, and he marched forward at the figure. Removing the silver Beretta from its holster, he pointed both it and the light's beam directly at the shadowy figure. Sweat dripped from his brow, and all of his senses were firing at the same time when he came to a sudden stop.

"Ha!" He laughed at his paranoia. "It's a statue. A fucking statue Jericho."

He moved in closer and shined the light across the eight-foot statue of Anubis that stood before him.

"Creepy-ass Anubis statue." He laughed again, easing his nerves. "But a statue, nonetheless."

But as his mind settled down, the realization hit him in the gut.

"Fuck me!" He ran his hand across the ancient stone likeness of the Egyptian god of the afterlife. "Egyptians...in the Grand Canyon."

SNAP

The noise rocketed Jericho's mind back into defensive mode and he spun around to his right to face the direction of the open tunnel. Motionless, he listened. He still couldn't see in front of him, and he resolved to remain still for the moment. His heart beat in his chest like the vibrations of a big bass drum. As he remained in his statuesque position his visual perception, deficient as it was, gave way to strengthening audible attenuation.

Still, he waited.

And finally, it came. The snapping sound. Loud and echoing through the chamber. Jericho unconsciously held his breath and remained still.

SNAP

The sound repeated, this time followed by a new and even more menacing dragging sound.

SNAP ... DRAG

Jericho's breathing escalated until he was panting. It was too much. What had Storm sent him into?

SNAP ... DRAG ... SNAP

Closer now, the fucking sounds were getting closer. Jericho wrinkled his nose in disgust. The stench! The stench was getting stronger as well.

SNAP ... DRAG ... SNAP

It was almost on him now. Just beyond the limits of his flashlight. It was coming for him. Of this he had no doubt. Nervously, he snapped his head around to look over his shoulder, but he could barely make out the curve of the tunnel behind him from the last remnants of sunlight entering the cavern.

Fight or flight, I guess. His mind raced—it would take him some time to secure himself to the lead line and get back to a rope that could get him out of there. In the meantime, his mission would be a fail. All based on some unknown threat. That wasn't going to fly. He was Frank Jericho, damn it. He had stared into the darkest depths of evil, both human and other worldly, and he had survived his traipses through Hell. He wasn't about to turn and hightail it out of there without at least sizing up the threat and making a logical decision based upon his chances for survival.

"Jesus Christ." His mind continued to race like a kid on cold medicine, spinning madly. "I sound like fucking Storm now."

Silently moving to the left side of the Anubis statue, he was able to obtain some degree of shelter, obfuscating him from the tunnel ahead.

SNAP ... DRAG ... SNAP

It was there. His deepest, darkest nightmares were about to materialize before his eyes.

SNAP ... DRAG ... SNAP

The foul stench was unbearable, and he fought with his lungs to suppress a cough.

"Storm. Well, if I'm thinking like Storm..."

SNAP ... DRAG ... SNAP

"I may as well *act* like Storm!"

Lurching forward from the shadows surrounding the Anubis statue, he ran directly at the harrowing noises.

Right into the snap, drag, snap of his worst nightmare, if such a thing existed.

It was then Frank Jericho saw it emerge from the darkness. It was then that Frank Jericho realized he had made a horrible mistake.

101

Moloch moved swiftly through the threshold of the altar room in Dalquharran Castle. With Naamah's limp and lifeless corpse draped over his shoulder, he reached out, and with a swipe of his free arm, wiped the altar free of candles and debris.

"Fucking Storm!" His words echoed through the stone chamber with unearthly pain.

Placing his hand at the base of Naamah's neck, he let her body fall forward, and he laid her gently on the stone slab. He slowly walked around the remains of her shattered body, peering down at the Medjai's handiwork with flames in his eyes. He could fix this, of course, but it would require a trip into Hell. And that was a journey he had hoped to avoid at this particular juncture in time. Walking to the top of the altar, Moloch reached his steely hands out to embrace Naamah's shoulders. Her head was all but gone. Blown clear off by the silver falcon's devastating assault. He had never expected to feel so strongly about such a thing. He felt no true love, except for himself and his own ambition. He had grown fond of Naamah, but she was as disposable to him as the night sheds the day, or so he thought. The feelings of loss—yes, true loss—had overcome him since they pulled through the portal. Desperation, almost panic, had overtaken his thoughts. He paused at the altar. This was a weakness, wasn't it? A chink in his armor that his enemies could, if they became aware of it, exploit.

"No matter," he thought to himself. He had grown to enjoy her company. He enjoyed their plotting, and he enjoyed their carnal adventures.

"Perdition it is," he said with a new sense of surety. Having argued both sides in his mind, he felt confident in his decision to revive Naamah and restore her earthly body.

Moloch moved to the center of the stone altar, and with quick, purposeful movements, he dropped his pants to his ankles and pulled his shirt over his head. Standing naked before Naamah's body, he outstretched both of his arms in front of him. Clenching his fists tightly, he began to chant ancient and forbidden words. Within seconds, he and the altar were encircled in a ring of green-hued flames.

He reached forward and firmly grasped both sides of her dress. Like a scissor cutting through a thin sheet of paper, Moloch tore Naamah's dress in two and pulled it away, exposing her naked body. The green flames intensified and danced around her, engulfing both her and the altar in a magical inferno of flickering cold heat.

"Bring her now!" Moloch shouted out through the chamber's threshold. In response to his command, two figures, hidden in the shadow of over-sized cloaks, entered the room of crumbling stone, leading an unwilling participant with them and delivered her to Moloch. Draped in a dark cloak as well, the girl struggled to get away from her captors before they reached the edge of the flames. It was too late. Moloch reached out and grabbed her wrist, pulling her through the flames and to him. She continued to kick and punch as Moloch wrapped his arm around her waist and hoisted her onto the stone slab, dropping her hard next to Naamah's body. A loud bang echoed over the hiss of the flames as the girl's head slammed onto the rock. Moloch watched as her eyes bounced and rolled up into her head. She was fading in and out of consciousness, and he reached out and violently shook her body.

"Stay with us," he whispered. "You must remain present."

The girl responded by wrinkling her brow as she tried to reorient herself.

"There, there. What a good girl." He chided her as a mother would to a child. "You'll be just fine."

The girl calmed and the fear seemed to drain from her body as she submitted to Moloch's intent.

"It will be okay," he continued as he crouched down and fiddled with something at the side of the altar.

The girl shook her head back and forth, trying to clear the thoughts in her mind. She looked at Moloch again but could only see the top of his head. Turning to her other side, she suddenly began to tremble. Her mouth fell open, but not a sound escaped as she gazed at the empty space where Naamah's head should have been. She turned back to Moloch just in time to see him rising back up at her side, a sick grin painted on his face as he grew unnaturally taller.

"There, there," he began again. "Good girl ... what a good girl you are." Smiling dementedly at her, he brought his hands up to expose a thick silver blade grasped tightly in his fists. The girl's eyes grew wide in terror at the sight of the dagger, and this time, when she opened her mouth, the screams blasted forth like ramparts. Moloch threw his head back as a maddening laugh emanated throughout the chamber. Lifting the dagger high above his head, he smiled at the destruction of innocence he was poised to unleash as his face morphed and changed. For a split second, the unwilling participant saw Moloch's true self—his Hell face, his black soul.

And then she saw no more as he drove the blade down into her chest with such power it plunged through her body and shattered into pieces against the stone below her. Hissing and spitting with primordial fury, Moloch watched as the flames expanded around them, the green tendrils licking at every corner of the chamber. Then, as quickly as the flames had expanded, they were sucked together around the altar, like smoke through a straw, finally disappearing altogether. Moloch, Naamah's body, and his sacrificial offering disappeared with them.

In what was mere seconds in the chamber, but hours in Hell, a bright red flame erupted across the barren rock altar. The flames quickly receded to expose the two bodies entwined within. Naamah shoved herself away from Moloch's broad chest and his embrace. Sitting up, she began to cough.

"Did they get the papyri?" she asked, turning to look at Moloch as he sat up to meet her.

Moloch smiled. "So nice to see you too, my dear."

"Did they get the stone serpent's papyri?" she shrieked viciously, and Moloch raised one eyebrow, eyeing her cautiously.

"No, they did not," he finally responded. "Safe and sound here in Dalquharran."

Naamah nodded with satisfaction and threw her legs over the side of the altar.

"You did a marvelous job of holding onto the prize," Moloch said in consolation.

"Fuck that!" Naamah arched her back and jumped down from the stone slab. "Death spasms held the prize in place."

"Ha ha!" Moloch's voice rang out loudly as he dismounted the table from the opposite side. "It really is wonderful to have your head back." He turned and grinned at her. "And that pretty little mouth that accompanies it."

Naamah said nothing, but instead stretched and turned her neck. Reaching up with her long fingers, she ran them around the circumference of her throat.

"Good as new, Naamah," he smirked. "No need to fret."

"That fucking Arabian witch!" her voice dragged from some guttural region within. "I am going to slaughter that cunt!" she howled as she moved around the altar until she was face to face with Moloch. "I'm going to peel the skin from her bones...and make Storm watch."

"Easy." Moloch extended his arms and pulled her to him, to which Naamah resisted just a bit. "All in good time, my dear."

Naamah opened her mouth in protest but was cut short by Moloch's finger across her lips.

"The prize, remember? Vengeance in due time."

Naamah nodded and pulled his hand away. "Vengeance in *soon* time," she said with a familiar smile.

Moloch grinned in return. "Shall we get to it, then?" he paused. "Or do you need a bit of time to get your head together?"

Naamah pushed away from him in pseudo disgust. "I'm glad you are enjoying this."

"Come now," he said and sympathetically extended a hand in truce. "We have much work to do."

Naamah paused momentarily, pouting, then snatched Moloch's hand in hers. Giving a hard tug, she pulled his body against hers and began to back up to toward the altar.

"We have a few moments, don't we?" Naamah unleashed her seductive voice on him, kissing his neck and shoulders, and he nodded.

"What say we test out this new mouth of mine, then?"

Moloch smiled devilishly at her, void of any protests, as she lowered herself down his body.

102

Jericho dove to his left and rolled to avoid the glowing spectral sword that sliced through the air within inches of his head. Hitting the wall of the cave's tunnel hard, his legs buckled as he tried to quickly spring to his feet. His mind raced as he struggled to steady himself and assess his options. The two phantom figures moved in unison as they spun to their left to face his fumbling body. Still crouched at the stone floor, he snapped his legs out like a frog and leapt to the center of the passage behind the ghastly pair.

"Holy shit." He huffed as he rose up to face his challengers. The inner sanctum of the cave was behind him, and he contemplated his chances if he turned tail and ran further in. What new hell lie in the depths of the dark passage? No, he didn't necessarily like that idea. His assailants turned, like wild dogs in a unified pack, to face him once more. He could make them out completely with the light of the day filtering in through the tunnel behind them. Towering heaps of rusted steel and leather, frayed decaying cloth dangling from their twisted bodies. Their faces concealed by the twisted and dented remains of archaic helmets whose open masks gave way to nothing beneath except unfathomable darkness.

"Knights," Jericho muttered to himself in disbelief as the pair readied themselves for onward assault once again.

SNAP

The demonic pair brought their swords up in unison with such force they split the air like a whip.

SNAP... DRAG

Stepping forward with their right legs, their left legs dragged across the floor in a combative maneuver. The forward advance appeared sluggish at first. Jericho's senses were tested, however, as the air surrounding the ghostly knights rippled and shifted. And they were on him.

SNAP

Inches from his head again!

"Mother fucker!" Jericho dropped, his rear-end hitting the ground hard. Springing up on his hands and feet, he immediately began to back pedal away like a crab running to the surf.

"Screw it!" Jumping to his feet, Jericho took off blindly into the passage, his light having been dropped in sheer panic somewhere on the other side of his pursuers. The tunnel seemed to grow tighter as he proceeded deeper into the cliff.

SNAP ... DRAG ... SNAP

"Crap! Oh, crap!" They were close already.

Using his fingers, he gauged his surroundings by running them along the stone wall, he was able to move quickly enough, but not fast enough to stay ahead of them for long.

Knights, he thought. *In the Grand Canyon. In an Egyptian tomb.*

Jericho continued his race through the winding tunnel, his mind reeling. Trying to analyze the situation, he whispered to himself, "Knights... Egypt...knights...Egypt..."

SNAP ... DRAG ... SNAP

Too close. Pulling his arm from the wall, he picked up his pace. Refusing to look behind, he squinted into the darkness ahead. Suddenly he caught a twinkle of light shimmering on the stone in front of him.

"Keep going...keep going," he chanted. It was light! Rounding a bend in the rock, he was instantly met with a warm amber glow filling the tunnel ahead of him.

SNAP ... DRAG ... SNAP

Jericho knew what lie ahead could be worse than what lay behind, but at least he would be able to see the form of the horrors that awaited.

"Egypt...knights," he continued repeating, and at that moment he completely scrapped the Grand Canyon issue—it made no sense. Then it hit him. Of course! Knights...Templar!

SNAP ... DRAG ... SNAP

The fiends were like choreographed robots in their repetitive movements. Stumbling forward into the light, his eyes were met with a flood of bright candle light as he threw himself into a large chamber. Quickly adjusting to his new surroundings, he realized the intensity of the light was not created solely by the candles that lined the walls of the oval catacomb, but by the vast array of treasures brilliantly reflecting the flickering glow. Gold and jewels. Rows of Egyptian sarcophagi that would put Tut's cache to shame. An enormous gold altar center and to the rear, surrounded by gilded gods and goddesses, a flame of unknown origin levitating above the altar's surface.

Jericho gasped at what must surely be the largest collection of ancient Egyptian treasures ever seen by a modern man.

SNAP ... DRAG ... SNAP

Close now. Their ghostly armaments rattling in their relentless pursuit. In order to bask in the glory of this find, he would first have to survive. He *must* focus. Darting to the side of the chamber, he spotted a jewel and gold-adorned sword glistening in the light cast off the altar. Kneeling to retrieve it, his eyes wandered in front of him to the inlayed gold eye of Horus set in the center of the floor.

"Templar...Egypt." He paused, the gears and cogs of his deductive mind spinning. "The riddle!"

Fumbling in the pocket of his shorts, he withdrew a crumpled-up scrap of paper and opened it. Tilting it to catch the light, he mouthed the words until he reached the last sentence.

"Once you find this cavern in time, follow its passage to the nights aligned. There you will find that which they guard, marked with Osiris's seal in a place so odd." Looking up to think, his eyes fell upon the ancient warriors who had finally come to call.

"Nights aligned!" he yelled, jumping to his feet, sword in hand. "*KNIGHTS* ...aligned."

SNAP ... DRAG

He dove across the Eye of Horus and ducked to the ground.

SNAP

I'm still here, a maddening voice jested from within him.

Rising to his feet, Jericho lifted the dazzling blade over one shoulder, and snapped into an attack stance. Peering down, he quickly took inventory of what lie beneath his feet. Taking two steps backward, he moved to one side of the Eye of Horus inlaid on the ground so it stood directly between him and the spectral knights.

SNAP

The air of the chamber whooshed around Jericho's face.

"Come on, you bastards!" His teeth were borne and spit flew from his lips and melded with the layer of sweat that engulfed his body.

DRAG

The knights moved forward, but did not metaphysically shift and cover the full space between them and Jericho. Standing stoically at the edge of the great eye inlay, their heads tilted as one toward the floor.

"That's right!" Jericho screamed, a maddening grin on his face. "Osiris's seal!"

The knights continued to gaze—with eyes that had ceased to exist eternities ago—at the golden symbol that separated them from their prey.

"Now align, goddamn it!" Jericho stiffened his arms as their heads rose in unison and fixated on him. "Whatever the fuck that means..." His voice trailed off into the darkness, his grin faded.

The haunted knight to his left moved first.

DRAG

Sliding into position atop the great seal, Jericho could hear the monster's armor bulge and groan as it prepared to deliver its killing blow.

"Oh, shit!" The words barely escaped Jericho's lips as he realized he had misinterpreted the riddle. He was going to die. There was no time for defensive maneuvers. There was no time for anything. He grimaced, eyes squinted, as he watched the wraith unleash its sword forward.

SNAP

Jericho felt an icy cold mist cross his face and his eyes popped open wide. Dropping his sword to his side, he began to run his hands over his face, head, and neck.

"Ha!" His laughter rang out uncontrollably. "Ha ha!" He jumped in place and gazed up at the Templar. Its body had dematerialized into an ethereal form. Lifting its misty sword up, its helmet twisted and turned as it inspected the weapon.

"Ha!" Jericho bellowed out again, leaning forward into it. Jericho couldn't contain himself. The knights dumbfounded movements struck him as comical.

SNAP ... SNAP

The ancient guardian brought the sword down across Jericho's chest, but it broke into mist across his body once more. Jericho jumped back as his heart skipped a beat.

"Oh, yeah!" He laughed, looking up. "Got me again, asshole! You got me again!"

SNAP ... DRAG

The sound rang out from beyond the seal and the vaporous ghoul turned to face its companion. Jericho's smile quickly faded as he seized the opportunity to reclaim the jeweled sword from the ground. Rising up, he was startled to find knight number two standing in the middle of Osiris's seal, sword raised high above its hulking metallic figure. The vaporized knight's body had merged with its physical counterpart, the mist of its form radiating from the advancing warrior's armor.

"Come on, fucker!" Jericho could take no more *"Align!"*

SNAP

Jericho lifted his sword to meet the onslaught this time, his face stern, his eyes fixed.

The two blades met in an awful clamor of metal on metal, and Jericho's hands exploded in pain. The burn radiated up his wrists and into his forearms as if a grenade had gone off in his hands, and he cried out in agony as he watched the demon's sword dematerialize and pass through his own.

A large sigh, from somewhere deep within his soul, escaped his body as he released his sword. Listening to the blade hit the floor and bounce several times, he stumbled back against the altar. The pain in his limbs was slowly subsiding, and he turned his attention to the seal of the great Egyptian deity.

Awestricken, he watched as the two ancient souls merged into one form and rose above the eye. The mist became a formless ball of smoke and fire. Without warning, it shot from its suspended prison above the seal in an explosive stream. Jericho dove from the altar as the spirit mass crashed into the hovering fire above it and dissipated into the flame.

Leaning against the majesty of the intricately designed sarcophagus he had fallen into, Jericho watched in sheer wonder as a stream of intense light projected from the altar flame. Shooting with laser precision, it traced the gold inlay of the Osiris seal which glowed like molten lava as the light passed over it. Once the entire outline had been irradiated, the light from the altar faded and disappeared, leaving a glowing eye of Horus in the center of the chamber.

"The knights aligned." Jericho whispered the words as he rose to his feet and walked toward the radiant seal. Without warning, the ground under his feet began to rumble, and he could make out the distinctive sounds of crushing and shifting rock. Sounds a cave explorer hope they never hear.

Steadying himself before the glorious display of magic, he watched as the seal revealed its secret. Parting down the center, it opened like the mouth of a great beast and exposed the eerie green glow within. Without further hesitation, Jericho leapt to the opening and peered over the edge.

"Bam!" he yelled out with great satisfaction as he plunged his hand into the hole. Grasping the small gold box within, he rose to his feet and lifted the prize to his face. Sliding the inlay top back, he smiled as he gazed down at the small papyrus within.

"Screw Storm!" he shouted to an audience of treasure and darkness that surrounded him, "I'm a god...damned...bad...ass!"

103

"Welcome, welcome." Alexander paced the area equatable to center stage in the castle's library anxiously. His entire troupe of actors in this epic performance now stood half-circle around him and Kate. All except Jericho, of course, but he didn't play well with others anyway, so Alexander considered his absence a blessing. Having walked some distance from the line of eagerly awaiting guests, he quickly pivoted on his heels and marched back to Kate's side.

"How are you doing, Decks?" he asked, eyeing Anika for a truthful response.

"I'll live," Decker said with a laugh and shifted pressure from one leg to the other. "Been through worse."

Alexander smiled at his friend. "Perhaps I should leave you here to rest with Kate. No?"

"Hell, no!"

Kate looked up at Decker with a questioning glance.

"No offense," responding to her expression, "just ready to go, that's all."

Kate smiled and nodded. She knew what he had meant.

"Excellent," said Alexander as he once again took to pacing. "We have had all our introductions. Everyone knows everyone now and all that." He paused once again, then continued, "And everyone will trust each other without question, as I now trust each of you. Am I clear?"

"Excuse me," Serket shot back at him.

"You heard me. Do you trust my judgment?"

Serket brought her hand up to her chin, pondering his question.

He asked, "Seriously?"

"Most of the time, Storm, yes, I trust your judgment."

"Fine. It's settled, then."

Serket closed her eyes and shook her head. "Glad we had this talk."

Storm's face grew stern. "There is quite literally no time for talk."

Serket sighed and looked back and forth to members of the group. They said nothing.

"Where is Jericho? Decided not to join us, I guess?"

"Jericho is busy at this moment, securing a scrap of ancient paper that may be the key to saving the entire planet from damnation and darkness."

"Oh," Serket looked down at her feet. "He's excused, then."

Alexander smirked and turned back to Kate. She was grabbing sheets of paper out of the printer. Spinning in her chair to face Alex, she sprang to her feet.

"Okay, so I went out of order as per your suggestion, and I started with riddle six, which reads as follows." Kate paused and turned to address the others as well. She wore her enthusiasm and her sense of accomplishment on her face for all to see.

"'A cage for an entire land, ripe with fury, stone and sand. A keep without a castle door, a home with frame and nothing more. When sixty-seven make it whole, the sixty-sixth is the one to know. A sacred serpent—'"

"Jesus Christ! Another fucking snake?" Lobo interrupted, shaking his head.

"Continue." Alexander cut further complaints short, giving the floor back to Kate.

She continued, "A sacred serpent guards this guard's retreat and guards the truth beneath its feet."

Kate looked up at her listeners and opened her arms.

"Yeah, I'm clueless," Keith responded to Kate's prodding for the riddle's *obvious* context.

"That's nothing new." Sam laughed, but none of the others joined in her juvenile banter. "Sorry."

Alexander nodded at Sam in recognition of the gravity of the present discussion.

"What have you surmised, Kate? Enlighten us." Alexander urged her on as he walked over and sat in her seat. "Give us the details of your findings, please."

"Okay," she began. "First, let me tell you what I believe it refers to. I think you'll all be able to follow along once you have that."

"Excellent idea. Continue, please."

"The Great Wall of China!" Kate shouted.

"A cage for an entire land!" Anika exclaimed illustrating her immediate conceptual grasp of Kate's reasoning.

Kate turned to address her directly. "Yes! So, I searched the number sixty-seven against the great wall and I came up with guard towers." She turned to Alexander and said, "There are sixty-seven guard towers along the wall at the section known as Jinshanling."

Alexander smiled. "Excellent work, Kate! And based on that finding, sixty-six, ironically, is our target, yes?" he said and winked at Decker, amused by the numerical irony.

"Exactly!"

"Jinsa...what?" Keith squinted and shook his head at the others.

"Quiet, Keith." Alexander was in no mood for infantile behavior.

Kate came to his rescue and explained. "Jinshanling. A section of the Great Wall located about 130 kilometers northeast of Beijing."

"Perfect!" Storm launched himself from the chair and leaned across the desk. "Serket, you are up. Take Keith and head to China. Find the serpent in the sixty-sixth guard house. You should be able to figure out the rest. I'll send Jericho to meet you if he should return in time."

"Wait," Keith started. "Shouldn't we hear the rest of—"

"No need," Alexander cut him off. "Serket, take your warrior waiting on the roof with you as well."

Serket nodded. "See ya', Storm." She turned to exit the library.

"Wait!" Kate called after her. "Take these copies of the riddle and my research."

Serket continued her exit. "Grab 'em, Keith, and let's go."

"Wh, wh, what?" His words stumbled forth.

Kate stepped forward and shoved the papers into his open hand. "You'll be fine. Stay in touch." Kate leaned forward and softly touched her lips to his. "Come back in one piece, okay?"

Keith smiled and said, "I shall return with your treasure, my lady." He turned to follow Serket with a renewed spring in his step. "Wait up!"

"I do like him," Alex said softly at Kate's side.

"Yeah," she sighed. "Me, too. She'll keep him alive, right?"

"She'll do her best...or die by his side."

104

Jericho's hand launched forward to grab the edge of the stone cliff. He was exhausted and thirsty thanks to the unrelenting sun directly overhead. Swinging his other hand up, he pulled himself hard against the side of the mountain. *One last burst of energy,* he thought to himself, and he heaved his body up and over the apex of the rocky wall. Once his knees passed over the precipice, he allowed his body to drop unsupported to the surface of the canyon peak.

"Jesus Christ," sweat sprayed from his goatee as he rolled to his side, "I'm getting too old for this shit."

Reaching behind his back, Jericho struggled to lift his pack over his head then let it drop to the rock beside him. He pulled his gloves off and shoved his hand into the bag, withdrew his phone, and dialed Storm.

"Jericho?" Storm answered before it even had the chance to ring.

"Jeez, Storm, what are you doing? Holding the phone in your hand?"

"Actually, I was." Alexander replied dryly. "I was just about to check on you."

"Ha," Jericho said as he sat up. "Mind meld."

"What?"

"Forget it, Storm." He grabbed his bag and placed it between his legs. "Good timing, that's all."

"Indeed. Any luck on your venture?"

"Well, let me tell you this, Storm. You need to work on your translations, okay?"

"Meaning?"

"Meaning 'night' wasn't night like *darkness*." Visions of the evil pair flashed across his mind's eye. "It meant 'knight.' Like a fucking *Templar* knight."

"Yes, I know," Alexander said before Jericho went any further. "I dictated the riddle to you over the phone, Jericho. You assumed the word 'knight' was 'night.'"

"Jesus, Storm, you didn't think that was a useful piece of info?"

"I honestly don't see how that would have helped you. To know there could be a knight? In the Grand Canyon? In an Egyptian temple? Would that have assisted you in your efforts?"

Jericho was silent.

"Jericho did you obtain the papyrus? It is rather pressing, and I must insist on—"

"I got it, Storm!"

"Spectacular news, Jericho! Absolutely wonderful!"

Jericho rose to his feet and withdrew the small box from his pack.

"I'm looking at it right now, and it's not even the greatest treasure in there. You need to send me some hands and transport. We gotta get everything out of there!"

"Nonsense!" Alexander shot him down. "Mark the coordinates in your GPS, and we shall return another day."

Jericho began to pace about. "Look, Storm, this is *the* treasure. I'm set. I'm not leaving here without it."

Storm's voice grew stern. "Mark the coordinates, Jericho, and prepare for transport."

Jericho suddenly heard the distant, dull drone of propellers. He looked to the eastern sky and squinted.

"Storm?"

"I'm not asking, Francis."

A military grade Black Hawk helicopter emerged from the ripple of heat in the distant sky, and Jericho shook his head.

"Storm?" he pleaded again.

"Get on the chopper, Jericho. That's an order!"

Alexander could hear him rustling about in exasperated desperation.

"Get on the chopper, and get the papyrus to the safety of the castle."

"Storm, if I leave this cache behind someone else may track it."

"Jericho ... if you don't secure that spell from the enemy, there will be no museums to display your find, no patrons to view it, no scientists to study it, no papers to report it or give you your due accolades. There will only be eternal darkness and suffering!"

Alexander could hear the hum of the rotors amplified through the phone.

"Do you hear me, Jericho?" Alexander shouted over the intensifying din in the background. "Do you understand?"

Suddenly, there was silence on the line, and he put the phone down on the desk in front of Kate.

"Excellent news!" he said to the remaining group. "Frank Jericho has obtained one of the papyri and is on his way to Dragon Loch as we speak!"

A roar of cheers broke out in the library and echoed throughout the castle.

Serket, who was halfway up the steps of the tower to the roof, paused as the sounds from the library reached her. Smirking and shaking her head, she looked down at her companion on the steps below.

"Looks like the pirate came through." She turned and continued her ascent. "Doesn't change our job, though. Let's go."

Back in the library, there was a renewed sense of hope as the remaining members of Alexander's group moved closer to him with excitement in their eyes.

Alexander smiled. "So, Kate. Where are *we* heading?"

105

"Ah, Cambodia," Alexander exclaimed as he sprang from the side of the dilapidated steam train before it came to a complete stop. His boots hit the ground with a plume of dust as he straightened his body and tilted his head to face the unforgiving Indochina sun. Pulling his fists to his chest and lifting his elbows upward, Alexander unleashed a huge stretch and turned to face the doorless exit of the train. Lobo appeared in the opening and nodded to Alex as he stepped down.

"Do you smell that, man?" Alexander asked, lifting his nose to the wind, breathing deeply, then exhaling with bravado. "Magnificent!"

The aromas of the surrounding villages lofted into the makeshift train station and filled the air with incense and exotic spices. Alexander's mind danced through the muddled array and tried to discern the exact source of the smells.

"Definitely frankincense." His eyes were shut, blocking one sense to enhance another. "Turmeric? Perhaps ginger?"

"Reciting a recipe?" Sam teased as she reached out to grasp Lobo's extended hand and jumped down to his side.

"A recipe?" Storm's eyes popped open. "Yes, my dear. An ancient recipe of unsurpassed value."

Samantha gave Alex a puzzled look and raised one eyebrow. He smirked at her and then looked at Abigail, who stood at the precipice of the train. Quickly moving past Sam and Lobo, Alexander extended his arms and grasped Abigail around the waist. Effortlessly, he hoisted her up and set her down gently beside him.

"Thank you, Mr. Storm." Abigail, taken somewhat by surprise, averted her eyes and stepped to Samantha's side.

Alexander turned from his companions to assess the dirt road to his left. The path was littered with locals, coming and going. Quickly shooing away the hordes of street vendors as they approached, Alexander began to move up the road.

"'In the holy city of the land, which in winter feeds the starving Mekong,'" he began as he walked, "'Seek ye out the ancestor of Brahma. In the temple where the trees eat the stone,'" he turned to ensure the others had fallen in behind him, "'locate that which should logically house what you desire. If perplexed by many, remember to always first center yourself. Find the stone with serpent's seal, the truth beneath Buddha had hoped to conceal.'"

"You get all that, Lobo?" Sam asked as the three caught up to Alexander.

"Sure," he replied without missing a beat.

Alexander stopped in his tracks and spun around to face them.

"Good." He smiled. "As there is sure to be a test."

After a moment's pause, he turned and continued down the road.

"It's a mile or so from our current location to good transport," Storm advised. "Shall I explain the riddle as we walk?"

"Yes," Abigail uncharacteristically blurted out as she quickened her pace to join Alex. She had hoped to avoid another snide comment from Sam, and Alex recognized her sentiment and appreciated it, and as such, flashed her a brief smile.

"Excellent." Alexander turned to Abigail as they strolled across the dusty road. "It's actually quite simple. Follow along. A holy land where the melting snow of the mountains feeds the Mekong rRiveriver." Alex paused and studied Abigail's face, waiting to see if the words were formulating anything in her mind. Smiling a crooked smile, she shook her head back and forth slowly.

"Okay." Alex comforted her with the voice of a teacher to pupil. "That's fine. It gets us here to Cambodia—the holy city—the largest man-made temple complex on the planet. Angkor Wat. The melting mountains feed the river."

"Simple enough." She smiled at Alexander. "Well, at least now that you've told me." The two laughed at their own amusement.

"The references to holy city and Brahma reiterate this sentiment, leading us to Angkor."

"Hey, man! Hey, man!" The shouts came from behind the duo, and he turned slightly to peer over his shoulder.

"Ah," he said with a touch of glee. "I believe our chariot approaches!"

The local continued to yell in his broken English and was waving his arms back and forth as he trotted toward them.

"Anyway," Alex continued as the four stood watching the man's approach, "'the temple where the trees eat the stone' can be only one place in the Angkor complex—Ta Prohm."

The local livery reached them at last, his tattered clothes hanging loosely on his slight frame. He arrived at the group of travelers huffing and sweating. His worn blue denim shorts were frayed and dirty, and his white T-shirt was stained an unsightly yellow. "Hey, man!" he called again through his gasps for air.

Alexander tapped him on the shoulder. "Yes, yes. Take a moment, will you?"

The villager looked up at Storm and smiled a mostly toothless grin. "Ruinz. Ruinz. I take."

"Now there's a smile only a mother could love," Sam mumbled under her breath, disgusted by the native's atrocious mouth hygiene.

"Shhh." Lobo shut her down before she got out of hand, as there was clearly sufficient ammo here to get her firing off rounds of humorous, and insulting, observations.

Alexander studied him a moment, tilting his head to one side. "English?" he finally blurted out. "English?"

The man smiled at the four and lifted his hand up, tilting it back and forth.

"A little aye?" Alexander smirked.

The man smirked back, "liddle."

"Ta Prohm?" Alexander barely got the words out when the man turned and whistled with his fingers to another man standing beside a long-past classic Ford pickup on the other side of the tracks. The driver quickly jumped in and gunned the truck right at them. Coming to a sharp stop in front of the party, the driver sprang from the truck and stood beside its open door, awaiting further instructions.

"How much?" Alexander asked, lifting his hand and rubbing his thumb and pointer together.

The man's face looked blank for a mere moment then sprang to life with understanding, once again displaying his gums to the group.

"Liddle," he said and laughed, shaking his head. "Liddle."

"Very well." Alexander motioned the group to the back of the pickup and the driver sprinted to the rear and dropped the gate. Lobo hopped up first and offered a hand to Abigail, pulling her up into the truck bed. She quickly took a seat on one of the crates that lined the sides posing as makeshift benches. Dusting off her knees, she winked at Lobo who then turned to pull in Sam. The driver, another sharply dressed and impeccably groomed individual, had already offered to help her.

"Back off!" she sternly ordered, and although the driver most likely didn't understand the words, he responded to Sam's body language and quickly fled to the driver's seat of the truck.

"Gimme your hand wildcat," Lobo said as he snickered.

"I got it, big guy," she replied and pulled herself up and past him, taking a crate across from Abi.

"You cool?" Sam whispered.

Abigail laughed. "This is amazing! Are you kidding?"

"Nerd alert!"

Alexander approached the rear of the truck with their toothless host and thanked him.

The man laughed, nodded, and pointed at his own chest. "Bill."

"Bill, huh?" Alex smirked. "Alexander," he replied, gesturing to himself.

The man nodded and gestured for Alex to climb up.

Alexander swiftly moved past the others and took a seat directly behind the glassless opening in the back of the cab. He watched as Bill shut the lift gate and walked past him to the passenger's seat.

"Ta Prohm!" Bill shouted with false enthusiasm as if the four of them were the first visitors he had ever taken into the jungle. "Ta Prohm!"

"Hold on!" Alexander shouted to the others.

"To what?" Samantha laughed.

"Your ass! Ha!" Lobo yelled over the gunned engine and spinning tires that shot puffs of dust and burning oil into the air behind them like white water in a boat's wake.

Once the truck had exited the sun-drenched roads of the town clearing and entered the jungle, the driver's pace slowed and the trip took on a pleasant serenity as the passengers admired their open-aired view of the surroundings splendor. The canopy of foliage above them offered a heavenly relief from the sun's rays. The shade, coupled with the breeze from the drive, lulled the passengers into a slow, albeit bumpy, calm.

Alexander caught their two hosts exchanging glances in the cab of the truck that made him uneasy. No words were spoken by the two, but their faces seemed transformed in some indiscernible manner that put Storm on his guard.

"Beautiful!" he leaned forward and yelled through the window at the two.

As if on cue, their faces broke into smiles, and they nodded at Alexander.

Alexander nodded back. His apprehension thoroughly masked.

"Ingilngeu," the driver shouted to Bill, still flashing his smile at Alexander through the rear window. "yYeung yk vea tow peak kantalophlauv yk avei del yeung chngban haey touk vea chaol nowknong prei."

Sam caught wind of the exchange from her position next to Alex, and she saw Alexander's demeanor change. His body tensed, and his neck tightened.

"What are those idiots yapping about?" She leaned forward to get a better look through the window.

Alexander quickly extended his arm and pushed her back into her seat. In the same motion, he came to rest on his knees at the window, his head partially in the cab of the truck.

"Sakalbong vea haey khnhom," he spoke to Bill through gritted teeth, then turned to the driver. "Nung rel bampngk robsa anak moun pel anak... chakchenh pi lan!"

The driver slammed on the brakes, throwing everyone forward off their seats. Someone crashed into Alex's back. He didn't move, but remained locked and unwavering from his position of advantage.

"You speak Khmer," Bill said with a nervous laugh.

"And you speak English...*Bill*." Alexander remained poised.

Slowly sliding both of his arms forward into the cab, Alexander's body stiffened and seemed to grow in bulk.

It was then Bill caught sight of metallic points emerging from Alexander's sleeves at his wrists.

"Try me," Alexander whispered to the pair.

Silence encapsulated the truck. No chattering of birds or click of silk worms. Even the truck's engine sounds seemed to have faded into a distant memory.

"Big mistake!" Bill yelled. "So sorry, friend. Big misunderstanding."

Bill reached over and slapped the driver on the shoulder.

"Go! Go!" he ordered. "Ta Prohm!" He turned to Alex with defeated and apologetic eyes. "Ta Prohm. No charge, my friend."

Alexander slowly withdrew from the cab and settled back into his seat, never taking his eyes off the pair.

"All good!" Bill was still shouting.

"What the fuck?" Samantha leaned into Alex.

Alexander's features softened a bit, as he was fairly confident they would have no more trouble with the pair of would-be-thieves.

"They said we were dumb tourists and that we knew nothing of their history." Alexander smiled at his three companions, and Lobo rolled his eyes in obvious disbelief.

"Yeah, right," Sam replied.

"No, really." Alexander laughed. "And I told them to 'try me,'" he added for effect.

"Sure." Abigail laughed. "We could have had a mobile Cambodian Jeopardy going, right?"

"Ha ha!" Alex clapped his hands together. "What a bizarre thought!"

"Twenty minutes, my friend," Bill shouted as the truck plunged through the jungle pass at breakneck speeds.

Alexander nodded to Bill.

Lobo chuckled. "Well, whatever you said to them, they obviously want your ass out of their truck."

"Yes, it would appear so." They laughed together as the truck took a hard bump, sending all four into the air off their crates. "Maybe something got lost in translation?"

"Yeah." Lobo shook his head. "I highly doubt that, Storm."

106

"Hey!" Jericho shouted as he touched Kate on her shoulder.

Kate screamed — loud — and jumped out of her seat, ripping the earbuds from her head.

"What the hell?"

"Sorry! Sorry!" Jericho advanced to comfort her, but she recoiled from his approach.

"Jericho," he said, tapping himself on the chest. "Frank Jericho."

Kate let out a burst of air in relief. "You scared the crap out of me! Francis, isn't it?"

"Hey," Jericho said as he dropped into her vacated seat. "Do you mind?" he asked pointing at the arm of the chair. "I'm a bit beat."

Kate regained her composure and leaned back against the desk.

"And it's Frank. Actually, it's Jericho," he instructed. "Don't go listening to Storm's happy horse shit, okay?"

Kate laughed. "Happy horse shit, huh?"

"Yup." Jericho leaned back in the chair.

"I'm Kate." She extended her hand, and Jericho stood to meet it. "Nice to meet you."

"I know. Asar sent me in here. Said you were lost in the library."

"I'm most certainly not lost," she replied. "Especially in a library."

"Figure of speech, I guess." Footsteps sounded the approach of a friend. Jericho turned around and said, "Asar, baby! Whatcha got there?"

Asar walked past Jericho, laboring with a large chest, which he set down gingerly on the desk next to Kate.

Taking a deep breath, he dusted his hands together and turned to face Jericho.

"Give it here, now, Francis," his said somewhat paternally.

"Damn, what's with this Francis crap?" He was getting annoyed. "Did Storm put you all up to this? Okay, joke's over."

"Give me the papyrus, Jericho."

Frank could see Asar was all business right now, and he reached into his jacket pocket and withdrew a clear plastic case. Kate could see the fragment of ancient paper within, and her eyes gleamed.

"My God!" She leapt forward toward Jericho. "Is that it?"

Jericho paused and then extended his hand and the case to Kate.

"Wanna check it out before grumpy here seals it in that titanium sarcophagus?"

Without hesitation, Kate gently took the plastic case from Jericho and held it up to the light. It was eons old, but the fine hieroglyphics seemed freshly drawn.

"The ink looks wet!" she exclaimed.

"Pretty awesome, huh?" Jericho laughed.

Kate studied the ancient script, and Asar could see the cogs in her head turning as she began to decipher the text. Her mind's work suddenly translated into speech as her lips parted, and she began to mouth the sacred words.

"*Stop!*" Asar screamed and snatched the case from her hands. Kate recoiled from him, shocked by his uncharacteristic aggression.

"Dude!" Jericho stepped to her side and braced her from backing into the desk behind her. "Don't you know not to read this stuff out loud?"

"No!" Kate snapped back. "I mean, yes," she stammered, "but I wasn't thinking."

"You must *always* be thinking now," Asar replied in a calm whisper as he carried the papyrus to the titanium box. "Always vigilant, always aware."

Reaching forward, he pressed his right thumb against a small flat square on the top of the box. A hidden green LED flashed three times and the chest popped open. Holding the plastic case between his fingers, he reverently placed it inside the chest and lowered the lid. The locking mechanisms churned and popped and seemed a bit extreme for the dimensions of the safe.

"Always ready," he continued, turning to face Kate. "Your life has changed forever, my dear." Asar paused and gently took her hand. "And in turn, you must change with it."

107

"Down! Now!" Serket ordered Keith and Amaat as she dove into the shadows of the wall. The early morning fog that clung to the newly budding trees and bushes offered a natural defense from eyes passing overhead. Keith scrambled on his hands and knees to get under the closest tuft of blanketing camouflage. The roar of the jet's engines was almost deafening, and Serket covered her ears with both hands and leaned into the stone. Keith watched her from his position on the grassy hill, fearful she was too exposed. Then, as if by some trick or illusion, Keith thought he saw Serket disappear. He blinked several times to clear the dust from his eyes.

"What the hell?" he said to himself as he watched her figure fade into the stone with a mesmerizing ripple that resembled radiating heat. He remained transfixed on her position as the jet's roar came and went, fading into the distance, echoing off of the mountain landscape of China. Then, as suddenly as she was gone, she was back and walking toward Keith.

"You okay?" she called out to him, waving her arms, beckoning him to join her. "We're good for some time, now. Won't be another patrol for a few hours."

Keith hopped to his feet and dusted the fragments of dried grass and debris from his jeans.

"Come on!" she yelled, turning back to the wall. "We're close!"

As Keith walked up the slight incline to Serket, he allowed his eyes to drift to the massive structure in front of him.

The Great Wall, he thought. *My God!*

The beauty and history of the structure was not lost on him, and he marveled at the sheer expanse of it. Like rivers of stone, it ran on in either direction, contouring with the land as it went.

"I can't believe where I am right now," he blurted out as he reached Serket.

She laughed and patted him on the back. "Soak it all in. Just do it quick, though, okay?"

"Well, there's a lot to take in!"

"Yes," she replied with a lack of enthusiasm and turned to face the wall.

"Wait!" he called out. "You must surely be moved by this?"

"Oh, I am." Serket turned her head slightly to reply. "But we've work to do."

Keith nodded. "Been here before, huh?"

"Yes," she replied. "A few times."

Serket began to walk along the wall to his right and Keith jogged over to catch up with her.

"What's the plan?"

"You know the plan." Her pace quickened as she continued. "We have discussed it many times on the way over and—"

"Wait!" Keith cried out, stopping Serket in her tracks. "Where's Amaat!"

Keith had lost sight of him when the jet passed over and had all but forgotten about him in his admiration of the wall.

"I'm up here!" Amaat yelled from above them.

She smiled when she saw Keith's jaw drop. "He's up there," Serket pointed and smiled at Keith, "why don't we get *up there* too."

Keith looked up in shock. "How the hell did he get up there, Serket?"

"He's a high jumper," she dryly replied without missing a beat.

"Ha ha. Go ahead, keep the guy with no super powers in the dark."

Serket stopped and looked at Keith. "And how do you know you have no super powers?" Her tone was eerily serious. "Perhaps you just have not been tested yet?"

With that, she turned and waved to Amaat. "Rope!"

Keith watched as Amaat lifted a large coil from the ground at his feet and tossed it over the side of the wall to them. He allowed it to come to rest between the separated stones that lined the top row of the wall like a tower in a castle. The heavy cord hit the ground with a slap, and Serket reached out and grabbed it firmly.

"Super heroes first." She ushered him to climb the rope.

Keith took it firmly in his hands and looked to Serket, who smiled.

"Hand over hand," she whispered. "Use the stone blocks like a ladder."

Keith nodded and climbed, ascending slowly. He found the spaces between the stone to be a perfect fit for the tips of his boots. Keith estimated the wall to be about twenty-five feet tall at their location, and he worked hard to cover the distance with some haste. But it was slow going all the same.

"You got it!" Amaat called out from above him.

"Don't say, 'don't look down,'" Keith mumbled to himself as he strained at the ropes.

"And don't look down," Amaat said, laughing.

"Well, I wasn't going to until you said something," Keith said with a huff.

He was almost there, Amaat's voice was close now.

"Look at me!" Amaat called out. "Get a good foot hold and grab my hand. I'll pull you the rest of the way over."

Keith wanted to say, "I got it, back off," but he didn't have it. In fact, he was quickly approaching the end of his rope.

"End of my rope," he said to himself with a laugh as his arms began to quiver.

"Give me your hand before you *can't*," Amaat demanded from right above.

Keith felt around with his feet and found a good spot to wedge his boot in. With a grunt, he let go of the rope with his right hand and swung it up to meet Amaat's, who clasped onto him at the wrist. With a swift jerk, Amaat brought him up and almost over the wall. Keith scrambled with his free hand and his legs and launched himself the rest of the way over. He twisted around and came to rest seated on the ground, his head on his knees in exhaustion.

"On your feet." Serket was standing beside him. "It's about a kilometer to the guard tower."

Keith looked up in shock. "How?"

"I'm a high jumper, too," Serket laughed.

108

"Long time, Jericho!" Decker extended his hand to greet him.

"Hey!" Jericho smiled and pulled him in for a hug. "How you doing, buddy?"

Decker let out a groan. "Easy, brother," he winced. "Had a rough night at the local tavern."

Frank relinquished his hold and dropped back. "Oh man, sorry. Sorry."

"It's fine." Decker grinned. "Just no bear hugs, okay?"

Jericho nodded and helped Decker over to the chair Kate offered him.

"Sit, Decker," a voice called from the recesses of the library.

"I am." Decker smiled, his voice mixed with appreciation and a tinge of annoyance.

Anika emerged from the shadowy edges of the library and walked toward them, a sly grin adorning her face. "I know," she mimicked. "You're fine."

"I am," Decker said as he dropped into Kate's chair with a muffled groan.

"Well, hello." Jericho turned on his charm, flashing Anika his pearly whites. "Wife?" he whispered out of the side of his mouth to Decker.

"No," he replied. "And she's not my nurse, either. Even though she thinks she is."

450 I ANTHONY DIPAOLO

"Nurse." Jericho moved from Decks's side toward Anika. "I'm hurt myself, you know."

"Fascinating." Anika walked past Jericho to Decker.

Decker laughed out loud as Anika bent and kissed his cheek softly.

"Don't mind him," he said, touching her arm. "He can't help it."

She extended her hand. "Anika. Nice to meet you."

"Charmed, I'm sure," Jericho replied in a comical British accent.

"Okay, enough." Kate walked between them and motioned to Jericho.

"You need to leave *now*. Keith is alone. In China."

Jericho threw his hands up with exaggeration. "Okay, okay, I'm going. And Keith is not *alone* by the way. He's with Serket, who I'm sure does not want or need my help."

Grimacing, he turned to Decker and Anika. "That woman really doesn't like me."

"Really?" Anika shot back. "I can't imagine why not."

"Ha ha." Jericho nodded and turned to leave. "She's a keeper, Decks. She's a keeper."

"See ya, Jericho," Decker called out after him.

"Not if I see you first."

"Hey," Decker added. "Don't get dead, huh?"

"I'll do my best, buddy."

"And Keith!" Kate called out to Jericho, taking a few nervous energy steps in the direction of his departure. "Same for Keith ...Make sure he doesn't get dead, too! Okay?"

109

"Why are we slowing?" Alexander leaned into the rear window of the truck, shocking both the driver and the passenger.

"Huh?" Bill shook off the terror that had crept across his face and turned to Storm. "Ta Prohm. Just ahead," he anxiously replied.

"Nonsense, Bill." Alexander once again extended himself further into the cab of the truck, causing the driver to come to a skidding halt.

"Wait! Wait!" Bill clamored about in his seat. "Wait! Secret entrance, my friend."

Leaning across the seat, he yelled something at his partner in crime in their native tongue and slapped him on the shoulder, causing the driver to accidentally gun the truck forward, sending Alexander tumbling back a bit into Lobo, who had sprung up to brace him.

"Many thanks." Storm huffed as he lurched forward into the rear window once more. He could see through the front windshield and watched as the truck skidded to a stop once more. Bill didn't even let the vehicle come to a complete stop before he threw his door open and stumbled out.

"Wait! Wait!" he screamed again. "Look, friend. Look!"

Alexander turned his eyes from the irate man to the section of overgrowth he was pointing to. Lush green leaves cluttered over tubular trunks spinning their way through the primitive landscape of the expansive jungle before them.

"Look!" Bill shouted.

Storm saw it—a thin path, lined with archaic stones, leading from the road to their right into a thin section of clearing within the jungle wall.

"Not west entrance." Bill's voice had relaxed some as he noted Alexander's hardened expression soften with the recognition of the path. "No tourists," he continued, softly. "Secret path to Prohm."

Alexander stood upright in the truck bed and adjusted his long coat, pulling his shirt sleeves down from beneath the flowing black fabric covering them.

"Very good, Bill," he said as one might speak to a newly trained dog. "Unlatch the back, please."

Bill moved as quickly as his could to the rear, his dirty twig-like legs trembling beneath his shorts. "Yes, yes."

Alexander helped Abigail to her feet and brought her to the back of the truck. He watched patiently as Bill fiddled with the latch, finally freeing it from its weathered mechanism.

"Step away," Alexander instructed as he jumped from the truck, hitting the jungle floor with a thud. Bill raised both his hands in figurative surrender and continued to walk backward, away from the truck. Alexander turned to his side and reached up to assist Abigail down. He helped her to the dusty jungle road then turned back to Bill, who was standing still.

"Ugh." Samantha hit the ground to his left and took Abigail's hand, swiftly leading her a safe distance from the truck.

"You got him?" Alex called up to Lobo, never taking his eyes off of Bill.

"Of course," Lobo replied calmly.

Alexander took a few steps toward Bill. "Tell the driver to shut the truck off and come out and join you—*friend.*"

Bill's cartoonish smile fled his face, and he took a deep breath. Alexander watched as his chest rose and fell several times. He was clearly contemplating the current situation and gauging his options. Alexander allowed this to continue for a bit, then he raised one eyebrow at the nervous man.

Bill's lips finally parted, and he called out to his cohort.

"You have chosen wisely," Alexander said evenly and without doubt or fear, and Bill nodded at him.

As the driver exited the vehicle, Lobo shadowed him from up above in the truck bed and followed him to the rear, jumping down next to Storm once he was clear of them.

"Plan?" Lobo inquired.

Alexander smiled. "Thank you for your hospitality, gentlemen." He began to pace slowly. "But this is where our paths must part. I'm sure you understand."

Bill nodded and began to walk toward the truck.

"Where are you going?" Alexander sprang toward him, blocking his forward progress. "Keys. Now," he commanded.

"Friend—" Bill began once more.

Alexander leaned into him and grasped his shoulder with powerful force. "Give me the keys and flee this place now," he whispered through grinding teeth, "or you will *never* leave."

Bill looked into Storm's eyes, which were ablaze with conviction, and wiggled from his grasp. Stepping backward once more, he signaled the driver to hand over the keys. Alexander watched as flashes of sunlight rhythmically moved across the would-be bandit's faces courtesy of the wind-blown foliage above. He could see the rivers of sweat flowing on both of them, and he could smell the fear radiating from their bodies. They knew, they were aware, they would comply.

Calling out to Lobo, the driver tossed the keys across the space between them and walked over to Bill.

"Gracias," Lobo swiped the keys from the air with a clang.

Without further word, the two locals turned and ran down the road from whence they had come.

Alexander smiled, serene once more, and turned to his companions. "Very well, then. Shall we get on with it?"

"And that's the way you do that ..." Lobo laughed out loud and fell in beside his employer.

"Is that okay?" Abigail questioned as they joined them. "Are they gonna make it in this heat?"

Alexander stopped and turned to her and Sam. "My dear, their intentions were to take us into the jungle, rob us, kill us, and who knows what else, so I quite honestly do not care what their futures hold."

"What did you say to them, Storm?" Sam prodded excitedly.

"I simply told them they would not be accomplishing their goals today."

"Ha," Sam spit out. "I'm sure you weren't so civilized."

"Civility is much like beauty," Alexander said. "It lies in the eye of the beholder."

"You don't say?" Samantha made a wide-eyed gesture to Abi.

Alexander turned and headed toward the obfuscated entrance ahead of them. "Besides," he quickly added, "a death at the hands of the jungle would be merciful in comparison to a death at my hands."

No one laughed this time. Even Samantha was silent.

110

Naamah danced atop the edge of the stone wall, spinning and swaying to some internal tune playing in her mind.

"Get down from there," Moloch commanded half-heartedly. "You'll fall to your death...again."

Naamah stopped her dark ballet and shot him a look.

"Really?" he asked rhetorically. "You did die at the last site, did you not?"

Naamah leapt from the stone façade, her black boots hitting the stone walkway with the snap of a whip.

"Death is relative, my lord," she spoke slyly and smirked. "And as long as I have you to protect little ole me, I shall never *die*."

Moloch laughed and began walking once more.

"You'd do well to remember that." His voice echoed in the gusts of wind that enveloped them every few seconds. "And heed my direction when I suggest you abstain from activities such as dancing on the edge."

Naamah laughed out loud at his word play and dashed forward to his side.

"You know how I feel about abstinence," she said as she reached up and ran her nails across his back.

"Yes," Moloch peered down at her with dark lust in his eyes.

Without any further discussion, the two marched forward atop the Great Wall, covering large distances in a metaphysical flash.

"Mistress?" The disincorporated call came from behind the demonic pair causing them to stop dead in their tracks.

Turning to face the sound of the voice, their eyes were met with a small tempest of smoke, light, and fire spinning, without earthly logic, on the path behind them.

Naamah smirked at the apparition and ran a finger across her lips, resting on her face in a call for silence.

"Shhh." The sound bellowed from deep within her and sent the smoke and fire fleeing, leaving in its wake a tall, darkly cloaked figure. Fierce, burning red eyes radiated from within the fathomless black beneath its hood. Outstretching its arms and tilting its head in a mocking manner, the figure stood obediently quiet and motionless.

"It's one of mine," Naamah said. "If you will excuse me a moment?"

Moloch watched as Naamah left his side and strutted to her demon soldier. She stood before it and was clearly engaged in discussion, although the demon remained motionless in its cruciform stance. Moloch strained to make out the conversation, but was unable to discern anything. Naamah had clearly used a spell to distort and obscure the conversation. She peered over her shoulder at him, concern on her face, and quickly averted her eyes back to the demonic messenger.

"What is it?" Moloch finally called out, walking slowly in their direction. Once Naamah caught wind of his approach, she took a step back from the demon and thrust her hand forward with an open fist, dispatching the evil entity in a flash of smoke and ash.

"What is it?" Moloch grew frustrated.

Distressed, Naamah spun on her heels to face him. "Storm is in Angkor."

Moloch laughed. "Yes, I know."

"And you said nothing?" Anger welled up inside her and spread like wildfire across her features. "Are we fucking partners here, or what?"

"Partners?" Moloch squinted at her, searching her mind for the part of the messenger's tale she was attempting to keep from him. "I suppose. But the roads and paths of a partnership run both ways, Naamah."

A look of shock, theatrical as it was, flashed across her face. "What are you implying?"

"You have knowledge." His lip curled in a snarl. "And I am not implying anything, *partner*. So, drop the tedious fucking act and divulge your emissary's words."

Naamah turned in a dramatic pout and strolled several steps away from him.

"Oh, please," he burst out. "Enough!"

Naamah turned to face him once more, smiling deviously. "Share and share alike," she whispered with exaggerated movements of her mouth. "That's what I say."

"Very well," Moloch hissed as he closed the distance between them in an instant. "Storm is in Angkor. I have dispatched all manner of nightmare to halt his progress and secure the location's hidden papyrus."

He paused, waiting for her to reciprocate. "And, should the opportunity present itself," he added to solidify his veracity, "they are to lay waste to that intolerable piece of shit's soul."

Naamah smiled a wide grin. "Wouldn't that be wonderful news?"

"Yes." His eyes relaxed slightly as the rushing gusts of wind howled about them, over and along the dusty stone wall. "And what of *your* news now, partner?"

Naamah's smile faded quickly. "Very well. It was my intention to share all along, anyway."

"Truly," Moloch mimicked?

"Truly." Naamah put on a sincere face. "Francis Jericho." She paused for effect as Moloch's eyes filled with rage at the mentioning of the name. "Under the direction of our dear Storm, has acquired one of the papyrus fragments and secured it at Dragon Loch."

"From whence did he acquire this?" Moloch's voice roared across the mountain range. "Pray tell...*partner*."

Naamah, sensing the end of her little word game, shrank back from the ancient demon. "The Grand Canyon," she whispered.

Moloch appeared startled. "Where?"

"A hidden cave in the sheer rock side of a mountain in the Grand Canyon."

Naamah watched Moloch's expressions as he filed through the riddles in his mind.

"'Ripped in the Earth...found in a place so odd,'" Moloch recited a portion of the riddle. "It is one of the two I have not been able to solve."

Moloch turned from Naamah and laughed. "Well done, Storm."

"What are we to do?" Naamah's concern was evident. "If we lack just one of the twelve spells, we are done here."

"What do we do?" he repeated her words. "Why, we go and take it, of course."

"In, into Dragon Loch Castle?" she stammered. "Are you mad?"

"Of course, I am!" he said, laughing, and turned to face her again.

"Alrighty then," she sighed, resigning herself to his lead.

"But first, my dear," he said, his face growing dark, as did the sky with an impending storm. "I believe right ahead of us you have a date with your dear friend, Serket."

"Stupid fucking bird-chucking bitch." Naamah's face shifted and contorted in anger at the thought, her words coupled with spit like a rabid dog's bark. "I'm going to rip her soul apart and leave her bleeding and broken for eternity."

111

Alexander led the way, pushing through overgrown vegetation and dried husks of curling branches that lined the narrow pathway Bill had brought them to. His bearings remained somewhat distorted, and he continued to question their location.

"I feel like we are off," he commented to no one in particular. "I estimated Ta Prohm another mile to the West at least."

Lobo, who followed last to protect the rear, spoke up somewhat empathetically so as not to insult Storm. "Let's move forward a bit and see where the path leads. It has to lead to something, right?"

"You are right," Alexander replied, never looking back at his followers.

Alexander walked another fifty feet or so and stopped in a small clearing. "Come up here, and join me," he beckoned.

Sam and Abigail quickly obeyed and tried to gauge what was to come. Lobo stepped into the clearing as well, but remained with his back to the group, watching the path they had just followed.

"What's up?" Sam finally asked. "What's wrong?"

"Nothing's wrong, per se," Alexander quickly replied, swatting at some jungle insect that had landed on his hand.

"Listen," Sam began in a tone more serious than Alex had ever heard before. And he did just that—listen.

"We are bound together now, Storm," she continued. "All of us. Not just those who are here now. We've all put our trust and complete faith in you and your decisions. We honestly have no idea what is real or illusion, and this is all beyond imagination. So, you need to tell us the truth from now on. The *whole* truth. You clearly feel that we can handle whatever comes, or we wouldn't be here with you."

Alexander nodded in surprise. "Clearly."

"Jesus Christ!" She was ready to burst with emotion after all that had transpired. "Say something, Storm! We're not your puppets, and we don't need protection. We need to be aware of what's coming, all right?"

"All right." Alexander finally acknowledged her, stepping closer to both her and Abigail. "You are in agreement, Abigail?"

Abigail smirked. "What she said."

Alexander turned and peered through the tree-line ahead. His pensive behavior was not helping the situation, and he knew it.

"All right." He spun around to face them again. "There is truth to what you say and to receiving the information you are entitled to." He paused but a moment, and he felt Sam getting ready to interrupt. "That being said, I will decide what you need to know, when you need to know it, and if the knowledge is truly something you can *handle*."

Alexander sighed and looked at Lobo, who had been through so many trials and adventures with Storm that even the absurd and fantastical seemed commonplace to him.

"It's time, Alex. They're all strong, and not one of them has questioned you or fled in fear. It is time to reveal their destiny, as well as yours."

"My destiny is not written!" Abigail quickly called out, clearly upset by the serious nature of the conversation. "I prefer to take Mr. Storm's lead and play it out *as* it plays out, if that's all right with you."

Alexander paused and looked at Abigail. "You are right, but at the same time, you cannot remain ignorant of the evil that surrounds us. You must taste the darkness to recognize it."

Tears welled up in her eyes. "I see the darkness, Alexander Storm. I have embraced it in one form or the other since I was a child." She looked at him with questioning eyes. "And I'm pretty sure you know that. It's why I'm here, right?"

"No." He moved closer to her. "You are here because through all the darkness you have been dealt, you have remained pure."

Alexander broke away for a moment to peer back into the tree-line before them.

This time, his words fell softly. "You are here, my dear child, because you are a warrior—a soldier for the light. Chosen from birth. And the powers you have been 'plagued' with all your life are but a small glimpse into what the future holds for you."

Abigail looked at Storm with disbelief. "I'm just a Southern girl who inherited some magic from my ancestors...that's all."

Alexander circled around her in the heat of the jungle.

"You are so much more. So very much more."

"You're freaking her out," Sam said, coming to Abi's rescue. "Cut the crap, Storm. Stop with your riddles and motivational speeches, okay?"

Alexander turned to Samantha and laughed. "And you, my insolent girl, are also a warrior."

"What the fuck, Storm?" Sam joined Abi to comfort her, as she was clearly confused and shaken by Alexander's words.

"Have you not known all along, Abigail?" He ignored Sam's pleas. "Have you not sensed the power? Felt it growing in you without an ascertainable outcome? Well, here we are. Time to become—"

Alexander's satellite phone rang from inside his jacket, like a bell that saved the boxer named Intensity, and he looked at Sam.

He laughed. "You will have to show me how to put this damn thing on silent. Otherwise, it will go off at the most inopportune moment and perhaps be the death of me."

Sam smiled. "Well, since you put it that way, I'll silence it for you." She paused and stared at Alex as the phone continued to ring and vibrate. "Truth be told, I've grown a bit fond of you, even though I can't understand you half the time and the other half I want to punch you." It was her turn to smirk at him. "But that being said, I'm pretty sure if you weren't here, the entire Earth would be on the brink of ruin. So, yes, I'll put your phone on silent."

"Your too kind," Alexander jested and handed his phone to her.

Samantha looked at the vibrating, bulky satellite phone then looked back at Alex, confused. "Aren't you going to answer it? The caller ID says it's you calling you."

Alexander snatched the phone back from Sam. "Yes, of course. It's Kate, I am sure."

Storm held the phone so he could see the function keys.

"Have you never used your satellite phone before, Mr. Storm," Sam laughed.

Alex shook his head. "Of course I have. I have a lot of information to remember, and these eyes are much older than you know." Alex paused and hit the green button to accept the call before he lost it.

"Hello?" Alex exaggerated his salutation to isolate everyone's attention. "Hello? Kate?"

"Yes, it's me." She paused. "Can you hear me okay?"

"Loud and clear." Alex raised a finger at the others, signaling them to hold their questions.

"Listen, I've been working on this obscure one." She paused and Alex could make out the sound of rustling papers. He waited a few moments and engaged her again.

"Kate!" he called into the phone. "You still there?"

After a moment, Alexander could hear her breathing on the other side again. "Yes, I'm sorry, Alex. I'm just trying to get this right, and I have all this evidence and articles and papers—it's insane."

Alexander lifted the phone closer to his face. "Take it easy, Kate," he said patiently. He looked at the others and lifted his eyebrows. "Catch your breath, collect your thoughts, and begin."

"Is she all right?" Sam stepped toward Alex, who raised a hand to the phone to cover the mouthpiece. "She's exasperated." He smiled at Sam, who looked puzzled. Alex shook his head. "She's excited. I am quite sure she has solved one of the difficult riddles."

Alexander turned slightly from Sam and looked up at Lobo.

His words were slow and precise. "We are all waiting. Enlighten us, please."

Kate cleared her throat and her mind and allowed the pieces of the riddle to coagulate into place. Alex placed the phone in the palm of his hand and pressed the speaker button.

"See?" Sam smiled. "You know what you're doing."

"Always," Alexander shot back at her with a somber expression. "Always—"

"Testing us," Sam finished his sentence for him.

Alexander's eyes narrowed, and he returned to the call.

"Okay," Kate began. "I went to the twelfth riddle, since I felt it had a direct reference to our fate as a whole." She laughed nervously. "With the 'our' being either the group, or the entire planet—not really sure—but it called to me."

"Kate, we are about to enter the temple in Angkor." He looked up at Lobo. "Not to rush you, but we can address the 'calling' at a later time, okay? Just give us the facts."

"I'm sorry," she quickly replied.

"No need," Alex was becoming tense for some reason. "We just have pressing matters before us, so please, tell me of the twelfth. It intrigues me as well."

"Okay," she began again. "Twelfth riddle reads as follows, 'In the olive-skinned land of all ports, beneath the whine and the hum of the sea, lies a world as above except void of sound and of love, but still they continue to be. As a pupil of Anubis might thrive, so, too, must the dead teach the live. Find him who has waited the longest, be sure that your math is true, for this is the last of the journey, a mistake may end all of you.'"

Kate paused as if waiting for some input.

"We defer to you, Kate," Alex spoke gently, "the hour grows late ... no need for debate."

Alexander was growing more and more anxious. Lobo noted his eyes darting back and forth between the group and the tree-line ahead of them.

"Right," she continued. "The 'olive skin' reference immediately made me think of the Mediterranean."

"Very good." Alexander said with both encouragement and prodding.

"Next, I thought the use of the words, 'all ports,' was deliberate and significant." She paused, shuffling papers again.

"Kate?" Alex did not hesitate this time.

"Yes," she replied softly.

"You don't need your notes or papers." He laughed slightly, he laughed nervously. "You know the details we seek. Just speak. I trust your conclusions."

"Panormus is ancient Greek for 'all ports.'" Her voice was strong and renewed. "However, Panormus was what the ancient Greeks called Palermo!"

"Of course!" Storm exclaimed. "The rest is obvious, now!"

"It is?" Kate asked from the other side of the world.

"Yes." Alexander signaled Lobo to the front of the group. "Excellent work!" Next, he motioned the woman to move behind him. "Got a few things to wrap up here. Shouldn't be long. We must go."

Alexander ended the call and spun to face Abigail and Sam.

"Whatever comes through those trees—" he started.

"Wait, what?" Sam attempted to interrupt.

Alexander silenced her with his eyes. "Whatever comes through those trees, *we can handle it,* understand?"

They both nodded, eyes darting around wildly. Alexander reciprocated the gesture, nodding in acceptance.

"Storm!" Lobo called from the front. "Storm!"

Alexander quickly darted to Lobo's side.

"What the hell is that?" Lobo whispered, his voice drenched in terror.

"Yes," Alexander whispered back. "Hell."

112

S erket swiftly ascended the dilapidated stone steps that led to the sixty-sixth guard house of the Jinshanling section of the Great Wall.

"This is it!" she yelled to her comrades trailing behind her. The words echoed back and forth on the walls of the lined stairway. The archway entrance lay just steps away from her, and she could feel the excitement welling up inside. "Is this the right one?"

"It's GPS marked, Serket," Amaat replied. "This is it."

She stood in the threshold and gazed around. "Ha ha! Absolutely beautiful."

Serket marveled at the stone-on-stone structure as she waited for them to join her. "No time to waste. Keith, get up here with those notes."

Keith quickly arrived at her side, huffing, but invigorated. Reaching deep into the pocket of his jeans, he withdrew a cluster of folded pages and opened them to review.

He began to recite the riddle from the notes. "A sacred serpent guards this guard's retreat and guards the truth beneath its feet."

Folding the papers back up, he turned to the others, smiling.

"Serpent it is!" Amaat shouted, opening his backpack to retrieve three LED lights. "We will need these," he advised, passing a light to Keith and Serket.

Keith depressed the button and flashed the beam into his eyes to confirm it was on. "You mean you can't see in the dark? I'm disappointed," he teased.

Serket smiled and turned to enter the guard house. The stone structure looked just that, a house. Equipped with doors and windows, built solidly, built to last the test of time. There were areas of the structure that appeared to be in distress, but the overall integrity of the nearly eight-hundred-year old marvel was impressive, to say the least.

"Time for a good old fashion snake hunt," she shouted and walked into the darkness.

Keith and Amaat quickly followed, each of them passing the beam of their lights over the walls, ceiling, and floor. The interior was essentially open and accessible.

"I've got a dragon and a lion I think," Keith called out to the others.

"Yes," Amaat quickly responded. "Same here. And elephants."

"Great," Serket replied with distraction in her voice. She was focusing on a square hole in the center of the ceiling above them. She walked directly under the opening, shined the light up into its recesses, and exclaimed, "A virtual zoo of stone."

"Where do you suppose they house the reptiles?" Keith joked.

Serket's voice resounded with reserved excitement. "Pretty sure they keep them up there."

Keith and Amaat joined her and shined their lights up into the opening as well. The vague images of bas reliefs on the upper walls could be viewed from below.

"I don't suppose you have a ladder in that pack?" Keith toyed with Amaat.

"Nope," he replied.

"Don't need it," Serket added.

Keith nodded. "I got it—high jumpers. You want me to step outside so you can do whatever it is you *do*."

"No need," Serket replied with a laugh. "Amaat, give me a boost up."

Amaat nodded and dropped to one knee below the hole in the ceiling. It was a good twelve feet above, Keith estimated.

Amaat extended his hands cupped together in front of him and nodded to Serket, who charged right at him. Leaping from the ground just as she got to him, her feet landed squarely in the center of his hands, and he sprang up and lifted his arms hoisting her high into the air. Keith held his breath as she sailed upward. Serket's hands slapped against the stone floor above, and she grasped hard to the edge, dangling for a moment, and then pulling herself up into the darkness.

"Holy crap." Keith finally exhaled. "That was awesome."

Amaat nodded and retrieved the rope from his pack. Tossing one end up, Serket's hand darted from the darkness and took hold of it.

"I'll tie it around my waist," she shouted, "and pull you up as you climb, Keith."

Keith took the rope from Amaat and waited for it to grow taught.

"Okay!" Serket yelled from above, no longer visible to them.

Keith struggled with the climb, but her technique had him to the top fast and he scrambled onto the safety of the stone floor. Turning his light on and toward Serket, he could see her body heaving forward with Amaat's weight as he quickly scaled the rope and pulled himself into the upper chamber of the guard house.

Serket hurriedly yanked the rope up and set it on the floor. The chamber was completely illuminated with the rays from their three lights, and they quickly returned to examining every surface of the upper room.

"I got it!" Keith yelled out almost immediately, and the others ran to his side. There, on the bottom stone, directly above the floor, was their serpent.

"A cobra, I believe," he said with self-congratulatory bravado.

Serket dropped to one knee and ran her hand across the raised relief of a snake. Looking up at Keith, she smiled. "Nice job, snake-man."

"Snake-man?" Keith replied.

"Yes," she said, laughing. "Finding snakes is your new superpower!"

Turning her attention back to the wall, she let her hands glide from the stone pictogram to the floor tile directly below it.

"And here," she said, tapping the tile. "Under here we should find our prize."

Amaat dropped down beside her. He had retrieved a hammer and pry bar from his bag and inserted the tapered end of the bar into the seam of the floor stone.

"Gently," Serket urged. "Whatever is under there is delicate, to say the least."

Amaat used the hammer to drive the bar farther into the space between the tiles. Applying slow and steady pressure, he raised the stone from its ancient resting place and slid it to one side. Serket pointed her light in the hole. There at the bottom of the hollowed-out space, amongst dust and debris, lay a thin stone cylinder. Reaching in, almost to her elbow, Serket quickly retrieved the vessel.

"Gotcha," she whispered.

Rising to her feet, she inspected the cylinder as Keith used his light to aid her.

The tube was adorned with shapes and lines, and it was stone corked on one end. It couldn't have been more than four inches long and an inch in circumference.

"That's odd," Serket studied the markings closer. "Looks like hieratic."

"Egyptian?" Keith knew it was.

"Very good," Serket replied without looking away from the tube. "But quite out of place here, no?"

"I'll say," Keith stepped forward to look closer. "Open it."

Serket nodded and grasped onto the stone stopper. Pulling with some force she was met with great resistance.

"I don't want to have this thing crumble in my hands," she announced, relinquishing her hold on the stopper.

"May I?" Keith asked as he took the tube from Serket's hand.

"Wait! You have to be gentle, Keith."

"Naturally," he said and laughed, then he brought the stone-stopped end to his mouth. Grasping the edge in his teeth, he began to twist and pull. Within seconds, the cylinder was opened, and he handed it back to Serket, smiling, stone stopper still between his teeth.

"Like a pirate and his rum!" She laughed.

Keith dropped the stone cork into the palm of his hand. "Yup."

Without further hesitation, Serket slid her slender finger up into the stone cylinder. A smile crept across her lips.

"I feel it," she whispered with force. "It's in there."

"Are you going to take it out, or what?" Keith asked moving closer.

Before she could respond, her eyes darted to the hole in the floor from where they had entered. Swiping the stone stop from Keith's hand, she placed it back securely and shoved the cylinder into Amaat's pack.

"We are no longer alone." Her voice was full of dread. "And if we don't get out of here, this place will become our tomb."

Amaat threw his pack on his back and scrambled to the hole. Dropping the rope down, he motioned for them both to go.

"No time for climbing!" she ordered Keith as he took hold of the rope at the edge of the opening. "Slide down! Now!"

But at that very moment, a voice echoed loudly through the guard house. "*Serket!*"

"Naamah," Serket said, moaning. "Go, Keith! Go!" she roared.

Keith loosened his grip—creating a cup around the rope—and slid hard to the floor below.

"The enemy cannot get that papyrus. No matter the cost."

Amaat nodded and motioned her down the rope. "I'll be right behind you! Figure a way out."

"Sure," she replied nervously. "I'll come up with something on my way down."

With that, she disappeared to the floor below. Amaat dropped the rope and crouched at the precipice. Letting himself propel off the edge, he dropped without support to the ground below, hitting with a thud. Keith watched, momentarily frozen, expecting Amaat to cry out in pain. Instead, he sprang to his feet, and the three charged toward the entrance opposite from whence they had come in.

"*Serket!*"

The demon's voice was directly behind them, and Serket stopped dead in her tracks. "The time for fleeing has passed." Serket extended her arms and stopped her companions. "Now is the time for battle!"

113

The jungle floor vibrated beneath their feet as the massive figure zig-zagged through the trees toward them. Alexander strained to make out its form, but the speed at which it traversed the Asiatic terrain, and the shadowy mist that surrounded it, made the task all but impossible.

"What is it?" Sam seemed to yell and whisper at the same time. "What do you guys see?"

Lobo and Alex remained silent, staring ahead into the overgrown vegetation.

"Hey!" Sam's voice grew louder.

Alexander's ears caught the faint sounds of twigs snapping as Sam began to inch forward. If they weren't going to explain what was going on, she was going to go see for herself. She took one more step forward as Alexander spun around to face her.

"Remain where I have placed you!" It was an order; it would be obeyed. Alex turned back to the approaching hulk. The figure was gaining momentum, no longer moving back and forth. It had locked on their position, probably thanks to the exchange with Samantha, and was barreling right toward them. Trunks and branches splintered under its force, and Alexander threw his arm out across Lobo's chest.

"Fall back," he whispered as the two walked backward to the girls.

"What is it, Mr. Storm?" Abigail implored. "What's coming?"

Alexander turned and looked at her, his face wore a sheen of terror. "I don't know yet my dear, but clearly it means us harm."

Without further word, Alexander thrust both of his arms down and out, forcing two long sword-like blades to extend from beneath the sleeves of his coat. Sam and Abi stepped backward in unison as the intermittent rays of sun gleamed off the blades.

Alexander looked at Lobo's holster and said, "I fear a firearm will be useless at this venture. What else have you in that bag of tricks?"

The cacophony of splintering and cracking was growing closer, and from where they stood in the clearing, it was difficult to make anything out through the thick rows of trees and plants.

Lobo swung his large pack off his back and unlatched its main compartment. Diving in with one muscular arm, he quickly withdrew an item that brought a smile to Storm's face.

"Crossbow? Silver tips, of course."

"Ha ha!" Alexander's mood changed instantly. "Well done, old friend."

Abigail's scream was deafening, and Alex and Lobo stumbled backward in surprise. Alexander turned to look at the tree-line before them, and in the distance, he found what Abi was reacting to. The center head had popped through into the clearing first. Immense and evil, as if chiseled in stone, ooze dripped from rows of fang-like teeth lining its sick smile, oblivion reflected in its dead eyes which were the size of dinner plates, and smoke billowed from its nostrils. At the centers of its giant pupils, flames danced and leapt. A wicked, curled mustache of wild black hair seemed to move above its mouth with a life of its own.

"Oh, my God. Oh, my God," Sam repeated, her voice riddled with fear and disbelief as the group of trapped adventurers watched rows of identical heads pop through the tree-line to the left and right of the first monster.

Alexander stood up and took a step forward. "Foul, hideous, abomination!" he shouted, and in return, the heads roared a deafening din in unison.

Alexander lifted his arms skyward and pivoted on his toes to face the others. He could smell their fear, he could taste their doubt. He needed to change that or they were done for.

Storm was shouting at the top of his lungs as the creature slowly continued to advance. "May I introduce you to The Demon King...Ravana!"

The demon reacted to the sound of its name, and its heads screamed tortured wails. Without warning, rows of giant arms slithered into the clearing, tearing the remaining trees from its path. Rising, it towered above Alexander at least twenty feet into the air. It was then the others realized what Alex already knew. All the heads and arms of the creature were connected to one massive body. Adorned in jewels and brightly painted with designs and symbols, the demon's skin shone with a deep, bright blue hue.

Alexander, appearing to cower, instead leaned into Lobo. "The demon's weakness is its bellybutton."

Lobo stared at Alex in complete and total disbelief. "Seriously? It's fucking *bellybutton?*"

Alexander stood up tall again. "Nope...*just* its bellybutton."

Lobo shook his head and studied the creature's torso. The beast was rapidly advancing on them.

"Kindly place one of your bow's bolts in his gut, will you?" Alexander barely finished his words before he dashed to Samantha and Abi.

"Ladies!" They were non-responsive as they stared at Ravana. "Ladies!" he shouted even louder this time, and Samantha looked at him for a moment before turning back to the towering servant of Hell.

"What?"

"It's time for you to make good your exit. I've recovered my bearings."

"Nice timing," Sam replied.

"Yes, well, the temple complex is about one hundred yards to your left through the overgrowth. We will distract the beast. Can you make it?"

"Yes," Sam said without even a thought. Of course, they could make it. Was there another choice?

"No," Alexander yelled. "You have no other choice!"

"Don't read my mind!" Sam shouted back.

"Don't think so loudly! Wait for my signal," he yelled in return, returning to Lobo's side.

"Don't leave me behind, girl," Abigail whispered to Sam, who shook her head in reply and grasped her hand tightly.

The creature was almost to Lobo, and he lifted his crossbow and leveled it at The Demon King's belly.

"Fire at will, old man," Storm shouted and turned to look at the rows of heads descending upon him. "And you...you filth. Tell Moloch I'll see him in Hell!"

Reacting to Alexander's words, the beast raised its arms in fanlike unison up into the sky. Its eyes blazed brighter, and growls and screams emanated from its snarling jaws.

Alexander heard the snap of the bow line, and without even watching to see if the bolt hit its mark, he turned to Sam and Abigail.

"Now!" he shouted with fierce conviction. They did not hesitate, but instead turned to their left and charged the creature's immense body, which still blocked their passage.

Before Alex could confirm Lobo's marksmanship, the demon let out a bloodcurdling roar. Lobo's aim was true. Alexander watched as the spawn of Hell's body convulsed and shrank. Focusing now on the rough, blue hued skin covering its abdominal region, Storm could make out the end of Lobo's bolt protruding from Ravana's bellybutton.

"Good show!" he yelled with congratulatory exuberance.

Lobo smirked and nodded at Alex.

"Go! Go!" Alexander pointed to the path cleared by the demon's shrinking body. They did not acknowledge his cries, but instead broke to run in the direction they had been instructed and quickly disappeared into the cover of the jungle.

Ravana had shrunk proportionally and stood not more than six feet tall, shriveled, and hunched before them.

"Now, to send you back from whence you came!" Alexander shouted as he approached the beast, raising the silver blade in his right hand, high above his head. The two locked eyes. "Khnhom thkaoltosa anak tow thanonorok!" Alexander whispered, and the beast responded.

"I condemn you to Hell!" Storm shouted.

"Thanonorok." The demon's voice rumbled deep and hollow, and Alexander watched as its snarl turned to smile as a horrid explosion of laughter burst forth. Soon, the laughter was mirrored by all of the demon's shrunken heads, echoing through the jungle like war drums beat in unison.

Alexander turned around and headed back to Lobo.

"What are you doing?" Lobo shouted. "Finish it, Storm!"

"I'm afraid there is more to come my friend," he replied, somber eyes still fixed on the monster whose body was shaking and burning, flames of blue and green enveloping it, radiating up from the jungle floor, up and over it into the sky.

Storm turned to Lobo. "Run!" he shouted, motioning toward the same route Abigail and Sam had taken.

Without question, Lobo took off and headed toward the edge of the clearing. Alexander turned to move as well, but his ears caught sound of a horrific din of ripping and tearing, and he turned to look at the demon once more.

"Run!" he shouted again. "Don't look back!"

Alexander watched through the multicolored hellfire that shrouded him as Ravana underwent his unholy metamorphosis. As if in the grasp of some unseen force, the demon's body was being pulled apart, split into individual Ravanas, each with a full body, arms, legs, and a head. Alexander continued to watch one...two...than three individual demons appeared before him, stretching and acclimating themselves to their new, independent form.

They turned to Alex, peering at him through the flames. Four...five...six bodies of Hell broke free of their maker. Storm had seen enough. Breaking to run in pursuit of the others, he dashed away from the clearing and battled the overgrowth of the jungle to escape. He could make out Lobo ahead by some length, and it energized his pace.

Crack!

To his rear, the creatures had completed their transformation and pursued him through the jungle. Alexander did not turn to look. Keeping an eye on his footing, he attempted to accelerate even more. Lobo was gone from view, and Alex could make out what appeared to be a large clearing ahead.

Snap!

They were close. Tearing apart the jungle behind him. Seeking to exact their revenge by devouring his soul.

Storm made it to the clearing, and he burst through into the light like a marathon runner hurling himself forward through the tape at the finish line. He emerged at the massive stone temple outskirts of Ta Prohm. Directly in front of him, a tall stone archway loomed, and at its center was a shrouded figure.

What the... Storm mouthed the words to himself as his vision came to rest on the figure. There, kneeling at the cloaked entity's feet, on the jungle floor, were Abigail, Samantha, and Lobo.

Alexander had no time to pause and assess his options; forward or back, it made no difference at this point. Behind him, he could hear the demons' thunderous crashing through the jungle into the temple's clearing. Quickening his pace once more, he covered the space to the others in seconds. Standing before the hooded figure in the archway entrance to Ta Prohm, he paused, chest heaving, eyes watering. The clamor behind him grew ever closer. Devastation and ruin had arrived.

Then, as calm and poised as rain falling softly in a meadow, the figure raised its arms and pulled back the hood that had hidden its face from the light.

Alexander understood then. Pressing his palms together in the form of prayer and peace, he bowed his head and closed his eyes, allowing fate to take hold of their future. For in that moment, he knew Hell—and the doom it carried— could not tread there.

114

Kate removed the phone from her ear and held it out in front of her. "He just hung up on me! I can't believe he just—"

"Hey, you!" The voice behind her startled Kate, and she dropped the phone into a pile of notes and printouts on the desk.

"You scared me!" She turned to see Decker and Anika coming around the far corner of the elaborate desks.

"How are you making out?" Anika asked as Decker walked over and picked up the phone and placed it on the charging dock.

"Good, good," she said. "I figured out we need to go to Palermo next."

"Ah, Italy!" Decker said jubilantly. "Was that Storm on the phone?" He lowered himself into one of the extra chairs that had been placed in the area and stretched his legs out in from of him.

"Yes," Kate replied, offering Anika the seat at the desk, which she waved off. "I was excited about my find regarding the riddle, but apparently they're in the middle of something. He hung up on me."

"Well, that could mean anything, especially since it's not unlike him to hang up the damn phone once he's said what he has to say, or once you've answered his questions."

Kate shook her head, "Yeah ... I kinda got the feeling they were in the middle of something."

"Don't sweat it, kid." Decker laughed. "Whatever they've gotten themselves into, Alex will get them out."

"Have you heard from Serket's team?" Anika asked softly, matter-of-factly. "Or from Keith?"

"Nope."

"No worries, I'm sure." Anika smiled and walked over to Decker's side.

"Seriously, Kate," Decker added. "Serket is probably more cautious than Alex. They'll be fine."

This time, Kate's nod was unconvincing.

"And," Decker said, "Jericho will get to them soon if he's not there already."

"I know." Kate sat hard in her chair and let her body slump. "It's just this isn't Keith's thing, you know? I hope this isn't too much for him."

Decker shook his head. "You ladies, always underestimating us guys."

Anika shook her head and rolled her eyes at Decker. "Why don't we help you take your mind off of it and work on one of the riddles with you?"

Kate perked up and smiled. "Okay! Sounds like a plan."

The idea of working on these with someone else appealed to Kate since she had been in the library, alone, almost continuously for the past few days, and the isolation was beginning to wear on her. Asar and Philip had taken turns sitting with her when they served her meals, but there was only so much conversation to be had with them. Asar had many intriguing, and often amusing, stories about Alexander and their adventures, while Philip resorted to comments on the weather and a history of certain parts of the castle and the island. Kate was fairly sure that Asar was always pretty close, in another part of the library, perhaps, or just on the other side of one of the doorways, keeping a watchful eye or ear on her. This was fine with Kate. Even if it was just her imagination, it didn't matter. It made her feel secure and allowed her to work without concern for her well-being.

"So," Decker slid his chair closer. "Whaddya got for us?"

Kate shuffled the papers on the desk around a bit and ran her hands along stacks to even and neaten them before moving them aside.

"Let's see," she replied, with new spunk in her voice.

She picked up an ornately bound, brown leather journal which had been exposed on the desk once all the loose sheets of paper were tossed aside and opened it to the front pages. Scanning the page, she shook her head several times.

"Nope...no...no..." She ran her finger down the page as she read.

Anika and Decker looked at each other and shrugged their shoulders.

"Bingo!" Kate finally found what she was looking for. "Let's try this one."

She retrieved two notebooks and pens from the large desk drawer to her left and handed them to Decker and Anika.

"What are we doing with these?" Decker inquired, opening the book to see if it contained anything.

Kate looked at him. "What do you mean? They're for notes."

"Oh, right." Decker pushed the back of the pen, exposing the tip. "Ready."

Kate sat back down and picked up the journal.

"Okay, I'll read slowly. Jot the riddle down so you can dissect it and stare at it, you know what I mean?"

Decker said nothing.

"Yes," Anika stepped forward. "We know what you mean. Excellent idea."

"Okay," Kate nodded and looked at the journal once more. "'South of Heaven, but within its walls no evil lies.'"

She paused and then repeated herself with greater assurance and understanding. "'South of Heaven, but within its walls no evil lies.'"

They seemed to understand, so she read the whole riddle.

"'South of Heaven, but within its walls no evil lies. Carved in a slayer's memory for helping a dragon meet his demise. From sky across—from land it's lost—within a holy altar does reside.'"

"Short and sweet," Decker commented as he wrote.

"Yes," Kate smiled. "That's why I picked it."

Kate repeated the riddle several times, allowing them to finish.

"So?" Kate began "Any thoughts?"

"Yes," Decker said with confidence. "St. George."

"St. George," Anika repeated.

"Yes," he said as he rose from his chair. "St. George slay the dragon."

"I know who St. George is," Anika said, smirking.

"Okay, so the line is fairly clear. 'A slayer's memory for helping a dragon meet his demise.' In other words, for killing a dragon." He paced toward Anika. "And the only one I know who's credited with killing a dragon is St. George."

"Ahem." Kate cleared her throat. "What about Bard the bowman?"

"Who?" Decker turned to face her.

"Bard killed Smaug. *The Hobbit*?" She laughed at his obvious confusion.

"I know who Smaug is," he said and grinned. "But I thought we were looking in the realms of reality with these."

"Oh, really?" Anika rolled her eyes. "So the dragon St. George killed was real? Of course, not like Smaug."

"Of course," Decker snapped back.

Both Anika and Kate giggled at his reaction.

"What?" he smiled.

"'Within its walls no evil lies.'" Anika decided to move on.

"Well, 'its walls' tells me it's a structure." Kate closed her eyes to picture the words.

"Very good." Anika slowly moved in Kate's direction. "So, theoretically a structure which is void of evil would be a—"

"Church," both Anika and Kate said at the same time.

"Yes," Decker said as he laughed. "Teamwork at its best."

Kate ignored his sly remark. "So, there must be hundreds, if not thousands of St. George churches or St. George cathedrals around the globe."

"That's probably true," Decker replied sympathetically. "However, there is one that is quite different from all the others."

Decker walked over to the computer keyboard and jiggled the mouse. The screen turned on. He opened the browser and typed in, "Church of St. George Ethiopia."

Kate and Anika gathered around the monitor as the search page results popped up.

"This should do." Decker clicked on the first image to enlarge it. "What do you think?"

"Holy crap, Decks," she whispered. "I think you got it, dude."

The Church of St. George, Ethiopia, is carved down into the ground. It's in the shape of a cross, which is only discernible if viewed from above.

"'South of Heaven.'" Anika looked at her notes. "Which, even though this could have several meanings, it clearly applies here as the church is carved down into the ground."

"Yes," Kate continued with growing excitement, "and the word 'across' is really a word play—'a cross' only visible from above, from the sky." Kate looked at Decker. "Jesus Christ, you got it!"

Decker laughed. "Don't beat yourself up, kid," he said, returning to his chair. "Been doin' this shit a long time."

"My hero." Anika winked at him, and Kate was pretty sure he blushed under his scruffy recovery beard.

"So, I assume there is an altar within the church." Anika walked to the keyboard.

"Yup," Decker quickly replied. "No need to search it."

"And you know this how?"

"Cause I've been there." Decker said smugly, wiping imaginary dust from his pant legs. "Friends with the caretaker, too."

"For real?" Kate shouted.

"For real." Decker laughed. "And a good thing, too, because we're gonna have to get inside that altar, which would have proven an issue otherwise. Still might."

"We?" Anika asked. "As in the collective 'we?'"

"Nope." Decker rose from the chair and walked over to the phone. "'We' as in you and me."

115

Naamah slowly strolled into the guard house, her tall black boots clicking on the stone ground beneath her. The dark cloak that surrounded her body ebbed and flowed in an imaginary breeze, exposing the naked skin of her thighs as it sailed about.

"My little Egyptian harlot. You should have made your exit when the chance presented itself." Naamah's eyes narrowed, and her lip curled to one side. "But then again, why prolong your inevitable fate?"

Serket stepped forward, back into the guard tower, leaving Keith and Amaat behind her.

"So be it." The words calmly passed her lips as she dashed to the far-left side of the room. Facing the wall, she placed the palms of her hands against the ancient stone and began to chant in ancient Egyptian.

"Rise, O' guardian. Swallower of the night! Protect your prize! Rise!"

Within seconds, the very foundation of the tower began to vibrate and hum. Dust that had gathered between the fine seams of the stones shook free and clouded the air around them.

"Are you going to put a stop to this vulgar display, my dear?" Moloch prodded Naamah as he entered the chamber behind her.

"I want to see what the witch is up to first," Naamah replied without turning to face her demonic companion.

As if responding to her curiosity, loud cracks and bangs began to emanate from the space above them. Naamah searched the ceiling for a moment before catching sight of the opening in the center above them. There was a deep amber glow radiating down from the space overhead, and she took a cautious step back toward Moloch.

"What have we here?" she said, smiling at Serket.

The sound of a rough, stone-on-stone, sliding movement echoed throughout the tower from above, causing Naamah to lean forward to get a better view.

"I wouldn't underestimate her." Moloch said sarcastically. "She *did* take your head in our last meeting, if you recall."

"Silence!" she commanded, reaching deep into the folds of her black cloak. Her hand came forth with one solitary stone, one of the remnants of Hell she collected all over the globe. Squeezing her fist tightly around it, she raised her hand to her lips and blew a glowing breath into the space created by the circular bend of her long fingers. Opening her mouth to speak, she fell silent as stone and debris generated by Serket's spell, spilled forth over her. Taking refuge in the entrance's threshold, she watched the space above as a glowing stone serpent coiled out of its lair and dropped with a crash to the floor in front of the demons. The cobra coiled back and rose up and over Naamah and Moloch, who stood motionless. The internal glow of the giant serpent cast light and shadow about the chamber as it rocked in rhythm over its intended prey.

"Well done." Naamah finally broke her silence and dashed to the side of the creature, causing it to bob back and forth between her and Moloch.

Serket seized the opportunity to turn to her companions while both demons were occupied.

Desperately, she cried, "You must flee! Now! Split apart and move on opposite sides of the wall ... NOW!" she cried loud enough to attract Moloch's attention from the other side of the tower.

He stared through the dusty dimness at the three, locking eyes on Amaat.

"That Medjai has the papyrus!" he called out over the serpent's hiss and grind. Naamah nodded and turned to face the head of the stone reptile. The serpent veered back in recoil and aligned itself directly across from

484 | ANTHONY DIPAOLO

her. With graceful poise, she brought her arms across her chest, like Osiris in his tomb, and lowered her head—but not her eyes. The snake shot forward at its target with speed and precision. It was, however, no match for the cunning demon. Effortlessly, Naamah leapt into the air above the serpent's head, which crashed into the wall of the tower behind her. The explosive force of its strike blew a hole in the stone. Naamah seemed to float momentarily in the space above the stone beast, finally dropping to its back beneath her.

"Ignis! Urere! Desolati!" she cried out, clutching the stone she had been holding above her head. "Ignite! Burn! Melt!"

The monolithic monster withdrew its head from the hole it had punched through the wall, but it was too late. Naamah cast the glowing stone against the serpent's side and jumped to the safety of the ground below.

Stone burning stone, the tiny rock entered the snake's body, and a pinpoint of light began to expand outward and throughout. They all felt the glowing heat of the magic as the serpent began to radiate like molten steel. Within moments, the hard rock shell turned into folds of molten rock spreading up and down, from head to tail, until it was nothing more than a cooling pool of glowing liquid on the tower floor.

Serket had not trailed behind to watch the demon's display of magical supremacy, and she was already running at Keith's side. Moloch and Naamah stepped out of the tower onto the wall just in time to see Serket take a diving hold of Keith as they both went over to the ground below.

Naamah, poised to follow the pair, was stopped by a firm hand on her shoulder.

"Papyrus travelled that way, my dear." He pointed to the grassy hillside on the opposite side. "We must not lose focus."

Naamah shook free of Moloch's grasp. "She is mine!"

Moloch smiled. "Yes." But his grin disappeared. "Get the papyrus, my dear. Now."

He wasn't asking, and she knew better than to cross him at this juncture.

She cried out in frustration and walked further down the edge. She could see Amaat fleeing fleet footed toward a wooded area in the opposite direction of Serket.

A low, strong hum suddenly filled the air above. Moloch watched as a chopper appeared above them, speeding toward Serket and Keith. The pair were sprinting across the open hillside in the opposite direction of his prize.

"Ignore them," he commanded, turning to Naamah. "Retrieve the scroll!"

Without further hesitation, Naamah pulled a small handful of stones from within her cloak and raised her fist above her head.

"Milites quo affliguntur damnati ortus!" she cried out, casting the stones down with demonic force against the floor of the Great Wall. "Rise, warriors of the damned!"

Like sprouting saplings, her soldiers came forth from the stone—six in all. Their tattered leather and cloth armor hung loosely over their rotted bones. Hair, skin, and sinew dangling putrid in the breeze, they turned in unison to their mistress for direction.

"Destroy him!" she ordered, pointing toward Amaat's escaping figure in the distance. "Bring me the Egyptian spell he carries!"

The horde of unholy servants sprang into action, leaping from the wall, sinking hard into the soil below. Without pause, they took to flight after the Medjai.

Serket grabbed Keith by the back of his shirt and spun him to a stop. The chopper was over them, and Keith looked up at the open side of the copter and the tall, dark man calling to Serket.

"Need a lift?" Jericho shouted, a smug smile betraying his dry, raspy voice.

Serket pulled Keith close to her side. "Great," she whispered. "Saved by the goddamned pirate."

The chopper was mere feet above the ground, and she hoisted Keith up to Jericho's reaching hands.

"I'm never gonna hear the end of this one," she said, huffing as Frank pulled her into the chopper.

"Nope," he replied, dropping into the seat across from her, his head rocking with the turbulence of the rising copter. A satisfied grin crept across his face.

116

"Check-in at terminal one in the international flights terminal." Kate was typing as she dictated the ticket information to Anika and Decker. "Ethiopian Airlines flight 766."

"Got it," Anika replied. "Can you send us—"

"On it already," Kate interrupted. "Boarding passes should be appearing in the wallet app on your cell as we speak."

Anika scrolled through her phone, tapped on the appropriate icon, and watched the screen.

"Yes," she assured Kate. "The tickets just popped up. Got it."

"You're not going to have much time to get through security." Kate, realizing she was probably adding to their stress, quickly said, "But you can do it. Just move quickly, okay?"

Anika's cell sat atop her thigh, and Kate's voice filled Alexander's Lincoln Navigator as it barreled down the Southern State Parkway toward JFK International Airport. Decker leaned forward and grasped Anika's leg, steadying the phone.

"We're working on it, Kate," Decker said, looking at Anika, who was smiling at his touch. "When's the next flight if we don't make this one?"

She clicked the mouse to confirm the information. "Not until late tomorrow night. You'll end up losing an entire day."

"No worries." Decker was shaking his head. "We'll make it," he added, winking at Anika.

He leaned forward and looked out the front windshield. "We're coming up on the exit, Kate." He reached over the seat and tapped the driver on the shoulder. "Nice job," he said, and sat back next to Anika.

The now familiar ring of Kate's satellite phone echoed through the truck from the other end of Anika's cell speaker.

"Is that Storm, Kate?" Decker hoped to hear from his friend before take-off.

"Looks like Jericho," Kate replied with both regret and excitement, as she knew Decker wanted to speak to Alex. But at the same time, she was hopeful Jericho had news about Keith.

"Go take it," Anika said. "I'll text you right before we go into airplane mode, okay?"

"Yup." Kate was already holding the satellite phone to her other ear. "Safe flight!" And she was gone.

Anika put her cell away and looked at Decker. "Poor girl. This must be nightmarish for her."

Decker smiled and tapped her on the leg. "Why? Because she's not accustomed to all of this? Pretty sure the same goes for you. But you're handling it like a champ."

Anika smiled at his compliment and leaned across the seat, positioning her face close to his.

"Yes," she whispered, their lips almost touching, eyes locked. "But I have you."

Decker reached up and gently wrapped his hand around the back of Anika's head, grasping her hair just enough to close the gap between their lips. They kissed passionately, and as the driver took the bending road through the airport at full speed, they found themselves firmly in each other's arms.

"Get ready, sir," the driver called from the front.

"On it," Decker replied as he assisted Anika up and back onto her side of the seat.

Turning to Decker with a smile, Anika caught sight of the bulge that had appeared in his pants. "Down, boy," she said and laughed. "Time for business."

Anika was sure she saw him blush as the car came to a jarring halt. The driver jumped out and was immediately accosted by airport security instructing him to move. He ignored their New Yorker shouts and opened Anika's door, which caused the din of their order barking to rise in volume. She quickly sprang from the vehicle and stepped to the curb, passing through the rows of stopped cars dropping passengers off. Decker had slid across the seat and was exiting the vehicle when the driver grabbed his upper arm and assisted him to out.

"You okay, sir?" the driver whispered, his voice vaguely familiar. Decker strained to make out his facial features, which were obscured by large aviators and a driver's cap pulled down low on his forehead.

"Yeah." Decker stumbled into his reply as the driver pushed him on toward Anika. "Hey, what's your name again?"

Without responding, the driver placed his hand over his ear and paused, an action that Decker immediately recognized. He said nothing and waited for the driver to relay the message he was receiving through his earpiece.

"Asar has dealt with security." He motioned Decker on, shaking his head. "Show your passports to the TSA Commander at the security control desk, and you should be good."

Decker smiled. "Very good," he said, and turned to Anika to give her a thumbs up. She shook her head in confusion, but smiled back nonetheless.

A siren let out a warning burst to their left, and both driver and passenger whipped around to the shrill call.

"Move it!" the Port Authority cop in the passenger seat was leaning out the window. "*Now!*" he ordered.

Decker's driver waved and nodded.

"Don't wave me off!" The cop huffed under his breath as he reached down and unlatched his door.

"Go! We're good."

Without warning, the driver reached over and wrapped his arm around Decker's back, pulling him in tight to his face. "You're not alone," he whispered with force. "They're all around us...now...as I speak."

Decker's face grew dark, his brow furrowed. "What?"

The driver ignored him and continued. "They will be with you from now on. They will be with you on the plane. They will be with you in Africa. They will be with you at the Church of the Dragon Slayer."

The Port Authority cop was almost to them. "Trust no one. Be vigilant and ready, or you will not survive this journey, *old friend*."

Decker pushed away from the driver in shock. *"Alexander?"* The chills ran from his head to his toes, and he stumbled back toward Anika. The driver was already gone, past the oncoming cop, entering the driver's side of the truck. He had sailed past everyone as if invisible to all except for Decker. The door slammed shut, and the truck was gone within seconds.

"What is it?" Anika took hold of Decker's arm and helped him to the curb. He was visibly shaken.

"What's going on?" She pressed harder. "What is it?"

Decker steadied himself and regained his composure.

He took Anika by the shoulders. "We're in danger. The forces of darkness are here with us—now—and they will do all in their power to stop us."

"What?"

"We must prepare!" Decker grasped her hand and scanned the droves of people moving like ants around them.

"Wait!" Anika's slight resistance to his grasp regained his focus on her, and he saw the terror in her eyes. "How do you know this?"

Decker turned to her; his face transformed in so many ways that Anika barely recognized his expression. "Alexander Storm just moved space and time to tell me."

117

L unging himself forward into the wooded hillside, Amaat did not pause to look behind. His sure-footed movements propelled him further into the stalks of barren trees and overgrowth. He did not need to see his pursuers. He could sense their presence. Digging and reaching, he worked his way further up the hill's incline. Amaat had heard the chopper zoom overhead. Whether it was Storm's bird or the Chinese government's mattered not. It meant safety in the sky, and he needed to get to the clearing at the top of the hill if he was to have any chance of escaping.

Amaat began to pick up the faint whispers of his pursuer's boney steps. Breaking twigs, rustling leaves, snapping branches.

"Amun," he whispered for divine intervention and increased his stride.

The evil horde was close now. Amaat realized he would not make it to the clearing in time. If he kept to his current course, they would take him down like a pack of wild dogs. Still continuing his ascent, he turned from side to side, looking for somewhere, anywhere, to take cover. A huge boulder jutting out of the hillside to Amaat's right looked promising. He changed course and dashed toward the stony sanctuary. As he grew closer, he was able to make out an indent in the earth below the enormous rock. A hole. He could make it if he pushed. Diving forward headfirst, his body plummeted into the ground, disappearing under the boulder. Grabbing at the ground ahead of him, he pulled himself further into the darkness until he could proceed forward no more. Amaat was confident his feet were concealed within the dark tunnel, and he lay motionless. Breathless. Waiting.

Only seconds had passed when he could distinctively make out the crashing sounds of his hunters approaching and fading again. They were moving past him!

Like a fox that takes refuge in a hole as the hounds saunter on their way, Amaat played the part well. He was resigned to lay motionless in the dark hole until nightfall. He would take no chances. Allowing his head to drop, his chin came to rest in the cool, damp soil.

Minutes passed, and whether sheer exhaustion or declining adrenaline were to blame, he began to doze off. Still vigilant, but in a relaxed state, relinquishing his being into the soft earth bed.

"Thank you, Amun." His lips let slide a whisper so faint only the god himself could have intercepted it from the windy air around the boulder. Or so he thought.

Without sound or warning, Amaat felt the rotted skeletal hands of one of Naamah's warriors grasp tightly around his ankles. A cry escaped his mouth as the creature began pulling and tugging him out into the light. He writhed and kicked, and he managed to spin onto his back. He wouldn't go out with his face buried in the dirt. He was an ancient Medjai, and he would fight until the last gasp of air left his lungs.

As Amaat's body exited the hole, he came face to face with the demons before him. Ragged, horrid creatures of bone and rot. Eyeless faces peered down at him from empty pits, and although he fought and struggled, they quickly overtook him. Four of the demons pinned his arms and legs down, while a fifth took hold of his head and immobilized him. He strained to look around, kicking and pulling. He tried to break free of their ghastly grip. It was useless. He was at their mercy. He was doomed.

The monster at his head took hold of his hair and pulled him up. With a sudden jerk, the demon slammed the back of his head back down with such force his vision hazed over, then slammed it again, and again, and again until Amaat was on the edge of consciousness.

Don't pass out, he cried within. *Don't pass out.*

The demon lifted his head again, and Amaat was sure this last slam would render him unconscious. But rather than delivering the incapacitating blow, the creature held his head in the upward position. Amaat strained his failing eyes to make out the approaching figure in front of him. A sixth warrior. Its size and stature appearing greater than its counterparts, and it wielded a heavy long sword in one hand. Standing at Amaat's feet, it dropped to one knee and brought its putrefied face close to the Medjai's ear.

"Amun cannot save you." It hissed and spit. "My steel will split your very soul."

With those final words, the demon sprang back upright above Amaat. Spinning its sword in hand to point down, it grasped the handle with both hands and drove it down into his helpless prisoner.

Amaat, the ancient warrior, did not cry out as the steel blade entered and exited the back of his body, burrowing deep into the ground beneath him. Nor did his emotions betray him by releasing a single tear from his bulging eyes. The creature stared down into Amaat's face, leaning its tattered body into the sword, twisting and driving it further. Sensing Amaat would offer no satisfaction to the demons in his suffering, the sixth relinquished its grip on the handle of the blade and stepped back from its handiwork.

"Find the scroll," it demanded. "Find the papyrus."

The creatures immediately obeyed; they released Amaat's limbs and took to searching his body.

Amaat watched through fading eyes as they tore and shredded his clothing looking for their objective. He felt the tension on the side of his backpack beneath him as they pulled and ripped it out from underneath. And he watched, with his last breath, as fingers of bone withdrew the stone cylinder from the pack and presented it to the sixth demon.

Then, although his warrior soul wished for anything but, peace found Amaat, and he was gone.

118

The mad discord of demon feet charging across the jungle floor ceased, and quiet serenity appeared to return to Ta Prohm. Alexander's eyes had remained closed in the presence of the revered monk. He opened them, turning to apprise the situation behind him and was relieved at what he saw.

Standing silent and still, at some unseen delineation in the ground, the many demons who had been born of one could proceed no further.

"Even if one commits the most abominable actions, if he is engaged in devotional services, he is to be considered saintly because he is properly situated in his determination. He quickly becomes righteous and attains lasting peace."

The monk's English was soft and true, and his words passed like feathers over Alexander's body. He turned to meet their savior's gaze.

Alex smiled and bowed once more. "Arise. Awake. Standup and fight."

The monk's laughter broke the tension. "You know your Krishna, my son."

Alexander nodded, his hands still folded, and he signaled for the others to rise and join him.

"Ravanah cannot pass into the land of peace, my friends." Alex said in an effort to ease their fears, but the others remained clearly disturbed by the row of stalled demons behind them.

Alexander stared at the monk, unable to gauge his age or stature in the holy community. His dark skin and shaved head were overtaken by a stunning pair of ice-blue eyes which radiated with light and knowledge. His garb was traditional. Long flowing robes of bright and dark orange covered his body, except for his hands and feet which were weathered and dry.

The monk offered a hand to Alexander. "Come. Let us find your ancient riddle from the eastern sands."

Storm, taken aback by the Monk's insight, stepped to him nonetheless and proceeded past the entrance to Ta Prohm temple. The others, remaining silent but relieved, fell in behind them.

As the group entered into the open courtyard of the temple, they were met with a complex in stunning disarray. The jungle had clearly claimed Ta Prohm. Banyan trees fused with stone. Long winding limbs danced over the temples, creating a spectacular display of Lovecraftian proportions. The structures had not been restored as they had been in most other parts of Angkor. Instead, the monks had preferred to allow the jungle and the temple complex to become one. Perhaps they had chosen to keep the temple in its original state to keep hidden that which it housed.

"Remarkable," Alexander commented and then smiled. "Simply breathtaking."

"Here, the spirits of jungle, stone, and man unite and hurtle forward through time intertwined."

As they walked closer to the temple structures, Sam was the first to break the silence, running her hands along a tree limb that was more akin to an elephant's trunk than a tree.

"Awesome," she said to the monk. "Supreme awesomeness."

"Indeed, young lady." He smiled and nodded.

The monk led them to a shaded area beneath an immense Banyan tree and sat down on the ground. The others followed suit and sat in a makeshift circle with him at the top.

"Ta Prohm," he said again, lifting his hands first to the sky and then to the large stone Buddha fashioned in stone to their left. "Your holy sanctuary. The Buddha told me you would come Mr. Storm. He told me of your needs, and he ordered me to assist you, so here I am. How may I assist you?"

Lobo laughed. "Heck, thanks for stopping the monsters out there, for starts."

The monk bowed and smiled. "I had nothing to do with that, my friend, so I cannot take credit for that which was not my doing."

"Well, thanks anyway," Lobo replied. "Credit or not."

"Yes," Abigail agreed. "Thank you. You saved our lives."

Again, the monk smiled. "It was your souls that were saved. But as I said, no action nor inaction of mine leant to your salvation."

Alexander grimaced and grabbed his forehead. He remained motion-less for several seconds and then looked up at the others, who had moved toward him in concern.

"There are pressing issues in my home." He held up a hand, staving off assistance and their questions for the moment. "I am sorry to impose upon your holiness, but the completion of our task here has just become a para-mount urgency."

The monk rose to his feet. "I understand."

He turned and walked to the center of the temple courtyard and motioned for Alexander to proceed.

"Thank you," Alex said softly and walked just beyond the monk's position.

Storm began to pace customarily. "The relevant part of our clue is as follows: 'locate that which should logically house what you desire. If perplexed by many remember to always first center yourself. Find the stone with serpent's seal, the truth beneath Buddha had hoped to conceal.'"

The monk pondered Alex's words, repeating them to himself as he gazed around the dimly lit temple complex at the various structures.

"Kate, okay?" Lobo whispered in Alex's ear.

"Not now." Storm ushered him away. "I must concentrate on the task at hand."

"Yes, yes!" the monk sang out.

Alexander sprinted to his side. "Illuminate me, please. Time is truly not on our side at the moment."

"Yes," the monk nodded with new-found knowledge. "What you seek is the written word—paper and ink."

Alexander nodded. "Correct."

The monk hurried toward a structure in the foremost corner of the courtyard. "Well, where does one keep the written word? The printed word?"

"A library?" Abigail called out, surprising herself in turn.

The monk stopped before a long twisting building, in severe disarray and partially gobbled up by the jungle, and offered his hands in prayer to the others.

"I present to you the temple structure known as..." He paused for effect, which under any other circumstances Alexander would have found amusing for such a humble holy man. "The Library. Yes."

"Well done!" Storm marched past the monk and crossed the threshold.

"No time to waste, my dear friends." He summoned the others. "Split up and find anything that could signify the 'serpent's seal.'"

One by one, they entered the Library and chose a wall to examine.

"What am I looking for?" Sam called out, already frustrated at her own ignorance.

"It is unclear," Alexander replied from a further recess of the stone edifice. "But I am fairly certain we will know when we find it."

"Totally non responsive," Sam muttered.

"What?" Alex was moving farther in.

"Nothing!" Lobo yelled out and made a face at Sam.

"What?" She shrugged.

"Not helpful!" Abigail shouted from across the room.

The monk had joined them, a perplexed look on his face. Alexander returned after having quickly examined the far end of the Library, and was rehashing areas the others had viewed already.

"What is it?" he called to the monk upon noticing his expression.

"Mr. Storm," the monk said, disappointed, "I do not recall ever seeing a serpent in these walls, nor anything I can equate with such a creature."

Alex approached the monk, whose eyes seemed saddened by his failure to assist further.

"What are we supposed to do now?" Sam said, cutting her way through the frustration that was quickly mounting. "Think, Storm. The answer is here. The answer is in the riddle."

Alexander paced around, eyes to the floor. "The answer is in the riddle." He repeated Sam's words. "The answer is in the..."

He suddenly shot forward into the Library. "Good show, Samantha!" he exclaimed. "Well done! Way to maintain focus!"

"Yay, me," she said, teasing.

Storm came to a stop midway through the structure and stood still. The others were running toward him, awaiting the fruits of his mental labors.

"'Center yourself!'" he cried out. "'If confused...*center yourself.*'"

"Always sound advice," the monk said dryly.

"We don't get it, Alex," Lobo finally blurted out.

"I counted the stones that line the floor from entrance to end."

"You did?" Abigail seemed doubtful.

"Yes, of course." He all but brushed her off. "I always keep track of my steps."

"You do?"

This time Alexander actually ignore her.

"Three hundred and thirteen stones," he said with a laugh. "And if one is to center oneself, it would be on the one- hundred-fifty-seventh stone."

Alexander pointed down at the tile below his feet.

"Lift your foot," Sam demanded.

She studied the stone intimately, then she withdrew.

"There's nothing there, Storm." She was confused.

"Of course not." He smiled and pointed to the ceiling above. "'One must center oneself' *and* look to the heavens for answers." He winked at the monk. "So states Krishna."

119

"Woah!" Jericho tapped the chopper pilot on the shoulder. "Don't fly too close to that pair!"

The pilot pulled the stick hard and veered the chopper out and off the path that would lead to Moloch and Naamah. Serket spun in her seat, trying to keep her eyes on the edge of the forest Amaat had fled into. Appraising the situation back on the wall, she reached across and tapped Jericho.

"This could get bad," she cried, pointing to Naamah, who was already whipping a cyclone of wind and fire up into the sky toward them.

"Get outta here!" Jericho ordered the pilot, who nodded in agreement.

"No!" Serket cried rising from her seat. "Head out and around back to the top of that clearing on the hill!"

Serket pointed out where she wanted the pilot to go after he took some evasive maneuvers. She knew Amaat was smart enough to head for the hilltop after hearing the chopper whiz overhead. She knew he would have only seconds to be picked up after he emerged from the tree-line, and she had every intention of being there to extract him from the grasp of Naamah's legions.

"Your mans on his own Serket," Jericho offered with sympathetic force. "If he's anything like you, he'll beat us home."

"Compliments?" Serket's eyes grew tight. "We must be in dire straits."

Jericho waved her off. "Whatever. I'm in charge of this bird, and I say we get out of here. Now!"

A bolt of fire whizzed past the left side of the helicopter, and the passengers were tossed to one side as the pilot made some maverick-like moves to avoid impact.

"*Now!*" Jericho screamed as he righted himself in his seat.

"Amaat has the papyrus," Serket almost whispered, staring into Jericho's eyes which responded with gentle understanding, stunning Serket once again.

"Get your ass to the hilltop," he ordered the pilot, who nodded and changed course once again.

Naamah turned to her companion. "Looks like you were correct. The Medjai has the scroll. They're not leaving him behind."

"Had you really any doubt?" He laughed and walked to the edge of the wall, peering hard into the forest.

"They will do as I have commanded," Naamah assured him. "They will retrieve the riddle from his cold, dead hands."

"No doubt." He spun to face her. "No doubt, my mistress. All do as you command."

She smiled slyly at him and turned to cast another bolt of fury at the chopper. The bird veered again and dropped below her magic fire.

"Are you missing on purpose?" He was at her side now, whispering in her ear.

Naamah did not turn to him, nor did she reply.

"Destroying Serket in *any* manner is beneficial to our cause." He hissed.

"No!" Namaah turned to face him. "She will die my way! The way I say. I will be gazing into her eyes as the life drains from them, and I will crush her soul as it departs to wherever Egyptian whore witches' souls travel to."

Moloch laughed slowly. "I would imagine they travel to the same place demon whore witches' souls do." He laughed again, infuriating Naamah.

"Splendid," she spit back. "Then I shall have eternity to torment her."

"As you wish." He turned and began to walk from her side. "Do as you will, but take heed. If this little display comes back to haunt us, I will show no mercy."

"Have you ever shown mercy, my lord?" she said seductively, having been granted her will.

"If she is so inclined, can the demon bitch open a portal for me now?"

Naamah removed one hand from the flowing rapture emanating from her fingertips and retrieved a stone from her cloak.

"Storm's castle?" she asked, catching sight of her warriors emerging from the forest.

Moloch nodded. "Your dogs return to their master."

She cast the stone, which burst and expanded into a swirling display of smoke and fire, cutting a pathway through time and space.

"Had you any doubt?" She laughed mockingly as she relinquished her onslaught on the chopper and turned to face Moloch.

"Never." Moloch winked and stepped into the portal, vanishing with the smoke and fire.

"Safe travels," Naamah said with a laugh at the empty space. *"For now..."*

120

Alexander emerged from the Library and stepped forth into the shaded light of the courtyard. Standing to one side, he watched as the others filed out and past him. Falling in next to the monk, Storm held him back a moment.

"I must speak with you in regard to matters quite urgent, your holiness."

The monk nodded and signaled him to walk on. Noticing them lingering, Samantha slowed until they had caught up to her.

"What does it say?" she asked, holding the glass case Alexander had provided to safeguard the papyrus up to the light.

Alexander smiled at her curiosity and removed the vessel from her hand.

"It says, in simplest terms of course..."

"Of course," Sam said jokingly. "That's me. A simple girl."

"Really?" Storm shot her a glance and continued, "Come in peace! Come in peace! Come in peace! Come in peace! O' thou, whose transformations are manifold, thy soul is in Hell, thy body is in the earth. It is thine own command, O' great one."

"Lovely." Abigail's distaste was evident as she turned from the words.

"The prose is, in fact, as eloquent as one would expect an ultimate invocation of Hell to be." He turned to each of them for agreement, but received questioning stares instead.

"Should you speak the words out loud?" Lobo finally asked nervously.

"Harmless mumbo jumbo." Alexander laughed. "Unless, of course, you combine the twelve and partake in the ritualistic behavior required to perfect their intent."

Lobo laughed nervously again.

"Like the components of a bomb, it is the engineered combination that makes them deadly."

Alexander offered the glass case back to Samantha.

"You want me to hold onto this?" The surprise in her voice was evident to all.

Alexander chuckled. "Naturally." He placed the papyrus back in her hand, and folding her fingers over the case, said, "You are now a guardian of the twelve. One of a long and powerful line. Protect it with your life."

Samantha said nothing, for once, and slid the case into the pocket of her jeans.

"I must speak with our host in private for a moment." He motioned for the others to continue into the courtyard. "We shall join you momentarily."

The three proceeded on their way, and Alexander turned to his guide.

"I am now required," he started, "for the effectuation of good, to call upon evil."

The monk showed no emotion and said nothing, but instead listened to Alex's words attentively.

"I am in a bit of a conundrum as our present locale would seem to exclude such communion." He paused and rubbed his chin in his hand. Alexander was all but too aware what he was asking was at the same time insulting to his host, and placing the very sanctuary in which they stood in dire jeopardy.

He bowed his head ever so slightly. "I would, selfishly, as it were ... wish to avoid having to leave the safety of your embrace to perform this task—"

"As I have told your companions," the monk interrupted Alex, "it is not I who protects you from the evil that is held at bay on our doorstep." He stepped close to Alex and took hold of his forearm. "It is you—each of you within, who have created the peace that protects us now."

Alexander smiled at the wisdom of the holy man. "I understand."

"I am sure that a mind as learned," the monk said, growing very close this time, "and *aged* as yours can conjure himself into the space he requires."

Alexander smiled at his host. "The quiet seclusion of the Library should proffer a sliver of space required to work safely."

"I agree." The monk nodded. "I shall occupy the minds of the others while you perform your dark task."

Alexander could not believe his arrogance. "The others? They cannot travel where I must go. I cannot afford to spend the—"

The monk raised his hand. "Say no more, my son. There is more than one way to depart Ta Prohm. I will lead them to safety. You will arrange transport, yes?"

"Yes. Keep them with you here in the temple until morning, if you will."

The monk nodded once more. "And of the papyrus. It is it to remain with—"

"Sam." Alexander did not let him finish. "It will remain with Samantha. It is as it must be, my friend."

"As you wish." He smiled at Alex. "I wish you luck, although I believe in it not. But I do believe the fate you have constructed will not fail you. This I hope, for all our sakes."

The monk slowly began to walk to the others. Stopping, he spoke without turning to face Alexander. "Until next we meet." He bowed his head, and he continued on.

"Until next we meet," Alexander softly replied as he turned toward the Library. Moving with lightning speed, he arrived at the entrance once more and disappeared into the darkness within.

"What's going on?" Lobo demanded as the monk arrived.

"Yeah," Samantha chimed in. "Where's he going?"

The monk looked to each of them. He could see the fear and doubt growing in their faces.

"You are quite safe," he consoled them. "Quite safe."

"Where is Storm going?" Samantha demanded again.

"My child." The monk extended a hand and placed it on Sam's shoulder, consuming her attention instantly. "Where he treads now — you dare not follow."

121

The tiny hairs on the back of Kate's neck stood up.

"Spidey senses." She joked to herself, trying to ease her nerves. "That's what Keith calls it."

She had just hung up with Jericho who, although appearing to be failing in his main quest, had secured Keith and was returning him to her. That was the last time she would allow Storm to separate them. They would meet their fate, whatever it may be, together. Besides, she wasn't built for this. She wasn't built for the worry that comes from silence and the unknown. At least as it pertained to him. Him. Keith. She laughed in her head. At least one thing had come from this separation. Kate had finally come to terms with the fact that her feelings for the boy were much more than she had ever allowed herself to admit. They were entwined, for lack of a better word. And although she would not dare to utter, even internally, the "L" word, she was all but too aware when she was unable to speak with him, to know he was safe, her heart hurt.

Lost in her pondering over one of life's great mysteries, she was snapped back to reality by a strange aroma that crept into her nostrils like a spider into a hole.

Her body tensed, and she bolted upright in her seat. Spinning in her chair, she peered out into all the visible corners of Storm's immense library.

She was unable to see anything beyond a certain point, and truthfully, darkness shielded most of the great hall from her eyes.

"Sulfur." The words left her lips like a bullet from a gun, and she jumped to her feet.

"Who's there?" she called out into the darkness surrounding her circle of artificial lamp light.

Silence responded, and she moved around the desk nervously. Asar had instructed her, at length as it were, about how she could control the lights throughout the library from the iPad on the far side of Alex's desk. She swept it up into her hands and began to fiddle with the icons.

"Chill out," she whispered reassuringly to herself and thought back to the large Egyptian's instructions. Recalling the navigational sequence, Kate quickly arrived at the main lighting screen, which was composed of rows of digital sliding controls. Reading the labels of each, her eyes darted to the top of the screen.

It read: "Master Lights."

She tapped the empty box next to the words and a check appeared under her finger. Below the label, a new sliding control appeared, and she slid her finger to it, inadvertently scrolling it in reverse, killing all the lights, including those around her.

"Shit!" she yelled, positioning her finger on the control again and dragging it all the way to the right.

Instantly, the entire library transformed from pitch black to blindingly intense brilliance. Kate squinted at the sudden and severe shock to her senses and slowly retracted the control to a comfortable level.

"Whose there?" she called out again with a renewed courage the light afforded her, "Asar? Philip?"

There was no reply, and she turned and headed back to her chair. This was Storm's castle. Evil would have to be mad to venture here. But Storm wasn't here, was he? She was, for all intents and purposes, completely and utterly alone. Kate's imagination began to spin a macabre spell through her mind. Asar and Philip could be dead already. Were there other workers in this castle, on this island? *My God, an island.* Not only was she deserted in an ancient castle, she was quite possibly the only occupant on a friggin' island.

Kate steadied herself and called out once more. No reply came. The air, however, seemed to take on a quality she was vaguely familiar with. Damp and misty like a swamp in summer, her breath became more labored. Whether caused by, or a reaction to, her changing environment, she found it harder and harder to catch her breath.

"Christ," she called out. The smell was growing even stronger, wrestling her nostrils into submission. She opened her mouth to bypass her nose and was ultimately met with the same sulfuric taste interpreted as smell by her nose.

Kate jumped to her feet once more. Her mind was reeling. Should she make a run for it? Should she barricade herself somewhere in the hidden recesses of the library? Should she...should she...call someone? Grabbing the phone from the desk, she hit the intercom button and pushed every extension available. Dead silence greeted her. Clicking on the button for an outside line, she held the phone to her ear and waited for a dial tone. Eerie silence echoed in her head yet again. Kate dropped the phone and grabbed her cell from the opposite desk. Yanking the charging plug violently from the port. She dropped into the corner the adjoining desks created and opened the keypad to dial out. Squeezing herself into the tight space, she dialed Keith, Samantha, even Storm. Dead air.

The tension was too much. The stink. The heaviness of the air surrounding her. She felt as if she was about to break, an escape from this reality that was horrifyingly upon her.

Suddenly all the lights in the library went dark. All save the small banker's lamp that sat upon the desk directly above Kate, its antique form casting an unnerving green glow upon her face.

"Jesus Christ!" she screamed, sobbing.

"No," a deep, reptilian voice hissed from the newly created darkness. "Not even close, my dear."

And with that, the last vestige of light in the library went black.

122

Serket stared somberly out the window of the chopper. China's landscape sped by at a dizzying pace, but her eyes were not trying to focus on the ancient land. Instead, it was her mind's eye that replayed the decisions and actions that had led to her dear friend's demise. How could she have allowed him to be alone with the papyrus as they fled? She had reacted and not planned. The events that had transpired would haunt her for the rest of her days.

"You okay?" Jericho reached across and touched her knee.

"Fine," she replied, withdrawing from his hand.

"What's next?" Keith interrupted the awkward exchange and adjusted his position to partially separate the two.

Neither Serket nor Jericho replied.

"Fuel!" the pilot called from the cockpit. "And back to Dragon Loch. Those are my instructions."

Jericho looked up at the pilot and nodded in agreement.

"What of the others?" Keith quickly added.

Jericho lifted the satellite phone from his lap and held it in the air. "I don't know! No one is picking up! Anywhere!"

"That's a problem," Serket interjected. "Don't you agree?"

"I do. But all we can do is return to the castle and await word or further instructions." Serket's mouth opened, but Jericho raised his voice and continued. "We can't go traipsing all over the globe without any direction or purpose."

"I disagree." Serket turned to address him directly. "We know where they were going from your last communiqué with Kate. Why not head to Cambodia and offer our assistance?"

"Because that's not what Storm wanted." He leaned forward into the space between them, causing Keith to sit back in his seat. "And goddamn it, if there's one thing I've learned from my years of dealing with Storm is that you do nothing but fail if you try to guess his plans, motivations, or the fifty moves ahead of you he already is."

Serket shook her head. She couldn't argue with his logic.

The momentary silence of the cabin was interrupted by Jericho's ringing phone.

"Kate? Kate?" he said with intensifying volume. "Kate?"

Pulling the phone from his ear, he allowed it to drop from his hand to the floor of the chopper. "What the fuck?"

"What is it?" Keith rose from his seat in panic. "Is it Kate? What's wrong?"

Serket moved with the speed of a viper and snatched the phone from the ground before Keith could retrieve it. She held a finger to her lips, commanding silence, and slowly raised the satellite phone to her ear. It rested against her head for a fraction of a second before she dropped it into the seat at her side.

Keith did not hesitate this time. Springing forward, he grabbed it and spun around and onto his knees in his seat, effectively blocking the others who were trying to remove the phone from his grasp.

"No! Stop!" they were yelling in virtual unison. "No, Keith!"

Keith ignored their pleas and brought the phone up to his ear.

"Kate!" he screamed into the mouthpiece, rolling around in his seat to face the others once more.

Keith's bulging eyes and blood red face made Jericho swat at the phone with an open palm, sending it crashing into the wall of the chopper.

"Hey!" the pilot called, reacting to the loud bang.

Keith slumped down in his seat. His body was trembling, and his eyes were tearing. "What...was...that?"

Serket jumped into the space next to Keith and put her arm around him, drawing him into her. He was on the verge of sobbing, and Jericho tapped his back in a compassionate rhythm.

"I can't say for sure," Jericho finally said, believing Keith was due some type of explanation. "But if I had to wager a guess, the screams and wails of the countless damned."

Keith shook his head and looked at Serket. "So what? We're getting calls from Hell now?"

Serket raised her head from the comforting embrace she had on Keith and exchanged glances with Jericho.

Keith caught their silent communication and demanded insight.

"What? Tell me!"

Jericho let out a large huff. "According to the caller ID, it wasn't Hell calling. It was Kate."

123

"Why would *I* bargain with *you*?" Bathin circled her summoner in the dim light of Ta Prohm's library.

Storm stepped toward her ethereal form. "Because we share a common enemy in Moloch, demon."

Bathin shifted and shot toward him. She floated face to face with him, her red locks drifting and encircling her cheeks.

"You hold me with six stones, Storm." Her eyes narrowed to slits. "And once free, I will gather my thirty legions and, at Lucifer's side, crush Moloch and his pet bitch."

Alexander shook his head and continued his attempts at bargaining with the beast. He had to get to Dragon Loch. He needed Serket with him. But he must keep four stones at all costs, and the demon was demanding he use three.

"I will make use of two stones, Bathin—"

"I love the way you say my name, Storm," she interrupted, smiling in mystical seduction. "I just roll off your tongue—"

"Leaving me only four left over you—"

"Or maybe your tongue rolls over me?"

"Enough, demon!" Alexander's voice changed and the slight shadow of his body cast by Bathin's unholy glow appeared to stretch and grow. The demon's eyes grew wide, and she withdrew from him.

"You *will* do as I command." The words spewed like fire from his lips. "You will take me to Serket, wherever she is, and then you will manifest safe passage for the two of us to Dragon Loch!"

Bathin growled and hissed in discordant disapproval.

"You will do this for me!" he stepped to her, and she recoiled. His voice lowered to a hum. "If not for your allegiance to Satan, then because if you do not obey my command, demon, I shall drop my last stone into the deepest, darkest crevice in the Earth." Storm reached out and grabbed the demon behind her head and pressed her face to his. "And you will remain trapped, my prisoner, for all eternity."

The demon stared into ageless eyes. Eyes she knew shared secrets too dark for light, and she nodded, causing Alexander to relinquish his grasp.

"You had my head in a firm grasp," Bathin whispered, attempting to dissolve the serious nature of Storm's words. "You could have directed my pretty little mouth anywhere you wanted."

"Well, it's a shame I didn't have a pig handy for you to kiss."

"What?" the demon laughed, genuinely shocked. "Poking fun? Joking with the enemy?" Bathin's full, ruby red lips curled into a smile. "I'll make you mine yet."

"Perhaps," Storm walked to the far wall, turning his back to the demon. "Perhaps not!"

"Well, if not a pig," she said with a huff, her voice showing signs of his insults, "I hope you brought something else to bleed for me, or you're not getting very far, Storm."

"I have brought myself." Alexander turned to face her, in one hand a silver blade, and in the palm of the other, two of the remaining demon stones. "Will that be sufficient?"

The demon rose up, and her excited laughter echoed through the ancient stones. "How delicious!" She cried out. "An exquisite treat."

With her acknowledgment of the validity of his offering, Alexander wasted no more time. Bathin watched, licking her lips, as he drew a red line across his hand with the razor-sharp blade. Blood immediately pooled out into his palm and soaked the stones.

Bathin threw her head back in sheer ecstasy as the smoke and mist of her black magic engulfed the space. And without further word or action, the two were gone from Ta Prom Temple.

124

Anika gazed out the oval window of the twin prop aircraft onto the surprisingly well-manicured tarmac of Ethiopia's Lalibela Airport. The trip had taken them more than a day. Stopping first at Bole International Airport, they left the security of the large Boeing aircraft and settled into the relatively cramped quarters of the Ethiopian Airlines dual prop for the remainder of the journey.

Decker stood up from his seat next to her and lifted his arms to the aircraft's ceiling, stretching his aching limbs with a smile.

"Well, that was fun," he said with a wink.

Anika smiled and peered out the window again. The mobile staircase came into view as an informally dressed local, with one foot propped up on the vehicle's dash, steered it alongside the plane.

"Well, at least the company was good." She turned back to Decker, motioning him forward. "The stairs are here. Let's get the hell off, though, huh?"

Decker nodded. "Gotcha," he said, and reached out to Anika. He took her hand and guided her into the row toward the plane's exit. Allowing her to walk first, he leaned forward and whispered into her ear.

"Listen," he started as they moved forward. "We're in danger, as I have explained—"

"Several times," she interjected without turning to face him.

"Yes, well, I'm a cautious man." He leaned in closer, guiding her by grasping her hips lightly as they moved forward. "And I have no idea what to expect, okay?"

She slowed slightly. "And you have been warned," she said, laughing. "I got it. You have been warned by Alexander Storm." She came to a full stop, and he released his grasp, expecting her to turn and face him. "Storm, who just so happened to be somewhere on the other side of the globe at the time."

"Move it," Decker grumbled, grasping her waist once more and edging her on. "That's the way it works with him."

She laughed again, nervously this time. "The mysterious Alexander Storm."

As the two reached the end of the aisle, they were stopped by a large figure as he rose from his seat in the first row. Turning slowly to face the pair, he presented to them a grotesquely exaggerated smile. Anika was caught off guard, and she took a step backward into Decker.

"My apologies, miss, if I startled you," he said with the easy-going accent of a local. Lifting his white brimmed hat, he exposed his clean-shaven head. His dark skin radiated with the hue of years in the African sun.

"But I could not help but hear you mention a common acquaintance." Decker squeezed her side keeping her nonreactive for the moment. "Mr. Alexander Storm."

"Who?" She fumbled the word.

"Come now, miss." His smile seemed to intensify a bit unnaturally.

"I'm afraid you're mistaken, friend." Decker grasped Anika's arm and shifted her to his rear. "That name's unfamiliar to us."

The man tilted his head to one side and stared at Decker silently for what seemed like an eternity. Decker returned the stranger's gaze, unwavering and contemplating their next move as they were clearly in a trapped condition.

"The rear," Decker whispered out the side of his mouth to Anika, who quickly responded by turning to look behind them. The line of passengers had accumulated, making it difficult to see their faces. Several women, some noisy children whining from the fatigue of the flight, men spread out intermittently along the line. Nothing and no one stood out to her.

"Clear, I think." She informed him, still scanning the rows. "Wait!" Her voice, although a whisper, carried the force of a scream. There, in the very back of the line, was a tall woman. Her features appeared Asian, and her long, flowing black hair cradled both sides of her face. She was staring. She was staring directly at Anika. How had she missed her on her first glance? The smile. The twisted, over-accentuated grin sent a chill down Anika's spine. She was moving. Pushing the other passengers to one side. Anika had almost failed to notice her advance, hypnotized by her eyes and that awful grimace.

"She's coming," Anika's voice was panicked, and Decker recognized it.

"Who?" he shot back at her. She was pressing him forward, fearful to gaze back at the advancing menace.

"I know you," the figure in front hissed at Decker through his exposed teeth. "I know..."

The ominous man's words seem to trail off, and Decker felt something wet splatter across his face and arms. His mind reeled as a figure shot across in front of him from the opposite seats. Looking down at his arm, he rubbed his finger across the wetness on his arm.

"Water?" He turned to grab Anika as the diving individual drove their aggressor back into the seat he had risen from. Anika watched in confusion as smoke and fire spat into the air from the first row. Their savior, rising to his feet, motioned toward the woman approaching from the back of the plane.

"Run, sir. Please." Decker could see the faint outlines of the individual under his monk-like hood, "please."

Decker hesitated no more. Grasping Anika's hand tightly, the two darted to the plane's exit. Anika could hear the man who had come to their assistance behind her. Or at least she hoped it was him. Squinting hard in the sunlight as they broke free of the prison of the plane, Decker and Anika ascended the stairs in record time. The man in the hood was at the top of the steps, screaming in the local dialect at the attendants surrounding the plane. The workers seemed unaffected by what surely must have been directions and orders—they remained motionless. Standing tall atop the mobile stairs, the man removed his hood, allowing all to see his face.

"Plague!" he yelled. "Seal it!"

Upon recognition of the individual making the commands, the entire crew sprang into action. Reaching into the folds of the robe that adorned him, the man withdrew a clear bottle, and without popping the cork, raised it above his head like a grenade. The smiling woman from the back of the plane had just reached the threshold, her face twisted and grotesque in the rays of the sun. The man launched the bottle against the floor at her feet, causing twisting puffs of smoke and fire to rise up around her as she fell back into the dark recesses of the plane. An attendant had already reached the top of the stairs and quickly slid the plane's door shut, sealing their pursuers inside.

"Jam it!" he ordered.

The attendant nodded and pulled a screwdriver from his belt. Grasping the release handle, he drove the screwdriver into the circular space around it and bent the tool back, snapping a wedge of steel in its track.

Gliding down the stairway in an almost spectral fashion, the short Ethiopian man approached Anika and Decker.

"I am the monk." His words were calm and precise, a hint of his French origins evident. "Marabou."

Anika was still stunned. "Pleasure. What's in the bottle?"

"Holy water," Decker and Marabou replied in unison.

"Ha ha!" Marabou turned to Decker with a smile that faded instantly. "We must depart immediately."

Marabou waved an arm over his head, causing a large truck, which resembled a Hummer, to take off toward them from the side of the runway.

"Who are you?" Decker asked as the monk gathered them together in anticipation of the vehicle's arrival.

"Marabou," he replied once again.

"But *who* are you?" Decker asked again, and the serious tone of his voice did not go without being noticed by their new friend.

Shattering glass and the twisting cries of metal being pounded and stretched stopped him from entertaining the question any further. The sides of the plane popped and protruded at the force of its inhabitants trying to escape their captivity.

"No time!" Marabou opened the back door of the truck, which had skidded to a stop beside them.

"Wait!" Decker put an arm across the doorway.

"Listen." Marabou shot Decker a dire glance. "You can take your chances with me." Marabou peered over his shoulder at the plane's side which was now falling to pieces. The head of the first demon pressed and poured its deformed features through a tear in the aircraft's side. The creature's eyes dangling detached from its skull, it continued to smile that horrid smile in their direction.

"Or...you can take your chances with them!"

Anika had already pushed Decker's arm over her head and was firmly seated as he and Marabou joined her.

"Go!" Marabou ordered the driver, rolling down his window as they pulled away. "Destroy the plane!" he shouted out the window to a newly gathered group of men dressed in bright white, hooded robes.

"Wait!" Anika yelled as the truck sped away. "The other passengers?"

Marabou shook his head and smiled sympathetically at Anika.

"What?" she demanded.

"The moment it departed Bole International, everyone on that plane, save you and Mr. Decker, were murdered by the two demons. Everything your eye's saw after that, was a lie."

125

"What the hell is that?" Keith was up from his seat and pointing at the far corner of the chopper. Serket followed his gaze to the spectral circle of smoke and fire which had appeared in the far upper corner of the passenger compartment. She, too, rose from her seat, joining Keith in the opposite corner.

"What?" Jericho was puzzled, his eyes darting back and forth between his huddled companions and the object of their terrified stares. Sliding across the back bench until he was next to Keith, his eyes grew wide as they fixed on the opening spiral of smoke and fury.

"What do we do?" Keith cried out.

"It's got to be Naamah," Serket replied, reaching across to grab her backpack from her seat.

Jericho pushed past Serket, tossing her pack to her as he advanced to the right of the pilot's seat.

"No matter what happens," he instructed the pilot, "you keep this bird up! You hear me?"

The pilot tried to peer behind him, but the chopper's inner structure blocked his line of sight to the area under siege by smoke and fire.

"Hey!" Jericho yelled. "Eyes forward," he instructed, pointing to his own eyes and then forward in the universal command. The pilot nodded and returned to navigating the chopper.

Jericho fell back into place next to his companions. Serket had averted her vigilance from portal and was rummaging through her pack when Keith grunted.

"What?" she cried out, looking up at the swirling mass of displaced time and space that was encompassing the entire side of the copter.

He didn't answer her.

"What?" she questioned Keith once more.

"Don't, don't you see it?" He stammered to get the words out.

Serket squinted into the black hole and leaned forward to try and catch a glimpse of what Keith was reacting to.

"I don't see what you're—"

Her words were cut short as pair of rotting, sore-ridden hands shot out of the darkness. She tried to veer away from the unholy onslaught, but the apparition's unnatural speed caught her before she could move. Long, boney hands wrapped around her throat, and she could feel the icy fingers clawing at her consciousness. Serket could make out the din of her companions' screams, and she lifted her eyes to peer upon her assailant. To her dismay, the blood was already draining from her optical nerves, and a blurry figure of light and shadow was all her brain could interpret. Her body rocked back and forth as the pilot, in panicked spasms, jerked the chopper across the cloudless blue sky. This was it, she feared. All her years, all her battles, and she had been caught off guard sailing through the open sky in Storm's chopper. Storm. Storm. Storm! Had she just heard his voice, or was it a final cruel illusion.

"Bathin!" Serket heard it clearer this time. The grasp was loosening. Was she dreaming?

A burst of air passed down her windpipe like tiny razors and smashed against the walls of her lungs. The aggressor had relinquished the choke hold, and she heard...laughter?

"What?" The word sputtered like a dying flame from her mouth as she gasped and coughed.

"Bathin!" *My god, it was Storm.* Her vision was rapidly clearing, and the features of the laughing demon came into focus. Serket dropped back into the security of the seat behind her as her own hands found her throat. Massaging the pain from her neck, she looked past Bathin to find Alexander standing before the portal chiding his "pet" demon like a child.

Bathin turned from Storm and drifted back into Serket's face. "You poor thing," she hissed through her bouts of laughter. "But since I have been abused by your fearless leader, I thought I would return the sentiment."

"What the fuck is going on, Storm?" Jericho had regained his composure.

"Long story, old friend." Alex walked past him and extended a hand to Serket. "Another time, perhaps."

"Another time?" he exclaimed.

"Yes. Time to go, my dear." He grasped Serket's hand and hoisted her to her feet, "time to go."

She continued to stumble over the formation of her words. "Why, why would you send her through first?"

"I had no choice," he explained, but was cut short by the demon.

"You're a moving target, sweetie." She turned to Jericho, who was clearly having trouble digesting the series of events that had just unfolded. "Not the easiest place to open a portal, you know?"

Jericho shrugged, deciding to play along with the creature's folly. "I'd imagine that would be a bitch."

The demon laughed. "Yes, Francis. Just like me."

Turning to address Storm, Bathin pointed at the spinning passageway. "Gotta go, Storm. Your dime's almost up."

Alexander nodded. "Jericho, fuel up and head to St. George church in Ethiopia."

"What?" Jericho shook his head. "Where?"

"Ethiopia," he instructed again, leading Serket to the portal. "Decker and Anika are in peril, I fear."

Jericho nodded. "Understood. Say no more."

"Fly high over the Sudan, good man," Alex called to the pilot who was doing a stellar job of concentrating on flying, "Be vigilant of ground fire, understood?"

"Yes, Mr. Storm," he replied without taking his eyes off of the path unfolding before him.

"Good." Alex turned to Serket. "We must go now, truly."

"Wait!" Keith called out. "Where are you two going?"

Alexander paused and finally turned to face the young man. "Home. Dragon Loch."

"What?" Keith rose from his seat and took a step forward. Jericho reached out and grabbed his arm.

"What's so urgent?" he demanded. "Is Kate in trouble?"

"Kate?" Alexander quickly laughed him off. "Oh, no. Nothing so concerning, I assure you. Some rodent problems, that's all." He smiled at Keith, who clearly wasn't buying it. "Old castles are filled with them, you know?"

"Rats?" Keith yelled and tried to tug away from Jericho, but to no avail. "I'm coming, Kate!" His emotions took the better of him.

"Nonsense. No need, my boy," Storm replied, pulling Serket into the spinning mouth of fog. "I've already got one of the most proficient exterminators I know right here."

"See you soon handsome." Bathin winked at Jericho, who cocked his head in surprise. Before he could respond, the demon disappeared into the portal with Storm and Serket, and in a brilliant flash of glowing light, they were gone.

126

"The ride to the church is quite short," Marabou said to his guests. "But I'm afraid also quite bumpy."

No sooner had the words left his mouth when the truck took a heavy patch of bumps, sending the three passengers sailing upward in their seats.

Marabou smiled. "My apologies, miss."

Anika waved him off. "No need." She smiled at Decker. "I'm quickly becoming used to bumpy rides."

The truck barreled down government road D31 toward their destination. Decker stared out the tinted windows at the terrain whipping by.

"It's been some time since I have been here," he said, reminiscing.

Marabou nodded and smiled. "Welcome back, then."

He turned to the monk. "Yes, well, is Father Mathias still hobbling around Saint George these days?"

Marabou laughed. "Yes, I imagine he is." A paternal smile appeared in the corner of his mouth. "But he passed some time ago, my friend."

"Oh." Decker's face saddened, and Anika reached over and touched his hand. "I'm sorry to hear that."

"Yes, the church wept, but then we rejoiced at his ascension to his heavenly father."

"Of course," Decker quickly agreed, rubbing his beard thoughtfully at the same time. "I should have liked to see him one last time. Speak to him once more," his words were solemn and he returned to the passing landscape.

"You will be afforded that chance when you are reunited in paradise." The monk folded his hands together in a peaceful gesture.

"Ha! From your mouth to God's ears, brother. From your mouth."

"Oh, surely you jest, Mr. Decker." The monk braced himself as the truck took a massive series of potholes. "You sound like your mentor."

"Who, Storm?" Decker smiled. "My mentor?"

"Yes, Master Storm." Marabou nodded in agreement.

"I taught that guy everything he knows!" Decker smirked and shook his head.

"Ha ha." Marabou seemed to find Decker's words extremely amusing and his exaggerated laughter verged on insult.

"Well?" Decker looked at Anika, who was smiling at the monk's display.

"You are very capable, Mr. Decker." The monk settled down. "I do not doubt this."

"Exactly," Decks replied, then redirected the conversation. "Who's the holy father at Saint George, now?"

Marabou sighed as if the laughter he had just experienced was much needed. "That would be Father Strehold." Marabou's jolliness ceased altogether. "An odd man, to say the least."

"How's that?"

"He subscribes to an old doctrine, and his followers teeter somewhere between mysticism and the occult." Marabou's voice grew quiet. "Outsiders are not welcome. Tourism is frowned upon, and many of the old congregation have turned elsewhere for their spiritual needs."

Decker leaned forward in his seat. "Unfortunate. Should we expect our visit to be a problem?"

"Oh, I imagine so."

"Really?" Anika was shocked by his response.

"Yes, my dear," he said and smiled. "I will have to devise a plan to get you in." He paused and corrected himself. "To get Mr. Decker in, that is. You must not leave the safety of the truck and my driver, understood?"

"What?" The truck slammed against the rough road again. "I'm to be confined to the truck?"

"Yes," Marabou replied without reserve. "It is for your safety, of course."

"Does he know what we seek?"

"Yes," Marabou's eyes grew cold and serious. "I imagine he knows why you have come and what you are bringing in your wake, leading to the very altar of his church."

Decker bowed his head in contemplation and dug into the front pocket of his vest. Unrolling the small sheet of paper Kate had given him, he extended his arms from his face and squinted.

"Really, Decks?" Anika reached over and withdrew a small pair of glasses from another pocket on his vest. She slid them onto his reluctant face.

"Distinguished," she said and smiled. "Stop being a baby."

"Ha ha!" Marabou once again bellowed a flurry of laughter. He held up his hand at Decker. "I'm not laughing at your expense, my friend. I'm laughing at her words. Ha! 'Baby!'"

"Okay, okay." Decker grumbled. "Do you guys want to hear this or not?"

"By all means, proceed." Marabou kept a straight face. "Baby man."

Marabou's laughter started all over again, and Decker waited for him to stop, embarrassment creeping into the monk's face. "Sorry. Proceed, please."

"'South of Heaven,'" Decker began, "'but within its walls no evil lies. Carved in a slayer's memory for helping a dragon meet his demise. From sky across—from land it's lost—within a holy altar does reside.'"

"Not much of a riddle," Marabou shrugged. "Your objective must be somewhere within the altar."

"Well," Anika quickly interjected, "I must give credit where it is due. Our associate Kate solved the riddle, which in this case was more about the locale than about the papyrus's hiding place within the church."

Marabou bowed his head. "I meant no disrespect, miss."

"Of course not," Anika said and smiled. "Just saying we know where the riddle is referring to, so it seems simple. However, taken in a vacuum of knowledge, it was actually one of the more elusive of the riddles as it was short and really non-descriptive."

"Yes, yes, I agree." The monk turned to Decker. "So our challenge will not only be to have access granted for you to explore the church, but also to create a diversion, allowing time and privacy for you to do as you must to the holy altar."

Decker nodded. "A problem?"

"No," Marabou smiled. "I have a plan."

"Excellent." Decker turned to Anika and then back to Marabou. "What is it?"

"The church is occupied by Strehold's initiates—zealots."

"Understood." Decker was still taken aback by the transformation of his old friend's church.

"They are the white-robed warriors from the airport, my friend."

Decker stared at Marabou in silence.

"Now you understand our dilemma."

"I do." He shifted in his seat. "Are they soldiers? Monks? What?"

"No, no, no, my friend." He smiled, putting Anika at ease. "They are demon hunters."

"What?" Anika blurted out.

"Yes." Marabou reached out and touched her hand. "Fear not, miss. We are not demons."

"They are of the Brotherhood of the Night Star," Marabou explained, "an Order promulgated by the sixteenth century Benedictine monk, Balthasar Von Dernbach."

"I am familiar with his work," Decker acknowledged, "but not of the Order."

"Yes, well that is who they are." He smiled softly.

"So," Decker leaned back in his seat. "How do you propose we distract these *demon hunters*?"

"Simple." Marabou laughed a deep and hearty laugh. "We conjure a demon for them to hunt."

127

"Oh, you poor thing." The softly whispered words crept out of the darkness and struck Kate's ears like the crack of a whip. Instinctively, she recoiled and a faint cry escaped her lips.

"Hush, child." Moloch's words were more defined — closer.

Kate's mind spun, as did her head, searching in the pitch black for the intruder. She was trapped. Hopeless in the dark. Warm tears welled up and cascaded down her cheeks, dropping from her face into the darkness.

"Hush." He was upon her now. She could taste his acrid breath mingling with hers.

"Fight or flight, my dear," he whispered as his steely fingers wiped away her salty tears. "That is the question, is it not?"

Kate cried out loud at the demon's unseen hands as they swept across her face.

Fight! Her mind screamed. Springing upright, she threw futile blows into the infinite night that surrounded her. Kicking and swinging, she backed up and sprang onto the desk.

"Impressive." His words were filled with patronizing laughter.

"Fuck you!" she screamed. "Show yourself, coward! Or are you afraid of a girl?"

Moloch's laughter ceased, and a solitary band of light, like a spotlight directed from above, split the dark. Kate's eyes grew wide at the awesome stature of the figure before her. Without warning, Moloch's hand shot out and grasped Kate's throat.

"A girl." Moloch lips were close to her face now, vibrating against her cheek. "Is that what Storm has been selling you? You are a *woman*, my dear."

Moloch's free hand reached behind Kate's head and jerked her from atop the desk until she was standing before him. Running down the back of her head, he allowed his hand to trace the lines of her figure.

"All woman." His words met with protest and struggling as Kate tried to break free from the demon's grasp. Her movements incited the tightening of his vice-like grip on her neck, and she paused to escape passing out.

"But, we will get to that." He relinquished all hold over her and stepped back. "Business first. I'm sorry, you will just have to control your carnal desires for the moment."

Kate cried out and dropped to her knees, gasping for air. Moloch lifted both of his hands to the heavens and spewed forth an incantation in a language Kate couldn't understand. Instantaneously, light expanded outward from his hands until the great hall was lit throughout. Lifting her head, she locked eyes with the beast. Moloch noted the rage in her eyes—the anger. Anger, not fear, filled her.

"Impressive." Moloch shook his head in approval. "I see what Storm sees in you."

Kate rose to her feet, and keeping an eye on Moloch, she assessed her options. A large dagger sat in a stand on the far end of the desk. She couldn't make out the ruins that covered it, nor had she any idea as to its origins, or its effectiveness on pure evil.

"Oh, stop." Moloch laughed and walked over to Alex's leather chair. "Its providence is Nordic." Looking away from Kate, he settled into the comfort of the chair. "Odin can't help you, Katherine."

A chill ran down her spine as her name dripped from his lips, twisting and turning like a serpent.

He winked at her. "If you don't believe me, give it a try. I shall be a compliant test subject."

Kate took a step toward the ancient knife and paused, looking at

Moloch once more. He remained motionless and seemingly at ease in the chair.

Bad idea, her inner voice screamed. *Stay put.*

"Come, Katherine," he hissed. "I feel your hate. Let it grow stronger. Do it!" His arms, which had been crossed over his chest, opened as if inviting a hug.

Silence filled the heavy air. She would not succumb to his prodding. Not because she was afraid to unleash on his ass. But because she was pretty sure she would just piss him off.

"This grows tiresome," he finally said as he rose from the chair. "And I have some much to do. Busy, busy bee." He smiled at Kate, allowing a shadow of his true self to shine through, and she withdrew, trembling.

"Jericho's papyrus, if you will." He extended a hand to her and stood rigid.

What was he, crazy? Did he think she was just going to fork the fucking thing over?

"It's not here!" Her voice rang true. At least to human ears, perhaps.

He stepped closer. "Oh, come now, my dear. Really?"

"It's with Storm!" she shouted. "He'll be returning soon if you'd like to wait."

"Ha ha ha!" Moloch couldn't help himself. "It is not with that miserable, wretched animal." His lip raised in a snarl. "And he will not be returning —ever."

"What?" The words escaped before she could check them.

"Oh, poor thing." The demon pursed his lips together. "Have you not heard yet? Storm is rotting in Hell, awaiting my eventual return, I surmise. Waiting for an eternity of damnation."

"What?" Damn. There it was again.

"Dead, my dear Katherine." The demon shook his head in mock sympathy. "Your hero—your savior—is dead."

"No!" she was confused, and her mind was spiraling.

"Yes!" he said and laughed maniacally. "Dead saviors seems to be a running theme here, no?"

"Fuck you!"

"There she is! My little warrior." Moloch began to explore the desk and its drawers.

"You lie," she cried out, fighting back her emotions.

"Yes." Moloch smiled. "Quite often...but not today."

Walking along the row of desks, Moloch scattered papers and books, knocking them to the floor.

Oh, shit, Kate thought as he approached the chest, still obscured by her piles of research and printouts that surrounded and covered it.

She knew she had to act quickly. "Wait! It's in the castle!"

Moloch paused to listen, intrigued by her comment.

"And I'll show you, but you have to promise to let me go."

Moloch remained motionless. What was he concentrating on? Damn it. Why was he not reacting to her words?

"I'm hot, huh?" He laughed and furiously swiped the remaining clutter from the desk, exposing the metal chest.

"No!" Kate cried out.

Moloch lifted the chest from the desk and exclaimed, "There you are! Sneaky little fox."

Kate launched forward in a futile attempt to reclaim the box and was met with the demon's magic, propelling her up and over the desk. She hit the floor hard and scrambled to regain her footing. Rising to her feet, she watched in horror as Moloch extended a solitary finger and gently tapped the fingerprint reader on the box.

"Oh, yes. I must speak the words," he mused. "Open sesame...right?"

Kate watched as the box gave way to the demon's touch and sprang open. Smiling a hideous grin, his face warping back and forth between true form and disguise, he reached in and withdrew the papyrus. Dropping the box to the floor of the library, Moloch looked back at Kate, who had already started to back away in retreat.

"Run!" he shouted, startling her into motion. "Run, little fox!"

Kate was moving as fast as her legs would carry her, and she sprinted through the center hall of the library. The demon's laughter echoed and followed in her path. She could see an exit ahead. She could make it...if he allowed her. *Almost there!*

"Boo!" Moloch appeared in front of her. She stumbled to a stop, and fell back away from the monster.

"Time to die!" His words were deep and unearthly. Extending his arm as if throwing a punch, his powers hauled Kate up and into the air, flinging her backward until her body slammed into the stone wall. She remained there, some fifteen feet off the ground, completely pinned. She could not scream. She could not cry. She could not break free and fight. She was frozen.

"I fear our little visit must come to an end now." Moloch tightened his fist further, and it shot pain coursing throughout her body. Her eyes were slowly giving way to unconsciousness, but she fought to stay present. What was that behind Moloch? There was movement. Kate strained to keep her eyes open against the demon's magic. Yes! There was movement. Mist and smoke, swirling, spinning, just like her head.

"Portal!" she thought she screamed, but no words left her mouth. The reality rippled around her like water hit by a stone, and she willed herself with all her might to focus on the figure—wait figures—emerging from the wormhole.

"Storm!" Moloch squinted at Kate. Her mind had revealed the potential surprise, and he spun around to face the new arrivals to his game.

The pressure suffocating Kate receded slightly and, although she remained pinned to the stone, she was able to observe the events unwinding below her.

"Storm," Moloch greeted them, "and Serket!" He snickered, "I know someone who is *dying* to get her hands on you!"

Alexander ignored the demon's banter and dashed forward into the center of the great hall of the library. Moloch watched him a moment, then turned back to Serket to check her location. She was advancing, but toward Kate, not him, so he returned to Storm.

Kate watched as Alex, on one knee, lifted his fist high into the air and slammed it down on the hard stone floor. Moloch tilted his head to one side, almost as if Storm's motions perplexed him.

"Exorcizamus te, omnis immundus spiritus!" The words bellowed from deep within Alexander. "Omnis satanica potestas, omnis incursio infernalis adversarii, omnis legio, omnis congregatio et secta diabolica!"

Moloch cried out in response to Alexander's Latin din, and he charged at him. Stepping back, Alex let the incantation come forth once again with greater fervor and all movement stopped. Kate watched as etched lines of glowing flame darted out in all directions. From her vantage point, she was able to quickly see that the lines were transmorphing into a definite set of shapes and symbols that ran up and down the walls, as well as across the floor and ceiling of the library.

An outer circle with glowing symbols along its lines encircled the entire hall. Inside the first circle was a large octagon shape, followed by an oddly shaped seven-pointed star at the center. Kate studied the star, trying to focus on its qualities, and she was met with confusion as she was unable to properly trace its lines with her eyes. She could not identify a start or a finish to the lines that comprised the star. As she tried to follow the under-lying shapes of the star, she was consistently thrown off track and unable to follow the shape through to the end.

"Now!" Alexander yelled to Serket, who darted to the center of the star. Kate watched the fiery etching reveal the shape of a scorpion in the stone below her feet.

"Scorpion to a Scorpion!" Alex yelled out to Moloch, who remained motionless. "And now, the devil is trapped!"

"Of course," Kate said to herself. "A devil's trap! The whole damn library is a magical trap."

Alex rushed at Moloch, and Serket tossed what appeared to be a snake to him as he passed her.

What the hell? Kate stared in astonishment at the act playing out before her. She watched Alexander grasp the serpent's head and stretch its body, from tip to tail, into a rigid, spear-like weapon.

Storm planted his feet firmly as he came to a stop just in front of Moloch. "When you get back to Hell," Alex whispered, "be sure to thank my old friend Solomon for his wisdom."

Alex reached his arm back, the serpent in hand, and stared into the demon's face. Unleashing, his forward motion came to a sudden stop midway to Moloch's chest, and all movement slowed to a crawl. From her vantage point, Kate saw it first. A circle of fire and smoke had appeared directly behind Moloch. It was electrically charged and banging and moaning in the air, clearly fighting through the ancient magic Alex and Serket had filled the room with.

Then, all three of them watched as a single hand jutted out from the darkness of the portal and grasped Moloch's shoulder. The arm, which had initially emerged as flesh, was burning and tearing away. It was Naamah, fighting through the sacred protection of the symbol to retrieve her master.

"Looks like we are even, old man." Her ruby lips were barely visible in the darkness of the void, but her words made Moloch's lips, which should not have been able to emote, curl into a grin.

Time snapped back to reality, and the demon sorceress plucked her counterpart through the portal, escaping the final motion of Storm's thrust. As the portal slammed shut, Kate dropped, slowly at first, then with a thud to the stone floor.

"No!" she cried out, springing to her feet. "No!"

Serket stepped in front of her and stopped her advance.

"Easy," she said, trying to comfort her. "Easy. You okay?"

"Stop them, Alex!" Kate cried out.

Alex nodded at her. "It's okay, Kate. We live to fight another day. All *three* of us. That's a win."

"Alex," Kate said through sobs and breaths as Serket continued to try to sooth her. "Moloch had Jericho's papyrus!"

Alexander said nothing, allowing his chin to drop to his chest as the fiery etchings of the devil trap faded into memory.

128

The monk led Decker through the deep-cut trench leading to the Church of St. George. Marveling at the mastery and beauty once again, Decker was taken back to the time he had spent among the ruins many years ago. The slowly descending trench transitioned into a tunnel, and Marabou paused in the secrecy of the covered section of their walk.

"So, what's in the matchbox?"

Decker smiled. "An Abiku."

"Truly?" The monk took a step back.

"Yup." Decks lifted the box adorned with dragon artwork and gave it a shake for effect. "Caught him myself."

Marabou took a quick glance behind to ensure they were still alone. "And you carry it about with you?" Like a, like a..."

The monk could not find the words to address his thoughts and threw his hands out.

"It's trapped in a rattlesnake's rattle," Decks said, offering the monk a view into the box. "Quite safe."

"I disagree. But no matter, now, as your prize will soon be destroyed, not trapped."

Decker nodded nonchalantly in agreement and slid the box closed.

"What's the plan?"

"Walk now." The monk turned and continued through the tunnel. "We will speak at the next section of tunnel."

Decker followed, stepping once more into the light of a section of trench. Peering up at the space above, he was startled to see a group of white-robed men had begun to congregate on both sides of the channel. They were watching the two outsiders proceed, assessing their purpose, he surmised. Decker noticed the monk's pace quicken, and he double stepped to keep up. Both men breathed a sigh of relief as they entered the shelter of the last run of tunnel leading downward to the church clearing.

Marabou motioned for Decks to hurry near. "Quickly. Has your recollection of the layout been refreshed, my friend?"

"Absolutely." Decker winked and said, "I'm good."

"Good." The monk let slide a slight smile. "The baptismal pool. Do you recall?"

Decker did recall the magnificent structure that was St. George. Built in the late twelfth or early thirteenth century, the church stood profound in an eighty-foot by eighty-foot wide pit that was carved out of solid volcanic rock. The construction of the church involved excavating a free-standing block of stone out of the bedrock and then removing all the waste material from around it. The stone masons then carefully chiseled away the church outline, shaping both the exterior and interior of the building as they went. They fashioned a simple yet exceptionally beautiful cruciform structure approximately forty-feet high that was spectacular at any angle, but especially from above.

The church contained three west-facing doorways, nine "blind" lower-level windows and twelve upper-row windows. A number of them were embellished with carved cross motifs, while the roof of the structure contained a sequence of Greek crosses in bas relief, one inside the other. The structure was accessed from ground level via the gradually sloping trench and tunnel system, which granted access to a sunken courtyard surrounding the building. Within the courtyard, outside of the actual church, lay a small baptismal pool.

Decker smiled. "Of course, I know the location of the pool. It's to the right of the main entrance."

"Good, good." The monk nodded. "That is where you will do your dirty work."

Decks grinned. "Dirty work, huh?"

"Storm said you have no problem with such activities."

"He did, did he?"

"Yes." The monk paused. "Was his assessment flawed?"

Decker shook his head and stepped past the monk.

"What's the plan?" he asked again, without turning to face Marabou.

"Simple. Cast the demon's imprisonment into the baptismal pool."

"Huh?"

"Throw the snake's tail into the water, sir. Is that a problem?"

Decks laughed. "Well, yeah. Pretty sure that will expunge it from our plane straight to Hades. The pool's filled with holy water."

"Ah, yes." The monk slowly proceeded onward. "The great enigma of baptismal waters. You are correct. However, you are mistaken at the same time. The pool contains holy water, and it *has* washed its initiates of their sins. So, in fact, it contains both holy water *and* the remnants of hundreds of years of sin."

Decker's eyes widened as the truth hit him.

"Throw it in, my son." Marabou smiled. "Let God worry about the rest."

"Whatever you say." Decker smirked and followed the monk through the rest of the length of tunnel.

Stopping at the crudely cut door, which opened into the church's courtyard, Marabou turned to Decker. "Be prepared. Inquiry and resistance awaits. Be ready to find your relic as soon as the spectacle begins."

Decker nodded as he fumbled with the matchbox, dumping the rattlesnake rattle into the palm of his hand. Closing his fist around the fragile serpent's tail, he indicated he was ready, and the two stepped out into the light.

Ten or so white-robed figures blocked the entrance to the monolithic shrine, and several of them advanced immediately.

"Speak not," Marabou whispered. "Work your way to the pool."

The splendor of the stone church was quickly torn from Decker by the insistent chattering of the guardians. Decker couldn't really make out much, but he did hear Marabou's name several times.

"Friends of yours?" He joked nervously.

"Shhh," Marabou demanded and urged him on to the baptismal pool.

Rather than turning and hightailing it to the water's edge, Decker backed himself farther into the courtyard, keeping eyes on both his companion and the white robes. Inadvertently gazing upward, he was surprised to see more than thirty of the brotherhood gathered around the top of the pit.

Clearly outnumbered, he said to himself. It was nothing new. He just hoped Marabou was correct in his assertion regarding the water's effect on the demon.

The monk was shouting, trying to overcome the onslaught of voices. Some of the white robes had surrounded him, brutally poking and prodding his body.

Decker shot a glance at his feet and the space behind him. He was at the pool. Nodding at Marabou, he tossed the demon's prison backward into the water.

Jesus Christ! He mouthed as he turned to make sure his aim was true. It wasn't. The rattlesnake rattle had landed in the soil and rock at the pool's edge. Looking back to the monk and the white robes, he noted two or three had moved from the entrance and were headed in his direction. Panicking, he looked around, teetering back to the edge.

"Fuck it." Turning to the rattle, he extended his foot and kicked a puff of dust and dirt at the baptismal pool. The snake tail sailed into the water with the surrounding debris.

Screams began to emanate from all sides, above and in the courtyard. Decker quickly figured out they had interpreted his actions as a disrespectful encroachment on the pool of holy water.

He stepped forward to meet Marabou, who was sprinting to his side.

"You might as well have spat in the water, my friend!" he shouted.

"Yeah, then I guess you'd better hope you're right about our little chemistry experiment!"

The robed figures were on them, clutching and grabbing at their limbs. Decker saw the distinctive flash of steel as a scarab emerged from beneath one of the robes.

"I think we have a problem!" Decker cried, struggling to get to his own blade which was strapped to his waist.

"Stand fast!" Marabou shouted. "Do not engage them boy!"

Decker's defenses and instinct to survive the battering mob of white robes kicked in; he lashed and flailed, desperately hitting whatever his fists could find. Then suddenly, all sound and motion stopped...except for the solitary scream of a woman from above.

I know that voice, Decker thought and looked up into the sky for its source.

Nothing. She wasn't there!

"Anika!" he screamed, uncontrollably. His heart was racing.

"*Demoon!*" the voice shouted again. This time Decker saw the outstretched hand of a white robe pointing down at the baptismal pool. "*Demoon!*"

"Anika?" Decker whispered in disbelief.

The attacking horde of holy men immediately turned to the scene developing behind Decker.

"Quite impressive, she is." Marabou smiled. "Go. Now. They will be efficient with their work. You haven't much time!"

Decker broke into a sprint and headed to the main entrance of the church. Stopping at the threshold, he turned to assess the results of his "dirty work," as Marabou so aptly phrased it. To his horror, he watched the demon rising up from the water, bloated and enormous, its belly fed by the centuries of sins it had absorbed. The white robes above were running to join their brethren; some were even dropping from ropes to hasten their assistance at the pool. Decker looked back to the beast that was slowly emerging from the water. Gazing up, he found the demon's eyes. Dead and blued over, like a body rotting in the water, they transfixed on Decker with an obvious note of recognition.

"Screw this!" Decker turned and entered the church, "I already danced that dance!"

Racing through the dimly lit stone hall of the church, Decker headed toward the altar. The deep burgundy carpets that were strewn over the temple's floors silenced his steps. Rounding a corner into the long hall that led to the altar, Decker stopped dead in his tracks. He had caught movement in his periphery and turned to face the new unknown.

Emerging from a small square space cut in the wall, a feeble monk twisted his body free and rose to his feet. Staring at Decker, he spoke not a word. Decker turned his head toward the screams and wails from the courtyard behind him. When he looked back, the monk was toe-to-toe with him, and Decker was completely confused.

He stepped back and attempted to plead with the holy man. "We mean no trouble. I just need something from the altar."

The monk squinted at Decker with an obvious lack of understanding.

"You don't understand." Decker tried a different approach. "Evil will come for it, I need to..."

Stepping back from Decker, the monk turned his body to allow him to pass.

"Guess you understood that, then." Decker smiled and dashed to the altar.

Evaluating the ancient stone, Decker wondered where the papyrus could be hidden in what appeared to be a solid slab. The riddle had offered no specifics besides its location at the altar. Colorful cloths and holy relics adorned the stone edifice and made investigation cumbersome. He lifted several hanging red and white pieces of material and ran his hands over the stone beneath. Nothing.

"Ahem," the monk said. Decker was surprised by his proximity, and he once again recoiled.

Smiling, the old monk approached the back of the altar and, extending his arms, yanked all the coverings away. He pointed to the top of the stone structure, then backed away and let him pass.

"I see." Decker turned and smiled at the monk. "Just like that, huh?"

Before him, in the center of the top of the altar, was a grooved square no more than a foot long on any side, set flush into the stone. Decker traced the edges with his finger and brushed away the centuries of dust. At the center of the square was a hole.

"A key," Decker whispered to himself. "I don't have a key."

Turning to face the old monk, Decker shrugged. "No key?"

What was he going to do now? Did Storm want him to desecrate the entire holy sanctum of the church *and* demolish the altar?

The monk again bowed his head slightly and reached into the folds of his robe. Withdrawing it quickly, he held up a tarnished, ornately decorated metal key, then laughed.

Decker couldn't help himself and laughed along with the old monk. The pair's mutual enjoyment was shattered by the cacophony of hideous screams bellowing in through the church's main entrance. Decker knew that sound. The white robes were verging on the end of their destruction of the demon.

Decker felt the old monk take his hand and place the key in his palm. Turning to him again, the now stoic monk motioned Decker to open the altar. Sensing the urgency, Decker plunged the key into the stone hole and turned it. As if situated on top of some ancient hydraulic platform, the square of stone rose rhythmically, exposing one open side to Decker. There, within the elevated stone cube, lay a clear, crystal vial, a cork pressed firmly in the top—the rolled papyrus visible within.

Shrieks echoed throughout the church.

"Shit!"

The monk frowned at Decker's profanity and pointed adamantly at the vial.

"Sorry." Decker gave the monk a repentant look and seized it from the stone cube.

Stepping back, Decker watched as the small seat the vial had rested on began to rise in a manner similar to the outer cube.

"Ha ha ha!" The monk laughed at Decker, whose face was filled with fear from the fast approaching white robes. Tugging on Decker's arm, he pointed to the rising mechanism on the altar, then directed Decker to a spot on the wall behind them. Decks heard the click from behind them and watched as a doorway slowly emerged from the solid stone wall. Stepping forward, the monk pushed the door inward, granting Decker access. He waved an arm across his body, guiding Decker into the darkness. Stepping past the old man, Decker placed the papyrus in his vest and withdrew his light.

Smiling once more, the monk motioned Decker to push the door shut behind him. Complying, Decker began to push the heavy stone back into the wall, watching the old monk as he did. The sound of the approaching guardians was loud. They were almost to him.

"Thank you," Decker paused and whispered to the monk. "I know you can't understand, but thank you."

The monk smiled and Decker pushed the stone forward to finish closing it. He prayed his path of exit would be obfuscated from the white robes who were entering the room.

"Godspeed, old friend." The monk's unmistakable words filled the secret tunnel as the door slammed shut, disappearing once more into the stone wall.

"Storm?"

129

Alexander carelessly tossed aside the papers and debris scattered around his desks by the demon, stopping when something caught his eye. Slowly turning toward Kate and Serket, he stared at them momentarily before looking back at the document he was holding.

Serket studied his expression carefully. Desperation radiated from his every muscle and his eyes wore a band of exhaustion she did not recall ever seeing before.

"Alex," she said, but he did not acknowledge her. "Alexander."

Alex held up a finger halting both her words and her approach. She turned to Kate and shrugged in response to her equally confused glance. The three stood in silence, and time ticked away for an eternity as Alexander looked from the page to the empty space before him. *361 His mind was obviously attempting to wrap itself around some fleeting thought, not unlike the way one grasps at a forgotten song title to accompany the vague tune dancing through their mind's ear.

Kate and Serket watched as the man before them suddenly appeared to straighten and grow in stature. The instant metamorphosis was followed by a sly and telling smile creeping across Alex's lips. He had it. Whatever *it* was —it was now his.

"Things looking up?" Serket mused, walking to his side and then past him.

"Of course, my dear." Storm nodded to Kate, offering her some semblance of relief from the guilt that filled her. "I was wrong to despair. We are warriors of the light, and the light will guide us."

Serket touched his shoulder. "Even in the dark."

"Especially in the dark."

Alex snapped his arm down, and the pages in his hand cascaded to the floor. They were no longer necessary.

"Come, now. There's much work to do."

A breath of relief escaped Kate's lips as she made her way to the desk.

"Pen to paper, my dear." Alex pointed to a pad on the desktop across from them. Kate grabbed it, ready to take notes.

"So, we are faced with an ever-increasing degree of challenge here. We seem to continue to fall short of the demonic scheming which has besieged us. But perhaps we are attempting to overcome challenges that the architects of the riddles had planned for. I do believe that is the case here. I believe our primary task's failure was, and is, inevitable."

"What?" Kate was puzzled. They were not destined to fail. This was the converse of all that Storm had preached up until this point, and now, she feared, he had been overcome by their seemingly endless failures.

Alexander smiled. "Don't fret, Kate. I have not lost possession of my faculties. It is quite the opposite. The endgame here is far too important not to have implemented a failsafe, if you will—a kill switch."

Serket smiled. "Of course."

Alexander turned to his old friend. "We will continue our quest to obtain and control, at the very least, one of the sacred riddles. But at the same time, we will delve deep into the remaining locations and find our *failsafe*. It's there—I have no doubt."

Kate smiled as she tapped the top of the pen on her teeth. "I guess it makes sense. Why create such elaborate safeguards in the riddles themselves and not offer some extra measure of security, just in case."

Alexander winked at her. "Just in case. Yes." Alexander drew them in closer. "So, Palermo...your last communication with us in Angkor...the catacombs."

"Yes!" the excitement rekindled in Kate. "The catacombs! And a warning."

"Yes. The warning. Perhaps therein lies the key."

"Do you have a copy?" Serket asked, not recalling all of the details.

Alexander reached down and picked up the documents he had dropped.

"Kate's mock up is both intuitive and poignant." Alex handed Kate's work to Serket. "Exquisitely done! The fuel for my cognitive fire."

Kate averted her eyes and her cheeks burned a slightly darker shade of red.

Serket studied the page Alex had presented to her.

"'In the olive-skinned land of all ports', means Palermo. The Greeks called it Panormus, meaning 'all-port.' 'Beneath the wine and the hum of the sea, lies a world as above except void of sound and of love, but still they continue to be'. 'As a pupil of Anubis might thrive.' Embalming— refers to mummification of one form or another. 'So, too, must the dead teach the live. Find him who has waited the longest, the first in the necropolis.' The catacombs came into being circa 1599 as a result of the resident monks performing a rudimentary mummification on one Silvestro of Gubbio, another local monk. The holy men wished to display Gubbio in a manner that would permit them to continue to pray in his presence. 'Be sure that your math is true, for this is the last of the journey, a mistake may end all of you.' Convento dei Cappuccini, or The Capuchin Monastery, was built over the remains of the original medieval church in 1623 and underwent modern restoration as late as the early twentieth century.

Capuchins' Catacombs of Palermo! Kate had written in bold at the bottom of the sheet. Serket looked up and smiled. First at Alexander, then at Kate. "Nice work."

"Thank you." Kate bore a proud face at the recognition of her toils.

Alexander cleared his throat and nodded to Serket. "Indeed, and of course, I chose her for this task. Did you doubt my—"

"Alex," Serket interrupted him. "Not now."

Kate spoke over their banter. "So, the question is, who is the oldest? Truly?"

"Correct," Alexander smiled, "and what is offered to the victor on this venture...I sense there is more to this locale."

"Well, there is only one way to find out." Serket adjusted the belted row of shinning knives hidden beneath her flowing garb.

"Indeed. That leaves four riddles for you to solve, Kate. Quickly, if you would."

"I would, I will," she stammered.

"Copan and Vatican City."

"What?" Kate tried to follow the apparent jump in topic.

"Write it down." Alexander tapped the pad. "A head start."

"Show off," Serket whispered as she passed by Alex.

"Complete the task." Alexander turned to grab a few items from the drawer of his desk. "When next we meet, you will join us to complete our journey."

"Really?" Kate's excitement was uncontainable.

"Of course," Alexander nodded. "Unless you would rather remain a spectator in this dusty old castle, with Asar's ancient bones, while the future of mankind plays out beyond these shores."

"Hell, no!"

Alexander smiled once more, his eyes alight with regained passion and purpose. "Where is the old goat, anyway?"

"Asar?" Serket asked.

Storm nodded. "Yes, Asar."

Serket flashed a devilish glance at Alex. "I sent him to Egypt."

"You what?" Alexander spun to face her.

"You're not the only one with a failsafe, Alexander Storm."

130

Decker's heart was pounding as he ascended the narrow steps in the dark passage. His mind was still reeling from the ancient monk's last words, which had echoed with the distant voice of Alexander Storm. He brushed the idea aside as he reached the apex of his climb and pushed at the dimly lit blackness before him. The stone wall gave way after some effort, and rays of light shot into the passage like bullets from a gun, and as he squinted to meet them, Decker's body quickly adjusted to his new surroundings. Hacking with his arms at the overgrowth that had consumed the opening, he emerged from passageway.

"Failed priest! Come quick priest!"

The shouts continued and filled the air like a serpent winding through the tall grass towards its unsuspecting prey.

"Priest, bring unto me!"

Decker rounded the corner at the top of the small hillside that had shielded his view of the hole in the earth. He found the source of the shrill cries, and his heart dropped like a lead sinker in a dark sea.

Naamah grasped Anika from behind with one arm across her chest. The other pressed a long, twisted dagger against her throat.

"Hello, Priest." Naamah smiled and ran her tongue across her teeth. "Join us, please."

"Wait!" Decker cried out as he approached the demon.

"Wait!" Naamah mimicked. "You mean, don't do this?"

"No!" Decker sprinted forward as Naamah applied just enough pressure to bring forth a thin line of blood from Anika's throat.

The demon laughed in pure delight at Decker's panic.

Decker came to a halt just in front of them and extended a hand outward. "Please, don't."

"Begging, huh?" Naamah's eyes narrowed. "You've aged well, priest. This pretty young creature must be good for your dark sinner's soul."

Anika shifted and was met with greater resistance. "Don't cut your own throat, sweetheart." Naamah laughed.

"Wait!" Decker cried out once more.

"Oh, stop." Naamah pushed Anika's body forward toward his pleas. "Unbecoming at best. Pathetic at worst."

Decker steadied himself and swallowed hard.

"What—"

"Don't even fucking, ask priest," Naamah hissed. "Hand it over, and maybe I'll let her live. The world will burn soon, anyway. Resist, and I'll carve her fucking heart out and feed it to you, you miserable shell of a man."

Decker reached into his vest, grabbed the papyrus, and held it up in front of him.

"No!" Anika struggled. "Don't, William!"

With a grotesque sense of mockery, Namaah said, "No, William. I'm a selfless whore. Just let me die. Save the world...blah blah blah." But she became driven by fury once more. "Give me the fucking papyrus priest! My blade is crying out to be fed!"

Decker leaned forward, his arm extended. "I can't," he whispered to Anika, whose eyes had welled up with tears of fear and desperation. "I can't let you go."

"How sweet." Naamah loosened her grasp slightly to retrieve her prize from Decker's hand.

"No!"

The shouts came from behind him, and Decker snatched the papyrus from Naamah and turned to see Marabou charging at them with a band of white robes.

Marabou yelled, "Do not offer unto the beast, my friend!"

Decker turned back to Naamah, who was smiling again, and said, "Now it's a party."

Marabou stopped several feet from them, and the white robes came to a halt at his side. They were with him now. Not chasing him, as Decker had first surmised.

"We must all sacrifice," Marabou said calmly.

"Not all." Naamah laughed. "Just you, priest. Give me the scrap of shit, and save your love. There is no other option, no other solution, no need to contemplate. Submit to my will, or I will send her soul to the infernal fires of Hell as you watch."

Marabou began to chant as he lowered his head and embraced his prayers.

Fire sprang to life in Naamah's eyes as she turned to meet his words.

"You grow tiresome, old fool." The words emanated from the deep bowels of Naamah's true self. "Begone!"

Naamah raised the blade to her mouth and grasped it between her teeth. Releasing the handle, the demon reached into her cloak and tossed something behind Marabou. A chill ran down the monk's spine as the wind and heat emanating from the space behind him met his skin. A din of invocation escaped Naamah's lips as she dropped the dagger back into her hand. Marabou turned to Decker, eyes filled with the revelation of his unavoidable fate.

The white robes, bewitched by the demon's words, took hold of Marabou and lifted him high above their heads.

"No!" Decker darted to Marabou's aid, but he was too late. The band of possessed holy warriors had succumbed to Naamah's instructions. Decker watched in horror as they tossed his guide into the burning wormhole she had opened. But she wasn't done yet. The demon's display of an unparalleled power of suggestion continued as she forced each of the white robes, one by one, emotionless, to follow their countryman into the abyss until they were no more.

"Last chance, priest. Then I toss her head and body, one at a time, into the portal! Straight to Hell!"

Decker said nothing more. With a trembling hand, he offered Naamah the papyrus.

"No, William!" Anika implored one last time.

"Shut up, bitch!" Naamah tossed Anika to the ground and snatched the cylinder from Decker's hand. "Nice doing business with you, failed priest."

Naamah stepped back from Decker and waved the portal closed.

"This one's a keeper, baby." The demon prodded Anika with the tip of her boot. "He's willing to sacrifice all of humanity for one more night between your legs."

"No..." Anika sobbed.

"Yes." Naamah replied. "Yes, yes, yes!" She rolled the words together in a sexual overture.

Decker and the demon simultaneously looked to the sky as the distant hum of rotors echoed through the air.

"Friends of yours?" Naamah scoffed and withdrew another hell stone from her cloak. Dropping it at her side, the demon threw her head back in laughter as wind and fire split open space and time at her beckoning. Her dark hair flowed in the air, and the glow of the portal caused shadow and light to bounce across her dark features like a torch in the night.

"Well, this was fun," she whispered at Decker as she disappeared into the wormhole. "Let's do it again real soon."

Anika struggled to her feet as the sound of Jericho's chopper rang out from above.

"I'm sorry." Decker touched Anika's hand and she turned to face him.

"Why?"

"Because I love you with every fiber of my being." He kissed her softly. "I'm sorry."

Without further word, Decker turned from Anika and charged the closing portal.

"No!" Anika screamed as the spinning mass of fire and smoke disappeared, and with it, William Decker.

131

"Death is lighter than a feather," Alex mused, as the two descended into the realm of the dead. "Duty, however? Heavier than a mountain."

The Capuchin Catacombs of Palermo, as they are known, are a series of open chambers and corridors, excavated from the earth and formed in stone and plaster. The friars of the same name created the necropolis beneath the church of Santa Maria della Pace in 1534 AD to house their brothers who had passed forth into the kingdom of God. What had begun as a simple project, with a chamber-like mass grave beneath the altar of Saint Anne, soon evolved into something much more. In 1594, after the small space had reached capacity, the monks decided to expand the burial area. Upon investigating the state of those who had been buried beneath the altar for over sixty years, the holy men were shocked to find very little decomposition had occurred. The faces, expressions, and clothing of the deceased had remained intact, and for all intents and purposes, the bodies were naturally mummified.

"Astonishingly morbid." Serket's eyes grew wide as they entered the first area of the catacombs.

"Indeed." Alexander moved quickly from side to side, marveling at the bodies. Some were hung prone and upright from the walls, while others were tucked, lying on their backs, into little grottos cut into the stone or open wooden coffins strewn across the floors. There were corpses housed in glass, corpses sitting and waiting, corpses smiling and corpses grimacing.

A chill ran over Serket's body. "Why is this creeping me so I wonder? I am no stranger to the reaper's work." She uttered the words softly while joining Alex in his investigation of the catacomb's occupants.

"Perhaps it's the life-like state of the dead." He turned and smiled at her. "Yes, I'm pretty sure the overall magnitude of the display is the culprit."

Serket shook off his words. "How will we know when we have located the 'oldest' occupant, Alexander?"

Alex paused and turned to his companion. "Well, as I explained, the body that was first housed in the catacomb was that of Silvestro da Gubbio."

Serket nodded. "I heard that, Storm. How will we know if we should happen to stumble upon Gubbio?"

"According to Kate's research, the illustrious Silvestro da Gubbio will be donned in a very smart brown robe accessorized with a faded blue headdress."

Serket laughed. Storm's charm could be quite amusing when he allowed himself to venture beyond his steadfast stoicism. It did not happen as often as she would like to see, but it was always seemed to surface when most necessary. What she was unaware of was the fact that Alexander allowed his guard down the most when he was in her presence.

"Well, gosh, Professor Storm," she said and laughed as she continued to investigate the corpses across from him, "that really narrows it down for me."

"Really?" Alexander stopped and turned to her once more. "Because I found the information rather useless since the description fits about half the holy men down here."

"Precisely, Storm," she mused and returned to her work. "My point precisely."

He continued his toying. "Death...feather...duty...mountain."

Serket threw her arms up. "Come on, Storm!"

Alexander veered to his left and darted to her side. "Would it be a little more useful to know that Gubbio is holding a sign?"

"What?"

"Yes. A sign. It states, 'Hey, I'm Gubbio.'"

"Cut it out, Alex."

"Seriously, my dear." He turned and lifted his chin high as he returned to his side of the catacomb. "Big sign. Gubbio. October 16, 1599. He's grasping it in his hands."

Serket rolled her eyes and spoke in her best Italian accent. "Yes, Professore. That is a useful sliver of info."

Alexander smiled with his back to her. Serket was, nonetheless, aware of his amusement over their banter. They moved silently, past the rows of the frozen dead, stalled there in time, the sands of the hourglass unaware of their existence. The vast corridors that made up the catacombs had been arranged by order of groupings. Friars, priests, men and women, a chapel housed the virgins; doctors, lawyers and the like had their own corridor, as well as areas set aside for prominent families.

Serket moved forward into the area known as the children's corridor and stopped before a glass covered casket.

"My God." The words rushed from her lips, and Alexander walked to her side.

"I see you have found Rosalia. The Sleeping Beauty of Palermo."

"She looks alive, Alex. How is this possible?"

"Well, this particular resident was embalmed in the 1920s, whereas many of the others lie in their natural state. Little Rosalia's father implored a man named Alfredo Salafia to, and I quote, "Make my daughter live forever.""

"Astonishing." Serket was overwhelmed by the surreal display. "Skill and artistry to rival that of the priests of Anubis."

"Oh, I think the old jackal clan could learn a trick or two from Salafia." Alex smiled and winked at his companion, soaking in her radiant beauty and the sheer essence of her curiosity that resonated about her face. Serket's exquisiteness to the eye was surpassed only by her stunning mind.

"Yes," she said slowly at first. "But I doubt it."

Storm marveled at her childlike qualities that often remained hidden behind her warrior's exterior. "Ha! Our friar is just up ahead. Shall we?"

Annoyed, she said, "Storm, we haven't time to play. If you knew where he was you—"

"Come now," Alexander brushed her off. "How often does one get to stroll the streets of a necropolis with a lovely woman by his side?"

Serket's response was stifled by the ground shaking explosion that rattled the corpses around them.

"What the hell?" she cried out, looking to Alex for explanation.

"I fear you very well may have been correct." Reaching out, he steadied her as another barrage of explosions echoed through the catacombs, sending dust and debris billowing at them from somewhere further in the catacombs. "Delay was a poor calculation on my part."

Alexander nodded at Serket, ensuring she was okay, then broke from her side and darted forward toward the blasts. Standing amidst the bodies of friars and death, Alexander quickly apprised the corridor for his objective. "There!" Serket was ahead of him now, "straight ahead!"

Alexander squinted through the plumes of dust and spotted the corpse Serket was referring to.

"Very good!" he shouted over yet another round of blasts. "And the sign?"

"Gubbio!" Serket turned and smiled. "October 16!"

Alexander had reached her side and was rummaging through the Friar's robe. It was immediately clear the holy man's clothing had already been disturbed, and not due to the explosions. Working his way to an inner pocket, Storm excitedly withdrew a small box and stepped back from Gubbio's corpse.

"Open it!" Serket shouted over the next wave of blasts.

Alexander cautiously lifted the small hinged lid and stared into the box. But excitement soon turned to horror when he looked back at Serket.

"What is it, Storm?" she shouted. "Is it the papyrus?"

Alexander said nothing, but instead reached into the box and held up its contents for Serket to see.

"What is that?"

"A holy relic!" He paused and lifted out a familiar worn medallion, letting it dangle from his fingers. "St. Peter."

"I don't understand." Serket looked nervously ahead of them toward the explosions that continued in the distance. "What does it mean, Storm?"

Alexander placed the medal back in the box, slowly closed the lid, and placed it in his jacket.

"It means our demonic adversaries have the papyrus." He started toward the exit of the Catacombs. "It also means they have William."

132

Decker cried out as his knees slammed into the cold, hard stone floor of the castle. The blinding light radiating behind him quickly faded to a dull glow and then disappeared altogether. He remained motionless, allowing his eyes to adjust to the darkness surrounding him. Listening like a thief, he rotated his head back and forth slowly searching for some indication of both his location and the whereabouts of the demon he had followed through the wormhole. Squeezing his eyes shut tight, he could still see Anika. Decker held his breath, soaking in the vanishing vestiges of her image before it, too, faded to black. Opening his eyes once more, he rose to his feet and searched his vest for a light. He fumbled through his pockets to no avail.

"Shit," he whispered to the darkness as he realized he might have dropped it to the floor at the top of the church's secret passage. Motionless once more, he searched for an alternative source of light. He no longer carried a lighter or matches since he'd quit the cancer sticks some years ago. Not the greatest of ideas, he mused to himself. The lack of a lighter, not the smokes that is.

Gotta remember to pack a lighter next time I plan on following the devil through a black hole, he thought, trying to soften his mood with internal humor. It didn't work.

"Bingo." He remembered the snap-and-glow stick he had stuck in the side pocket of the vest.

Holding the plastic tube up in front of his eyes, Decker bent the ends, bending it into illumination. A dim, green glow quickly began to emanate from the stick. Grasping it in one hand, he vigorously shook the tube, causing the chemicals inside to blend. The ancient stone blocks beneath his feet became apparent in the eerie green light. Raising the glow stick up in front of him, Decker pivoted around to try and make out his surroundings before taking a step.

"Hello, darling." The words froze Decker in place as he watched Naamah emerge from the darkness into the green hue before him. "Welcome to oblivion!"

133

K ate's heart skipped a beat as the low, muffled drone of the chopper's rotors met her ears. Springing from her seat, she darted across the library and up the long, twisting stairs to the heliport. Flinging the large wooden door at the top open, Kate practically stumbled out onto the landing pad, her eyes immediately fixed on the incoming helicopter above. Using her hand as a visor, she shielded herself from the sun's awesome late day blaze. Apprehension filled her heart as she watched the chopper descended to the castle. The whirlwind blew her long hair about her face, causing strands to snap in and out of her eyes and mouth like flashes of light.

"They are sure to be famished."

The voice startled Kate, who jumped and cried out. Turning quickly, she was soon put at ease by the crooked smile that met her.

"Philip?" she said with an uneasy smile.

"Pardon me, young lady." His apologetic expression was sincere.

"Where have you been?" Kate asked, glancing over her shoulder just in time to see the chopper touch down.

"Here." His eyes twinkled with confusion. "I'm always here."

"Could have used a hand some time ago," she said with unintentional annoyance.

"You are fine." He began to head to the opening door of the chopper. "I am always here. And if you *really* need me, I am there."

Kate chuckled and shook off the odd old man's enigmatic words, joining him to approach the helicopter. Sam and Abigail were the first to exit, waving at Kate as they moved from the decreasing wind of the rotors as the humming engine turned off. Anika slid out behind them, her face blank and her stare empty. Decker wasn't at her side as Kate would have expected. Lobo appeared next, quickly followed by Jericho, who turned to retrieve a large bag from the floor. Slinging the sack over his shoulder, he glanced at Kate. His expression was stoic and unreadable. Kate's heart dropped again, and she felt panic creep over her. Where was Keith?

"Hey!" Keith shouted as the passenger door of the helicopter popped open. "Shotgun is so cool!"

Tears of relief filled Kate's eyes as she laughed out loud at Keith's foolish ignorance. Lowering himself down from the cockpit, he quickly leaned back into the compartment and high-fived the pilot.

"Thanks, dude! That was sick!"

Kate dashed toward Keith as he trotted toward her. She passed the others, oblivious to their presence, and arrived toe-to-toe with him.

"That was awesome," he started. "Jim—that's the pilot...he's a military pilot—he let me fly! He actually let—"

Keith's words were cut short by Kate's lips as she locked her fingers behind his head and pulled him down to her.

Sam whistled, but neither of them heard Sam's obnoxious overture. They were lost in the moment. Time and space stood still as he brought his palms gently to her cheeks and reciprocated her embrace.

"Miss me much?" He winked as their lips parted.

She laughed through the tears that were streaming down her cheeks, and he reached out and gently brushed them away.

"Hey, hey." His words were soft and mature. "I'm not going anywhere. You're stuck with me. Always."

Kate wrapped her arms around him and squeezed with all her might. She had missed him more than he could ever have imagined.

"I love you," he whispered in her ear. "Do you love me, Kate?"

"You know I do." She laughed, playfully biting his ear lobe.

"Hey!"

"What? You don't like that?"

"Never said anything like that!" Keith smiled down at her.

"Keith?"

"Yeah?" A look of concern washed across his face.

"You smell!" She winked and said, "Hit the showers, okay?"

Lobo jumped in. "Show's over! How come I don't get a welcome like that?" He joked to Jericho as they walked, leading the others into the castle.

Jericho cracked a slight smirk and slid his free arm around Philip, who was at his side.

"I missed you, baby!" His dry, raspy voice echoed off the stones of the castle. Philip did his best to escape Jericho's grasp, but to no avail, and instead was met with a solid kiss to the cheek.

"Good God, man," Philip blurted out, finally able to push away. "Get a hold of yourself."

"What's a matter," Jericho shrugged, "didn't you miss me horribly."

Philip turned and quickly moved through the doorway into the castle.

"Fool," he was mumbling under his breath as he disappeared down the stairs.

Jericho laughed and turned to Lobo. "Let's eat, huh?"

"You made his day, brother!" Lobo slapped him on the back.

"Yeah, well," Jericho said as his smile quickly faded and reality crept back in. "Probably be the last time any of us smile for some time."

134

Asar crouched down and touched the warm Egyptian sand. He grasped a handful and allowed it to run between his fingers back to the desert floor. His strong brown eyes peered across the distant landscape from beneath white linen wraps that covered his head and body. In the dying rays of the western sun, he could make out faint clouds of dust on the horizon. It wasn't long before the heavy thump of approaching horses sounded, and Asar could feel the galloping fury sending shockwaves through the sand.

Rising to his feet, he watched as the riders grew closer. The fading silhouette of Cheop's pyramid visible behind him reflected the last light of the dying sun. Leaning down, he retrieved the torch that was protruding from the sand and set it ablaze. Holding it up to the sky, he waved the torch back and forth, signaling the horseman to his location. The wrath of their approach continued to increase steadily until at last they were upon him. Breaking off, the riders formed a circle of thirty or more around Asar, who lowered his facial wraps.

"Welcome, brothers," Asar spoke in Egyptian as he thrust the torch into the desert sand.

"And sisters!" a woman's voice called out from somewhere within the ranks.

"And sisters." Asar laughed. "My deepest apologies, noble warrior."

The riders silently acknowledged his apology.

"You have been summoned," he began, walking toward the lead horse in front of him, "and you have answered."

"We are the Medjai," the lead horseman spoke up. "Our fate is written, our purpose known."

"Honorable is your path." Asar walked closer. "But death will now shadow your every step."

The horseman leaned down. "It always has, brother. Serket has called, we answered. It is a clear and unambiguous purpose."

Asar nodded at the horseman's words.

"Your time is at hand." Asar took a step back and shouted to the heavens. "Medjai, it is time to honor your oaths! We must prepare! For behind me, in the ancient ruins of our ancestors, the greatest battle of our time will rage! Failure is not an option!"

A chorus of cheers and cries broke out in unison in response to his words. Waving their blades in the air above them, Asar watched as the solitary light of his torch danced across their steel.

"To war!" Asar screamed. "To war!" The riders broke from their formation and headed past him toward the Giza complex.

Stopping at his side, the lead horseman extended a hand down to Asar, who took firm hold of it. Hoisting him to the back of the equestrian beast, the rider prodded the horse to a gallop and joined the others as they raced toward their fiery destiny.

135

L obo yanked the bag off Jericho's shoulder and dropped it onto the only empty space on Alexander's desk.

"Been busy, Kate?" He joked, surveying the state of disarray that was now Storm's once immaculate work area.

"What the hell happened here, girl?" Jericho quickly chimed in, lifting a stack of scattered documents and perusing them carelessly.

"Exactly," Kate snapped, snatching the documents from his hands and placing them back down.

Jericho shot her a surprised glance and looked at Lobo. "Exactly what?"

"Hell." She was ushering them away from her work. "Hell happened."

Lobo shook his head at Jericho, waving further inquiry off for the time being. "Making any headway then? On the riddles?"

Kate smiled at the change of topic. "Of course."

She quickly slid into the chair in front of the keyboard and tapped a key, bringing the monitor to life. Jericho looked at the large bag on the desk and undid the flaps that secured the main compartment closed.

"So," Kate began as Lobo moved in behind her and squinted at the words and images on the bright screen. "The riddle I've been working on is centered in Rome."

"How do you know that?" Jericho asked half-heartedly, his arm buried almost to his shoulder within the leather bag.

"A little bird." Kate looked over her shoulder at Frank. "A little bird directed me in the right direction."

"Oh," Jericho replied, still rummaging through the bag. "Where'd you put Sam's papyrus, Lobo?"

"It's in there."

"Yeah?"

"Yeah," he said, clearly annoyed with Jericho's interruption. "Keep looking."

"What's the riddle?" he asked Kate.

"It's an interesting one! I'll read it to you!"

Using the computer's mouse, she quickly navigated to a minimized window and clicked the riddle's text into the foreground.

"It says, I am the fisherman, Simon. One of the twelve. Visit with me beneath the eighth Clement. Hesitate not and begin your further descent. Move quickly through the darkness to the tomb of the Nile, find the West-erners bird and remove its perching tile. Take the prize and rise like the Morning Star. Search your quarters and you will find a space for all and the answer you seek."

Kate turned to Lobo and smiled. "Amazing, right?"

"I suppose." He wrinkled his forehead. "You got Rome from that?"

Jericho slammed the bag down. "She got Rome from Storm, man!" He was clearly agitated, and both Kate and Lobo turned in his direction. "Where's the fucking papyrus, brother?"

"It's in there." He waved a dismissive hand at Jericho. "So, what do you think?" He returned to Kate, genuinely interested in her analysis.

"Goddamn it, Lobo." Jericho walked to Kate's other side and peered down at the screen. "Simon? Twelve? The apostles? Simon is Peter! The tomb of St. Peter is located beneath the altar of St. Clement the eighth." He stared at their shocked expressions, shaking his head. "St. Peter's? Rome? Descend through the altar to the Roman catacombs beneath St. Peter's?"

Kate's mouth hung open.

"Come on guys, seriously?"

Kate and Lobo remained silent.

"Pull up a map of the catacombs on your fancy machine, sweetheart," he said, directing her with a nod.

Kate spun around and did just that, quickly locating a map of the necropolis. Jericho leaned in over her and studied the map, which was accompanied by a legend that identified the various rooms and chambers located beneath the ancient church.

"There," he pointed at the screen. "The chamber labeled 'Z' is for the Egyptians, which I imagine is the 'tomb of the Nile' referred to in the riddle." Jericho continued to look back and forth between the text of the riddle and the map of the catacombs.

"Ha!" He pointed at the screen once more as Kate did her best to mimic his thought processes.

"I see it!" she shouted, pleased with her own skills. Her competitive nature had kicked in, and she was game to race Jericho to the finish line.

"Morning Star!" she blurted out before Frank could spoil her reveal. "The chamber labeled 'U' is Lucifer's room!"

Jericho laughed. "That a girl! Mystery solved!"

"Huh?" Lobo remained somewhat lost.

"I got it, Lobo." Jericho moved back to the bag. "No worries. What I don't have is the fucking papyrus from Angkor."

"Language!" Kate laughed, still elated by their quick work of the riddle.

"Let me," Lobo demanded, pulling the opening of the bag to him.

"By all means." Jericho raised the palms of his hands, symbolically relinquishing control of the search to Lobo.

"It's in here." His muscular arm began to swipe through the bag at an ever-increasing pace, and Jericho watched the panic spread across his face.

"It *ain't* in there, brother," Frank whispered through gritting teeth.

Lobo shook his head and continued his fruitless search through the internal folds and pockets of the leather bag.

"It ain't in here!" He suddenly stopped his search and withdrew his arm.

"That's what I said, big guy!"

"I get it. But I put it in there myself. It hasn't been out of our sight."

"What?" Kate leapt from her chair. "Are you guys busting my chops?"

The two men ignored her interjection and stared at each other, puzzled at the quickly unfurling dilemma.

"Hey!" she shouted.

"Wait!" they both shouted in unison, silencing her inquiry.

"I don't understand." Kate was at the bag, opening every pocket and compartment in the convoluted sack's interior. "How does this happen? In front of all of you!"

"Really," Jericho finally responded to her, sidelining what was surely about to become a verbal onslaught. "Put that stone away, baby. Everyone's glass shatters the same, right?"

Kate shied away from his words, recognizing the truth of his assertions.

"I don't understand," Lobo started, but his words were cut short by the dull hum of rotors emanating from above them.

He looked at Jericho. "Where's the pilot? What's his name? Jim?"

Jericho said nothing, but instead closed his eyes and shook his head.

"He *was* with us!" Kate cried out. "He ate with us all in the dining room!"

"Well, he's not with us now." Jericho was already turning for the exit leading to the helipad. "And he's about to take the fuck off with the papyrus!"

136

The small brass bell above the door rang with tinny elegance as Naamah entered the small rare bookstore on Windsor Street. The balmy cold of Halifax, Nova Scotia was not to her liking, and she shook the damp air from her limbs as she proceeded further into the shop.

"Hello, hello!" An ancient voice, garbed with whispers of French origin, called from somewhere within the stacks.

"Hello to you." Naamah smirked at the entire setting, a bookstore from a storybook.

She watched as wisps of curly gray hair appeared slowly from the far side of one of the shelves that lined the entrance hall. The aged, yet vibrant hair, was soon followed by the entire head of a distinguished-looking gentleman. His round reading spectacles lowered to the tip of his nose to allow his eyes to focus on his guest. The man's robust, neatly manicured goatee gave way to a large grin.

"My, my." He rose from behind the bookshelf and stepped out. "She wasn't doing a thing that I could see, except standing there leaning on the balcony railing, holding the universe together with her beauty."

Naamah laughed at the romantic's words. "Salinger," she whispered, seductively soft, causing the old man to giggle like a child. "Or at least *mostly* Salinger."

"Partial plagiarism at its best. Now you have my mind as well as my heart."

Naamah nodded and strolled toward him. The man turned and set the bundle of books he was still clutching absently under his arm down on the main counter. Turning back to meet her, he symbolically dusted his hands off and extended one in greeting.

"Jack Molay at your service, miss." Naamah extended her hand to meet his with a sly smirk.

"Charmed, I'm sure," she replied with a delicate Southern drawl, diving wholeheartedly into the theatrical scene playing out in the old bookshop.

"Ha, splendid!" Jack lifted her hand to his lips and kissed it gently, "splendid."

Naamah stepped back and scanned the rows of shelves that surrounded her. As she looked closer, she quickly surmised there was no discernible order to the arrangement of the volumes. Nothing was alphabetized, either by author or title. Genres were clearly mingled together as well. Budge beside Tolkien, Hemingway boxing King in on either side.

"Insurance," Jack quickly piped up, noticing the dilemma hanging from her wrinkled brow.

"How's that?" Naamah smiled.

"Insurance," he repeated. "It's the way I *insure* that beautiful young ladies require my assistance to find anything. The cataloging is in here." He smiled, pointing at his cranium.

"Well," Naamah said and smiled deviously at her host, "I guess I will just have to do some picking then." The thought made her bite her lip in anticipation.

"Fire away!" Jack turned and directed her further into the shop.

"Very well." Naamah moved past him with floating grace. Her long legs, wrapped tightly in the dark leather of her tall boots, caught the old-timer's eye as she did.

"Lovely morning, indeed," he said as he drew in a hearty breath.

Naamah stopped suddenly and turned to face the shopkeeper. She was several inches taller than him, and she gazed down into his eyes.

"I am a bit of an amateur historian, you might say."

"Aren't we all?" Jack replied, peering over the top of his glasses for effect, clearly unshaken by his proximity to the demon's beauty.

Naamah laughed at his quick wit. "Yes, well, your name—Molay—has some rather interesting historical significance."

Jack's expression changed ever so slightly. So slight many would not have noticed, but it did not escape the demon's senses.

"You don't say?" Jack backed off slightly. "Do tell." He tried to hide his words in laughter, but their inflection had lost some of the preceding jolliness.

"Yes, indeed." Naamah toyed with him "And *in* deed."

"I'm sorry, I don't follow, young lady." The uneasy feeling that had crept its way into his spine, at the base of his skull, began to spread across his body.

"de Molay," she said as if to a child. "Jacques de Molay. Surely you know of whom I speak?"

"I'm afraid my namesake's identity escapes me, my dear." The tone of his words fell stale as he moved further from what he now perceived as danger.

"Come now," Naamah smiled. "You were doing *sooo* well."

Jack shook his head, remaining true to his assertion of ignorance.

"The last Grand Master," Naamah said with a scowl as she moved at him, "of the Templar."

Jack had moved behind the counter, his eyes never veering from her stare.

"You are he, one and the same, and this shop was once known as Creighton's Bookstore, was it not?"

"Blasphemous fiend!" He reached under the counter and retrieved an archaic sword from its recesses. "Fire will take you!"

Naamah laughed. "I half expected a shotgun! What do you propose to do with that, old man?"

He leveled the ancient blade at her and cried out, "This is *The Flame of Corpus Christi*, the very nails of the crucifixion melted and forged into its steel!"

"I am here for the Ninety-Foot Stone, old man," Naamah hissed at the revelation of the sword's origin, "and I shall have it!"

The ancient knight's arms moved with the strength and speed of youth as he leaned over the counter and swiped at the demon. As if passing through a hologram, the sword met no flesh, but instead swept from one side of Naamah to the other, throwing de Molay off balance. The demon seized the opportunity created by the knight's imbalance and effortlessly leapt up onto the counter before him.

"The stone!" she repeated.

Sensing the immediate danger of Naamah's proximity, de Molay threw himself back, away from her reach, and stumbled. Extending one hand out before her, Naamah took control of Jack's body. Her invisible grasp lifted him upright and several inches off the floor. Waving her other hand, she caused the mighty knight's blade to break free from his hands. It swung and sailed across the shop, coming to rest with force in the far wall.

"You remain pathetic until the end!" she spat. "Clement, possessed of my lord, did his best to rid the world of your wretched brotherhood."

With labored breaths, he cried, "He failed. He will always fail against the power of God."

Naamah rose above the counter, and like a streak of lightning, levitated face to face with the Templar Knight.

"Not today he won't, old fool." Her eyes were ablaze with fury. "The stone!"

"Never," de Molay said, choking on the word.

"Riddle upon riddle!" she screamed. "I have had enough of this! One riddle brings us to the accursed island, but then we need the stone; the Ninety-Foot Stone brings us to our prize. I *will* have the stone!"

"Never!" the knight cried out once more through the crushing force of her invisible grasp, "Nev—"

Closing her fist tight, de Molay's mouth slammed shut with such force his teeth shattered and splintered into his throat. He stared into her eyes defiantly, his own bulging from their sockets with pain and pressure.

"Well, then," she whispered as her face twisted and danced in shadows. "You offered me your heart." de Molay's eyes grew wide, "I accept!"

Thrusting her fist forward, she plunged it through the Templar's chest, ripping past skin and bone until her fingers rested upon the contracting muscle of his heart. Evil excitement aglow in her face, she opened her fingers within his chest cavity and wrapped them around the ageless muscle.

"How beautiful am I now?" she hissed. "Now I bid you—the last Templar Knight—adieu."

As if plucking a feather from a bird, Naamah yanked the ancient knight's heart from his chest and let his limp, dead body fall to the floor. With her blood lust satiated by the knight's execution, her composure quickly returned. Floating gently back down to the floor, she stood above de Molay's lifeless body.

"Guess we will have to do this the old-fashioned way," she said, jesting to the empty space as she surveyed her surroundings before beginning the search for the stone. Spying an old chest to the left rear of the shop, Naamah smiled.

"Could it be that easy?"

She took a step forward and immediately froze as the wooden plank beneath her foot creaked and shifted with her weight. Taking a step back, she kicked the wobbly board with the tip of her boot and it lifted to one side

"Even easier." She smiled, de Molay's heart still in hand.

137

"She's resting now." Abigail's voice startled both Keith and Kate, who spun in their seats to face her. "Sorry. I'm so sorry."

Kate smiled. "That's good. We'll go to her if we hear any news on Decker."

"Yup." Abi pulled a third seat over to her companions. "That's what I told her. Philips milling around by her. He'll keep an eye out."

Keith nodded for a moment then returned to his work.

"So," Abigail said. "How's it going?"

"Not bad." Kate wrinkled her nose, betraying her words. "Could be better, I guess. Lots of distractions at this point."

"I hear ya."

"Right." Kate nudged Keith, who shot her a sorry attempt at a smile. "He's getting discouraged."

Abi shifted forward. "Nonsense. The two of you can do this—a team."

Kate nodded. She was right. How many research projects and paper investigations had she and Keith worked on through the years? Too many to count. This was no different.

"You just need to have some faith, guys."

"Faith?" Keith stood up and exclaimed, "We're battling the very forces of evil here, and you want me to have faith? In what? A God who is offering zero assistance? We have nothing, Abi. Anything we had is now gone."

"No assistance?" Abigail's face grew serious. "How do you figure that? We have survived the unimaginable. We—you and me and Kate—have done battle with those forces and have survived!"

Keith took a deep breath and dropped back into his seat.

"Let's focus." Kate reached out and grabbed a sheet of paper off the desk. "We have three riddles left. Let's work as a team, the three of us, and get this done...for Alex and the others."

Keith's head fell into his hand, and he began to rub his forehead slowly.

"We can do it." Abigail encouraged him. "We *can.*"

Lifting his head, Keith nodded and let the hint of a smile escape his lips.

"That's the spirit! What do you have, Kate?"

"These are the last of them," she noted, rustling the page in her hand. "Ready?"

Abi clapped her hands together. "Fire away! Give 'em to me, baby!"

Keith couldn't help himself, and he laughed at Abigail's exaggerated enthusiasm. "Man, you're such a nerd!"

"Whatever. This coming from super nerd." She looked at Kate and nodded to Keith. "Turn around. You got your Space Invaders shirt on?"

Keith smiled. "Sadly, not today."

"Ha! He's really got one?"

"Space Invaders." Kate rolled her eyes and looked down at the paper. "The boy wears it every other day."

"Whatever." Keith feigned annoyance. "Can we get on with it, please?"

Their spirits lifted; Kate began to read the remaining riddles. "'Cast upon my shores a broken oar, a broken winch, a broken hole, a broken thief may add his gold to my treasure which has always been on the side of the broken hole six men down and fifty-five men home.'"

"Wait!" Keith shouted, leaning forward to the computer keyboard. "Let's try simple: 'winch hole treasure.'"

He typed the phrase and hit return. The search returned a bunch of random results that seemed to have no bearing on their quest.

"Crap." Keith moved from the keyboard.

"Wait. Expand it. Try adding 'pirate' and 'gold.'"

Keith leaned forward and did as she suggested.

"Oak Island!" they shouted in unison as Keith scrolled through the results.

"OMG!" Kate laughed.

"Right?" Keith smiled at Abigail. "Seems incredibly obvious now, huh?"

"Yeah, sure." Abi wrinkled one eyebrow. "Whatever you say, super nerds."

"Let's see if we can run through the other two riddles the same way," Keith said with renewed purpose.

"I bet the authors of these riddles never imagined Google!" Abigail tapped him without thinking and froze with her hand resting on his shoulder. She waited...waited for the flood of visions and emotions that would consume her. Nothing. She released the air that had been locked in her lungs and smiled at Kate with disbelief. Nothing.

"What is it, Abi?"

She laughed. "Nothing. He's a keeper, my friend."

"Yeah." Kate turned back to the remaining riddles. "I'll keep him around a bit longer."

"Come on!" Keith prodded her; his fingers poised above the system's keyboard like a maestro about to begin a grand performance.

"Wait. What the hell does 'six and fifty-five' mean?"

"Who knows?" Keith was ready to go.

"We just have to get them there, Abigail." Kate looked up from the page. "They'll figure out the rest."

Abigail shrugged and motioned for her to continue.

"'Floating south in the Caribbean lies a city of heroes, their skulls carved in stone built by the architects of zero. Within this jungle a city does rise to conquer the beasts of stone and serpents of vines. A wise man, a sacrificed man, a holy man will find his demon knelt on a throne and steal his royal scepter, cracking the T in stone.'"

"Okay." Keith began to hit the keys. "'South Caribbean'...'hero'...'skulls'...'zero'—"

"Wait!" Abi jumped from her seat, eager to chime in. "'Architects of zero'...'creators of zero.' That's the—"

"Mayans," Kate finished with a wink.

"Of course!" Keith shook his head in agreement. "Good one, Abi."

"Ancient aliens." She smirked in response.

"So, 'south Caribbean'…'hero'…'skulls'…'Mayans'—"

"Too vague." Kate scanned the search results over Keith's shoulder. "Add 'jungle city'…'stone'…'vines.'"

Keith typed her suggestions and hit enter.

"Results look nearly the same." Abi took the riddles from Kate and read the paragraph again in silence.

"Try taking some stuff away," she finally said. "Get rid of 'south Caribbean' and 'skulls.'"

Keith nodded and made the changes. Nothing.

"Pull up a map of the Caribbean," Kate instructed, and Keith opened another window. Studying it, she whispered to herself.

"What is it, Kate?"

"Try 'Honduras.'"

"Why?"

"Beause I said, Keith."

"Fair enough!" He laughed and began to type the changes. Before he could finish, he froze and turned to Kate with a smile.

"Copan," he said, and she leaned over as the words left his mouth and kissed him on the head.

"Copan," she whispered in agreement.

"You all sure?"

"Yes, Abi, we're sure. The jungle city of Copan—stone and vines—it's as obvious as Oak Island now."

Elated, Keith cried out, "We're on a fucking roll! Next!"

"Easy there, Einstein." Abi laughed.

Keith turned to her and smiled. "Man, you're channeling Sam…big time."

Abigail smirked and focused him back to the keyboard with a pointing finger.

"Okay." Kate's enthusiasm was as evident as Keith's. "Last," she paused and smiled at him, "*fucking* one baby."

"Yeah!" he shouted. "That's the spirit!"

"Looking down on all the world, wondering if it will ever rest, lies the land of the wild horse, with the lair of the kat to the northwest. Find the caves, many they are, hidden by time, forgotten by all. Search through each until one finds a prophet marked by sorrow his treasure hid behind."

"Jesus," Keith slowly reacted, "save the best for last, huh?"

"Nonsense." Kate hip checked his chair and it rolled out from in front of the keyboard. Dropping to one knee, she set out typing in the search bar.

Keith read the words aloud as she went. "'Kat'— 'caves'— 'wild horses.'" She stopped and looked up at him with exaggerated goofy wide eyes and lifted one extended finger out over the enter key.

"Hit it, sister," Abi cried out, relishing in the pace and results of their little game.

"Bang!" Kate yelled with cool confidence. But nothing useful appeared on the screen.

"Oh, man," She moaned and got up, letting Keith return to the throne of searches.

"That's right," Keith said, playfully as he slid back into position.

"'Kat' with a 'K' is significant, —no?" Abigail proposed to the others.

Keith nodded. "I think so. Let's see what it gives us by itself."

"An evergreen shrub from Arabia and Africa." Abi read the words out loud. "Maybe?"

"Very vague, but you may be on to something," Kate said without looking up from the page she was once again studying.

"Anything?" Keith grew impatient, hoping to return to the stride of their previous results. Kate lifted a hand and hushed him.

"Sorry," he responded with exaggerated offense to her gesture.

"'Looking down on all the world, wondering if it will ever rest.' Yes! 'Looking down on all the world, wondering if it will ever rest,'" she repeated the sentence over and over. "'Looking down...down.'"

Keith sat up in his seat. He could see the spark of revelation forming on Kate's beautiful face, kicking and clawing its way to her consciousness. He nodded at her, driving her on.

"'Looking down'— 'Ever rest'— 'Ever rest.' 'Ever'—*Everest!*"

"Yes!" Keith jumped up and grabbed her around the waist. "That's my girl!" Kate responded by raising one eyebrow, off putting his embrace slightly, and then she smiled and kissed him, bringing him back to her.

"Get a room!" Abi laughed and walked toward the computer keyboard.

Keith relinquished his hold of Kate. "*Really* channeling her now."

"Shut up!" Abigail laughed as she typed.

"Type 'kat'— 'Everest'— 'caves'," Kate started and was quickly shut down.

Abi said, "I got it! You did the heavy lifting! I got it."

The results popped up, and Kate stepped forward to review them.

"Nepal! Of course! Kathmandu! 'Kat!'"

"Look at this one." Abi clicked on one of the results. "Newly discovered caves in the Himalayan North are the 'entrance to inner earth.' That's got to be our location!"

Keith scanned the article and nodded. "I think you're right, Abi. And I bet there's a crying Buddha in one of them," he said and laughed.

"Okay." Kate grabbed a pen and jotted down the names of the last three locations. "Newly discovered Himalayan caves in Nepal, Copan Ruins, Honduras, and Oak Island, Nova Scotia."

The silence that followed Kate's words was instantly shattered by slow clapping which echoed from the darkness at the front of the library. Keith reached out and grabbed Abigail by the arm and yanked her behind him, alongside Kate. His eyes fixated on the location the clapping was emanating from. Squinting hard to see beyond the wall of dark, he finally caught a faint glimmer of movement from within the shadows.

Kate watched as his body relaxed and a gasp of relief left his mouth. She stepped forward and watched Anika come into view.

"Nice job, guys." Anika congratulated the trio on their work. "Sorry to startle you. Who did you think I was, Keith?" She laughed at his obviously stressed reaction.

"The Devil." Keith dryly replied. "I thought you were the fucking Devil."

138

Naamah walked slowly across the southeasterly shoreline of Oak Island. The small, 140-acre island was one of 360 of its kind found throughout Mahone Bay in Novia Scotia, Canada. She headed north toward a small clearing located just south of Oak Island Drive. She could see Moloch waiting there and lifted her stone prize above her head. Moloch clapped his hands together and let a slight laugh escape his oft apathetic lips, and she smiled in response to his pleasure. After a momentary pause, Moloch lifted a small bronze sword up into the air. The sword was of Roman origin and had been discovered decades before, just off Oak Island's coast. It represented clear proof that Romans had visited the land long before the pirates of legend. It also presented the possibility that the famous treasure pit on the island had existed thousands of years earlier than first thought. The sword, covered with the green patina of time, depicted a man on the end of the hilt. The figure's arms outstretched above him, clasping a strange rectangular block and holding it up to the heavens.

"You see?" Moloch laughed as Naamah arrived at his side. He reached out and relieved her of the Ninety-Foot Stone, and in exchange, handed her the Roman sword. She held the dull blade up to the light and studied it briefly.

"Difficult to retrieve?" she asked inquisitively.

"Not at all, my dear," he replied. He was studying the strange symbols carved in the stone.

"And you?" he finally inquired without looking up from the stone.

"Ha. No problems. As a bonus," she said, then paused for maximum effect, "the last Templar Knight is no more."

"Really?" Moloch looked up. "de Molay? That is wonderful news!" He took a step toward Naamah. "I know many a dark soul who will be elated by this turn of events."

Naamah nodded in agreement and lifted the sword, hilt end up, into the air between them.

"You see, my dear?" Moloch raised the Ninety-Foot Stone above his head with both hands, mimicking the brass representation on the end of the Roman blade.

"Yes handsome," Naamah said, purring. "I see."

The stone held high above the demon's head was a perfect replica, in both shape and scale, to that held by the figure on the handle of the warrior's blade. Moloch lowered the stone and handed it back to his demonic companion.

"Shall we proceed?" Moloch turned and walked several feet farther inland, stopping at a large oval beach stone protruding from the ground at his feet. The demons stood over the area known by Oak Island aficionados as the 'Stone Triangle.' Discovered in 1897 and located just above the high-water mark, a patch of beach stones formed an equilateral triangle pointing true north.

Naamah watched intently as Moloch waved his hands back and forth over the area on the ground, causing the grass and debris around the stones to scatter and fly into the island breeze.

"The stone, if you please."

Naamah handed the Ninety-Foot Stone back to him and watched as he once again studied the symbols etched into its surface. Running his fingers across the faded markings, he traced the lines they formed. Naamah watched as his lips parted and formed words without any sounds.

"The sword is the key to the stone," he finally said, noticing her perplexed gaze. "It's nothing more than a simple symbol cypher. However, the key is in the translated language. In this case, Latin."

"Can you read it, my lord?" she asked with anticipation, albeit an ego appeasing performance since she had solved the riddle of the stone's words back in the bookshop. "What does it speak of?"

"It is the key to the triangle." He signaled for her to take a few steps back. "And it reads, 'Ad astra per aspera.'"

No sooner had the words left his mouth than the ground beneath their feet began to tremble and vibrate. Moloch's eyes, ablaze with flames of revelation, stared down at the stone formed triangle at their feet. The individual stones comprising the shape, twenty-nine in all, began to roll and dislodge from their footing in the soil. As they broke free of the Earth's crust, the velocity of the stones spin increased to a feverish pace and the sheer inertia created lifted the stones up into the air. Maintaining their originally formed shape, the stones began to glow and smoke.

"Spectacular!" Moloch shouted over the din of the whirling rocks. "Absolutely spectacular!"

As if situated atop a potter's wheel, the triangle formed by the stones began to turn in midair from true north toward the West. As the glowing red intensity of the rocks peaked, the rotating arrow point of the triangle came to a stop. All at once, the sounds of life that radiated from the island ceased, as if sucked into a vacuum. The silence was broken seconds later as the stones shattered into a glowing beam of red light, whose concentration was evident by the hue it cast over all in its path.

"Ad astra per aspera." Moloch repeated the inscription once more for the mere satisfaction of his accomplishment.

"A rough road leads to the stars," Naamah translated with a wink.

"Indeed, it does." Moloch stretched his hand in the direction of the beam's path. "Shall we?"

"We shall." Naamah stepped passed her companion and out on the crudely paved road to the north of the beam's origin.

"We are heading in the opposite direction of the so-called 'Money Pit,'" Naamah said as they walked.

"A ruse." Moloch laughed. "An unsolvable puzzle for greedy little monkeys to waste an eternity attempting to solve."

"How clever." Naamah was truly impressed with the ingenuity of the riddle guardians' planning and foresight.

Moloch changed the subject as they continued to follow the glowing red beam, passing the mid-point of the island. "How did you fare in Palermo?"

"Our objective was accomplished," Naamah replied after a brief hesitation. "The papyrus was recovered without incident."

"Storm was there?" Moloch's voice was different. Did the ancient demon suspect something afoul in his companions' behavior? Was her subversive plotting becoming evident she wondered?

"He was." Even staring straight ahead, she could feel his gaze upon her cheek. "He escaped my trappings, unfortunately, and I did not feel I had sufficient time to play cat and mouse with the piece of shit."

Moloch reached out and took hold of her wrist, stopping their forward progress momentarily. "I was not questioning you, my dear. Simply making small talk, as it were."

Naamah forced a smile to form on her artistically chiseled lips, and he released his hold on her. He most certainly was not just making small talk.

Pressing on, the pair finally emerged from the overgrown vegetation into yet another clearing on the northern tip of the island. Pausing once more, Moloch spied the end of the red beam on the surface of a boulder across the clearing from them.

"You had assistance?" His words shocked her, although she did not allow her emotions to be a tell. "Locals, I believe?"

"Yes, local initiates."

"And explosives abound?"

"Yes." She smiled and turned to face him. "Yes, they love their bang."

Moloch laughed. "Yes, don't we all?" He stepped from her toward the ray's endpoint ahead. "I trust they satisfied their mistress?"

"Extensively," she said, toying with him as she moved in closer. "Over and over again."

"Ha!" He was always pleased with their word play. "We have reached our prize, my pet."

Moloch reached out. "Give those to me."

Naamah handed the sword and the stone to Moloch and waited for what she hoped were further instructions, nothing more.

He nodded up. "Elevate, my dear. See what we have here."

Naamah, relieved by the command, twisted her hands and pressed, palms face down. Her body instantly took flight and she sailed straight up into the air above Moloch. Turning about, midair, she smiled down at her waiting companion.

"A cross!" She shouted down to him. "The beam's endpoint is the headstone! Six stones in all!"

Naamah mentally locked location of the rocks and gently lowered herself back to the earth. Moloch was already walking toward the beam's endpoint.

"Hurry now," he called after her.

Naamah shot forward with supernatural speed to his side as the two arrived at its headstone.

"Hold this, my dear." Moloch handed the Roman sword to Naamah and quickly scaled the large boulder that was located at the topmost point of the aerially viewed cross.

Standing atop the rock, he bent over and dropped the Ninety-Foot Stone into a precisely carved compartment located in the boulder's surface. It snapped into place with a sharp crack, and the beam of intense red light immediately disappeared and then reappeared, but this time it traveled only between the headstone and the center stone a short distance away.

Without saying a word, Moloch jumped down from the rock and snatched the sword from Naamah's hands. Dashing twenty or so feet forward, he quickly made his way to the large rock that was the center of the cross—the crossroad of the two intersecting lines. With one fluid motion, he sprang up onto the boulder and dropped to a knee in order to run his hands over the rough landscape of the rock's upper surface.

Naamah once again lifted herself from the ground and levitated to Moloch's right, watching as he proceeded to blow the dirt and dust from a small rectangular hole with the great force of his breath.

Moloch, having cleared the opening, stood upright and positioned the sword down into a thrusting position. With a growl, he drove the Roman blade into the opening on top of the boulder. It penetrated the stone as he drove the ancient metal to the hilt. Relinquishing his grasp of the handle, he gingerly stepped off the rock and came to a thud on the island floor.

Naamah dropped to his side, and the pair stepped back as the great boulder, without sound or sigh, split into two halves. The halves rolled onto their sides, the newly exposed inner surfaces facing up to the sky.

Moloch stretched his hand, inviting for Naamah to do the honors. Scaling the sides with a mixture of physical and metaphysical ingenuity, she quickly spied the small, notched out space on one of the stone halves. Dropping to one knee, she reached down into the shallow hole and retrieved the stone vessel containing the small fragment of papyrus.

"Excellent team work, you are an archaeological vixen." Moloch laughed as she dropped down to join him.

Nodding in agreement, she studied the ancient fragment in her hand.

He was close to her; she could feel his intense power. "We are, in fact, a team after all— aren't we?"

Naamah smiled at him, offering no hint to the inner storm of fear brewing within her. "Of course, my prince." She smiled seductively. "Together unto the bitter end."

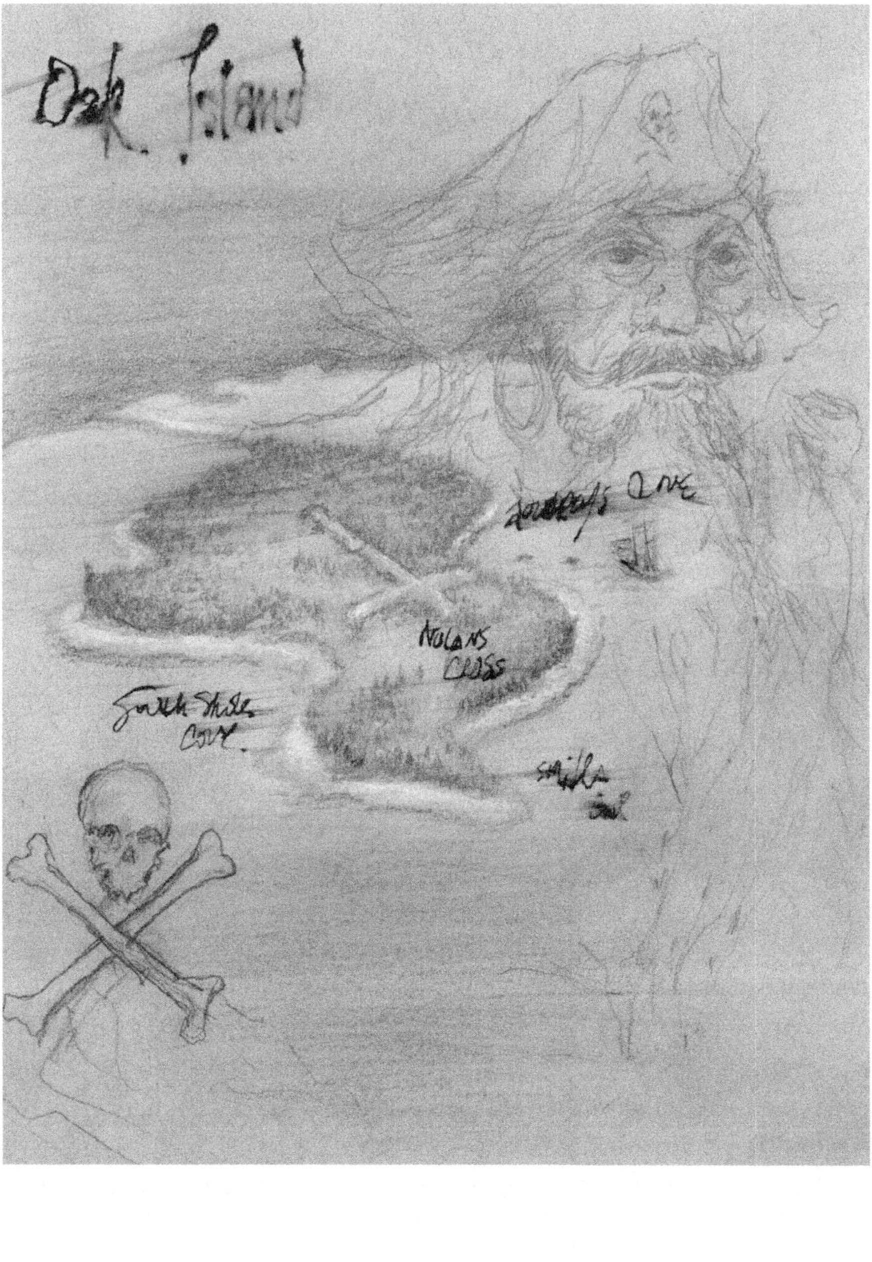
Oak Island
NOLANS
CROSS

139

"Where are the fools?" Alexander pounded his fist on the wooden desktop and Kate impulsively jumped and took a step away from his wrath.

"On their way to St. Peter's," she stammered. "The catacombs."

"Who directed them to do anything further?" His fury intensified.

"Easy ..." Serket attempted to get control of the situation before Storm got out of hand. "Easy—"

"Silence!" he snapped at her before she could say more.

"We had the one thing we needed to stave off this assault on humanity." He turned to Keith, who quickly averted his eyes. "We could have spent eternity protecting this one fragment, and it would have been sufficient to protect mankind from an onslaught by the armies of darkness."

Alex felt his blood pounding in his temples, and he caught himself, if not but for a moment, and allowed some semblance of serenity to return.

"Here," he continued, regaining his composure. "Here, in my castle, in the sanctuary of mankind, we allowed evil to enter and take that which was ours." He turned to Kate and screamed, "*Twice!*"

"Alexander!" Serket had had enough, and she rushed to his side. "Easy does it, Alexander. They are kids, for God's sake."

"They are soldiers. Warriors. The chosen ones!"

"Chosen by whom?" she pressed. "Again, they are kids."

Alex leaned down, almost touching Serket's face with his own. "Not me," he whispered cautiously.

Storm's words hit home, and she immediately understood her old friend's confusion. As that was exactly what it was. Why put forth this cast of characters for Storm if they were not up to the task?

"Get it now?" Alexander chided her.

Serket nodded. She did understand. She saw the turmoil in his eyes. She would not allow him to break, or to fall apart now.

"Stop thinking," she demanded.

"What?"

"Shut it off." Serket stepped toward the others. "Clear your thoughts. We need you. We require your guidance and insight, your knowledge. This is a powerful team." She smiled. "And you, my dear friend, are our sails, our wheel, our compass, and our sexton."

"Wow." Abigail couldn't help herself.

Serket turned to her and winked, to which Abi smiled and looked at the others.

Keith nodded. "Mr. Storm, Serket isn't wrong, man. We can do this, but you have to keep us going, okay?"

Alexander closed his eyes and stretched his neck from side to side. When at last he opened them, they were once again ablaze with the light of inspiration.

"Did you ever really doubt my dedication?" Storm rhetorically asked as he squeezed Keith's shoulder in assurance.

Serket smiled. "Never."

Kate joined in. "Nope."

Abi followed. "No. Never."

Keith reached up and placed his hand over Alex's, which remained perched on his shoulder. "I haven't doubted you since the very first moment we met. You give us the same optimism and trust."

Alexander smiled at him and then looked at Kate. "What do you have for us?"

Kate, relieved the moment had passed, snatched the loose sheet of paper from the desk. "We."

"Hmm?" Alexander looked puzzled at her reply.

"What *we* have for you. It was a true group effort."

Alex laughed. "Very good."

Kate nodded in response to Alexander's approval and quickly began reading her notes. Along the way, she was sure to explain the simple process they used to ascertain the locations of the last three riddles; being sure to give credit where it was due in an effort to alleviate some of the negative marks against her comrades.

"Kate." Alex reached out and touched her hand softly. "Time is of the essence as I am sure you are well aware. You are welcome to elaborate on the process over a fine wine and perhaps a lamb dinner in the not so distant future—"

"Lamb?" Kate wrinkled her nose.

"Pardon. Cheeseburgers and beer?"

"That's better."

Alex pensively nodded. "The locations now, if you will?"

"Right. Oak Island, Copan Ruins, Nepal." She looked up at Storm. "The recently discovered cave complex in Nepal."

"Excellent, Kate." Alex saw the words forming in her mind and headed her off at the pass. "Excellent Abi, Keith."

Turning back to her, he said, "And Decker, Anika?"

"No." Abigail said the word with a stiff inflection that caused Alex to turn to her with concern.

"What is it, Abigail? Speak."

"Anika is here. She returned to her room right before the two of you arrived."

"Decker? The papyrus from St. George?" His voice was laced with growing panic.

Abigail shook her head slowly.

It took every ounce of forced composure to push the words forth. "Dead?"

"We don't know," Kate called out before suspense and speculation could take hold of Alex. "They were ambushed in Ethiopia — by Naamah."

"Scarlet whore." Alex symbolically spit to the ground. "The papyrus?"

"Found and lost," Keith replied.

"Anika says he followed Naamah through her worm hole," Kate continued.

"Naamah's?" Alex clarified, terror mounting.

"Yes, but that doesn't mean he is—"

Storm waved her off. "We proceed as planned. I firmly believe Decks can handle whatever scenario he has found himself in. If anyone can survive skulking about a demon's lair, it is he." Alex turned to the others. "I'm no longer worried. My concerns have abated," he assured them.

"Truly?" Serket strolled to his side.

"Yes," he replied. "Decker will be fine, and, his position could very well prove to be an advantage, actually. Only time will tell."

Serket wasn't buying it. "Alex, we need to go get him. Now."

"While I appreciate your concern, and I, of course, share in the sentiment, I would prefer him here with us — we have neither the time nor the means to track his whereabouts and retrieve him from the diabolical clutches of Naamah."

"There is one who could find him," she leaned in and whispered. "The one of which I speak could take you to him and bring you both back."

Alexander shot her a silencing glance. "The remaining stones cannot be used. They are required — all that remain are required."

"I don't understand, Storm." She pleaded with him. "It's Decks."

"*He* would, though," Alexander shot back. "Decker would understand."

Serket shook her head in disbelief.

"Trust me." His voice was soft and assuring.

"Always, and unwaveringly," she replied, and her eyes morphed into a squint as she gazed into his, trying to see into the machinations driving his mind, the processes he kept so well hidden, "unwavering."

"Yes, well." Alex smiled. "How about 'un'questioning as well?"

"Don't push it, Storm," she scowled, "you wouldn't appreciate that now would you — really?"

He turned to the others. "We remain together from this point forward." Alex lowered his body into the large leather reading chair. "From here on out, I will require a concerted effort in the field. Gather what you need. *385 Remember, we may be gone from Dragon Loch for some time—forever, perhaps—so take what you need and meet Serket and me in the kitchen. She and I require sustenance before departing."

"It *has* been forty-eight hours," Serket said with a laugh.

The others nodded in agreement.

"Where are we heading first?" Kate was excited, even under the present circumstances. She needed to get out of the stuffy stone fortress. "Oak Island?"

"Not Oak Island." Alex shook his head without making eye contact with her.

"Why?" Kate wanted to see the small island desperately. "Our interpretation of the riddle is—"

"Dead on," Storm finished. "However, its treasure is now lost."

"What?" Kate's voice echoed with disbelief. "How can that be?"

Storm turned to exit the library. "It is. The darkness has already solved the mystery of Oak Island."

"How do you know?" she demanded.

Alexander turned back to her; one eyebrow raised. Kate's growing tension subsided quickly as a result of Storm's stare. "I know. Is that not enough?"

She said nothing in reply.

"The sands of time are truly dropping their last vestiges — their final grains — into the glass of the bottom chamber." He turned to Serket. "We are now about to embark on the final leg of this, a journey inspired by the likes of Dante and Bosch. We must not fail — we cannot waiver — and we must be willing to sacrifice all in our efforts — understood?"

The group nodded in silent unison.

"Excellent." He smiled a forced expression. "Collect Anika on your way back and meet us in the kitchen. We shall decide between Copan and Nepal together. We will pray the others are successful in Rome. We will not surrender the day to the darkness, understood?"

Again, the nods came, this time accompanied by vocalized approval.

Alexander turned toward the exit once more, Serket trailing closely at his side. "Inspiring the masses, Alexander Storm?" she whispered, to which he slowly closed his eyes in painful desperation.

~

"*A*lexander?" Anika entered the kitchen and nodded to him listlessly. Storm stared at her, not saying a word. She ignored his glance and took the seat next to Serket.

"How you doing, honey?" Serket rubbed her back. "William is an amazing man — resourceful and strong."

"I know," Anika waved her off with a forced smile that begged Serket to stop before the tears started to flow once more.

Serket nodded, inhaled a breath of understanding, and respectably said nothing more.

"Where are we going?" Kate burst into the kitchen. "Have you decided?"

Alexander, although looking in her direction, was focused on the large screen mounted on the wall behind her.

"I would be happy to debate the benefits. The pros and cons, I've made a list, of each location," she continued, unaware that Storm was fixated on the news broadcast playing out behind her on the television.

"I would say Copan is closest in terms of travel," she continued. "I mean, that's obvious. I'm sure you've considered this — probably the paramount factor, already. However—"

Alex soared from his seat and lifted a hand, silencing Kate. "Turn it up! Turn the program up, Keith!"

Confused, Kate looked back and forth between Alex and Keith, who had snatched up the remote from the table and had begun to turn the volume up.

A reporter announced, *Authorities are baffled by the strange phenomena which appears to have swallowed an entire pond in Palermo, Italy overnight.*

Alexander hastily moved closer to the hanging screen.

The report continued, *Authorities and locals report that a large pond, known locally as Alexophil, located less than a kilometer from the famed and morbidly curious Cappuccini catacombs, emptied into the Earth under the cover of night, leaving behind a large crater in the landscape. Experts are able to offer no explanation for the strange series of events in the region, which also include a barrage of eruptions or explosions emanating from below ground less than a day ago. Scientists claim no seismic activity in the area over the last forty-eight-hour period.*

Alexander took the remote from Keith and muted the report. He stood motionless as the others watched him for an inclination as to what was going on.

"Grab your gear!" he suddenly called out. "Our transport is fueled and ready."

Kate returned to her previous discussion as she hurried along with the group, "So, Nepal or Copan?"

"Neither," Alexander stopped dead in his tracks and smiled at Kate.

"What? Did I miss something?"

"Yes," he replied.

"I don't understand," she continued as they exited the castle onto the roof.

"Where are we headed, Storm?" Serket spoke up over Kate.

"Palermo!" he shouted with heartfelt enthusiasm over the whirl of the newly arrived chopper. "We missed something!"

"What?" Serket yelled, grabbing hold of his jacket and spinning him to her. "What did we miss, Storm?"

"The failsafe my dear," he said with a hearty laugh. "We missed the failsafe."

140

"**B**rother!" Jericho called out to the sharply dressed gentleman from across the crowd in Saint Peter's Square.

"Who's that?" Sam asked, tugging on Jericho's jacket like a child. "You know him?"

Jericho ignored Samantha and began to make his way through the crowds of tourists and pilgrims flooding The Square.

"Go." Lobo tapped her shoulder, encouraging Sam to follow Jericho.

"Hey!" she shouted, throwing him a cross look. "Easy there, Rambo."

"Oh, please." Lobo walked past Sam, following after Jericho. "I barely touched you."

Sam watched a moment as he marched away. "Yeah, but do you *want* to touch me?" she shouted, jogging to catch up to him.

"You're cute." Lobo smiled down at her then looked back up just in time to see their companion shake hands with the man from the crowd.

"Cute?" Sam shouted. "Really?"

Without breaking his stride, Lobo shook his head. "Jeez! You know what I mean!" She could see the pink in his cheeks. "Not now, Samantha."

They got to Jericho, and he said, "I would like to introduce you to an old friend. Commander Pierre Le'Strat."

Lobo reached out and offered his hand in greeting. Le'Strat grasped it firmly and spoke with a low, gravelly voice. "Pleasure."

Samantha allowed the voice to resonate in her ears. His rich French accent was musical in its cadence and tenor. "And you my dear? Who might you be?"

"Sam. Um, Samantha."

Lobo thought she was a little too giddy as Le'Strat took her hand and kissed it gingerly.

She repeated herself, a bit lost in the moment. "I'm Samantha."

"Yes, you are." Le'Strat smiled a devilish grin, which she found difficult to interpret. His mysterious nature wasn't limited to his dialogue, though. His expensive gray vested suit and impeccable shoes were contradicted by the faded brown fedora upon his head and the mirrored aviators on his face. Bizarre, she thought.

"Commander of what?" she finally piped up.

She watched Jericho wait for approval from Le'Strat before answering.

"Pierre is the High Commander of the Pope's Gendarmerie Corps," he said, then paused momentarily.

"The Blue Line?" Lobo interjected, to Jericho's surprise.

"The Blue Line," Jericho repeated, shaking his head with pleasure. "You got it, man."

"Which *is*?" Sam was still confused. The monikers meant nothing to her.

"I am commander of his Holiness's private police."

"Oh," Sam smiled. "That is, um, something."

She smiled awkwardly. *Something*? Really? That was the best she could do? Her embarrassment at her weak discourse was quickly alleviated by the comforting wink Pierre shot her from beneath his raised glasses.

"Why are you here, my friend?" the commander asked, turning to Jericho.

"You mean a leisurely visit to see an old friend isn't a sufficient reason?"

Pierre laughed. "Seriously, Jericho?"

"Not buying it, huh?"

"No, my friend." They strolled toward the south side of The Square. "It is a nice thought — but no."

He ushered them to a small space niched into the brick-layered wall. Reaching into his pants, he withdrew a ring of keys, which also contained several odd-shaped plastic fobs. The others watched as Le'Strat waved one of the key fobs over a brick, causing the top layer, a façade of some sort, to slide over, exposing a glass square beneath. The commander placed his right thumb over the small space exposed in the wall. After a moment, an audible beep emanated from somewhere within, and a small doorway slid open in the wall before them.

"Fancy," Jericho said and smirked.

"It's the Vatican, my friend," said the commander as he ushered the three companions inside. "There have always been secret passages and doorways, tunnels and rooms."

"Yes," Jericho replied dryly. "The holy city has always had its share of secrets."

"Oh, come now." Le'Strat seemed defensive as he closed the door behind them. "Even though you make light of my words — the structural secrets I speak of are necessitated by the eternal threat, which is always present."

Jericho nodded in agreement, "I didn't mean any offense, man."

"I know, Frank." Le'Strat stopped and turned to him. "But these are not the streets of Manhattan. These are the halls and spires of history, of God— the stronghold, like it or not, of man's never-ending struggle to keep the light shining and the night at bay. And although we are plagued with centuries of man's imperfections and sin (we are, after all, men) and for every hundred saint-like individuals who have roamed these hallowed corridors — there must also be, peppered in, a fair number of sinners. A fact of life as we know it. But in no way should it detract from the big picture, if you will."

"Sorry," Jericho said with solemn and genuine remorse. "I meant no disrespect. You know how I am."

"I know." He squinted his eyes to make his point unquestionable. "But remember where you are and perhaps allow it to humble the great Frank Jericho — just a slight bit, aye?"

"Point taken. Let's not flog a dead horse."

Le'Strat threw his hands up and walked past Jericho.

Sam, normally quite comfortable with crude wisecracks and the occasional double entendre, pushed past Jericho and joined Pierre.

"I haven't known him long, but he is clearly an idiot." She laughed as she met up with him.

"No, he's not," Le'Strat replied firmly.

"No, he's not," Sam parroted. "What I meant is, I'm impressed by the hidden entrance and the tunnel we are in. This is incredible engineering."

Pierre smiled. "Yes, it is. And some of it dates back centuries. We are constantly evolving, though, making use of the old-world designs and the latest technology and advances."

"I can see that." Sam was working her way into her wheelhouse, "I am a techie. For real. Not just goofing around—it's my job."

"You work for Storm?"

"No," she answered with a bit of surprise. "Not at all."

"Did you think I didn't know whose errand you were on?"

"I really didn't think about it either way," she said matter-of-factly. "We're just following Jericho's lead right now."

"I see," Le'Strat sounded unconvinced, but the reason for it escaped Sam.

"Is that how you know Jericho?" she asked.

"How's that?"

"Through Alexander Storm?"

"Oh, no. We worked together on a case some time ago."

"Here?" Sam was confused. "Or in New York?"

"No, in New York."

Samantha peered over her shoulder at Frank, who was several footsteps behind them, Lobo at his side. Nodding his head at her in acknowledgment, she gave him a quick smirk and turned back to Le'Strat.

"What kind of case requires the Pope's chief of police and an NYPD homicide detective?" she asked the host.

"A very important one," he replied without missing a step.

"Attempt on the Pope kind of thing?"

"No, something along the lines of Storm's specialties." He looked at her to see if she was following him. "But it is a tale for another day, yes?"

"Oh," she replied, no longer wanting to know the details of a battle in a war she had been happily ignorant of but a short time ago.

"At the conclusion of our work," he continued, "the Holy Father thought it best for Francis to return with me. To spend some time here to... recover, for lack of a better word."

"Oh." Her simple response let Le'Strat made him aware of her understanding of the underlying meaning of his words.

"He was here, with you, for a while then?"

"Over a year, my dear."

Le'Strat came to a halt as he and Sam reached the end of the tunnel, which split in two directions to the left and the right. He waited for the others to catch up and then pointed to the dark tunnel to the right.

"A little history," he said, turning to Jericho. "And if you know this one, don't spoil my fun, please."

Frank nodded with a smile. "Wouldn't dream of it."

"That tunnel has quite a history, and it relates to our brother order, the Swiss Guard."

Sam nodded her head in a scholarly fashion to which Lobo leaned down and spoke right in her ear, "the Pope's army."

She shot him a glance, which caused him to back away. "Just saying."

"Yes, the Pope's Army, for lack of a better description," he continued. "Anyway, the Guard, which has been in service for over five hundred years, used this very tunnel in their first major battle. On May 6, in the year 1527, Emperor Charles V's soldiers were attacking Rome. When they attempted to invade Saint Peter's Basilica, they were met by the comparatively tiny Swiss Guard force. The Guard held back the massive onslaught long enough for Pope Clement VII to escape through this secret passageway to Castel Sant'Angelo."

"Wow," Samantha responded to the commander's tale. "That's amazing."

"What's amazing is your reference to Clement." Jericho shifted where he stood.

"Really?" Le'Strat raised his hand to cradle his chin, waiting for his friend to finally reveal the purpose behind their visit.

"Yeah," Jericho laughed nervously. "We need to go see him."

141

"Astonishing!" Kate gazed out across the vast crater that had once been Lake Alexophil with excitement in her eyes.

"Truly," Alexander replied softly as he leaned over the edge and peered some thirty meters sloping down into the hole.

"What does it mean, Alexander? What is your theory?" She continued to prod him for answers, to which he remained non-responsive.

Keith lingered with Abigail some distance behind them. A safe distance. Alexander was fine with that. He had too much on his plate to be distracted by the fumbling boy; nor did he wish for his powerful neophyte to be placed in harm's way. Turning to his right, he watched Anika slowly walk the edge, Serket at her side, surveying both the dried lake bed and the diminishing light of the horizon before her. Alex was sure her mind was almost exclusively latched to thoughts of Decker's safety and well-being.

"He will be fine," Serket finally said, breaking the long silence the two had shared. "Alex's lack of action here proves it to me."

"How is that, Serket?" Anika snapped at her. "How does inaction equate to well-being, may I ask?"

"I know Storm," Serket said with unmistakable sincerity. "I know his relationship with William. He would not forgo retrieving him unless he was confident in his ability to survive until the time is right."

"That's nonsense, and you know it!"

Serket could see new tears forming in Anika's eyes, preparing to retrace the salty tracks that had dried on her cheeks. "Storm is concerned with one thing only—stopping whatever this is!"

"The end of humanity," Serket whispered.

"What?"

"He is concerned with saving humanity, Anika. This is true. But his concerns, his worries, and his responsibilities are many and—"

"And Decker's safety is just one of a multitude of concerns, amounting to nothing more than a checklist of tasks to perform. I get it."

"That is *not* what I said." The annoyance in the Medjai's voice intensified.

"Enough!" yelled Alexander, who had moved in behind them without their knowledge. "William and I are connected—"

"What?" Anika tried to interject.

"Silence!" he demanded. "I knew when he was injured in the desert. I have known when he was in danger. I even knew he was in peril at the church of the dragon slayer." He lowered his tone and grew close to Anika. "And I sense now, wherever he is, whatever he is doing, he is safe and secure and in no immediate danger. The topic is, therefore, closed."

"But—"

Anika was silenced by Storm's stare. "I repeat. The subject is closed...for now."

Alexander nodded to Anika, who said nothing, and he returned to Kate.

"She all right?"

"No, Kate," Alexander responded in an uncharacteristically harsh manner, which took her by surprise. "William takes refuge amongst demons and she knows it. She is most definitely *not* okay."

Kate reached out, taking hold of his hand in hers. "Are *you* all right, Alex?"

Alexander's heart slowed, and a soft breath escaped his lips. "Yes, my dear. I am. We are. Thank you."

Kate released her hold and pointed across the barren lake to the shoreline opposite from them. "Seems to be some activity over there."

Alexander strained his vision in the dying light, squinting for clarity.

"Yes," he started. "Curious locals, I presume."

Something or someone caught his eye, and they popped open wide as he sprang into action.

"To me!" he called, dashing halfway between the lake's dried up shoreline and Keith and Abigail. "Quickly now!"

His commands were met with immediate compliance and within seconds they all reached his side.

"My friends, we are under the gun now, if you will. We must act quickly."

Serket needed answers. "Why are we here, Storm? The papyrus is already lost."

"Fine," Alexander acknowledged, conceding that their burning desire to know what the hell was going on should finally be satiated. "Quick synopsis. Naamah used blasting charges at the far end of the catacombs. Not to destroy us, but to expose something that was hidden for centuries. As we surmised, there was more to this location than just the riddled papyrus."

"What is it?" Keith asked when Alex paused to take a lungful of air. Storm shot him a glance, to which Keith nodded. "Shut up. I got it."

"First, I am not sure what the missing puzzle piece is. I have some ideas, but they are nothing more than that. Second, I am fairly sure Naamah knows what she is searching for, and the fact that there is a horde of demonic soldiers, not curious locals, across the way as I speak tells me she has not yet acquired said object."

The entire group turned in unison, fear taking root in their eyes, and stared across the lake bed into complete darkness. Since they had now lost all traces of the Sun, nothing was visible besides the occasional beam of light, the others could no longer ascertain the position or quantity of Naamah's horde.

"Focus," Storm whispered harshly. "Here. Now."

When he was sure he had regained their complete attention, he continued.

"Keith, you will take Abigail and guard her well."

"Hey!" Abi objected at the implication she needed an inordinate amount of protection.

Alex spoke over her protests and repeated the command.

"You will take her back to the truck, and you will bring the truck down here. Understood?"

"Yes," Keith replied.

"Don't drive into the lake bed. Don't get too close to the edge, understand?" Alex extended the tip of his boot and tapped the earth around him to illustrate the possibly fragile nature of the Earth's crust where there was once water.

"I got it," Keith said, swiping the truck keys from Alex's hand. "Jeez, I'm not dense."

"Oh, yeah," Kate whispered. "Not at all."

Her playful giggling was silenced by a dirty look from Anika.

"Sorry," she swiftly responded to the glance, realizing their banter was probably inappropriate at this point in time.

"Yes, well," Alexander continued, "you two will come with me, and we will enter the catacombs anew and proceed into the uncharted areas located in the recesses of the passageways. If all goes well and my bearings are accurate Keith, I expect to exit right there." He turned and pointed into the darkness of the dry lake bed. "I noticed a hole toward the bottom and suspect the water drained through there into the newly exposed hidden compartment of the catacombs."

"Wont the tombs be flooded?" Anika asked.

"A good question." He smiled at her renewed interest in the planning, hoping it signaled an end to her worry. "I suspect Naamah, or her cohorts at the very least, engineered the explosions in such a manner that should they breach the floor of the lake, the water would be forced to empty somewhere other than the illucid hidden chamber. Any other scenario would risk destruction or loss of whatever lie secreted away in the veiled chamber of the catacombs."

Anika nodded. "So, no scuba gear, then?"

"I should hope not, as I haven't got any scuba gear right this moment."

Anika let a slight smile form and it further set Alex's mind at ease. "You may join us, or you may accompany Keith and Abi. Your call."

"Well, if it's all the same to you—"

"Be it known now; I will not permit you to engage in a dialogue with

Naamah should we cross paths with the venomous creature. Understood? Her words will only spread through your mind like poison. Her truths are lies and can serve you in no manner."

Anika rolled her eyes, but finally agreed. "I will be with you then, okay?"

"Agreed." Alexander started for the small hill that led to the catacombs across and below. Kate, Serket, and Anika quickly fell in line at his side, and within minutes they were at the service entrance to the church.

"We will have to break in, I am afraid, my fellow burglars." Alex withdrew several tools from within the hidden recesses of his long coat and set to work on the lock.

"Ahem." Serket caught Alexander's attention just in time for him to shift to one side as her foot planted heavily against the old wooden door. The door gave way instantly under her force and flew open into the dim light of the empty church.

"Time is—"

"Of the essence," Alexander finished with a wink.

Alexander and Serket charged across the church to the entrance to the catacombs below. Kate and Anika followed closely behind, and soon the four were ascending into the ancient burial chambers.

"Silence is requisite from this point forward," Alexander demanded as they gathered at the start of the labyrinth of the dead. "A demon's sense of hearing is akin to that of a rabbit; if she has not already sensed our presence, I do not want to signal her with unnecessary noise or chatter."

Alexander used hand gestures to direct Kate and Anika, keeping them close to the walls on either side of him, while he and Serket moved furtively down the center of the pathway. Alexander noticed Kate suddenly become excited at something she had encountered along the route. He watched pensively as she pointed, eyes bulging, at one of the residents of the ancient mausoleum. Alexander was overcome with an inordinate amount of comical relief as he watched her struggle with every fiber of her being to not vocalize her find.

Later, he finally mouthed to her and signaled her onward.

As the group neared the end of the "professional's room," the section of tomb that counted lawyers, doctors, and the like amongst its inhabitants, their ears pricked up to the sound of indiscernible chatter and movement ahead. Alexander motioned to the others to pick up the pace as they quickly passed through the remaining chambers and arrived at the huge blast hole in the far wall of the catacombs.

Alexander retrieved a tarnished, well-weathered compass, and held it up before him in the direction of the shrine's gaping void. *West-southwest, runs right at the dried lake basin,* he thought to himself and smiled at the others. Holding a hand up to keep them at bay, he stepped through the hole into the musty cavity beyond the known space of the catacombs. Storm was about to signal the others to enter as well, when he perceived all sound had ceased. Dead silence filled the air, and he feared they were found out. The three watched as Alexander's hand shot out from the darkness back at them, his palm turned out, gesturing them to halt.

Once he was certain the others understood his command, Alexander turned and ventured further into the dark, damp orifice. After traveling a hundred feet or so, he arrived at a most unusual phenomenon. A wall of water blocked his path, stretching from floor to ceiling, side to side, as if suspended in midair in the passageway. He quickly surmised that his nemesis was on the other side, and that was why the sounds they had heard earlier had ceased. Naamah had made good use of her accomplices skills with regard to stone blasting.

Without attempting to proceed further, he hastily made his way back to the others.

"Come," he said in a low whisper, to each of their surprise. "Follow me."

"What is it?" Kate asked, reaching out to touch the cascade.

Alex grabbed her hand before it found the water, and he shook his head. Kate withdrew it and took a step back. "Sorry," she said, the words barely audible.

Alex paid her no mind and huddled the others together so he could address them at a nearly inaudible level.

"The water that drained from the lake must be trapped above here and flowing down, running through a cut in the ceiling of the chamber to the opening in the floor directly beneath. Its flow is being throttled by the tight space, and thus will continue to create an illusion of a wall of water until the entire lake, which is trapped somewhere within the Earth above us, drains to the cavern below us. Or floods these catacombs," he added gravely.

Serket nodded, clearly impressed by the illusion.

"I don't know how thick the wall is," he continued, "nor what lies on the other side, so we must be prepared."

Without further hesitancy, Alex thrust his arm into the flowing water. It passed through the stream and finally came into contact with the cool, balmy air on the other side. Turning to the others with a smile, he launched his body through the water wall and stumbled upon the hard rock floor on the other side. Quickly apprising the situation, he rose and walked about, surveying the chamber. It was barren except for the tremendous, intricately carved white sarcophagus at the center. Alex's eyes widened as they took in the incredible sight before him. Running his hands over its surface reliefs, he circled the stone coffin. His attentions were momentarily diverted as Serket passed through the aquatic barrier to join him. Her companions swiftly followed suit, shaking the soaking water from their vestments as they came clear of the deluge from above. All immediately feel under the trance of the great white sarcophagus at the chamber's center. Serket moved closer and studied the complex design of the battle scenes that comprised the side of the ivory-like cask. Soldiers on horseback engaged in battle with foot soldiers, lions, dogs and an antlered creature all adorned the stone vessel in brilliant detail.

"Amazing," Kate finally broke the awe inspired silence that had befallen the group. "Is this what we're looking for?"

"Quite assuredly, my dear," Alex replied as he moved closer to the stone artifact. "We must slide the top. Quickly."

Serket rushed to his side. "Alex. Alex, do you realize what this is?"

"I do," he replied as he pushed the top slab. "The last resting place of Alexander the Great— help me open it, if you will."

"Oh my God," Kate repeated over and over. "We just found the tomb of Alexander the Great! Oh my God. I can't breathe!"

"Breathe, please. Come here and help," Storm prodded, fully appreciating her enthusiasm over the find, but needing them to make haste nonetheless.

It took a tremendous amount of force and leverage, but eventually the stone top gradually gave way. The sound of sliding stone on stone echoed against the rush of water in the background. Particles of dust and ancient debris danced in the air as Alexander sprang up onto the edge of the vessel and peered down at its contents.

"He is in here!" he announced with more than a modicum of pride, no longer concealing his excitement.

"Oh my God!" Kate screamed again, hoisting herself up next to Alex with the grace of a gymnast. She stared down at the well-preserved face of the great warrior. Only then was she rendered speechless.

"His arms are out of place." Storm reached down into the sarcophagus and gently felt about, trying his best to not disturb the revered warrior.

"What?" Serket called to him.

"Out of place," he repeated. "This tomb has already been desecrated!"

An uneasy feeling crept over him, and he leaped down. As his feet thumped against the stone and soil below, his heightened senses caused him to scan his surroundings.

"Looking for this, Storm?" Naamah's laughter echoed throughout the small chamber.

Serket reached up and snatched Kate down to the floor. She grabbed Anika's arm with her free hand and dragged them both to cover at the rear of the sarcophagus.

"Stay put," she directed them both. "Don't move a muscle."

Once she was sure they understood the gravity of the situation, she emerged from the shelter of the stone vessel to Storm's side.

"Seems you are late once again, Alexander Storm!" Naamah goaded him as she pranced about the chamber, never taking her eyes off the pair. "Another failure, I'm afraid."

Alexander apprised the situation as he tried to make out the long, flowing object folded over her arm. Naamah caught sight of his inquisitive eyes and laughed.

"You don't even know what you were looking for," she hissed. "You fucking fool."

She stopped her manic pacing, then grasped the object in her arms and held it up to the light. "Look familiar, Storm?"

Alexander strained to make out the object, when all at once its pattern and shape became clear.

Naamah laughed once more, realizing he had finally figured it out.

"What is it, Alex?" Serket asked.

"It is an ancient cloak," he replied, his voice drained of all emotion, defeated.

"Ding ding!" Naamah toyed. "Give that man a prize!"

"You will burn," Alexander said as he moved toward the demon.

"Not likely," she replied. "Your scorpion bitch still looks a bit confused."

Alex looked at Serket. "It is the cloak of the great serpent, fashioned from the gift of his skin."

Serket understood instantly—she was well acquainted with the ancient Egyptian tale.

"It is the key to all, Storm." Red flames danced in the demon's eyes, her face shifted and pulled. "And it is mine!"

Alexander stepped forward and thrust his arms to his sides, exposing the long blades which had been concealed beneath his sleeves.

"Although it was my intention to tear you limb from limb, scorpion," Naamah said and smiled a most terrible smile directly at Serket, "I must take my leave before I am missed."

"Give it your best, whore of Lucifer!" Serket cried out, hoping to stall the demon's departure.

"If I were *you two*, I would be more concerned with the *other two* you left up top," Naamah said with a cruel laugh. "I am sure my wolves have already had their feast!"

"I shall end this now!" Alexander cried, launching toward the demon with his blades. Swiping both in opposite unison across Naamah's torso, he was sure he heard her scream out in pain before she vanished into the worm hole that had opened behind her.

Anika stood at the side of the sarcophagus, ready to charge. "Follow her! Follow her to William!" she implored.

Alexander ignored her cries and dashed further into the unexplored chamber, exiting out into the tunnel the demon had entered from. The others were doing their best to keep pace with him.

"The exit into the lake basin should be right ahead," he called out, "that is how the demon arrived so surreptitiously at our repose beside the sarcophagus."

Kate's head was spinning. How could she have left him after swearing to herself they would never be separated during this quest again?

"Up ahead!" Alex pointed at the hole leading to the surface which was opening up before him.

One by one they passed through the exit hole into the cool Mediterranean night air only to be overtaken by the stench of burning chemicals and plastics and the sight of their truck, ablaze in a hellish inferno.

142

Decker dove across the dimly lit room of stone, retreating back into the shallow hole in the wall he had found. The room was dark and concealed his location well. He had ventured out to survey his surroundings, as well as a cluster of the rooms close to his, several times in the past few days. He had concluded that he was in the subterranean quarters of an archaic stone structure, most likely a castle. The architecture and design of the areas he had explored leant to European origins, but he remained unsure of his exact location. He had been sure Naamah had him when he first exited the portal and he thought she was speaking to his shadowed figure. However, it seemed she was figuratively addressing the papyrus in her hand and not him. After coming into view momentarily, she had exited the room and he had not seen her since. Although he heard commotion and muffled voices at various times throughout the day, no one else had entered the room since his arrival. Decker had quickly located the cracked section of wall in the corner of the room. His safe haven was not only cracked, but was also missing several stones which afforded him plenty of room to secret his body away. His concealment was amplified by the large stone altar which stood between him and the doorway. He had decided to stay put until a definitive advantage presented itself. He was no fool, and was not about to sacrifice himself for a mere attempt on Naamah or

Moloch. It would have to be a sure thing. He was willing to perish in the pursuit of destroying his unaware captors, but only if he was sure to take one or both of them with him.

Decker had whittled away several hours performing a complete inventory of the items he was carrying. Among his most useful finds were a vial of holy water, a small antique crucifix from the time of the plague, a zippo lighter etched with skull and crossbones, three shotgun shells, a gravity knife, and a shard of pottery from ancient Assyria depicting a full-blown devil's trap in relief form. What any or all of these items would amount to was beyond him at this point. But he wanted the objects fresh in his mind should a situation arise which called for some good old exorcist ingenuity.

Decker peered out of the recesses of his hideaway as the fire and smoke that had triggered his retreat grew and filled the room with light. This might be the chance he had been waiting for. A portal was opening. Reaching into his vest, he grabbed the vial of blessed water and inched his way toward the edge of the opening. *400 Twisting his body around one-hundred and eighty degrees, he allowed his feet to drop to the floor, the rest of his body squirming and inching behind. The room was still aglow with the rapture of the wormhole, and he slid up against the side of the stone altar. Moving slowly and silently, he peered around the corner into the room.

It was Naamah. She was carrying something. A robe or dress of some kind. Its material shimmered in the fading light of the closing wormhole. Decker ducked back out of sight as the demon turned and moved toward the altar. Had she seen him? Had she sensed his presence? As he lay there wondering if he was going to be forced into what most likely would be a losing battle, he heard the large stone slab above him grind and slide as she pushed it ajar, exposing a hollowed-out chamber within. Decker could make out part of her through the space between the altar's top and its base frame, and he watched as she placed the item she was carrying into the compartment. He dropped flat on the floor as the demon took hold of the altar's top and slid it back into place. He remained still until he heard Naamah's heels click away toward the door, at which time he stuck his head out again. He watched her slender artistically strut across the room and reach for the ornate brass door handle. Her hand froze on the handle, and she remained motionless. Her chin rose slightly, and she remained still, listening, he surmised, for a moment. That was it. Her supernatural senses had picked up on his shallow breathes. Or maybe even his beating heart, racing away in his chest; because although he could command the rhythm of his breathing, he held no control over this muscle's cadence.

Releasing the handle, Naamah backed into the center of the room and quickly undid her long cloak, allowing it to drop to the floor at her feet. Puzzled, Decker watched as the rest of her clothes followed her cloak to the cold stone below. He marveled at the perfection of her body, which was more than evident, even in the poor light of the room. What was she up to? If she knew he was there, why not just dispatch him? Did she seek to seduce him over to the dark?

Quickly, Naamah moved to the far wall of the room opposite Decker, and with a bout of reverse physics, blew the candle on the wall alight. The flame grew strong, causing shadows to dance across the chamber's walls and the demon's flawless features.

Damn, Decker thought to himself and laughed. *I hope she's not going the seduction route.* His humor in the face of fear was soon dismissed when the door flew open, and Moloch stepped over the threshold into the candlelight.

"There you are!" Moloch strolled toward his evil counterpart. "My black angel—where ever have you been?"

"About," she answered playfully, teasing her hair with her fingers. "Where have *you* been?"

Decker's blood froze as Moloch moved to her in a fraction of a second, grasping her long locks in his hand and yanking her head back.

With a low, guttural wolf's growl, he said, "I asked you a question, bitch. And I will be answered. *Now.*"

Naamah's hand shot out into Moloch's side as she drove her long nails through his clothes and into his skin, causing him to recoil ever-so slightly. His retraction was sufficient enough for her to wiggle free of his grasp, and she took a step back toward Decker.

"I thought your inquiry was in jest," Naamah blurted out as Moloch moved at her again. "Where do you *think* I have been?"

Moloch stood motionless, very close to her nude body and stared into her eyes.

"I do not know. That is why I asked." His voice had returned to some semblance of normality. "You have been secretive in your movements as of late. Lucifer has granted you the power to come and go at will, making it impossible to track you."

"A free spirit," she replied.

"Yes." Moloch laughed as he walked to the altar and leaned his back against the cold stone. His position made him invisible from Decker's vantage point.

"So, humor me. This room is filled with the acrid scent of Hell. A portal was open in here. Where have you returned from?"

Decker hadn't noticed the aroma of sulfur, but now, upon the suggestive words of Moloch, the stinging scent filled his nose and lungs.

"I return from the sands of Osiris, my prince." Naamah's tone was melodic, and her tongue darted from her lips as she spoke. "We are close now, are we not?"

"We are." He walked to the wall across from the altar and back into Decker's view. "So close I can taste the culmination of our efforts."

"*Our* efforts," Naamah purred as she began to pace back and forth in front of the muscular demon, his eyes following every curve and muscle flex of her legs.

"That is what I said," Moloch barked.

"I was making preparations, my lord." Her exaggerated movements drew him to her body and not her words. "Gathering the soldiers we require to ensure our ritual proceeds uninterrupted and without issue."

"Clever girl." Moloch laughed.

"What did you think I was up to?" She stopped, eyes squinting, lips pouting. "Are we not the perfect team? Baptized by fire, entwined by our bodies and our mutual desire to cast the world into darkness."

Bravo, Decker thought. He had to control his desire to stand and clap at this performance. She was now the master. She had reversed their roles with but a few words and even less clothing. She was playing him. The ancient Prince of Hell was putty in her hands. Decker had a mind to rise and demand Moloch retrieve her secret from within the altar. But he was unsure how that would play out, and he was pretty sure however it went, he would be annihilated at the end of it. Nope. He would remain hidden and enjoy the show.

"Come to me," Moloch commanded her, and she responded. Dropping to her knees in front of him, she looked up into his eyes with all the winds and fires of Hell radiating from her beauty.

"I am your servant, my prince." She undid his pants as she spoke. "There is no need to doubt my allegiance. I am with you until the end and beyond into the great and long night."

Moloch reached out and grasped her hair once again, this time with forceful passion.

"I do not doubt you," he whispered, "but you must be kept in check, my dear. Of that I have no doubt, either."

"Only *you* have the fortitude to do so." Naamah smiled up at him.

"Enough talk." Moloch pulled his shirt over his head and threw it to the side, landing in front of Decker.

"If you wish to silence me, master," she said, biting her lip between words, "shove something in my mouth."

Oh, Christ, Decker thought to himself as he dropped back into full seclusion behind the altar. He sat there in silence as the room filled with the moans and howls of the demons' copulation.

After what felt like an eternity, Decker shifted his position and peered around the corner of the altar. *Just a peek. No harm in that.*

He watched as their bodies thrusted in kinetic unison. Naamah's head moved about in the rhythmic motion of their furious passion. Her lips parted, echoing sounds of erotic delight in response to each drive of Moloch's hips. Her eyes—her eyes did not move at all. They were locked on Decker's, staring straight into his soul.

143

"The subterranean world below St. Peter's consists of two layers," Le'Strat informed his captive audience. "The grottoes, which are directly below us, and the ancient necropolis, which lies below the grottoes."

He raised one hand flat and placed the other on top of it mimicking the layers. Nodding to Sam, he continued, "The necropolis dates back to the Romans and still holds evidence of the pagan ancestors who first marked this land."

"Wow." Samantha was genuinely intrigued by the tale. "So, one of the most holy Christian locations in the world—"

"Catholic," Jericho corrected.

"*Catholic*," she repeated, slicing at him with enunciation tantamount to a verbal knife. Jericho stared at her, waiting a second before smirking. His smile was returned with a wink. He was definitely rough around the edges, of that there was no doubt. And yet, at the same time, there was something gentle, even innocently reserved about him at times. Sam couldn't help but like him. She didn't care what scorpion lady thought. She could recognize a good man when she saw one.

"Continue." Le'Strat was visibly pleased to engage in any historical conversation regarding his home.

Sam nodded and continued. "As I was saying, the most holy place is built upon the foundations of paganism. Fascinating."

Lobo chuckled. "Fascinating, huh?"

"For real? Right now?" Samantha looked back and forth between her two companions. "Are you guys five years old, or what?"

"Young lady," Le'Strat interjected, "you must forgive them their Western ignorance. It may be the age of your country that is reflected in the behavior and mannerisms of your American men."

"Woah there, Prince Charles." Sam's demeanor quickly morphed. "Pretty sure American men are the bravest, smartest, most creative, and driven men in the world."

"American women," Jericho nodded.

"What?" Samantha snarled in his direction.

"I said American women." He took a step toward her. "American men *and* women."

"Oh." Sam smiled. "Yes...sorry."

"No problem, kiddo," he said and laughed as he walked past her toward the great metal doors, flicking her earlobe as he did.

"Then you go and ruin it." She rubbed her ear and didn't turn to face him.

"See?" Le'Strat smiled. "Like the Three Stooges."

"Yeah, I got nothing." Samantha returned to her inquiry. "So, all this is built upon the foundations of the Roman gods, and the church is okay with that?"

"Don't open the door yet, Francis," Le'Strat ordered. Jericho dropped his hands and leaned an ear against the door. "Wait, please."

"Yes, the church is fine with this." He walked to Sam's side. "It is the foundation—the root of our beliefs. In the days after Christ, the church shunned those roots because the fear of the pagan ways reestablishing themselves was a valid threat. Today we do not fear such things, and we find embracing the history and the evolution of the Church is most effective."

"Maybe the church should reevaluate that stance," Jericho turned, "those pagan ways are doing their best to reemerge."

"There is a vast difference between Satanism and Paganism my friend,"

Le'Strat pointed out, joining him at the pair of oversized double doors. "These are known as the Doors of Death."

"Why do you call them that?" Lobo joined the others, eager to lend to the inquiry Sam was finding so *fascinating*.

"Nothing so dramatic as the name would suggest, I'm afraid. Funeral processions entered through this way."

Lobo nodded. "Ah, makes sense."

Le'Strat checked the time on his cell phone and urged the others to back away from the doors.

"Very good." He signaled for them to retreat to the darker corner of the hall. "Let me ensure our path is clear, and we will proceed."

"Are we entering through the altar?" Sam smiled. The idea of such a secret entrance, in the middle of such a historic and well-visited place, sparked her curiosity.

She frowned at his reply. "No, there is a less conspicuous manner of entry. Sorry to disappoint."

Le'Strat unlocked the Doors of Death and pulled the right side open slightly. Peering in through the crack, he did his best to surveil the main hall of St. Peter's. The church was usually empty during this time of night. All of the tourists were gone, and the guards and clergy were at dinner or retired to their rooms.

"Looks good," he motioned the others, "let's go— mirror my path, if you will."

The group swiftly made their way through the church behind Le'Strat's lead. He was forced to make Sam focus once or twice along the way, as the grandeur of her surroundings acted as the perfect distraction.

Stopping before the stunning monument of Pope Alexander VII, Le'Strat pointed to the small wooden door below the celebrated sculpture.

"Who is that?" Sam whispered at his side.

"Alexander VII," he replied as he fumbled with a large ring of keys. *403 "The sculpture depicts the pope, on his knees, engaged in deep prayer. Death appears to his holiness, holding an hour-glass to signify the threat of time. Alexander VII remains stoic, unfazed by the reaper's message."

"Appropriate," Jericho said with his back to them as he scanned the church for any strays.

"Quite." Le'Strat inserted the ancient skeleton key into the lock, and it responded with an audible click. "Shall we enter the realm of death?"

The three said nothing as they walked past him over the threshold. Le'Strat followed, then shut and locked the heavy oak door behind them. After giving them the signal to stay put, he disappeared into the darkness ahead. But soon, the strange thump and click of a switch sounded. The stone-encased hall soon grew aglow with the artificial lights that lined it.

"That's better, no?" Le'Strat smiled at his handiwork.

"I'll say," Sam joked. "I wasn't going in there, otherwise."

Le'Strat laughed. "Nothing here to fear, my dear. Just the dead, sleeping the eternal sleep."

"Whatever." She shot Lobo a skeptical look. "Not sure I believe that load of crap anymore." Lobo winked in agreement.

"Le'Strat knows better as well." Jericho walked to his friend and tapped him on the back. "'That is not dead which can eternal lie' and all that mumbo jumbo, right."

"Lovecraft," Sam blurted out to Frank's obvious surprise. "Don't looked so shocked. I can read, you know?"

"Never doubted it for a moment."

Le'Strat changed the subject back to the matter at hand. "Tell me where we must visit first. We have limited time. Unless you want to spend the night down here."

"Nope." Sam looked at their guide. "Tomb of Osiris."

Le'Strat squinted in thought for a moment and then smiled. "Egyptians, of course."

"That's right," Jericho confirmed. "Up ahead, yes?"

"Yes, about midway through."

Sam marveled at their surroundings. The brick and stone walled walkway ran ahead of them and out of sight. The walls were constructed from an amalgam of blocks of all shapes and sizes, each with a different shade of red or brown. The layering of the mortared rocks lacked perfection, and various stones jutted out or sank too deeply in. To the left and right were doorways and passages to tombs, many adorned with arches or similar designating designs. The underbelly of the grottoes above created the ceiling of the hall they were in which was scattered with holes leading to the sacred tombs above. The overall effect of the catacombs was that of a quaint village road at night. It was surreal, and Sam felt a strange sensation deep in her gut, as if she had stepped into some ancient city where all the inhabitants were tucked away in their beds.

As the group proceeded further into the tombs, they came across stone sarcophaguses housed in protective glass or plexiglass.

"Each of these rooms we are passing were either contracted by the wealthy patrons of the church for their family shrines or for high officials of the church."

"It really is something," Lobo called out as he stuck his head through a doorway on their right. The interior was lined with niches in the stone for the placement of corpses. The walls, crafted of white stone and plaster, still held the faint remnants of colorful murals and paintings that had graced the crypts.

"That is the tomb of L. Tullius Zethus," Le'Strat called out. "It is one of the most decorative, lined with mosaics and stone urns. You should all take a look."

"No time for sightseeing," Jericho continued forward towards their objective. Peering back over his shoulder, he called out again for Sam and Lobo to catch up.

"You are right, my friend." Le'Strat picked up the pace with Jericho. "We have a schedule."

After passing several more entrances leading to tombs of various sizes and designs, they finally arrived at the tomb of the Egyptians, which lie to their left. The entire front façade of the room was missing, which allowed the four of them to look inside at once.

"Well," Le'Strat broke the silence. "What's next, my friend?"

Jericho reached into his pocket and extracted a small piece of paper. "Let's see—"

"'Find the Westerners' bird,'" Sam said, "'and remove its perching tile.'"

Jericho read the scrap and looked up. "Yeah, she's got it."

"Told you I could read." Sam smiled.

"Yes, yes." Le'Strat stepped forward and snatched the riddle from Frank. "Let us see."

The three stood silently while Le'Strat read the words and then looked at the interior of the tomb. He walked about a bit within while the others watched pensively.

"What is it?" Lobo asked.

"Anything?" Jericho added, stepping into the tomb as well.

"There!" Le'Strat called out, pointing to some artistry on the center of the north wall. "There's your bird, Jericho!"

Sam and Lobo quickly joined their companions and found the image their guide was referring to—a brilliantly painted rendition of Horus, the ancient Egyptian falcon-headed god.

"Kinda outta place down here," Frank said. But Le'Strat only looked at him, saying nothing.

"You sure it's what we're looking for?"

"Yup." Jericho ran his hand gently over the image. "Horus is the son of Osiris, and he is associated with the realms of the dead."

"Okay, obviously." Sam didn't see the connection to the riddle besides the fact that Horus was winged.

Jericho shook his head with slight annoyance. "Ancient Egyptians buried their dead on the west side of the Nile and lived on the eastern shores. They eventually began to call their dead, 'Westerners,' in honor of this tradition."

"Ahh," Sam understood. "'Westerner's bird.'"

"Bingo!" Jericho yanked a small blade from his belt and snapped it open.

"What are you doing, Francis?" Le'Strat stepped toward him. "You said no damage, no desecration."

He acted before his old friend could stop him. "I need this stone! The little birdie's perch!"

Jericho inserted his blade into the groove of an oddly situated tile below the image of Horus and pried it free. He let the stone to drop to the ground, exposing a dark hole beneath. Reaching in with his fingers, the others watched as he felt around.

"Anything?" Sam exclaimed. "Let me try! My hands are smaller."

Jericho looked back and nodded her over. He watched as she inserted her hand up to her wrist.

"I feel something!" Sam shouted. "I almost can—got it!" she cried, withdrawing her closed fist.

"What is it?" Jericho demanded.

Sam opened her hand, and in the center of her palm was a finely etched, red glass star.

"'The Morning Star,'" Le'Strat said, peering down at the sheet of paper still in his hand. "Looks like we visit Satan next."

"What?" Lobo asked as he reached around to the small pistol concealed at his back.

"Easy, cowboy." Jericho jumped forward and pushed Lobo's muscular arm back to his side. "What do you mean?"

"Mausoleum U." Le'Strat was already heading farther into the catacombs. "It is known as Lucifer's Tomb because of the painting of Lucifer—The Morning Star—on the back wall."

"Rise like the Morning Star," Sam called out after Le'Strat.

The four explorers moved quickly through the maze of catacombs, with Le'Strat in the lead.

"Here!" He pointed, finally coming to a stop before a tomb that was almost completely obfuscated by the foundations from above. "There, on the wall, Jericho."

Frank stepped passed him and into the relatively small chamber. On the back wall of white, centered in a large painted square of red, was Satan himself, atop a bucking wild horse.

"Holy crap." Sam stood on her tiptoes to see over Le'Strat's shoulders. "What the hell is that doing under the Vatican?"

And once again, Le'Strat said nothing with regard to the seemingly out of place depictions. Instead, he stepped into the tight quarters and turned to Sam. "May I have a look, young lady?"

Jericho nodded to Sam in agreement. Le'Strat lifted the star up to the light and was able to see through the opaque glass that comprised it. There were, however, several deep etches of symbols scattered about within the glass itself.

"Here, look." Le'Strat offered the star to Jericho.

"I see it. What does it mean?"

Sam and Lobo shifted and shimmied into the small tomb to lend to the investigation. Stopping in front of the eerie fresco, Lobo brought his face to within inches of its surface. Reaching out, he ran his hand over the ancient art and realized that, contrary to first glance, the painting was not flaking. Instead, when viewed at close range, the system of odd shapes and squiggles on the surface were, in fact, part of the painting. He thought for a few moments and then turned to Jericho.

"Hey." He beckoned him to the painting. "Hold the star up and get close to the surface."

Jericho, unsure of Lobo's intentions, complied nonetheless since there were no other viable options at that point. Raising the star to eye level, Jericho studied the surface through the red lens. Suddenly, he understood Lobo's insight.

"I see!" he yelled. "Just gotta line the marks up, —yes?"

"That's the idea!" Lobo laughed, pleased with what he hoped would be a solid assist.

"Very good!" Le'Strat tapped Lobo on the back. "Well done."

"Yeah," Sam joined in the praise by flashing her pearly whites at Lobo, "nice job, rockst—"

"*Got it!*" Frank shouted, unable to contain his excitement. "Now what?"

"Try pressing it against the wall," Lobo said, driven by his successful insight into the first phase of the riddle. "Keep the symbols lined up."

Jericho shrugged. "Makes sense."

The others watched as Frank, still eyeing up the star by looking through it, moved it forward into its mirrored position in the portrait of Lucifer. *406 Suddenly, the star flew from Jericho's hand and came to rest firmly against the wall. The others watched as the deep ruby glass began to take on a chilling glow. Suddenly, the floating star of glass began to spin, the rate of its rotation quickly picking up pace.

Jericho took a step back to the others and watched in awe. Looking around to check their surroundings, he huddled them closer together. No way he was going through another bout of the shit he went through in the Canyon. At least not alone, anyway.

The spinning red star morphed into a circular blur, rotating in place furiously.

"Perhaps we should exit?" Le'Strat grabbed Jericho's arm.

Before he could respond, the stars circling came to an abrupt halt and burst, shattering across the room into a finite number of pieces, spraying them with a mist of red dust.

"What manner of magic is this?" Le'Strat cried out, visibly disturbed by the events unfolding before him.

Jericho grabbed his shoulder to steady him. "Old magic, brother. Very old magic."

As the four turned to escape the unknown, a low, powerful, grinding sound began to emanate from the red and backed mural of Satan. Sam and the others watched as the squared outline of the image broke free of the wall, separating from the stone, and rose several inches from the surface, suspended in the air, unfettered. Not a breath or sigh could be heard until the stillness was broken by the thunderous smashing of the fresco to the floor. The force of the impact was so great that it turned the archaic imagery to dust at their feet.

There, inside the space of missing wall where the mural had once been, lay the papyrus.

"Lobo!" Jericho waved him in. "I think you should do the honors, buddy."

Lobo proudly stepped up, eyes darting from side-to-side, and retrieved the clear crystal cylinder containing the riddle's prize.

"We must move now," Le'Strat prodded them, his voice barely a whisper. "Our window to escape unnoticed is closing fast."

Jericho nodded and turned to usher the others out of Lucifer's Tomb. A strange wind brushed against his checks. Gentle wisps at first, swiftly turned to frigid gusts rushing into the small opening of the room; stopping them all dead in their tracks. The draft chilled the stone chamber and ushered in air that was thick and heavy.

"Where's that coming from?" Sam asked, looking about the rocky ruins for the source.

Jericho spoke not a word at first, trying to measure the gravity of their circumstances. Scanning his surroundings, he searched for venues of retreat and gauged the sustainability of areas of cover. His eyes continued to traverse the ancient necropolis, searching for both the source of the chilling wind, as well as the best route to flee what was surely about to escalate into a cataclysmic event for the small group of subterranean investigators. Although it was Jericho's eyes which were currently employed in the task of resolving their current predicament, it was the sharp senses of his nose that caused those same eyes to bulge in fear as he uttered a single word.

"*Sulfur!*"

Lucifer Locus

144

"Feel better?" Naamah inquired with a grin as Moloch lifted himself and sat on the ground between her spread legs. She already knew the answer of course.

"Immensely!" He laughed and slapped Naamah's inner thigh playfully. "But there is work to be done, my dear."

Before Naamah could respond, a solid fist rapped against the chamber door. Moloch looked in its direction and then back to Naamah, who remained motionless.

"See?"

Naamah rolled her eyes. "So insightful, my lord."

"That I am."

The knocking upon the door came once more. "What is it?" Moloch demanded.

The rusty creak of the ancient doorknob resounded throughout the stone room, and Moloch responded with frustration, "I did not say enter!"

"My apologies, Great One."

"Speak now," Naamah called out, "or be gone."

"A dispatch from Rome, my lord." The voice, partially muffled by the door's wooden barrier, sounded desperate. "There is something amiss at Saint Peter's."

"Something?" Moloch echoed, struggling free of Naamah's long legs that were attempting to ensnare his body. He rose to his feet. "Amiss?"

"Yes, my king."

"Did my imbedded offer anything more?" he asked, gathering his clothes that had been strewn about the chamber.

"They instructed I tell you a solitary word."

"Yes? Damn it— speak!" Moloch's impatience swelled as he headed to the door.

"Storm!" The voice called out. "Storm!"

Moloch stopped in his tracks and turned to Naamah, who had laid back, flat on the floor. "I must away to Rome."

"Shall I join you?"

"No." He paused a moment to think.

"My lord!" the voice bellowed from beyond the door once more.

"Silence!" the demon demanded, and the messenger complied.

"You will head to Nepal, my dear," he directed Naamah. "I will deal with Rome and make my way to the Copan ruins."

"As you wish," she whispered.

"We shall join each other at the journey's end to perform the ritual."

Naamah smiled. "We are so very close."

"Soon the darkness will creep across all lands— consuming all men— and the eternal night will be all— and all will be night."

Naamah closed her eyes and let a hearty laugh escape her lips. "Soon, my prince."

Moloch turned his back to her, facing the far wall of the room. "If you would be so kind?"

"Rome?" she confirmed.

"Saint Peter's Square."

Without rising, Naamah fumbled through the inner lining of her long cloak which lined the floor beneath her.

"When in Rome," she said musingly and tossed the stone in front of Moloch, causing the fire and smoke of a wormhole to burst open before him.

"Murder the Romans," he finished as he stepped through the succubus's portal and disappeared.

Decker stared at the walls around him as the reflecting light of the magical transport's flames faded and disappeared. He remained motionless and out of sight.

"My lord?" The voice came from beyond the door once more.

"Begone!" Naamah screamed. "Now!"

Decker could hear the messenger's footsteps on the stone ground beyond the room fade into the distance. They were alone. Perhaps he had imagined their connection. Maybe she had just been staring into the darkness and not deep into the recesses of his soul.

"Did you enjoy that, priest?"

Decker, against his better judgment, leaned around the corner of the altar to Naamah's prone body.

"Did you enjoy watching him fuck me, priest?" she asked, rising unnaturally, without the use of her hands and arms, to a seated position.

Decker snickered as he stepped out from behind the altar. "I'm pretty sure *you* were fucking *him*."

The demon rose to her feet. "Ha! Let me assure you, your sharp words are not lost on me."

Stepping to the side and turning her back to Decker, Naamah bent over at her hips to retrieve the cloak at her feet. "Clever priest."

Decker, sensing it could be his only chance, charged to the center of the chamber.

"How many times must I tell you, bitch," he cried, lifting his arm over his head and to the side like a pitcher about to unleash a fast ball. "*I am no priest!*"

Decker's arm snapped forward as she turned to face him. With little, if any, effort, the demon shifted slightly to the side as Decker's vial of holy water sailed past her and shattered on the wall behind her.

"Really?" she smirked, raising one brow at him. "I thought we were proceeding civilly here—for a spell?"

Decker, sensing she was serious, quickly replied, "Sorry. Force of habit."

She laughed again and Decks watched her bare stomach muscles tighten from between her parted cloak.

"Habit. Was that purposeful, priest?" She was enjoying the word play.

"Jeez." Decker shook his head. "I...am not...a priest."

Naamah said nothing, but instead walked to the corner of the chamber, opposite of Decker's current position, to a small wood table he was sure had not been there seconds before. Picking up a decanter, she pulled the glass stop and poured herself a goblet of wine. Raising the chalice to her lips, she took a hearty gulp and turned to Decker. Raising the glass to him, he nodded and walk cautiously to her side. Picking up another goblet, Naamah poured a tall drink and reached out to hand it to Decker. Just before his fingers wrapped around the stem of the cup, Naamah pulled it away.

"What do we say?" she whispered seductively.

Decker, who had not eaten or drank anything for at least forty-eight hours, did not hesitate. "Please and fucking thank you?"

"Brilliant," Naamah said and laughed as she gave him the drink and watched him guzzle its contents down with two giant gulps.

"May I have another, kind sir?" He said in his best broken old English accent.

Smiling, the demon refilled his glass and placed the decanter down. "You can pour yourself the next one, priest," she replied.

"I told you—"

"I know, I know," she interrupted. "But it pisses you off, so..."

Decker shook his head and took another swig of the red wine. It was fermented to perfection. The flavors—a mixture of dry and wet, sweet and savory—tickled his parched tongue like diamonds in the rough of a mine.

Naamah was eyeing him, her partially naked body still visible through her parted cloak. "I am quite sure you truly are not a priest."

"How's that?" Decker asked, his mind, fueled by the wine in his empty stomach, began to swim about.

"Any of the priests that pass our way would have either seized the opportunity to align themselves with Moloch," she said, then paused as Decker rocked his head back and forth, pondering the suggestion. "Or," she continued, "they would have joined in our little orgy."

Decker's eyes peered at her from above the goblet that was once again at his lips. He watched as her long fingers traced the contours of her body from breast to belly.

"Well, demon," he started, lowering his cup. "That is not the majority... at all."

"So, you say," she whispered casually.

Decker took the final gulp of his wine and set the glass down.

"What is this exactly?"

"This *is* whatever I want it to be."

"Meaning?"

Naamah said nothing and gathered up the rest of her clothes. Dressing, she nodded to the altar.

"I know you saw."

Decker said nothing.

"You didn't really believe I did not know you followed me through the wormhole, did you?" She studied his face. "Oh my— you did! Silly prie—" she stopped herself. "Silly boy."

Fully dressed, the demon walked over to the altar and effortlessly slid the top over on an angle so it rested on the walls of the main body below.

"You could have been a bird," she said, smiling a dangerous smile, "and sang your tale to Moloch— exposing my deception "

Decker nodded and acknowledged her assumption was true. "I did not wish to protect you, make no mistake. I simply felt it was against my best interests to make my presence known to your master."

"Master?" Naamah chuckled. "Are all men truly so stupid?"

Decker shrugged, exposing his clear ignorance of both the arrangement between the demons as well as the purpose of the interaction that was presently ensuing.

"Stop trying so hard!" Naamah laughed. "You're going to hurt yourself."

Decker, feeling quite tipsy, took a few steps toward the demon.

"William," Naamah whispered. "Decker...are you going to try and kiss me?"

Decker spit to his side. "No. I was going to attempt to slay you again."

"With what? A lighter and a shotgun shell?" Her own words amused her, and she leaned over in laughter. "No," she finally emerged from her self-induced bout of laughter, "I spared you because you did right by me. For whatever purpose— it matters not."

"Self-preservation," Decker assured her once more.

"Whatever," she interrupted and turned and reached into the open altar compartment and withdrew the long cloak. "The serpent's skin remains safe. That is all that matters."

"The what?" Decker amplified his ignorance for effect, hoping to coax more information from the demon.

"The skin of the Great Serpent from the islands that hide in plain sight."

"Oh," he stuttered. "Thanks. Now I understand."

"I am sure you do not," she replied, tucking the mysterious garment into a bag, that, like the table and wine, suddenly appeared at her feet.

"In you go, William." She directed him to the open altar.

"What?" he protested. "I'm not getting in there!"

Naamah stepped toward him. "Very well," she replied as she removed a long-twisted dagger from her garb.

Decker said nothing. Realizing he had no choice, he quickly moved to the edge of the altar.

Naamah motioned him in and he followed her direction, hoisting himself up and into the huge stone vessel.

"I shall not forget about you, William Decker." Her eyes were ablaze once more, and he averted his own from her gaze. "When the world is consumed in darkness, I shall come for you. I find you oddly intriguing— for the time being. A choice will be offered. Choose wisely."

"Now or then," he hissed, "my choice will be the same, demon."

"So say you. Lie down in the altar, William. It must be closed. Oh. I almost forgot," she said as she leaned over to retrieve a leather pouch from the floor. Tossing it into the altar, she returned to sliding the stone top.

"I'm afraid it is only water...*priest*." Her face was taught and drawn, transforming as Decker stared up and out at her. "But you will have plenty of time and solitude to petition your God to transform it to wine for you."

145

Naamah stood still on the white sands that lined the ground at the base of the Himalayan marvel known as the Sky Caves. The sheer cliff rising up into the Nepal sky was littered with dozens of rough man-made openings of square and rectangle design. Like windows in an ancient skyscraper, the caves appeared inaccessible since there was no steps or pathways leading to them. Carved by hand, peering out on the Himalayan landscape, each led deep into the mountainside, opening to all manner of chambers, halls, and temples within. The Mustang Kingdom, as it was known, bordering the Tibetan plateau, was one of the most remote and isolated regions of the country of Nepal. And as such, the demon stood alone, in silence, with only the moaning mountain winds to speak to her with their ancient voices.

Naamah smiled to herself. She had no time to search the caves alone. The task would be quite tedious, and she was unaccustomed to such boring duties. She had an idea that would assist her two-fold. She was preparing for battle, after all. An unholy war was slated to be waged very soon. And what else does an unholy war need but an unholy army?

"Resurgemus! Resurgemus!" she cried in Latin, lifting her hands from her sides to the sky repeatedly. "Resurgemus! Resurgemus! Exercitus quo affliguntur damnati! Resurgemus! Resurgemus! Rise, my army of the damned!"

Suddenly, the silence of the mountain-scape was broken. Sounds of bursting earth and cracking rock echoed all around her from the ground, the hills, and the mountains. The blasphemous rhythm swiftly chased away the whispers of the highland wind's voices, giving way to the shrieks and cries of the rising dead.

Naamah watched as all manner of man and women rallied around her. Some bore the garbs of the local monks, others were cast in tethered scraps of cloth bearing the stench of thousands of years of passing time, and still others were from more modern times in pants and jackets. Even here, in one of the most remote locales on the globe, hundreds had not escaped the reaper's hand. All the dead within earshot of her voice joined the call. The eons had amassed her an army, and she was prepared for the gloom at hand. They dropped in around her at supernatural speeds, falling from peaks above and in from paths behind. The dead even crawled from the very caves of her focus and defied the laws of nature as they scurried down the sheer cliffside on all fours.

They encircled Naamah, their enchanting reanimator. Broken, eyeless skulls stared at her for direction, for purpose in their awakening.

"*Seek!*" she cried out. "Seek that which I lust! Seek that which I covet!" The papyrus was hidden somewhere in the caves, and she was hell-bent on finding it without Moloch.

As quickly as they had assembled around their queen, they broke away. Clambering, scaling, crawling up the dizzying heights to the Sky Caves, ascending in search of their mistress's prize. Her thoughts filled their hollow skulls, her eyes substituted their vision. "Find me the 'prophet marked by sorrow!'"

Naamah watched as her newly risen legion piled in and out of each of the cave entrances. They reminded her of busy little worker ants, running to and fro in organized chaos to please their queen. Their movements so extreme that pieces of stone from the mountainside began to crack and crumble under the toil of their march.

Her attention was drawn to one of her soldiers who stood at the entrance to a large cave. He appeared to be a Northman—a Viking, she surmised, his long red locks still clinging to his split skull. Naamah watched as his jawbone opened and emanated a growl akin to that of a great grizzly bear. She nodded to her follower and scaled the cliffside in a slow, single bound. The dead Viking retreated into the cave to allow his master's entry, ushering her to a wall where she found several paintings of the living Buddha.

"A prophet," she hissed. "Lame as all the others."

The redheaded soldier tapped the time-yellowed bones of his hand over one particular rendition of the Buddha, and Naamah moved in for a closer look. There she found a joyful young man, laughing, surrounded by all manner of beast and bird.

"Sorrow!" she belted out. "'Marked by sorrow!'"

She lifted an open palm in the Viking's direction as she prepared to send him back to oblivion. Stepping forward, he closed his skeletal digits over Naamah's hand and reached over and pointed to a particular spot on the Buddha's chest.

Brushing his hand from hers, Naamah humored him, amused by his perseverance, and leaned in to view the area of the painting his bony finger rested on.

"Ha ha ha!" Naamah turned to her soldier. "Brilliant, old Northman!"

The Viking continued to point at the faint image of a skull and bones the Buddha was brandishing on his chest.

"Death is sorrow, is it not? At least for the living anyway. Brilliant."

The Viking nodded its decaying head and stepped back, awaiting further instructions.

"Break it open! Smash the prophet to pieces!"

Without hesitation, he stepped to the wall and bashed through the painting with ease, revealing the hollow chamber behind it. Stepping aside to allow Naamah access, he once again lowered his head and awaited further instruction.

Naamah approached the wall and inserted her slender arm up to her elbow. Feeling around, her fingers found their purpose and she grasped the stone cylinder tightly.

"Well done." She smiled, turning to the Viking, papyrus in hand. "For your insightfulness, I grant you speech. For your loyalty, I rise you up."

The Viking dropped to one knee before Naamah, head bowed.

"Rise, my commander, my general. Rise and take the reins of your legion. Gather my army—prepare them for travel and war."

The Viking rose to his feet. "Yes." The word echoed off his dry, skeletal throat. "Yes, my queen."

146

L obo's blood ran cold as he turned from Jericho's cries to look out of the entrance. There, before him, stood Moloch. Fire flickering in the demon's pupils, his face chiseled in stone, he smiled at Lobo.

"Run!" Samantha screamed from somewhere behind him. "Fucking run!"

"Silence, child!" Moloch waved a hand, and Sam's mouth was paralyzed. Her eyes darted around as her hands fumbled at her jaw. Lobo was frozen solid, unable to take a step.

Moloch gazed down at Lobo's hands, clenching the stone cylinder tightly. "What have you got there?"

Lobo said nothing. He heard the rustling to his left and watched as the demon's gaze shifted toward the movement behind him.

"Run! Run now!" Le'Strat commanded as he stepped forward, brandishing his bulky Glock in hand. His forward advance swiftly stalled as he noticed the room remained motionless.

"Everybody stay cool." Jericho tried to keep control of what he saw as an escalating situation which, if handled improperly, was only going to get them all killed.

Le'Strat paid his pleas no regard and decidedly opened fire on the demon. The powerful gun's slugs ripped through Moloch's shirt, burning holes in the white linen that covered his broad chest.

The percussive report of the gun fire was deafening, echoing through Lucifer's Room.

Lobo's body finally unfroze as he tried to dart around Moloch, but was stopped instantly by an outstretched arm which took hold of the heroic pilot.

The muzzle flare intensified as Le'Strat walked toward his intended victim, firing repeatedly as he did. It was hopeless. The bullets damaged the demon's wardrobe and nothing more.

"Enough games," Moloch hissed, his features contorting and changing, exposing the true visage under the human façade. Still grasping Lobo in the hand of his outstretched arm, he lifted him into the air and dropped him back in front of him. Swiping his free hand across the room, Moloch sent Le'Strat sailing into the wall face first, splitting his skull completely with an awful crack.

"No!" Jericho screamed and tried to run to his friend's assistance. He was stopped dead in his tracks as he watched Moloch lift Lobo up again, cocking his free hand back. Without further hesitation, he thrust his fist forward into Lobo's chest and out the back. Samantha's knees buckled and she dropped to the ground at the sight of Moloch's bloody hand waving to her through Lobo's body. He released his grasp, but kept Lobo up, impaled on his arm. Reaching down, Moloch pried open Lobo's death grip and retrieved the papyrus.

"Nice to see you, Francis." The demon smiled at Jericho as he yanked his arm from Lobo's body, allowing the lifeless corpse to flop to the earth at his feet. "Been a while."

Jericho tried to form words, but his mind was reeling. Spying Samantha on the ground, he took a few steps to her side and bent down to help her to her feet. Supporting her, he turned back to Moloch.

"I don't know you, fucker!" The words came hard and squeaked and broken as they left Jericho's lips.

"Oh, we have met, Jericho." Moloch turned his back on them and began to walk away. "Many years ago—Frank Jericho and Michael Witcher."

"My partner?" Jericho was trying to move Samantha toward Le'Strat to render assistance if there was any to be given.

"Cold New York winter." Moloch turned and smiled at them. "All those young girls. All that blood desecrating the pure white snow."

Jericho's heart skipped a beat, and his stomach dropped. "You fucking piece of shit!"

Moloch smiled once more and slowly backed into the growing darkness. "See you soon, Samantha," he whispered as he faded away.

Jericho remained locked on the space where Moloch last stood. His trance was suddenly broken by Sam's screams. Dropping from Jericho, she crawled across the floor to Lobo's side. Her uncontrollable sobbing consumed the small space, and Jericho knew he needed to get them out—as fast as possible.

With tender desperation, Jericho said, "We've got to go, girl. We have to."

"I'm not leaving him!" Her tears flowed down onto Lobo's cheek as she held him tightly in her arms. "I'm not leaving him here to rot in this awful place!"

Jericho took the opportunity presented by her grief to run to Le'Strat. Dropping to one knee, he attempted to look beyond the bloody brain matter scattered about his head and placed the tips of his fingers against his comrade's throat in search of signs of life. Nothing. He grasped Le'Strat's wrist in his hand and searched for a pulse. Not even the faintest rhythm flowed through his old friend's veins. He was gone. Jericho reached up and lowered Le'Strat's eyelids to cover his clouding pupils.

He sprang up and screamed at Samantha, "Now! Right fucking now! Get to your feet!"

Jericho grabbed her under her arms and pulled her up and away from Lobo. Shoving her forward, he bent down and lifted Lobo's limp body up and over his shoulder.

"Move—the way we came!" he demanded through strained words.

Sam responded to his directions this time and started out through the catacombs. They hurried down the narrow walkway, Sam leading, Jericho on her heels.

"Frank," she whispered as they reached the exit.

"Yeah?"

"I'm scared, Frank."

"Yeah, kiddo." He empathized as he struggled to keep Lobo's blood drenched body positioned over his shoulder. "I'm scared, too."

147

Jericho peered out onto the narrow road behind St. Peter's. Crouching down, he swapped his gaze between the sliver of space produced by the slightly ajar door and Samantha. She was behind him, cradling Lobo's fallen body in her lap. They had returned through the Door of Death to a small passageway at the back of the room. Jericho had recalled Le'Strat explaining how the undertakers brought the dead in from outside through a door down the hall. He explained how the death dealers would work very quietly, secretively even, so as to not to disturb the sanctity of their surroundings.

"You okay?" he whispered across the dimly lit room.

Sam looked up at him and said nothing. They stared at each other for a moment before she dropped her head in despair.

Rain had begun to fall from the sky, and it splattered up off the ground, hitting Frank's face, gently mixing with his sweat and Lobo's blood. Leaning a tad forward out the door, he allowed the cool, cleansing water to thoroughly drench him. Lifting his head skyward, he closed his eyes, and soaked in the soothing musical percussion of the beating drops.

Jericho's iota of peace was shattered by the screeching brakes of the black van that had managed to arrive without him realizing it. Alex had come to rescue them.

"Fuck," he whispered to himself. "You're losing it, old man."

Rising to his feet, he summoned Sam. She didn't move.

He needed her to move, but he knew she was frozen by her grief. "Sam," his voice slightly elevated now. "Get in the goddamn van, please."

She looked up, and once again, said nothing.

"I'll bring him." He walked to her side and reached down to touch her shoulder. "But I need you to get in first."

Samantha slid Lobo's body off her lap and laid him gently on the marble floor. Rising silently, she walked toward the exit. Jericho followed her and slipped past her to open the door. Alexander stood on the other side, soaked by the falling rain, a cloud of sorrow on his face.

"Come, my dear." Storm extended a hand, beckoning Sam. "There is the comfort of your companions within."

Samantha took Alex's hand, and he helped her up to the open side door into the waiting arms of Keith and Kate.

"I'm sorry," Kate whispered, hugging her friend tightly.

Sam nodded and allowed them to seat her on one of the van's benches.

"Unlock the back, Serket," Alex instructed and slid the door shut, blocking the others' view from Jericho, who was emerging from the church with Lobo slumped over his shoulder.

"Lay him in here." Alexander stepped aside and allowed Frank to lower the body into the rear cargo space of the van.

"I'm sorry, man," Jericho said humbly, offering his condolences.

"It is not your fault, my friend," Alexander reached out and placed an open palm on Lobo's chest. "It is the greatest risk of war, casualties. No one knew that better than him."

Jericho nodded.

"Get yourself out of the downpour. I'll be right with you."

Jericho turned to leave when Alexander reached out and grasped his arm. "Samantha?"

"Not great, but she's tough."

Alex nodded. "Yes, she is. They had grown quite fond of each other, I understand?"

"It would appear that way, brother."

"Yes." Storm smiled. "I could see why that attraction was there. Very good."

Alex released Jericho and waited for the click of the closing door of the van behind him. Bending down to Lobo's corpse, Storm leaned forward and kissed his friend's forehead gently.

"Sleep, guardian of the light. Perhaps we shall meet again. Very shortly I surmise, if fate deems it so."

~

"Copan and Nepal," Alexander shouted from the passenger seat of the van as it barreled through the paved streets of Rome with Serket at its helm. "These are all that remain."

"Where's Decker?" Sam finally broke her silence, rising up in her seat.

"With them," Anika said, leaning over her seat toward Sam.

"Them?"

"The demons. He's with the demons."

"Why aren't we going to him?" Sam demanded, turning to Alex.

"Because it is a strategical distraction, that's why."

"Distraction?" Anika screamed, the jumped up and kneeled on her seat. "Is that what he is to you?"

"We don't have time to rehash this." Alexander all but waved her off. "Time is coming to an end."

"*Our* time," Keith sought to clarify for panic's purposes.

"Time." Storm's voice left no room for speculation.

Jericho sat up in his seat. "Let's split up. You guys take Nepal. I'll head to Copan."

"No!" Alexander firmly denied the plan.

"No?"

"We are together now until the end."

"Except for William," Anika snidely chimed in.

"Except for Decker." Storm was done with this line of discussion.

Anika shrugged and slammed herself back into her seat cushion.

"We only need one of the papyruses to stop them," Alexander began. "Nothing has changed. It is what we have always said. We will stay together and head to Copan. We will abandon Nepal. It is too far and the terrain is too dangerous."

He looked at the faces before him for acknowledgment and acceptance of his plans. There was none forthcoming.

"Copan," Serket finally called out. "We all head to Copan and put an end to this once and for all."

Jericho nodded in agreement, and Alexander turned face forward in his seat.

"I hope you know what you are doing," Serket whispered almost silently as she swerved the van around a bending group of turns in the road.

"So do I my dear," Alexander whispered back. "So do I."

148

Alexander led the others across the runway of Ciampino Airport toward a row of large jets. They needed to leave Rome quickly, not only to get to Copan, but also to escape the bureaucratic shit-storm that was about to hit in Vatican City. They had left death and destruction in their wake, and Alex did not want to be in Rome when the inquisitors came to call.

"Where are we going?" Kate asked as she tried to keep stride with Alex.

He did not respond. The question had been answered on the way over and he was not about to stop and waste time with the details of their departure.

"Alex? Hey!" she called to him. "Where are we going?"

Without stopping, Alex turned to her. "To that plane!"

"Ha ha. Okay." She was not willing to take such a snide remark as an answer. "*After* we get on the plane, where are we going?"

Storm stopped abruptly. "Up in the air." He then spun on his heels to face those to his rear. "We are boarding this jet. Please settle in, and we will discuss our plans once in the air. Any questions?"

"Yes!" Kate called out from his side.

"Good." He once again ignored her. "Let's go."

"I'm not too keen on taking a commercial flight, as I am sure you can understand," Anika said quietly as not to panic her fellow travelers.

"I heard of your difficulties in Africa." He continued on his forward advance without slowing his pace. "This, however, is not a commercial flight. Just us and a pilot."

Alexander's heart ached at the thought of a pilot. Lobo should have been in the cockpit like so many times before. But he was gone.

"There!" Storm pointed to the large Boeing aircraft before them. "Up the stairs, please. We need to get in the air immediately."

Alex could hear the approaching wail of sirens; there was very little time. He was not concerned so much with the end result of an encounter with authorities as he was with the delay their detainment would cause. An unrecoverable delay.

Anika looked at the large jet with the Egyptair logo painted across its body, an artistic rendition of the god Horus below the name. "This *is* a commercial flight, Alex!" she said, panicked. "You said—"

He cut her off and ushered her to the steps. "I said this is a private flight, and it is."

"A charter?"

"Mine." Alex winked at her, nodding her on, expressing the first traces of anything but mourning and sorrow since the news of his friend's death.

Standing at the bottom of the steps, he hurriedly fell in behind Keith, who was last up. Alexander whispered to him, "Keep an eye on her, you hear? Very soon we will be pilgrims in an unholy land."

As the words left his mouth, he tapped his jacket pocket and listened for the low rattle of the remaining portal stones. *Pilgrim*, he repeated in his mind, recalling conversations with the demon, Bathin. Perhaps her often used moniker for him was not so odd after all. Perhaps her foresight was right on point.

Storm stopped at the doorway of the jet and turned to seal the door when his eye caught sight of the flashing lights of the approaching Italian police force. Sealing the aircraft without further delay, he called into the cockpit for the pilot to taxi for takeoff. "Close communication with the tower!" he commanded. "They will reroute other flights! Get this bird in the air now!"

Storm moved into the main cabin as the plane took to the runway in a burst of speed which sent the others falling about their seats.

"Sit! Belt in!" he called, and they did their best to comply as the plane took a hard turn onto the runway for takeoff. "We will talk when we are airborne!"

Alex left his companions to the task of securing themselves and turned back to the cockpit. Leaning forward into the pilot's door, hands resting on either side of the doorway, he peered out the aircraft's front windshield across the airfield. The cluster of flashing lights at the end of the runway impelled Alex to rush the cockpit into the co-pilot's seat.

"What's your name?" Alex kept his voice even keeled as he turned to the pilot.

"Doc," the young pilot replied, glancing once at Alex then back to the impending collision ahead. "Friends call me Doc. You Mr. Storm?"

"Yes," Alex locked into the seat. "You got this?"

The pilot snickered. "Don't worry Mr. Storm. I'm not as young as I look."

Alex nodded. Doc appeared calm and in control.

"Care to unlock me, and I can assist in the ascent?" Alex reached out and grabbed the co-pilot's yolk.

The pilot nodded. Collision seemed imminent, and they'd need to start the climb immediately to avoid the horde of police and emergency vehicles that continued to gather at the runway's end.

"Start pulling!" Doc called out, an adrenaline-fueled smile across his face. "What did you do, Mr. Storm?" he asked as the two began to pull their yolks back, forcing the jetliner to hop across the tarmac.

"Nothing," Alexander replied dryly.

Doc laughed. "Big turnout for nothing! What do they *think* you did?"

"They believe some of my associates were complacent in the death of the Pope's private police commander. They were not."

"Le'Strat?" Doc asked sharply, the smile leaving his face.

"That's right. Pull, son!" Alexander reminded him that they needed to get the bird off the ground immediately.

Doc grunted, and the two of them got the plane airborne as Alex reached out and slammed the thruster control all the way forward. The jet trembled and moaned as the wheels on the landing gear rolled across the roofs of several of the tallest vehicles they passed over with a series of shakes and grinds.

"That was close!" Alex popped the latch on his seatbelt as the familiar sound of the pneumatics of the landing gear retracting signaled they were underway safely. "Thank you."

"I've had closer calls—No problem."

Alexander studied his face; it looked more concerned than before, even though they had just eluded a horrific collision.

"We good, Doc?" Alexander asked, rising from his seat to head back to the others.

"Yeah," the young pilot replied. His tone was troubling Alex, and he was not prepared to leave the cockpit just yet.

"So, what's Doc short for?" Storm asked, hoping to engage the pilot in a bit more conversation in order to evaluate his new pilot a bit deeper.

"Just a nickname," he said, and smirked without looking up. "Name's Alfonse." He turned and offered a tight-gripped handshake. "Alfonse Le'Strat."

Alexander stood in the center of the two cockpit seats still grasping Doc's hand, his face remained stoic and void of reaction. "And Commander Le'Strat was your—"

"Uncle." Doc released Alex's hand. "Raised me after my parents died in an auto accident when I was ten."

"I am very sorry for your loss. Your uncle was assisting my people. We had no part in his demise except that it occurred due to the fact that he was rendering my associate's assistance in a dangerous task." Alex was caught off guard and tried to find the words that would both convey his condolences and ascertain the pilot's stability after hearing such grave news. This flight must reach its destination, even if it meant removing the pilot, by force, and landing the plane himself.

"I'll deal with it when we are on the ground, Mr. Storm."

Alex nodded and patted him on the shoulder, recognizing the professionalism of his tone. "I must confer with the others now. We are good, are we not?"

"We are." He looked Alexander straight in the eye, conveying his steadfast determination. "I'll have you to Honduras in about thirteen hours give or take."

Alex turned to exit the cockpit, and Doc said, "Hey."

Alexander paused but did not face the pilot.

"So, you guys didn't have anything to do with it, right?"

"No." Storm didn't allow a second to elapse before responding.

"Who did?"

"An unholy creature." Alex was unsure of Doc's understanding or belief in the supernatural aspects of the world. Just because his uncle was who he was, and thus privy to knowledge that was not fit for most people's understanding, did not mean Doc bore the same insight.

"This creature brutally murdered a dear friend of mine at the same time your uncle met his end. My pilot, which is why you are there in that seat. You are taking us on the course that will eventually lead us to the perpetrator of all this misery. He will be called to answer for his crimes—against your uncle—against my friend—and against humanity."

Doc nodded. "Good. Sounds like our paths crossing was fate. Perhaps I'll join you in the hunt."

Alexander smiled; Doc was clearly familiar with the darker side of reality. "Perhaps you will."

The chopper set down in a large patch of open grass in the sweltering Honduran jungle. Grass as green as a field of emeralds, seemingly unscathed by the brutal equatorial sun. Alex reached out and slid the side door of the helicopter open. Jumping out, he landed firmly on the ground and stood right outside of the ruins of Copan. Doc had remained with the jet on the small, but sufficient, jungle runway they had landed on. He would refuel and protect their means of escape. Alexander had commissioned a local tourist pilot to whirlybird them to the ruins, and once their task was complete, get them back safely to their jet.

"Quickly, now!" he called to the others, who filed out behind him. Swiftly assessing their surroundings, he directed them to the stone remains of the fallen city and waved the chopper pilot off. Alexander's deep black hair blew wildly as the copter departed and disappeared from view. Silence soon christened the barren ruins.

Storm began reviewing the riddle once he had the silence of the still jungle on his side. "A wise man, a sacrificed man, a holy man will find his demon knelt on a throne and steal his royal scepter, cracking the T in stone.'"

"We're in search of a demon?" Kate called out.

Alexander nodded. "I would guess the riddle refers to one of the many stone figures scattered throughout the ruins. It may appear, as many of the deities here will, as a monster or a demon."

Serket stepped forward and ushered the others to follow her between a barricade of trees through to the ruins on the other side.

"The scepter is the key," Kate said loudly, for all to hear, although she was directing her analysis at Storm who had fallen in at her side.

"A key to a lock?" Abigail asked from in front of them.

"No, no," Kate replied. "The key to the riddle. The characteristic which will allow us to identify the right stone figure."

Alexander nodded and smiled at Kate. "I think you may very well be correct." He stopped and lifted a hand to the great stone complex before them. "Welcome to Copan. Let us make haste and find Kate's royal scepter."

Breaking into small groups, they attacked the location as quickly as possible, weaving around the stout stone pyramids and temple monuments that littered the forgotten jungle city. Kate and Alex broke off into a subgroup, leaving Abigail and Sam wandering behind.

"Did you know this is a Mayan city?" Kate said as she scaled the small pyramid beside Storm. "But its name is Aztec."

Alex smiled at her enthusiasm. "Yes, I did know that." He laughed.

"Of course, you did." She shook her head as they began their descent after reaching the apex of the small stone monument.

Finally reaching the grassy ground at the base, Kate turned to study the strange entranceway at ground level behind her. Stepping forward, she snickered and stopped dead in her tracks.

"Hey, Storm!" she called after him. He had already begun to proceed to the next cluster of stone wonders ahead of them. "I bet you didn't know *this* fact."

Alex slowed down. "What's that?"

"This complex houses two very unique statues—The Simian Kings!"

Storm came to a full stop. "The monkey kings."

"Right. Okay, you may have already known that." The excitement was radiating from her voice, and Alexander turned and walked back in her direction. She continued, "Did you also know they have scepters in their hands?"

"I did not," he replied as he arrived at her side.

"Or that this one in front of me is brandishing a scepter embellished with a very discernible 'T' right there in the center?"

Alexander followed her pointing finger to the hand of the menacing primate. He laughed out loud. "Yes, I do believe you've got it, Kate."

Alexander scrambled up the random stones that lined the floor and sides of the large stone sculpture until the scepter was in arm's reach.

"Get the others," he whispered. "Quickly!"

Alexander sensed the change in the light and scent of the jungle. They were no longer alone. Reaching out, he touched the face of the stone scepter, tracing the relief that formed a "T" with his finger.

"What do ya got, Storm?" Jericho called up to him.

"Possibly the end of this long journey, my friend." He turned to face Frank. "But we are no longer alone, Jericho."

Frank turned from side to side, in subdued panic, as the others arrived beside him. The sky was definitely growing darker, the blazing jungle sun was now beaming with an eerie silver luminescence that reminded him of a cold winter sky right before snow begins to fall.

"Hey!" Jericho called up to Storm, retrieving a field kit hammer from the small pack on his back. "Smash the mother fucker! Now!" he demanded, tossing it up to Alexander.

Lifting the hammer above his head, Alexander's damning blow was stopped by the crushing pain radiating down his other arm. Turning toward the source of his agony, he was met with the blue icy stare of the Monkey King. Fully animated, the stone creature held Storm's arm tightly in its grip, lifting him upward as it struggled to break free of its rock prison.

Alexander ignored the screams from below. He ignored the pain of his bones being crushed in his arm, and he let loose a powerful blow on the Monkey King's other arm.

The beast released its grasp, dropping Alex to the jungle floor with a mighty growl, its teeth bared, exposing huge, stone points as it howled. The creature continued to writhe about in agony as the small crack Storm had created spread and split the scepter from its arm.

Dropping into Jericho's waiting hands below, the stone was heavy, and he dropped it almost instantaneously.

"Leave it!" Sam cried.

"No!" Alexander dropped to the scepter on the ground and delivered a second stone-crushing blow with his bare fist on the "T" symbol. Alexander's efforts were rewarded when the front of it popped open like a hinged box.

"Run!" he cried, reaching down to grasp the crystal vessel from within the scepter's hidden compartment. "Flee! We have it!" His fingers did not make it to the prize, however. His body was jerked backward and thrown like a rag doll across the Mayan complex.

Stunned, he quickly regained his composure and rose to his feet. Despair drenched his soul when he saw Moloch, standing over the broken scepter, papyrus in hand.

"Many thanks Storm," he laughed, waving the prize above his head, mocking their failure once again.

"Destroy him!" the demon demanded, and the Monkey King responded. Charging at Storm on all fours, it hurtled its massive body of stone at its intended target.

Moloch didn't linger to ensure the monster's success, but instead disappeared into the jungle landscape. He was gone, as was the final piece of the puzzle.

Alexander saw the beast galloping at him with murder in its icy eyes. Dropping to one knee, Storm, without any room for escape, braced for the creature's deadly impact and shut his eyes.

But instead of the bone thrashing explosion of rock on flesh, he was met with a stinging spray of sand and dust. He opened his eyes and there, standing several yards from him, stood Abigail, her arms and hands stretched out before her. He smiled at her and rose to his feet, brushing the dust and debris from his long black coat as he walked to her side.

"You are beginning to make a habit of this, my dear."

"How's that?" Abigail replied, somewhat shaken from the burst of psychic energy she had just released.

"Saving my hide," he said and winked. "Saving *our* hides."

150

"Where is she? Where is that conspiratorial bitch?"

Decker's eyes struggled to adjust to the light. He struggled to speak; the sound of the sliding stone top had shocked him from the meditative sleep he had entered within his prison of rock. "I—I don't know."

Decker felt a large hand grasp his clothing tightly and yank him up and out of the altar. Moloch dropped him to the ground and delivered a stunning blow to Decker's side with his boot.

"Wait! Wait!" Decks held up his hands to stave off another blow. The kick had hurt, but he was fairly certain it was at the very low end of Moloch's strength meter. "I can tell you what she said—"

"Go on," Moloch took a step back. "Let's see if the tongue can save the neck."

Decker struggled to his feet and stood before the hulking demon. He felt the anger sparked by betrayal radiating from every pore of the monster's being. He quickly relayed the crux of his conversation with the she-demon, leaving out several key details.

"So, she *does* seek to usurp me. She is nefarious to a flaw, I'm afraid." He snickered and walked to the altar to survey the interior.

Decker's apprehension, with regard to the demon's wrath, diminished as he sensed a change in both his tone and demeanor. He may have a chance here. A chance to survive.

"You are a priest, no?"

Decker cleared his throat. "No, I'm not."

Moloch turned to face him, staring down into his eyes. "You most certainly *are* an exorcist—Do you deny this fact?"

"I do not."

"Many have lamented over your name—your rituals."

Decker stood silent, unsure of how to respond. Moloch's lip curled into a snarl, his teeth gnashing, eyes ablaze.

"I should rip you limb from limb. Crush you into an indiscernible mound of piss and blood."

Decker swallowed hard at the thought, his body going rigid as the demon crossed the room and stood toe-to-toe with him. Decker's eyes darted from side to side in avoidance, not wishing to enrage his nemesis further through insolence.

"There is nowhere to run, little man." Moloch leaned down to him. "So tell me, why did that treacherous bitch seal you in there rather than destroying you?"

"I don't know," Decks quickly replied. "She said she would come back to me after—"

"After?"

"Yes. That's what she said. After the darkness."

"Why would she do that? It makes no sense, little man."

"I don't know. Perhaps she planned to prolong my suffering? I honestly don't know. I wasn't going to look the gift of time in the mouth of horse." Decker shook his head as the words escaped fumbled and confused.

Moloch walked back to the stone altar and peered in once more.

"Something is amiss here." He reached in and ran his hands over the smooth stone interior. "I was unaware this space was here. How did she know?"

"Maybe she's been here before? Who chose the location?"

"I did!" he snapped, angered by the suggestion he was being directed by Naamah.

Moloch marched at Decker, who jumped to the side as the demon passed by him and headed to the door to the chamber. Whipping it open, he called out into the dimly lit hall, and within seconds, a dark figure appeared.

"Bring them to me!" he commanded the figure, handing him an object Decker instantly recognized as one of the crystal vessels containing a portion of the sacred papyrus. The figure nodded and disappeared into the shadows. Shutting the door sharply, Moloch turned back to Decker.

"I shall require your assistance." Moloch returned to the altar and effortlessly slid the stone top back into place. "Come here. Now."

Decker stood frozen. "What can I do for you, exactly?"

Moloch moved across the room with supernatural speed, took hold of the back of Decker's neck, and pushed him alongside the altar, all in the space of a second.

"You can bleed for me," he hissed, raising a clenched dagger above his head.

Decker's veins ran cold. This was it—this was the end. Moloch brought the dagger down hard, stopping as the tip touched the skin on his face. Pulling Decker's arm over the altar, Moloch laughed as he cut a deep gash across the palm of his hand. Milking the wound in his mighty grasp, Moloch soaked the top of the altar in Decker's blood. He struggled, but the demon pulled him closer and extended a long serpentine tongue across his wounded hand. Decker watched in disgust as it passed over the gaping slash, sealing the wound as it passed over.

"There," he said, laughing at Decker's fear. "Good as new. You'll live...for now."

Moloch threw Decks to the side and climbed onto the altar. Raising his hands above him, the demon began to chant. Low at first, but it quickly gained volume and momentum. Decker struggled to understand the words, but couldn't follow. It wasn't Latin, but it was hauntingly familiar. He watched as the air around Moloch changed. It became dense with a rippling wave of heat and smoke, spiraling about the summoner.

Aramaic? Decker posited the question to himself, and answered it as well. *Yes, yes. Why Aramaic? It made no sense.*

The spiral of wind and smog focused on the pool of scarlet blood atop the altar, atomizing the liquid as it went, and funneling the mist into the air in front of Moloch.

"My God," Decker whispered as he watched a figure materialize before his eyes, his own blood a conduit for evil!

Steam radiated from the tall, slender figure that stood face to face with Moloch. Decker could not discern if it was male or female. The long, blue-gray hair suggested a woman, while the boyish figure lacking breasts or hips suggested a masculine entity. It clearly was not Naamah, of that he was sure.

Hopping down from his stone perch, Moloch introduced their visitor from Hell.

"Introductions are needed," Moloch said and smiled. "May I present Succorbenoth—the great and powerful Gatekeeper."

"Oh, fuck me!" Decker let the words slip as the beast snapped its head in his direction.

"My Lord," it growled, greeting Moloch. "No introduction needed for this piece of filth." Its black saucer eyes tore at William, who physically shied away from the stare. "He has been tormenting our kind for decades. William fucking Decker—failed priest—failed man—servant of the miserable Dragon Storm. Why is his heart still pumping? I shall rip it from his chest and burn him into Hell!"

Succorbenoth flew across the air and thrust its hand toward Decker's chest.

"No!" Moloch cried out, stopping the demon's hand in midair.

"My lord." The demon subserviently backed off its attack and awaited Moloch's command.

"There will be a time for that, I promise to you. But I have been betrayed, and that must be dealt with first. His role in that betrayal," Moloch said, pointing at Decker's cowering body, "I am not yet sure of—so he travels with us."

"As you command," Succorbenoth agreed in fealty.

Decker heard the wooden door behind him creak open, and a cold chill crept across his sweat-drenched skin.

"My lord," a low hiss called out, as the dark figure from the hall drifted across the room like a shadow to its master.

Decker peeked from beneath his tightly squeezed eyelids just enough to see the shadowy figure hand an ornately decorated box to Moloch. It appeared to be comprised of gold and silver, but he was unsure in the dim light if that analysis was accurate. He also didn't think it really mattered.

"Excellent," the high demon laughed, tucking the box under his arm. "Shall we?" Moloch rhetorically asked as he grabbed Decker with his free hand and dragged him across the room to Succorbenoth.

"To where do we travel, my lord?" The demon of the gates was already conjuring a wormhole, and Decker watched as the empty space, cut in time, opened and expanded before them.

"Giza," Moloch snapped. "Your home."

"Perfect." Succorbenoth nodded and gestured for them to pass into the portal.

"Now, exorcist," Moloch said and smiled an evil grin as he tugged Decker into the worm hole. "Let us see what the miserable cunt is up to —shall we?"

151

Serket stood in the aisle ahead of the others in their seats and clapped at them to get their attention. Most had dozed off at the onset of the long flight from Honduras and awoke to the sound of Serket's clamor. Keith smiled to himself as he pictured her performing the customary preflight informational skit in a flight attendant's uniform. Displaced as his humor was, he just didn't care at this point.

"Now, in case of demonic infestation," Keith said playfully, "a holy relic will drop from above. Be sure to destroy your demon first before tending to any of your fellow travelers' demons."

"Keith?" Serket said. "You with me?"

"Yes ma'am." He shifted and sat up straight in his seat.

"Pay attention!" Kate demanded, backhanding his shoulder lightly with her fingers.

Alexander, who sat in the seat just to the left of Serket, leaned around to face the others. "We are headed back to the start—Egypt. Giza, to be precise." Although he could not see Kate's face directly, he felt her questions forming. "Please, just listen. Kate—"

"Hey!" She called out from behind Jericho's seat, but he continued, ignoring her displeasure at being singled out.

"As I was saying, the Giza Plateau is our destination. You must prepare yourselves—Moloch and Naamah now possess the complete papyrus, and we are left with no other option besides open war. Listen to Serket. She is going to bring everyone up to speed."

Serket took her cue from Alexander and began. She explained how the papyrus fragments formed the complete *Book of Gates*, an ancient Egyptian text. That if the twelve chapters, which represented the twelve hours of the night, were recited while performing the requisite rituals—at the proper location—a gateway to the underworld would be opened; and Hell would be unleashed on Earth.

"The texts were written to guide a soul through the hours of darkness—the night—and then back out the other side of morning," Serket explained to her captive audience. "However, the disciples of Hell have contrived a plan for one to travel this path and not only pick up stowaways on the journey, but also a way to prop the final hour open, if you will, allowing the ethereal world, the underworld, passage into our plane of being."

"Fuck. Me," Jericho said slowly, annunciating his concern.

"Language!" Alexander called out from his seat.

"Language?" Jericho didn't care about Storm's objection at all. "Come on, Storm. Pretty sure this situation, this one in particular, calls for some 'Fuck me's,'—'Holy fuck's,'—or even the ever appropriate—'Jesus fucking Christ's,'—wouldn't you say?"

Alexander rose from his seat and turned to Frank. "Actually, I would not, my friend. I would say the current situation calls for something entirely different—civility to start—actions *and* words that are pure and true will guide us through this terrible ordeal—"

Alexander's diatribe was cut short by the crackle of the plane's intercom coming to life. "Mr. Storm, prepare for landing."

"Words that are pure." Jericho stood to face his accuser, taking quick advantage of Doc's interruption. "Do you really think God cares if I say *fuck*, Alexander? He just tossed a stone monkey king at you, brother."

"God?" Alexander stared hard into Jericho's weathered eyes. "I have no idea what God cares about, honestly. And I don't care to know. I know what I care about. I know what you care about. And that my friend, that is the crux of my argument—*isn't it?*"

Jericho shook his head. It was useless discourse at this point, serving no purpose as far as he was concerned, and he was not about to allow it to come between the two of them at such a critical point in their mission. And perhaps, although he would never admit it aloud, the fact the Storm was correct played a part in the end to the exchange. Waving Alexander off, he fell back into his seat.

"You heard the man," Storm said to his companions. "Strap in. I expect the ride will become quite rough from this point forward." Following his own instructions, he strapped the belt across his waist as well. "Quite rough indeed," he whispered to himself and cast a momentary, *questioning* glance to the heavens above them.

152

Between the ancient stone paws of the immortal Sphinx, time and space parted as Naamah's precisely placed wormhole opened into the cool night air of the Giza plateau. Stepping out onto the desert sand, the demon peered over her shoulder at the immortal trio of pyramids, decoratively lit for tourists, in the near distance.

"Splendid," she whispered to the breezy Egyptian night. Stretching her arms out as if to embrace some unseen friend, Naamah took a deep breath of the fragrant air and sighed a purposefully dramatic sigh. Smiling at the culmination of her planning, she walked out from the protection of the lion's legs.

"Come forth," she commanded, turning back to face the void she had created. "Come forth and serve your queen!"

Without the need for further command, the Viking skull general emerged from the portal and joined his mistress at her side.

"Bring forth my legion!" she instructed the commander, who nodded and called forth the army, ordering the ghosts of Nepal to assemble for battle on the Egyptian plateau.

One by one, her militia of the dead passed through the wormhole and fell into organized ranks before them. Their silent skeletal remains stood in blasphemous splendor awaiting Naamah's instructions. The demon watched as the last of the warriors emerged. Stepping forward, she waved a hand and slammed the portal closed.

"Collect your warriors around the great pyramid," she instructed the Northman, pointing to the largest of the ancient wonders for clarification.

"No one is to approach the structure once our ritual has begun—understood? Form me a barricade of the damned!"

The Viking skull nodded. "Understood, my queen. Nothing shall pass."

"Tonight," Naamah began, turning to face the throngs of the dead. "What we conjure tonight—will reverberate through all time! Darkness will engulf the souls of men! Heaven shall crash from on high—shattered and splintered at my feet. Shadow will take them all, and with it—"

Naamah's voice suddenly fell silent, and she turned to the Viking to see if he had heard it, too. The pounding upon the Earth. Nodding to her, the skeletal commander drew his tarnished and marred steel from the rotten leather sheath that hung loosely from his bony hips. His motion, to arm himself, was sufficient to cause the hordes of the dead to brandish their own weapons, raised in unison for battle.

The rhythmic pounding of hooves on the desert sand intensified and echoed all around them as the horsemen grew closer.

"Protect your mistress!" The Viking growled, and they fell in and wrapped around Naamah, forming a circle of bone and rot.

She could see the approaching droves of horsemen now. Her keen vision immediately identified the mounts as the bitch's soldiers—the Medjai of Deshret, the Red Scorpions. Their fighting skills were legendary amongst men—but her warriors were no longer men.

"Destroy them!" she cried, sending her horde into a frenzy of gnashing bone and clanging steel.

Breaking from her, they charged out to meet the horsemen who had advanced between the pyramid complex and the Sphinx. Within seconds, the crashing din of blade on bone rang out across the desert night as the massive militia of the departed threw themselves with abandon against, the slight by comparison, swarm of Medjai.

Asar, mounted on his own steed, yanked the reins tightly. Veering his stallion hard, the mighty Egyptian skated around the farthest reaches of Naamah's army. Passing them at a breakneck gallop, he headed toward the Sphinx.

Screams and wails of pain filled the night as the demon army overtook the horseman through sheer numbers, bringing the magnificent horses to bloody thuds in the sand and then slaughtering the fallen riders.

Naamah watched from her vantage point next to the Sphinx, her Viking skull at her side.

"What a disappointing effort," she hissed. "Pathetic—anticlimactic even."

Her lips grew silent as she felt the hot, thick air splash across her back. She knew the origins of this telltale sensation, and she quickly turned to greet the great beast as he emerged from the wormhole. His face was twisted and cruel as he charged at her.

"Moloch—my prince." She smiled seductively, hoping to bewitch him before it was too late. "You are just in time to—"

Her words were silenced as the formidable demon took hold of her throat and lifted her petite body up over the waning heat of the dessert sands.

"What are you up to, whore?" he demanded, refusing to loosen his grasp to afford her an opportunity to respond. "You think you can overtake me? Surpass me? Proceed without the great and powerful Moloch? I will twist your filthy form into oblivion, bitch!"

Naamah's bulging eyes caught sight of Decker as he stumbled forward through Moloch's portal, dropping to his knees in the sand. Leaning over, hands on his legs, Decker convulsed and gagged until he vomited, and it splashed onto the sand at his knees.

Panicked at the arrival of the priest, she turned her attentions back to her captor and struggled to speak, but the grasp of the demon prince was unrelenting. Without warning, Moloch released her and arched his back. Naamah thumped to the ground and looked up just in time to see her Viking skull deliver a second blow to Moloch's back. She smiled at her ardent warrior, but her sense of ill-placed pride was quickly replaced by dread as Moloch spun around and snatched the dead warrior's blade from his hands. Raising the ragged steel over his shoulder, Moloch swung it hard at the would-be slayer, removing the Viking's skull from its shoulders like a warm knife through butter. The once again lifeless body dropped into a pile at his feet.

Turning to Naamah, Moloch hoisted the ancient blade up once more to deliver a devastating blow, this time, to Naamah's kneeling body.

Naamah raised her hands up defensively. "Wait my lord! Wait!"

As if on cue to save the embattled she-demon's skin, the furious commotion around Moloch at last attracted his attention—there was a great battle taking place around him that had escaped his rage fueled senses up to this point. Naamah's army was devastating the ancient order of the Red Scorpion in a fight that stretched across the entire complex.

"What is this?" he demanded, lowering the sword to his side.

"It is for you, my lord. For us."

"Explain yourself," he demanded, "and be quick about it."

"I learned of this treachery that awaited us from one of my many whisperers." She rose to her feet slowly, monitoring his reaction closely. "And I took steps to thwart it for you. I am a faithful servant. I beg of you, do not banish me when we have come so far...*together.*"

Moloch studied her eyes, searching for some semblance of the truth behind their beckoning gaze. He looked at Decker. "And what of this filth? Why did you secret him away? Let him live? Tell me that, then?"

"My prince," she softened her voice even more and walked to his side, running her finger over his chest as she passed. "Insurance, my lord. Nothing more."

Moloch allowed the thought to churn around his mind, relaxing his paranoid inclinations. "Meaning precisely what, my dear?"

"Meaning if either of us was unsuccessful in acquiring the last pieces of papyrus, we could use the priest to arrange a trade. He is precious to Storm —I thought his life may prove useful to our purposes, my lord. That is all— nothing more."

She purred in Moloch's ear. "I am sorry if I have overstepped my boundaries, but it seemed like a solid plan. My clandestine movements were nothing more than self-serving. I do relish in it when I surprise you with an advantageous move or strategy. I bathe in your praise and admiration. Gets me hot."

She had him now. Naamah could read it on his face. She could see it in his eyes.

"Great one!" she cried out over the continuing din of swords and pain which resonated just beyond their vantage point before the timeless Sphinx. "Look what I have done for you! I have amassed an army of the damned—I have secured a valuable prisoner—and," she said, reaching into her cleavage and withdrawing the Nepal papyrus, "I have retrieved the last piece of the incantation for you."

Moloch dropped the sword to the ground, thoroughly convinced as to Naamah's loyalties, and pulled her to him—embracing her tightly.

"Forgive my ignorance, my queen." He smiled down at her inviting face and retrieved the final hour of *The Book of Gates* from her offering grasp. "I believe your *secret* army has the situation in hand—Shall we begin the *end*? Do me the honor and accompany me on high."

Smiling at her victory, although Moloch clearly thought the sentiment to be for him, she nodded in agreement. "Let the *end* begin, master."

He started toward the Great Pyramid of Giza, Naamah's hand in his, but came to an abrupt halt.

"The priest?" He headed back to Decker.

Decker backed away from Moloch's advance like a crab on all fours. He turned to Naamah, who quickly understood the failed priest was looking for salvation at her hands having kept her secrets.

"My lord," she stepped between the two of them. "He may still be of use to us, and if not, he will make a wonderful gift of sacrifice and torment for our new king on Earth. Our unholy messiah."

"Wise as ever." Moloch searched the floor of the desert around him. "Especially since that approaching rotors are no doubt Alexander Storm."

Without further hesitation, Moloch grabbed the first thing he could find and raised it above his head. "Can't let the foul priest scurry away into the night, though. So unless it is your intention to carry the pathetic bag-of-bones," he laughed, and smashed Decker into unconsciousness with the broken Viking's skull.

153

Alexander dashed across the sand toward the shadow of the Sphinx. He had been able to discern the cries and clamor of the great battle as soon as the noise of the departing chopper was cleared from his ears. With the others doing their best to keep up, he quickly scaled the great desert lion and looked down on the conflict between the Medjai and Naamah's dead. The ghostly warriors clearly held an advantage in both numbers and endurance—they were hard to kill again, after all.

Serket arrived at the Sphinx with Jericho at her side.

"Oh, fuck!" Jericho called out, catching sight of Decker's blood-drenched body in the sand. He dropped down and checked for signs of life as Anika quickly joined him on her knees.

"William! William!" she cried and embraced him tightly to her chest.

"There!" Serket yelled, pointing to the center of the Great Pyramid.

Alexander looked at the metaphysical display that had overtaken the ancient Egyptian monument. The internal, center rows of stones around the area known as the Grand Gallery were separating and levitating out and up. The display created an otherworldly show. Stones weighing hundreds of tons danced in circles in the air, giving way to an open and exposed interior of the pyramid.

"Oh my God," Alex heard Abigail call from below and immediately jumped down beside her.

"We have run out of time, my dear." Grasping her hand, he led her to the edge of the Sphinx platform, overlooking the great battle below. "You and I must act, and act *now!*"

Alexander reached into the recesses of his long, black coat and retrieved a small bottle. It appeared to be glass, with a dark green hue. Metal fibers wrapped around the bottle in all directions, and a cork sat upon the neck.

Alex spoke in a hypnotizing cadence. "Abigail, I will require your assistance now—your power."

"What?" Abigail was still dazed by the madness she was surrounded by at every side.

"Focus." His words met her ears like a charm, like a spell. "Focus on the task at hand."

Alex held the bottle out in front of him and reached for the cork.

Out of nowhere, a voice said, "Hello, old friend." Alex and Abigail jumped back, startled by the large form that fell forward, addressing them with such familiarity.

Storm's eyes focused as the man dropped into the sand at their feet, beaten and bleeding.

"*Asar!*"

Turning back to the others who were seeking shelter in the protection of the Sphinx's arms, Alex called out for Jericho.

"Francis! Now!"

Jericho ran toward them, the group's newest member, Doc, in tow.

"Francis, it is Asar." His voice remained calm. "Take him back with the others and stay there until the end. Your work, the rest of you, is done. You can render no further assistance."

"Like hell!" Jericho defiantly responded.

"Jericho," Storm said softly and grabbed his attention wholeheartedly this time. "The rest must be left to us. Keep the others safe, my friend. That is the task I charge you with."

This time, Frank complied, and with the help of Doc, moved Asar to safe haven with the others.

"Shall we try this again, my dear?"

Abigail nodded, having no idea what *this* was. Alexander raised the bottle again and yanked the cork from the top. Abigail watched as a green mist instantly emanated and formed around the opening, then he bent down and wedged the bottle securely in the sand. Standing upright, he raised his arms up and shouted, "Draco, arise!"

Like a lit rocket unleashed from its base, a steady stream of the mist and smoke shot out high into the sky. The gaseous form spun and expanded, and quickly took form before Abigail's eyes. First the head, then the body, then the massive wings of emerald vapor emerged out into the dark Egyptian night. An immense and powerful dragon formed and finally took flight through the sky, its body whole, its eyes aglow and fixated on the army of the dead below.

"Give it the power Abigail! Give it the force of your will!"

"What? I don't know—"

"Do it!" Alexander cried. "Or all will perish!"

Abigail dropped to her knees. Her eyes slammed shut and squeezed together. Her body tensed and convulsed as the power built within her, ready to burst. Then her mouth sprang open, and a white-hot beam of pure psychic energy radiated from her to the flying serpent. It filled the winged beast's body, and Alex watched as it dove toward the battle below. Opening its jaws in a silent roar, the smoke dragon unleashed on Naamah's army, destroying her soldiers with every pass.

Alex turned to Serket, who was still atop the Sphinx, and signaled for her to head to the Great Pyramid. Reaching for Abi's hand, he hoisted her up and fell in behind Serket.

The three arrived at the pyramid just in time, and they leapt upon stones, which were levitating free from the base and floating up toward the demons.

"Jump!" Alex yelled, tossing Abigail to Serket who was already on an ascending stone block. Alex jumped to the next passing stone, and they rose up together. As they reached the exposed Grand Gallery, Alexander jumped into the pyramid first and quickly turned for Serket to help Abi clear the space to get her to Alex.

"Don't look down!" Serket said.

"Ohhh," Abigail complained. "Now you know I'm going to look!"

"Jump!" Storm yelled again, and with a combination of push and jump, Abigail made it safely to his arms.

"I'll get it on the way down." Serket had no choice. The stone she stood upon was already too far above Alexander. The massive rocks were traveling on a circular course to the peak of the pyramid and then back down in a continuous cycle and she was now forced to wait before she could render assistance to the pair.

Alex waved her off and turned to Naamah and Moloch, who were standing naked before a large stone altar located within the interior of the Grand Gallery.

The ancient papyri laid out before him, Moloch was reaching the final hour of the incantation, and the air around him was alight with sparks and flashes.

"You're too late, Storm!" Naamah laughed upon seeing them. "My master is about to free the one destined to be the master of all!"

Moloch raised his hands high as he recited the words of the final hour of the night. Taking a slight step back, he was attempting to steer clear of the burning, fiery air around him. But he couldn't, and the flames followed him about the Gallery, eventually igniting his skin.

Alex watched the confusion and panic take hold in his eyes as his true form became known. Shedding his human form, the reptilian behemoth shrieked in pain. Massive webbed wings attempted to open as the creature scrambled in bewilderment, hoping to take flight and escape the wrath of flames which seemed intent on his demise. But it was too late for Moloch, and the fires of oblivion engulfed him. In the blink of an eye—he was gone.

Serket, finally reaching the others on her descent, dropped in from above.

"What's going on, Alex?"

She had caught the last glimpses of Moloch's body burning away into the netherworld.

"I believe we have encountered the results of the failsafe you and I so wisely assumed existed," he whispered.

"You have encountered me!" Naamah yelled to them. "The inevitable me!"

After reaching down behind the altar, Naamah rose up with the long, snakeskin cloak in her arms. She quickly draped it over her body and spun her hands in a circle over her head. Before Alex or Serket could react, a ring of blue flame encircled the demon, affording her impassable security.

All the three holy warriors could do was watch as she began the ritual anew. Reading quickly from the papyrus fragments, she arrived at the point that proved the end for Moloch. This time, however, the flames of oblivion bounced from the snakeskin cloak like raindrops on glass.

The three watched as the flames ceased their fruitless attack on Naamah and changed form to create a gate of fire. Naamah took a step toward the burning passage and reached out, pulling the gate open.

Alex had not noticed Abigail had dropped to the ground and was lost in deep psychic meditation. His eyes, like Serket's, were fixed on the massive creature emerging from the darkness. Samael, the great demon, second in command of Hell, stepped from the flaming threshold and spread his mammoth wings.

Suddenly, a furious scream escaped from deep within Abi. She had done it. She had destroyed the protective ring of blue flames that surrounded Naamah.

This was his chance. Reaching into his jacket, he retrieved the last three portal stones and ran toward Serket, who already had her palm out in sudden burst of insight. *436 With his dagger drawn, he clutched her hand in his, fingers folded together in a symbolic gesture, and slid his blade between, slicing both of their palms in unison. Blood flowed from their union and he dropped the stones between them. In that instant, Bathin appeared to them in all her glorious and seductive form.

"Oh, my! What the fuck is going on here?" She laughed.

Alexander grabbed her behind the neck and pulled her to him. Whispering in her ear as she squirmed and shrieked, the demon suddenly withdrew from his relaxed grasp, her face drenched in fear.

"I will not, Alexander Storm," she cried! "I will not open a portal to there!"

Storm's face grew dark, and his eyes grew thin and tight. "You will open that portal—you will open it now—or I will end you mark my words—I will end you!"

Unable to deny his request because she knew he had the power to destroy her, the reluctant demon nodded to Alex and carved a wormhole into the space behind Naamah and Samael.

"Until the end of forever, my dear." Alex kissed Serket's hand, and a solitary tear ran down his cheek. Before she could respond, he turned and raced toward the stone altar. Leaping atop the platform, his long coat flying behind him in trail of agility, he swiped the papyrus up into his hands and dove off the altar at Naamah and Samael. Lost in their own revelry, they did not see the Storm headed right for them. Diving headfirst, he wrapped his arms around their bodies and drove the three of them into the wormhole. Bathin followed reluctantly, slamming shut the portal behind her, winking at Serket's tearing eyes as she dematerialized in wormhole.

~

*A*lexander tried to open his eyes, but the blinding white light kept them to a squint. A sweet, earthy aroma filled the air, entering his nose, calming him. A peaceful tranquility overtook him, and he fought again to open his eyes against the intense radiance. This time, it seemed to diminish enough for him to view his confused companions searching about the empty space they lay in.

"What the fuck, Storm?" Naamah screamed. "Where the fuck are we?"

Samael had risen to his feet as well and was walking toward Naamah in the illuminated haze.

He suddenly stopped, and his body transformed. The monstrous features that defined him began to soften, and a smile crept across his lip. Within moments his figure transformed into handsome, muscular man.

"My father," he began, addressing the empty space around him. "I see you father."

Alexander tried discern what Samael saw, but there only emptiness.

"Forgive me father—Yes—thank you, father." Alexander scrambled to his feet as the transformed body of Samael shed its gravitational restraints and ascended up into the brighter light above them. Alexander watched as he slowly faded away, and then he was gone.

Soon, Naamah greeted the unseen visitor as well, speaking to someone or something that Alex was unable to perceive. He watched as the demon began to radiate a lightness of being that Storm could not quite classify, but was sure was occurring. Seemingly, overcome by what he could only categorize as grace, she, too, faded into the light, extending her hand to some unseen force that lifted her away.

"Looks like it's me and you, Storm," Bathin said, joking. "No more stones, my pretty pilgrim. I am free, and you are trapped."

"So be it," Alexander turned from her, uninterested, and scanned the space before him again, trying to understand what had just transpired.

"Goodbye Storm—I must be—" Bathin's words, like those of the others, faded and changed, her sin and contempt melting away. So too, she drifted up and was gone.

Alexander paced about, frustration mounting, searching through the glow that surrounded him to no avail. Finally, faced with the reality of his situation, he dropped to one knee and bowed his head.

"Truly," he whispered, "am I to spend eternity here? Without you even acknowledging my existence?"

No reply came. No change in vision, no change in sound. No voices or welcoming greetings. Nothing. For the second time that day, Alexander Storm shed a solitary tear. Rising to his feet in dismay, everything suddenly went black. He lost his balance then, falling forward into the warm night sands of the Egyptian desert.

"Storm!" Jericho yelled from several yards away. "There you are, brother! We good? Did you personally deliver those bastards back to Hell?"

"Yes, Francis," he replied, shielding the others from his confusion and consternation, "I believe we are good. All are where they should be."

Alexander walked over to the shelter of the Sphinx and sat in the sand, leaning his back against the Dream Stele between its paws. Serket, busy helping the others, walked past him, gently running her hand over the top his hair.

"Knew I'd see you again," she said and smiled. "I never doubted you."

Alex nodded, and they understood their private exchange.

Abigail walked to his side and sat beside him. She stared at him pensively for a moment, able to feel the emotion radiating from the guise of his visually calm exterior. "So...I wasn't aware Hell was so darn bright and beautiful."

Alexander lifted his face from his hands and smiled at her. "Having visions through my eyes, huh?"

"Perhaps," Abi said and smiled. "Perhaps."

He looked down at the sand below him. "As I said, all are where they should be."

Abigail touched his hand and stood up. Taking a step toward the others, she stopped and turned back to Alex.

"Hey," she said with a puzzled look on her face. "I thought you only had three of Bathin's stones left?"

"That's right," he replied.

"Well," she paused and leaned down. "How did you get back, then?"

Alexander took in a deep breath and winked at Abigail. "That, my dear, is apparently a tale for another day."

HE END

ABOUT THE AUTHOR

~

Anthony DiPaolo is an emerging author in the genre of Archaeo-horror. This is Anthony's first book in The Dragon Storm series. An attorney from New York, he lives on Long Island with his wife, Michelle, his two sons, Anthony and Thomas, and his K-9 writing companions, Frodo and Sam.

~

The Dragon Storm Web

www.DragonStormNovel.com

Made in the USA
Coppell, TX
07 February 2022